VICTOR LODATO is a playwright and the author of the novel *Mathilda Savitch*, winner of the PEN Center USA Award for fiction. His stories and essays have appeared in *The New Yorker*, *The New York Times*, *Granta*, and *Best American Short Stories*. He is the recipient of fellowships from the Guggenheim Foundation and the National Endowment for the Arts. Victor was born and raised in New Jersey and currently divides his time between Ashland, Oregon, and Tucson, Arizona.

ALSO BY VICTOR LODATO

Mathilda Savitch

EDGAR
AND
LUCY

VICTOR LODATO

PICADOR   ST. MARTIN'S PRESS   NEW YORK

in memory of my grandmothers, Jo and Tess—
who read no books,
but who taught me everything

———————

EDGAR AND LUCY. Copyright © 2017 by Victor Lodato. All rights reserved. Printed in the United States of America. For information, address Picador, 175 Fifth Avenue, New York, N.Y. 10010.

picadorusa.com • picadorbookroom.tumblr.com
twitter.com/picadorusa • facebook.com/picadorusa

Picador® is a U.S. registered trademark and is used by Macmillan Publishing Group, LLC, under license from Pan Books Limited.

For book club information, please visit facebook.com/picadorbookclub or email marketing@picadorusa.com.

Designed by Steven Seighman

The Library of Congress has cataloged the St. Martin's Press edition as follows:

Names: Lodato, Victor, author.
Title: Edgar and Lucy : a novel / Victor Lodato.
Description: First edition. | New York : St. Martin's Press, 2017.
Identifiers: LCCN 2016044041 | ISBN 9781250096982 (hardcover) | ISBN 9781250097002 (ebook)
Subjects: Mothers and sons—Fiction. | Single mothers—Fiction. | GSAFD: Suspense fiction. | Love stories.
Classification: LCC PS3612.O33 E34 2017 | DDC 813'.6—dc23
LC record available at https://lccn.loc.gov/2016044041

Picador Paperback ISBN 978-1-250-09699-9

Our books may be purchased in bulk for promotional, educational, or business use. Please contact your local bookseller or the Macmillan Corporate and Premium Sales Department at 1-800-221-7945, extension 5442, or by email at MacmillanSpecialMarkets@macmillan.com.

First published by St. Martin's Press

First Picador Edition: February 2018

10 9 8 7 6 5 4 3 2 1

There is no place for grief in a house that serves the muse.

—Sappho

BOOK ONE

THE AGE OF FLORENCE

She poured out Swann's tea, inquired "Lemon or cream?" and, on his answering "Cream, please," said to him with a laugh: "A cloud!"

—MARCEL PROUST

1

Chanel N° 5

Having a life meant having a story. Even at eight, Edgar knew this.

What he didn't know was his own beginning. Newborn brains were mushy. If you wanted to know how your life had started, you had to get this information from other people.

But what if these people were liars?

"I kept falling asleep," said Lucy. She was speaking of Edgar's birth. The boy liked this particular story, and so he made sure to roll his head in feigned boredom. "Even with all the pain, I was, like—" Lucy opened her mouth and made a stupendous snore sound worthy of a cartoon character. "It was nearly three in the morning when you decided to show your face."

She tossed back her hair and turned to the mirror. "And you didn't make a fuss, either. Doctor said he'd never seen a kid care less about being born. Slip, slap, and back to sleep."

"And then they put me in the box, right? In the glass box?"

"Yup. Because you were so small. And you didn't wake up for a week."

Edgar didn't remember any of it.

"Size of a dinner roll," Lucy said with a slight shudder. "And so white, I thought you were a friggin' ghost."

The boy looked up as his mother swiped a pink stick the color of cake frosting across her lips.

"Are you going out, Ma?"

"Yes, I am," she said. "Yes, I am."

She had a habit of answering certain questions twice. The first time, full voice, part of normal conversation; the second time, a more private matter, as if she were gauging the truth or untruth of what she'd said. She repeated words to see if she could believe them. The second round lacked conviction. To Edgar, the echo always seemed tainted by sadness.

None of this mattered to him, though. He liked to listen to her, even though he knew she was slippery. He knew the story of his sleepy birth was nothing more than a ploy to soften him toward bed. Edgar didn't hold it against her. Her tricks were the tricks of a child. Transparent. If she lied, so what? At least she wasn't boring. From her mouth shot forbidden words with a marksman's precision. And she had red hair—and, as far as Edgar was concerned, there wasn't another person on the whole of Earth who had red hair. No one, anyway, who could lay claim to what his mother possessed.

Plus, she had the most delicious voice. Like the lady on the peanut butter commercial, Edgar thought. You could actually hear the peanuts in her voice. You could practically *taste* them. Watching his mother fuss with her makeup, Edgar wanted to bark like a dog. He'd done it before, he was good at it. Sometimes it made her laugh, if she was in the right mood.

But she wasn't in the right mood. Edgar could tell. It wasn't just the candied lips (the unabashed color highlighting his mother's natural pout), it was the dress as well—so tight it made her breathless, like his grandmother when she climbed the stairs. His mother was nervous. And now she was putting on the shoes that sank hopelessly into lawns, if she wore them to picnics—which she did sometimes, to the old woman's chagrin. The shoes were red, shiny as plastic apples. Dorothy's shoes, Edgar thought. The good witch! The bark erupted, beyond his control.

"Stop that," Lucy said. "You wanna wake up you-know-who?"

"No," said Edgar. But then he did it again, this time adding a growl.

Even as Lucy glared at him, the boy could detect the smile held in check.

"You shouldn't even be up," she said. "But since you're here." She did a little turn in front of him. "How do I look?"

Bark.

Lucy smiled now without reservation, and then grazed the boy's cheek with her sticky mouth. "And I don't want you snooping around when Mr. S gets here. You hear me?"

They were always initials, the men. In respect for his father, Edgar supposed. His father who was dead, and who was always *Frank*. The other men were reduced to single letters, black flies over the bulk of his father's body. This was his mother's second date with Mr. S, who was a butcher. Edgar was astonished upon hearing it. It was like his mother was going out with a pig—or, even worse, a killer of pigs. From television, Edgar knew that there were machines one could employ to detect the microscopic bits of blood that were no doubt hiding on Mr. S's clothing. After committing a murder, a criminal always washed vigorously, but there was always a spot left somewhere, some glimmer of evidence, if you knew where to look.

Poor Ma, thought Edgar. A butcher, a killer of pigs.

"Are you cooking him dinner?"

"Don't be ridiculous. Does it look like I'm cooking him dinner? We're going out."

"Bed," she said, swatting the boy's bottom.

Edgar sauntered away in mock desolation, dragging his feet. When he turned to look at her from the doorway, she was lost again in the mirror, applying a second layer of frosting.

* * *

Edgar looked at himself in his own mirror. Pale skin, white hair, tired eyes a sea-glass shade of green. I should have oinked, he thought. He tried it out, but it wasn't nearly as good as the dog. He'd have to practice the pig. With his index finger he pushed up his nose. It was stunningly effective.

He was a small boy, skinny, with knobby knees that were constantly bumping into things. Wrists so thin the bones rose like the lurky eyes of an alligator. In movement he was awkward; in stillness he possessed a natural grace, remarkable van Eyck hands, a long neck worthy of Pontormo. But in the mirror all the boy saw was an insect. He didn't make sense; not to himself. Though he understood his paleness was a disease, it often seemed a curse. People stared. Plus, he lacked the meat of his fellow humans, the meat of his mother, his grandmother. He was more like the dead. More like his father.

"You don't eat," Lucy was always saying.

But he did eat. He made an effort, anyway.

"One pea at a time," Lucy once said to a friend.

"I do not!" Edgar had shouted. "I eat lots of peas at the *same* time."

When both women laughed, the boy stormed out of the room, nearly sick from the ferocity of his blushing.

"Leave him alone," the grandmother would say. She was even larger than his mother, but she didn't mind Edgar's bones. She didn't mind that he was more like the dead, considering the fact that the dead man in question, Edgar's father, was her own son.

The boy tiptoed into the hallway and peered into the old woman's room. She was asleep on her back, her great Jiffy-Pop bosom moving up and down with comforting regularity. He walked straight into the dark bedroom without making a sound. One of the good things about being an insect, Edgar thought: no one can hear you when you walk across the floor. Most people made a lot of noise. Most people stomped. His mother was a stomper. And, with one footfall heavier than the other—a telltale limp for which Edgar knew no tale—the sound was hers, and hers alone. You always knew when she was coming.

The old woman, on the other hand, for all her heft, could appear suddenly behind you, out of nowhere. If she weren't a person you loved, she might terrify you. "The creeper," Lucy called her. Sometimes Lucy jolted at the creeper's unexpected materializations and Edgar would have to suppress a laugh. It was funny to see his fearless mother jump at the sight of a fat old lady. It was a great routine. It never failed. Edgar wondered if the two of them rehearsed it while he was at school.

Entering his grandmother's bedroom at night (he'd done it before) felt like entering a cave where animals lived. He wasn't scared. A small white votive candle housed in a blue glass cup burned at all hours, and at night threw a living splash of light on the face of Mary. The whole room was enlivened in a gentle but peculiar way. The room seemed larger, and then smaller, and then, if you stood very still, you could feel the light moving on your body, making you part of the mysterious scheme. The candlelight was up to something, Edgar knew. He could feel its miraculous little brain ticking away.

The boy touched Mary's small plaster head. He liked the way her clasped hands warmed themselves over the fire, like the bums on Tulaney Avenue when the weather turned cold. Great sparking flames leaping from trash cans. "Don't stare," his grandmother would say if the two of them were walking by. But Edgar couldn't help himself. To him, the bums seemed wonderful, living, as they were, in their play town of cardboard boxes and rags and plastic bags. They were like Boy Scouts gone bad. One afternoon Edgar had locked eyes with a particularly ravaged man in a yellow ski jacket—a fringy red scarf wrapped around his head like a pirate. He'd winked at Edgar, making the boy blush. It almost felt as if the man had kissed him.

Now he waited for the Virgin to wink at him, and when she didn't (she never did), he made his way toward the old woman's bed. He was barely touching the earth. On nights like this, gravity had no power over Edgar. The laws were the laws of space: quixotic, effortless, dangerous. One wrong move, one wrong thought, and the world as you knew it would be whisked away, replaced by some grinning immensity. When he finally willed himself down, it was to the floor beside the bed. The thing he liked best was here: a night-light, a small disk of frosted glass, bearing, in delicate relief, the figure of an angel on a bridge. A tiny lightbulb the size of an almond, cleverly concealed behind the glass, brought the scene to life. The angel's dainty foot, toe pointed, hovered just above the bridge. It was a still picture, but Edgar didn't see it that way. He saw movement. He saw the angel descend, he saw her breathe.

Edgar rarely thought about his father when he looked at the angel, even though he knew—but only vaguely, a borrowed memory—that his father had died on a bridge. But that was a long time ago, before Edgar had yet to utter his first word. And so, to the boy, the father remained in the lump and shadow of a half-lived dream. His father was something at the edge of things, but he wasn't a person, exactly. There wasn't enough light behind him to cast his undoing into a satisfactory story. When his mother and grandmother talked about Frank, it was confusing. It was like the two women were talking about an imaginary friend—and there seemed to be some ongoing argument about ownership. Edgar couldn't participate in the game; he had no credentials, no leverage. It was infuriating.

In private, alone with her son, Lucy never mentioned Frank. The grandmother, on the other hand, was less cooperative. Sometimes she cornered the boy and spoke, in theatrical whispers, about her dead son. It was like a fairy tale. *Frankie*, she called him, sometimes *Francesco*—often with a cockeyed expression on her face. At such moments, Edgar wondered if his grandmother was a little dim, or possibly she was mad. "When he was your age," she would say, or, "When your father was little . . ." It made Edgar dizzy. It was like the old woman was playing with a time machine—and, even worse, she was trying to tempt Edgar inside. But Edgar didn't want to go with her to where this other boy lived, this fairy-tale boy who was supposedly his father: a lump, a limp body on a dark road the old woman was trying to flood with light.

"Uh-huh," Edgar would say. "Can I go outside?"

He didn't like to think about that stuff.

But now, as he sat before the night-light, he found himself wondering: what was the point of an angel on a bridge unless she was there to *save* you? Otherwise, she was just holding up traffic.

The old woman stirred in bed, but didn't wake. Edgar turned and watched her breathe. He could have easily climbed under the covers with her (she never minded), but, instead, he floated over to the bureau and opened the top drawer. *Don't creak,* he prayed, glancing at the Virgin for support. The top drawer was skinnier than the rest, like the pencil drawer in a desk, and it was filled with cards. Prayer cards. Small laminated rectangles, each with a flashy saint on one side, and, on the other, a name, some dates, and a prayer. They were all dead people! And though his grandmother was generally a very neat person, the cards in the drawer were a helter-skelter mess, as if she'd been playing a game of Go Fish. Edgar joined in the fun and shuffled them a bit, before picking one at random and slipping it into his pocket. Why? No reason. The drunkenness of not sleeping when you should be sleeping. It was his first theft.

After that, there was no stopping him. His eyes went straight to the bottle of Chanel N° 5. He loved its solid shape, the heavy glass stopper, the simple lettering, black on white. It could have said *Arsenic* or *Sulfur,* it belonged in a laboratory, or a storybook; it could have said DRINK ME. His grandmother had had it forever. It was ancient. Edgar knew this was something special. The amber liquid inside the hollow ice cube came from a source that no longer existed. It had to be preserved, which is why, he supposed, his grandmother never used it. For as long as he could remember, the bottle had remained half full. The level never varied. Still, half full meant half empty, which meant his grandmother had been less careful in the past, more certain things would last.

Edgar didn't *think* these things, exactly; he *felt* them. He felt that his grandmother had a past, sometimes merely by the way she turned her head, as if there were a breeze blowing through her hair. But there was no breeze—and certainly there was no hair. His grandmother was nearly bald and regularly wore a bandana on her head like a hoodlum.

The past was also in her closet, where there were outrageous dresses—some with tiny sparkles sewn in, some with beads. Dresses that, if she were to put on now, she'd split open like the Incredible Hulk when he turned green. Among the many photos on top of his grandmother's bureau, there was one in which the old woman was young and impossibly slim, with a cigarette in her hand and a sharp-fanged fox wrapped around her neck. It was all so strange. His grandmother had been alive such a long time that she had traded one face for another. Or perhaps someone had stolen the first one. Edgar knew nothing. The only feat of logic he managed (a good one) was that there had once been perfume-wearing days, and that, now, they were over. Anyway, she wouldn't miss a few drops.

As soon as Edgar touched the bottle (it was cold!), the old woman awoke, as if the boy had put his hand on her.

"What are you doing?"

"Nothing." He retracted his fingers.

"Why aren't you in bed? Is something wrong?"

The boy shook his head and drifted toward the old woman. There was no fear. He touched the blanket where it covered her arm.

"Where's your mother? She go out?"

Edgar knew better than to answer this question. He shrugged languorously. His grandmother didn't approve of the men. *Suitors,* she called them, even though most of them wore jeans. If she was ever downstairs when one of them came to claim Lucy, she retreated into the kitchen and made a very loud cup of instant coffee, clanging the spoon like a Salvation Army Santa wielding a bell.

Her pudgy red hand emerged from under the blanket and covered the boy's cold fingers with a blissful warmth. "Get me a glass of water, would you, sweetheart? That Chinese was salty."

Florence was referring to the cartons of food that Lucy had brought home for dinner. Such surprise attacks of to-go fare irked the old woman. She was the cook in the family, she cooked beautifully—who could deny it?—and the idea of restaurant food in her own house, well, it bordered on insult. Why couldn't she be permitted to cook every single meal of their lives? She was willing to do it. It was her joy.

At least the Chinese was tasty. She'd give it that. The old woman liked a little fire now and then, and had consumed the incendiary broccoli in chili sauce with formidable gusto. When she sat up, a prolonged burp rolled out of her. "*Oh,* it's repeating on me."

Edgar turned on the light in Florence's bathroom.

"Let the tap run for a minute," she called out, "or it'll be full of clouds."

Edgar knew the rules. When he returned with the water, it was crystalline. He sat on the edge of the bed while she drank the entire glass.

"*Ahhhh,* that hits the spot." The old woman's tongue darted in and out of her mouth in an intriguing lizard-like fashion.

"Tomorrow, I'm going to make meatballs," she said.

But tomorrow wasn't Sunday. Meatballs on a Thursday? Edgar sensed the competition. He knew his mother didn't care for meatballs. Too much fat. Once, she'd tried to convince the old woman to make them out of ground turkey, and the old woman had looked at his mother like she was insane. "Turkey? What do you mean?" It was as if Lucy had suggested she make them out of socks, out of sawdust. For days after the suggestion, when Lucy wasn't around, the old woman, in Edgar's presence, would shake her head and mutter, "Turkey, my foot."

Anyway, Edgar liked the meatballs. When his grandmother made them, she always put one, freshly fried, on a small white plate, before delivering the rest into the bubbling sauce. A special gift. A naked sauceless meatball, just for him.

"You're turning him into a real Italian," Lucy once joked.

"He *is* Italian," the old woman replied without levity.

"Half Italian," Lucy corrected. "I'm not Italian."

"No, you're not, dear." Upon which, the old woman put her hand on the boy's head and watched him eat his naked meatball.

Lucy was never up to fighting for her own team. The Polish. What had the Polacks ever done for her? These Italians had taken care of her, at least. And, besides, this was the old woman's house. Lucy had never meant to stay here all these years after her husband's death, but here she was. And there was the boy, happy, eating.

Actually, the boy was not undilutedly happy. His mother, his grandmother, yes, it was true: to be alone with either of them was sweetness itself. But combine them and things tightened, a constriction Edgar felt in his sensitive, divining throat. When the two women spoke to each other, Edgar felt their untrue voices somehow coming from inside his own body, as if he were the liar. But what was it all about? Why did their voices change in each other's presence? He saw a great deal at 21 Cressida Drive, but understood little. The first time he did the math and realized that there was no actual blood shared by his mother and his grandmother, it frightened him. Technically, they were strangers.

If Frank were around maybe it wouldn't be so bad, thought Edgar. Frank could take on some of the responsibility. But Frank was dead—and, as far as Edgar could see, dead people didn't do anything except get whispered about in kitchens. If there was a ghost, it was the name itself, hissed or swallowed, breathy air between the two women.

Both were widows. Another complexity they had in common. Edgar remembered the old woman's husband better than he remembered his own father, which wasn't saying much. Still, there were a few things he could manage to recall: the thick cloud of cigar smoke around his grandfather's La-Z-Boy; how the old man never called him by his name but referred to him only as *boy,* the word often shouted in a fairly startling tone. Sometimes the old man walked in circles in the yard, talking, it seemed, to himself. Edgar would watch from his bedroom window on the second floor. Even at five, the boy knew it was possible the old man wasn't talking to himself, but to Frank.

People were still talking about Frank, in one way or another. Edgar wasn't easily fooled. Brought up in a haunted house, he had a keen sense of when someone was conversing with the dead. A person could be stirring red sauce or putting on lipstick when, in fact, what she was *really* doing was walking through a cemetery. Widows! They were almost like witches, weren't they? They were deathy. They had secrets.

Edgar reflected on the fact that he had never seen his mother, *not once,* set foot in his grandmother's bedroom. Edgar couldn't even imagine her here, especially at night, with the Virgin rubbing her hands over the flame and the angel floating in her dress of light. He knew it was not an atmosphere in which his mother would be able to breathe. He knew, if she walked in here, she would immediately fall dead.

"What are you thinking about, Mr. Big Eyes?"

He looked at the old woman from his perch at the side of the bed. She was already falling back asleep.

"Gramma?"

"Yes?" she said. She was patient with the boy, with his silent staring spells. With his darling little thoughts, which is how she imagined the things that moved inside his head. In fact, she saw them, the boy's thoughts, little blue wheels rolling over sunny pastures. She was drifting off.

"Tell me," the old woman said. But her eyes were already closed.

"Can I have some of the perfume?" Edgar whispered.

"Mmmmh," the old woman sighed, fading.

"I can?"

Edgar knew she was gone. Her breathing changed. He watched her bosom float away on sea-waves. There was no embarrassment. He knew her body better than his own. Better than his mother's, certainly. It was the old woman's bed he climbed into after a bad dream. Nightmares weren't uncommon with the boy, and the old woman always welcomed him, should he gently wake her, at any hour, with his delicate hand.

Lucy knew. Sometimes she'd hear the boy gasp, coming out of one of his dreams. She'd hear his bed creak as he got up to find comfort, not with her.

She didn't mind the boy's choice. She had enough trouble sleeping as it was. The old woman slept like a stone. Not that Lucy would ever prevent the boy from climbing into her bed. She would accept her duty, gladly, should Edgar ever call her to it. But he spent more time with the old woman; certain tracks got laid, certain habits. Was Lucy jealous? No. No. She didn't mind the physical fact of Edgar's choice, but sometimes she just didn't care for the *idea* of it. There were nights, of course, when she craved a body next to her. Yet, even then, she knew the boy wouldn't be enough to ease her loneliness. He might make it worse, his skinny sleeping body instinctively burrowing into hers for warmth. What room did she have for such innocence? The bodies she craved tended toward violence.

Edgar eased himself off his grandmother's bed and went straight for the bottle. He had permission, didn't he? He touched it (still cold); he lifted it and pressed it to his cheek. The ghost of a scent lingered on the glass. When he removed the stopper and pointed his nose toward the opening, he knew to close his eyes. Powder and flowers and spice—and now sweet grass, sweet sweat. He tilted the bottle and wet his finger, quickly carrying the precious fluid to the taut skin just behind his right ear, then behind his left, as he'd seen women do on television. The liquid tingled, a subtle electrification, as the scent changed, bloomed, became an extension of the boy himself. It was Edgar; Edgar electrified by flowers. The charge was exhilarating, and he could feel the rush of his blood. He stole some more, just a bit, and swiped it across the front of his neck.

Time stopped, as it rarely does. The boy breathed, unnoticed by life or death. Breathed himself into himself. It was as if there were two of him, and each kissed the other, agreeing on something. Exactly what, neither could say. They could only say: yes, this. *This.*

* * *

He stood in the hallway. Eight years old, sleepy—someone should have sent him to bed. He looked toward his room, and sent himself.

But wait. A burble of laughter. Or was it an owl? Edgar leaned against the wall, listening. The sound was coming from downstairs. He moved toward the banister. The owl was his mother.

But the sound was wrong. His mother's real laugh was something else, flames shooting from a ten-story building. Nothing could put it out but the fire itself. And if you stood too close, you were doomed. It was a leaping, contagious cackle. But downstairs, now, it sounded like a doll's laugh. High-pitched but breathy, like a paper horn, spiking at intervals, steady and mechanical. Maybe it wasn't his mother. As he walked down the stairs, he wondered if he was in the right house. Sleepiness was doing funny things to the pictures on the walls. Where there should have been a painting of a sailboat, there was now a painting of a huge sunlit cleaver emerging from the sea. At the bottom of the stairs, he caught a glimpse of his grandmother's black piano, an impeccably polished upright that seemed to have gained some weight since last he saw it. He regarded it as if for the first time—the keys like loose teeth, bright whites and rotting blacks that could fall out at any moment. Maybe that's why no one played it anymore. Someone, he noticed, had turned down a few of the framed photographs that rested on top.

And the boy could smell cigarettes, and cigarettes weren't allowed in the house. After the old man had died, Florence had said, *enough* (her exact words were "I'm done with that stink."). His mother was supposed to smoke on the porch.

Hee hee hee, went the doll, as Edgar entered the living room. Mr. S quickly pulled his meaty hand from between Lucy's legs.

"Eddie," he boomed from the couch. "Eddie, my man!"

Lucy tugged at her dress. There was a sweating bottle of booze on the coffee table, the vodka she kept in the freezer (it never froze, to Edgar's amazement).

"What are you doing up? What did I tell you?" Lucy brushed back her hair with her fingers. Her pink lips were slightly smeared.

"I thought you were going out." Edgar didn't look at his mother. He watched the cigarette in the ashtray, watched the forbidden smoke rise in curls of script. "I wasn't spying on you. I didn't know it was you."

"Who else would it be?" said Lucy, standing, putting her hands on her hips like a sixteen-year-old.

How old was she anyway? Edgar wasn't sure. Thirty, maybe, but she looked a lot younger, standing like that, and with her lips smeared like she'd been eating jam.

The butcher stood, as well. Edgar couldn't see any blood on his clothing. Still, he wasn't pleased when the man moved toward him.

"He's all right. Just checking on his mom."

The man touched the boy's head with the same hand that had been between Lucy's legs. As well as inside pigs and chickens and cows. Edgar froze.

"*Whoa,*" the butcher said. "What do you smell like?" He leaned in and began to sniff.

"Na-nothing," Edgar stuttered, taking two steps back.

But the butcher pursued him. "Is that perfume?"

"No. I spilled something."

Edgar suddenly wished he could fart. He had heard that there was a boy in his school who could fart on command. Edgar couldn't even manufacture a burp, a skill that every other boy in the world seemed to possess. Supposedly it was just a matter of swallowing air, but how did one swallow air? Edgar pressed his knees together and prayed for flatulence.

Lucy was sniffing now, too. The boy waited for a snotty comment from a sixteen-year-old, but, instead, his mother smiled. Her face relaxed, as if something important had been clarified. A tiny *whoosh* of air streamed from her nose. Was she laughing at him? She leaned down and kissed the boy's lips. She stared into his eyes and stroked his hair. Edgar knew she was drunk. They had shared odd moments like this before—moments in which the world dropped away and it was just the two of them, half asleep, with a nervous red thread quivering between their chests.

"Oh, baby," she said, shaking her head. More air came out of her nose, three short bursts of it. Sometimes, to Lucy, it all seemed so absurd. Again, she kissed the boy. Her burden. Her funny little albino fruitcake.

"I should get going," the butcher said.

"Hold your horses," Lucy barked. And then sweetly, softly, to Edgar: "Would you please go to fucking bed?"

The boy nodded, but didn't move. Why was his face burning? Why did he feel like crying?

Lucy turned, put out her cigarette, and grabbed the butcher's arm. "Come on. I want to go to Larson's."

"We can have a drink at my place," he suggested.

"I don't want to be in a *house*," Lucy said. "I want to be *out*." She heard her voice—sharp and ridiculous—as if it were coming from a woman standing beside her. Why was she getting so riled up? The man was going to think she was a bitch. She adjusted her dress and, in an effort to get back on track, slipped two fingers between the buttons of the butcher's shirt and caressed his belly.

Edgar watched them as they put on their coats in the foyer. He waited for his mother to look back, but she didn't. Only the butcher looked back. He stared at the boy and offered no discernible gesture of farewell. Edgar closed his eyes, hoping the man could no longer smell the scent that, amazingly, almost diabolically, still lingered upon his skin.

2

Two Wineglasses and a Banana

Annabelle ("Nelly") Tortelli (b. 1934–d. 1946). Edgar looked at the prayer card and did the math: twelve years old. Possibly eleven, if she'd died before her birthday. Death was no softy; he might have claimed Nelly the night before her party—the ice cream cake (*Happy 12th!*) already in the freezer. The thought of such an unfortunately timed demise stuck in the boy's mind. He pictured a white-faced girl, arms crossed in a coffin, surrounded by stacks of elaborately wrapped presents. Surely God would let Nelly open them after the mourners had left. The girl's white fingers undoing the red ribbons; the ripped paper thrown into the convenient wastebasket of the coffin. It was possible. What the dead did behind the backs of the living was anyone's guess.

At breakfast, Edgar was prepared to ask his grandmother about the girl, but as soon as he placed the card on the table he remembered that he'd filched it. It was a small treason; still, he couldn't risk its exposure. His grandmother was smart. Give her one clue and she kept sniffing. Of course, he'd washed thoroughly this morning, but it was impossible to know if all traces of the perfume had been erased. His moment with the butcher had left him with a peculiar sense that it might be wise to keep secrets. A person's desires, the things a person found beautiful, were probably best kept to oneself. Hadn't he learned that already? You couldn't just say, "Oh, how pretty," when you saw the daffodils on your teacher's desk, which is exactly what he'd done one morning last spring. The words had popped out of his mouth unexpectedly—a genuine rush of delight and admiration overcoming his native shyness. He hadn't realized he'd said the words to anyone but the daffodils until Ralphie Francovilla clasped his hands together and exclaimed, in a fluty voice and with a flourish of limp wrists, "Oh yes, very pretty!" Three boys standing behind Ralphie had leaned their heads together to form a tight coven of laughter.

Boys could not use the word *pretty*. Nor could they mess with Chanel Nº 5. Edgar knew that now by the way the butcher had practically recoiled at the sudden loveliness of his aroma. As the old woman approached with a carton of milk, Edgar reclaimed the prayer card and slipped it into his pocket.

She poured the milk over the boy's cereal and sat down beside him, with her cup of coffee, to watch him eat. It was a habit of hers Edgar generally found endearing, but today he was uncomfortable under her gaze, nervous. Even those who loved you best were bound to find the flaws if they stared long enough. To lose his grandmother's favor would be the end of everything. Unlike his mother, whose light flashed on him only intermittently, like the beam of a lighthouse, the old woman was nothing less than the sun. The idea that she might think less of him filled the boy with shame.

How could he have known that were he to desire more of the perfume, she would have given him every last drop? She would have rinsed his white hair with it. She would have taken her time machine back to the beginning and asked the priest to christen the boy in the stuff. If Edgar wanted Chanel Nº 5 on his cereal instead of milk, she would have found the request difficult to deny. More than anything, she wanted the boy to be happy. The way her son had not been happy. Well, yes, he'd been a cheerful child. A clever boy with a great capacity for wonder, not unlike Edgar. It was the end, and the road approaching it, that had been so disastrous—a shadowy chaos that, still, she could not penetrate. When she awakened this morning, Frank was clearly in the house—some part of him pulsing in the darkness.

"Happy birthday," she'd said. One had to mark such occasions, even if the words felt like nothing more than a stone dropped into a bottomless well. She wondered if Lucy would even remember. The girl was getting more and more forgetful, it seemed, where Frank was concerned.

"Do you want more milk on that?" The flakes in Edgar's bowl were looking a little dry.

The boy shook his head—a pale replica of his father.

"Have more," the old woman said, pouring the milk. "You'll choke on it if you don't have enough liquid."

That Edgar looked so much like the young Frank was a complicated blessing. It felt like a second chance. But it felt dangerous, as well, like a time bomb. The last few months of Frank's life, his face had become unrecognizable— warped, the old woman supposed, from the weight of the terrible invisibles that had pursued him.

But what were they, these thoughts that had made her son's hands tremble?

Even his eyes had trembled, like compass needles turning in dread toward some dark and unimpeachable north.

After the fact, people had always put it too simply. Frank Fini had gone crazy. Florence resented it when it was summed up in this way. Too tidy. As if you could put your son's death in a filing cabinet and be done with it. Even her ancient cousin Sabina, Frank's godmother and a woman stitched from kindness itself, had succumbed to the cruel conveniences of such language. *Pazzo pazzo pazzo,* almost as if she were spitting into the boy's grave. It was a ridiculous word. Who wasn't a little crazy? No one, that's who. The old woman had her eyes open. She saw the housewives talking to themselves in grocery stores, the businessmen gesturing and shouting as they walked alone down the street. "They're on the phone," Edgar would tell her, but she could never *see* a phone. "It's in their *ear*," Edgar would say. The boy had a vivid imagination.

She looked at him now, across the table, eating his cereal in such a deliberate and careful way. *Oh,* if she could have a tall glass of this child every morning, she would live forever. Sometimes she worried that her love for Edgar was too strong, a covetous earthly love, a love against God, a love to reclaim lost things. But what love wasn't that? What love wasn't a reward to counter an old wrong? Anyway, it wasn't something she could control. How she felt about the boy was how she felt. Love was love, and it was always a monster.

She thought of the others. Her dear sisters, all gone. Edna in the car crash with Jimmy. Gussie, peacefully in her bed just two years ago. Cynthia, horribly, with that cancer in her womanhood. Her childhood friends, Grace, Pauline, Nelly—sweet Nelly! The old woman hadn't thought of her in years. The dead girl's face fluttered across Edgar's, and then vanished.

Oh, and Pio, of course, her husband. She tended to forget about him, God rest his soul. It was a devil of a thing to admit, but Pio was not the great love of her life. The boy was. This boy, here at the table. Pio was stormy, quick-tempered, with a foul mouth. Frank had been the same.

That this quiet child had come from wolves was something the old woman marveled over. He was like one of those tiny figurines in the gift shops: a boy in a straw hat sitting on the edge of a wishing well, a fragile and lovely apparition made of porcelain. The old woman's heart used to leap when Frank would toss the infant into the air, practically to the ceiling—or in the yard, high enough to scare the birds from the trees. "Up we go!" Frank would shout—Lucy watching from the sidelines, sipping at something. "Up we go!" The baby smiling, oblivious to the danger. After three or four throws, the old woman was always a nervous wreck. "Stop," she'd plead. But Frank wouldn't let up. "Make him stop," she'd say, turning to Lucy for support. But the girl was of no use. She'd been no more than a child herself back then, and the old woman could see that she loved her husband best when he veered toward danger. Frank turned on all the girl's lights and made her blind. "I can't make him stop," she would say, smiling, shrugging. And it was true, she couldn't. No one could stop him. Frank had had a mind of his own. Even at five, he'd been his own boss. A terror, really, when she thought about it. His teenage years had practically killed her.

Lucy had been wild, too—was still wild—there was no denying that. She'd been fuel to Frank's fire. Her son would have been better off with a cold woman, not with such a burning mess. When she was first going with Frank, the girl always looked like she had a fever, hot from something that raged inside her, a force that seemed half joy and half desperation. Frank had something like this, as well, and the two of them set each other off. Bonnie and Clyde! Passion was good up to a point, but too much of it was asking for trouble. Who's to say Lucy hadn't spurred him on? Not intentionally, of course; but with all her natural lustiness and her feverish love for Frank, it made too much seem possible, and then a man was bound to become disappointed. There had been something animal-like about their love, something primitive. Whenever Frank latched on to Lucy's waist in that seize-the-world way of his, the girl would erupt into a shriek of laughter that disturbed the old woman.

Florence had never been to the mountaintop of sexual love, as she imagined Frank and Lucy had. Once, in Dr. Faustini's waiting room, the old woman read an article that suggested the finale was like a great wave, and that a woman could ride it very high indeed. But when Florence had sex with Pio, she always managed to stay on the boat, no matter how furiously her husband rocked her. She refused to go into the water, to lose herself in babbling liquidity. She feared that kind of abandonment. From her locked perspective she'd only seen danger in what Lucy had drawn out of her son. Plus, the girl was younger than Frank by a good five years. And with that red hair, well, who wouldn't be bewitched?

Not that she blamed the girl, really. There was no one to blame. That was the only way to look at it, if you wanted to get on with things. The girl was still in the house, after all. The girl was the boy's mother. And she'd had a hard time, supposedly, as a child. Frank had mentioned something once about the girl's father not being kind. When Florence had gently pressed her son for more details, Frank had said, "Let's just leave it at that."

Unkind. The old woman shook her head. The word still weighed on her after all these years. She wondered about her own cruelties. Had there been any? Well, kindness wasn't always the easiest thing in the world. Sometimes it took a lifetime to learn.

Why was his grandmother looking at him so oddly, with her mouth slack and slightly crooked? Edgar was aware of the fact that, sometimes, something popped in old people's brains, and they just froze, unable to move or speak. He'd seen a "Health Corner" segment on the evening news in which there'd been an interview with a man who'd survived one of these brain pops. The man could only talk out of one side of his mouth, like a bad ventriloquist.

"You okay, Gramma?"

The old woman smiled. The little mind reader, he didn't miss a trick. She slapped her hands against the tops of her thighs, willing her horse into the future. "*So.* What are you doing in school today? Tell me."

The boy lifted the nub of his left shoulder and then let it drop. "Nothing."

"You must be doing something."

"I have *Art.*" His eyes went big with the awfulness of this fact.

"I thought you liked Art," the old woman said.

"I like to *doodle,*" Edgar explained. "I don't like to *draw.*"

"Oh, okay." She nodded. "What's the difference?"

How could he make her understand? It was complicated. He sighed, looked the old woman straight in the eye.

"She makes us—"

"She who, the teacher?"

"Yes. Mrs. Blessum."

"That's her name?"

"*Gramma.*"

"What?"

"I'm trying to *explain.*"

"Sorry, I'll zip it." She did the zipper thing across her mouth, which the boy appreciated.

"She makes us do pictures of things she puts on a table. A teapot, or last week it was two wineglasses and a *banana.*"

Edgar waited for his grandmother to respond to this absurdity, but she only murmured through tightly pressed lips.

"That's *drawing*," the boy continued. "Having to do what's on the table. Doodling is when you make stuff up."

The old woman widened her eyes into fonts of understanding and offered a sympathetic grunt. In truth, she had no idea what the child was talking about. *Two wineglasses and a banana?* Is that what he'd said? As she watched the boy gesture, so serious to make his point, the world shifted again. An old scene with Frank, in this very kitchen, rushed at her. He, too, had said something incomprehensible. Something about his teeth, about how the teeth inside his mouth were not his, that someone had put them there. At first she'd thought her son was making a joke. But it wasn't a joke. To Frank, the teeth apparently had been a matter of life or death. He'd grown frantic. Some gesture of Edgar's, a sharp chopping motion of his hand, was familiar. The old woman's heart stopped for what seemed like several seconds.

"You can talk now," the boy said. What was going on with her today? He didn't like it when she had trouble breathing.

"Gramma."

"Yes, yes," she snapped. "I heard you."

She was scolding the wrong child. She came to her senses and softened her voice. "You better just do what this Mrs. Blessus—"

"Bless-*um*."

She tapped the boy's hand. "You better just do what the teacher says. Why make trouble?"

Edgar knew his grandmother was right. Besides, he'd be incapable of contradicting Blessum. He was frightened of her. She had wrinkles, oddly, only on one side of her face. She also had long red nails that she tapped on her desk while waiting impatiently for everyone to draw the exact same thing (it was like a drawing factory!). When she finally made her inspections, she'd point a single red nail at your picture and say things like, *Why is your banana so big? It makes the wineglasses look like eye cups.* This exact criticism had been directed at Edgar. Blessum had no sympathy for interpretation—and what were eye cups anyway?

"I always do what she says," said Edgar. And yet, it was torture, *torture,* having to draw what was in front of you. It was almost worse than having to write about what you did during the summer, or being asked to do a book report. Edgar felt uneasy when forced by adults to look backwards, to give his attention to what he'd already done or seen. Sometimes a teacher would spend hours talking about things that happened hundreds of years before you were even born. Edgar preferred the future. He thought of the old woman's time machine, and right there, at the breakfast table, he made a deal with himself: were he ever to get his hands on such a device, he would program it only to go forward.

"You can draw your own things at home," his grandmother said. "I'll get you some more of those big pads you like."

"Not the real big ones," Edgar said. Because, once, his grandmother had given him an extra-large sketch pad, almost as big as a tabletop, and the boy had felt overwhelmed. His tiny drawings had seemed to float in the middle of a huge white emptiness. Faces and horses and flowers, all looking like they'd just been ejected from a spaceship. He'd felt compelled to draw decorative borders, like fences, to protect them. It never occurred to him to make larger pictures. The pieces of the world, as Edgar saw them, were small and precise. He was, by nature, a miniaturist.

"The pads I like are about this big." He showed her with his hands.

"And the ones I like are about *this* big," the old woman replied, placing her hands on both sides of the boy's head and kissing him. It was true affection, as well as a sly move to change the subject. Because, on second thought, maybe the boy didn't need any more sketch pads. He spent too much time scribbling as it was. On his bed for hours, with his head down and his pencil scratch-scratch-scratching like a dog with fleas. Too much time alone wasn't good for anyone. The old woman tried to recall if Frank had been a scribbler. Nothing came to mind. Though, of course, as a child, Frank had always kept his bedroom door shut (half the time it was locked), and so who knew what the hell he'd been doing in there. And back then she hadn't been a snooper, as she was now. It was a skill Florence picked up late in life.

During the day, when Edgar was at school and Lucy off at work, the old woman cleaned the house—and, really, the only way to do a good job was to go through everything thoroughly. It was inevitable you were going to cross a line into other people's private realms. People kept messy drawers; someone had to tidy them. But not too much, or there'd be accusations. Sometimes Florence found herself lazily fingering Lucy's undergarments. The girl had a number of fancy pieces with lacy edits the old woman suspected had little to do with ventilation. The stuff looked cheap, but probably cost an arm and a leg.

One day, the old woman lifted an unfolded T-shirt, wrongly stored in the top drawer of Lucy's bedside table, and was confronted by one of those devices shaped like a man's thing. She stared at it, shocked by its unnecessary realism and vascular detail. Using the T-shirt as protection, she picked it up cautiously, as if touching the thing might arouse it further. When her hands began to shake, she wondered if she'd forgotten to take her blood pressure pills. She allowed no other reason for her unsteadiness. She thrust the device back into the drawer and covered it with the T-shirt. By now her legs were shaking, too. She sat down on Lucy's bed.

Did the girl think of Frank when she used it? Or was it simply a nameless appendage, simply pleasure itself, untethered from humanity? Florence put her hand over her mouth, as if the shame and squalor of the world were contagious. There was something wanton, ruthless, about stealing pleasure for yourself alone, without the body of the beloved upon you. No matter that you might no longer love the beloved, or that he might not exist anymore. He was still her husband, he still had his rights—even after death he had them.

For several weeks after discovering the man-thing, Florence was covertly furious at Lucy and unable to look her in the eye. When she would see the girl leave the house in some provocative getup (the red silk sheath or that glittery gum-wrapper miniskirt), the old woman was beside herself with rage—which only partially diverted her awareness from the obvious hypocrisy. Because, of course, Florence had dressed differently once. When she was younger, she wouldn't have been caught dead in these shapeless muumuus of her later years.

Long ago—it seemed another lifetime—Florence had made her own dresses. Brilliant creations modeled after outfits she'd seen in movie magazines. Everyone had remarked on them. She was gifted, all the girls said. *Look how she put that one line of beads at a jaunty angle. Look at that marvelous stitching on the padded shoulders, almost like butterfly wings. Would you make one for me, Flo?*—how many times had she heard that? Who knows, she might have made a name for herself. *House of Florence.* She'd had a pipe dream once. Occasionally, she'd made a piece for someone else, selling it for barely enough to cover her expenses. That tarty rich girl, Honey Fasinga, had ordered nearly a dozen, and had been gung-ho to help Florence open a shop.

Blond, stick-thin Honey, who seemed to exist in a mysteriously mobile blur of Hollywood mood lighting, had even convinced her terrifyingly mustachioed mafioso father to agree to a loan. But the truth was, Florence had little interest in the marketplace. She was simply a plain girl who wanted the pleasure of a few extra sequins.

She'd looked good, though. Plus, she'd always worn gloves, which was of course quite stylish—though her real motive had been to cover her ruined hands, boiled red from her job at Consolidated Laundry. When Pio was courting her, he told her she was the best-dressed girl he'd ever seen—and he'd seen the French girls in Paris after the war.

But once they were married, whenever she would put on one of her creations, he said she looked like a harlot; what would the other husbands think? And so, slowly, over time, she found things less flattering to her figure—and her figure, ignored for so many years, finally packed up and trotted off, leaving her with a body she didn't recognize, a body that was best covered by a dress that was little more than a tent.

Yet, when she regarded Lucy in something flattering (too flattering, perhaps), she always noted to herself the difference between the girl's sartorial impulse and that of her own youth. For Florence, the dresses had been merely skins, they'd had nothing to do with any deeper desires; when she'd put on such dresses, she certainly never planned on taking them off in the presence of a man. But Lucy wore her dresses as if they were nakedness itself. The girl's body wrapped in fabrics that would no doubt dissolve in the rain or blow off in a stiff breeze. Often the word *harlot* came to mind, and Florence was nothing if not confused by the shell game of her memory. When clarity descended it came down like law. A widow was a widow, no matter how young. You had to give up certain things. Put out the lights, cut your hair, hang your old skins at the back of the closet.

Later, in the midst of another deep cleaning, she finds a picture in the girl's room, hidden under a neat pile of tennis socks. A hazy snapshot, the young lovers in bathing suits, their backs to a wind-pitched sea; Lucy's hair blowing straight into Frank's face, their mouths open wide, as if shrieking, and their bodies bent by a laughter so forceful that Florence is tempted to put the photograph to her ear like a seashell. Such a lovely picture of her son—and Lucy had saved it. For this, she forgives the girl all the rest—for a while, at least. She only wishes she had found the photograph in the same drawer as the male appendage—though she stops herself from reflecting on why this should seem proper.

After the photo, she vowed that she would never snoop again. Only innocently in Edgar's room, where it was her duty. When she cleaned the boy's sunny little room that faced the garden, she hunted out not only dust and dirty socks, but demons as well. The sins of the father. Evidence of inappropriate tendencies—or what did they call them now, *genes*—that might have slipped like an infinitesimal school of fish into the boy's body. Which is precisely why she regretted having offered to buy the child more of those sketch pads. One afternoon she had paused the vacuum and leaned down to pick one up from beside his bed. She paged through the boy's fancies—quickly at first, but then with a vague, slow-moving dread. The sketches seemed innocent enough, but the years of Frank's illness had turned the old woman into a dark magpie, always on the lookout for any bright rumple of strangeness, any flash or glitter of unwholesomeness in the people she loved. Edgar did seem to have a fondness for drawing men with beards. Was that normal? Who did he know with a beard? Florence couldn't think of anyone. Well, they might not be real men; the boy might have made them up—a thought that offered little relief. On various pages of the pad, there were at least a dozen attempts at the subject, most of them crossed out with distressing, multi-lined *X*s. When she came, at last, to a lovely hilly landscape with oversized flowers and a generous sun whose rays stretched all the way to the hills, she allowed herself to smile. For heaven's sake, there was nothing to worry about. She knew instinctively that there was only goodness in this child. His thoughts were pure; you could smell it on him. A freshness like white sheets baked in the sun.

Still, she had to remain vigilant. There were forces that came from beyond the logical, malevolent forces that preyed on the innocent. Frank's unraveling had had the effect of turning Florence's mildly superstitious Christianity into something darker, more medieval. Happy children, especially the dreamy ones, were watched and waited for by a ruinous vengefulness that existed below the threshold of the human. She knew this because she had seen it. She had suffered it.

In this way, her thoughts went back and forth: between worry and faith, between the black buzz of Frank's illness (an invisible insect still trapped in the house) and the clear bell-tone of Edgar's purity. At the center of this schism lay the clear understanding that it was her job to keep the boy safe, to stand between him and all things of questionable merit. She felt she had the power to accomplish this because she was now an old woman and free from all cares relating to herself. Her life was lived in service to the child, and in this humility she believed herself invincible. Sometimes her blood surged with such thunderous devotion that all fear disintegrated, as if struck by Zeus's lightning bolt. Let the boy doodle, she decided magnanimously. His clever little scribbles had nothing to do with Frank. Why, he probably gets his talent from me, she thought, remembering her dresses.

Edgar watched Florence's face twitch, and wondered if it had something to do with his mother. It often did. Before he'd come downstairs for breakfast, he'd poked his nose into his mother's bedroom—and though it was much too early for her to be up, she'd already made her bed and left the house.

* * *

Actually, Lucy hadn't made it home yet. She was still with the butcher. As Edgar walked out the front door, heading for school, Lucy opened her eyes for the first time that day. She was wrapped in ham-colored sheets, marred here and there with pale blotches from a careless use of bleach. Lucy noted the damage and wondered if Ron slept with lots of women. Not that it mattered. He'd worn a condom—and the sheets, though blotchy, smelled clean. Lucy slipped out from under the man's tremendous arm and shimmied over to fetch her cigarettes from the nightstand. She smoked, and felt unexpectedly well. The sex had been good—loud and buoyant—and she could tell, from the only moderate throbbing in her temples, that the hangover would be manageable.

Why was it, Lucy wondered, that sex after drinking always seemed to temper the next day's sickness? As if the sex somehow burned away the poison. Or maybe what it burned away was the sadness, the feeling of waste. More likely, it was simply the collision of bodies, the violence of it, that brought a mind back to its senses. Lucy imagined the effect would be pretty much the same if, after a few too many drinks, you were to drive your car into a tree. You might wake up with a broken arm and a gruesome gash across your forehead, but the hangover would probably be minimal.

Lucy turned to look at the tree she'd run into last night. Ron Salvatore, the butcher. *Salvatore's Meats.* Lucy giggled. Would she ever be able to drive by that sign again without blushing? She always felt girlish after sex. Somehow it enabled her to stretch her mind gently toward the future. Not stupidly, of course, not with any great ambition or specific longing, but with a more general feeling that her moment had not passed, that the angels (or, at least, men) were still watching her.

Ha! She couldn't believe she'd slept with a fat man. Well, he wasn't fat, exactly. He was just extremely large. But it was all firm—even muscular. And at nearly seven feet tall (to Lucy's five foot five), he was practically a giant. Not to mention another Italian. She couldn't escape these people. New Jersey was full of them. She flicked her ash into an empty wineglass and smiled. The way he'd growled unabashedly during their multiple collisions. It was exactly what she'd needed. She hadn't had sex this good since Frank died. There had been other men, of course, in the last few years, but they lacked skill. For all of Frankie's faults and weaknesses, he was a master of pleasure— knew how to inflict it. Lucy ran her free hand slowly over her belly in the same way her husband used to do, so lightly that it caused her whole body to shiver. She lit another cigarette and dragged deeply. Time had passed so quickly, while she wasn't looking. How old was she now, anyway? Thirty-four?

That's exactly what she was, but she pretended she couldn't remember.

God, she'd been so innocent, practically a virgin, when she'd first slept with Frank. Even after all these years—seven since he'd died—he still seemed to have possession of her. There'd been only one boy before Frank—a single incident at a party—but Lucy never counted that. The sex had been unpleasant; she'd barely been conscious. But with Frank she'd felt like a treasure chest, full of exquisite things she'd never fathomed were inside her. She was a richness into which he'd plunged his hands, his tongue, his cock. It was strange, at first, to be the object of someone's greed. To be idolized, adored. Over time, it had actually changed the shape of her face. Before Frank, she hadn't been beautiful. It was a gift the bastard had given her. If he was glaring down at her now as she lay beside a virile giant, well, it was his own damn fault. He could have stayed. She would never have strayed from his bed.

She shrugged off these thoughts. Her body was still a marvel of contentment. Someone had touched her again in a way that made birds fly through her stomach. Not butterflies; it was more than a nervous flutter. These were big-winged creatures swooping down off high cliffs. She glanced at the clock. An hour yet before she had to be at work. Maybe she'd get up and make some breakfast. Surely there'd be some nice bacon in the butcher's fridge. Ron lived just above his shop. A man with a good supply of meat in barking distance from the bedroom—not a damn thing wrong with that, she thought, as she swung herself lightly off the bed and slapped her hips with an easy, offhanded affection. The angels, who had thought this affection dead, took note of it, and followed Lucy into the kitchen.

*　*　*

Distracted momentarily with the mother, the guardians ignored the child, and he tripped, dropping the prayer card he was trying to read as he walked.

> *God of all mystery, whose ways are beyond understanding,*
> *Lead us, who grieve at this untimely death—*

Toni-Ann Hefti dashed from her yard and snatched up the card, which had slid across the pavement. "Mine," she said. "Mine now."

Edgar stood, brushed himself off. "No, Toni-Ann," he said, holding out his hand and waiting for the girl to return his property.

The girl shook her head and smiled. She had a terrifying, freewheeling face that stretched expressions to their limits. Her smile showed too much of the inside of her mouth. Her tongue, today, was purple. Grape juice, hoped Edgar. Though, with retarded people, who knew? It might be house paint.

"It's my grandmother's," said Edgar.

"Find-uz keep-uz," said the girl.

"But you didn't find it. I dropped it."

Such logic, though, didn't work on Toni-Ann. She smiled again and tilted her massive head. She was more like an animal than a person. Edgar leaned back, hoping she wasn't going to touch him.

Toni-Ann liked Edgar, even though he'd never done anything to claim her affection. Sometimes the girl snuck up from behind and hugged him, lifting the little boy and planting a wet kiss on the back of his neck. It horrified Edgar. Retarded people had terrible manners. She was probably at least fourteen, but his grandmother had explained that people like Toni-Ann had the minds of infants. She also had told Edgar that such people were dangerous. The Heftis lived next to the Finis, and the old woman always warned the boy to steer clear of the fence if Toni-Ann happened to be playing in her yard.

"Ed-guh," she said now, running a hand through her hair like a demented movie star. She had a weird kind of power, a booming voice, painfully strong hands, and a hairline that seemed to start just above her eyes. "Sign of an idiot," the grandmother once noted. "They tend to be hairy."

Still, Edgar was fascinated by the girl. Though why did she always have to get so close? At the right distance, he'd be able to love her more, the way he knew he should. Because you have to have pity on poor souls like that, his grandmother always said.

Toni-Ann was looking at the prayer card now, scanning the text. Could idiots read? Edgar wasn't sure.

"Nelly," she suddenly said with astonishing clarity. But then she faltered. "To . . . To . . . Torrrrrr," dragging out the *r* like a car that wouldn't start.

Edgar watched her struggle, but it was too painful. "Tortelli," he finally said. "Nelly Tortelli."

Toni-Ann giggled. And, really, Edgar had to agree: it was a funny name. As he smiled at the girl, her own smile doubled in size, and her laughter increased to frightening proportions. It was like water shooting out of the ground, like a geyser—a kind of joy Edgar could barely comprehend.

"Toni-Ann, get your ass in here!" Mrs. Hefti called from the doorway. She was wearing a bulky yellow robe that looked like something made from inflated swimming pool rafts. "Toni-Ann!"

The girl's face went blank. She put the edge of the prayer card into her purple mouth and scurried off toward the house. Edgar watched her slip past her mother, who continued to stand in the doorway, looking up as if she had a question about the trees.

"How are you, Edgar?" she called out.

The boy offered a little wave and opened his mouth. But he was too shy to shout across the immense green sea of the woman's lawn.

"What?" Mrs. Hefti said, putting her hand to her ear as if she were going deaf.

Edgar shook his head and moved his lips to no effect.

"I can't hear you, honey."

"Nothing," he said. He didn't mean it to sound rude, but it did. That was the problem with shouting.

"Okay then," Mrs. Hefti said, as if any further interaction would be useless. "You have a nice day."

What a strange slip of a boy, she thought—and *so white*. Something wasn't right about him. Of course, he might have been damaged in the womb. The mother was quite a drinker, from all accounts. Mary Hefti sighed, whisked her puffy robe back into the house like an antebellum hoop skirt, and shut the door.

At the sound of knocking, Edgar looked up to see Toni-Ann thumping her fist against one of the upstairs windows. What did she want now? She was banging so hard Edgar was afraid she'd break the glass. He shook his head to warn her and then ran off. There was nothing he could do to help. Her house was her house, just as his was his. Inside of which a person had to face his problems alone.

3

Beards

There was the truck again: a pale green pickup with mud-crusted tires. The streams of rust that flowed down the dented hood made Edgar think of tears—but only painted-on, like a clown's. For all its mars and pocks, the truck seemed oddly happy. You couldn't say the same about the man sitting inside. There was something serious about the way he stared out the window and watched the kids smashing into bags of chips and chomping on candy bars. Every few days the truck was there, parked across the street from the Mark-O-Market. The convenience store was just down the block from Edgar's school. He often bought a Coke there on his way home—a beverage his grandmother frowned upon. Usually he sat on one of the red benches outside the Mark-O, the bottle of forbidden nectar clutched solemnly between his hands.

Today, under late summer sun, Edgar sipped and stretched out his legs. There was a terrific slant of light bearing down on the truck, but the man wasn't wearing sunglasses, like he usually did. Even from across the street you could see his blue eyes. They were unnaturally bright, as if they were plugged in somehow, or operated by batteries. The man's hair fell from his head in complicated locks. Blondish-brown. The beard, neatly trimmed, was darker. It was hard to tell from a distance, but sometimes it seemed to Edgar that the man was looking directly at him. It didn't make the boy nervous, because there were lots of other kids around—and the man looked at them, too. He looked at everything (the treetops, the clouds), or he just leaned his head back as if to study the inside roof of the truck. Every now and then he seemed to have fallen asleep. Once it looked like he was laughing behind the rolled-up windows. Strange, Edgar had thought. People usually didn't laugh like that—with jerky, shoulder-heaving shudders—when they were alone. Which made Edgar wonder if maybe the man was crying.

Did the other kids see him? No one else ever seemed to be looking in that direction. But the man was right there, in broad daylight. It wasn't like he was a man hiding in the dark—a thing Edgar knew about. A long time ago he'd had a friend, Jack, who'd shown up at odd hours to camp in his bedroom closet. If Edgar wanted to speak with him, he had to go into the tiny room with a flashlight and a box of cookies (Jack was always starving). Even then, Edgar never saw Jack's face. The man was always standing up, his face lost among the hanging clothes. Conversation was little more than a brief exchange of hums and squeaks—a bird language—after which Edgar and Jack would lean against each other silently, often with the buffer of Edgar's blue peacoat between them. When his grandmother would find him, he'd be sound asleep, still on his feet, propped up inside the dense rack of clothing.

Today, outside the market, Sara Prokoff, a classmate, was sitting on the bench beside Edgar. He was inclined to mention how it was now exactly five times that he'd seen the green pickup across the street—and did she think that strange? But, as he looked at Sara, who was manipulating a straw to loudly hoover up the stubborn dregs of her frozen Berry Blast, he decided to keep the man to himself. Edgar wondered, though, if he was breaking some law by doing this, because it was a major rule these days to report anything you saw that was out of the ordinary. The man clearly wasn't a terrorist, though; he had blond hair and a blue shirt like someone who worked at a gas station. Though he did have a curious bumper sticker on the back of his truck.

GUN CONTROL IS HITTING YOUR TARGET

Edgar noticed it as the man was pulling away. He wasn't sure what it meant, though he knew guns were generally a bad thing. Still, he looked forward to the bearded man's visits. He was one of the few men in Edgar's life, and the boy didn't want him to go away.

Besides, Edgar knew from experience the cost of disclosure. When he'd finally mentioned Jack to his grandmother, that was the end of it. Jack never came back. No doubt he was off with some other boy who knew how to keep a secret. Edgar refused to make the same mistake twice.

Whenever the man in the truck waved at him, Edgar waved back—and no one needed to know.

* * *

The sweating bottle of vodka had sat overnight on the coffee table, and now there was a huge ring on the wood. Florence stared at it. She'd cleaned the table this morning, cleared away the glasses, the ashtray with one, two, *three* butts in it. Luckily she'd been up early and had set it all to rights before the boy had come down for breakfast. That's the last thing the child needed, waking up to evidence of his mother's debauchery—not only the vodka and the cigarettes, but the couch cushions suspiciously atumble, the whole damn living room looking like Who-Did-It-and-Ran. She'd have to polish the table again. Rings were stubborn. As she headed to the hall closet for the oil soap and the rag, she noticed the photographs on top of the piano: three of the frames placed facedown. *Och.* This was the last straw. One by one she lifted them, begging God for some insight into the girl's twisted mind. A photo of Pio and Frank at the boy's high school graduation; one of Frank, alone, on his cousin Vincenzo's motorcycle; and the third photo, not Frank at all, but Lucy herself—yes, of course—in her wedding dress. The old woman shook her head. What was the girl trying to pretend with these men of hers? That she had no past? That she was a blank slate? Well, she was fooling herself if she thought her history wasn't written all over her face.

Florence sat down on the piano bench, exhausted at ten in the morning. The girl had been good for so long. No drinking, no men; she had stopped her foolish attempt at dating. The old woman had thought, with relief, the girl was finally settling down. But now, it seemed, she was out twice a week—and that wasn't counting the weekends. She'd have to have another talk with her.

Why was it so hard for people to get used to their loneliness? Why did they fight it so much? At a certain age, you had to throw in the towel. Not that she wished loneliness upon Lucy; but *ha,* what else was there? What was the silly girl hoping for? And with the kind of men she dated. Florence wouldn't give fifty cents for any of them. From the looks of them, they were sure to give the girl a high time and not much more. She thought of the waves again in Dr. Faustini's magazine. With too much force, she slammed the lid over the piano keys. Who was always opening this? No one even played the stupid thing anymore. She should get rid of it, donate it to people who would appreciate it. These days, she could barely stand to look at the contraption. When she dusted it, she couldn't get past the feeling that she was dusting a huge black casket shoved up against the wall. An empty casket, no less, just waiting for her to climb inside. Once a month she polished it. Absurd! A woman forced to polish her own coffin, like something out of a fairy tale.

But she'd loved this piano once. When her father had brought it home, she'd been ecstatic. Her mother had burst into tears: *"Ora si vive così bene,"* she'd cried, her hands covering her face. "In English," her father had scolded, and her mother had ventured it slowly, turning to Florence like a nervous schoolchild. "We live so good now?" The girl nodded; it was close enough. When she sat down on the bench, her parents joined her, but no one dared touch a single key. Florence was afraid she might insult this noble creature that had come into her house and whose language she did not yet speak. But after a single lesson, her trembling fingers could make a song—a simple lullaby about a star. And for years then, every Friday, Ms. Bernice Tilling, a beautiful giraffe of a woman with pearl earrings, ducked her head through the front door, carrying a new batch of sheet music. It was an hour of unadulterated bliss. Florence played beautifully, studying for seven years straight—until Pio arrived, and suddenly there seemed to be no time for anything but the idylls and anxieties of romance. Later she tried to encourage Frank to play, but he never cottoned to it. Which was infuriating, because he had so many other ridiculous ambitions. It would have been a lovely thing to see the boy—his feral hands put to good use—playing "Clair de lune" or "Beautiful Dreamer." How she'd loved those songs. It would be nice to hear them again, though she knew she could never bear to play them herself. Maybe Edgar, one day, she thought—but then she brushed the thought aside, parsimonious as she had become with her hopes. She closed her already drooping eyes while her fingers sought out the lovely fleur-de-lis carved into the center of the lid. Like a blind woman, she could read her whole life on that raised figure. There was the left petal, there was the right, and now her finger traced the great rising center of the flower—sharp still at the tip, after all these years.

"No," the old woman muttered, nodding off, confused. Why did they always leave her alone? She wanted the boy back. It was his birthday, wasn't it? Where had he gone? And where was that mother of his? *Harlot.* Leaving a ring on the wood. *No,* she cried from the depths, her leg suddenly twitching—*not in my house!*

*   *   *

After Pio died, Florence had gone on exactly one date. Lunch with Dominic Sparra. He'd worked with Pio, a lifetime ago, in the tunnels—another
of the craftsmen hired to tile the inside of those huge passageways that allowed drivers to travel safely underwater into the city. They had always frightened Florence, the tunnels, and she would worry every time Pio had to go
off to that inhuman place. When, just two years back, she ran into Dominic at the cheese counter at Corrado's, she felt an immediate affection for
him, recalling the danger he'd shared with her husband. And she knew that
his wife, Mary, always sickly, had died suddenly of flu, the winter before—
the same winter Pio had passed away.

"How are you, Nicky?" she said, falling easily into the name of his youth.
"Menza menz," he said, tilting his gray head; and then he said her name in
the old way, too. "Florie." The shock of hearing that, and the brief song of the
old language rising into an air already rich with the smell of excellent cheese,
must have been the reason she said yes when he asked her to join him the
next week for a cup of coffee.

But instead of coffee, he took her to a nice restaurant at which she felt
embarrassingly underdressed (a beige sweater coat over a plain brown frock).
All around them, handsome young men in blue suits and skinny women in
silk chemises pointed tiny forks at silver towers of *frutti di mare*. It must be
a special, Florence thought, amazed at the midday extravagance. Nicky
ordered a bottle of wine, even though, when he'd suggested it, she'd said,
"No. No wine." When it came to the table, she had to say no again to the
waiter; and then a third time when Nicky pointed out that it might go well
with her soup. She shook her hand, but he poured it anyway, filling the
glass to the rim like a peasant. Florence was so nervous by then, she allowed
herself a few sips, with full knowledge that her face would turn beet red,
which it always did when she drank. Pio used to call her Blushy Magee.
And then she would titter, helplessly, in that high-pitched way of hers.

The wine softened Florence, and soon she was beaming like a Christmas
tree bulb as she listened to Nicky talk about the old days, the years with Pio
in the tunnel. He was a good storyteller; he had a wonderful voice. And there
were so many things she'd forgotten. The time the four of them, Nicky and
Mary and she and Pio, had driven impulsively one Friday night to Seaside Heights. All the hotels were full and the two couples—both still

newlyweds—had stayed on the beach practically the whole night, talking and eating and swimming in the dark water. They'd changed into their bathing suits under a towel. Impossible that such a thing could be true, but it *was* true. As Nicky spoke, Florence could see every detail again. How poor Mary had fallen asleep, and how the boys had covered her up to the neck in sand. What a lark it had been. Mary crying, "Get me out, get me out, I have to pee!" Florence remembered all of it—and before long she heard the laughter, the old sound of it. It was a few seconds before she realized that it was her own titter, flapping foolishly like a trapped bird in the brightly lit restaurant. She swallowed, coughed. Before she could raise her hand, a boy appeared to pour her more water. She drank it slowly, raveling herself back to reality. Here she was, a widow in a public place, giggling like an idiot and sharing a bottle of wine with a dapper loudmouth who was already a good deal more than tipsy. She coughed again, for effect, and touched her throat, somehow trying to let Nicky know that perhaps they had better lower their voices.

Oh, but he wouldn't shut up!—talking incessantly and with no discretion, even as the waiter brought a second bottle of wine, pouring it so slowly he was sure to overhear every word. Nicky leaned past the waiter's hand and brayed at her. *Did she remember how he and Pio had stolen some of the surplus tile from the tunnel; had come home one afternoon with the backseat of Pio's car piled high with the shiny white squares? Didn't you use them in your bathroom, Florie?*

Oh, for heaven's sake! Florence looked around in distress. She always knew she'd be arrested eventually for the theft—because it was true: the downstairs bathroom, as well as the bathroom in her own bedroom, had been tiled with stolen property. *Property of the Port Authority of New York and New Jersey.* It was printed right on the back of the tiles. If anyone cared to pull them off the wall, the incriminating evidence would probably still be legible. For years, as a newlywed, Florence was terrified whenever she took a bath. Looking up at the white tiles that belonged in the tunnel, she would often imagine the bathroom as a place underwater, a makeshift limbo—the separation between air and liquid meekly provisional. As she smoothed the soap over her legs, she knew it was only a matter of time before the water burst through the walls and entombed her. The wrath of the Hudson.

And there was Nicky, telling the whole world her husband had been a thief, and laughing about it with a piece of food trembling above his chin, stuck in that silly beard of his. At the cheese counter she'd thought the facial hair becoming, but now she realized it was nothing more than an old man's laziness. Her mother had always said, never trust a bearded man. Wisdom from the grave. She made a distinct noise with her chair.

"Shall we have dessert?" Dominic said, and Florence fluttered a hand in the general direction of her lower regions. "I think I may be sick."

"Have a seltzer. Do you want a seltzer?" The old man signaled for the waiter.

No, she did not want a seltzer. She wanted to go home, she wanted to lie down on her bed and sleep, and not dream, and be done with it. "Wipe your mouth," she said. "You have a clam on your chin."

Dominic dabbed at his face. "On the other side," Florence said. He attempted to clear the deck two more times, with no success, and finally Florence reached over and wiped the old man's chin.

"Thank you, Florie." He said it quietly, and he held her eye in such a way that Florence suspected the man harbored some vague hope that she might be wiping other clams off his chin in the future. Her hands suddenly felt swollen and hot; her heartbeat pulsed in her fingertips like a series of tiny clocks. "I really do feel sick," she said. "I'm sorry."

After he signed the check, they stood. Florence allowed him the courtesy of pulling out her chair and helping with her coat. But when they were outside and he touched her shoulder, she flinched. "I have a grandson," she said sharply.

He drove her home unevenly, slurring through stop signs. After a blessed spell of silence that lasted six blocks, he suggested they go out to a movie some night. *He wasn't doing anything on Friday. Was she?*

What an idiotic question; what would she be doing on Friday? Painting her nails, she should have said, for heaven's sake. He was talking to her like she was some kind of teeny-bopper. In reply to his question, Florence only said that she was very sorry about Mary. *Such a nice woman, Dominic, so devoted. A pity she was always so frail.* That shut the man up for the rest of the drive, and then, at last, they were back in Ferryfield, pulling into her driveway.

"That grandson of yours. That's Frank's son, right?"

It couldn't have been a real question. He knew exactly who the child was. Why bring up Frank now, just as she was about to step out of the car?

"He doing okay? The kid. Adjusting and everything? After what happened to him, *my God*. Does he remember any of that?"

Florence was abashed, and wondered if such rude questions were a weak effort at retaliation in the face of rejection. Or perhaps it was simply a drunken man's unthinking blather.

"I take good care of him. He wants for nothing."

"Light of my life," she added. And then she was sorry she'd said it, remembering that Dominic and Mary had produced no children; though surely they must have tried.

"You're very lucky," he said, and Florence replied, "We all have our burdens." She patted the man's knee as lightly as she could. She didn't want to end the afternoon at odds with him. The poor man, so desperate he had wanted her. A fat old woman. An Italian widow with a crucifix around her neck. He should have known better than anyone that he was barking up the wrong tree. A mail-order bride from Russia is what he needed; or perhaps he should join a bowling league. Old men had to do terrible things. It had nothing to do with her.

She told him to take good care of himself. Kind words, but laced with a prick of finality. Yes, she thought, getting out of the car, she had handled that just right.

After Dominic pulled away, she went behind the house, into the garden, and picked a tomato. She carried it to her bedroom, and she was crying before she reached the bed. She held the tomato carefully so as not to break the delicate skin and stain the pillowcase. Frail Mary, the poor childless woman. Florence held the fruit to her nose and smelled the greeny place where the stem had been. She felt a weight on her shoulder. Dominic's hand still pressing there. She changed position, rolling onto her back.

But then came the thought of the boy from the grocery store. Just the week before, he'd dashed outside to find her in the parking lot and touched her arm. "Ma'am." The way his hand had lingered there on her bare skin. "You forgot your purse," he said blandly—and there it was, her patent leather clutch, in his other hand. He held it out, but Florence didn't take it immediately. Let the boy think she was dotty. She'd wanted to be near him a moment longer. As she lay in bed, she could still feel the warmth of their closeness, the way something had bloomed in her chest, hopeful—but frightening, too, like blood unfurling in water.

But why? Why should she want this boy to touch her, while she had refused the affection of the old man? Somehow (and here Florence's finger gently punctured the skin of the tomato) it was as if the boy had the power to make life start again—or as if the life whose end she was now approaching was not her real existence, but something badly imagined. The boy seemed to possess some ingenious secret concerning time. There had been an error, but the boy could correct it. She turned her head on the pillow, moaning.

4

Best in NJ

At Celestial Styles, the sole salon in Ferryfield, Lucy was cutting Audrey Fenning's hair—though her greater attention was on herself, in the mirror. Under her work smock (purposely left untied), she was still wearing the pretty silk wraparound she'd put on for the butcher. A little thrill ran through her. The thrill of seeing herself in yesterday's dress. There was no shame; in fact, she felt quite the opposite. As Lucy reflected on her outrageous behavior of the night before, the memory only served to draw her upward, like a flower toward the sun. It was one of Lucy's gifts, to recognize the intelligence of her body and the utter impossibility of denying it. No matter how many times her father had said it would ruin her, she'd always known that her carnal appetite was the one thing capable of saving her. If she believed in God, it was here. Surely, He'd given us such appetites so that we'd stay—for a while at least—on our side of the fence. Without the force of the body, its compulsions, what would prevent a person from sprouting wings before his time and demanding entrance to paradise?

Yes, her cleavage looked excellent. Customers and co-workers were no doubt wondering about Lucy's attire—the glam-slut dress wildly inappropriate in the grim salon, a grooming station for a dying breed of wash-and-set dowagers and second-marriage dye-jobs. The worst were the golden-anniversary types, women with the cachet of having been married to the same man for more than half a century, and whose thin speckled fingers were burdened with an excess of diamonds—the wreckage, Lucy suspected, of years without sex. It was a horror show—a friggin' wax museum. Well, at least one's vanity never suffered here. Lucy pushed out her chest and noted the success of the gesture in the large mirror.

"Ow!" Mrs. Fenning said. "Watch what you're doing."

"Oh my God," Lucy muttered, looking down and seeing a dot of blood on the old woman's ear.

"What?" Mrs. Fenning asked in alarm. "Did you cut me?"

"No, no," Lucy said, quickly wiping the woman's ear with a towel.

"You jabbed me."

"I am so sorry. It's a tricky spot."

"It's an *ear*." Mrs. Fenning reached up her hand. "What's dripping there?"

"It's just water," Lucy said, blocking the woman's arm. "Here, let me . . ." She pressed the towel against the earlobe. "All dry." It was only the tiniest of scratches, thank God, and the blood seemed to have stopped. "What do you think of the bangs?" Lucy said brightly, in an effort to change the subject. She could not afford to lose this job.

"Maybe a little shorter," Mrs. Fenning said, pursing her lips.

Lucy turned the chair a bit, to impede the woman's view of her left ear, and then concentrated with an exaggerated studiousness on her work. The attention cajoled the old woman back into place. She sighed, and then closed her eyes regally, as if meditating.

It was so much easier to cut people's hair when they didn't talk to you. But Lucy knew it wouldn't last. It was physically impossible for Audrey Fenning to keep her mouth shut.

"Did I tell you Lou and I went to Florida?"

Lucy smiled tightly, suppressing a yawn.

"That's why you didn't see me for two months. Our daughter lives down there. Karen. She works for the space people."

"For who?" Lucy thought of the small set of rubber aliens—green, with bendable limbs—that she'd purchased for Edgar recently at the dollar store.

"For the government," Mrs. Fenning said irritably, as if it taxed her to have to explain herself. "Satellites, outer space, that sort of thing."

"Oh, wow." Lucy glanced at the ear; it was still a touch red.

"Very smart girl, let me tell you. "

"So, what is she, an astronaut?"

"Karen? Oh God, no. Can you imagine that? That's just suicide, if you ask me. No, she does numbers and stuff for them. Calculations for the orbits. They hired her right out of college and she's been there twenty years now."

Lucy wondered if Karen was overweight. Perhaps, after a day of numbers, she liked to come home and eat a box of chocolate donuts in front of the television.

"Makes a good living, let me tell you. Bought a new house, couple of years ago. Orange trees, swimming pool, the whole shebang. Two hops and you're on the beach."

"You look like you got a tan."

"That's just the bronzer. It rained practically the whole time we were down there. Weather was crap. We saw a lot of movies. We saw the one about the dog. Did you see that?"

"No," replied Lucy, losing steam. She wasn't good at these kinds of conversations. Privy to the dullness of others' lives, she often worried about her own. Were we all like this? Tape recorders that had run out of available space long ago? After a certain age, it was all replay—an endless loop. This wasn't the first time Audrey had told her about Karen's new house in Florida. Florence did this, too, repeating the same old stories until you wanted to scream, or knock over a lamp. And the worst part of it was, the dullness of others rubbed off on you; it was contagious. Lucy glanced at herself in the mirror and noted with dismay that the dress was losing its power. A lock of Fenning's hair was clinging to the skirt. She brushed it off as if it were feces.

"Oh, and did I tell you about the salon I went to down there? I needed a trim because with all the humidity my hair grows like a spider plant—it gets very big, you know, very *puffbally*. So Karen says, 'Go where I go, Mom.' Place was amazing. Spotless, everybody in white. I said, what do they do, surgery here? But I mean it was gorgeous. Big vases of flowers everywhere. You want fresh fruit, they got fresh fruit. Hispanic girl in the back making cappuccino. And they give you a *massage* before they cut your hair."

Lucy wished she were still in bed with the butcher. She wanted those hairy arms around her again, that big body on hers, blocking out the sun. The salon suddenly seemed too bright.

"And not *bing bang boom*. The girl rubbed me for a good ten minutes."

"Maybe you should move to Florida," suggested Lucy.

The woman's quick eyes darted upward, gauging the girl's level of flippancy.

"I'd move there in a second," Lucy said, with as much innocence as she could muster.

I'd move anywhere, she thought. She glanced impatiently toward the front of the salon, as if she were waiting for someone who was very late. She could see the street beyond the windows, the buildings across the way, the small municipal trees in their individual metal corrals—each component of the scene so familiar it seemed to return her gaze. Lucy had grown up not far from Ferryfield—just two towns over, in West Mill, across the river. Seventeen years in a dark house with dreary furniture and too many clocks, a conspiracy of clocks that had slowed down time in an effort to forestall the future. She couldn't wait to be free of that house, of her father—to live as far away as possible. Frank had wanted the same thing, and the two of them had often spent hours over a six-pack or a bottle of wine, discussing the options. Frenzied, youthful conversations that had left them breathless—the idea of escape so potent it sucked the oxygen from the room. Once, the plan had been to live nowhere at all. They would simply drive all day and then spend every night at a different roadside hotel—dirty sex and clean sheets, tiny soaps wrapped in paper. She'd never met a boy with so many ideas—and the laughter, she'd never laughed harder with anyone. They could be happy anywhere, even in a car going nowhere. Maybe they'd head south, toward Mexico. Frank had managed to make her believe in such things. His fantasies were inspiring, life-giving. Until they weren't. Until they somehow became the exact opposite. A line of thought that carried her husband straight out of the world.

Lucy resented Mrs. Fenning's mobility, even if it was nothing more than a geriatric gambol in Boca Raton—or wherever it was the space people conducted their business. Why should this old woman with canary-yellow hair and the beginning of a goatee have more freedom than she did? Lucy was suddenly furious. She took a deep breath. A molecule of perfume rose from her breasts, offering a brief comfort. "It might be nice," she said dutifully. "Florida."

"I don't know." Mrs. Fenning scrunched up her nose. "You can't really do Christmas down there. The lights just look stupid."

Lucy plugged in the blow-dryer.

"Wait." The old woman held up her hand and wiggled her fingers. "Let me see the back before you dry it."

Lucy passed her a small mirror and turned the chair. Mrs. Fenning made a thorough inspection. It seemed she was satisfied when suddenly she brought the glass closer to the left side of her face.

"I knew it."

"What?"

"There's a mark there."

Lucy leaned in as if she couldn't see it. "Where?"

"Where do you think? On my *ear*."

"Sorry," said Lucy. "Hands of a surgeon usually."

"Well, don't expect a tip." Audrey brushed a snip of yellow hair off her lap. "I mean, you do a nice job, but half the time you seem very distracted."

She snagged Lucy's eyes in the mirror. "And news flash, *news flash,* Ms. Fini—those scissors are sharp!"

Lucy agreed. They were still in her hand; she pressed the cushion of her index finger against the tip. Very sharp, indeed. You could kill a person with these scissors. You really could.

As soon as Fenning left, Lucy checked her phone. There were no messages.

Well, what did she expect? Men were men. They were slow, prideful; they had a thing about calling too soon. Often they were cruel. A man who chopped up animals for a living was certainly no exception.

Yet, for all his evident aggressiveness, there was something tender, almost bashful, about the butcher's eyes. She'd noticed that right away. Of course, it was possible he was hiding something. Bashful eyes were often indistinguishable from lying ones. Not that it mattered, either way. It was just sex. Still, there'd been a spark. And even though he'd declined to eat the breakfast she'd made, claiming an early meat delivery, the butcher had grabbed her as she was leaving. He'd brandished his unshaven face over hers, holding the threat for a delicious few seconds, before kissing her, point-blank, on the mouth.

Well, Lucy knew how to take charge, too. She dialed his number, and with each ring tapped a cherry-red shoe against the linoleum.

There was no answer. She hung up, pointed her toe, and improved her posture—a sort of advance guard to ward off despair. Maybe she should call him at the shop. Just to say hello. Or was it better to wait a few hours?

Shit, her next appointment was already here. She waved at the oddly tilted Mrs. D'Angelo and held up a one-minute finger.

She marched to the front desk, past Celeste, the owner. She pulled the phone book from the bottom left drawer, quickly paging through it to find the number. *Q, R, S. Salvage Solutions, Salvation Army*—and yes, there it was—*Salvatore's Meats,* the listing in its own little box, demanding attention. "Best in NJ," the ad proclaimed—the endorsement attributed to a former mayor who, if Lucy was remembering correctly, had been indicted on racketeering charges. Or perhaps this was that other politician, the one who'd slapped the black prostitute in Newark. Either way, it was a nice little ad. Above the name of the shop, like a garland, was a crudely sketched dangle of sausages. Fucking adorable. Lucy smiled, happy again, and punched the numbers into the phone.

5

Fat and Skinny

From a perilously swaying branch, a squirrel looked down at Edgar, who was sitting on the ground in a small clearing. The animal blinked, cocked its head, and dashed to the end of the white oak's arm. When a gust of wind swept through the upper air, the squirrel, as if lifted by wires, leapt to the arm of a neighboring tree—an astounding feat whose only cost was the loss of a single acorn.

It landed at Edgar's feet. He regarded it solemnly as another rush of air moved through the treetops. The congress of leaves shivered and rolled, a voluptuous tossing that culminated in a vigorous nodding, as if all the trees agreed on something. The decision was unanimous; the answer: *yes*.

But what was the question?

The world was speaking to Edgar in a language he did not fully understand. But he knew enough to take the fallen acorn and put it in his pocket. He liked acorns—chestnuts, too. It was only mid-September, but he already had a large collection of both, which he kept in separate brown grocery bags in a cubbyhole at the back of the garage. The nuts were irresistible—perfectly polished, wonderfully hard. They clacked like wampum whenever Edgar ran his hands through his stash. In terms of acorns, he was a millionaire.

Edgar loved the woods. There was a good-sized forest—or so it seemed to Edgar—that he could enter just behind the Mark-O-Market, only to emerge, some time later, less than twenty paces from his own backyard. Somewhere along the route, he always forgot where he had come from and where he was going. Deep in the clutch of green the world stopped, and Edgar walked on a plain of breath and slatted light, above the crunch of his own footsteps. He had weight here—but no witnesses. It was a place where nothing happened and everything happened, the contradiction of nature. The handsome tree trunks standing apart, huddled but separate, like soldiers—and then, to look up and see the canopy, the great spreading and branched flowering of the leaves; and how, in the upper air, it was all one thing—the treetops messing into each other with an easy affection, the loosed dreams of the steady soldiers below.

So unlike humans. Trees had perfect lives. They knew how to be alone and together at the same time, without sadness. Edgar sat in the clearing with no idea that he was lonely. He only knew that there was something between himself and other people; it was like a heavy curtain—all the more troubling for the fact that you could *see through* this curtain. His mother had told him that when he was a baby the doctor had thought he might be deaf, or even something worse. Apparently he'd rarely made eye contact, and often he didn't look up when someone called his name. And, later, when he started to rock his body or hide at the back of his closet, his grandmother always tried to stop him—even though the rocking made him feel so much better.

Closing his eyes, he fingered the acorn in his pocket. He thought of the spaceship again: a great silver mushroom cap with an iridescent underbelly like an electric jellyfish. The ship would come and he would go away with it. The door would open, and he'd walk up the mile-long plank, just like the boy in the movie. He would miss Gran, of course. He would miss his mother, too. Inside his head, as if in a fortune-teller's crystal ball, he saw her, standing on the lawn in front of the house, calling his name. She was wearing her cherry dress, her cherry shoes. But it was too late. *You live with us now,* the aliens said, touching him gently with their praying-mantis fingers. Edgar pushed the acorn deeper into his pocket and caressed its smooth cheek. He laid his head on a flat rock and stretched out his legs. As the spaceship picked up speed, he ran his thumb over the acorn's point to steady himself.

"What's he doing?"

"Oh my God, he's jacking off!"

Edgar's heart leapt as he opened his eyes. Two boys had materialized in the clearing. Thomas Pittimore and Jarell Lester. They stood less than ten feet away, snickering like scruffy cartoon wolves. Thomas swung his nylon knapsack three times and then released it. Edgar watched it fly high into the air and then descend, alarmingly, in his direction. He flinched and covered his head. Thomas, in perfect timing with the bag's landing (two inches from Edgar's foot), produced the phlegmy sound of a great explosion. *"Pkkkhhhuuulll!"* And then, in a mechanical voice like a robot: "Kill the mas-tur-ba-tor!" Jarell, the lesser beast, only smiled, and scratched his knee through a hole in his jeans.

Edgar's face flushed, even though what Thomas had said wasn't true. He wasn't doing that; he'd never done it. In fact, he was a little cloudy as to what, precisely, *it* was. But he knew better than to deny the accusation. Denying it would only enflame his inquisitors and prolong the agony. Say nothing; that was always the best strategy.

The boys moved closer. They were older, twelve or thirteen. Edgar had noticed them before, outside the Mark-O. They were often together, though they seemed to have no matching parts. Jarell was tall, and moved with an exaggerated but convincing swagger. He had black skin, but the blood that moved beneath the dark pigment made him seem almost purple—like an eggplant. Thomas, on the other hand, was pale like Edgar, but doughy; there was something vaguely wet about him, some mist that seemed to be the private weather of his corpulence. Edgar could smell him as he approached. For, in truth, it was Edgar who was the wolf. His tendency toward silence enhanced his senses and gave him the eyes and the ears—and above all, the nose—of an animal. Thomas smelled like bread not yet baked, with a top note of ripe banana. Jarell had the scent of pennies.

Thomas stared at Edgar, while Jarell looked down into his phone—the light from the display panel intermittently evident on the dark screen of the boy's face. In one quick glance into Thomas's eyes, Edgar saw everything: how this breathless, sweating boy was grossly unafraid, bent on the prospect of some perfect disaster. He was equally mesmerizing and repulsive, the human equivalent of a car accident.

"What do you have in your pocket?" asked Thomas.

Edgar shook his head, feeling the fear begin, as it always did, like a stream of octopus ink seeping into his belly. "Nuh-hee," he said, inaudibly, from the back of his throat.

Thomas squinted his eyes and grimaced. "What? Speak up."

"Nuh-theen," Edgar said, in over-articulate compensation for his previous failure in communication. "An acorn."

"You sound like you're from Australia." The fat boy sneered. "Doesn't he sound Australian?" He hit Jarell's arm, causing his friend to drop the phone.

"Hey, don't be obnoxious. I'm texting Bethany."

"*Breast*-any," Thomas said, pushing jauntily at his own mammaric protrusions.

Jarell flashed his extraordinary teeth in a brief smile, and then retrieved the phone to resume his thumb-punching. Thomas, ignored, turned his attention back to Edgar.

"You sure you're not from *Australia*?" He seemed to be fixated on this concept. Edgar wondered if there was a secret meaning; if perhaps under the word lay an insult. Edgar was aware of his speech impediment. He had trouble with his *R*s. An acorn became an a-cawn. A pearl was a peh-wol. The world, a wold—a treeless rolling plain that offered nowhere to hide. The northern New Jersey accent, which often lent a toughness to the voices of the locals, only served, in Edgar's case, to exaggerate the preciousness of his speech.

Edgar shook his head, denying any connection to the continent down under. He stood and held up his hand to signal that he was leaving. A twig snapped under his feet as he turned.

"Where are you going?"

It was Thomas, pretending to be friendly.

"We know what you were doing."

Edgar bit his lip, which was the best way to stop oneself from crying.

"It's rude to stand with your back to someone," Thomas said.

Florence had told Edgar the same thing, and so he turned, biting his lip harder. He kept his eyes down. Thomas's shoes were a dusty black, wrinkled in places like the skin of an elephant.

"What are you staring at my feet for? Look at me. I'm not gonna *do* anything."

Edgar had succeeded in not crying, and bravely lifted his head.

"Dude, *gross*—you got blood on your face."

Jarell glanced up from his phone.

Edgar, confused, wiped at his cheek.

"On your mouth," Jarell said helpfully, and Edgar quickly licked it away.

"Gross," Thomas said again.

"I only bit my lip," the little boy ventured in his own defense.

"Would you stop looking at my freaking feet? Come on, I want to show you something." He turned to Jarell. "Give me your phone." He pulled it from his friend's grip.

"Ass-wipe. Use your own."

"Battery's dead. I'll give it right back."

"I don't want your paw prints all over it," Jarell said.

"Dude, just give me one second." Thomas had moved away slightly and was now leaning against a tree, diligently typing something into the keypad. Jarell watched him impatiently, but did nothing. This was surprising to Edgar because Jarell was clearly the stronger of the two. He could have

easily pounced on the fat boy and reclaimed his property. But he kept his distance, as if Thomas Pittimore possessed a power that had nothing to do with physical strength. Edgar could see it, too. Something about Thomas was foolish, but there was also something monstrous, something dangerous. He was the kind of boy who might pull out a gun in the school cafeteria. In fact, just two towns over, a boy had done exactly that. He'd shot down two teachers and six students, and three of them had died. Edgar had seen his picture on television. Like Thomas, the boy was fat—though how blubber was related to violence, Edgar wasn't sure.

"*Tom,*" Jarell said. "You're gonna use up my charge." He reached for the phone.

"Wait wait wait," Thomas said, laughing as he turned away. "I just want to find the right one."

Edgar felt relieved by the tension between the two boys, which afforded him his favorite status: invisibility. Slowly he made a move toward the trail.

"Stay where you are, Egg-roll." Thomas spoke without looking up from the phone.

"Leave the kid alone," Jarell said. "He's like six years old."

Edgar blushed—partly from gratitude and partly from shame: Jarell's infantilizing subtraction of two years from his age. Edgar accepted it, though, without injury; he knew he was a shrimp. He'd been born too early.

Jarell knew all about this. His mother had helped Mrs. Fini when she was pregnant. Back then, that's what his mother had done for money—help women deliver babies. In fact, Jarell had been at the Finis' house when Edgar was born. So they had some history.

Plus, being one of only two black kids at his school, Jarell sympathized with Edgar's predicament. Even though the kid was white—he was *so* white it almost qualified as a different color.

"Here, look, *look.*" Thomas bounced over to Jarell and showed him the phone.

"Oh, man." Jarell began to laugh. "You're twisted."

The two friends stared into the machine, smiling. Suddenly, they both said, "*Ohhhh,*" at the same time, as if they'd jumped, hand in hand, into a pool of cold water.

What were they watching? Edgar was curious now. Jarell's mouth was wide open with a shocking lack of self-consciousness; he held back none of his teeth, which were large and gleamingly white. Thomas snickered, baring his much smaller endowment—pointy little things with too much space between them, the color of unpopped corn.

Jarell sobered suddenly. "I better not have to pay for this shit."

"Don't worry, dude, it's free."

"Are you sure?"

"Yeah, I watch them all the time. Okay, look at this. Watch watch watch!"

"Ohhh," the boys said again.

Edgar could hear someone in pain, a small mouse of a sound, tinny, coming from the phone. Thomas and Jarell were locked in place. Their initial volatile excitement softened into a kind of dull fascination. They looked into the black device with the slack, expectant faces of infants. Edgar sometimes saw this expression on his grandmother at church, when she stared up at Jesus on the cross.

The boys' smiles rose and faded, their mouths twitched like dreaming dogs. Finally, Thomas snickered, a staccato sound like machine-gun fire that startled Jarell from his reverie. "Okay, that's enough. You're gonna kill my battery."

"One more minute. I wanna show him."

"Who? The kid?" Jarell guffawed. "No fucking way."

"Yes way." Thomas turned to Edgar. "Come here, dickweed."

Another gust of wind blew through the treetops.

Jarell was laughing so hard now he looked like he might pee his pants. "Shit," he said. "Don't show him."

Edgar both wanted and didn't want to see. He could still hear the mouse in pain. But the boys were laughing—so how terrible could it be?

What Edgar feared most was that it might have something to do with *Faces of Death,* a movie he'd overheard some boys talking about at school, in which you could watch people die in all sorts of horrible ways—car crashes and plane wrecks and mountain-climbing accidents. And it wasn't fake; it was all real people who'd had the misfortune of having their final disfiguring moments caught on camera. Richie DiGeneva had said that he'd stolen the DVD from his older brother's room and that there was a "totally amazing scene of a man's head being crushed by a freaked-out horse," and Jason Zittle had replied that you didn't need a DVD to see shit like that, you could see even better stuff online. Edgar was terrified that, were he ever to watch *Faces of Death,* he might see the face of his father.

Thomas turned the shiny black rectangle and held the screen in front of

Edgar's nose. The image was so bright it was like a flashbulb going off. The boy blinked, and then focused. At first he wasn't sure what he was seeing. Some sort of natural disaster. Strangely moving hills and valleys, golden-colored, with a dark patch of heaving grass. As Edgar stepped back to better understand the tumult, he gasped. It was two women on top of each other, kissing! They were naked, tossing and turning, their fingers moving between each other's legs. From their mouths came, stereophonically, the sound of the suffering mouse. Edgar, astonished, looked up at the boys, who were shrieking with laughter. It was safer to look at the screen, which was a window the women had failed to shut. Did they know someone was watching them? Their thighs were splayed terribly now—unabashedly, like toddlers. One of them had a beard between her legs; the other was bald. They both had ballooning chests that looked dangerously close to bursting. It didn't seem wise, the way one of the women was pinching the tips of the other's overblown mounds. Edgar braced for an explosion just as a man—golden-colored like the women—entered the scene. He stood in the doorway with a profound weight between his legs. His thing was nothing like Edgar's. What hung from the man's thighs was a thug, thick and powerful.

"Look, he's enjoying it. The little pervert."

Edgar was not, in fact, enjoying it; but he couldn't turn away from the pretty women in pain and the man who'd come to—*what?*—rescue them? The writhing women were like drowning dolls, clutching each other to stay afloat; and the man, with his tanned skin and muscular body, did look like a lifeguard, albeit one who'd lost his trunks. When he approached the bed, his thug in tow, the mouse-women whined louder. It was clearly a cry for help. One of them reached out her hand and latched on to the growing rope between the man's legs. Edgar felt something funny in his stomach. Is this what his mother did with the butcher?

"What part are you at?"

The boys were still there. It was Thomas speaking. Edgar didn't know where to turn. There was a tremendous heat on his face, and he looked up to see a sun that wasn't there. The woods had fallen into shadow.

"What's the matter?" Jarell said. "Are you cold?"

Edgar's teeth were chattering. His hands were shaking, as well. Thomas pulled back the phone and turned the screen to his own face. "Oh, this is the part where she blows him."

Jarell feigned indifference but allowed his eyes to wander back to the movie. There was a shifting of cloth in his pants. He made a quick adjustment before snatching the phone from Thomas and pressing a rigid finger into the device, ending the transmission. "I've seen this shit before," he said.

"It's better on a big screen anyway," Thomas said. He turned to Edgar and smiled, raising his eyebrows. "Now you have something to think about next time you jack off." He laughed in his mirthless way, and then leaned forward to let a long drool of spit fall from his mouth. It landed on Edgar's sneaker.

Edgar said nothing, wishing he could bash a rock against the fat boy's popcorn teeth. Or, even better: to unleash vengeance without lifting a finger. Using telekinesis, he would levitate Thomas into the air and make him spin like a rag doll until blood flew from his bulging eyeballs. As a rule, Edgar abhorred violence, but with boys like Thomas it was different. When a villain was destroyed, stabbed through the heart or crushed by a boulder, there was a kind of joy that bubbled up inside you. Edgar had experienced the feeling in dozens of movies—the thrill of power, as if he had killed the villain himself. Here in the woods, though, Edgar could see no way of prevailing. His great success, for which he gave himself no credit, was that he didn't run or cry.

Thomas, of course, had hoped for tears; was, in fact, hungry for them. It was a taste for which he'd developed an addiction—having consumed them for so long, at the cost of smaller boys. Over the years he'd made lots of little faggots cry; it was easy, it was fun.

But Edgar remained mum—and his martial silence made the fat boy nervous.

Thomas reached for his knapsack, unzipped it, and pulled out a pen. He took hold of Edgar's arm, gripping it with some violence. He uncapped the pen with his mouth and, as Edgar squirmed, began to write on the boy's forearm.

"Don't hurt him," Jarell said from the shadows.

"I'm not hurting him." And then, ferociously, to Edgar: "Stop moving or I'll jab you with this fucking pen."

Edgar froze as Thomas completed his scrawl, pressing with unnecessary force. The little boy moaned—not only in pain, but with a horrible sense that something like this had been done to him before. Someone with a pen, or maybe a knife. A long time ago, when he was a baby.

"Okay, all done." Thomas tossed away Edgar's skinny limb as if it were something distasteful.

Despite a rush of vertigo, Edgar's curiosity took him straight to his stinging arm. *Supersluts.com* was written there, in large letters that traveled from elbow to wrist.

"Just in case you get the urge," said Thomas.

Edgar was confused.

"The website, dickweed. For the naked chicks."

"Come on," Jarell said. "Leave him alone."

"Buh-bye," Thomas said, waving maniacally in a parody of sweetness.

Edgar watched the boys move off into the trees. Jarell glanced back with a face that was not unkind—and though he made a gesture with his hand, it was too small to mean anything.

Edgar could no longer see the boys now; he could only hear the murmur of their voices, the fading crunch of their footsteps.

Then there was silence—and into the silence fell the sounds of birds and wind-jostled leaves. The end of human voices was a comfort. Edgar kneeled in the clearing. The sun was setting, and the trees were leaking long tarry shadows—a surreptitious doubling that was vaguely sinister. He should get up, go home; his grandmother would be worried. Yet he didn't move. The little blue wheels of thought were turning—but in slow motion now, vexed by the weight of some profound human gravity. Golden bodies and their strangely ecstatic sufferings. When the man and the mouse-women had moaned, it was not without pleasure. Edgar recalled something his grandmother had told him about Jesus; that Jesus *wanted* to suffer.

Maybe normal people wanted to suffer, too. Why else would his mother date a butcher, or his grandmother collect dead people in a drawer? Why else would a person with telekinetic superpowers not stand up to a bully?

Edgar felt confused. He wanted a cookie, the forgetfulness of sugar. Perhaps Jarell will come back, he thought. Without Thomas to fox him, Jarell might sit beside Edgar and patiently explain any number of things—his purple lips pausing now and then to make sure Edgar had understood. Life was complicated, and dangerous. Edgar needed a teacher. Someone, like the aliens, who could extend long fingers into his brain and adjust the dials, rearrange the chaos of dots until the picture was marvelous and clear, and with no effort at all you would understand why you'd been born in a place where the rain of information never ceased, and where every person was a baffling conceit.

Edgar looked down at the tip of his sneaker where Thomas had spit; a slug trail of wetness still glistened. It made no sense. What was the point of a boy like Thomas Pittimore—and what was he doing in Edgar's story? The fat boy suddenly seemed, to Edgar, more than simply an unpleasant bully. Thomas Pittimore was a dragon, a foul-smelling beast—a challenge Edgar had to either engage or decline.

Maybe the man in the green truck could help.

Gun control is hitting your target.

As the boy curled up on the ground, some other words came to mind, something useful that someone—maybe the man in the closet—had taught him a long time ago.

Fat and Skinny had a race
all around the United States.
Fat fell down and broke his face
and Skinny won the race.

As Edgar recited the poem—his voice barely a whisper—the squirrel (who had by now safely ensconced himself in the crook of another white oak) looked down. He watched the boy's moving lips, and—being a creature of supreme hunger—misunderstood, and wondered only what the boy might be eating. Before Edgar had finished his incantation, the squirrel had made his way to the bottom of the trunk and was moving toward the small human, in search of crumbs.

6

Pinocchio

When Edgar walked in the door, his grandmother let out a sharp yelp. The boy was startled but had enough presence of mind to hide his tattooed arm. Though he'd tried to rub off Thomas's savage engraving with some damp leaves, the text was still flagrantly legible. Why had he worn short sleeves in September? Stupid!

"Where have you been? I almost called the police."

Edgar saw the clock in the hallway. He was two hours late.

Florence had been frantic. Not only had the boy been kidnapped (she was sure of it), but, to add insult to injury, that wandering mother of his still hadn't telephoned. This wasn't the first time Lucy had stayed out all night, but at least she should have had the common courtesy to call—even if it was only to lie, say her car had broken down, she'd slept at a friend's. Florence just wanted to be sure the girl wasn't in some kind of trouble. With the boy, it was even worse. He was defenseless, a bit of butter under a hot sun.

"It's almost five o'clock." The bandana on the old woman's head was dark blue, with a scattering of pink and yellow daisies—a happy concoction of Chagall-like exuberance that undermined the distress in her eyes.

"I was in the woods," Edgar said—immediately wishing he'd fibbed.

"I told you, I don't want you walking in there. What if you get lost?"

"I wouldn't get lost."

"Or something could bite you. You don't know."

"There's nothing to—"

"*Animals,*" the grandmother said with a scolding severity, before reaching out to draw the boy into her bosom.

"I have to pee," he said, slipping away and dashing up the stairs.

Florence watched his effortless flight, the flash of his white head, his pale shirt. Her heart raced. He was too fast sometimes. A little Speedy Gonzales, just like Frank.

"I have to *'go to the bathroom,'*" she called after him, correcting his manners. How many times had she told the child that *pee* was not a word polite people used; *pee* was something that came out of your privates, not out of your mouth. She stood at the bottom of the stairs, shaking her head. *Not home two seconds, and already he's gone.* She needed him by her side today, not flitting off into the woods.

During the long afternoon alone in the house, an old fear had stabbed at Florence's heart: that it was Lucy who'd kidnapped the child. Scooped him up and driven off, God knows where, in that zippy little coupe of hers. It was something Florence used to worry about when Edgar was an infant. All day she'd had the sense that she must prepare for something terrible. It had started as soon as she opened her eyes this morning, when she'd felt the presence of Frank, a subtle turbulence stirring the edges of her room. Ever since then, nothing had been right.

"Edgar Allan!" she called out. What was he doing up there? There was a perfectly fine powder room downstairs. She should have kept him home from school today. Without the boy, the day had passed too slowly. Each corner of the house, each piece of furniture, every object, seemed strained by its own history. Frank's birthday was always a difficult day. The day one's dead son was born: it seemed a kind of complicated math, a riddle Florence felt she was required to solve—though each attempt only raised more questions.

In years past, she would bake a cake and give Edgar a little present, without offering any explanation to the child. If he asked the reason for the cake, the present, Florence would simply reply that she was in the mood for a party. When the boy was five, Lucy (who'd spent the afternoon commemorating her dead husband's birthday with a flask in a parking lot) had come home earlier than usual and found Edgar and Florence in party hats. The girl had made a big stink about it. She'd dragged the old woman into the hallway and told her that if she ever did anything like that again, she'd have Florence committed. Of course, that was hogwash; but Florence chose to respect the wishes of the boy's mother (the girl had been absolutely livid with rage), and for the last three years there'd been no party, no cake.

Now she was alone with it—and today, for some reason, had been worse than last year. She'd moved around the house in a bleary torpor. She'd made a ham sandwich for lunch and then sat before it, immobile, for nearly forty-five minutes. When her consciousness had returned to the food, it appeared vile, the ham dangling from the edges of the bread. She'd sniffed it and decided it'd gone bad. After she'd tossed the sandwich in the garbage, she took the rest of the ham from the refrigerator and discarded that as well—not remembering that she'd purchased it only the day before.

And earlier, when she'd gone into the yard to water her tomatoes, the spastic girl next door had been playing near the fence. Well, she wasn't a spastic exactly—but she moved erratically and was soft in the head. Florence didn't like the girl. A hairy beast who always had something in her mouth. Today she was chewing on a small piece of paper as she marched around a tree in some sort of demented trance. She was chanting, too, saying the same words over and over. At first, Florence couldn't make out what the child was saying—but then it struck her, clear as a bell.

"*Nel*-ly Tor-*tell*-i, *Nel*-ly Tor-*tell*-i."

Florence had dropped her watering can and nearly fallen into the tomatoes. She'd clutched her chest, fearing she might be dying. Just this morning she'd thought of her childhood friend—and now the spastic girl was chanting Nelly's name like a mob about to burn down a building.

When Toni-Ann had finally stopped her mad circuit around the tree, she'd turned to Florence and smiled, her huge teeth the color of violets. The old woman, aghast, had gone back into the house, sweating. And though she'd tried to forget, the name of the dead girl had stayed with her, stitching a black thread across her mind.

* * *

Edgar flicked on the bathroom light and locked the door. He looked down at his forearm. Thomas had pressed so hard that the lines of black ink were now dimensional, rising on red ridges of irritation. The boy felt stung, branded. He turned on the hot water, soaped up his arm, and scrubbed—first with his hand and then with a small towel. When he rinsed the suds away, he could still see the letters. A pang of anxiety shot through him. What if he could never wash it off? What if *Supersluts.com* remained on his skin for the rest of his life, like the eagle on his grandfather's shoulder? Supposedly someone had needled it onto the old man's skin when he was twenty, and it was still there on the day he died. Edgar had never liked the eagle—a deranged-looking bird that lurked behind the brush of the old man's arm hair. As for the creature's persistence unto his grandfather's final day, Edgar knew this for a fact. It was Edgar who'd found the lifeless old man in the bathtub, a forbidden cigar floating in the gray water.

Edgar scrubbed again. After three scourings, he accomplished only to blur the black ink, making the letters appear even larger; and now his entire forearm was bright red. His grandmother was sure to notice.

When he came downstairs wearing a long-sleeved T-shirt, she asked if he was cold. "A little," he said, and she felt his forehead.

"You feel fine."

"I *am,*" he insisted. "I'm fine." A lie that struck with jarring force against its polar opposite, the raw sadness that filled his lungs. He felt the rush of tears behind his eyes. But his mother would be home soon, and he didn't want her to see him like that, a baby crying in his grandmother's arms. His mother, the stomper, didn't care for such displays. Tears—Florence's or Edgar's—always sent her straight to the porch with a pack of cigarettes. Where she went with her own tears, if she had any, the boy didn't know.

A funny smell drifted from the kitchen, a burning odor that seemed a perfect way to change the subject. "Are you cooking, Gramma?"

"Oh!" she said with a stagey slap to her forehead. Edgar followed her into the kitchen; watched as she turned down the sauce and wiped up the smoking ooze that had bubbled over. "Just in the nick of time. What would I do without your sniffer?" She tapped the boy's nose. Having him near again changed everything. She could actually feel something like a small flame warming the inside of her chest. Edgar felt something similar in his own body.

"Are you making meatballs, Gramma?"

"I told you I was, didn't I?"

"We have leftover Chinese," Edgar reminded her.

"I threw it out. Stinky the next day—and gloopy. *Uccch.*" His grandmother made a face of supreme disgust that encouraged the boy to smile.

All the lights were on in the kitchen, and it was warm and bright. Darkness had already begun to creep up outside the window, like a beggar. They would not let him in. The room was fragrant with mint and oregano, nutmeg and garlic, and these things belonged to them. Edgar stuck his nose into a pile of chopped parsley on the cutting board and inhaled the clippings of a freshly mown lawn. With a little bit of dish soap, his grandmother twisted off her rings—her wedding band and engagement ring—and set them on the counter. She washed and dried her hands, then tossed the tiny leaves and grated cheese into the bowl of meat, added the nutmeg and the garlic and the stale bread, twirled the black pepper, pinched the salt, broke the single egg on top of it all, before plunging her fingers into the mix, gently pressing and turning the ingredients until the various became the singular.

As Edgar watched her work, he reached for the wet rings on the counter. So big! Like the rings of a giant. He could see the places where the jeweler had cut the shanks and added flat bars, spacers to accommodate the old woman's swollen fingers. As he slipped them onto one of his own thin digits, they jangled together. He shook his hand and listened to the sound of metal against metal. His grandmother didn't mind.

You couldn't break a diamond anyway. A diamond was harder than a brick, harder than glass. And if you did break it, it wouldn't come apart in pieces that would fall to the floor; it would come apart in bits of light that would fly about the room, ghost bugs of various color, the shattered nest of a prism. Edgar watched his grandmother cook while, distractedly, he moved the rings up and down his finger like an abacus.

"I worry," she said, as if the cooking were only a dream and now she was awake. "That's all."

Edgar touched the bowl, which was the same as touching her. Sometimes she seemed to need something from him, but it wasn't anything you could find in your pocket or in a shop. It was more like a promise, or a kidney. "I'm home," he said. And he was.

The old woman nodded, satisfied, and with a light humming began to call back the dream, which hadn't strayed far.

But Edgar couldn't fall into it again. As his grandmother resumed her preparations—filling the large pasta pot with water, pouring the golden oil into the skillet, removing a bunch of broccoli rabe from the refrigerator (an alien bouquet of green stalks held together with a hot-pink rubber band)— the boy looked to the window, which was much blacker now, and much hungrier. It was a wonder the darkness didn't just smash itself into the kitchen. Black was tricky. Like a diamond, it wasn't one thing, one color, but many. Thomas Pittimore was out there in the darkness. The man in the rusty green truck was there, along with tomorrow's math test. Then came the butcher, the stolen prayer card, Toni-Ann's purple mouth. At the edges of the darkness, most obscured—but clearly the ringleader—was Edgar's father. It was too much—too many people, too many questions.

He looked at the rings dangling from his finger. If there was a war between a diamond and darkness, who would win? Would a diamond cut through the blackness to open up seams of light? Or would the darkness cover the stone with a tar-like ooze, trapping the gem for another million years? Edgar was pretty sure a diamond would win—especially since aliens often used them to power their ships.

"Here you go," said his grandmother. She set the white saucer with its single meatball on the table.

"Can I have my other fork?"

From the back of the cutlery drawer, Florence found one of the tiny oyster forks the boy favored. He handed her the large fork and she, in return, gave him the little one shaped like Neptune's trident.

As he nibbled, he watched his grandmother drop the *farfalle,* his favorite, into the steaming cauldron. Her face flushed as she drowned the butterflies with the ancient wooden spoon, whose long handle looked to Edgar exactly like Pinocchio's nose. Everything was so familiar it seemed strange, as if it were only pretending to be ordinary so as to better hide its secrets.

The old woman was wearing slippers and the boy could see the cracked backs of her feet. Sometimes she asked him to rub Keri lotion on them after she'd had a bath. She'd settle into her armchair, wearing the shiny quilted robe embossed with swirling paramecia-like paisley, and the boy would kneel before her, the jar of Keri lotion in his hands. The moisture barely penetrated the skin, which was thick and dry like the peel of an orange. Rubbing lotion into his grandmother's feet was like polishing a pair of shoes. But there was no repulsion. He marveled over those feet, cracked and swollen. The feet of a dinosaur. Had she once walked barefoot through a desert? Through a fire? Her hands, too, were damaged—so red they looked burned. Clearly his grandmother had been through some things, too. The writing wasn't on her arm, though; it was on her hands, her feet.

The room tilted, even before Edgar asked the question.

"How did he die, Gramma?"

Florence was certain she hadn't heard him correctly. She pushed at some *farfalle* that had stuck to the bottom of the pot.

The kitchen was warm and Edgar was under its spell, believing himself and all that he loved safe from whatever lay beyond the dark window. One could speak of terrible things, it seemed, and still not abandon safety. Somehow, the confusions and terrors of the last day distilled themselves into this:

"Did someone kill him?"

The words floated from the boy's mouth without effort.

Edgar had never asked before. He'd never wanted to know, never imagined that he *could* know. But at this precise moment a strange synthesis took place;

from dozens of overheard conversations a single bell seemed to toll: someone had pursued his father on the bridge, someone had pushed him. The world outside the house—Edgar was an expert now—was a dangerous place. The kitchen continued to tilt until it reached a precipitous angle. His grandmother slid away from the stove. Pinocchio's nose dripped onto the floor.

Did someone kill him?

Silence, for as long as you can imagine. A rosary of silence the old woman counted with a chain of memory, and the boy counted with the beats of his heart.

"Gramma?"

But there was no reaction. The kitchen had reached complete inversion, and Florence miraculously held her ground until a full turn had been completed and the room clicked back into place.

"My father, I mean," the boy said.

Florence wondered if the child had somehow figured out that it was Frank's birthday; why else would he be asking such questions? Suddenly the ghost was in the room—a glare off the refrigerator vexing Florence's wits. What would *he* want Edgar to know? Surely, he would want the boy to know the truth.

"Yes," she said, nodding to herself vacantly. She spoke quietly, but loudly enough for the boy to hear. "Someone killed him."

Edgar made a small sound, like a pigeon.

Florence looked into her grandson's face. There was no turning back. "Yes," she said again. "Yes."

7

Francesco

It wasn't a lie. Not entirely. Even Father Reginald, in private consultation, had hinted at the word *murder*. According to certain theologians, the killing of one's self was no different from a man killing his brother. Nothing brilliant here; Florence had always known that there were two Franks, and one of them—the shadow Frank, the impostor—had murdered the innocent flesh-and-blood Francesco.

But Father Reginald had stopped short before any suggestion of innocence. He talked about moral ambiguity and permanent solutions to temporary problems. Florence resented the priest's fancy philosophical tap dance, when all she'd wanted from him was that he locate her son's soul, stick the black pin of it on the map of God's mercy. But all the holy man did was drop the pin into a void, claiming it was God's to catch. Or not. Much of what he said was clearly damning. *We are stewards, not owners, of the life God has entrusted to us. It is not ours to dispose of.* Though he did mention that the Lord made concessions—concessions!—for grave psychological disturbance. Such disturbance would diminish her son's responsibility. Responsibility for what? she'd asked; to which Father Reginald had replied—rather cagily, Florence thought—that taking one's own life was a tragic loss of hope. To abandon hope, he said, was to abandon God.

Florence recalled how the priest had laid his shriveled hand on her own, and, no doubt thinking himself kind, had said she was welcome to have the funeral Mass at St. Margaret's (the church where Frank had been christened, communed, confirmed, *and* married); he'd officiate the Mass himself, if she liked—but he needed her to know that, in his eulogy, he would not be able to refer to the everlasting glory and eternal life of the deceased. It was not hopeless, he assured her; it just wasn't his to say. When Florence had left the rectory, a wave of vertigo overtook her, and she nearly fell in the street.

The boy at the table was staring at her with his impossible green eyes. The boy who, with his startling little question, seemed to have toppled the floodwall Florence had built between tragedy and innocence. She had built it for herself so she could rest, for brief moments, in the sunny garden of Frank's childhood, unassaulted by shadows. And she had built it for Edgar. Of what use would the truth be to him? A storybook father was preferable to the real McCoy, especially in Frank's case. The floodwall was no different from Pio's tunnel, a way to move through an element inhospitable to humans. But as the water rushed inside her now, it produced a feeling that was not altogether unpleasant.

She suddenly had an urge to tell the little boy everything, to confide in him. The impulse was dangerously strong; she could feel the great wave of it in her chest, like a hunger that had been denied for too long. After Frank's death, Pio had refused to speak about their son. So many times she'd tried to draw her husband into the private maze of her confusion. Perhaps he could help her find a way out; they could help each other. But whenever she'd broached the subject, Pio would shake his head and turn away, as if she were a stranger on the street trying to hand him a flyer. He'd leave the house, wander into the yard, smoke one of his horse-manure cigars—the whole time never ceasing to shake his head, as if to ward off any subsequent approach by Florence.

As for the girl: in the first few months after it had happened, Lucy's grief had been as great, if not greater, than Florence's. The young widow had wept with such sickening force that she often needed to run into the bathroom to vomit. It was as if grief had impregnated her, the dark seed of it a living havoc in her belly. The two women had been closest then, almost like sisters, in those underwater weeks after Frank's death. Florence would sit with Lucy on the porch, would hold the girl's hand. Once, she'd kissed her daughter-in-law's face when it had been wet with tears; had actually *eaten* the tears off her cheeks—a strange kind of sustenance, but that's exactly what it had been.

Unfortunately, the communion between the two women hadn't lasted very long. When the first mad flush of mourning had passed, and the faculty of speech returned to Florence, Lucy had no interest in conversation. Florence—who was ready to trade in her howls and sobs in return for a small piece of meaning—took up the mantle of Grand Inquisitor. Why had this happened? Who was to blame? What might have been done to prevent the tragedy? And, above all, there was the unresolved issue of Frank's soul. Lucy seemed indifferent to such questions. Occasionally, there was outright hostility. "What the fuck does it matter?" Lucy had screamed at her once. "He's not here!" A statement she'd cruelly repeated three times before retreating to her room. Lucy's tears retreated there, as well. She began to cry selfishly, locked away, preventing Florence's consumption of her grief. It was almost as if the girl were hoarding it. A starved Florence would stand by the door, listening—just as once (it was something for which she would never forgive herself) she had paused in the hall outside the young couple's bedroom when she'd heard the muffled sounds of an incomprehensible passion.

Within a year, the girl's crying had stopped. She began to grow hard, not unlike Pio. Often she took long rides in her car and skulked in late, long after the old woman had put Edgar to bed. If the child cried in the night, it was Florence who went to the boy's crib.

More than once Lucy had scooped up the toddler and taken him with her in the car. The old woman would be on pins and needles until the two of them arrived home safely. When pressed for information about where they'd been, Lucy would always say the same thing. "Nowhere." Well, Florence didn't like the sound of that. Nowhere was no place for a child, a baby. If Lucy wanted to go nowhere, she should go by herself. Florence's greatest fear (the one that had returned today) was that the girl would leave with the baby and not return. That the mother would *steal* the child. It was not too strong a word. The child belonged to all of them.

As she regarded Edgar's infinitely patient face at the table now, the tiny trident still in his hand, Florence felt confused. What had she told him already? Only pleasant stories of his father's youth. She'd never spoken of Frank's later years. For the child, she had kept Frank a child, a neat package of diverting anecdotes. If she'd sugared it up a bit, there was no harm in that. That was the privilege of memory—to edit, even to lie.

"Why are you crossing yourself, Gramma?"

She'd done it reflexively—and felt a prick of shame now, as if she'd been caught biting her nails. "Sometimes you do that for your thoughts," she said casually.

To which Edgar of course responded: "What were you thinking?"

She had to keep her story straight. There was a certain history of Frank she'd already recorded inside the boy's head. After her son's death, she'd recognized exactly what Edgar was: a blank slate. He was useful to her. Through him she had reinvented not only Frank's life, but her own. Were it not for the boy, she might have died, too. Edgar was nothing less than a second heart, to replace the one that had been ripped from inside her. There was no mad science here. The transaction was simple. Grief loves innocence, above all else. Over time, Florence's queen-like sadness was humbled; it bowed down before the opportunity that was Edgar. She put all her chips into the child's crib, amazed by how much she had left in her coffers to spend; and even more amazed by the extravagance of the profit. Loving Edgar had turned out to be a wise investment.

She could never understand why the boy's mother, or her husband for that matter, had not used the child in the same way. *Used* was not the right word. It wasn't strategy, it simply happened, it was nature itself. Love *streamed*, no different from tears. The girl's grief, Pio's, had turned in on itself and made them—it had to be said—less than human. What could be simpler than loving a child? Lucy and Pio had deprived the boy, but they had also short-changed themselves. The old woman felt this with a sadness that was torn in every direction, for all parties. How had her husband and Lucy managed to withhold what, to Florence, seemed so basic, so inalienable? Somehow grief had stripped them of their rights. After Frank's death, the two of them were no longer citizens of the world. Nomads, head-shakers, drivers without destination, they refused to come to rest, as if under the mistaken belief that one could stake a claim in love's ground only once. But hadn't they seen Florence's example, how she had set a tent on the windy hill of grief, and before long had rebuilt her home?

Had she lied to herself? Why was her breath coming up short? She moved toward the boy, who was clutching his three-pronged fork somewhat anxiously. A little god of the sea, uncertain of his power. But Florence could feel the trident stirring the water. She noted again the rush in her chest and, for the life of her, could not locate her heart. She had no sense, suddenly, if she were heartbroken or happy; if the house she'd rebuilt on love's hill was salvation or nothing more than a shack set on a graveyard. The waters tossed; a body thrashed in the undercurrent—Frank's body, which had never been recovered.

She wanted to tell the boy to put down the fork; he seemed to be pointing it right at her. Soon—she could already feel it in her throat—she would be crying out her son's name, as if seven years had not passed since his departure. The glassy eyes of the child were unrelenting, exposing the fragility of some unspoken agreement she'd made with him—with herself. Grief and confusion were just below the surface, buried under Edgar's loveliness. A shadow ran across the room. Florence made a small sound. And then it happened: the dead borrowed the child's face—and there was Frank, flashing like light off a mirror.

Save me.

But what could she have done? She'd done everything possible. Hadn't she?

Suddenly the anger rose again, against her husband and Lucy, who had refused to help Florence make sense of the disaster. With a small groan, she lowered herself into a chair beside Edgar. He set down Neptune's trident, but it was too late. She had no choice but to tell him everything.

"It's okay," she said. The boy was paler than usual. She wiped her hand across his cheek to erase the last bit of ghostly residue.

Edgar saw his grandmother's unhappy face and regretted whatever he'd done to cause it.

"I'm sorry," he said.

To which she responded, "Not you."

She grabbed his hand and held it so tightly that the boy knew he had no right to speak.

8

The Man in the Closet

There was so much she wanted to say. But it wasn't something you could say in five minutes to a priest in a box. Plus, she didn't have the words for it, she wasn't an educated woman. She gripped her grandson's hand and closed her eyes. The story had been locked inside her for so long it was part of her blood now. A roaring only she could hear.

The way Frank's sickness had progressed so stealthily no one had seen the monster of it until it was too late. It had taken advantage of what was best in her son. So smart, so handsome. Reckless, of course, as a teenager—but even that had seemed natural. Pio had said it was as simple as a boy becoming a man, nothing to worry about. By eighteen Frank had a thuggish swagger and a voice deeper than his father's. By twenty he'd quit the state college, claiming it was "bullshit." By twenty-two he'd been involved in four minor car accidents and had burned through at least a dozen jobs, all of which he professed were "physically killing him." He felt he was meant for better; said he wanted to write books! The boy was a confusing mess of ambition and laziness, arrogance and uncertainty. He slept too much, and when he was awake he was snappish, often downright belligerent. Scowling, unshaven, muttering about something, the twenty-two-year-old boy seemed, to his mother, more like an old man on the brink of senility.

But the next year, everything changed. Frank met Lucy. The two of them walked into 21 Cressida Drive, that first day, giggling like they'd just eaten a box of feathers—and then, for years it seemed, there was nothing but laughter in the house. Love took Frank out of himself; all that mattered now was that he make the girl happy. Always a jokester, his comic timing improved with Lucy in the audience. At dinner he had them all in stitches. The girl—who couldn't have been more than seventeen—seemed to give the household back its youth. Dinners were long again, as they'd been in the old days. Even

Pio lingered at the table, asking for more espresso and telling his own stories to the girl, in a kind of loving competition with his suddenly gregarious and clean-shaven son. It was a happy time. Lucy was a blessing.

But, behind Florence's back, the girl was encouraging the boy's old dreams. They planned to buy a motorcycle and ride from the Jersey Shore to Fisherman's Wharf—with a backpack full of nothing but almonds and dried apricots.

Almonds and apricots, my foot! What really kept them going, Florence realized, was shtupping and vodka. When Frank finally did buy a motorcycle, it took him exactly three days to run it into a tree. Luckily Lucy wasn't on board at the time, and Frank had fallen off the infernal chopper before it crashed against a hundred-year-old maple and burst into flames. Frank, badly bruised but miraculously unbroken, had taken them all to see the black scar on the tree—a blurry char whose shape suggested, to Florence's eyes anyway, a huge rat standing on its hind legs. It had filled her with dread—but Frank, standing before the seared tree trunk, had appeared elated.

A few weeks after the crash, he was all abuzz about a trip to Peru, to some steep green mountains where people who no longer existed had built a city. Frank had shown everyone pictures. To Florence it had looked bleak, cubicles of stone with no roofs; but Frank talked about the place as if it were the Vatican. He and Lucy—newlyweds now—were going to spend some time there. "Communing with the ancients" was how he'd put it. Pipe dream after pipe dream, until a person could barely see through the smoke. One day Frank announced he was going to be a professional gambler in Atlantic City; by the next morning the plan was to write a science fiction novel about alien vampires. Lucy had stood beside her young husband as he explained the gobbledygook of a plot, saying, *What great ideas he has, he really could be famous.* Encouraging Frank, egging him on, when the responsible thing to do—the duty of any decent wife—would have been to gently *discourage* him, or at least ignore him. But what did Florence expect from a child? Lucy had too much energy, combined with a stunning ignorance concerning what one could expect from life. The girl's youth had seemed, at first blush, like safety, a place where Frank could rest—but she'd turned out to be a wild horse upon which her son had resumed his old reckless habits.

Happy years, she supposed, for the two of them, running around, making their plans, doing whatever it was they did in their bedroom.

But when the boy's dreams crashed a second time, a strange stillness overtook him—a sullenness that Florence stupidly accepted with relief. She was glad to have a little peace and quiet. Frank began to read voraciously. He'd always been a smart boy; she was pleased to see him using his brain again—even if the piles of books grew to unmanageable proportions. Half of them were library books, grossly overdue—stories by writers long dead, with covers of faded black cloth in which dust seemed to have permanently settled. Others were curling secondhand paperbacks that smelled like mold and sported brightly aggressive covers with renderings of birds and castles and women in shimmering togas. He would read to Lucy sometimes—her body neatly folded up on his lap. Other times, he would wander off into the garden with his head drooping over the pages like a spent rose. And even though Florence could see, from the window, the odd expressions on her son's face, she thought to herself: at least he's focused.

Books were a mystery to Florence; she had had very little schooling herself—but she approved of education. She arranged Frank's books in neat piles. Such interesting names: Hesse, Huxley, Asimov, Nabokov, Vonnegut, Poe—plus one woman with the nutritious name of Rice. For a while, a blessed silence overtook the house—a silence ruled by the power of Frank's new-found inwardness. But this stillness had been deceptive. It was apparently a dark basement in which Frank had been tending even stranger thoughts—the evidence of which began to pop up everywhere, like black mushrooms. The thoughts were often so odd that when Frank gave voice to them, Florence wondered if they might not be a kind of humor she was not sophisticated enough to understand. There had been that nonsense about his teeth, about people coming at night and stealing things. Sometimes he counted the spoons.

She got to observe him more than the others. With Pio off at work and Lucy at beauty school, Florence spent the day with her jobless son, watching him wander around the house like he'd misplaced the Hope Diamond. Often he was in a tiff about frivolous matters: drips from a faucet; birds in the rain gutters; the Dominican mailman who wore a nylon head stocking and too much cologne. Whenever Florence opened the front door to fetch the mail, the smell of cologne would waft into the hallway, and Frank, who regularly observed the black man's movements from the living room window, would shout: "That's illegal!"

Florence often noted—sometimes only from the corner of her eye—how Frank clenched his jaw and flinched at the precise moment the mailbox was slammed shut. Noise seemed to be at the center of Frank's growing concerns.

At first, his condition didn't seem so much like madness, but simply touchiness, or possibly too much caffeine.

It was hard to know what was really going on in the boy's head. He never explained anything, never confided in Florence; though she would always say, "Frankie, talk to me. What do you need?" Still, it wasn't the end of the world. Florence knew it was a phase, it would pass. The boy was simply irritated with life, the way many among his generation seemed to be. The right job, that's all he needed—and then he'd come home exhausted, without the energy to nitpick the million little faults that were simply part of life. Because really, that's all it was, in Florence's opinion: a smart boy at odds with an imperfect world. She couldn't imagine, at that point, the power of the chaos tendrilling out from the center of Frank's brain. Later, she'd marvel darkly over the stealth of the shadow: a puppet show behind a scrim that took nearly ten years to arrive at its wretched conclusion.

When Lucy gave birth to Edgar, Florence hoped it would bring Frank back to his senses, but, sadly, the child had been born into the worst of it.

What had started out as foolish concerns and petty irritations became anxieties—which, in the last awful year, bloomed into full-fledged terror. Frank crouched on the floor of the baby's closet, tapping his fingers against the wall as if sending a telegram. Sometimes, when they found him there, he had Edgar with him—the child's eyes strangely placid or even closed, while Frank's were wide with fear. It was always Lucy who managed to coax him out, only Lucy whom he'd listen to. "Come on, baby," she would say. "Come on." Repeating the words until Frank stopped tapping and turned to look at her. She'd hold out her arms and wait for him to hand over Edgar. Florence, wiping her tears in the doorway, would watch as the mother laid the child in his crib and then went back to the closet for the man, who sometimes wouldn't step out of the tiny room for another half hour. It was not a rare occurrence to see the girl crawl into the closet beside Frank and whisper into his ear. Florence could never hear what the girl said, but whatever it was, it worked. Eventually, husband and wife—still so young, Lucy in her mid-twenties, Frank barely thirty—would emerge from the closet. A silent Florence stepped back to let them pass, hesitant to even touch her son on the shoulder. Though she would always touch the girl, in a glancing way, to mark her confused gratitude.

Lucy would lead Frank to their bedroom. They said nothing to one another as they walked down the hallway, but later Florence would hear them.

How was it possible, after what had just happened—and sometimes at two in the morning—that the two of them could sink into carnal activity? Sobs and ecstasies indistinguishable; it made no sense. And it wasn't right to mix love into nightmare. In Florence's mind, such disrespect for boundaries only added to the chaos that filled the house in those days. In bed, Florence would reach out in dismay and grab Pio's hand. "What's wrong?" he would say. "You don't hear them?" she'd ask him—at which point he'd take back his hand and tell Florence to go to sleep, it was over.

At the kitchen table, Edgar tried to pull his own hand away from his grandmother's.

"Stop fidgeting," she said. "Sit with Grandma." A sharp tone had crept into her voice.

Edgar looked at the stove, at the blue flames under the steaming pots and pans. His grandmother was ignoring the food. She'd been holding him captive for nearly five minutes now without saying a single word. It was stupid of him to have mentioned his father. His grandmother was going to burn down the house. The meatballs would be ruined.

Florence saw the consternation on the boy's face and released his hand. She held out the wooden spoon. "Give the pasta a stir, would you? Grandma needs to catch her breath." She offered him a smile—a stunning accomplishment, considering the tsunami in her chest.

As Edgar moved toward the stove, it was no longer familiar. What he'd always regarded as simplicity itself—the place where his grandmother produced meals with no discernible effort—now appeared to be the site of a very complicated scientific experiment. On tiptoes—for he was very small—the boy stirred the large silver pot. But that was the least of his problems. "The meatballs," he said. His grandmother's *pièce de résistance* appeared to be burning, judging from the smell and the demonic spitting of the olive oil.

"Turn them," the old woman said.

It was a strange inversion: Edgar cooking while his grandmother, in a fit of distraction, sat at the table. Is this what life would be like in the future, the boy wondered—when the old woman was too old to make their food? His mother certainly wouldn't do it.

Gently, Edgar turned the meatballs. A surprisingly difficult task—but he was glad to have the job. The science of it cleared his head of all other thoughts.

* * *

Such a good boy. *Mine,* the old woman thought as she watched him. Who would protect the poor child, if not her? After a half dozen or so episodes of Frank camping in Edgar's closet, Florence had put a padlock on the nursery door—the key for which she'd kept in her apron pocket. At seven o'clock every evening she would lock it. Lucy didn't object—nor did she argue with Florence when the old woman moved the speaker to the baby monitor into her own room. She kept it on the bureau beside the Virgin. At night she was comforted by the baby's sleeping sighs carried to her room by the miracle of invisible wires. Both she and Lucy agreed that possibly it was these very sighs—almost otherworldly in their animal loveliness—that might have tempted Frank to slip from his bed and go to the boy. Who—afflicted by late-night fears—would not want to clutch such sweet-smelling innocence to his chest? Florence herself knew it to be potent medicine. Still, they couldn't have Frank, in his altered states, swooping into the boy's room with unknowable intentions.

Luckily Edgar remembered none of it. Florence was greatly relieved when she read—another magazine article in Dr. Faustini's waiting room—that children did not form reliable, lasting memories before two years of age. Prior to that, it was as if they didn't exist—to themselves anyway. Florence did nothing to disabuse Edgar of a dull and empty beginning to his life on Earth. When she offered him tales of his early days, she offered him lies and blandishments. He accepted all of it without question.

Of course, there'd been that business, years later: Edgar's imaginary friend in the closet. But it couldn't have been Frank the boy was remembering; Florence felt sure of this. The boy always spoke of his invisible playmate with affection, not fear. Also, the closet man's name was John, or Jack—something with a *J.* Nothing to do with Frank. A made-up man to whom Edgar had fed cookies. Still, Florence had put a stop to it, had yelled at the boy—a thing she never did—and then, when no one was looking, had sprinkled a vial of holy water in the closet.

"They're stuck," Edgar said, referring to the meatballs.

"Use the spatula," instructed Florence, rising briefly from her reverie to help prevent culinary disaster.

As Edgar slowly shepherded the meatballs out of the pan, he did so with the care of a surgeon, as if the steaming balls were living things with beating hearts. Florence watched him. What an exquisite child. She was flooding again, her own meaty heart bobbing up briefly to the surface before sinking, once more, into the depths.

Foolish idea! To have put a padlock on the nursery door. Cruelty itself. Keeping the boy locked in, keeping his father out. And, really, what had Frank done? He'd never hurt the child, only held him. The padlock had been a mistake—Florence knew that now; it was a gun pointed in Frank's face. He'd absorbed the rebuff with a rage that was indistinguishable from shame. What had been intended simply to keep Frank in his own room proved to have the opposite effect. He took his night fears straight out of the house. When everyone was sleeping, he'd slip away, often without his shoes. When he returned, usually in the early morning, filthy as a coal miner, he would say nothing, ignoring everyone as he took the stairs, one retaliatory step at a time, back to his room.

Florence had often tortured herself with the thought that perhaps Frank's life might not have ended as it had if they'd only let him continue to clutch his son in a dark closet. Terrible as that was, worse things were yet to come. In the closet Frank had never seemed dangerous in any way—but not long after the insult of the padlock, the boy's rage finally erupted. One night he barged into the house, screaming. Florence woke with a start. She slapped Pio's head to wake him and jumped out of bed.

Lucy, in a cut-off T-shirt and pink panties, stood in the hallway, her hands on Frank's shoulders. He was banging on the padlocked door, shouting incomprehensibly in some wolf-howl language none of them could decipher. *"Gome fruk in there!"* he was saying. That's what Florence heard, anyway. *Gome fruk in there! Gome fruk in there!*—over and over, pounding his fist with enough force that the old woman was afraid he'd break the door. Lucy tried to stop him, but Frank kept shrugging her off. She persisted until a powerful shrug—practically a punch from Frank's shoulder—knocked her to the floor.

"Francesco," Florence shouted. "Enough!"

The madman turned to face his mother. *"You,"* he said, quite clearly, in hissing condemnation, before the more horrifying, if unintelligible, *"My owe weem kill me, huh?"* Florence hoped he was drunk. As he moved toward her, there was the threat of violence, and she saw, for the first time, that the man in front of her was not Francesco, but the other one, the impostor; a fact that allowed her to say something she could never have said to her own son. "Get out of my house." The words came from her mouth with surprising calmness, but as Frank continued to move toward her with his wolf eyes and his clenched fists, her consciousness enlarged to take in, once again, the infant—whose imprisoned cry had reached a throat-tearing pitch. No one was going to torture that child, not on her watch. Florence's second eviction notice shot out like a war cry: *"Get out of my house!"*

Lucy was still on the floor as Pio entered the fray, wearing the white terry-cloth bathrobe and matching slippers Florence had given him for his birthday. "What the fuck are you doing?" he said to Frank. Then answered his own question by slapping the boy's face. "You fucking bum, coming in here, middle of the fucking night, waking up your kid, waking up your mother."

Frank, stunned, looked for a moment as if some good sense had been knocked into him. His face went blank. Florence, seeing a quick flash of the real Frank, rushed in to touch her son's arm. Instantaneously, as if his mother's hand were a live wire—something entirely more dreadful than his father's slap—Frank fell to his knees. His mouth opened wide enough to show his silver fillings, and as his body began to convulse it was unclear whether he was laughing or crying. Florence knew something irrevocable was happening.

"You think this is funny?" Pio said. "You think this is a joke?"

Florence, now quite certain that the boy was not laughing, turned to her husband to warn him. But Pio was just beginning.

"Coming in here drunk," he scoffed—telling himself the same lie Florence had tried to tell herself. This was not drunkenness, though; it was something far worse. But Pio, a frightened old man standing at the edge of an abyss, chose to yell at his son. "You know what I think you are, Frankie? I think you're full of shit. What is this, three years now, this is going on? 'I don't feel well' or 'I'm confused,' and then you had to go to that friggin' *pazzo* doctor. You're lazy is what you are. You pretend you can't get up in the morning—but guess what, Cheech? We all gotta get up and do our job—and are we confused or not don't fucking matter!"

Florence could see her husband shaking as the anger moved through his frail body. In the last few months he'd practically stopped eating, complaining of a constant *agita*. Whereas Florence's worry for her son struck her straight in the heart, Pio's grief had burrowed into his stomach and hardened into an indigestible rage. Now it was coming up. Maybe this was good. Clearly Pio needed to get some things off his chest—and though his tone was cruel and his curses unnecessary, Florence essentially agreed with what her husband was saying. What did Frank have to be unhappy about? Yes, she understood, from what the doctor had said, that this was an illness—but still, it was hard not to see it as willfulness.

Pio was still shouting.

"What do you want out of life, huh? You want something special? You want it to be easy? You think your mother and I had it easy?"

Frank stared at his hands as if they were the source of his father's voice.

"You're a fucking disgrace."

"No," Lucy said quietly, tears in her eyes.

Pio, who'd never spoken harshly to the girl, told her to shut up. "You coddle him. You make him think he's some fucking hotshot."

Florence grabbed her husband's arm, warning him to go no further. As he pulled away from her, he lost his balance. The next thing Florence knew, Pio was lying on the floor.

How odd, she thought, noticing that she was the only person still standing. Frank was on his knees; Lucy, on her butt; and Pio, flat on his back. And though they all seemed far away, she could hear them distinctly: Pio moaning, Lucy softly crying, and her son mumbling a steady stream of nonsense. He raised his face to look at her. He was smiling now, though he was clearly not happy. Even his face was losing meaning.

"Ma," he said.

Tears came to Florence's eyes, to hear her name—a small scrap of sense in the boy's shattered language.

"Yes?" she said.

"Did you ever eat raw eggs?"

It seemed a burning question (the boy's hands were shaking), but before Florence could reply, Frank began to drill her with more nonsense.

"I had a, what-do-you-call-it, when it's blue, you know when you have a toothache, not blue, not blue, uh, not milk, because he's filthy, right?"

Florence closed her eyes.

"Did you ever wear a dress, Ma? A nice dress?"

Yes, the old woman thought. *I did. Made it myself.* Some part of her almost felt like laughing. She put her hand against the wall to feel something solid. Frank's voice rose hard again, chafing her flesh like gravel.

"And then they put them in there and they shit on everything, they puddle up the car."

"Come on, Frank. *Frankie.*" It was Lucy. She crawled over to him and touched his face. He didn't flinch. Florence felt a dart of jealousy. "I'll take him to bed," the girl said, and the old woman nodded.

"Come on, baby." He stood for her. When she kissed him, he kissed her back, even as the stream of words continued to fall from his mouth. The girl led her husband down the hallway. Before she followed him into their bedroom, she turned back to Florence and gestured toward Edgar's room. The old woman understood. *Take care of the baby.*

When they were gone, she looked at Pio. He wasn't dead, but he wasn't moving, either. His white robe had fallen open and she could see his hairy belly. "Daddy?" Frank had once asked his father. "Why do you have so much hair all over your body?" It was summer, and they'd taken the boy to Seaside Heights to swim in the ocean. "Because I'm a bear," Pio had said, lifting the child and growling into his ear until Frank was shaking with laughter—unabashed squeals that shot from the boy's mouth with operatic power. There had been so much laughter once. What a richness it now seemed, a jewel beyond measure. Florence could still hear the boy on the beach, squealing with a force that seemed too potent to have come from such a little body.

The baby was still crying. What was she doing, loitering in the hallway? She touched Pio lightly with her foot, but he didn't move. When she asked if he was okay, he replied, with a wave of his hand, that she should leave him alone. She stepped over his body and hurried down to the kitchen. She took the key from her apron pocket, came back upstairs, stepped again over her fallen husband, and inserted the key into the padlock.

The air in the room was humid, as if the child's cries were a kind of weather. Florence locked the door. When she picked up Edgar and bounced him lightly in her arms, the worst of his wailing stopped, though his face remained a terrible red shrivel and his breathing jerked in and out like a tiny handsaw. The child looked up at the old woman. What could she say? She kissed him three times on his forehead. With each kiss, she willed peace into his brain. It was late, the child needed to sleep. As she set him down in his crib, he flailed his arms with agitation and trumpeted his discontent. "Oh, no no no," she said. "Nana's here"—lifting him again and carrying him to the soft nursing chair by the window. Only then did she realize she'd forgotten the bottle of Lucy's pumped milk from the refrigerator. It didn't matter, though; the child wasn't hungry—Florence could tell. He simply needed to be held. "It's okay," she said. She kissed him again. "Silly people, all gone," she reassured him.

The room was sweltering. Holding Edgar carefully with one arm, she undid the top buttons of her nightgown. The baby watched her. "Nana's melting," she said. *Nana* was the name she'd given herself, but, later, when the boy began to speak, he seemed to prefer *Gramma*. He'd learned it from Lucy. *Go to Gramma; give it to Gramma; Mommy's going out for a bit, stay with Gramma.*

Florence felt better now with her nightgown open. The child reached out the white dumpling of his hand and knocked at the loosed flaps. "What do you need?" she asked. A tear fell from her eye and landed on the baby's lips. He flailed his arms more insistently.

Florence, understanding, undid her nightgown more fully. Damn them all.

No milk came, but as the boy suckled he looked at his grandmother with a profound expression of relief. Florence closed her eyes.

> *Stella stellina,*
> *la notte si avvicina,*
> *la fiamma traballa,*
> *la mucca é nella stalla.*

From the stove, Edgar could hear his grandmother singing behind him. As he turned to look at her, he was astonished to see that she was touching one of her boobies. The song seemed familiar, though it wasn't in English. Sometimes, for no reason, his grandmother spoke her other language. Edgar didn't like it. It sounded kooky. As he set the platter of blackened meatballs on the table, his grandmother opened her eyes and burst into tears.

Edgar was about to apologize for his poor cooking skills when he heard the front door open—and then the peanut-buttery voice of his mother. "I'm home!"

Lucy gasped when she entered the kitchen and saw Florence crying and the boy's shirt covered with a huge blood-red splotch. "Oh my God, what happened?" She rushed over to the table and touched Edgar's tomato-sauce wound. As if she'd pressed a secret button, the boy, too, erupted into tears.

"I burnt the meatballs," he wailed.

"He's fine," the old woman said, pulling herself together. She reached out her hand and patted Edgar's face. "Aren't you fine?"

Edgar nodded, rubbing his eyes. "She was teaching me to cook," he squeaked to his mother.

"Yes," Florence said, going with Edgar's story. "He has to learn sometime."

Lucy glanced around the room, checking for party hats (she knew it was Frank's birthday and suspected Florence might be up to her old games). "I have to pee," she said, leaving the kitchen.

"We have to talk," Florence called out. And then she turned to the boy, stroked his hair. "But first we'll eat this lovely dinner you made us."

"It won't be any good," he said, still sniffling.

"It'll be delicious," the old woman replied. "Here"—she handed him a napkin. "Wipe your nose."

9

Boo-Boo Bag

Driving at night was a loneliness made bearable. Lucy liked it best, very late, when all the porch lights and lampposts were dark, as if whatever virtue existed in other people's houses had been snuffed out, too. At such hours there was a democracy of loneliness; one felt the smog of it to be equitably distributed.

Lucy reached across to the passenger seat and pulled her handbag closer. Earlier she'd cashed her paycheck; the money was in her wallet. That, on top of the day's tips, added up to something. She could stop driving whenever she wanted, should she get thirsty. She could go to Nicky's or the Red Hen or Slaphappy's. She could even get on the Turnpike, make her way to one of the airport hotels, join the company of those lucky insomniacs waiting for an early-morning flight. At airport bars, you could pretend to be anyone. *Who, me? I'm off to Brazil,* she'd say to the businessman next to her. *I love Brazil,* he'd reply, slurring enthusiastically—*Brazil is fucking amazing.*

Maybe she wouldn't spend the money on booze, but rather on a few tanks of gas. Drive aimlessly until she was thoroughly lost, unable to find her way home. Drive until there were cornfields and cows and old men on tractors.

Every time she dreamed of escape, though, something twinged in her side: that damned elastic strap that connected her to Florence's house. It seemed capable of stretching endlessly; though surely, at some point, it would break—the loosed cord snapping back to hit the old woman flat in the face.

The nerve of the old bitch. Treating Lucy like she was a teenager in need of a curfew or a cold shower. Florence needed to get a fucking hobby, something other than Edgar. Other than sticking her nose into Lucy's private affairs.

Earlier, when Florence had brought up the fact that Lucy hadn't come home the night before, Florence had tried her best to pass it off as concern.

"Everything all right, dear?" When Lucy replied, "Just a date," the old woman had smiled affably and said, "Oh, very nice."

All through dinner Florence had maintained a thin veneer of pleasantness—though Lucy could see the effort it cost her. After the meal—a disgusting offering of mushy pasta and burnt meatballs—Edgar was excused, and Florence suggested that she and Lucy have some demitasse. At the mention of it, Lucy knew she was in trouble. Since Pio had passed away, Florence rarely made demitasse. Lucy understood the old-world politeness to be, in this case, the equivalent of one last cigarette before she was shoved before the firing squad. In the living room, with the tiny cups in their hands, Florence began her interrogation. The questions were short and direct, and Lucy, in turn, delivered her answers in as few words as possible.

"And who is this man?"

"A butcher."

"From where?"

"Not far."

Florence sipped. Lucy sipped.

"What's his name?"

"Ron."

"Ron what?"

"Salvatore. He owns the shop."

"Salvatore's Meats?" The old woman pursed her lips.

Lucy nodded. "That's the one."

"We don't get our meat there," Florence said.

"Would you prefer I date your butcher?" replied Lucy.

"Haven't you?"

It went on like this, quip for quip, until the two women were speaking in strangely high voices that sounded, to Edgar—who was hiding at the top of the stairs—exactly like Beep and Tweep, the rivalrous cartoon parakeets from *The Beep and Tweep Show*. The tension had started while the two women were attempting to eat the horrible dinner Edgar had prepared. When the old woman first bit into one of the shriveled meatballs, she smacked her lips approvingly but suggested a salad might be in order. She sent Edgar into the yard with a flashlight to pick some tomatoes. Soon they'd be gone, she said. "Pick as many as you can find." When the boy returned with three enormous beauties, his mother and grandmother looked up at him with such phony smiles that Edgar was certain they were going to kill each other before the meal was through. As the boy watched them chew and swallow, dutifully eating what was indisputably inedible, he felt sick to his stomach—even as he spit each of his own small bites discreetly into a napkin. Dinner had passed slowly, in eerie civility. But later, from the top of the stairs, Edgar clenched his fists as all hell broke loose below.

"Should I never fuck someone again?" Beep said.

"Language," said Tweep.

"You want everyone to live in a friggin' wax museum."

"I want respect. This is my house."

"I help pay for this shit."

"Keep your voice down, Lucille."

"Why? As if the kid doesn't know what's going on."

"Well, you don't have to rub his face in it."

"What did I—"

"Vodka on the coffee table, *cigarettes.* Is that what you want him to see? What are you teaching him with things like that? What's he supposed to think?"

"Whatever you tell him, I guess."

"I keep my mouth shut. I don't say a word."

"Please. You twist his fucking mind."

"Again with the language!"

Edgar felt that perhaps he should be writing all of this down, like one of those ladies in the corner of a courtroom. What if somebody wanted to know, one day, the story of his life? He'd have to remember things like this.

"What were the two of you up to when I got home?" he heard his mother say.

"I told you, I was teaching him to cook."

"Why was he crying?"

"He's a crier, he's *sensitive.*"

"Having another little party, were you?"

"What are you talking about?"

"Don't play games. I know what day it is, Florence."

"Oh, do you? Is that why you went out with some stranger? Is that how you pay your respects? Staying out all night. Acting like a . . ."

"Like a what?"

"Not like a wife, that's all I know."

"Don't you dare—"

"Not like a mother."

"Fuck you."

When Edgar heard the slap, he jumped. Before he knew what he was doing, he was running down the stairs. In the living room he saw the tiny cup on the floor, the brown stain on the pale carpet. The women looked up at him. Both their faces were red; it was impossible to tell who'd been slapped. Edgar hesitated, not knowing if he should move any closer. His mother's hands were trembling, and his grandmother wasn't breathing right. He looked from one to the other, and then back to the doll cup on the floor. When he lifted his head again for an answer of some sort, habit and instinct returned him to the old woman's face. His mother was a burning planet to his left. Edgar felt the heat.

"That's right," Lucy said. "Go to Grandma."

Something was peculiar about how she'd said it. When Edgar turned to her, she spoke again, her voice strikingly unkind. "Go on. *Go to her.*"

But Edgar didn't move. He kept his eyes on his mother now, even as the horror-movie sound of his grandmother's breath troubled his ear.

"I'm leaving," Lucy said, turning away.

"No." Edgar rushed to her side. After everything that had happened today, he had a funny feeling. What if she meant *forever*? He grabbed her hand.

"Leave her alone," the old woman hissed, and the boy, to everyone's surprise, obeyed.

Strangely, the gesture of releasing his mother's hand seemed to have more power to hold her in the room than when he'd clutched her. She stopped moving and turned to him. In the silence between them, Edgar felt like an actor who'd forgotten his line.

Was his mother crying? It was hard to tell. The tears were just enough to fill her eyes, but not enough to fall. Worse than the tears, though, was the way his mother shook her head in disgust. It was exactly how Mr. Brunelli, the phys ed teacher, shook his head when Edgar tripped or fumbled a ball.

He should not have let go of his mother's hand. He knew that now. It was a terrible terrible mistake. The boy had an urge to punch himself in the stomach to prove his loyalty.

Florence, watching the scene, felt that all of it had happened before. The boy, the mother, the dark stain on the carpet. If not this slap, this violence, then another one. She felt, suddenly, a fear that all things, all people, were interchangeable in the cruel mechanics of the universe. As she collapsed into the armchair, an almost painful boredom seared her heart. The endless repetitions within a single life, like some bedeviling trick with mirrors. When she heard a car pulling away, Florence returned to her body, only to realize she was now alone in the room.

"Edgar!" She tried to stand, but her knees locked.

Had she really slapped the girl? Strangely, the aftermath of her small violence was a wish to wrap Lucy in her arms, to clutch her until all desire for flight had been exhausted.

But the girl was already gone. Why, Florence wondered, were people so impatient? Didn't they realize that love was slow, shy, baffled half the time by pride? The girl should have recognized what was in Florence's heart, even if Florence had not yet expressed it.

"Edgar!" she cried out again, now certain that the girl had taken him.

When the boy reappeared, Florence wheezed with relief. She held out her hand. "Come here, baby. Help me up."

But the boy stayed where he was, hovering like a dark elf in the shadow of the entryway. She couldn't see his face. Again she shook her hand, demanding he move out of the darkness and come to where the light was better.

Edgar watched her breathe in fits and starts, and wondered if she was pretending. If it was just some trick to make him go to her.

"Go to Grandma," his mother had said, as if she knew him better than he knew himself, as if everything he would ever do was already written.

"She left," the boy said, keeping his distance.

"Yes. It's okay. Come here."

"Did you hit her?"

"What? No, of course not."

Edgar stared at the old woman, waiting for an explanation.

"This is between grown-ups," she said. "It's"—hiccup of breath—"nothing for you to worry about."

"Why are you doing that?" the boy said with sudden force. He couldn't stand another minute of his grandmother panting like a dog.

"What am I doing? And stop hovering in the doorway, I can hardly see you."

"She drove away."

"She'll be back."

"How do you know?"

"Doesn't she always come back?"

Edgar barely shrugged.

"Of course she does."

"She made *marks* on the driveway," the boy said, his voice rising again.

"Where are you going? *Edgar.*"

The boy returned to the front door, which was still open. In the glare of the outdoor lights, he looked again at the black chars on the driveway. His grandmother was shouting something behind him. When he returned to the living room, she was standing, leaning on the chair for support.

"What's gotten into you?" she said.

Edgar lifted his foot to stamp it, but only held it there before letting it fall gently back to the carpet.

"They could kill her, too."

"Kill who?" The old woman touched her neck, which was damp with sweat.

"Her," the boy insisted.

"Your mother?"

Air rushed from the boy's mouth. "If they killed *him.*"

"Oh my God," Florence said, falling back into the soft chair with a thud. "No one's killing anyone tonight." What had she said to the boy? She couldn't remember now.

"Did they ever catch who did it?"

"Oh my God," Florence said again. "You just forget about all that." She closed her eyes and begged silently for forgiveness. Whatever seed she'd planted in the boy's mind had already bolted into bloom. "You don't know anything," she said softly, as if she could mesmer, the boy into forgetfulness.

But Edgar took umbrage. "I know things," he said sharply.

"Of course you do. I'm only saying there's nothing to worry about."

Edgar was suddenly beside himself with fury. He marched over to the old woman and pulled up his sleeve. "Look," he said.

"What? What are you doing?"

"Look!" He brandished *Supersluts.com* right before Florence's face.

"What is that? I can't see. Get me my glasses."

Edgar, regretting his rashness, tried to pull away. But the old woman held tight. She leaned in to inspect his arm.

"Did you cut yourself?"

"No," he said, still trying to extricate himself.

"You scratched yourself in the woods, didn't you? What did I tell you about traipsing around in there?"

"It's not *scratches.*"

"I can see it," she said. "It's all red. Why didn't you show me this when you got home? Do you want to get an infection?"

"I'm not hurt!"

"Go and get my boo-boo bag," his grandmother ordered.

Edgar's rage slumped into exhaustion before the insult of his grandmother's blindness. "It's not *scratches,*" he said again, but with less conviction. "It's words."

"I can't hear you when you mumble. Go and get my bag."

When the boy returned with the little Macy's shopping bag his grandmother kept under the sink in the downstairs bathroom, he watched dolefully as she removed the contents and lined them up on the table beside her chair. Cotton balls, gauze pads, Band-Aids, a needle-nosed tube of ointment, a large bottle of hydrogen peroxide, a tiny one of Mercurochrome. The old woman took nothing more seriously than an injury to Edgar's person. Even a mosquito bite was cause for alarm, requiring treatment with a cold compress, followed by calamine lotion.

"Give me your arm."

This was all wrong. He wasn't hurt; his mother in all likelihood was the injured party. Still, Edgar gave up his arm and watched, in detached horror, as his grandmother soaked a cotton ball in hydrogen peroxide and then swiped it across every letter of *Supersluts.com.*

"Some scratches you got here, Mister Explorer. Those brambles did a number on you, huh?"

Edgar nodded, confused, as the tears fell down his cheeks. He wiped them away quickly, but the old woman saw the gesture.

"Am I hurting you? I'm almost done."

She wet another cotton ball and cleaned the last of the letters. Miraculously, the hydrogen peroxide had removed some of Thomas Pittimore's ink. When she applied the Mercurochrome from an ancient-looking dark glass bottle, all meaning was abolished behind a stain of reddish-brown. A large gauze pad was put over the wound, and held in place with surgical tape.

Someone, Edgar thought, should be putting a cool washcloth on his mother's cheek.

"All done, soldier," his grandmother said, lifting his hand to kiss it. She held his fingers to her mouth, and her little kisses sounded like words. She was using his fingers the way she used her rosary beads at church—holding them before mumbling lips that offered up some secret prayer. Edgar pulled away.

She didn't seem to notice, though. Her eyes were closed. When she opened them a few moments later, she looked confused. She looked sad. "We're still here, huh?"

Edgar, who could think of no lie, said, "Yes."

"Well, that's no good. Let's get ourselves into bed." She held out her arm, and the boy had no choice but to take it.

"Up up up," she said—and Edgar pulled.

10

Saint Christopher

Lucy's hands were shaking as she pulled over and parked in the dark lot outside Slaphappy's. Damn them all, she thought. Even Ron. Earlier, from work, she'd called the butcher shop. Ron had answered with a rough, "Yeah?" Even after hearing Lucy's voice, he'd remained just as gruff. "I have customers coming out of my ass. I'll get back to you later." But, of course, he hadn't.

Get back to her later? Only now did she recognize the cool brush-off couched in those words.

She'd wanted to spend the night with him again, crushed under his massive body, lobotomized by the knife blade of sex. Now she was alone in a dark parking lot. The light from the dash glinted off the Saint Christopher medal Florence had hung, years ago, from the rearview mirror. She'd installed one in Frank's car as well—and a lot of fucking good that had done. Impulsively Lucy reached up and tore the medal away. She buzzed down the window and flung the patron saint of travelers onto the blacktop. It landed with a tinkle, strangely musical in the darkness. Lucy felt a small stab of fear, similar to what she'd felt two months after Frank's death when she'd thrown her wedding ring into the Hudson River.

She closed the window and pulled down the visor flap to check her face in the mirror. Eyes monstrously green, trapped inside rims of fire. Delicate wrinkles flared outward from each temple, like a child's drawing of seagulls. A subtle falling of the cheeks secured a permanent frown. Frank probably wouldn't even recognize her were his ghost to stroll past the car. She'd changed so much since he left. *Because* he left. Lucy leaned on the horn and let it blare into the empty parking lot.

God, how she missed him—the part of him that was good, that had saved her from her father, protected her. She missed the boy who kissed her so deeply he could taste her anger—and yet he'd never turned away, never spit it out. He'd swallowed her whole. What the two of them had, it wasn't something she could explain. It was just everything.

To be honest, she hadn't remembered it was Frankie's birthday until she'd seen Florence blubbering in the kitchen and Edgar covered in red sauce. Even if she *had* remembered, it was unlikely she would have acted differently. She would have still gone out with Ron, still fucked him three times on his ham-colored sheets. Wouldn't Frank have wanted that? That she keep herself going somehow? To hell with Florence's judgment about what was right and what was wrong. After what had happened to all of them, it was clear to Lucy that such lines couldn't be drawn. One had permission to do anything, live however one chose. If there was any law, it was the law of chaos.

There was no place, though, for such wildness in the immaculate house of her dead husband's mother, a frigid old woman of seething politeness who Lucy often felt hated her more than her own father—and for similar reasons. Lucy's bent toward pleasure seemed to threaten them. Most days she felt she had to move through Florence's house with her head bowed, so as not to be blinded by the glare of the old woman's piety. It was a house of glass—of ice. Of course, Florence and Edgar had made a private circle of fire, into which Lucy had never been invited, and inside of which the two of them seemed to exist in a kind of contented silence.

What ordered beings she lived with! Even with their occasional fits of tears, their days for the most part unfolded under the influence of steadier rhythms. The old woman and the boy moved through the rooms with such ease, with such clear intentions and purpose, that their paths achieved an almost perceptible pattern, a web inside of which Lucy often felt trapped. The house was theirs, its very fiber an extension of their bodies. After living there for almost fifteen years, Lucy still stumbled, confused, over the laws of the territory. If she tried to help with the housekeeping, she always got it wrong. "This vase lives here," Florence would say, taking it from where Lucy had put it and placing it on the correct shelf. Just last week, she'd been stripping her bed, only to have Edgar poke his head in her doorway and say, "Sheet day is Tuesday, Ma." She'd watch from the sidelines as the boy held up the corner of an area rug so that Florence could vacuum underneath; or the way the pair of them moved apart and then together as they folded a sheet, their fingers touching at each inward sweep, until the distance between them closed and a perfect rectangle rested in Florence's hands. The customs of some foreign country. The way the old woman tugged at the boy's left ear as she kissed the top of his head.

Lucy wanted to touch her son more than she did, but he was babied enough by the other one. She'd kissed him last night though, hadn't she? When she'd smelled the perfume on his neck. What a strange kid. Even his occasional larks and bursts of zaniness, like his recent habit of barking like a dog, seemed to rise not from a playful ease, but from a kind of gothic nervousness.

A doctor had once said that the boy might be borderline autistic. He'd wanted to do more tests, but Lucy had refused. The stigma of albinism was enough. Besides, Lucy knew there were other reasons for the boy's oddness— first and foremost the shock he'd suffered on the day of his father's death. She could also blame the kid's strangeness on the ridiculous name Frank had given him.

After the boy's birth, Frank had fallen into a spell of manic excitement, during which he'd insisted that the child be named Edgar. They'd already decided on Frank Jr., but Frank, looking at the newborn's unnaturally white face, had said it was impossible. Lucy resisted for weeks—a limbo in which the child had remained nameless. Florence, too, had spoken up. *"Edgar?"* she'd said. "What kind of name is that?" When Frank tried to explain the genius of the author whose namesake Edgar would be, Florence—who only knew the blood-drenched movie versions of this author's works, starring Vincent Price—was aghast: "You want to name him after a man who hangs knives from the ceiling?" But Frank had been adamant—and since they all knew it was unwise to stand in his way when he was dead set on something, the boy had become Edgar. *Edgar Allan Fini.*

Lucy reached for her handbag, in need of a cigarette.

Most of the time she simply didn't know how to relate to the kid. He was nothing like her. Well, he was beautiful, as she'd once been. But even their beauty was different. Edgar was a large-eyed, rail-thin prince from some animated Japanese fantasy. Lucy was top-heavy and ample thighed, with seastorm hair. And the boy was timid. When he spoke it was like someone had trapped his voice under a glass bell. Lucy, with her limp, clonked into a room and had fearsome lungs. Her words were rarely misunderstood.

Edgar was afraid to ask for things, whereas Lucy, at her best, had no compunction against demanding, grabbing, or, if necessary, stealing. Life was short, people were selfish; sometimes one had to hold an antagonist upside down and shake the change from his pockets. Lucy imagined her son wouldn't even steal a penny from his grandmother's purse.

How could the boy have come from her? Lucy was an open-faced sandwich; Edgar, a closed book. She ate like a day at the races—competitively; Edgar chewed cautiously, food taster to the king. Once, on a plane (Lucy taking a five-year-old Edgar to visit a cousin in Michigan), a stewardess had given them individually wrapped packets of cookies. Lucy immediately ripped open the foil and scarfed down the two dry wafers. Edgar, on the other hand, ate only one before resealing the bag with an origamically precise fold. When Lucy asked why he wasn't eating the other cookie, the boy replied that he was "saving it for later." The answer had made her head spin. *Save for later?* The concept was beyond Lucy's understanding; she spent or devoured life without delay. Frank had been the same. When Edgar had fallen asleep, thousands of miles in the air, Lucy slowly wriggled the foil bag from her son's hand and polished off the remaining biscuit.

She was a terrible mother, she wasn't going to deny it. So kill me, she thought—right here in the parking lot of this sleazy fucking bar.

Immediately came a loud rapping against the window.

Lucy jumped, and turned to see a silhouette standing outside the car. It was exactly Frank's height. Lucy gasped and quickly locked the door.

"Are you okay?" The man leaned in, close to the window.

"I'm fine. Just don't . . ."

"I didn't mean to scare you, sorry. I saw you sitting there, I thought maybe you were having car trouble."

When she realized that her face was illuminated by the small light in the visor mirror, she quickly snapped it shut, putting both herself and the man in a more equal darkness. "Do I know you?" she ventured cautiously.

"I don't know, do you?"

"I can't see your face," Lucy said. "I'm not a fucking owl."

"Oh, sorry." The man pulled a cigarette lighter from his jacket pocket and lit it a few inches from his nose. The jack-o'-lantern glow showed pale skin, blond hair.

"You shouldn't knock on people's windows like that," Lucy snapped, emboldened by the fact that the man outside the car was not her dead husband.

And then, because the Zippo-wielding stalker was not unattractive, she softened a bit, shifting blame to the establishment. "I don't know why they don't put better lights in this parking lot."

"It's a shit hole," the man agreed.

"I didn't even see your car pull in," Lucy said.

"Yeah, you looked like you were praying or something."

"I don't pray," scoffed Lucy.

"No, but I mean you were like totally in a trance or whatever."

The flame from the lighter went out. *"Ow,"* the man said. "Burned my finger on this bitch." His face was in shadow again.

But Lucy had seen enough to know what she was dealing with. He was a boy, twenty-five, twenty-six. Jacked up on something, but obviously harmless.

"I'm James, by the way."

He was speaking loudly, probably in compensation for the darkness, and for the fact that there was a closed window between them.

Lucy buzzed down the glass and extended a hand toward Jimmy (surely that's what his friends called him). "Lucy," she said.

The handshake extended beyond its measure of politeness, but neither made the first move to release the other.

"My palms get sweaty," Jimmy said shyly.

"Yes," Lucy replied, noting in particular how the heat of the Zippo still lingered on the boy's thumb.

*   *   *

A distraught Edgar had trouble falling asleep, but he refused to seek refuge in Florence's room. After checking under his bed three times, and the closet once (no one was hiding in either place), he crawled under the sheets and began the secret process that often helped him to drift off. By gently rubbing his index finger in steady circles against the palm of his other hand, he slowly unwound himself from thought (*someone killed my father*) into abstraction (*acorns falling into black water*). Absorbed by the fluid cosmos of intersecting ripples, he successfully shed his body and drifted into the underlight.

Only to dream of two men fighting on the rooftop of a skyscraper, a lavishly budgeted enterprise in which a basalt-black cityscape was twinkle-lit with the power of a million unleashed brain cells. If he had escaped his own body, he could not escape the others. One of the men had the face of his father. The other, the murderer, took no face at all—a blind spot in Edgar's consciousness that persisted even here, in the all-possible. As the violent tango on the rooftop veered into edge-taunting dips, its very intensity caused it to dissolve, as is the dreamer's fickle right. A field of falling leaves, and then falling itself, until the boy was safe in the deepest chamber of sleep, the bottomland below emotion.

In the bedroom down the hall, Florence was falling, too. This after an hour of burning indigestion, a slow poisoning—not of her stomach, it seemed, but of her heart. She had prayed for all of them, but the words only served to blow the evening's embers back to flame. One couldn't pray when one was angry. When she finally fell asleep, her rest did not take her to the depth Edgar achieved. She stayed on the fiery plain of emotion, the haunt of the living, where the dead visit only in chains.

He would come, though, if she were patient—come as he was, without redemption or hope. But he would come.

* * *

When Lucy stumbled from the bar, her new friend was perfectly sober. He'd nursed a single pint while Lucy made her way through four bourbons with a beer back. Jimmy was an odd duck, a little twitchy, and the longer they'd sat at the bar the more nervous he'd become. His inability to relax—the tapping foot, the subtle spice of his perspiration—had made Lucy feel like she needed to drink for both of them. Jimmy was not being clear about what he wanted—and someone, Lucy felt, had to bring the crisis of flirtation to a head. The alcohol helped, as it always did, but she feared she was camping it up too much for the boy's comfort. At one point, he'd glanced around the bar and said, "Shit, we're the only people in here," and Lucy, in reply, had put her hand on the boy's thigh and slurred, in her best older-woman voice: "The only two people in the world, baby." When Jimmy saw the generous tip she'd left the bartender from her leafy pile of hard-earned cash, he asked with an anxious titter if she was a mobster. "*No-oh,* baby," she whispered, patting his smooth cheek. "You're the mobster. I'm the moll." The word had taxed his vocabulary. "Cool, yeah," he said. "Maybe I better get you home."

A few steps outside the establishment, in the dark parking lot, Lucy stepped on a stone, causing her ankle to go wonky. As she tipped to the left, she crashed into her companion and clutched him ineffectively, as if his thin body were a slippery flagpole. "I can't . . . oh shit, I . . ." She wanted to laugh, but it really wasn't funny. Finally she felt the boy's strong arms stopping her descent and the next thing she knew, she was upright again—and then the boy was lifting her like a bride. "No," she said, "I'm fine." But he already had her fully in his arms and was carrying her across the parking lot. "I'm too heavy," she sighed. But the boy's muscles didn't seem strained. She gave in and laid her head on the tautly upholstered bones of his shoulder. In an instant, she traded in the hirsute cleaver-wielding giant she'd slept with the night before for this sturdy and nervous usurper. When he put her down in front of his car, she leaned, face-forward, against the back-door window. The glass felt cool on her cheek.

"You're really wasted," the boy said, and Lucy's rebuttal ("No-um-nah") only confirmed that she was. Her eyes slowly focused on the inside of the boy's car, which was jam-packed with the shadowy lumps of his belongings. There appeared to be piles of clothing, a collection of overstuffed shopping bags, and something that looked like a folded-up tent. On the floor lay a computer and a baseball bat—or maybe an ice chest and a rifle. It was hard to tell in the darkness.

"You've got a lotta shit in there," Lucy said.

The boy said nothing as he placed his fingers on her shoulder.

"Are you going on a rip?"

"A what?"

"A *trip*," Lucy enunciated.

Again, Jimmy offered no reply—but at least he was touching her. Lucy leaned into the car and moaned as the boy's hand slid down her side. "We should go someplace," she suggested. For all her boldness, Lucy was not one for sex in public places. Not since she'd been fined for it, years ago, with Frank. "You live close by?"

"It's okay," Jimmy said, as his hand worked more quickly to position her as he wanted. When he yanked Lucy's arm away from her body, she realized he was getting tangled up in her handbag.

"Is that in your way, baby?" She pushed away from the car to unstrap the bag from her shoulder.

Immediately he pushed her back and told her not to move.

She'd not expected such forcefulness from the boy.

"At least let's get in the car," she said. "Or my car, there'll be more—"

"Shut up for two goddamn seconds, will you." It was a voice she hadn't heard from him before—but since she wasn't opposed to a little aggression in a man, she flattened herself agreeably against the door. When she felt his hand again, it wasn't on her hip, but inside her bag.

"I don't have a condom," Lucy said. "Is that what you're—"

Mid-sentence, she snapped awake. *"Hey,"* she shouted. "What the fuck are you doing?" When she turned, the boy had her wallet in his hand and was pulling out the cash. "You little piece of shit." Unsteadily she lunged at him, but with one easy push he knocked her to the ground. She felt the damage, a burning scrape across her knees.

"Sorry," he said.

"James," she said gently—as if there'd been some mistake, as if he'd forgotten they were friends.

"That's not my name. Get a fucking life."

She felt the empty wallet hit her on the back of the head—an insult so great that, as the boy drove away, she could not bring herself to look up to note the license plate. Neither did she call out for the bartender. She vomited, wiped her mouth. The empty wallet was beside her, and she retrieved it before crawling toward her car. Shame, more than drunkenness, prevented her from standing. The pain in her knees was sobering.

She felt a coin under her hand as she crawled. The boy had stolen all her money. What would she tell Florence? She usually gave the old woman half her paycheck. Lucy picked up the dime, but it wasn't a dime. It was Saint Christopher. The man who'd carried the Christ child across a swollen river. She only knew the story because she'd overheard Florence tell it to Edgar.

Lucy gripped the medal in her hand and then flung it with all her strength toward some bushes at the edge of the lot. All she wanted now was to get in the car and drive. Disappear.

When the phone in her bag began to ring, she was afraid. She knew it was the old woman. But what could Lucy tell her? She could say a friend was ill, she'd be gone a few days. Buy herself some time.

She blindly pulled the phone from her bag and answered it. Her lips were trembling, though, and no words came.

"Lucy?"

It was the butcher.

The sound that suddenly burst from her mouth could not be stopped.

"What's wrong?" the butcher said. "Are you all right?"

"I'm . . . yeah, I'm . . ." She held the phone away from her face so that he wouldn't hear her crying.

"Did I wake you up?" Ron was saying as she brought the phone back to her ear.

"Don't worry about it."

"So, do you feel like it?" he said.

"Feel like what?"

"What I just said. Come over, if it's not too late."

A shaking Lucy covered her mouth.

"You don't want to?"

"I want to," she said quickly.

"Good," said the butcher—and Lucy repeated the word with the shrill lilt of a mockingbird.

11

Vesuvius

Edgar woke with a start. There was something cold on his chest, as if someone had dropped an icy coin there. He slipped his hand under his pajama top and then looked up to see if the roof was leaking (it had happened before). The only thing entering the room, though, was the sun, oozing through a crack in the baby-blue curtains. The light was thick, a bright yellow-orange like hot lava.

Edgar's mind flashed to something he'd seen on television. Figures encased in ash. People trying to run from a volcano's wrath; families huddled together, even a dog—all of them simultaneously killed and preserved by the hot goo that had rained down upon them. Edgar sympathized. He lifted his hands against the sun-lava pulsing between the curtains, feeling certain he'd achieved the perfect gesture of mortal terror. To any onlooker, though, the boy's pose—jazz hands and angelic O-mouth—might have suggested that Mount Vesuvius had splattered its juice upon an amateur production of *Annie*!

Edgar climbed out of bed and scuffed his feet against the thick carpet, slowly making his way across the room. Before entering the hallway, he stopped, pointed a finger, and touched the copper doorknob. When it sparked, he let out a small, satisfied squeal. It was his habit to greet the doorknob in this manner every morning. Today's shock was particularly potent, and Edgar was wide awake as he made his way down the stairs. When he heard a clang in the kitchen, he hoped his grandmother was making waffles. He was *starving*.

* * *

She'd told the butcher she'd been out drinking with a few gals from work. "One too many?" he'd said, noticing the scraped knees. "Angie kept ordering pitchers of margaritas," she'd replied, padding the story. Luckily he'd pried no further about her injury—though if he needed more specifics, she'd prepared a line about an uneven sidewalk outside a Mexican restaurant. When the butcher kissed her boozy mouth, it was with a slow seriousness that had made her swallow her lies and fall silent. In the bathroom he'd told her to sit on the edge of the tub—after which he'd knelt down to clean the cuts with alcohol poured onto a wad of toilet paper.

Now they were sleeping. They'd had sex only once—rather uncomfortably in the bathtub. When Lucy had first arrived, the butcher noted the shaking hands and strained smile, not to mention the roughed-up knees—and he'd pretty much abandoned the idea of fucking her. But after he'd cleaned the cuts, she'd leaned forward and bitten his ear—and his ears were his weakness. She bit and licked and flicked her tongue until he was moaning like a little girl. When she tugged him into the empty tub, it was like some fumbling reenactment of a boyhood fantasy. "I'm crushing you," he kept saying—and the girl kept saying, "Yes." He pulled up her dress and entered her unsheathed, pumped until he shot his warmth into her. It wasn't until later, lying in bed beside his gently snoring lover, that he realized this was the first time he'd ever come inside a woman. A terminus of latex had always limited his fulfillment. Nearly forty years old, and it was not until tonight that he'd experienced the full flower of sex. When he exploded unimpeded within Lucy, he felt a shock of expansion, an astronaut's weightless bliss.

Plus, the girl was beautiful. He'd never had a piece of ass this fine. And now he'd had her two nights in a row. She was not without some damage, of course—and though she clearly had a past, she wasted no time in the present, the little fire-starter. Red hair, holy shit, above and below. He turned in the bed and laid his large hand on her belly. Feeling his fingers rise and fall with each of the girl's breaths, he closed his eyes and fell asleep.

*   *   *

The old woman was chasing a small animal. At first she thought it was a cat—but *no,* the tail was too long. Maybe it was a monkey. Were there monkeys in New Jersey? She wouldn't be a bit surprised. The world had changed so much; there were no proper borders anymore. Well, whatever the creature was, it was sure to get at the tomatoes, the perfect end-of-season beauties.

With the sun just coming up, the old woman ran across the yard, amazed at the animal's speed. More amazing was her own speed; the fact that she could keep up with the beast. It hesitated for a moment at the fence, and the old woman leapt for it, landing on her chest with a thud that made the breath bark out of her. She slid across the lawn until, miraculously, she had the animal in her hands. She pressed her fingers into its pliant, muscular midsection, and when it turned its head and bared its teeth, she saw that it was something extraordinary. She gasped and, as she opened her eyes, reached her arm upward toward the ceiling, where the candlelight was flickering in the most deliberate and insistent manner. Her arm was heavy, but she kept it aloft, even as the pain shot through it. The light on the ceiling was lovely— its clever arabesques bringing to mind the pair of pretty orange guppies her mother had kept in a glass bowl in the parlor, when Florence was a girl.

She felt her heart, as she'd never felt it before—as if she were meeting it for the first time, this beating striver, monster and angel of her life. Even the old embers (her sewing machine, the piano, the touch of Pio's hand), things she had thought long extinguished, suddenly flared into an overwhelming chaos. When she turned her heard toward the Virgin, she could barely breathe. She tried to call out for the boy, but nothing came from her lips. Edgar, she thought. *My Edgar.* The boy's mother was flooding her chest, as well. Poor sweet Lucy, she had always been such a beautiful girl, and the old woman was sorry for all of it, all the pettiness between them. The tears came to her eyes, and as her heart grew to unmanageable proportions, she sank below the surface of the room and returned to the animal in the yard.

It was still there, still looking at her. It smiled benevolently, with its white fangs gleaming and its gray fur flashing needles of silver. For a moment, the old woman clutched it tighter—victorious, proud. But then she let it go, she relinquished everything. It was so much easier than she would have guessed; complicated for a moment only by the great tug of love for the child. But that love, at the same time, spurred her onward, and she slipped into a black coolness that stripped her of all pain.

She passed through her mother's parlor again, but now the whole room was filled with water—the fish swimming freely, drawing complicated circles that seemed to possess and define her whole life, circles that seemed to live at the threshold of music. As she sank farther down, she knew where she was going. She knew this was the water she'd been trying to plumb for years, the water below the bridge at Shepherd's Junction, from which no body had ever been recovered. When her feet touched the sandy bottom, she stood, at last, before the gold Chrysler LeBaron. Amazingly it was still in excellent condition. The driver's window was open and Frank sat at the wheel, staring ahead, unchanged. He didn't turn to look at his mother. And, for the first time, she did not ask, *Why?* A question that, since her son's death, had plagued her like a fly trapped in an airless room—*tap tap tap* against the sealed glass. The question, like the fly, had never grown weary, but had persisted with a savage lunacy.

Now there was only silence. She was strangely absent of questions. She leaned her head forward into the car's interior and kissed Frank's surprisingly warm cheek. Immediately, as if she'd clicked a switch, her course shifted and she began to rise, speedily, through the cool water. She looked up and saw the light-riddled undersurface rushing toward her, and when she broke through it, she dissolved into a kind of perfect laughter. A rippling white denouement that tore her apart. The relief was profound, and shamelessly erotic. Not bad at all, she thought. Her first orgasm, in death.

* * *

Edgar sat at the table, waiting for his breakfast to appear. That's how it happened: he sat down and his grandmother brought him food. When he'd walked into the kitchen, he realized that it wasn't his grandmother he'd heard, but a pan that had fallen from its hook on the wall. The hook had fallen out as well, leaving a crusty hole in the plaster and white dust on the floor.

After sitting awhile, Edgar decides to make himself useful. He stands and collects the dust, throws it into the sink. Then he picks up the pan, his grandmother's ancient fryer—a blackened and dented thing the size of a trash-can lid. He groans when he lifts it, ashamed of his weakness.

Edgar, though, is not weak. Edgar is gentle. The subtlety of this eludes him, though.

With a grunt, he swings the frying pan and lets it crash onto the counter. Where *is* everyone? He's hungry. It's a quarter past seven already. His mother's a famous sleepyhead, but not his grandmother. Should he go upstairs and wake her?

And then he remembers the women's argument from last night. His mother had left the house, had driven away. Edgar feels the familiar dread of octopus ink in his belly—which sends him straight to the cupboard for some cookies. He takes them into the living room. Sugar and television— that often does the trick. Edgar picks up the remote and, after several clicks, lands on an early-morning children's show. A tall man in a rainbow-colored top hat and fluffy bedroom slippers is dancing a funny little dance—except it isn't funny at all. The man looks like he has to pee. When he finally stops dancing, he claps his hands three times. At each clap, a child appears—all three of them hamming it up with over-actory faces *(Whoa! How did I get here?)*. Edgar makes his own face, one of distaste. He knows fake magic when he sees it. Real magicians don't wear rainbow-colored top hats. They don't wear top hats at all. Real magicians, Edgar knows, wear the same clothes as everyone else. Plus, they don't do their tricks on television. Real magicians do their stuff at home, in private—or in the woods, at night.

Edgar clicks off the television with a huff and turns his head toward the hall. And though he isn't supposed to shout in the house, he shouts, calling out for the one person who always comes when he calls. It isn't magic, how she appears; it's simply his life.

BOOK TWO

TIME REGAINED

Wild, wild horses, couldn't drag me away.

—THE ROLLING STONES

12

L.O.V.E.

It wasn't her. It was a person made of wax, made to look like his grandmother. Edgar was kneeling before the ornate silver casket that seemed to him like a giant butter dish. Inside lay the woman who was no longer his, nestled in a froth of scrunched-up fabric shimmery as his mother's underwear. A vandal had put slashes of red paint across his grandmother's lips and on her cheeks.

"She looks nice, doesn't she?" said Lucy, standing behind her son.

Edgar didn't say yes and he didn't say no. He could hear his mother clicking her nails, something she did when she was nervous.

"She looks peaceful." Lucy tapped the boy's shoulder, encouraging him to get up. He'd been kneeling there for a while.

"Stop saying *she*."

"Stop saying what?"

"Don't say *she*."

"What am I supposed to say?"

Edgar shrugged and wished his mother would go away. He wished everyone would go away. There were too many people in the room, and Edgar knew he'd need to be alone with the old woman to get her to open her eyes. He was too shy to say the magic words in public. *(I love you. I'm sorry.)* And though he knew he was betraying his grandmother by remaining silent, he could not do otherwise.

It was awful. Death would think itself real without an official protest from the dead person's greatest ally. Edgar hated the tears that ran down his face; they were a giving in to a reality bereft of imagination. He brushed the warm trails from his cheeks with a feeling of shame.

At least he'd worn the sneakers with the lights in them. When you stepped firmly on the heel, tiny blue lights danced around the edge of the sole; and when you pointed your toe, a beam of red light pulsed from the tip. He was standing now in front of the casket. With a nimble movement of his feet, he activated the lights—both the blue blips and the red beams.

"What the hell are you wearing?" said Lucy. "I told you to put on your Buster Browns."

"I know," Edgar said glumly. But he'd worn the sneakers for a good reason: his grandmother had hated them. And he was old enough to know that there was something even stronger than love to get people to notice you—and that was irritation. Edgar directed the red beams directly at the casket.

"*Turn them off*," Lucy whispered.

"You can't turn them off. They turn off by themselves."

"When?"

"When they're *finished*," sassed Edgar. "It's on a program."

Lucy took hold of her son's arm and suggested he move away from the box.

Where was he supposed to go, he asked her.

"Just sit down for a while," she said. "Out in the audience."

"It's not a *play*," replied Edgar.

"Don't be rude, baby. Other people need to come up and say goodbye."

Goodbye? Edgar pulled his arm back from his mother's grip. "Did you do that to her face?"

"Do what?"

"The red stuff."

"Of course not."

Lucy glanced at Florence in the butter dish; really looked at the dead woman for the first time. The boy's distress was legitimate. The funeral parlor had obviously hired someone from Ringling Brothers to do the makeup.

"You said she looked *nice*."

"I lied."

Edgar was relieved to hear his mother admit it. "Because she doesn't look like that."

Lucy agreed. Even the hair was wrong. For the past fifteen years, Lucy had cut and set the old woman's wispy frizz, always managing to make it look elegant. She reached into the coffin and adjusted Florence's coif, relieving her of the awful spit curls someone had pasted down on her fore-head.

"That's better," said Edgar. "Push it back more."

The room was preposterously full, considering the fact that, other than the boy and his mother, Florence had no living relatives. Well, yes, there was Pio's brother's family, but those bonds had dissolved in rancor when it was discovered that Frank's cousin Vincenzo had been selling drugs to Frank. Lucy hoped Vincenzo might show up. She wouldn't mind scoring a little pot. The next few weeks would be tough.

Many in attendance were strangers to Lucy. Throughout the interminable hours of the wake, it was the boy who had to inform her, with discreet whispers: "That's Mr. Wong from the fish store" or "That's Mrs. Collucci from where we get the bread." Edgar referred to one ancient man with whiskered nostrils as *the peddler*. "What do you get from him?" Lucy asked. "Different things," the boy said. "Peppers, artichokes. Sometimes buttons. He has a cart." Lucy felt dizzy. There was a whole world she knew nothing about. Henry and Netty Schlip who ran a "dry-goods" store. The Fortunato brothers who sold pots and sharpened knives. A black cobbler with the unlikely name of Willie Marchwell. It was as if the boy had lived with Florence in some other century. *Peddler, cobbler, dry goods.* Hard to believe such things still existed.

"And that's Mrs. List from where we get the flowers."

"Okay," Lucy said, unable to keep track.

"The house flowers," the boy added. "Not the *cemetery* flowers."

"Do you go to the cemetery?" Lucy asked, amazed.

"Sometimes," the boy said.

"How do you get there?"

"Mr. DePinto from down the street takes us. His wife is there."

Lucy found an empty seat and sank into it, feeling a sudden anger at Florence. How dare she take Edgar to the cemetery without asking permission. She pulled the boy into her lap.

"You go there to see Pio?"

The boy nodded and shyly took hold of his mother's fingers. His father's name was carved on the gravestone, too, right below his grandfather's. *Francesco Lorenzo Fini.*

Ridiculous, Lucy had always thought, to put Frank's name there without a body to go with it. She wondered how much the kid knew. What combination of lies and truth had Florence fed him? In time, hopefully, he'd forget whatever stories the old woman had concocted. History would be erased. There'd be no more visits to the cemetery, or to fucking peddlers or cobblers. If Edgar wore down a pair of shoes, they'd throw the damn things out and drive straight to some civilized department store.

But these valiant thoughts only brought Lucy to a troublesome cul-de-sac. Because what was she to do with the boy, really? Who was going to take care of him? He had nightmares and food issues and exceptionally pale skin that required a pharmaceutical-grade sunscreen. Florence had seen to all those things. Florence had been the one to tend to him after school, and on Saturdays when Lucy was at work. And what if she wanted to go out in the evening? How many times a week could she afford a babysitter? Did she even make enough to cover basic expenses? She had no idea. Every week, she'd given cash to Florence, and Florence had taken care of the bills. But now there'd be no pension check from Pio. Would she have to sell the house? But certainly Florence had left it to Edgar. It would have to be his decision. Oh my God, she'd be trapped there until he was eighteen.

"Ow!"

"What?" Lucy looked at the eight-year-old still on her lap.

"You're digging your nails into me."

Lucy let go of his hand. "We shouldn't be sitting here anyway. We should talk to some of these people, don't you think?"

"I guess," replied Edgar, unconvinced. "Mr. S is here."

"Who?"

"Your *friend.*" In his head, he heard his grandmother say *suitor,* because for once the old woman's word had hit the nail on the head.

Lucy glanced across the room and saw the butcher, in a dark blue suit, standing awkwardly beside a squadron of lilies. What the hell was he doing here? She'd told him not to come. Florence had always accused her of dancing on Frank's grave. She didn't want to be accused of dancing on Florence's, as well.

The butcher caught her eye and lifted his hand. Lucy returned the wave meekly, with disastrous timing. Through the archway, just behind the butcher, emerged the last person in the world she wanted to see. Her father. He caught the last flutter of Lucy's wave, and thinking it for him, grimaced and made his way into the room.

No. No. He had no right to be here. Lucy started to shake.

"Edgar, why don't you go talk to the Heftis?"

"I don't want to talk to Toni-Ann."

"Edgar, please. Just go say hi. I'll be right back." She gently pushed the boy off her lap. Both the butcher and her father had come a few steps closer. Lucy marched toward them, colliding with the butcher first. He took her arm firmly.

"Luce, I just wanted to stop by and—"

"Ron, thanks, yeah, that was nice of you but—"

"I wanted to pay my respects."

She nodded cordially but could feel her face flush with an inexplicable fury. "It's not like you knew her."

"No, I know, I just—"

"This is really not a good time."

"Of course not." The butcher squeezed her arm tighter.

Lucy could see her father lurking, waiting for his moment. The closer he came the weaker her limbs felt, as if all they remembered now was submission and defeat. She'd have to face him immediately, before all her strength was sapped.

But the butcher persisted, indefatigably condolent. "I had a meat platter sent over to your house, for afterwards."

"I'm not having a get-together. I don't even know half these people."

"If you want me to stop by later . . ."

What did he want from her? What did either of them want?

"No, I'll be fine. Thank you."

"When my mother died . . ." the butcher said.

"She wasn't my mother," Lucy said in a somewhat hysterical voice—and the shrunken Schlip couple, who were standing nearby, turned to her with their dried-apple faces.

"Okay," the butcher said, "you're upset. Why don't you sit down?" He took more of her body in his warm hands. The fact that she wanted to give in to him so badly only made her lash out more.

"Stop it. Get off me. *Get off.*"

"Is this man bothering you?" Lucy's father stepped forward and placed a hand on his daughter's body, which was now at liberty.

If her recoil from the butcher's ministrations was demonstrative, it was nothing compared to how she lurched back now: a great swooping movement involving a side-flung arm that struck Netty Schlip under the chin.

Lucy was too flustered to apologize. She turned to her father, a short stout man in a brown suit, and lifted her fists with bar-brawl bravado.

"Touch me again and I'll knock your goddamned teeth out."

"Lucy, please." His voice was the same as ever, gravelly but strangely high-pitched.

"*Please?* Please what? Please knock your teeth out?"

Netty Schlip wished the girl would stop saying that. Though she'd not been injured by Lucy's hit to the chin, her dentures had slipped. Her husband was tending to her mortifications behind a crucifix of yellow roses.

Walter Bubko was close enough that his daughter could smell the sham mint of his breath. "I saw the obituary and I thought maybe . . ."

Lucy lowered her fists and waited, while the man swayed on his feet like a buoy in a stiff breeze. He ran a palm over his slicked-back black hair, as if to steady himself. "I felt it was time." The man bowed his head. "I thought maybe I could meet the boy."

"I would like you to leave." She stood straight and made an effort not to shout. *"Now."*

"Lucille." Her name in his mouth was ruin itself. And there she was again in that house, with that fear, the man's arm lifted at the merest excuse.

"What makes you think you can come here?" She was now shaking so visibly that Mr. Wong, compelled by a sense of propriety, closed his eyes.

"I'm sorry for your loss," her father said.

She'd not spoken to this man in nearly fifteen years. Even at her mother's funeral, more than a decade ago, she'd kept her distance. Frank had been by her side that day. Florence had been there, too. Perhaps if she'd talked to her father then, when she was still young, surrounded by the Finis, who loved her—perhaps then she might have found it in herself to forgive him. But it was too late now. Time was the thing that ripped out your heart and left you cold. With a haughty lift of her chin, belied by quivering lips, she turned to the butcher.

"Ron, would you please make this man leave?"

"You don't need to do that," her father said. "I'll just sit in the back. If the boy wants to talk to me, that's where I'll be."

"He's not talking to you."

"That's for him to decide."

"No, actually, it's not. He will *never* talk to you. He doesn't need a fucked-up drunk in his life."

Her father smiled, as if to better show the waste of his face, the contours of his skull. "He's already got one of those, huh?"

Lucy smiled back—her raised lips a kind of shield. How awful that their faces could meet like this and recognize each other. But it was good, too, because she could see, beyond the blight of his aging (something for which she might have had sympathy), that he was the same man from her childhood, the same evil fuck.

"Come on now," he said, "let's not be like this. I'm sorry." He reached for her hand again, but Lucy discreetly pulled it back.

"No. This is it, Dad. You leave. You just . . . you leave."

Walter Bubko turned toward the casket. "I'll just go up and say my piece to Mrs. Fini."

"Don't even try." That her father could imagine he had any right to stand in the old woman's presence was absurd. Lucy felt the shaking return to her legs. Florence was dead. *Florence was dead*—and her father was in the room, alive, flesh and blood, making demands. Though Lucy had no experience in such matters, she knew it was up to her to preserve the sanctity of the old woman's farewell. At the same time, she wished the old woman would rise from the coffin to protect her, as she had done in the past. Florence or Pio or Frank, sometimes all three of them, standing on the porch, telling the drunken man who'd come for Lucy to go away; go away or they'd call the police. "She doesn't want to see you."

Her father made a move toward the front of the room.

"Ron, stop that man. *Ron.*"

The butcher was unsure what was expected of him. He turned toward the sloshed man in the brown suit. "Sir."

"Always acting brave when you have a boyfriend around, huh?" her father said. When the giant man did nothing to physically impede him, Walter Bubko proceeded toward the coffin.

"*Ron,*" Lucy begged again.

The butcher was still uncertain. But then Lucy gave him a look of such pleading belligerence, a look that was shocking to see on the face of someone who wasn't a child.

"Sir." The butcher put his hand on the man's shoulder.

"Get your paw out of my way." He shrugged off the familiar grip of the bouncer. "Still go for the guineas, huh, Lucy?"

Okay, the butcher thought, assessment complete: *asshole*. No one called him a guinea, especially not some drunken Polack. Ron Salvatore would do his part, despite the occasion. He grabbed the short man by the shoulders.

As Walter Bubko was dragged away, muttering obscenities, the peddler turned to the cobbler. "Redheads."

The cobbler nodded, in agreement that surely it must be the pretty girl who lay at the root of the trouble. "Sad day," he said. "Florence was a nice lady."

"Eyes like a hawk," the peddler added. "Could spot a bad artichoke from a mile away."

Wearily the men turned their gaze from Lucy to the casket, where that miniature child was hovering again. How the old woman had adored him. Both merchants would tell, if asked, how she'd often arrived with the boy in hand, only letting go of him when absolutely necessary. Even then, he would stay close to her, lingering like a little white cloud. Like a ghost.

Lucy didn't watch as her father was removed. Standing alone, she surrendered to the kind of tears she'd managed to keep at bay for nearly seven years. In a cold funeral parlor in Ferryfield, New Jersey—viewing room 2—Lucy choked before the blaze of her own history. The Finis were gone; they were finished. Florence and Pio and Frank.

She looked at her son. He was kneeling once more at the front of the room, a blemish of brightness in her already dazed world. A spotlight meant for Florence's body was shining on his white hair.

Edgar Allan. Well, he was a Fini, too, wasn't he?

And what the hell was he putting in the coffin?

* * *

Earlier, before the floor show *(Netty Schlip Slapped! Drunk Dragged Away!)*, Edgar had obliged his mother and talked to the neighbors. Toni-Ann Hefti, in a puffy green dress, sat hunched over between her very erect parents. When she saw Edgar, she looked down and put her wet fingers farther into her mouth.

"Hello, dear," Mrs. Hefti said.

"Hello." Edgar pulled at the collar of his shirt, which had started to feel a bit strangly.

"Sit up, Toni-Ann." The girl's mother gave her a tiny whack on the back. "What did the doctor tell you about posture?"

"We're very sorry," Mr. Hefti said.

"About your *grandmother*," his wife added.

Edgar wondered if she talked to everyone like they were an idiot.

"Didn't you want to say something, honey?" Mrs. Hefti whacked the girl's back again, as if that's where the controls were.

Toni-Ann shook her head.

"She's never been to one of these before," Mr. Hefti said. "We thought she should experience it."

"I like your sneakers, Ed-guh."

Mrs. Hefti frowned and patted her daughter's leg. "We told her people die. Yes, they do. People die."

Edgar hoped Mrs. Hefti wouldn't say it a third time.

"Right, Toni-Ann—what did we tell you?"

"People die," the girl parroted.

"That's right. It's just part of life."

Edgar didn't think this was the kind of thing you should tell a retarded person. He barely wanted to hear it himself. Mrs. Hefti was probably a terrible mother. Maybe all mothers were like this—bossy shovers, miffed that their kids were less than perfect. Plus, he didn't like the way the woman was using his grandmother's death to make a lesson for someone who drooled.

"Flow-rinse," Toni-Ann said quietly.

"That's right. The old lady."

"Always gave us tomatoes," Mr. Hefti said to the girl, as if to jog her memory.

"I know," Toni-Ann said grumblingly to the floor. "You don't have to tell me."

"She didn't sleep well last night," Mrs. Hefti explained.

"I have dreams," Toni-Ann said, leaning in toward Edgar. "You know how they get *big* sometimes?"

Mrs. Hefti patted the girl's leg again. Obviously, it was a back whack that turned her on and a leg pat that shut her off. Toni-Ann slouched, deflated.

"Well, she was a good neighbor," Mr. Hefti said, wrapping things up. "A good person."

"She's at peace now, that's all that matters," Mrs. Hefti concluded in a pained whisper. Both she and her husband nodded in a way that made Edgar think they might be doing long division in their heads.

"I love her!" Toni-Ann blurted suddenly.

"You love who?" Mrs. Hefti asked.

"Flow-rinse."

"Don't be dramatic, Toni-Ann."

"I *love* her." The girl rocked her chair.

"*Loved,* sweetheart," Mr. Hefti corrected. "Past tense. When someone's not here anymore—"

"Don't encourage her, Bill, for God's sake. You didn't *love* her, Toni-Ann." Mrs. Hefti turned to Edgar. "She gets like this. What she means is she *liked* your grandmother."

Toni-Ann shook her head and rocked her chair with greater fury. "L.O.V.E."

"If you're going to be like this, we're taking you home."

"No!" Toni-Ann said. "I have to talk to Ed-guh."

Before her parents could protest, Toni-Ann stood and dragged the boy a few feet away. Tears welled in her sleepless eyes.

"I'm sorry. I'm sorry, Ed-guh. I give it back, okay?" From a pocket in her puffy green dress, she produced the prayer card, streaked now with purple stains. Edgar felt dizzy, slapped in the head by time.

Had it really been only four days since he'd walked from his house and tripped and dropped the card? Just four days since Toni-Ann had snatched up his grandmother's property—which he himself had stolen only five days ago? Could so much happen in so little time?

Because his life had changed utterly—a fact that struck him only now, standing before the dimwit girl. Edgar gulped as Toni-Ann pushed the prayer card toward him.

"Nelly To-to-to . . ."

"Tortelli," Edgar said quietly.

"Yes," said Toni-Ann. "Funny."

She was crying now—her face a mess. She smeared its wetness into Edgar's cheek.

The girl's parents detached her and led her away. Edgar watched them leave the room without a word to his mother, who was still arguing with the red-faced man with greasy hair. There was nothing to do but go back to the woman in the giant butter dish. Edgar knelt and placed the prayer card deep in the shimmery folds of her nest.

"She said she was sorry," he whispered—apologizing as best he could for everyone.

"Flow-rinse." His final prayer, and the first time he'd ever spoken his grandmother's Christian name.

* * *

People came and went; mostly went, as it was getting late. For Lucy and the boy it was all the same now, a half-bodied dream of the sort that comes in late-afternoon naps or in fever.

When Dominic Sparra arrived, dressed spiffily in a black suit, with his beard neatly trimmed, he went straight up to the coffin and kneeled before it. He was a stranger to Edgar and Lucy. Florence, of course, had never mentioned her disastrous date with the man—and her prior history with him had happened long before Edgar and Lucy were born. Dominic knew a different Florence from the one they knew. He had different regrets, different joys to relinquish. He reached into the coffin and took Florence's hand.

"He's touching her," Edgar said. "Ma, he's touching her."

"What do you want me to do?" said Lucy.

"He's gonna mess her up."

But Lucy only shrugged, exhausted, and closed her eyes.

"Belle gambe," Dominic Sparra said; not to the dolled-up corpse in front of him, but to a memory he had of a younger Florence. A girl standing at water's edge in a bathing suit—a bathing suit she'd made herself, with fabric flowers stitched fetchingly over the breast. *"Bella figura."*

The old man crossed himself in the name of a father and a son and a holy spirit whose existence he no longer accepted. But he knew Florence's belief had persisted—pious to the very end, just like his own wife. Dominic often wondered if Florie had married Pio for his name as much as anything—as if it were some seal of approval from the Almighty, a promise of the man's worth. But Dominic knew otherwise. Pious Pio had cheated on his wife endlessly. Had Dominic beat him to win Florence's hand, he would never have betrayed her. And he would have given her healthy children, a pack of them. Poor Florie. A handful of miscarriages, and then, finally, that *pazzo* Frankie, late in life. Pio's infidelities had cursed him, if one believed in that sort of thing.

Dominic thought of the tunnel, that otherworldly realm where he and his friend had worked as young men. Death, to an unbeliever, was probably like being trapped in such a place—moving endlessly past the dim amber lights without ever being released to the pleasures of New York City or the homeward-leaning Weehawken. Dominic suspected it was where he'd end up when he croaked—underwater, in that exhaust-filled tube forever.

Distractedly, he thumbed Florence's hand, removing some of the camel cream concealer the undertaker had neglected to set with powder.

"Come faccio a dire arrivederci?"

And now he did the unthinkable (Edgar was still watching him like a hawk): he leaned down into the butter dish and kissed Florence's face.

When he finally stood, it was not without difficulty. He touched his lips and moved away from the casket. When he saw the redhead and the little bird-boy beside her, he knew who they were. Yet he said not a word. A small nod of the head—returned, in kind, by the woman. The boy only furrowed his brow.

"I guess we can go now," said Lucy. "Are you ready?"

Edgar considered the question, but could find no reasonable answer. The room seemed a hundred times heavier, like it was filling with sand. When his mother stood, he did the same. It was so strange, though, to be leaving Florence up there in a box. Where would they take her now? *Who* would take her? And would they be nice, would they treat her gently? Or would they knock her about like the men who loaded trucks?

"I'll be right back," said Lucy.

Edgar was surprised to see his mother return to the casket. She proceeded slowly, her limp more pronounced than usual. As she stood before Florence, Edgar could see her shoulders moving up and down like they were being jerked by strings. The boy stopped his own tears so that his mother could take her turn.

The butcher was waiting at the back of the room, just outside the archway. He stepped forward as Lucy and Edgar made their way to the exit.

"You're still here?" Lucy said, with more confusion than gratitude.

"I wanted to make sure that guy didn't come back. How you doing, Eddie?"

Lucy replied for the boy, who was crying again. "We're good now, Ron. Thanks for . . . doing that before." She just wanted to get past him, get outside. A quick cig in the parking lot, and then home, and sleep. The kid was dead on his feet, she could tell. "It's way past his bedtime," she said to the butcher.

"No it's not," said Edgar, sniffling. He had no wish to sleep, afraid to find his grandmother gone in his dreams, too.

Lucy brushed the boy's hair from his eyes. When she turned back to Ron, he was looking at her with a sad affection that seemed genuine.

"I'll give you a call," he said. "Maybe, like, in a few days? Give you a few days to . . ."

"I'm gonna have a lot to do, so . . ." Lucy hesitated. "We'll just play it by ear."

As the butcher leaned in toward her, she lifted her shoulders in defense. "Not in front of . . ." She gestured vaguely, not sure who she was referring to. The living or the dead.

The butcher backed off.

After a formal goodbye, shaked hands all around, mother and son headed off into the *Phantom of the Opera* lobby, with its Empire urns and ornamental candlesticks. Gloomy lighting emanated from shaded wall sconces, while a dusty unlit chandelier gently tinkled in a flow of refrigerated air.

"I'm going to stay up when we get home, okay? Okay, Mom?"

"What, baby?"

"I'm going to stay up, okay? I don't have to go to sleep."

Lucy stopped in the middle of the room. The child obviously needed something from her. She suddenly felt anxious. Because what would they do, the two of them, at home?

"We could have some tea," Edgar said.

"What?" Lucy said. "When?"

"When we get home."

"You drink tea?"

"Not the keep-you-up stuff," the boy said. "The kind with flowers on the box."

Lucy smiled tightly and touched her brow. She was sure to make a mess of things.

"Ron," Lucy called out. He was standing by the entrance, talking to Henry and Netty Schlip.

"It's *herbal*," the boy said.

"One second, baby. *Ron*." She called louder this time, and the man turned.

"Something wrong?" he said.

"No, I'm sorry, I just . . ."

The butcher waited patiently.

"No, I was just, uh, wondering about the meat."

"The what?"

"That you sent to the house."

"Oh, yeah. Sorry about that. I thought you were having a repast afterwards, so . . ."

"No. No. It's just gonna be the two of us."

"I guess you can freeze some of it."

"The freezer's full," Edgar said quietly.

"What's that, Eddie?" the butcher said.

"Nothing." The boy looked down.

"I mean, if you wanna come over and have something," Lucy said. "Have a drink or . . ."

Edgar's heart sank.

"I could do that," the butcher said.

"Otherwise it's gonna be a waste. This one eats like a bird."

The boy yanked his hand away from his mother's. A comment like that deserved retaliation. "And they can come, too, can't they?"

"Who?" said Lucy.

"Mr. and Mrs. *Schlip*," the boy said with aggressive enunciation.

"Oh." Lucy saw that they were standing right there, looking at her. "Oh yeah, of course. Yeah, yeah. Would you two like to . . ." She wanted to strangle the kid.

"It's late," Henry Schlip replied.

"Yes, I guess it is," Lucy said, relieved.

"But we could come for a little while, I suppose. What do you think, Annette?"

"Well, if it's no imposition . . ."

"Not at all," Lucy said, smiling as she fell into the pit. "Florence would have . . ."

Henry nodded. "A very gracious woman."

"You know, dear," Netty said quietly, approaching Lucy, "I just wanted to say that I understand that people get upset at these things . . ."

As Netty faltered, Henry forged ahead. "What she's trying to say is, she knows you didn't *mean* to hit her before."

"On purpose," added Netty.

"Of course not," said Lucy.

The Schlips looked at each other and visibly relaxed. "Yes, oh good, well, that's what we thought," said Netty. "And Henry and I do hope you'll continue to come to the shop. Florence always got her slippers there."

"Sheets and towels, too," said Henry.

"We don't get too many customers these days," explained Netty.

The butcher rolled his eyes—and for this Lucy was grateful.

As the adults made their plans, Edgar drifted away. He crossed the lobby and wandered down a short corridor until he came upon the entrance to viewing room 1. How had he not noticed it before? Not far from his grandmother, there was a whole other catastrophe being staged, with a completely different cast. It appeared to be a much better show. Ten times more crying—and all of it spilling out into an enormous room with newer carpet and a stained-glass window that appeared to have lightbulbs behind it. The man in the coffin was wearing a tuxedo—while his grandmother had been dressed in something that looked like a gray blanket with sleeves. For the first time in his life, Edgar wondered if he was poor.

"There you are," his mother said, striding down the corridor. "Come on, we're leaving."

"It's not fair," said Edgar.

"What's not fair, kiddo?"

"There's another coffin here."

"Other people die, Edgar."

"On the same day? How can *he* be dead on the same day?"

"Do the math," said Lucy.

As she took the boy's arm, a tall woman in a diamond necklace emerged from viewing room 1.

Edgar gasped.

"Stop playing games," said Lucy.

"I'll be right back," the boy said. "I forgot something."

"*Edgar.*"

But he was off and running.

"I'm not chasing you," Lucy shouted. "I'm going to the car. I want you outside in *two* minutes."

13

Honey

"Stealing is a sin."

Edgar froze, but did not drop Florence's hand, from which he'd been trying, without success, to remove her rings. Certainly his grandmother would have wanted him to have them—the diamond, especially.

"I'm not stealing." Without looking behind him, he made one last attempt to twist off the jewelry. His nose was running; he wiped it with his shoulder.

"I may be old, but I'm not blind."

It was a line Edgar had heard before, from the very woman whose cold hand he was now trying to maneuver back into its placid, hand-over-hand arrangement.

When he turned to face his accuser, he was already defeated—a self-hating sinner, all the more so for failing to accomplish his sin. He was certain it was a man who'd caught him, due to the husk of the voice—but he'd been deceived.

The old woman approached slowly, relying heavily on a scratched-up rubber-tipped cane. It was her only unfortunate accessory. Earrings of dangling pearls and a tiny veiled hat, sparkly bracelets and hard-candy rings, all gave proper honor to her dress: a spectacular black gown bandaged at the waist with a swath of pink silk—artfully knotted in a huge butterfly bow. On the shoulders, delicate embroidered wings echoed the lines of the bow and infused the dress with a touch of poetry.

As the decrepit woman made her way to the front of the room, Edgar stepped aside to let her peer into the coffin.

"I see you've made a mess of her," she said, bending down awkwardly to straighten Florence's sleeve.

"I didn't do it," said Edgar.

The woman turned. Even through the veil, he could see the suspicion in her eyes.

"An old man did it," Edgar mumbled. "He touched her first."

"I can't hear you, child."

"An old man," the boy repeated with as much force as he could muster. "He *kissed* her."

"Did he?" The visitor harrumphed. "Well, she always had a lot of admirers. Even with those awful hands. Pity she had to work in that laundry. A real sweatshop. I knew a girl—lost a finger there."

Edgar followed the woman's gaze; watched how it moved up and down the length of the coffin as if his grandmother's body were something on a sale rack. It was true: his grandmother's jewelry was nothing compared to the splendid stones on the visitor's twiggy fingers. Still, he'd desperately wanted that small diamond on Florence's hand. Possessing it seemed a matter of life or death. Without it, nothing would stand in the way of a darkness that was spreading across the Earth with alarming speed.

"Horrible dress," the visitor said.

Edgar wondered if the woman had strayed into the wrong room. Maybe she'd meant to go to viewing room 1, where the rich people were.

"Smells like mothballs." The woman reached into her purse, pulled out a small bottle of perfume, and spritzed it into the air over the coffin. "Mothballs are *poison*. One should always use cedar."

The boy felt a wayward droplet of the perfume land on his cheek. It was not Chanel No 5.

"Though perhaps the best thing would have been to let the moths eat that dreadful *shmata*." The woman shook her head and turned to Edgar. "Did you know Florence?"

What an extraordinary question. "Yes," the boy said, confused. "She—"

"Speak up, speak up. It's bad manners to mumble."

"I know her," Edgar said. "I'm *related* to her."

"Are you? And what is your *relation* to the deceased?"

"To who?"

"To *her,*" the interrogator said, pointing a pink-lacquered finger that matched the bow of her dress.

"I'm her grandson," Edgar replied.

"*Oh.* Yes yes yes, of course. Oh my goodness. I read about you in the paper."

"About me?"

"Years ago. That awful accident. Oh my goodness. You're a very lucky young man."

Edgar suspected she was confusing him for Frank. "I'm her *grandson*," he repeated.

"Yes, yes, I heard you the first time." The old woman extended her hand. "I'm Honey. Honey Fasinga."

Edgar stared at the tan bejeweled fingers wiggling in his direction.

"If you were brought up by this one, I'm sure you were taught better manners. When a lady offers you her hand . . ." She wiggled her fingers again, and a cautious Edgar latched on to a single digit and shook it.

"From what I read, your mother saved your life."

Edgar wondered if the woman was drunk. He knew drunk from his mother. Honey seemed to be in that early, chatty stage of drunkenness that often resulted in inappropriate confidences. Once, his mother, at a similar level of inebriation, had told him she was worried her boobies were too big.

"You know, I haven't seen Florence in years. We were never really *friends,* but we knew each other as girls. Didn't we, dear?" Honey turned to the casket and tapped the rubber-tipped cane lightly against its side.

"Don't hurt it," Edgar said.

"Trust me, darling—I can do no more damage than has already been done."

But Edgar didn't trust her—mostly because of the veil, which covered her face and complicated her wrinkly eyes with a fine web of tiny felt dots.

"Are you looking at my hat? You know, your grandmother made this hat. A long time ago, when veils weren't just for weddings or funerals." She patted the pillbox affectionately. "Do you like it?"

"It's pink," said Edgar, aware that certain colors were inappropriate in the face of death.

"Yes, to match the dress, silly. Which still fits me perfectly." With the aid of her cane, the woman did a lopsided turn to better present the gown's splendor. Her impressively high heels, clamped onto shaking legs, added to the death-defying breathlessness of the fashion show. At the halfway point, Edgar was shocked to see a plunging V that exposed a large portion of Honey's tanned, chicken-boned back.

"She made this, too, you know."

"Made what?"

"The dress," Honey said, completing her clackety turn. "You're a little slow, aren't you, dear? But I like you, don't get me wrong. That hair! You know, I used to have platinum locks myself. Not shock-white like yours, of course. A nice shade, though. Winter Wheat or something. Well, we were all bottle blondes back then."

The woman's thick hair was currently the color of chestnuts, unnaturally lustrous.

"Yes, it's a wig, dear. Otherwise, I'd have hair like this one." She gestured breezily toward Florence. "And who, may I ask, put her in that getup? The fabric looks like something you'd cover a couch with."

"She's not a couch," muttered Edgar.

"See, you're doing it again. Why must you mumble? If you have something to say, just say it. The thing is, darling, the mumbling makes you seem mentally defective. If you want to avoid giving people that impression, I suggest you speak up, argue your case. If people don't like what you have to say, screw them."

"I said, she's not—"

"*Up up up,* louder. With gusto!"

"She's not a couch!"

"Excellent. *Bravo.* Who's not a couch?"

Edgar felt trapped, a contestant on some evil game show. The ancient hostess with the pink wings leaned in, waiting for an answer.

"You said her dress looked like something you'd cover a couch with."

"Well, doesn't it? What a pity to put her in that. Does she not make her own clothes anymore?"

"She doesn't make clothes," Edgar said.

"Oh, but she did. She did. Wonderful, wonderful things. Such a talented girl."

Edgar was close to tears again. He thought to call for his mother, but he was exhausted.

"I bought a number of her dresses over the years. She used to do them for a few girls, for extra money. And she charged almost nothing! I would have bought a hundred of them—but unfortunately we had a little *malentendu.* Before that, though, I actually suggested we open a shop. Didn't I, Flo?" Here, she turned again to the casket, proving to be as effortlessly loquacious with the dead as she was with the living. "I wanted to call it the Butterfly Boutique, *ha ha ha,* but you were horrified, oh my goodness, you looked at me like I was *insane.* But it made perfect sense, you see," she said to Edgar. "Because your grandmother—you said she was your grandmother, yes?"

The boy had barely opened his mouth before the woman plowed on.

"Well, you see, she often put these little stitched wings on her dresses. Look here, on mine, near the shoulders, these little *swoopy* things. Lovely, aren't they? Well, they were Florence's *thing*—what do you call it?—her emblem. Her *signature*. She really was a genius, your grandmother, when it came to style. Quite the contrast to her social persona. She was very proper, you know, a bit uptight. We're speaking here as friends, I hope. Because I respected her. I just didn't have the patience for all that self-effacing non-sense the lower-class Italian girls were brought up with. She was just so damn *timid*. And the absurd thing was, she was prettier than any of us, had every right to own the world, but she had that light-under-a-bushel problem a lot of Catholic girls have. I mean, I was Catholic, too, but my family was never *medieval* about it or anything. And then I was exposed to rather advanced spiritual ideas when I went to Bryn Mawr. Do you know Bryn Mawr?"

Edgar wondered if it was a school for witches. There was something vaguely sinister about the oversized pink bow and the black veil.

"And the funny thing is, for all her hemming and hawing, I could tell the idea intrigued her. A little shop of her own. And we could have done it easily. My father would have given us the money in a heartbeat. Rather ridiculous, really, that I was suggesting a partnership with Snow White here—but we both loved clothing." Honey sighed. "I could have been her great impresario. *Nous aurions été formidable!*"

Edgar took a step back, considering a dash for the lobby.

"But then, of course, Little Miss I-Can't-Make-Up-My-Own-Mind discussed my proposal with her father, and with Pio. And the fools discouraged her. He was a real knucklehead, that Pio. Cute as all get out, but a knucklehead first-class."

Cute? His grandfather? Edgar thought of the hairy grumbler who'd once lived with him. He took another step back, accidentally igniting his sneakers.

"Oh, *ha ha ha*," Honey said. "Aren't those adorable?"

"I'm sorry," said Edgar—and though he knew there was no way to turn them off, he attempted to do so by tapping them several times against the floor.

"I can see from your choice of footwear that you, too, are a person of style. Sneakers with a suit—very modish. I still keep up with the trends, you know. In fact this dress is *in* again. Girls stop me on the street when I wear it. *Oh, how amazing. How cool. Where can I get one?* And I love telling them, well, *ha,* you can't."

Honey turned from camera #1 (Edgar) to camera #2 (Florence) to deliver the final bit of this particular dramatic arc. Edgar had seen the technique before on the soap operas his grandmother used to watch.

"And I always say your name. I say this dress was made by the designer Florence Alba Veronese. I never call you by your married name. *Never*." The woman sighed loudly. "Such a pity to end up like this." Another quick turn to Edgar: "Has she been obese for a while?"

The word filled Edgar with a rush of heat. He blushed.

"When I started to get chunky a few years ago, I went straight to my doctor and he gave me the most wonderful pills. Completely banishes your appetite. Plus, they give you a nice burst of energy." The woman bumped her hips. "Pio always liked his women skinny."

Edgar thought of the photo of his grandmother—the one with the cigarette in her mouth and a fox around her neck.

"You know, when I ran into your grandfather on one of my summers back from Bryn Mawr, I gave him a piece of my mind. 'How dare you stop your wife'—because they were married at that point—'how *dare* you stand in the way of Florie's destiny.' I really gave it to him. 'Did you not notice how talented the woman is?' And he said, 'She sews.' *She sews!* As if what she did were the equivalent of making a pot roast. 'It's a great deal more than that,' I said. 'She's an artist.' But the more I sang her praises, the more he laughed at me. 'Are you trying to seduce my wife?' he said. Oh, he was horrible. I don't know how we ended up *en coït*. And it was only that one time. But somehow Florence found out. I think it was that dwarf Angela Carini, little bitch with a big mouth."

"I have to go," said Edgar.

The woman turned to him and miraculously fell silent—a silence so thick it prevented any movement on Edgar's part.

"Of course you do," said Honey. "Would you like to see my face?"

Edgar was crying now.

"Here, don't be afraid." She lifted the black veil and gingerly laid it over the pink crown of the hat. "Just so you know who you're dealing with."

Edgar wasn't sure what he was looking at. He'd never seen a face like this before. It was old and young at the same time. A taut upswing of wrinkles around the eyes, as if someone were pulling Honey's hair. The rest of the face was strangely smooth, but lumpy, like there were mashed potatoes under the skin. Her large pink lips were frozen in a greedy pucker. She had the look of someone who'd been waiting for a kiss for so long that it had turned her into a monster.

"Will you remember me? Will you remember Honey Fasinga?"

Edgar wiped his eyes and nodded.

"Good," Honey said. "I'm glad."

When Edgar turned, he did so carefully, wary of his sneakers.

"Wait!" Honey cried. "Shall we try a little hand cream?"

For what? thought Edgar. He wondered if she was going to put it on her face.

"I think I have some in my purse."

"No, thank you," said Edgar. No candy from strangers (Florence's rule) probably also meant no hand cream.

"Come on, come on, you only live once."

Edgar was petrified now as Honey unclasped her little pink purse and pulled out a small plastic tube. "Here." She extended it toward him.

"I don't need any," he said.

"What? Do you want me to do it for you?" asked Honey. "Stop crying or someone will hear us. And wipe your nose."

Edgar did as he was told.

Honey glanced toward the doorway to check for intruders. "Okay, let's do this."

She took up Florence's hand. When she squirted the cream, it made a horrible prolonged fart sound. "Excuse me," said Honey, as if she'd made the sound herself.

Edgar felt sick as he watched the old woman lube up his grandmother's fingers.

"Make sure no one's coming," she said.

Edgar pulled at his tie, panicked.

"Do you want both of them?" asked Honey.

"I don't know," said Edgar.

"Well, decide, decide, we're not exactly in the realm of legality here."

"Just the diamond," Edgar said.

"Wise choice," said Honey.

"Hurry," whispered Edgar.

"Ooof." Honey yanked and stumbled back a little. "Jackpot."

When she opened her palm, it held the wedding band and the diamond engagement ring.

"You got both of them," the boy said, astonished.

"Beginner's luck," said Honey. "Take them, take them. Put them in your pocket."

Edgar hesitated.

"What, you don't want them now? You were quite the little thief when I came in here."

Edgar took the diamond. "Put the other one back."

"Oh, for Pete's sake," Honey said. "You really want to get us arrested, don't you?"

"We should leave her one."

"She'll make do without it."

Edgar groaned in frustration.

"If we get caught, I'm blaming you." Honey, more wobbly than before, turned to Florence and snatched up her moist hand.

"*Stop,*" cried Edgar.

"Make up your mind," Honey said. "Am I putting this back or not? Well?"

"Let me do it," said the boy. He stepped forward.

"Yes. Of course." Honey softened as she transferred the dead woman's hand to Edgar. "It's only right that you should . . ."

Edgar took the wedding band and slipped it back onto his grandmother's finger.

"It's all right, it's all right," Honey said. "Shhh." She touched the boy's exquisite hair. "You must never feel bad about what we've done, do you understand me? Child, child, look at me. What is your name?"

"Edgar."

"Edgar, *ha,* perfect. Edgar, tell me . . . did you love her?"

The boy nodded. His vision blurred.

"And she loved you?"

Again, he nodded.

"Then, there's no problem here. Okay? Because if what you say is true, then you deserve that ring. A person can steal things that he deserves. So, that lets one of us off the hook."

Edgar stifled a sob and wiped his nose.

"Enough of that. Stop sniffling. And don't use your sleeve. I'm sure your mother tells you that all the time."

"No, she doesn't," Edgar said, crying some more.

"Well, then I'm telling you. A person of style does not use his sleeve. Here's a tissue. *Goodness gracious.* Are you generally a crier? It doesn't do any good, you know. You won't get far on an ocean of tears."

Edgar dried his face with Honey's pink, perfume-scented tissue.

"Because no matter what has happened, you're still here. I mean, after what I read about you, I would have thought you'd be covered in scars. But your skin is flawless. And with that floppy hair, you're quite beautiful, quite angelic really. You rather look like a girl. Oh my goodness, are you blushing?"

"No," said Edgar.

"Aren't you priceless? Listen to me, darling: if anyone ever tries any funny business with you again, you know what you do? Look, watch me. You take your knee and you—well, it's hard for me to lift my leg in this dress. Here, pretend this is my leg." She lifted her cane and swung it. "And you jam it right *smack* into their balls."

Edgar covered his mouth.

"Aha!" Honey cried. "Now I know how to make you laugh. *Balls!*"

Edgar laughed again.

"Ha ha ha," said Honey. "Balls, balls, balls."

She was so different from his grandmother. But maybe this was what his mother would be like when she was older. Except with a nicer face. But he didn't want his mother to get old. Because then she'd end up in a butter dish, too.

"Uh uh uh, what did I tell you about the tears?"

Edgar sucked them in obligingly.

"Anyway, from what I've heard, it's nothing like we imagine. Death, I mean. One of my spiritual mentors once told me it's quite a trip. The darkness is apparently quite lively. I wouldn't be surprised if this one here"—again she tapped the coffin with the cane—"came to pay us a little visit now and then." Honey smiled and her face trembled a bit as she looked at Florence. "Thank you for the dresses, dear."

"She has other nice ones," Edgar said. "In her closet."

"Does she? Well, I should like to see them sometime."

"My mother says my gramma has no fashion sense."

"And who is your mother?"

"She has red hair."

"The woman I saw in the lobby?" said Honey. "With the strappy black dress?"

Edgar nodded.

"Darling, your *mother* is the one with no fashion sense. Listen, let me give you my card. It has my number on it." She dug again in her pink purse. *"Voilà."*

Edgar looked at the small white rectangle with pink lettering: *Honey Fasinga, Bon Vivant.* "What does that mean?" he asked.

"Bon Vivant? It's French. Literally: a person who lives well. Loosely: a loose woman, *ha.* No, but seriously. I should like to see those dresses . . . if your family ever feels like parting with them."

"We might want to keep them," Edgar said, trying his best to represent the Finis' interests.

"Certainly, young man. I completely understand. But do feel free to call at any time, for whatever reason. I would welcome the opportunity to speak with you again."

"Okay," said Edgar.

"Honestly, anytime. Whenever the mood strikes you. And please don't hesitate if the hour is late." Honey gently replaced the veil over her face and sighed. "I rarely sleep anymore."

14

Flow-Rinse

After the initial burst of ecstasy, there was a long haul through other less appealing states. Irritation came first, as if she were moving through a cloud of sharp-beaked birds that hungered for something inside her body—though she had no body, as far as she could tell. Still, things were being taken from her. Irritation swelled into anger, which collapsed into confusion, and then panic. She was traveling very fast, deafened by echoes that possessed the eerie familiarity of her own voice. A ghastly cacophony of a life bowed by emotion and regret. Overwhelming anguish, a dense black curtain of it, and then—as if some unseen hand were playing a game of peek-a-boo with her—the complete lifting of anguish. A deadly amusement that continued for several rounds, until, at last, the black curtain did not fall and she peered directly into the face of her master, which was nothing more than her own unmasked joy. It was incomprehensible, really. The birds were gone now, and though their work had been violent, the old woman felt nothing but an enthralled gratitude. The panic was happening somewhere else. Below her, it seemed, there was a terrific commotion, a nervous storm composed of pinpricks of light. One was particularly insistent, with the power to pull her attention from what was inevitable. She willed that some of what the birds had taken from her be delivered to the boy, hoping the creatures were intelligent enough to separate the wheat from the chaff. Perhaps there was something there the child could use, should he find himself in danger again. Let it fall now, she thought, suddenly aware that she might never be able to return. As she continued forward, there was no music, there was no one to greet her—not even Frank or Pio. But she did not wish it otherwise. The solitude was a triumph—as was the silence.

15

Save for Later

On the drive home, it hit Edgar like a bird against a window.

Something was wrong with time.

It had been wrong for years; maybe since the day he was born. His life was unfolding too slowly—more like a book, when *obviously* life was a movie. He could see how his grandmother lay at the root of the problem. The way she'd made weeks out of minutes, and years out of days. His mother did it, too—falling into silences that had the bleak ardor of black-and-white photographs. The error with time was something he'd learned from them. And it seemed that today, the saddest day of the boy's life, time might stop completely.

In the car, Edgar felt something like panic. The air itself was turning to cement. He didn't understand that this imprisonment was an illusion, a phantasm of grief. He truly believed that life might be over, that all stories would unfold only in the already-lived, the sole place in which his grandmother was not dead.

But as he looked out the window, he saw how the landscape moved by so fast that it blurred. Trees and billboards slapped past his consciousness with the clicking intensity of a roulette wheel. Edgar felt a desire for something else. Perhaps there were other arrangements a person could make with time.

His grandmother was gone—and, sad as that was, it might be less sad in the future. He pressed his foot against an imaginary pedal. A race-car growl rose from his throat.

"What are you doing?" asked Lucy. "Singing?"

"No," replied Edgar.

"You're not crying, are you?"

"No."

"You're probably tired, huh?"

Edgar shook his head. "No."

"Brilliant vocabulary you got there, kiddo."

She'd meant it as a joke, but the boy didn't smile. He pressed harder on the imaginary pedal and unlatched his seat belt.

"What are you doing? Put that back on. *Edgar.*"

"I don't need it."

"Do you want me to stop the car? Put on your goddamned seat belt."

"Why should I?" the boy said. "You're not wearing yours. You never wear it."

Lucy reached for the buckle and pulled it across her chest.

"You're just doing that for now," the boy said.

"Meaning what?"

"You're just *pretending* to be safe."

"I'm stopping the car."

"No, *don't.* I'll put it on." Edgar pulled and clicked. Then, after some time: "How come I don't have any scars?"

"From what?"

"I don't know. You have them. On your leg."

"We're different people, Edgar."

"I know that. I'm just saying, I should know things."

"What things?"

"If something *happened* to me. If I was in the *newspaper.*"

"I don't know what you're talking about, baby. Did your grandmother say something to you?"

Edgar turned to his mother in horror. "How can she say something?"

"I meant, from before. It doesn't matter. Listen, from now on, we wear our seat belts, okay?"

The boy sighed, gripping the diamond in his pocket. "I'm not getting married," he informed his mother.

"I didn't know you were engaged."

"I'm not," replied Edgar. "Not everyone *gets* married."

Lucy reached out her hand and touched the boy's head.

"I don't have a fever. Besides, you can't tell like that. It has to be done with a thermometer, to be accurate."

"Okay, Doc."

"Mom, you're slowing down."

"Sorry. You in a rush?"

"Yes," said Edgar. "I am."

* * *

"Did you make all this yourself?" Netty Schlip asked the butcher, helping herself to some Chicken Carciofi.

"My sister Izzy helps out. But I made the sausage and peppers and the eggplant rollatini. Oh, and the cavatelli and broccoli."

In addition to the promised cold-cut platter, the truck from Salvatore's Meats had delivered several enormous trays of cooked food, along with the racks and Sternos to heat them. This surprise attack of generosity put Lucy on edge. It was a tricky business, accepting Ron's feast in Florence's name. She hardly knew the man, and to what extent she wished to become entangled with him she couldn't say.

For Edgar, the catered fare was upsetting for more haunted reasons: its disturbing similarity to dishes regularly prepared by Florence. Plus, cavatelli and broccoli was his favorite. It was impossible to look at it and not feel a kind of nauseous hunger. The little party of five was sitting in the dining room—a narrow, ill-lit rectangle with a faux-candle chandelier that offered the greater part of its light to the ceiling, while leaving the under-gatherers in a cloud of luminous neglect. The dining room was used exclusively for holidays, when the wedding-dress tablecloth was unfolded and the special plates with the little purple flowers came out of the china closet. And yet, today—the very opposite of a holiday—he and his mother and three guests were scattered around the large oval table, eating off Styrofoam plates with plastic forks—all supplied by the butcher. "No fuss, no muss," he'd said. Even the napkins were the butcher's: thin paper squares printed with the message "Let us *MEAT* your needs!"

Lucy sipped wine from a plastic cup. "I didn't know you did catering, Ron."

"It's a new thing," he said. "I like to cook, so . . ."

"Who doesn't like to cook?" Netty Schlip said.

Edgar looked at his mother, who met his eyes and made a funny face. He adored her again. Love was so exhausting, the way it spun you around. Edgar made a funny face back at her. Maybe she'd let him stay in her bed tonight.

"Eddie—why don't you try one of these?" The butcher had lifted a rollatini from the tray and was extending it toward the boy's empty plate.

"No, thank you."

"Take it," Lucy said. "You have to eat something."

The butcher plopped down the neatly rolled eggplant, and Edgar jumped back at the slight spattering of sauce, afraid it might get on his white shirt.

"What's the matter?" the man asked.

"Nothing," replied Edgar.

And now everyone was watching, waiting for him to take a bite.

"He's a picky eater, huh?" Henry Schlip said, leaning toward Lucy.

"We tried to give him some halvah once," Netty said. "But he wouldn't eat it. You remember that, Edgar?"

The boy felt the heat come to his face. He nodded at his plate. The halvah had looked like one of the large rubber erasers Blessum used in art class.

Edgar liked the Schlips, though it was strange to have them in his house, where they made less sense. In their shop they achieved meaning, surrounded by their vast array of goods—sheets and towels, slippers and bath salts, curtains, lightbulbs, extension cords; there were knitting needles and mason jars, buckets and brooms. Edgar especially appreciated the tiny scented pillows that Netty made herself—"to put in your drawer," she'd told him, "not under your head." Henry was constantly rearranging the displays, as if to make the items more comfortable. To Edgar, the Schlips seemed the wistful parents of an extensive brood of inanimate objects. Dry goods. "Is *everything* dry?" Edgar once asked them. "Show me something wet," Henry had replied. The boy had taken the quest seriously, had kept it up for months, but failed to locate a single moist product.

His grandmother had always seemed to enjoy the Schlips' company. They were not really friends, but there was genuine affection. Shopkeepers existed in a liminal zone between family and strangers. It was easy to be with them because the rules were so clear—unlike the complicated business of family or friends, or even strangers, for that matter. Stopping for a little while in a shop with his grandmother had been a kind of safety. Edgar felt calm in these places. He liked to watch his grandmother talk with the Schlips—an intriguing language of sighs and nods and wistful shakes of the head. The bird business of old people. Sometimes they all laughed about little things long gone.

All this being said, Edgar was fairly certain that his grandmother would never have invited Henry and Netty Schlip into her house, to sit around the dining room table on a Monday night. The fact that they were here could only mean that the Earth had swung off course. The Schlips must have felt it, too. They weren't themselves; they were nervous, and as hopeless as everyone else in regard to how to keep the conversation moving.

"So, what is halvah, exactly?" the butcher finally asked.

"That's the name of God," Henry said.

"Halvah," Netty shouted at Henry, before turning back to the butcher. "He can't hear. It's sesame seeds and sugar. Delicious."

"Very good," agreed Henry, spooning up some cavatelli.

"You wanna try the sausage and peppers?" the butcher asked the old man. Henry held up his hand.

"We don't eat pork," Netty said.

"But you eat chicken?" asked the butcher.

"Oh yes—and beef. And most fish."

"We're not fanatics," Henry said.

"Never understood what you people have against pigs."

Edgar looked up from his plate—relieved to see that the butcher hadn't pulled a cleaver from his pocket.

"Cloven hooves," said Henry. "Animal has to have toes."

"Pigs have toes," said the butcher.

"But they don't ruminate," said Netty.

"They don't what?"

"Chew their cud," Henry said loudly.

"You're shouting again." Netty leaned over and adjusted the old man's hearing aid. "The animal has to have cloven hooves *and* chew its cud," she said to the butcher.

Henry nodded, still chewing.

Edgar felt nauseous. All this talk of food. It was too much, considering the fact that it might have been a serving of burnt meatballs, made by *him,* that had killed his grandmother. Of course, his mother was to blame, too. She'd yelled at the old woman the night before she'd died.

"Can I be excused?" said Edgar.

"Where do you wanna go?" asked Lucy. "You haven't even touched your plate."

"We should have a salad," the boy said. "I could pick some tomatoes." Any excuse to get out of the house.

"He wants to pick tomatoes," Lucy said, shaking her head, and everyone laughed in a polite but infuriating way. To Edgar, it all seemed like a dream. Maybe there wasn't even a garden behind the house. Maybe he'd only imagined it.

"I just want to see if there's any left," he said in a militant whisper to his mother.

"Season's over," she said. "Eat your rollatini."

He could tell she was tipsy by the way she said *rollatini*—as if the word had fallen asleep halfway out of her mouth. The butcher was drinking, too. As were the Schlips. It was what grown-ups did when they were nervous.

"We still have a few left in our garden," Netty said. "But Florence's were always the best."

"Such a nice woman," Henry said. "You're going to miss her, aren't you?"

"Henry, don't upset the boy. I, for one, wouldn't mind a tomato," she said, winking at Edgar.

"Fine," said Lucy, turning to her son. "Knock yourself out."

Edgar got up from the table.

"And take a flashlight."

"I know," said Edgar. He'd been in the garden at night before, with Florence. She'd said it was better to water the plants in the dark, especially when the moon was up. Because the moon was full of water and it talked to the water on Earth. Edgar had asked his grandmother to explain the science of this further, but she'd said, "What science? It's got nothing to do with science."

"This wine is very red," Henry said, holding his glass up toward the chandelier.

"That's the way we like it," said Lucy.

"She likes to put water in my wine." Henry cocked his head toward Netty.

"I do not," she said. "Two drops, maybe."

"What kind of wine is this?" Henry asked the butcher.

"Which one are you drinking?" There were three different bottles on the table.

"Who the hell knows?" Henry released a long sigh, dabbed his face with a paper napkin. "Florence was always very particular about her towels. White or cream. Had to be white or cream."

"But then she bought the pink ones, remember?" said Netty. "For the girl's bathroom. She said you like pink."

Lucy met the woman's eyes and tried to smile.

"Now, you know, dear—Edgar's always welcome to come by the store. We'd be happy to watch him when you're busy."

"Same goes for me," said the butcher. "After school, whatever."

"See," Netty said. "You have friends."

"I could teach him how to make sausage," the butcher said with a wink, and the Schlips laughed—but only briefly.

Lucy had a sudden desire to fling a plate across the room. How dare these people—strangers—suggest taking care of her son. She suddenly wanted only Florence. Who knew better than Florence what the boy needed? At Frank's funeral, it had been the old woman who'd held Edgar. Lucy, still injured, had barely been able to stand.

"We don't have any grandchildren," Netty said.

"No," murmured Henry. "Our daughter's a what-do-you-call-it?"

"Henry. *Farmakh dos moyl.*"

"*Lesbijka,*" Henry blurted, and the butcher spit.

"That's right. You said it." Henry reexamined his wine by the light of the chandelier. "Terrible to have a child like that."

Lucy stood. "I'll get some coffee."

"We've upset you, dear."

"Not at all. Caffeine all right?"

"Caffeine is good," said Netty.

"Let me help you," offered the butcher.

"No," Lucy said. "Stay with the . . ."

"The Schlips," Henry said.

"No. What *Schlips?*" said Netty. "Henry and Netty. Florence was like family to us."

Just before stepping out the back door, Edgar noticed a large beetle crawling on the inside of the kitchen window. He fetched a paper towel and moved toward the bug, an emerald-green scarab whose armor shimmered with flashes of gold. Edgar wasn't afraid of insects. In fact, he admired them. Their compact intelligence, spectacular colors, and the sense that they had lost something they were single-mindedly though hopelessly trying to find—all these qualities encouraged the boy's sympathy. He didn't like to kill them. With a quick movement he encased the beetle in the paper towel—crumpling it carefully to trap the bug without smushing it. He dashed outside and threw the buzzing wad onto the dark lawn. He pulled the flashlight from his pocket and watched as the frazzled creature shuddered inside the paper nautilus. It looked like a beating heart and sounded like an electric chair. When the beetle emerged, flying toward the house, Edgar gasped and dropped the flashlight. He swatted at his face; but there was nothing. He could hear the wings zoom past him, the sound fading above the dark trees. Suddenly he was furious. Why hadn't he put the insect in a jar? An emerald-green scarab was probably a rare specimen. He might never see anything like it again.

He walked toward the tomatoes, stepping over the beam of the fallen flashlight. He didn't need it anyway; his eyes had adjusted to the darkness. He looked at the six plants, knowing their days were numbered. His grandmother had to put in new ones every summer, because, every fall, the bushes froze. Luckily the plants hadn't yet turned yellow, but Edgar could see the places where caterpillars had dined, leaving behind frayed leaves that had the mad perfection of lace. There would be no tomatoes; he knew that. He'd picked the last three just a few days ago, the night of the murderous meatballs.

Edgar knelt before the plants, rubbing a leaf to draw out its smell—a dusty, pungent freshness even more miraculous than Chanel N° 5. As he leaned in closer, he saw the dense black orb at the heart of the vines. Was it really there? He reached in and touched it.

"What are you doing?"

It was the butcher. He'd picked up the flashlight and was moving toward the garden.

Edgar tried to hide the tomato, but it was too large.

"Your mom wanted me to check on you. Hey, look at that." The butcher aimed the flashlight directly at the tomato. "Good job."

Edgar moved the fruit back into the darkness.

"Watch this," the butcher said, turning the flashlight and shining it under his chin. "My uncle Gus used to do this when I was little. Looks weird, right?"

It made the man look more like a pig. "You can stop doing that," said Edgar.

"Come on—your mother wants you inside."

Edgar didn't move.

"Inside—you will come inside," the butcher droned, shining the light on the boy's chest and making it move in crazy circles.

"Why are you doing that?"

"I'm hypnotizing you."

"No you're not."

"Come on—I'm your friend, Eddie." The butcher redirected the light toward the lawn. "Hey, listen, I told your mother if you ever wanna come by the shop after school, that's cool. She can pick you up when she gets off work."

Edgar was speechless.

"I really want to help you guys. Do what I can. You know, I had a really nice grandmother, too."

Edgar looked up from the man's tasseled loafers. "Where is she now?"

"She's, uh, you know, with yours."

"Were they friends?"

"No, but I mean, they're both . . ."

Edgar waited.

"My mother, too," the butcher said quietly.

"Dead?" asked Edgar. He was still amazed, and somewhat annoyed, that this was a problem shared by other people.

The butcher nodded, swung the beam of light into the trees—the oak and the elm and the dogwoods. "You know where the dead go, don't you?"

"Yes," said Edgar. He thought of the beetle.

"Happens just like that." The butcher clicked off the flashlight. "And there's nothing you can do about it."

The man's voice sounded different now, like he was talking to himself. Edgar stood with him in the darkness, and then set the tomato on the ground.

"What are you doing?"

"It's the last one," said Edgar.

"So bring it inside. We can have it for dessert."

When Edgar walked into the house with the tomato, the butcher held up the boy's arm. "And the winner is . . ."

Netty Schlip clapped her hands. "Oh, isn't that a beauty."

"Who wants a slice?" said the butcher.

It's my tomato, thought Edgar. He was not planning to share it.

"I'd love a slice," said Netty. "My mouth is watering already."

"Lucy?"

"I'll pass." His mother was still sipping wine from a plastic cup, even as she made coffee.

Edgar found some relief in the fact that everyone was in the kitchen now. The light was brighter, and the yellow Formica table with its blue vase of week-old asters was as familiar as the sun. A safe place, it seemed, until the butcher snatched the tomato from the boy's hand.

"Where's your cutting board?" he asked.

"I'll do it," said Edgar. He extended his hand, but the butcher seemed reluctant to concede the fruit.

"Is he allowed, Luce?"

"I'm allowed," said Edgar with some force.

"He's tired," said Netty. "Poor thing."

"I cut things all the time," the boy insisted. "May I have it back, please?"

The butcher swung his arm as if to toss the tomato across the room.

"Don't," said Edgar.

"I'm kidding. Here you go, buddy." He gently placed it in the boy's palm.

"He doesn't have a sense of humor," Lucy said.

"Yes I do. But not with *tomatoes.*"

The butcher mussed the boy's hair and then poured himself more wine. He stood beside Lucy as she served the coffee. "You two like sambuca?" he said to the Schlips. "You got any sambuca, Lucy?"

"One step ahead of you." She pointed to the bottle on the table.

Edgar stood at the cutting board with his back to everyone.

"I don't think anyone's gonna have that now," Lucy said to him. "Sit with us. I poured you a glass of milk."

When he turned, he saw the butcher's hand on his mother's back, and Netty Schlip sniffing the open bottle of sambuca.

"Smells like licorice," she said.

"Anise, actually," the butcher said.

"Is there a difference?" asked Netty.

"I believe anise has cloven hooves," said the butcher.

"Ha," barked Henry. "Then I'll try it."

"Maybe you've had enough?" Netty tapped the old man's arm.

"You want to insult the people? This is their custom."

"I'll give him just a drop," said Lucy, pouring the clear liquid into Henry's coffee.

"Caffè corretto," said the butcher.

Lucy smiled, remembering the expression from Pio. *Corrected coffee.* Without warning, the tears came to her eyes.

"Oh, sweetheart," Netty said. "Sneaks up on you, doesn't it?"

Lucy wiped her cheeks and poured a healthy dose of sambuca into her own cup.

"I guess I'll have a splash, too," said Netty. "For Florence."

"That's my girl," said Henry.

The butcher lifted his glass. "To Florence."

Edgar clenched his fists. The man didn't even know her. He was a *suitor*. A killer of pigs. Definitely not a person his grandmother would want sitting in her kitchen. Plus, the man's blubbery hand had found its way to Lucy's knee.

His mother seemed oblivious to all of it. She was falling asleep at the table. Edgar was tired, too. He had the feeling, once again, that he was moving through a dream. Some crumbs on the counter leapt to the size of boulders. When he looked away, he saw the wall calendar his grandmother bought every year from St. Margaret's. The image for September was, inexplicably, a white rabbit beside a bucket of apples. In the box that marked the date of his grandmother's death, someone had drawn a circle—inside of which was a tiny *F*. Edgar reached out and touched the letter, realizing something awful.

"She died on his birthday."

Lucy stirred. "What did you say?"

"Whose birthday?" said the butcher.

"Just ignore him," said Lucy. "He's in a mood."

"I'm not in a mood," Edgar said quietly.

"Do you want me to put him to bed?" asked Netty.

"He's fine." Lucy grabbed the bottle of sambuca. "Here, let me pour you a little more."

Netty shook her hand. "No, thank you, dear."

"Think of it like sugar," slurred Lucy.

As Netty accepted what could not be refused, she looked up and smiled at Edgar with an unfathomable sadness. The boy smiled back as best as his lips would allow—and Netty settled the transaction with one of her famous winks.

Slowly, the adults went back to sipping their corrected coffee and chatting. Edgar reached up and tried to smear the tiny *F*. His father suddenly seemed a thief, someone who'd been stealing things for a long time—and who'd now taken something irreplaceable. Maybe that's what death was—a kind of kidnapping, perpetrated by ghosts.

The boy stared at the tomato on the cutting board. He pulled the serrated knife from the wooden block and brought it to the fruit, letting the blade's teeth touch the skin without piercing it. When eating a tomato raw, his grandmother liked to parse it into thick slices; but Edgar decided it would be best to cut as many slivers as possible, making the most of what was possibly the last of its kind. He'd serve it simply, with salt: the best way to eat a Jersey beefsteak, the old woman had always said.

It was almost painful, making the first incision. The fruit bled. Edgar proceeded slowly, sawing gently at the base.

"What are you doing—brain surgery?" The butcher appeared at the boy's side. "You gotta cut it thicker. And if you do it too slow, you mutilate the poor thing. Here, let me show you."

The man pulled another knife from the block, and Edgar—propelled by a small nudge—stepped aside.

"That's the wrong knife," the boy said. The butcher had unsheathed the large chopper that was used for onions and carrots.

"There's no right or wrong, Eddie. Whatever does the job."

"Let him show you," Lucy said from the sidelines.

"But we don't use that knife for *tomatoes*."

"Watch," the butcher said. He lifted the silver blade and came down with an easy yet significant force. Edgar flinched, fearing the worst. But, miraculously, the tomato fell apart in two perfect halves, with hardly any loss of water. "See that?"

Perhaps the man was right. Perhaps his method caused the tomato less pain.

"Now you try it." The butcher placed one of the halves in the center of the cutting board, and offered Edgar the large knife. "Quarter it." Like a tennis coach, he lifted the boy's skinny arm. "You wanna get a little height so you can put some force behind it."

Edgar looked at the half-tomato—the seeds like teeth trapped under a bloody glacier. Never before had he realized the extent to which a tomato was a living thing.

"*Down*," the butcher said, and the boy, against his better judgment, followed the man's command. He closed his eyes, and when he opened them he saw that he'd quartered the fruit perfectly.

"Good man! Give this guy a drink."

Lucy got up from the table, bringing the boy's milk.

Edgar felt giddy. The room spun. Something like a laugh came from his mouth, as his mother set the glass beside the cutting board.

"I'll do the other half," said Edgar.

"Go for it," said the butcher. "I'm gonna give this kid a job."

Edgar saw the man lean in and kiss his mother.

Lucy was thoroughly sodden; the butcher only a notch less. Edgar was drunk, too—intoxicated by a potent cocktail of exhaustion and grief, spiked with an exhilarating desire for revenge. As he lifted the knife, he thought of

Thomas Pittimore. Across the room, his mother, whom he could see from the corner of his eye, pressed her body into the butcher's. Her hand strayed suspiciously downward. *Supersluts.com* flickered across Edgar's mind—and once again he felt the painful branding of Thomas's pen.

He lifted the knife higher and brought it down with uncharacteristic force. His form was excellent—a gesture of martial severity that would have guaranteed success had he not forgotten to move his other hand that held the tomato in place.

The pain was profound and prevented Edgar from hearing his own scream. When his mother heard it, she briefly mistook the boy's cry for a shout of triumph. But then she saw the blood—and the way Edgar's hand jerked away from the cutting board, scattering the tomato pieces onto the floor.

A thin fountain arced high into the air and, as the boy turned in a strange faltering spin, the red liquid spattered across Lucy's dress. Netty Schlip gasped and leapt from her chair. The boy was missing the tip of his finger.

Lucy, paralyzed, began to lose her feet. The butcher, having to choose, reached out to stop the boy from falling. Lucy collapsed to her knees, and Netty Schlip raced across the room with a towel.

"Where is it?" cried Edgar.

"Where's what?" said Henry.

From the floor, Lucy saw it under the table. She looked from the person-less finger to the fingerless person—a simple equation that her mind refused to factor.

"Pick it up," yelled Netty.

"Ice," said the butcher. He set the boy in a chair and sprinted to the re-frigerator. "Where do you keep your plastic bags? *Lucy.*"

"Henry," Netty shouted. "My rain cap. In my pocketbook."

The old man dumped the contents of his wife's bag onto the table and located the see-through plastic kerchief. He passed it to the butcher.

Edgar watched for as long as he could; watched as the rain cap was filled with ice; as his blood bloomed through the cream-colored dishtowel; as his mother picked up a piece of him off the floor and dropped it into Netty's kerchief. He even watched long enough to hear Lucy say, "Please don't die."

"Nobody's going to die," the butcher said.

Edgar didn't have the strength to correct him. He watched his mother pass out, and then, only seconds later, he followed her.

"I'll drive them to the hospital," the butcher said.

"We'll come with you," said Netty.

The butcher carried Edgar from the kitchen, leaving Lucy to the Schlips.

"Henry, take her other arm."

"Got it."

"Ready?" said Netty. "Now *pull*."

"*Oooh,*" Henry said. "She's no feather."

Netty gently slapped the girl's face. "Come on, dear. We need to get you in the car."

16

In the Car

A horrible brightness, as if the car were on fire. Where were her sunglasses?

"Slow down," Lucy said, shielding her eyes. Her husband was driving too fast, and Edgar was crying. "Frank, *slow down,* you're scaring him."

The car made a sudden sharp turn, and Lucy, not wearing her seat belt, slammed into the door.

"Please, baby, just pull over. I won't let anything happen to you."

"Don't fucking lie to me," screamed Frank.

As the car flew at alarming speed, Lucy wrapped her arms tightly around Edgar. She looked up at the Saint Christopher medal swinging from the rearview mirror—and though it was another woman's magic, she prayed to it.

"What are you saying?" Frank said. *"Why are you whispering?"*

But she didn't answer him. She moved her hand as slowly as possible toward the lock on the door and clicked it open. She had to get out of the car. *Now.*

Entry #1

She feels the boy's pain, though she has no body. She calls to him, though she has no voice. And though she feels all-powerful, she feels, as well, as if she's someone else's dream. It's not as easy as she'd imagined—being dead. Being bloodless, while all that blood fills her kitchen. If only she could write something there, something the boy might see. Three words on the red floor:

I am here.

17

Percocet-Demi

Edgar woke with a throbbing pain in his hand, and his mother's arm strapped to his chest. In the boy's twin bed, the two were jammed together—Edgar's butt to Lucy's belly. The room was dark, spooked by Lucy's high-pitched snoring. When Edgar tried to move, he found that his body had doubled, tripled, in weight. Maybe he'd been lying too long beside his mother. Was drunkenness something you could catch?

He felt as if he'd been sleeping for a hundred years, and yet he was exhausted. He rolled to the floor and examined his hand in the glow of his spaceship night-light. One of his fingers was so bundled in gauze it looked like a corn dog. The pain was strange: it was definitely *there,* but at the same time it was far away. The throbbing came through like a kind of intergalactic static.

What had happened, exactly? The last thing he remembered was his mother dropping his finger into a shower cap. Edgar gently pressed the tip of the bandage, uncertain what was underneath. Had someone managed to put him back together? He felt a rising in his throat, recalling the blood in the kitchen. His grandmother would be furious.

And then he remembered the larger problem.

He went to her room and, as he feared, she wasn't there. He touched the bedspread—patted it down as if looking for a lost coin rather than a large body. He pulled the blankets off the bed, and then the sheets, until he was staring at a naked mattress. It looked strange, like Wonder Bread. His brain seemed the same: flat, mushy.

In the closet, he tugged a few housedresses off their hangers—headless but surprisingly vivid versions of his grandmother. He did not forget the ones in the back, with the sequins and the beads. He carried the mishmash of dresses to the bed and arranged them in a long pile. He picked up the sheet

from the floor, covered the mound, and looked at the clock. It was five A.M.—
early enough for optimism. His grandmother didn't usually rise until six.

He wandered down the hall and ducked into the bathroom. His face was
whiter than usual, covered in a sheen of perspiration. Why was he so thirsty?
As he reached for the water glass, he saw the small bottle of pills. His name
was on the label, as well as a second, more exotic name. *Percocet-Demi.*

Take one-half tablet, as needed, for pain.

The bottle was open. Maybe he'd taken some already. Just to be safe,
though, he shook out one of the little pink pills and swallowed it with some
water.

"Oh," he said, slapping his head (he'd forgotten to break the little pink
pill in half). A few seconds later he giggled—a delayed reaction to the head-
clonking gesture he'd witnessed in the mirror. It seemed funny now—like
he wasn't really Edgar, only playing Edgar on television. After another slug
of water, he dug out two more pills and slipped them into his pants—a gesture modeled after Florence, who always had an aspirin at the ready in the
pocket of her housedress.

He stood outside the kitchen, reluctant to enter. There was a lot of blood.
Two sets of smeary red footprints, one large and one small, faded like ghosts
as they traveled toward the living room. The crime scene lacked nothing but
yellow tape and the outline of a body. Apparently, the police hadn't arrived
yet. If he worked quickly, he could remove the evidence. What had happened
was clearly the butcher's fault, but Edgar wasn't worried about him. The boy
knew, from the storylines of various police shows, that a careless mother could
also be dragged away in cuffs.

It was obvious what he had to do. He'd seen his grandmother do it a thousand times. He went to the hall closet and retrieved the bucket and the mop
and the scrub brush. From under the kitchen sink he got the rags and the
spray cleaner, as well as a spare roll of paper towels.

He rinsed the stained knife, wiped the cutting board—the ruined tomato
like chunks of guts. Cleaning the floor took some muscle. When he finished
mopping, he went out to the yard and poured the bloody water over the
anemic tomatoes. The sun was just coming up. He needed to get ready for
school.

Or was he supposed to stay home today? There was no one to ask. Upstairs, his mother was still asleep. He looked at the books on his desk; the
scattered pens; the yellow backpack hanging from the chair. These things
seemed to belong to some other Edgar. An expansive light-headedness washed

away all sense of familiarity. Plus, the room was spinning. When he looked out the window, the trees were spinning, too—confirming that the phenomenon was of global concern.

With some difficulty he put on a clean shirt, before heading down the hall to check on the progress of his experiment. He pressed on the mound of dresses, but there was no change—no Florence. He'd have to let it sit for a few more hours. From the bottom drawer of the bureau, he took a votive candle (his grandmother bought them in bulk from the Schlips). He dropped the candle into the blue glass cup at the Virgin's feet, and then struck a match from the box of chopstick-length matches he was forbidden to touch. When he left the house, he was still wearing his slippers.

*   *   *

Lucy woke to the smell of overcooked pancakes.

"Edgar?" She felt for the boy in the small bed and then drifted off again, to join Frank at a stock car race. A lowrider skidded against the wall of the track, flipping three times before bursting into flame. Frank cheered, and Lucy jumped from the bed, coughing.

"*Shit.*"

She ran down the hallway, following the smell. In Florence's bedroom she stood paralyzed before the implausible vision of two-foot flames rising before the Virgin Mary. When she darted to the bed to grab a pillow with which to swat the blaze, she screamed, seeing the body under the sheet. It was not until she felt the heat on her back that she turned again to the fire. It had fully consumed the doily under the statue and was now creeping up the wall.

In the bathroom she filled a glass with water. When she threw it in the Virgin's face, the liquid's only effect was to split the fire in two. Half of it set to work on Florence's wedding portrait, and half of it leapt to the undernourished leaves of the tall potted ficus beside the bureau. Lucy pulled open a random drawer and grabbed a pair of Florence's bloomers. As she slapped them over the fire they instantly ignited. She dropped the burning underwear and tore off her sweatshirt. After a minute of desperate swatting that knocked the Virgin from the bureau and the wedding portrait from the wall, Lucy managed to extinguish everything but the obvious culprit: the tiny candle in the blue glass cup. She leaned over and blew it out, before collapsing onto the floor.

Again she looked at the bed, at the large lump under the covers. What the hell was going on? *"Edgar?"*

She crawled toward the mattress and pulled away the sheet. She gasped— even though it was nothing but a pile of clothing.

"Edgar! Do you think this is funny?"

It was a strain to shout, and she fell into another fit of coughing. Even after opening the window, she found it hard to breathe. Smoke moved about in shifting eddies.

Lucy hated this room. Whenever she walked past the door and saw the flickering light, it annoyed her. The candle was part of the old woman's lunacy—some twisted hope that Frank might still be alive. But Lucy knew better; she'd been there at the end. Of course, whenever she'd tried to talk with Florence about what had happened at Shepherd's Junction, the old woman would hold up her hand like a traffic cop. "I don't want to hear it."

Lucy picked up the head of the shattered Virgin and stared at the black char on the wall. She reached for one of the dresses—a slinky green cocktail gown adorned with a fringe of orange beads. Eventually, she'd have to sort through all this stuff. Who knew what the old woman had stashed in here? Even now, she could see, in the drawer from which she'd pulled the bloomers, a black metal box tied shut with twine.

When she poked her head into Edgar's room, she saw that his schoolbooks were gone, his backpack.

Fuck.

The doctor had said the kid had suffered a serious shock. He'd also said the pills might make him confused. In the bathroom, Lucy splashed some cold water over her face. They had to be at the funeral by noon. She picked up the bottle of painkillers and shook out two. She'd suffered a serious shock, as well.

The phone was ringing. Lucy vaguely recalled that it had been ringing all night. By the time she got to the extension in her room, no one was there. It was probably Ron. What an idiot he'd been, with his fucking Benihana knife routine. And now, if the reattachment failed, her son would be permanently disfigured.

Reattachment? The word echoed in Lucy's head, growing less sensible with each repetition.

A hot shower is what she needed—and then she'd drive to the school and pick up the kid.

*   *   *

Outside the Mark-O-Market, a scrap of paper blew against Edgar's leg. He leaned down to pluck it from his pants. *Eggs, Tampons, Frosting.* A grocery list, no doubt, but Edgar, in his altered state, suspected it might be some kind of message from Florence—though he wasn't exactly sure what eggs and tampons and frosting had to do with his grandmother. Still, he put the list in his pocket before floating into the store.

When he set the bottle of Coke on the counter, Mr. Zhong, who owned the place, said, "Dollar twenty-five."

"What?" asked Edgar.

"Dollar twenty-five," repeated Mr. Zhong.

"Oh, right."

Digging for change, Edgar pulled the grocery list from his pocket, and then—since he was wearing the same pants he'd worn to the wake—he pulled out his grandmother's engagement ring.

"Oh, look at that!" Mr. Zhong said. "You getting married? *Ha ha ha.* You getting married today?"

Mr. Zhong was a tiny man with a screeching voice. Edgar only now understood that the proprietor of the Mark-O-Market was actually a monkey.

"I . . ." Edgar put his hand in his other pocket, but there was nothing.

"Okay, okay," Mr. Zhong said, "you pay me tomorrow."

Edgar reclaimed his property and walked away.

"Big shot, big shot, you forget your soda."

Outside, the sun was bright, and Edgar, wondering where his soda was, closed his eyes. He continued walking until he slammed into a strangely soft wall.

"Well, hello to you, too, *dahhling.*"

It was Thomas Pittimore.

Some boys nearby laughed.

Edgar scrunched up his nose. The fat boy smelled hideous.

"Oh my God!" Thomas cried. "What happened to your finger?"

The concern in the boy's voice made Edgar turn.

"Were you *masturbating* again?" The audience of boys snickered, and Edgar blinked. Things had started to spin again, and Thomas seemed to be on every side of him at once. Edgar took a step backwards into the road. A car flashed by, blaring its horn.

"You're gonna get creamed," Thomas said, yanking Edgar onto the sidewalk.

"Where's Jarell?" asked Edgar, noting with anxiety that the eggplant-colored boy wasn't among Thomas's posse.

In response to Edgar's question, the fat boy leaned over and, as he'd done before—as if it were simply the customary greeting of his tribe—released a thin rope of spit. It was surprisingly elastic, stretching a long way before snapping into a compact unit and landing on the little boy's foot. "Nice shoes," said Thomas.

"Oh," said Edgar, noticing for the first time that he was still wearing his slippers. He looked up into the fat boy's face. "You smell."

"What did you say?"

"You *smell*," Edgar enunciated—not with meanness, but with the necessary force to overcome the torpor of intoxication. He tapped his nose to further convey his point—adding, in case his meaning wasn't clear: "Like *poop*."

Thomas grabbed the boy's bandaged finger.

If this hurt, Edgar wasn't sure. It seemed to be happening to someone else.

"Say it again," Thomas said, squeezing harder. The pain made a brief but shocking appearance.

"*Ow.*"

"That's what I want to hear."

As Thomas began to twist the finger, Edgar panicked. "*Stop.* You're going to pull it off again."

"You mean *whack* it off?"

"Please," Edgar said. "I don't feel so good."

"*Leave him alone, you fat fuck.*"

Thomas looked up, but held fast to Edgar's finger.

"What did I just say?" The man grabbed Thomas by the shoulders and shoved him backwards.

"Don't touch me," Thomas cried, kicking. "You can't touch *children*. I'll call the police."

"You should," the man said. "Here, let me get my phone. In fact, I know a few guys down at the station. You want me to call for you? Or do you want to do it?" He extended the phone, tightening his grip on the boy's shoulder.

"Pervert." Thomas sneered and kicked again.

The man easily sidestepped Thomas's foot, before throwing a quick backhanded slap to the fat boy's face.

Edgar vomited onto the pavement.

The man gently touched the little boy's head, and then turned back to Thomas. "I think you better get out of here before my buddies from the station get here and we find out who the real pervert is."

Thomas's lips were quivering. "I wasn't going to hurt him."

"But you did hurt him."

"I only—"

"What did I say? Take your fat ass—and get the fuck out of here."

Feeling the tears in his eyes, Thomas turned away.

"Did I not say *run?*" the man barked—and Edgar watched in amazement as the fat boy did what he was told, only stopping when he'd reached the corner.

"I have a gun," Thomas shouted.

"I have one, too," the man shouted back, as Thomas disappeared around the bend.

Edgar looked up into his savior's face. Something was familiar. The blondish-brown hair. The beard.

"Gross," one of the boys said, passing the vomit.

"What's the fat kid's name?" asked the man.

A few of the boys laughed. "Thomas," one of them said.

"Thomas what?"

"Pittimore," another said, feeling no sense of betrayal. Thomas was amusing, but they all knew he was a shit. He stole tater-tots, flat-tired shoes, and had a nasty habit of grabbing a person's pen and licking it.

The bearded man took a small pad from his pocket and scribbled a note. "Move on, guys. Show's over." Slowly, the boys ambled away.

"Are you a policeman?" asked Edgar.

"Here." The man pulled a handkerchief from his pocket and wiped the boy's face.

Edgar swayed on his feet. "I don't feel so good."

"Come on, I'll give you a ride home."

"I'm going to school," said Edgar.

"I don't think so, my friend. You can hardly stand up."

"I'm . . ." Edgar's head rolled to the side. Things that shouldn't be moving were moving again, including the green pickup truck parked across the street. "Oh," Edgar said—and then he turned back to the man. "You're . . ."

"Yes," the man said, catching Edgar as he fell.

18

~~Tuesday~~

She dressed quickly: a pair of gray slacks and a midnight-blue turtleneck—an untouched ensemble Florence had given her last Christmas. It was the nearest to sober she could find, now that her one black dress was covered in Edgar's blood.

Lucy was dreading the funeral—could already hear the organ, the Ave Maria. Already, there was a knot in her throat. She hoped the priest wouldn't mention Frank.

She phoned the school, telling the secretary she'd be coming in to pick up Edgar. "He shouldn't be there today. He's ill."

"I'll pull him from class," the woman said. "When are you coming?"

"I'll be there in twenty minutes."

Outside the bedroom, the air seemed blurry. Lucy wasn't sure whether to blame the fire or the Percocet. Downstairs, she was shocked to find the kitchen spotless, as if Florence's ghost had stopped by with a mop.

Had any of it really happened? The tomato, the finger, the three hours in the emergency room before Edgar was carted away to surgery. Ron and the Schlips had waited with her. Afterwards, the doctor had been optimistic. "With kids that young, you could put a fingertip back on with Scotch tape and it would probably work." When Lucy had looked at the baby-faced doctor with a distinct lack of amusement, he'd added: "But, no, I mean, we did a lot more than that. I'd say there's an eighty percent chance it'll take."

On the drive to Edgar's school, Lucy felt nauseous and decided to stop at the salon to use the bathroom. Plus, she should probably tell Celeste, the owner, what was going on. When Lucy had called, several days ago, to request Thursday through Tuesday off, she'd simply said it was for "personal reasons." She hadn't mentioned anything about Florence.

When Lucy arrived, Audrey Fenning was by the front desk, speaking with Celeste. At the sound of the entrance bell, Mrs. Fenning turned. She had a large patch over her left ear.

"Good morning," Lucy said tentatively.

"Speak of the devil," said Fenning.

Staring at the white bandage taped to the woman's face, Lucy could think of nothing but her son's finger. In her drugged state, she struggled to comprehend how Edgar's injury had leapt to the old woman's ear.

"It's infected," said Fenning.

Lucy looked at Celeste as if she were an interpreter; but Celeste only shrugged and closed her eyes.

"There was pus. I had to have a shot." Mrs. Fenning zeroed in on the proprietress. "If this is the kind of shop you run, I don't think your doors are going to stay open for long."

"We've been here for almost *tree* years," replied Celeste—her Jamaican accent rising with her pride.

"Well, if you want to go for four, I suggest—"

Celeste held up a densely bangled arm. "We don't even know that this was caused by—"

"She *poked* me with a pair of dirty scissors."

"They weren't dirty," said Lucy.

"Oh, but you're not denying you *poked* me?"

A rush of air that was not entirely free of laughter issued from Lucy's mouth.

"See what she's like?" Fenning bristled. "Makes a joke out of everything. Look at her, she's smiling."

"I'm not smiling," said Lucy.

"What is that on your face then?"

"It's my face, all right? I said I was sorry, didn't I?"

"You're a smirker. From day one, you've been a smirker."

"We'll have another stylist take care of you the next time," Celeste offered.

"That's not the issue. The issue is the girl's attitude. The issue is my *ear*."

"Let me see it," Lucy said. She reached her hand toward the white bandage.

Fenning chirped and stepped back. "What are you doing?"

"I want to see it. Take it off."

"*Lucy,*" Celeste warned. "Ladies, why don't we go in the back? We can talk in the break room."

"As far as I'm concerned," Fenning said, "there's nothing more to discuss. Either you take disciplinary action . . ."

Lucy snorted.

". . . or I will file a formal complaint."

"It was a scratch. How many times do you want me to apologize?"

"It's not a matter of *apology,* it's a matter of *infection.* Plus, I have a wedding next week, and now I have to wear this." She touched the ear patch and winced.

Lucy sighed and turned to Celeste. "It was a fucking scratch."

Audrey Fenning shook her head sadly. "You know, I feel sorry for you, Ms. Fini."

"*Mrs.* Fini," Lucy corrected.

"I've been in this town a long time, *Mrs.* Fini, and I've seen a lot of girls like you. Mean types, unpleasant. My daughter Karen used to be taunted by girls like you. I mean, obviously you have problems, you have *issues*— and that's none of my business. But you know what? A person has to work things out. Take Karen, she didn't have it easy, and now she—"

"Yeah, yeah, I know—the space people. You tell me every friggin' time you come in here."

Mrs. Fenning sniffed and turned to Celeste. "For this language alone, she should be fired."

"Lucy," Celeste said quietly. "Please."

"You can't reason with people like her," Mrs. Fenning said, shaking her head.

"I will take care of it, ma'am," Celeste said. "I'm sorry for your trouble."

"And I expect a free haircut the next time I come in."

"Of course."

Mrs. Fenning touched her bandaged ear again. "You know, Mrs. Fini, I'm a reasonable woman. I only ask to be treated with respect."

Florence had often said the same thing. Lucy looked at Fenning coolly, though with a sudden desire to explain. "I had a bad night."

"We all have bad nights. It's no excuse for bad manners." Audrey Fenning adjusted the shoulder strap of her pocketbook and nodded at Celeste. "Good day."

When the coast was clear, Celeste set her hands on the ledges of her wide hips. "*Christmas,* girl! What you got stuck up your ass this week?"

Lucy rubbed her face and began to walk away.

"Where the hell are you going?"

"I'm sorry, I—I'll be right back." Lucy grabbed her stomach and rushed toward the bathroom.

Bracing herself against the sink, she hovered between nausea and tears. The two forces seemed to act at odds with each other, preventing either from flourishing. Finally, the scent from a large dish of cinnamon-orange potpourri gave an advantage to the nausea. Lucy leaned over the toilet, but no relief came.

Through the flimsy door drifted the sounds of the salon. A murmur of voices, the hum of a dryer, the insect-like clicking of a pair of scissors. Someone was muttering along to an Elton John song on the radio, singing both parts of a duet like a lunatic. *Don't go breaking my heart. I couldn't if I tried.*

Trapped in the tiny bathroom of Celestial Styles, what erupted finally from Lucy's body was neither sickness nor tears. It was fury—a particularly potent strain that had visited her before in the years since Frank's death. The bastard had abandoned her—had left her with broken bones and a baby. The wounds seemed fresh in light of Florence's departure. The old woman should have stayed—for Edgar, if for nothing else.

Lucy took a breath. She had better call the school—let them know she was running late. When she reached for her cell, though, she realized that she'd left it at home.

"Lucy, what you doing in there?"

"I'm doing what a person does in here."

"Don't get snippy with me," Celeste said—her voice still rabidly Jamaican. "We need to talk."

When Lucy emerged and phoned the school from the reception desk, Celeste waited with crossed arms.

"This is Mrs. Fini. I called earlier about my son."

"Yes," the woman said. "We left several messages on your cell."

"Yeah, I didn't get them. Could you just tell Edgar I'll pick him up in about ten minutes?"

"I'm sorry," the woman said. "He's not here."

"What do you mean, he's not there?"

"He didn't come in today."

"Yes he did. He took his books, his backpack."

"Did you drive him here?"

"What does that have to do with anything?"

"I mean, did you see him enter the school?"

"Why don't you check the bathrooms? He's probably—"

"Mrs. Fini, we've looked everywhere. So, you did drive him here?"

"No."

"Okay, so did he take the bus? Or does he usually walk?"

"I . . ." Lucy realized she had no idea how the kid got to school.

"If he walks," the secretary asked, "do you know who his Ped-Pal is?"

"His what?"

"We always recommend the children who walk have a companion. If you give me the name of his Ped-Pal, I can ask him if Edgar walked with him this morning."

Lucy rubbed her face and stared out the window of the salon. Florence should have given her a fucking file. *Ped-Pals?*

"If you want, Mrs. Fini, I can let you talk to the assistant principal."

Lucy felt an old fear, as if she were the one in trouble. Bad student, check. Bad mother, double check.

"Should I put you through to Mr.—"

"No— *Oh my God, here he is.* He just walked in the door."

Celeste scrunched up her face, looking from Lucy to the imaginary person who'd supposedly just entered the salon.

"Oh, thank goodness," the woman on the phone said.

"Yes," Lucy said. "Thank you so much."

She'd just have to get in the car and find Edgar herself. There was no need to get the authorities involved.

Celeste's arms were still folded. "What kinda games you playing, missy?"

"Nothing. It's just . . ."

Celeste widened her eyes, waiting.

"It's too hard to explain."

"Try," Celeste said gravely.

"It's really not any of your business," Lucy said.

"Not my business, huh? This *is* my business, missy. Where you think you standing? Whose phone you lying on?"

"Celeste—"

"Poking the customers, and now you come in late, doing some fish story on my phone."

"I'm not late—I told you I couldn't work today. I said I'd be back on Wednesday."

"Exactly," said Celeste.

"Exactly," mimicked Lucy. "It's friggin' Tuesday."

"On what planet? Look at the daybook, girl. It's *Wednesday.*" Celeste pointed to the appointment calendar on her desk.

Lucy stared at the black *X* drawn over the day through which she thought she was moving. She felt nauseous again. "I'm sorry, can we talk about this later?"

"Where are you going now?"

"I have to get home."

"You have six appointments today."

"I'm sorry—I can't stay."

"Is something wrong with your boy?"

"No, I just have to . . ." Lucy's hands were shaking. "Maybe you could just reschedule everyone for tomorrow?"

"This is ridiculous," Celeste said. "We can't do this anymore."

"Do what?"

"Let's step outside for a moment, shall we?"

"Celeste . . ."

"I know that woman's a bitch, but it's not just her. Some of the others have complained, too."

"They're all bitches."

"Well, that may be. But our job is to cater to them." Celeste touched Lucy's arm. "Come on, let's talk outside."

"What? Are you afraid I'm gonna make a scene?" Lucy pulled away. "Talk to me here."

The two women looked at each other. Celeste, who'd braved her share of heartache (a hurricane in Kingston had killed her youngest brother), could see the small tremors of fear compromising Lucy's swagger. "What's going on, girl?"

Lucy liked Celeste, too. She wasn't a liar or a pushover, like most women. Still, some heavy anchor stopped Lucy from moving toward Celeste's proffer of kindness. "Nothing," Lucy said flatly.

"That's all you have to say to me?"

"What do you want me to say?" The thought of breaking down here at the front of the salon, of falling into the vanilla-musk of Celeste's cleavage, brought up the bitter pride of a girl who'd learned to spurn her mother's kisses after her father had beaten her. "I'm sorry," she said. "I have to go."

Celeste nodded. "You can come back later to pick up your things."

Lucy made the sound that others often mistook for laughter.

Before she was out the door, Celeste stopped her. "There's just been too many complaints. Listen, girl, I'll see if my man can get you something at the restaurant."

"No, thank you," said Lucy.

As she stepped out of the salon into the bright sun, she leaned against the building to keep herself from falling.

Wednesday?

Some part of her knew it was true. She'd slept for a whole day once before—after Frank had died.

But what about Edgar? Had he gone to yesterday's funeral without her? She pictured him climbing into Florence's coffin; saw the two of them being lowered into the ground together.

Fuck fuck fuck.

Lucy slipped on her sunglasses, and ran.

19

Tuesday

"We should probably begin," Father Reginald said to the twenty or so people gathered in the front pews.

He'd waited as long as possible. Several calls had been made to the family's house; a large man, a friend of the young lady's, had even driven to the residence and knocked on the door—but, for all intents and purposes, Lucy Fini and her son seemed to have vanished. Florence's soul would have to be prayerfully entrusted to the eternal without them. There was a marriage to be performed later in the afternoon; the floral crucifixes would need to make way for garlands of pink delphiniums.

"Let us bow our heads," Father Reginald intoned.

Among those that did so were the Jews, Henry and Netty Schlip. In fact, a large number of the mourners were Ferryfield shopkeeps. Willie Marchwell, Leonard Wong, Teresa Collucci. The knife sharpeners, Richie and Enzo Fortunato, were in attendance, wearing identical suits and sitting so close to each other that their brotherhood appeared Siamese. Florence's old friends, Honey Fasinga and Dominic Sparra, also bowed their heads, as did the Heftis. When the butcher looked down, it was to discreetly text into his phone: *Where are you??? Funeral!!! Is Edgar okay?*

Father Reginald felt out of sorts. He hoped he wasn't coming down with Father Manuel's cold. He stared at the silver casket and tried to focus his mind. When Mrs. Fini's son had died, he'd offered the grieving woman counsel. He'd shown kindness, without sacrificing honesty in regard to the Church's view on suicide. He'd even given a nice little Mass for the disturbed young man.

But ever since then, Father Reginald had felt a chill from Florence. Of course, she'd continued to come to Mass every Sunday, listening attentively to his sermons as she sat beside her little albinoid grandson. It was a tragic family in so many ways.

"Let us pray."

He was rushing a bit; he knew that. He was also nervous. It was assumed the daughter-in-law would give a eulogy of some sort. In her absence, Father Reginald felt compelled to offer a little more than the standard fare—something more heartfelt and personal. Though, with his throat already aching, he felt less than inspired. Perhaps he'd simply read the poem printed on the back of Florence's prayer card—though, one had to admit, it was rather juvenile. Well, Florence Fini was not a literate woman. Not long ago, she'd sent a note to St. Margaret's regarding the donation of a piano, and her handwriting and grammar had been atrocious. Still, she deserved respect for a life of piety in the face of suffering.

"Bore her struggles with a stony grace," Father Reginald said at one point, rather pleased with the phrase, which he'd come up with extemporaneously. Of course, the Fini woman hadn't been a stone the day of her son's funeral. In lieu of a coffin there'd been a large photograph of the young man, surrounded by a profusion of roses that, considering the circumstances of the boy's death, seemed excessive. But the Italians were like that—the poor ones, especially. At one point during her son's Mass, right after Communion, Florence Fini had collapsed in front of the photograph, wailing. Her husband had had to practically carry her back to her seat.

"Florence Fini was a devoted wife, a fiercely loving mother and grandmother, a lesson, in many ways, to all of us. How does one manage to hold Christ in his heart after—*ha-ha-ha* . . ."

The small crowd waited. Toni-Ann Hefti leaned back in her seat, grimacing at what appeared to be an approaching tsunami.

"*Ha-choo!*"

Father Reginald clenched his fists. Unforgivable, the way Father Manuel never covered his mouth when he coughed.

"Excuse me. A lesson to all of us. A woman who kept Christ in her heart, and through His good influence led a quiet humble life, impoverished perhaps by worldly standards, but rich in the glory of the Spirit."

Dominic Sparra groaned. At his wife's funeral, a different priest had said nearly the exact same things, meaningless nonsense that had little to do with the complicated reality that had been Mary—and now Florence. Dominic had an urge to make his way to the podium and tell everyone about the girl in the flowered bathing suit, the girl who grew red-faced from two sips of wine and played "Clair de lune" like an angel. If some shred of her spirit was still hovering nearby, listening, someone should have the decency to say something that mattered.

"I think, in many ways, the simplicity of Florence's spirit can be summed up with the charming prayer on the back of her remembrance card. I'm told that she chose the poem herself. Apparently, she'd made her final arrangements in advance—wishing to spare her family any added hardship. A real trouper, we might say." Father Reginald lifted the prayer card from the podium. "If I may . . ."

You have come to my heart, dearest Jesus,
I am holding you close to my breast.
I'm telling You over and over,
You are welcome, Little White Guest.

And when I shall meet You in Heaven,
My soul then will lean on your breast;
And You will recall our fond meetings,
When You were my Little White Guest.

The priest tilted his head, bewildered suddenly by the poem and its odd central metaphor. Was it a reference to the Holy Ghost? The confusion was contagious. It moved quietly through the room until Toni-Ann released it.

"Ed-guh," she sobbed. At which point, Netty Schlip lost it and collapsed into a fit of tears worthy of the heart of the deceased.

Florence paid none of it any mind. She had nearly reached the place of infinite rest when a distraction far worse than the tears of shopkeepers harnessed her attention. There was a small white light, trapped, it seemed, in the confines of an airless green box. The little boy—something wasn't right. And though she had no idea what she could do about it, her consciousness snagged like a drifting weed caught in the roots of a riverbank.

All around her life went on. Even those close to death pretended otherwise. After the service, Honey Fasinga stopped Dominic Sparra on the sidewalk. "Excuse me, but I believe we had a moment once, many years ago." She lifted her veil.

Dominic's face remained blank for several seconds before his mouth fell open. "Well, I'll be damned. *Honey?*"

"On the *money*," Honey replied, tapping her cane firmly against the cement.

20

Kev

The child was asleep, the sun shining on the unnaturally pale face. The man pulled around to the back of a supermarket and parked in a nearly deserted lot by the delivery bay. Turning off the engine seemed an act of commitment, encouraging him to reach out and brush a flop of hair from the child's eyes. The delicate skin had already started to pink. When the man lowered the sun visor, a shadow fell, cutting the tiny face in half.

The kid looked a bit like the other one. The same green eyes (hiding now), the same stoically perturbed lips—endearing in one whose sufferings were no doubt slight. This child was smaller, though—younger. And the other had had dark hair. Maybe this one didn't look anything at all like the other one.

At this point, the man wasn't even certain if he was in the company of a boy or a girl. What he knew, though, was that this was the right one.

He'd understood this immediately when he'd first seen the child, weeks ago, in front of the market. The hesitancy; the self-doubt apparent in every one of the kid's gestures; the genuine innocence of the gaze, as if nothing in the world had yet been named; the silent consternation; the titanic gentleness; all these things had drawn the man's blinkered attention and encouraged him. The child seemed to be giving him permission.

The little bandaged finger was a sign, as well. Also a warning. The white gauze showed a spot of red—probably from the fat boy's assault. Something old turned in the man's stomach. With Kevin, there'd been a lot of blood.

The child moaned, achy but agreeable, as the man repositioned him to lie along the seat. "I just need to get you out of the sun." The child was breathing, right there below him. That people breathed seemed the most remarkable thing. The man put his hand by the kid's mouth to feel the living current.

Before he opened his eyes, Edgar returned to the world with his nose. He smelled grease, dog, dirty laundry, and something sweetly spicy, like oranges mixed with cinnamon. When his lids fluttered open, he saw a blue-jeaned knee and a shadowy recess with three black pedals. Turning his head slightly, he saw the wheel.

The man could feel the child tense. "Don't worry. It's okay."

Edgar's exhaustion pressed down upon his fear. He closed his eyes, but when he remembered the not-nice dream he'd been having, he opened them again. With his brain still swamped by Percocet, his thoughts arrived in parcels that took a long time to unwrap.

"Here, let me help you up," the man said.

"You can't touch me," protested Edgar.

"Okay, okay," the man said. "I'm not touching you."

The boy leaned his back against the passenger-side door, as far away from the man as possible. Abruptly sitting up had given him a rush of vertigo. Through the windshield, he could see the snout of the rusty green truck extending before him. It was as strange as waking up in his closet after a visit from Jack. When he glanced at the man again, he took in the blue eyes, the beard. As far as he could remember, though, Jack had never had a beard.

"Why am I in here?" Edgar said, confused.

"You passed out. You don't remember?"

Edgar shook his head.

The man scratched his chin. "I thought you'd be safer in here."

"I know you," said Edgar.

The boy had said it without sentiment, only in vague recognition; but the man took it to mean something more. "I know you, too," he replied.

Edgar knew he had to get out of the car. He tried the door, but it was locked.

"Let me drive you home," the man said quickly.

"I'm not allowed," said Edgar

"Not allowed to what?" asked the man.

"Get into a car with a stranger."

"But you're already here."

Edgar felt like he was going to cry. "I'm not *allowed*."

"But you said you know me, right? So I'm not a stranger. Right?" The man was desperate that the child not take back what he'd said. "I took care of that kid for you. That Thomas fellow." The man looked out the window, scanning the lot. "He's probably still out there."

Edgar looked out the window, too. Not very far away, a large truck was backing up to an open delivery bay like it had to go to the bathroom. Everything looked strange—and smelled even stranger. "Do you have a dog?" asked Edgar.

"I do," the man said. "How did you know?"

Edgar shrugged. It would be rude to say that he could smell the animal, a scent like crackers mixed with sweat. "I just guessed," he said quietly.

The man smiled. "You like dogs?"

"I don't have one," said Edgar.

"But do you like them?"

"I don't really know any."

The man pulled at his damp shirt, releasing more of the orange-cinnamon of his deodorant.

"I like all animals, pretty much," Edgar said shyly, holding his bandaged finger protectively against his chest. "I have to go home."

"Does it hurt?" asked the man.

Edgar looked down at the corn dog of his finger. "I'm not sure."

"Did Thomas do that to you?"

Edgar shook his head. His brain felt funny. "I have to put my medicine on."

"Take your medicine, you mean?"

"I'm not supposed to go in the sun without it." Edgar had started to feel the burn on his skin. He'd left the house without putting on his cream. Outside the truck, the day blazed like a sea full of sharks. "Can you drive me home?"

"Of course." The man put his hand on the ignition key without turning it. "I'm sorry, I just . . . you're a boy, right?"

Edgar blushed and said, "Yes."

As they drove, the man made an effort to keep his chatter to a minimum. The silence was broken mostly by the child, saying when to turn left and when to turn right. After ten minutes, the boy seemed sleepy again, his little head lolling as if he were drunk.

"You can put your seat back," the man said. "You want to?"

The child made no reply. His unresponsiveness excited the man, who wondered what else he might say to the boy. Silence, of course, guaranteed the greatest safety—but the man gambled against it.

"You always liked playing with that seat—sliding it back and forth."

And then he took a larger risk.

"You nearly broke it that one time. You remember that, Kev?"

The boy made a small, vague sound.

Perhaps the child could be swayed. Children believed in so little; or they believed in too much. Either way, they ended up confused. It was the responsibility of their caretakers to provide a clear accounting of the truth; to tell the tiny creatures who they were and where they'd come from. Sometimes, for the sake of kindness, the truth needed to be knitted from tiny lies, like the strings of a net. One had to capture a child's imagination gently, like a butterfly.

"Stop," the boy said—and the man felt a prick of shame, as if his thoughts had been overheard.

"*Stop,*" repeated Edgar. "I live here."

The man pulled over, gripping the wheel to keep his hands from shaking. "This one here?"—gesturing with his head toward a blue house on his right.

"No. That one." The boy pointed at a white house on the opposite side of the street. The air around the property was hazy, especially near an open window on the second floor.

As the boy unlocked the door of the truck, the man touched his arm. "You said you know me, right?" It was difficult to restrain himself. He wanted to grab the child—but what if he screamed? Everything they'd built together would dissolve.

"Let me just give you something, okay?"

But it was too late. Sirens disturbed the air.

"They're coming," said Edgar.

"Yes," said the man. "I know."

21

Superslut

As the fire truck clamored to a stop before 21 Cressida Drive, Edgar stood dazed across the street. The green pickup had pulled away only moments before.

It had been Toni-Ann Hefti, waiting for her special bus, who'd returned to the kitchen of 19 Cressida Drive to inform her mother that the Finis were on fire. Now, the Hefti women stood outside their door, watching the commotion. Mrs. Hefti smoked, flicking ashes onto the lawn, while Toni-Ann shook her hands anxiously, as if trying to dry nail polish. Neither saw Edgar, whose thin frame was blocked by the trunk of an adolescent poplar.

One fireman pounded on the door, and when no one answered it, another of the monstrously cloaked men proceeded to charge against it with a battering ram.

"No," cried Edgar, rushing toward the house.

A third fireman held him back. "Is anyone in there?"

"Yes. But don't hurt the door."

It was too late. The white oak cracked as it swung open.

"Who's in there?" the fireman asked. "How many people?"

"Two," said Edgar. "Let go of me!"

"Easy does it, bruiser."

Adrenaline had brought the boy back to life. He extricated himself from the grip of the fat-mitted fireman and sped toward the open door.

"Edgar!"

The voice stopped him. He turned to see his mother rising from her little red car.

"Get over here!" she yelled.

He was relieved to see that she hadn't been burnt to a crisp. Still, he ignored her and turned back to the house. From upstairs came the voices of men and the ticking and mewling of the floorboards under their insensitive boots. The smoke smelled like cigarettes and hot dogs—horrible.

"What the hell's going on?" Lucy clicked up the path in heels. Her sunglasses and trench coat, combined with haywire hair (she'd driven here at high speed with the windows down) made her look like some harried Fellini heroine.

"Fire, ma'am. Step back, please."

"There's no fire."

"We're checking things out."

"I just told you," Lucy said, flattening her hair, "there's no fire. I already put it out." She lit a cigarette. "It's just smoke."

"Things have a tendency to reignite," said the man.

"I didn't even call. Who called you guys?"

"Must have been a neighbor."

Lucy glanced over at the Heftis' property. Mrs. Hefti raised her chin in a meaningless gesture, while Toni-Ann waved fervently. Lucy turned back to the fireman. "And who's gonna pay for the door?"

"Yeah, sorry about that. They don't usually crack."

Lucy huffed and removed her sunglasses.

The fireman tilted his head and smiled. "Lucy?"

She pulled back her face and scowled, as if her name were bad breath coming from the man's mouth. "Do I know you?"

He took off his helmet and goggles and offered a more prominent smile. "William."

She couldn't place him.

At which point, he leaned in and offered, sotto voce, what he hoped might jog her memory. "Will-*yummy*?" His eyebrows lifted like a puppet's.

Lucy felt nauseous again.

"Nicky's Tavern?" he continued. "Like six months ago? I mean, it was just that one time but, *wow*, how are you?"

"I've had better days."

"Is that your son?" the man whispered, pointing at Edgar's back.

Lucy smiled tensely. "I didn't know you were a fireman."

"Just volunteer."

Lucy took a final drag from her cigarette before tossing it onto the lawn.

"Step on it," said Edgar.

"You really should always extinguish them," Will-yummy concurred.

"Excuse me a minute, would you?" she said, pulling Edgar aside. Decency required more distance between her son and her dimly remembered hookup.

The man held an imaginary phone to his ear and did the puppet eyebrows again. Lucy nodded vaguely. As if she still had his friggin' number!

No one had stepped on the smoldering cigarette yet, and so Edgar did it.

"Why are you wearing slippers?" Lucy said, kneeling on the grass in front of her son. "And where have you been? I've been looking for you all morning."

"You were sleeping," said Edgar.

She touched his flushed face. "Come on, we need to get you out of the sun. Can we go inside now?" she asked the fireman.

"Let me see what's going on," he said, trotting away.

Edgar kicked the flattened cigarette toward his mother. "Were you smoking in the house?"

"No, of course not. Why—you think this is my fault?"

Edgar shrugged and looked up at the open window of his grandmother's bedroom. He had a vague recollection of standing before the Virgin Mary with a match in his hand. "I didn't do it, either," he insisted.

Lucy followed the boy's gaze to Florence's window. A puff of smoke, the size of a person, lingered there.

"Why doesn't it disappear?" asked Edgar.

Lucy, eyeing the fat cloud, wondered the same thing.

* * *

All the windows and doors were open now (as recommended by the boys from Friendship Hook and Ladder No. 3). Lucy and Edgar sat in the dark living room under a single blanket, watching television. Earlier, when Lucy had informed Edgar about the missed funeral and the entire day stolen by sleep, the boy's reaction had frightened her. He'd walked in small, stimming circles, knocking a fist against his head. "You mean she's in the ground already?"—at which point both of them had started to cry. When Edgar hid behind the couch and proceeded to rock, she'd given him another Percocet-Demi (a proper half-tablet dose), and then, thoroughly chastened by the day, had allowed herself nothing more than the other half.

"Are you cold?" she asked Edgar, who was now resting quietly on the couch.

"A little," he said. "Are you?"

"A little." She pulled up the cover, and Edgar snuggled closer. He rubbed the satin trim of the blanket against his chapped lips. When they'd first gotten home, Lucy had smeared the boy's red face with some anti-wrinkle cream she'd recently purchased.

Florence's method for treating a sunburn had been decidedly more peasant: a few splashes of apple cider vinegar followed by a spoonful of olive oil, as if she were making a salad out of the boy's face. It worked better than the wrinkle cream, but Edgar didn't tell his mother this. The wrinkle cream smelled nice, like pink roses.

Lucy's stomach growled. For dinner, all they'd eaten were bowls of Frosted Mini-Wheats (neither could face the leftovers from the butcher). The sun had set over an hour ago, but no hand had yet reached to click on a lamp. The strength to locate the remote and change the TV channel eluded them, as well. They stared, mesmerized, at a seemingly endless infomercial about a food dehydrator. A stoned Edgar was impressed by the contraption's myriad skills. It did so much more than dry fruits and vegetables. It could raise bread dough and recrisp crackers; it could warm mittens, as well as dry a person's delicate hand-washables. With a shallow pan of water, it became a humidifier—and at Christmastime you could put in sprigs of pine to add a festive fragrance to any room.

"We should get one," Edgar said sleepily.

Lucy, equally exhausted, grunted.

When a door slammed upstairs, it startled them. Edgar's hand found Lucy's; she gave it a squeeze. "It's just the wind, baby. We can probably shut some of the windows now."

"The fireman said we could get asphyxiated."

"Edgar, there's hardly any more smoke. We'll be fine."

"I can still smell it."

Another door slammed—this time, the front one. Edgar sat up.

"Come on, lie back down."

"We won't be able to lock it," Edgar said. "They broke it."

"I'll put some tape on it so it doesn't blow open."

"Tape won't keep people out."

"Who's coming? No one's coming. Lie down. You're gonna wake yourself up."

"I was never sleeping."

"Ma . . ."

"What? . . . What?"

"Did he ever have a beard?"

"Who?"

Edgar examined the weave of the brown sofa. "My father," he said, picking at a loose thread.

"Why are you asking stupid questions?"

"It's not stupid."

"No. He never had a beard."

"Like hair on his face, I mean."

"I know what a beard is, Edgar. And what did I just say?"

"Sometimes you have to be asked twice."

"Is that so?"

Edgar shrugged.

"He might have had one a couple of times," said Lucy. "But not on purpose."

"You can't get a beard by *accident*," said Edgar.

"You can if you're lazy. Sometimes he didn't shave. And why are we talking about this?"

Lucy wondered if maybe the drugs were too strong for the boy. He never asked about his father.

"I'd like to see pictures," Edgar said.

"Pictures of what?"

Edgar's fingers worked the loose thread.

"They're right there," Lucy said, gesturing toward the piano.

"But I want to see when he was older."

"He never *got* older, Edgar."

"And those are all blurry. You can't really see his face. Do you have other pictures?"

"Somewhere. I don't know. Come on, lie down."

"I know Gramma has his baby pictures. We can look in her room."

"Tomorrow," Lucy said. "I want you to sleep now."

The boy scooted down and stretched out his legs. "But what are we going to do?"

"About what?"

"I'm freezing," Edgar said, hunching up his shoulders.

"We'll be fine. Close your eyes."

"We can stay on the couch, right?"

"Sure."

"Two bodies have a better chance anyway," Edgar said.

Lucy was glad to see the boy's eyes fluttering again.

"Mr. Levinson, my science teacher, says that's how homeless people stay alive. And birds, too."

Lucy smiled in spite of herself.

"It's not funny," said Edgar.

"I didn't say anything."

"You smiled."

Lucy slid under the cover, closer to Edgar. "It was an accident."

When the boy was asleep, she kissed his white hair before peeling away her half of the blanket. The front door had blown open again. She stood there and saw how close the night was, how close it had always been. Even during the day, it was never far. Florence had managed to keep it away, like some clever cavewoman, with candles and night-lights, with warm milk and early bedtimes. Lucy let it in now. Night was her element. She walked outside, onto the lawn, in her bare feet—the firm, cold blades deceiving her soles with a sensation of wetness. Nighttime had always meant a respite from Florence, from the boy. But now the old woman was too far away, and Lucy was afraid.

Keeping her promise to Edgar, she found some duct tape and sealed the front door. In the kitchen she shifted the tin trays of leftovers in the refrigerator, hunting for a beer. Florence kept the brown bottles at the back of the bottom shelf, like Negroes on a bus. Lucy moved them up to the front. She opened one and took a swig.

Pio had liked his beer, too. After Frank was gone, she sometimes shared a six-pack with the old man on the porch (though the split was often four to two in Lucy's favor). Florence would bring out salted nuts or buttered breadsticks because it was unhealthy, she claimed, to drink without eating. Sometimes, after Edgar was asleep, Florence would join Lucy and Pio on the porch, eat a nut, and eventually succumb to Pio's insistence that she take one goddamned sip. "Just to wash the salt out of my mouth," she'd say. A particularly salty nut might require two sips, but then her face would turn as red as Edgar's after too much sun.

Lucy downed her beer. Florence's departure meant a lot of terrible things—one of which was that Lucy needed to be a mother now, a job she'd been able to put off for years. Florence had been so much better at it. Lucy hadn't even wanted a child, but Frank had been insistent. "It's time," he kept saying. And then when she'd finally given him one—within a year, he was gone.

The sadness in her belly pulsed like a second heart. Luckily, the gentle buzz of the beer and the lingering bloom of Percocet kept the harshest realities muffled. She grabbed another bottle from the fridge and walked upstairs.

At some point, she'd have to look through Florence's room—not for the photographs Edgar had asked for, but for things that had real value. She'd need to find the will, though surely there'd be no surprises there. The house was Edgar's. What the old woman had in the bank Lucy wasn't sure. The jewelry, for the most part, was junk. She'd been an idiot to let Florence go down wearing that diamond engagement ring. She should have slipped it off the old woman's finger when no one was looking.

Her cell was ringing. She stood in the doorway of her dark bedroom and watched it glow on the nightstand. With each ring, a breath of weak light suffused the air, as if the call were coming from the bottom of the sea—or the grave.

She clicked on the lamp, in need of a cigarette. When she couldn't find the pack she kept at the front of her nightstand drawer, she dug deeper, excavating the rolled-up Pogues T-shirt shoved to the back. They were a band Frank had liked; he'd often played them during sex.

Lucy placed the T-shirt on the bed and unrolled it. The vibrator hidden inside had become a faithful friend—but it seemed ridiculous now, like a rubber chicken or a set of wind-up dentures. Lucy lifted the thing and shook it (it had a slight wiggle factor). She laughed and shook it harder. When the dick slipped from her grip and fell to the floor, she blanched, thinking of Edgar's finger.

The phone was ringing again. This time she answered it.

"Why are you calling so late?"

"It's not that late," the butcher said. "Were you sleeping?"

Lucy said that she was, and the butcher apologized. "You know, we were all waiting for you yesterday at the—"

"I know, I'm sorry. It was . . . not a good day."

"I've called, like, twenty times. Are you okay? Everyone was worried."

"I'm fine."

"How's the kid doing?"

"He's not your kid, Ron."

"I didn't say he was."

They were both quiet now. Lucy sat on the bed and closed her eyes. The butcher, in boxers, stood by his living room window. Neither hung up.

"You guys need anything?" the butcher ventured.

"Why are you calling, Ron?"

"I don't know." He scratched his belly. "I was feeling you."

"*Feeling* me? Are you drunk?"

"No. Are you?"

"I have a sick kid here—what do you think?"

"You need to relax."

"I don't have time to relax." Lucy reclined on the bed.

"I really was feeling you."

"Stop staying that. That's a friggin' Santana song. I hate Santana."

"The man's a genius. Why, who do you like?"

Lucy pulled the Pogues T-shirt from under her thigh. "I don't have a favorite band. What are we, in high school?"

"Yeah, why not? You could put on a little cheerleader skirt for me."

Lucy was still wearing the gray slacks gifted by Florence. Slowly, she slipped them off, anticipating the butcher's agenda.

"What are you wearing right now?" he asked.

"I'm naked," Lucy replied flatly.

They were quiet again. Lucy worked off the rest of her garments, bringing reality up to speed with her lie. The butcher looked at the sky through his window—and though he rarely noticed such things, he considered the colors of the stars. They weren't all white. Some were a little yellow, some a little red. He touched his crotch.

"Are you outside?" he asked Lucy.

"Why would I be outside?"

"I don't know. I can hear the wind."

"My window's open."

"Better shut it before you go to sleep. Supposed to frost tonight."

"It's not even October," Lucy grumbled.

"I know," the butcher said. "Why don't you put your finger in your pussy?"

He said it simply, and Lucy liked the sound of his voice, the deep, thuggish rumble of it.

"You got it there?"

"Yes," Lucy said. She wasn't lying.

The butcher rubbed himself through his boxers. "Are you wet?"

"Taste it," Lucy said—and the butcher made an exaggerated slurp.

"Rub your clit."

"Are you hard?"

"This isn't about me," the butcher said. "Get that finger in deeper."

Lucy did as she was told.

"Now take it out and pinch your nipples."

Lucy moaned even before her hand reached her chest. "Bite them," she said.

The butcher growled. "I'm devouring those fucking pink fuckers."

Lucy shivered and pinched as the voice in her ear went hoggish with desire. *"Mmmm-ahhhh-rah-rah-rah-rah-schllluuuup."*

He teased her, making her go back and forth between her nipples and her crotch. His words were not terribly original, but the timbre of his voice and his unabashed growls and slurps threw Lucy into a panic of thrusting, digging for something she'd lost, something she needed to find.

Finally, he fucked her hard—or so he said—and his grunting increased.

"Yes," she said. "Do it. Fuck me, you fucking ape."

He took no offense. To the contrary, Lucy's words seemed to inspire him, and he gave her more of what she needed, became more of a beast—but there was no cruelty, only a wild and devouring kindness. In fact, when the animal next broke from its gutturals and offered human words, it said it was kissing her. *"Mmmmmm,* yeah. Kissing that beautiful fucking mouth of yours."

"Yes," Lucy said as she worked her finger deeper. "Kiss me."

The butcher complied with absurdly wet, fruit-eating slurps.

"Grunt," she demanded. *"Grunt."*

"Ghhhuuurrrr-rah."

"Oh my God," cried Lucy.

"Yes," the butcher said. "Get it, get it, make it pop."

With her eyes closed, she began to feel the weight of the man on top of her, and when she came, she lifted her head and stretched her tongue into his invisible mouth, her whole body shivering under the burning presence of a man who wasn't there. She turned her head into the pillow to muffle her cry. Frank had often put his hand over Lucy's mouth, laughing, saying, *"Shhhh, shhhh,* my mother."

But the old woman was gone, and the kid downstairs was blotto from drugs. Lucy allowed herself one last uncensored cry.

"Fuck," she said, with the innocent ardor of a child uttering its first word.

The butcher sighed, for he'd spent himself, too—mostly in his hand, but a little had splattered the curtains, which he was now wiping with his boxers.

"Marry me," he said.

Lucy swallowed; opened her eyes. "Very funny."

Silence.

"I'm not kidding. I want you to marry me."

Lucy stiffened, feeling a mixture of fury and mortification.

"Are you there?" the butcher said.

Lucy paused for only a moment, before hanging up the phone.

Downstairs, Edgar was still sleeping, his face damp with sweat. Gently, she lifted him, carried him to his room. She was too tired to change the bandage (once a day, the doctor had said), but at least she'd get him undressed. When she slipped off his long-sleeved jersey, she noticed the pale blue lines on his arm. For a moment she was worried that some sort of infection had set in, something to do with his finger. She turned the arm toward the nightlight, and then dropped it in horror. A ghostly blur of letters seemed to spell out the word *Superslut*.

It was like something from *The* friggin' *Exorcist*. And it was hard not to take the demon's name-calling personally. Lucy threw a blanket over Edgar and backed away.

She had to stop taking the kid's Percocet; it was making her crazy. In her own room she retrieved the dildo from the floor and tossed it out the open window.

22

Salvashon

The Chanel bottle was black, and the Virgin had lost her head. The wedding portrait showed seared streaks, giving the impression of shadows—unseen beasts moving toward a young Florence and Pio.

"What's that?" Edgar said of a gooey patch of ash that resembled a flattened crow.

"Underwear," replied Lucy.

"Whose underwear?"

"Your grandmother's. Her bloomers."

Edgar touched the remains with a clothes hanger. "How did they—"

"Don't worry about it," Lucy said briskly. "Let's just clean this place up, okay?"

Edgar opened the Chanel N° 5 and sniffed. Luckily the fire had done no damage to the fragrance.

With the old woman's fabric shears, Lucy cut the burnt branches from the ficus. She tossed the fried scraps into a garbage bag, then reached for the body of the Virgin.

"Don't throw her out," said Edgar.

"It's broken, honey."

"We can glue it." The way his mother was chucking things, right and left, into a black plastic bag was making him angry. "Don't you have to go to work?" he asked.

"I'm off today."

"You always work on Saturday."

"What did I say? I'm off. I took the day off. Are you gonna help me or not?"

As the two of them tried to spruce things up, they saw that it was hopeless. The wall needed to be repainted; the curtains, replaced; the antique bureau was beyond repair. Ash had drifted everywhere, like the molted wings of insects; when you tried to wipe them up, they crumbled, leaving behind tarry blurs. Lucy and Edgar did the best they could with a vacuum and some rags. "I'll get a painter next week, " Lucy said. "Maybe we could make this into an exercise room or something."

"You don't exercise," Edgar reminded her.

"I should," she said, turning to the window. The butcher had been right about the frost. The lawn and bushes were glazed with white. It had been the same for the past three days, a deep morning freeze followed by brilliant sun. Lucy and Edgar had left the house only once since Thursday—a quick drive to Edgar's school so the boy could drop off some homework. "You'll be excused," Lucy had told him—but the boy had begged, claiming if he didn't turn in his extra-credit assignment to Mr. Levinson on time, it wouldn't be counted. It was creepy, thought Lucy, to see the boy at his desk, scribbling his homework under a haze of narcotics.

Ron had phoned several times since the night of the phone-bone marriage proposal, but Lucy hadn't taken his calls. Her cell was on vibrate now, and she could feel it buzzing again in her pocket.

Glancing at the burnt bureau, the Virgin's former resting place, Edgar was troubled by the absence of candlelight. His whole life, he'd known this room to exist under the constant vigilance of a small flame in a blue glass cup. The room was dead now, and, by extension, the entire house—as if the pilot light that empowered everything had gone out.

"Can I light another candle?" he asked his mother.

"Are you fucking kidding me?" She was kneeling on the floor, going through Florence's dresser.

Edgar began to snoop, as well, though not without trepidation. He sensed the mound of clothes on his grandmother's bed watching him. He wondered if he should call the woman who'd helped him steal the diamond. It would be nice to hear more about the dresses and what his grandmother had been like when she was young and skinny. The woman had referred to her as *Florie*, and had said she was prettier than all of them. Edgar ran his fingers across the old woman's pillow. It was all so sad it made you wonder why people were even born in the first place.

From drawers, Lucy pulled out lavender sachets and brand-new nightgowns still wrapped in tissue paper; a tiny pouch of French coins; neatly pressed handkerchiefs. There was a collection of unfamiliar baby clothes, possibly Frank's, that made Lucy's stomach rise. Edgar found a batch of unused postcards with pictures of Niagara Falls; a red lacquer box filled with dozens of derelict keys; an assortment of dried and flattened corsages in Ziploc bags. Under one of his grandmother's housedresses, he uncovered a small but surprisingly heavy cast-iron crucifix.

Explorers in an abandoned city—archeologists, looters, desecrators— Edgar and Lucy understood the violation they were perpetrating, though neither could stop digging. Partners in crime, it seemed, though they were looking for very different things: Lucy was looking for money; Edgar was looking for the Ark of the Covenant.

"That's not yours," he said, when he saw his mother reach her hand into Florence's black pocketbook.

"It's not anybody's now," Lucy replied. "Do you know where your grand-mother keeps her important papers?"

Edgar only stared at his mother as she pulled from the pocketbook tissues and eyeglasses—and then coupons and mints and money.

"I'm not stealing," explained Lucy. "We have to do this."

Edgar did know where Florence kept her bankbooks and her roll of money, but he didn't say. He sat on the floor and went through the bottom drawer of another bureau. The only item of interest was a latched box up-holstered in black silk, embroidered with a Chinese dragon. From inside it, he pulled a long length of braided black hair, tied at both ends with dark green ribbon.

"*Eww,*" Lucy said. "What is that?"

Edgar knew it was his grandmother's. She'd shown him pictures of her-self when she'd had long hair, though she'd never mentioned that she'd cut it all off in one fell swoop, and then had kept the evidence in a black silk box, like some voodoo princess. Edgar was astonished by how dark it was, so different from his own hair. He went to the mirror and held it behind his ear, letting the long braid fall across his shoulder.

"What are you doing?"

"Did you know her when she had long hair?" Edgar asked his mother.

"No. Put that away—and wash your hands."

"It's not dirty," said Edgar. "I'm keeping it."

"It's gross, Edgar." Having worked for so many years in a salon, Lucy had no romance about other people's hair.

"It's not gross."

"Honey, why don't you go downstairs and watch TV, and let me finish in here, okay?"

"I'm helping you."

"Yes, you are, but this is just upsetting you. It'll be faster if I do it by myself."

"Why does it have to be fast?"

"Edgar, please—this is grown-up stuff."

"You're not even *related* to her," snapped Edgar.

It was as if the boy had kicked her in the gut. She and the old woman had had their differences, certainly. The last few years, especially, had not been good. But once they'd fought side by side, allies in the same war. Despite everything that had gone wrong, Florence was still her family. "I loved her, Edgar."

"No you didn't," the boy said quietly.

Lucy took a deep, audible breath. "Go downstairs," she said, in a voice even quieter than Edgar's.

The boy pulled a chair over to the little shelf where Florence kept her collection of ornamental teacups. From his perch, he reached his hand into a blue cup with a faux-Dutch design and pulled out the roll of cash. After stepping carefully off the chair, he placed the bundle in front of his mother.

Lucy watched him go, shutting the door behind him like a warden.

Edgar went around the house and got the rest of it. Into a Savers shopping sack, he poured the change from the bowl in the kitchen cupboard, and then he found the small fold of singles tucked into Florence's sewing kit. Finally, he topped it off with the fifty-dollar bill his grandmother had taped, along with the number of the cab service, to the inside of the broom-closet door. "If your mother's not home and we need to get to the hospital," she'd always instructed him. When he'd mentioned that there were ambulances for such situations, Florence had replied something about the sirens, how it wasn't anyone's business if they had to make a trip to the hospital. Why announce it to the whole neighborhood? There'd been enough gossip in the past, she'd said, cryptically.

After all of Florence's secret stashes had been collected, the boy emptied his pockets and added an additional forty-nine cents to the Savers sack. He set the bag outside of Florence's room—inside of which he could hear his mother crying. "Stop with the waterworks," he should have shouted. She'd often said it to him. When he walked into his own room, he locked the door—something he'd never done before.

From his desktop, he picked up the prayer card—a small laminated rectangle with a picture of a fat baby Jesus reclining on a marshmallow cloud. The other side contained an incomprehensible poem, as well as the dates. The day his grandmother was born, and the day she died. At the cemetery, he knew it would be even worse: the dates would be carved in stone.

Four hundred and fifteen dollars. Lucy looked down at the bills—curled from having been rolled up inside a teacup for who knows how long. She recalled the wad of bills she'd stolen years ago from Pio, the day she and Frank had fled with the baby. Those bills had been rolled up, too—in a Chock full o'Nuts can in the basement.

Soon, Lucy will find Edgar's little gift bag outside the door; she'll find the bankbooks, too—the grand total of Florence's savings coming to fourteen thousand, eight hundred, sixty-seven dollars, and fifty-two cents. Not a fortune, but it'll be enough for Lucy to catch her breath. No need to rush around town yet, filling out job applications.

As she lay back on the carpet, the curled bills strewn around her like tiny cabbages, she reached her hand toward the bed and pulled down one of the dresses: a delicate, pink silk number whose narrow skirt flared into a flirtatious ruffle. Florence had been skinny once—part of a past that Lucy could barely imagine. She turned her head to look at the damaged wedding portrait on the wall.

Suddenly she sat up, remembering the black metal box. She'd seen it in Florence's underwear drawer, the day of the fire. It was still there—a dented lockbox wrapped excessively in twine. When her fingers failed to undo the riddle of knots, she took up the fabric shears and snipped the twine in several places. From the collection of keys Edgar had discovered earlier, Lucy found the one that fit the lock.

The disappointment of finding the box nearly empty—two thin envelopes and no cash—was relieved by the fact that the first envelope she opened contained the will.

It took Lucy's breath away to see it, handwritten in pencil like one of the old woman's semi-literate grocery lists. It seemed to be the work of a child—the words printed, the letters uneven, tilting variously to the left and to the right. Though barely half a page, Lucy could see the effort, the time it must have taken for Florence to write it. Here and there, a forgotten letter was inserted tightly between two others. Even with all the misspellings and peculiar grammar, there was nothing to be misunderstood.

I am the Florence Fini.
I live in 21 Cressida Drive in Ferryfield, New Jersey.
I say this now while I am well.
I give house to the boy Edgar and to his mother Lucille.
I give the money in my bank to the boy Edgar. For ejucate.
I give the jewlry and what she wants to Lucille.
All house things go with the house to the both remaning.
Clothes can donate to Saint Margaret (NOT SALVASHON ARMY!!!)
There is nothing else. If ther is it go to the boy Edgar.
The letter go to the boy Edgar when Lucille wants.
The letter she gonna find in the box too.

And then, in blue ink, as if added later—and with a shakier hand:

If the Lucille remary, the house go all of it to the boy Edgar.
This is Florence Fini.

Lucy shuddered as she set down the will. In her head, she could hear the old woman's voice, the little bell of it, the breathlessness. The bequest was more than she'd expected.

She stood and looked out the window. The frost was gone, the sun shining on the lawn as if nothing had happened. The boy was standing by the curb. *The boy Edgar.* He peered to the right and then to the left, as if looking for someone. Lucy opened the window.

"You have your sunscreen on?" she yelled down.

Edgar turned and said, "Yes."

"I'll be down soon. You okay?"

"We have to change my bandage," the boy said.

"Five minutes. Don't wander." Lucy closed the window and sat on the bed among Florence's dresses. Perfume, mothballs, dust. A ray of light touched the skeletal ficus.

The letter she gonna find in the box too.

Lucy went back to the bureau. She knelt before the lockbox and pulled out the second envelope. On the front, written in a different hand: *Edgar, I want you to have this.* Lucy immediately dropped the envelope, as if it were covered with worms. The handwriting was Frank's.

She felt hot, unable to stand—a sudden pain in her leg from when she'd fallen onto the rocks, the day of Frank's death. She looked at the letter and saw that the top of the envelope was torn. Someone—no doubt Florence—had already opened it. Lucy's hands were shaking so violently that they played a drum roll against the metal box. Why had she never been told about this?

As she picked up the envelope again, she moaned. Her thumb rested against the name of her son, as written by her husband. Suddenly, though nothing was visible there, she thrust her other hand into the metal box, scratching against the interior. She felt for a flap or a latch, a false bottom—a desperate pawing, like a starving animal digging for a bone. Why would Frank have left something for Edgar but not for her? Where was *her* letter?

She opened the envelope and pulled out the folded paper. The first thing she saw was the date: just three days before the accident. Lucy felt something waking inside of her, a chaos of old questions.

Had Frank known what he was going to do? Had he planned it? And did she finally hold in her hand the official note that everyone, even the police, had asked about?

There's nothing, he left nothing, Lucy would always say to people—as would Florence. Lucy's jaw tightened. The old woman had lied. All these years, she had lied.

Lucy took a deep breath, and read.

Dear Edgar. Your mother and I are gone now, I'm sorry. We went together. If this is a happy thought, I don't know. You don't remember us, I suppose. But we were your parents, Frank and Lucy Fini.

Lucy stopped. She read the lines again—the shaking that had started in her hands now taking over her entire body.

We loved each other and we loved you, Edgar Allan Fini. That is a good name. Don't let anyone take it from you. They will try. They have hooks

*and ladders and even mirrors. It can be very confusing. Your mother and
I are free, but you are not.*

Lucy could barely breathe. What did this mean? That Frank had planned
to take her with him? That he planned to . . .

Now that we're gone, you have to be careful.

*When they come, if they come to hurt you, they will look like anyone,
you will think you know them. Some of them are yours but some of them
are not. For the most part you can trust my mother, your grandmother,
but it is not 100% clean. Be more careful around the other one, my
father. He's spent a lot of time in the tunnels. If he wants to take you for
a drive to show you the yellow lights and the city on the other side, refuse.
The tunnel doesn't go to where he says. Most people are liars, even the
ones you come from. I'm telling you the truth but you <u>cannot</u> believe me.*

*If someone wants to take you away, make sure you understand what
you're dealing with. I went away once in a red car and another time in a
green car and it made a big difference. But don't try to find us. If you
find us, it will be by accident. Your mother and I are not where you
think we are, not where Nana tells you. You were born with almost no
hair on your head, which means you'll be smart. And you were so white
the doctor called you a cunt. But I'm not worried about you.*

*They fucked us, don't let them fuck you. It's not against the law to
carry a gun. It's not my way, I decided. You can make up your own
mind. Your mother and I are not to be hated, almost the opposite. You
would have liked your mother, she is was unbroken. She ate out of my
hand, though.*

*I've left some holes in the yard. If a door opens, go in. If it's locked, be
clever. When they used to keep me from you, I climbed in your window.*

I love you and your mother loves you and it's not over.

*I'll leave this under the cushion in your crib, where Nana will find
it. If she doesn't give it to you, I will get in touch through other means.
Remain calm.*

Your father, Francesco Lorenzo Fini

Lucy looked up from the letter. When she lifted her arm toward a slant
of illuminated dust, her hand passed right through it, as if she didn't exist.

* * *

Downstairs, Edgar's finger was throbbing. He sat on the couch with Florence's boo-boo bag beside him, waiting for his mother. By now, his grandmother would have changed the bandage three times. Lucy hadn't changed it once.

Edgar worried the tape on the gauze until it came undone. Slowly, he began to unwind the bandage—but then stopped, not wanting to see the damage. Besides, it was only right that someone else should take care of his finger—tell him that everything was going to be okay. Whenever Florence had cleaned a cut, she'd always told him to turn his head away and think of pickles. Edgar didn't even like pickles, but it was a funny word and saying it somehow lessened the pain.

Edgar winced. It felt like his whole heart was in the tip of his finger. It hurt more than before. Probably it was time to take another pill. He uncapped the bottle and fished one out. In the kitchen, he swallowed it with a glass of milk. Maybe, after his mother changed his bandage, she could drive him to the cemetery. He'd make her stop at Sylvan's to get some flowers. It wouldn't be fun, but going there was important. *If you don't visit them,* his grandmother always said, *they forget you.* There were rules when it came to dead people. Edgar would have to explain all this to his mother.

A half hour later, though, she still hadn't come down, and Edgar was too dizzy to climb the stairs. As soon as he put his foot on the first step, the staircase began to move like an escalator—though, strangely, Edgar stayed in the same place. He sniffed. It seemed that something was burning again.

"Ma," he said—though why was he whispering? He said the word again, repeating it over and over with increasing speed until it became something abstract—the end of each *Ma* blurring into the beginning of the next: *mamamamamama.* A quiet, droning chant. Then he slowed it down, like a robot losing power. He uttered one last, long *maaaaaa,* and let his head droop, as if kapooped. He laughed. His body felt limp.

Sliding his feet across the carpet, he made his way to the broken front door. The duct tape had come undone again, and the door had blown open. A few yellowed leaves littered the hallway, confusing inside with outside. Plus, it seemed too early for the leaves to have turned color. Was it autumn already?

In the sunlight, Edgar squinted. Across the street was the green truck.

The boy moved closer until he could see the man inside, sitting there with his eyes shut. Had he been watching the house? But what was there to see? Edgar turned, taking a few steps backwards to better consider 21 Cressida Drive.

It was nothing special, a white house surrounded by trees. But maybe other people saw something different when they looked at it. Edgar tried to imagine being someone else, someone who didn't live there. It wasn't possible, of course, to believe this entirely; but in his present state of mind he was able to inhabit a doubleness that was not completely implausible. Edgar regarded the house as if he were both the boy on the lawn as well as the boy inside—the main difference being that the boy inside was a child, and the one on the lawn was bigger. Inside-Edgar was doing the same things he'd always done, but outside-Edgar was unpredictable.

He looked at the house as the aliens might, if they were to pass overhead or land on the lawn. The aliens would see everything that had ever happened. They'd see Florence with long black hair and a fox around her neck; a man with an eagle on his arm smoking cigars in the bathtub; a redheaded woman bringing home a baby the size of a dinner roll. They'd see the man hiding in the closet. Outside-Edgar told inside-Edgar not to be afraid.

When he turned, he saw that the door of the spaceship was open. The man leaned over toward the passenger seat and asked Edgar if he wanted to take a ride.

"Is that a real beard?" Edgar said softly.

The man smiled. "I dare you to pull it off."

Edgar shook his head and looked down.

"We could just sit," the man said quickly. "We don't have to go anywhere."

Edgar glanced back at his house.

"Are you home by yourself?"

Edgar wasn't sure how to answer this question. "I got hurt," he said, shyly holding up his hand.

"I know," the man said. "You told me."

"When?"

"Last time we saw each other."

Edgar was confused. He knew that he'd been in the truck before, but it seemed more like something from a dream.

"We had a big day," the man said. "You don't remember?"

"I have to go," Edgar said. "I have to change my bandage."

"Well, you're in luck," the man crooned, snapping his fingers. "I have a first-aid kit in the truck."

"It's not just a scratch," said Edgar. "It's serious."

"Don't worry. I used to be married to a nurse. I'll have you fixed up in no time."

The boy sighed.

"Come on, I promise we won't go anywhere. We'll stay parked right here in front of your house."

"But where would we go?" asked Edgar.

"Nowhere. We'll just sit in the truck."

"No, but I mean . . ." Edgar was afraid to say it. "Where *would* we go, if we did go somewhere?"

"Oh," the man said, his voice cracking a little. "I . . . I don't know. Was there someplace you wanted to go?"

*   *   *

Lucy gently swept the ashes of the burned letter onto a Niagara Falls postcard. By the time she reached the window, Edgar was already in the truck. She paid no mind to the vehicle as it pulled away—focused, as she was, on scattering the remains of Frank's letter onto the lawn.

Done, she thought. *Finished.*

But as she flicked the last bits of ash off the postcard, a wind came—and a large flake, like a black moth, flew straight into her mouth.

BOOK THREE

THE LAST DAY OF FRANCESCO LORENZO FINI

I like to think the moon is there even if I am not looking at it.

—ALBERT EINSTEIN

23

Ten Minutes

Lucy wakes to Frank standing naked beside the bed.

"Where have you been?" he asks in a tight whisper.

"Sleeping," she says, reaching out to touch her husband's thigh. "Why don't you get into bed, baby? Come on."

Frank shakes his head and moves about the room, pulling at his ears like they don't fit properly. For the last few days, he's hardly slept, fearing what he refers to as "slippage," a phenomenon that supposedly happens at night—and which, if left unchecked, might lead to "a total fucking quantum derailment." He's warned Lucy not to spend so much time in bed, claiming the damage she's already suffered might be irreversible. "I can't even hear you anymore, Lu."

Even if this is nonsense, it makes Lucy sad. "You can hear me," she tells him. But he explains that, no, someone has put something in his ear—*"not an insect,"* he insists, as if this might be the conclusion Lucy's jumped to. When he puts the side of his head close to his wife's face and asks her to look, she isn't sure what to tell him. There's nothing there, of course, but, still, she slides two fingers into Frank's ear, pretends to pull something out—a horrible version of some game you'd play with a child, acting as if you'd removed their nose by holding the tip of your thumb between two fingers.

"I got it," she says—and when Frank asks her what it is, she tells him, "a piece of silver." A good answer, she thinks, since, in addition to assaults by ice and mirrors, Frank's fantasies often involve metal and wires and tiny magnets. Lucy's relieved that Frank doesn't ask to see what she's extracted—but just in case he demands to examine it later, she goes to the window and chucks out the imaginary scrap of metal.

The doctors say she should never play along with her husband's fantasies—but it works sometimes; it calms him down. Besides, the doctors, in Lucy's opinion, are either distracted or exhausted. Frank is one of too many patients, a fill-in-the-blank slot they fill with pills—which work for a while, and then don't. And when they do work, it's almost worse. Frank is a zombie; dull, neutered, empty. It makes sense, to Lucy, why her husband sometimes refuses to take his meds. In the hospital, the nurses had techniques to make a person swallow, but Lucy isn't going to force poison down her husband's throat in his own house. And terrible as it is to see Frank like this—the truth is, there's something here still recognizable as Frank, unlike the pathetic wet mop of a man, when drugged.

Even Florence is confused about the pills. "I don't know, Lucille. They know more than we do," she says of the doctors. Still, Lucy can see how it breaks the old woman's heart to watch her son flattened by the medication—hunched over on the couch, mute, voided of desire, refusing even her ricotta cheesecake, his favorite.

Lucy and Florence have to work as a team to keep Frank steady. He's been home from the hospital for over a week now, and he seems worse than ever. On his first day back from Trenton, the two women had cut his nails, which had grown horrifyingly long. Lucy had worked the clippers, and with each snip Frank had winced as if she were performing surgery without anesthesia. Florence had stood above her son, stroking his hair and telling him to think of pickles.

"*Shhh,*" he says suddenly in the bedroom, even though Lucy hasn't spoken. "Do you hear them?"

In the nursery, Edgar's begun to cry—a sound that Frank often misinterprets as sirens.

"It's okay," Lucy says. "It's the baby."

"Do we have to fix him?" he asks, and Lucy tells him, no—that Florence will take care of it.

Frank's still naked. He rubs his dick anxiously. "Why did it come out of me like that?"

"It's nobody's fault," Lucy assures her husband, who, each day, seems to grow more troubled by the child's whiteness. "It's just something that happens. He won't die from it."

Frank nods slowly, as if satisfied. Lucy nods, too, and tries to smile. She walks over to him and kneels down, doing something that always gives him comfort. Florence has faith in food; Lucy, in another kind of pleasure. She puts her mouth over Frank's dick and begins to suck. He leans against the wall, moans. His hand finds Lucy's head and caresses it with a gentleness that makes her wet. She sucks harder, devotedly, and has achieved a perfect rhythm when there's a knock at the door.

"Everything okay in there?" Florence's timing is always impeccable. Lucy wipes her lips and says, "Yes, we're fine."

"Do you need anything? I made some French toast, if you're hungry."

A naked and very erect Frank looks down at his kneeling wife and puts his hand over his mouth, like a little boy trying to keep himself from giggling. Seeing the sweetness of her husband's face, Lucy bursts out laughing.

"What's so funny?" Florence says.

"Nothing," replies Lucy.

"Well, come downstairs and we'll have a nice breakfast. There's bacon, too. You hear me, Frankie?"

Lucy can detect the anxiety in the old woman's voice, and worries that it might upset Frank—who often confuses concern for conspiracy.

"Give us five minutes," says Lucy.

After she hears the slap of the old woman's slippers moving away, she tries to resume pleasuring Frank, but he refuses her. She snaps a Pogues CD into the player. "Come on, Frankie, let's get into bed." When she takes his hand, he pulls away and clicks off the music.

Lucy will always regret not having this last moment with Frank, this final fuck. She knows it isn't bacon or cheesecake that Frank needs—or Florence's prayers and saints, for that matter. He doesn't need pills or cold baths or, according to Pio, a "project" or a decent haircut. Frank needs her; and he needs sex—and Lucy will torture herself for almost her whole life with the belief that she could have saved her husband if, on that last day, she'd somehow managed to get her lips back on his dick.

Because they wouldn't have stopped. The sex would have gone on all day, all night, until it dawned on them that they'd spent their entire lives in that bed, and Frank had missed his death.

*   *   *

At breakfast, the whole family is at the table—Lucy, Frank, Pio, Florence with the baby on her lap. She feeds him stewed apples, and Frank watches. "What is that you're giving him?"

"Fruit," Florence says. "Would you like some?" she asks, noticing that her son hasn't touched his French toast.

Frank only stares at her, but Florence, unable to help herself, extends the baby spoon toward her grown son's mouth. He pushes back his chair as if a dead rat's been thrust in his face.

Pio, who barely speaks anymore, lifts his head from his hand, says nothing. Why doesn't he take control of the situation? Lucy wonders. But Pio is stunned by a kind of regret that Lucy is still too young to fathom.

The baby's hand taps gently against Florence's arm. The old woman regains her composure and redirects the spoonful of stewed apples to a mouth that appreciates it. Edgar eats the warm fruit, oblivious (or so it seems) to the plight of his father. Florence gives the child too much, and the food runs down his chin.

"We don't all have to stop eating," Florence says with a false brightness. "Lucy, Pio. Go on."

Pio refuses, but Lucy makes a dumb show of eating a slice of the sweet toast.

"It's good, isn't it?" Florence says theatrically to Lucy, and Lucy says, "Yes, it's good, Florence. It's good, Frank." Her voice is shaky.

She can barely swallow, feeling like a traitor. This is not how she'd pictured her life—her child in another woman's arms, her husband recoiling from a spoonful of baby food. She and Frank were supposed to have been in San Francisco by now, or Peru, or in a cheap hotel along a highway, destination unknown.

This is why, for the last week, when Frank whispers to her about going away, she listens and doesn't stop him. Part of Lucy knows it's a lie, but she's still a girl, only in her twenties, and susceptible to a poetry of escape and adventure and an all-consuming love that will prevail over every obstacle.

Also, she's exhausted with this world—and the places that Frank has been whispering about lately seem more than just dots on a map. They no longer have names like Peru or San Francisco; their terrains are wholly emotional, places where, Frank says, *"they would never find us"* or where *"it's all one thing, one story."*

She knows she has to be careful how she responds when he talks like this. Little murmurs of agreement are best, because if she says too much, Frank can see that she doesn't fully comprehend the complicated rules and logic, and he gets upset. When she said, just the other day, "We can leave tomorrow. Let's pack our bags," Frank pushed her away and shouted, "Do you think they're gonna let you through with bags? They'll probably weigh us, see what's in our stomachs."

"Right, right," Lucy said, as if she remembered the rules, the plan. Frank said they shouldn't even eat for several days before leaving. "Not even a glass of milk."

In her chest, Lucy feels a kind of pre-travel jitters, even though she knows they aren't going anywhere. Where could they go with a baby and no money—and, if Frank had his way, no food in their stomachs? Still, within her, there remains a shimmery, abrasive grain of hope. She often feels it at night, scratching against her heart—especially when he kisses her neck and calls her his red star, his Alpha Orionis.

*   *   *

In the kitchen, Frank watches his family. They look strange to him. His so-called father, eyes lowered, tapping his finger against a stained napkin, signaling in some secret code to his so-called mother, who's also tapping—her whole hand against the baby's back, forcing tiny iridescent bubbles from its mouth. What does it all mean? The steady movements of each person working together like a kind of factory or assembly line, whose end product seems to be the tiny bubbles that come from the baby's mouth. As each one bursts, the atmosphere in the room changes. Some subtle gas is being released. Everyone's breathing normally, though—so maybe it's not poisonous.

Frank stares at the baby's mouth, so pink inside—shockingly so, opening as it does out of the chalk-white face. Even the redhead—his so-called wife—leans in toward the baby. Frank notices that her blouse is wet around the nipples. He watches as she reaches to take the child from its grandmother.

"No," Frank says. "Give him to me."

Everyone's heart jumps, even Pio's.

"Can I have the baby, please?" Frank's voice is quiet, but clear.

"Have the what?" Florence says.

"I just want to hold him," Frank says. "Just talk to him."

"He can't understand you," Florence says with a brush of her hand. "He doesn't have the language."

"What language?" Frank says, confused.

"Any language." The old woman pulls the baby closer to her chest. "Why don't you just drink your juice, Francesco, eat a little something?"

But Frank wants to make sure the baby remembers him. Time is flying out the window like a swarm of bees. "Edgar," he says, and the boy turns.

Pio crushes the napkin in his fist. Lucy's breasts feel cold; her mouth is dry.

"Edgar," Frank croons sweetly, and the baby responds, uttering a small squeal of contentment as he stretches out his arm to touch the stubble on his father's face. Frank hasn't shaved in days. Despite everything, Lucy thinks he looks gorgeous.

Father and son. French toast. The yellow kitchen. For a moment it all seems natural, almost normal.

"Maybe it's okay," Lucy says quietly, touching Florence's arm. Keeping the baby from Frank the last time, behind a padlocked door, had proved a disaster. "Here, give him to me," she says.

But the old woman won't let go.

"Florence," the girl says more firmly. "I need to feed him."

"He just ate. He's fine."

"He's not your kid," Lucy says to the old woman, but Frank reacts as if she's said these words to him.

"Did you fuck a dead person?" he shouts.

"Language," Florence scolds. She shifts position, obscuring the child in the folds of his blanket.

"No," Frank says. "Show it to me." He moves toward the baby.

Florence makes an unexpected sound, like a hiss, and Frank freezes.

"You can't have all-all-all the air," he stutters, "all the food."

"There's food on your plate, you idiot," Pio says.

"Sta' zitto," Florence whispers harshly to her husband.

Frank's frenzied attentions land on the brown napkin in his father's fist. "Don't try to hide it," he says.

"Hide what?" asks Pio. "What are we hiding?"

"Try to feed me a plate of shit."

"This is shit? This is *shit*?" Pio says, picking up a slice of French toast and waving it in the air. The bread breaks, and a good-sized chunk flies across the room. Frank steps back and makes a strangled sound as if he can't breathe. He sits on the floor and begins to rock his body.

Everyone watches him, even the baby.

When the moaning begins, from deep inside Frank's throat, Edgar accompanies the sound with a sharp wail.

"I'm not doing this again," Pio mutters, hiding his tears inside a sickened growl. He gets up from the table and leaves the room.

Lucy begins to shake. This is all too similar to the morning that Frank was taken to Trenton. He'd been found in the garden before dawn, filthy, moaning. The yard a mess—a series of holes, as if Frank were planning to inter a litter of kittens. When Lucy discovered him, he was sitting before the largest hole, the baby asleep in his arms. Pio had called the police.

In the kitchen, Lucy wonders if Pio is doing it again, calling the cops from the other room. Suddenly she's afraid she's going to lose Frank—that they'll drag him back to Trenton. Pio has made threats. Even Florence seems more concerned about the baby than about Frank. Clearly his parents no longer care about him like she does. In her gut, she knows that if Florence and Pio weren't here, overreacting to everything, she could make her husband well.

Frank had rescued her from her own parents, from a father far worse than Pio; and now she would rescue Frank. Why she loves him so much is beyond her understanding. But she knows that this terrible pain of his is something only she can touch, only she can heal.

Frank stops moaning and approaches her. Sometimes it's like he can read her mind. He seems calm, seems his old self again. Even the baby is quiet. Lucy leans over to wipe a curdle of snot from the child's face. Florence allows it.

"It's time," Frank says. "We have to go."

Lucy nods.

"Go?" Florence says. "Go where?"

"Just for a drive," Frank says so smoothly it almost makes Lucy smile. But then he walks away from her, toward the back door.

"Frankie?" she says nervously.

"I just want to check something," he says.

"Stay in the yard," Florence calls out as if to a child.

Lucy wanders to the refrigerator in an attempt to steer clear of the old woman's eyes.

"He can't go anywhere, Lucille. You hear me? You make him stay here."

Lucy stares at a carton of milk. Her hands are shaking.

"What's he doing out there?" asks Florence.

Lucy looks out the window. Frank is standing in the garden, among the tomatoes.

"I don't like him out there," Florence says. "He's not digging, is he?"

"No."

The old woman sighs loudly. "At least I have the baby. Thank God for that."

*   *   *

Frank checks the holes. No one's messed with them since he's filled them back in. Soon it will seem like he's never been here at all. His wife is watching him from the window. He lifts his hand to her because he remembers her now. She's the girl who said she'd come with him, that he wouldn't have to go alone. She's his safety, his constant. His red star. Frank kneels in the garden. The stars have been dead a long time, he thinks. Sometimes the helpless love he feels for the girl, and the awful gratitude that swells in him in the presence of the baby, pins his heart to the wall. He tears off a tiny tomato leaf and places it under his tongue.

"What you doing?" The voice flies over the garden, a happy bird. "Mistah Feen, what you doing?"

Frank turns to see the little koala-faced girl from next door, standing on her side of the white fence. She's smiling, tapping her fists together as if trying to produce a spark.

"Where the baby, Mistah Feen?"

Frank gets up and studies the girl. She must be six or seven by now. He's known her since she came here from wherever children come from; he can't recall anymore. He's always been nervous around this squat, thick-limbed creature with the flattened face, but as he stares at her now, he's astounded by the way her skin absorbs the light. She's a beautiful child.

Toenail, she seems to be saying to him.

Frank shakes his head.

"Tone-Ann," she enunciates. "Memba?"

Frank turns away, moves toward the house.

"Where you going, Mistah Feen?"

Frank stops, but is unable to look at her. The beauty of the child is too painful.

"I see a ow-a out here sometimes," the girl says. "You know, a ow-a?"

Frank keeps his back to her, but listens carefully. He's been thinking a lot about time lately. Seconds, minutes, *ow-as*. Timing is so important.

"Fly ova the house sometimes. A big ow-a." The girl makes the sound of it. *"Hoo hoo hoooo."*

Frank closes his eyes and breathes.

"Is it your ow-a, Mistah Feen?"

*   *   *

Lucy's gone to the basement, where Pio hides his dirty magazines. Also his money. She removes the yellow plastic lid from the Chock full o'Nuts can labeled "screws and nails" and pulls out the roll of bills. It's huge—enough, she imagines, for a few months' expenses: hotel rooms and diapers and gas. Maybe even enough for a deposit, when they find a place to rent. Stuffed into the pocket of her jeans, the money makes a ridiculous mannish lump. At the bottom of the stairs, she hesitates, feeling dizzy. Her excitement borders on nausea.

Upstairs, Frank is waiting in the living room, the car keys in his hand.

"Lucy, thank goodness," Florence says when the girl returns. "Tell him to give you the keys. He won't listen to me."

"It's okay," Lucy says. "We'll just drive around town and come right back. Ready?" she says to Frank; but he only stands there, staring at the wall. Lucy sees that it's up to her to keep things moving.

"Come here, kiddo," she says to Edgar, who's still packed inside the old woman's arms.

"I've got him," Florence says. "Stop—what are you doing? Don't tug at him like that."

"Well, let go then." Lucy pulls harder.

"Gah, gah." Florence gurgles as if Lucy's choking her. "Pio!" she shouts. But it's too late. Lucy's claimed Edgar and is moving toward the door.

"Fine," Florence says breathlessly. "The two of you go for your drive. But you leave the baby here."

"You can't keep him cooped up in the house," Lucy says. "He needs some air."

"It's too sunny," Florence says. "He'll *burn.*"

As the women argue, Frank swoops in and snatches Edgar, who's crying now. He carries the baby to the couch, arranges him gently between two throw pillows. *"Here,"* Frank tells the women. "He stays *here.*"

"No," Lucy says with a ferocious smile, doing her best to remain calm. "He's coming with us."

"He's not a toy for whenever you're in the mood," chides Florence.

"I can take my son for a fucking drive," snaps Lucy.

Both women freeze. It's the first time that Lucy has cursed at Florence. A moment passes before either realizes that Frank is gone. Lucy grabs the baby and flies out the door.

Why is he getting into Pio's car? she wonders. Lucy hates the tacky gold LeBaron. "Let's take our car," she says, sliding temporarily into the old man's Chrysler.

"It's too small," Frank says, not looking at her.

When Lucy spots Florence huffing toward the driveway, she quickly locks her door and then leans across Frank's body to lock his.

"Francesco," Florence shouts. "Open this door. *Francesco.*" She comes around to the other side and bangs some more. *"Lucille."*

"Give her the baby," Frank says.

"We'll be back soon," Lucy says to Florence through the glass.

"Give her the baby," Frank says again.

"Don't be an asshole, Frankie."

Frank turns to her. He looks terrified. "You want him to come with us?" he says.

"Yes," Lucy tells him. "Of course."

Frank is silent, and Lucy says, "Go."

When Frank turns the key, Florence steps back, startled by the engine's roar.

"Francesco."

Edgar turns to the familiar voice. The old woman stands on the lawn, her fat red hand glued to her forehead. The light strikes the diamond, catching the baby's eye. Pio watches everything from above, framed in an ellipsis of burgundy curtains.

Lucy wants to say goodbye to them. She wants to say *thank you* and *I'm sorry*—and something else she's never said to Florence and Pio. That she loves them. But all she can manage is one last lie. "Ten minutes," she shouts as Frank pulls away. "We'll be back in ten minutes!"

Entry #2

It's strange, but not at all unpleasant—the way she knows everything now. The "past" (she recognizes the unreality of this word) is a crystal she can turn in her hand and see from endless angles, in varying degrees of light and darkness. The crystal is almost too brilliant with sadness, but spectacular in a way she is not at liberty to discuss. "Then," as the living say—"then," she had stood on the lawn of a place called 21 Cressida Drive. She'd watched the boy and the girl drive away in the car—the baby with them. The picture had stopped there. But now, if she wants—and sometimes she does—she is with them in the gold LeBaron, moving from body to body, feeling everything. It's astounding, this ingress she has into their hearts. The way their pain is legible.

If only the dead could write books, she thinks with a laugh.

The living, she knows, would prefer this story not to be told. She is aware—but does not care—that flesh-and-blood will think her and her kind cold and indiscreet. Flesh-and-blood would round up the ghosts, if they could, and put them in camps; seal their lips or take out their tongues.

Still, she speaks, knowing that some will listen.

Of course, she'll have to make it easy for them. Unversed in simultaneity, they will require a more strict adherence to the facts. It happened like this. *This, then that.* Cause and effect. She knows, though, that there is no line, no path, no "time."

All things happen at once.

24

Shepherd's Junction

Frank drives, not speaking to the girl. It's a cloudless spring day shot through with clear yellow light. The air is cool and fresh—though, for some reason, Frank won't let the girl open the windows. She looks out at the scrubby oaks and beeches rushing by at the side of the Parkway. Tiny new leaves filter the late-morning sun; the black road is freckled with quavering pools of brightness.

"So we're going north?" Lucy asks after another long silence.

Frank doesn't answer; and now she's getting angry—but she doesn't argue, because the baby, finally, is asleep. She holds him tightly on her lap, since there'd been no time to grab the car seat. They can buy a new one later with Pio's money. For now she keeps Edgar down low in case a trooper spots them. *Reckless endangerment of a child.* God knows what the fine is for that. She takes the bottom of her blouse and half covers the baby's head.

"Why are you doing that?" asks Frank.

"His skin," she says. "Plus, I don't want anyone to see him."

What Frank hears is: *people are watching us.* Slowly, strategically, he begins to increase his speed—only an extra mile or so every few minutes, so that the observers won't immediately notice the variance. Frank's thoughts, too, are increasing in velocity. Though the car's speed helps him to outrun some of them, others—such as his mother's words, *he'll burn in the sun*—pop up again and again along the road, like mile markers.

Despite Frank's silence, Lucy continues to talk. It makes her feel calmer. She lays out her plan. Frank can drive for a few more hours; when he's tired, she'll take over. A car seat and diapers at the next big town; and then, when it's dark, a cheap motel. Part of her wants to say *Let's go home,* but she scolds her fear and touches her husband's arm. "We're gonna be okay," she tells him.

Frank pulls away. "Why did you bring him?"

Lucy says, "Relax. We can do this, Frankie."

When she sees that his hands are shaking, she asks him if he'd like her to drive. "You can hold the baby," she says, hoping to placate him. Plus, she wants him to know something that she isn't sure of herself: that she trusts him. "You and Edgar can sit in the back and rest."

"No," he says. "I don't want him here. It's your fault."

"What's my fault?" the girl asks—thinking, *You made me have this baby, you can't change your fucking mind now.*

"The two of us," Frank says.

"*The three of us,*" Lucy says sharply. "We're doing this."

The girl doesn't say anything else, because she's having trouble breathing. She listens to the sound of it; it's strange, like the breath of an old woman—as if, instead of forty miles, they've traveled forty years. The labored breathing suddenly reminds her of Florence, and Lucy turns to the backseat, half expecting to see her mother-in-law.

"I have to open the window," she says. "Okay?"

"What's wrong with him?" Frank asks, pointing his chin toward Edgar. "Why doesn't he say anything?"

"He's sleeping," says Lucy.

When Frank asks if she's sure the baby isn't dead, Lucy's breath constricts a little more. She rolls down the window, despite Frank's protests, and takes in a big gulp of air. "The baby's fine," she says, closing her eyes.

The channeled air streams across her face with a pleasing roughness. It clears her head and blows back her red hair—the tips of which flutter against Frank's neck. She can smell green things. She can smell water.

"Feel that, Frankie? Doesn't that feel nice?" She puts her hand on his thigh. This time, he doesn't pull away. When a raindrop falls into the car, she opens her eyes, confused, squinting at the cloudless day. When she feels another drop—on the hand that rests on Frank's leg—she realizes that he's crying. For some reason she can't bring herself to look at him.

"Hush," she says, using Florence's word. She tells the boy that she loves him.

"I love *you*," he says, contradicting her—as if only one of them could be in love, and Lucy were somehow a liar.

Sometimes it's better to say nothing when he gets like this.

She keeps her hand on Frank's thigh, caressing it softly, letting her mind go flat. Ten, twenty, thirty minutes pass in a turtle shell, before her consciousness sticks out its head again, and she hears the eager sound of air rushing through the LeBaron.

Where are they now? The trees are bigger, wilder; there are hills in the near distance, almost mountains. The car rolls along a snaking local road; beside it, a wide sparkling river—the water high and gushy from the spring melt. Lucy's pretty sure it's the Hudson. She thinks of Pio's tunnel, the stories he used to tell her: how the air inside had made the workers giddy, like they were drunk; how he and a friend had stolen a trunk load of tiles from the jobsite and installed them in the bathrooms of 21 Cressida Drive.

The breeze is suddenly cooler, and Lucy rolls up the window. Huge fair-weather clouds have appeared. Cliffs and rocky slopes and *Flintstones* boulders make Lucy feel like she's flying through a kind of prehistoric outer space. Everything feels enormous—and at the same time, the whole landscape is perfected in miniature in the side-view mirror.

Lucy realizes that this might be the most beautiful place she and Frank have ever been. On their honeymoon, they'd stayed at a hotel in Atlantic City, in a suite with a pink hot tub shaped like a heart. Where they are now—where they're going—might turn out to be just as sweet.

Relax, she tells herself, pushing down to where the innocence is.

For a while, the girl drifts in and out of sleep. Frank listens to her soft snoring. He takes one hand off the wheel and slips a finger into the baby's mouth. It's warm—not at all the temperature he'd expected to find inside the white face. The baby looks up with his pale sea-glass eyes—and Frank notes how the boy's gaze is clenched, as if he's looking at Frank from a distance.

This is when Frank realizes that there's something separating him and his son—though the problem isn't so much one of space, but of time. Edgar, Frank realizes, is in a different car, yet somehow the two vehicles have blurred together, a kind of quantum crash.

Neither of us are really here, Frank thinks. Which makes the moment more precious, being an act of science. *I'm already dead,* he remembers. He understands, now, that his finger isn't in the boy's mouth; it's in the dirt behind 21 Cressida Drive, in the black hole. Frank has his finger in the mouth of time. He can feel it sucking. He can feel how hungry it is. How warm it is, when all his calculations had predicted ice.

Lucy stirs, but doesn't wake. Frank can't understand how her dead hands can remember to hold the baby. Why doesn't the baby fall? Frank wonders if the boy's dead, too—and with a sudden dread he pulls his finger from the baby's mouth and presses down on the gas.

He can see the two bridges in the distance: a smaller one that goes over a stream, and then the larger one that goes over the river. He recognizes them, even though he's never seen them before. The LeBaron sails admirably around a sharp curve. The future opens its fist.

But what if he's wrong? What if the crash of time that brought them together—that spliced Edgar's story into his—breaks apart again into separate tracks? How can he be sure their lives won't unspool in the underneath, where there will be confusion, blindness, terror? His family might never be able to find each other again. That's why he'd wanted to leave the child behind, so that he could wait in the closet, in the darkness of 21 Cressida Drive—the lighthouse of his face beaming into the future, where Frank and Lucy will find him when they're ready.

Only he and his wife are supposed to go into the water.

Suddenly, a hot plume of fury rises up again against the girl. Why, Frank wonders, would she want to kill the baby—the one thing capable of preserving them across time? If the child falls, too, there will be nothing left in this world to guide Frank back to Lucy's arms, should he lose her in the underneath. Is that what she wants, to be lost from him forever?

He'll have to test her.

Frank speeds toward the first bridge, and Lucy wakes from the *thump thump thump* of the tires against the metal seams. She takes in the rock walls and the stream below. Her stomach jumps; she clutches the baby. "Slow down," she says.

When they arrive safely on the other side, Lucy sees the larger bridge in the distance, arching over the bright river. "Frank, did you hear me? Slow down."

Frank guns it for a second, but as soon as he hears the baby's cry, he remembers what he has to do. He applies the brakes and brings the car to an only slightly jarring stop. The baby falls silent again.

"What's the matter?" Lucy says. "Why are we stopping?"

"Look." Frank gestures toward the second bridge. He's certain that she, too, must recognize this place from her own dreams.

"It's beautiful," she says, taking it all in: the clean blue sky, the fleet of identical white clouds receding into the distance, the shimmering trees, the silver bridge high above the foaming river.

"Put the baby out of the car," Frank says.

Lucy smiles sleepily at what she assumes is a joke. "Does he need to be changed?" Frank has always had an acute sense of smell. She's about to remind him that they need to buy diapers when he says more forcefully, *"Put him out of the car, Lu."* He points to the side of the road. "Over there. You see those plants with the . . ."

Lucy glances at some bushes blistered with red-orange berries.

"We'll write his name on his clothes," Frank says. "Or on his—"

"What are you talking about? Why would we . . ." Lucy suddenly feels blinded; she needs her sunglasses. How stupid to have left the house with *nothing.* She digs noisily through the glove box. "Have you seen my sunglasses?"

"Look at me," Frank says.

"No," Lucy says. "Not if you're going to say stupid things. Please, can we just go?"

"You want to go?"

"Yes."

"With the baby?"

"Yes, Frank, *with the baby.* What the fuck?"

She touches her husband's face. "Listen to me, Frankie. We've come this far, right? We're not gonna stop now. Come on, *no,* why are you crying?"

When she tries to kiss him, he screams.

"Get out of the car!"

Vertigo strikes. Lucy's mouth tastes like metal. "Frank—"

"Both of you!"

Lucy shields her eyes. "Baby, why don't we just rest for a little while, okay?" She gestures weakly toward a tree. "We can pull the car over there, in the shade, and just . . ."

She can barely hear her voice. Frank is screaming again. When he accuses her of wanting to kill the child, Lucy's body levitates on a wave of nausea. She opens the door and hangs out her head. Her husband's condemnations are so strong that, finally, she steps out of the car. *"Shhh shhh shhh,"* she says to the crying baby. And now Lucy is crying, too.

"He's fine," she tells her husband. "Please, let's just go."

"Put him on the ground," Frank says.

Lucy stands with Edgar in the yellow sunlight; it seems like a dream.

"Put him on the ground." Frank peels off his shirt. "Here." He tosses it out of the car. "Put him on this."

It's the denim shirt she gave him years ago, knowing how good he'd look wearing it on his motorcycle. The motorcycle on which they were going to ride to San Francisco, live by the ocean. Her legs go weak at the memory.

"Frank," she cries—feeling dreams she's been clutching for so long, with all her heart and muscle, slipping away.

"Spread it out underneath him."

"I think I hear sirens," Lucy lies, in an attempt to disrupt Frank's preoccupation with the baby.

"I know," he says, pulling at his ears. *"Do it."*

Lucy kneels in the dirt. She brushes away some small stones before spreading the blue shirt on the ground. Maybe we've come far enough, she thinks desperately, her mind spinning. We could just live here at the side of a road; forget California. Live in a shed, a shack. She tries to reduce her hope to something so small, so humble, that it would be too cruel for the wish not to be granted. She's sorry if, before, she'd asked for too much.

"Make sure he's in the shade," Frank says.

Shivering, Lucy does as she's told, following a logic that's beyond her comprehension, but seems to be understood by the baby, who's no longer crying.

"Write his name," Frank says.

A black pen lands in the dirt.

"On his hand," Frank says—and then, *"No*—on his arm."

Lucy touches the child's soft unmarred skin. His face and body glow strangely blue in the shadows.

"Write his name, Lu."

"No." She pushes away the pen and lies in the dirt next to the baby, crying so quietly it's as if she's melting.

Frank is beside her now. He takes the tiny pale forearm, and Lucy watches as, slowly, the words appear on the baby's skin.

Edgar Allan Fini.

Frank kisses the boy's arm. He rests his stubbled cheek against Edgar's face. *I'll come back to find you,* he confesses. *I don't know when.*

Then, he grabs the girl's hand. "Get back in the car."

He pulls, and a dazed Lucy stumbles to her feet. He pushes her inside the door. The quiet child turns toward her vanishing and wails.

As Frank gets behind the wheel, Lucy sits with her legs still dangling on the ground. She's lost a shoe. She stares at the crying baby, confused. How could he even be there? She'd made an appointment at the clinic, hadn't she? She remembers the lights, the table.

"Shut the door," Frank says.

Someone had *forced* her to have this baby.

Frank starts the engine, and Lucy sobs.

"Shut the door!"

She shuts the door.

They'll find you, she thinks. *They'll take you home to Nana.*

For a moment the wheels turn on the rutted dirt without making traction. The car bounces violently in place. When it suddenly lurches forward, Frank touches Lucy's leg.

She sees the sign (SHEPHERD'S JUNCTION) and the large metal bridge. Soon they'll be across it, on their way to another life—and Edgar will be gone; he'll be the past. A living cord inside her stretches away from her baby. The pain is beyond anything she's ever felt.

"Stop the car," she whispers.

But it only moves faster.

"Stop," she screams. "I don't want to go! *Stop!*"

When Frank slams the brakes and the car skids to a halt, there's an awful silence, broken only by the ticking of Saint Christopher swinging from the rearview mirror. Frank reaches out his hand to stop it, as if it were the pendulum of a clock.

The lovers shake. Neither speaks, nor looks at the other.

When they do speak, the conversation is like something happening at the bottom of a well.

"Can't we take him?" Lucy asks quietly.

"No."

"Why?"

The only answer is an atmospheric disturbance in the distance. A green pickup truck flashes on the bridge, coming from the opposite direction. As it zooms past Pio's LeBaron, it makes a sound like a candle being blown out.

The girl feels the first flutter of doom.

"Please, let's just go back," she begs.

"No," the boy says. He says it three times, like a child.

"Edgar," says the girl.

"You have to choose," says the boy.

Lucy stares at him in disbelief. She opens her mouth, but there are no words.

Her stunned silence confirms Frank's worst fear.

"You don't love me," he says.

And even though she knows—the doctors have explained—that Frank says things like this only because something is misfiring in his brain, she's suddenly furious. For the first time she understands Pio's anger, his dismissal of Frank's illness as nothing more than willfulness.

But maybe Frank's right. Maybe she doesn't love him anymore. Because suddenly the love she feels for him is so violent it's a kind of hatred.

"You stupid fuck," she says, hitting him, slamming her fist into his arm. "You *stupid stupid* fuck. You know I love you!"

"Then come with me," he says.

"I'm not leaving him by the side of the road!"

But Frank doesn't relent, telling her again that she has to choose.

And though Lucy can see the tears in her husband's eyes, she hits him again before turning to open the door.

"You want me to get out, Frankie? Is that what you want?"

He looks at her, seeing an incontestable beauty. *My love.* These words are in his head, but the hole they make is in his chest. This girl he will remember. He almost wants to have her again, to fuck her right now in the car, her red hair falling over his face. It's not a lie when their bodies crash together; it always works.

But it never lasts.

In the end, everything is drawn into the machine, a painful contraption that picks you apart until you're so far away from other humans that words like *help me* or *hold me* lose all meaning.

Frank says nothing.

"I'm getting out of the car," the girl cries, poised at the open door, "Is that what you want?"

"Yes," he says.

A single fear grips them both.

"That's what you want?" she asks again, her voice small now.

Frank nods, not looking at her.

"Fuck you," she says, kicking her way out of the car. "I wasn't going to choose you anyway." She's crying now on the blacktop.

Frank closes his eyes and tries to breathe.

Lucy is bent over—the barked sobs jackknifing her body.

It's better this way, Frank decides. The girl needs to stay and take care of the baby.

"What are you waiting for?" she says, kicking the side of the car. *"Go."*

But he wants to give her something before he leaves. Except he can't find the right thing inside his head. On the front seat, only a silver gum wrapper.

"Go!" She slams shut the door of the car. *"See how far you get without me."*

When he turns to look at the girl one last time, she's already gone. He sees her in the rearview mirror, walking away in a single shoe, growing smaller and smaller.

"Lu," he says.

But she can't hear him.

Frank touches his neck, revs the engine.

Hearing it, Lucy rushes toward the berry bushes. *If he sees her holding the child, if he sees the two of them standing by the side of the road . . .*

Frank picks up the silver wrapper, and though the procedure terrifies him, he crushes it and pushes it into his ear. He doesn't want to leave any metal behind. He wants to remove all traces of the machine.

When Lucy hears the wheels of the LeBaron scream against the blacktop, she kicks off her remaining shoe and scrambles into the bushes, grabs the baby and carries him to the side of the road.

Lucy doesn't cry out as she sees the LeBaron moving away at breathtaking speed. She's still certain Frank will turn around. For one second, as she sees the car swerve, she utters a breathless sound of relief. But as the car crosses into the wrong lane just before the bridge, her voice corrects itself.

Edgar lifts his head at his mother's cry, a huge sound that consumes his entire attention. He doesn't see the car hurtling toward the first low guardrail.

Only Lucy watches Pio's LeBaron smash against the metal posts; watches how the metal spins the car around so that Frank, horribly, is facing her as he flies backwards off the edge of the Earth—the car floating for an impossibly long moment before thudding down the slope.

"Frankie."

She's running now with the baby in her arms.

She's standing at the edge of the bridge, oblivious to the stopped cars. All she can see is a golden rectangle: the roof of the LeBaron bobbing on the surface of the water. She moves past the fractured rail, trying to find her footing on the slope. She needs to get down onto the rocks, make her way to the water. Why is someone grabbing her arm?

"Stop. You're going to fall."

And she does fall.

But not far enough.

Only a few feet, onto a wide flat stone like a balcony, from which she has a perfect view. A final flash of gold, and then the car is gone, the water closing seamlessly around it.

Only air is coming from her mouth, like in the dreams she had as a child. There are voices on the bridge, shouting.

On the stone, where she's fallen with her leg awkwardly splayed behind her, there's blood. She doesn't feel the pain of the broken bone; nor does she recognize the bird-cry of the child.

She looks around at the overlit landscape. Trees, stones, water—all of it projected, it seems, onto a huge curved screen. What has just happened could not have happened. She looks at the baby still in her arms—his white skin burning. She can't pass out or she'll drop him.

"Hand him to me," someone says. "Miss. *Up here!* Hand him to me."

No. She clutches the baby, and slowly—painfully now—slides back from the edge of the rock. Her position is precarious.

"Don't move. We'll help you."

She presses her back against a large concrete pillar and tries to breathe. Her mind fills with spiders.

She looks at Edgar and then holds him up to a man reaching down from the bridge.

Hands are touching her now, like pulleys, lifting her body from the stone balcony. She keeps her eyes on the river, which she realizes is a road on which Frank is still driving.

All rivers lead to the sea.

At the thought her body goes limp, and her mind black.

Entry #3

The question now, as always, is whether to stay in the dark consciousness of the girl; or to travel underneath the water with the boy, who will continue to breathe for several minutes more; or to coil like smoke inside the screaming lungs of the child.

It's possible, of course, to be all places at once. Or to be nowhere at all, in the empty splendor outside of human affairs.

To accept the rules of tragedy, or to usurp them.

She's tempted to stay with the boy, the one who dies. But since this tale is for the living, she'll return to the girl—whose blackout hints at the absolute, without compromising what is most human: the desire to forget.

BOOK FOUR

BETRAYAL

The heart changes, and it is our worst sorrow.

—MARCEL PROUST

25

Holes

Lucy brushes the ash from her sweatshirt and tries to breathe. Though she's destroyed Frank's letter, his intentions remain.

Your mother and I are gone now.

She looks at herself in Florence's mirror. The light from the window is unforgiving and shows the deepening lines around her eyes and mouth. She isn't sure if she's more furious at Frank for wanting to kill her or for having left her behind to grow old, alone.

We were your parents, Frank and Lucy Fini.

For years, she's told herself that if she'd stayed in the LeBaron, she and Frank would now be living a new life somewhere; that he'd killed himself only because she'd spurned him.

But surely she wasn't that stupid; she must have known where they were heading. That there was no life past that bridge. Frank clearly knew it, and had no qualms about taking her with him. She thinks of the holes he made in the yard, a few weeks before he died. Everything seems meaningless.

Still, she needs to pull herself together. She needs to go downstairs, give the kid some food, give him his pill. Part of her thinks to get a shovel from the garage and take it to the yard. See what she can find. Pretend there's a story, when she knows there are only holes.

* * *

The green truck was parked in the same lot behind the supermarket. In the glove compartment was everything that was needed to change Edgar's bandage: gauze and sterilized cotton, a pair of little silver scissors; there were individually wrapped packets of alcohol-soaked pads; antibacterial ointment; white surgical tape. When the man asked Edgar to give him his hand, he reminded the boy that he'd been married to a nurse. Edgar noticed the man used the past tense a lot when referring to other people.

"I'm just going to cut this old bandage off," he said. "You can look away if you want."

Edgar did.

Maybe this was a bad idea. Being married to a nurse didn't make you a doctor. It didn't even make you a nurse.

"Hold still," the man said.

"My mother usually changes it," Edgar lied.

"But you said she was pretty busy, right?"

Edgar could feel the tips of the tiny scissors moving against his skin. He closed his eyes. "We had a fire at our house," he said.

"Is that right?"

"Some of our stuff got black," Edgar rambled on. "My grandmother's stuff. It got burned. But that doesn't mean we have to throw it out."

He was more talkative than usual. It was partially nervousness, and partially the Percocet—which not only made Edgar's thoughts turn in funny ways, but also made these thoughts slip from his mouth before he could think to stop them. "Even the head can be glued back on," he said, thinking of the Virgin.

He stopped speaking when he felt the bandage slip from his finger.

"*Oooh,*" the man said.

"What?"

"Nothing. You just—you really did a number on yourself, huh?"

"Is it all there?"

"Yes," the man laughed. "It's all there."

Edgar asked if he should look, and the man said it was probably better not to. "But don't worry, buddy. I've seen worse."

The boy kept his face turned away as the man cleaned the finger, applied the ointment. Out the window a small band of litter—two plastic bags, a Styrofoam cup, and a candy wrapper—raced toward a chain-link fence. Edgar knew that these things were garbage, but at the same time he could feel their tiny breathless souls.

"All done," the man said.

Edgar turned. A fresh white bandage was secured with a generous cross-hatching of surgical tape.

"You have to clean it every day," the man said. "That's very important. I've always got the kit here if you need it."

Edgar tapped his bundled finger gently against the dashboard. Amazingly, there was still no pain. Those little pink pills worked like magic.

"Did you want to go for a drive now?" The man had begun to tap his fingers, too—softly against the steering wheel. "Or I could take you home." It was important the boy know that he had some choice in the matter.

Edgar glanced at the dark caverns of the loading docks. He was feeling sleepy again and when he spoke it was barely more than a whisper. "Your name is Jack?"

"No," the man said, smiling. "That's my dog's name."

Edgar sniffed, picking up the scent again. "Oh yeah."

"But if you want, you could call me that, too."

"What?"

"Same as the dog."

Edgar blushed. "I just made a mistake."

"I wouldn't mind," the man said.

"But it's not your name, you said."

"Sometimes it is. I mean, it could be. I wouldn't mind having a nickname. Do you have a nickname?"

Edgar shook his head. Sometimes the boys at school called him *milk-face* or *mayonnaise* or *Snow White.*

"I could make one up for you," the man said.

"I don't know," said Edgar. "Like what?"

The man tried to keep his breathing calm, his voice steady.

"I could call you, I don't know, like maybe Kevin, or . . . yeah, Kevin's a cool name, huh?"

Edgar shrugged.

"Or maybe just Kev, for short. *Hey, Kev.* That's not bad. What do you think?" The man tapped his fingers faster against the steering wheel. "Unless you like your real name better?"

Edgar looked down and grimaced. "I don't *love* it."

* * *

"Edgar!" Lucy called from the front door.

Sometimes, when he was in a mood, he hid behind a bush. She directed her voice toward the Heftis' large hydrangea. "Edgar, I know you can hear me."

The porch steps were covered with yellow birch leaves, and the ones still on the tree quivered like a flock of nervous parakeets.

"If you're hungry, we'll order some Chinese! Come inside and look at the menu."

She fussed with the duct tape on the door, which still hadn't been repaired. Maybe she'd give that Will-yummy, the fireman, a call. His crew had broken the damn thing; the least he could do was come back and fix it. Not that she wanted a man around the house—but there was a lot to do.

In the living room, she picked up the bottle of Edgar's Percocet and shook it—taking some comfort in the fact that there was still a fair amount left. She might need one later. Who knew what she'd find in the yard?

* * *

Frank had dug the holes in the spring, when Florence's garden was full of irises and tulips and lilies. Now, on the first day of October, Lucy stood before pale chrysanthemums and limp asters, some loose-petaled orange roses. The delicate impatiens, zapped by last night's frost, looked like a patch of fried calamari.

She scanned the yard, trying to recall exactly where Frank had dug. Even after seven years, she couldn't forget the spot by the elm, where she'd found him sitting before an opened patch of dirt, the baby in his arms.

"I'm just showing him," Frank had explained. "So he knows where it is."

"Where what is?" she'd asked.

"The river," he'd said.

That had been the largest hole, the deepest. The others had been smaller excavations. One by the large oak and one by each of the dogwoods—and then a series of holes closer to the fence, where Florence grew her tomatoes.

Lucy knelt before the elm and tore at the cold grass. She began slowly, but the more she dug, the angrier she felt. Had she really been so deluded that she'd believed she and Frank could escape, end up in a little house in upstate New York? As she scooped up the dirt, there seemed to be no bottom to the hatred she felt—for herself most of all. When she broke a nail, she stopped her clawing, picked up the shovel, and moved toward the tomatoes.

* * *

Toni-Ann watched anxiously from her bedroom window. Mrs. Feen was digging up Mr. Feen's holes. The girl remembered them from when she was little. She'd seen Mr. Feen making them early one morning, after she'd woken from a nightmare about the flying monkeys in the pillbox hats.

As Lucy sank the shovel into the dirt under the tomato plants, Toni-Ann chewed her fingers. The day Mr. Feen had dug up the yard, he'd been taken away in a police car—his wrists locked in big silver bracelets. Mrs. Feen and Flow-rinse had followed in another car. There'd been a lot of crying.

Toni-Ann had never told anyone about the gun she'd seen Mr. Feen bury. She wasn't a tattletale. Plus, why make things worse for the people next door? Sometimes she wished she could make time go backwards for them. Because they hadn't always been sad.

In the old days, on summer nights, the Feens ate their dinner in the yard under Christmas-tree lights. They were always laughing. One time, the old man gave Toni-Ann a sip of wine from across the fence. "Don't bother the people," her mother used to tell her. But one of the Feens would always say, "It's no bother, Mary."

Sometimes they even used to let Toni-Ann come into their yard. Mr. Feen would lift her over the fence. He was skinny but strong, and when he told stories he used his hands like an actor on television. He was always kissing Mrs. Feen. Toni-Ann had never seen a bigger pair of smoochers. It was nice over there, back then. Flow-rinse was always pushing a piece of food into Toni-Ann's mouth. Soft, salty mounds of snow-white cheese, paper-thin ham over cantaloupe canoes, spaghetti that tasted like the ocean. Once, when Ed-guh was a baby, Mrs. Feen had let Toni-Ann hold him—and ever since then, she'd loved him best.

Of course, that was when things got bad for the Feens. After the baby came, Mr. Feen started to shout a lot, and he was always wandering around the yard like he'd lost his keys. When he'd finally gone away for good, the Feens pretty much stopped talking to Toni-Ann—though Flow-rinse would always send over a box of tomatoes in the summer.

The priest had said that Flow-rinse would watch over them now. Toni-Ann pictured a slow-moving blimp circling the neighborhood. But whenever she looked up at the sky, all she ever saw were birds or airplanes or clouds—and none of them had the right face.

26
Egg

Frank Fini buys the gun on a Tuesday morning. He pays cash, handing it directly to his cousin Vincenzo, who deals in small to midsized firearms—a business he conducts from the back of a motorcycle shop. There's no paperwork, no application forms, it's easy. Frank tells Vincenzo that he needs to protect his family—and Vincenzo nods, licks a blackened thumb to count the money. He's never liked Frankie (too handsome, too smart, too lucky—married that sexy Polack, who Vincenzo still hopes to screw one day). "You want me to load it for you?" he asks, and Frank says, "Please."

Vincenzo sees that his cousin's hands are shaking and how his eyes dart around the room. "If you're in trouble," Vincenzo says, "I don't want to know."

Frank says nothing, and takes the gun.

When he gets home, Florence is scrubbing the dishes. She speaks over her shoulder, telling him the baby is sleeping.

"Wash your hands, Frankie, and I'll make you a sandwich."

"No," he says. "I have a . . ." He gestures vaguely toward his belly.

"Have a ginger ale," Florence says. "You want a ginger ale?"

Frank can tell that she's afraid of him, the way she repeats herself.

"I'll pour you a ginger ale," she says as he's walking away.

Sometimes, he's afraid of her, too—this woman who sneaks garlic into sick children's ears and sprinkles holy water on her garden.

Upstairs, he peers into the crib and watches the alien form of his son— the white face twitching with visions. It occurs to him that this newborn has been with him forever, watching, taking notes. Frank feels ashamed— and worries how he'll be remembered. When he looks at the gun, it seems impossible now. He doesn't want to leave his family yet. In the closet he unzips the plastic cover that protects his old wedding tux, hides the gun in the left pocket of the jacket. Later he'll put it somewhere safer, somewhere he might forget.

Besides, it's not the only way.

When Lucy gets home from work, he fucks her quietly on the floor beside the crib—and then the three of them sleep for nearly two hours, until Florence wakes them for dinner. There's ricotta cheesecake. Pio pours sambuca into everyone's coffee; he's in a good mood, having won two hundred bucks this morning with a Pick 6 lottery ticket. The dollar-store banner (I JUST GOT PROMOTED TO GRANDPA!) still hangs in the kitchen.

Later, Florence brings three slices of cheesecake to the Heftis, to thank Mary for the egg (she'd been one short for her recipe). Mary asks how things are, and Florence, still flushed from the sambuca, says they couldn't be better.

Frank, who'd barely touched his dinner, sits on the porch until nearly two in the morning. Lucy stays with him the whole time, stroking his neck. Her touch is the only thing that still works. "Don't stop," he says.

She doesn't.

It's cold outside; they're wearing coats.

"We'll figure it out," he says, staring at the sky. He points to her star and she smiles.

She tells him how much she's been saving up in tips.

Every now and then he turns toward her, and they kiss.

27

Harvest

The man stopped the truck at the corner of Cressida and Laurel, claiming it would be better if the boy arrived home by foot. "That way you won't get in trouble."

At first the comment confused Edgar, but then he realized the man was right. If anyone had done something wrong, it was himself, for imposing on the kindness of a stranger. It wasn't the man's job to take care of his stupid finger. "I'm sorry if I bothered you."

"Not at all," the man said. "Bother me anytime. If you want, I can give you my number."

He'd been debating whether or not to take this risk. Not that he wanted to do anything more than talk to the boy again—and maybe, one day, to drive him to the house where the other boy had been, just to see what that would feel like. "Let me just . . ." The man fished a pen from the ashtray. "Do you have a piece of paper?"

Edgar felt inside his pocket. He pulled out the stray grocery list he'd found on the street (*Eggs, Tampons, Frosting*). He'd been carrying it around for days, still imagining it might be some kind of message from Florence.

For Kev, the man wrote at the bottom. When he put down the numbers, he proceeded slowly, making sure his fours looked like fours, instead of nines. His wife had always said that his penmanship was worse than a doctor's.

"You mentioned something about a cemetery," the man said. "I could maybe take you there sometime. If you want."

The boy shrugged, but the man felt encouraged by how carefully the kid folded the telephone number—so carefully, in fact, that he seemed to be performing a magic trick.

"I just"—the boy blushed—"I don't like it when the folds mess up the writing."

"Yes," the man said. "You're very clever."

* * *

Edgar hesitated by the hydrangea, wondering how he'd explain the fresh bandage to his mother. Also, he wanted to understand what Mrs. Hefti was up to. Her yard had been raked clean of fallen leaves—but now she was standing on a stepladder, actually *picking* the remaining leaves from the lower branches of a small tree.

"Stubborn," she said, noticing Edgar. "Stupid things won't fall."

She picked a few more. "Be a doll and take these from me, would you?" Edgar came closer to receive a handful of blazing leaves. "Better to get them off the tree now, before they make a mess. You can put them right there in that plastic bag, dear."

"Can I keep this one?" asked Edgar, holding up a particularly stunning specimen—a five-pointed beauty whose mottled reds and yellows made the leaf seem as if it had been plucked out of a sunset.

"Be my guest. They are pretty, I'll give 'em that. Toni-Ann always wants to save them, too. Puts them in water, like they were flowers."

Edgar planned to give the rescued leaf to his mother. It was only fair to forgive her for her meanness (digging through his grandmother's purse; trying to throw out the braid of hair, not to mention the Virgin's head). The truth was, he'd been mean to her, too (telling her that she didn't really love Florence). The leaf would be an apology. He'd give it to her and then the two of them could start the day over. Maybe they could drive to Van-Dervoort Park to see the swans.

Edgar stopped at the bottom of the front steps, noticing something in the rhododendrons. The tip of whatever it was stuck out from the green leaves like a snout—a small, shining cylinder. Kneeling on the pavement, Edgar reached for it—then gasped.

It was a boy's pee-pee. Well, no, not a boy's at all—it was extremely large, made of rubber or plastic. Edgar's mind flashed to the images on Jarell Lester's phone. *Supersluts.com.*

The boy wondered if someone were playing a joke on him. He turned and peered about the yard in case Thomas and Jarell were hiding in the bushes.

The coast seemed clear, and so he examined the oversized appendage more closely, wondering if his own thing would look like this one day. He knew that it had to get big to make babies. But *this* big? He'd need longer legs. Sometimes it seemed ridiculous to have a body; why couldn't people be more like clams, with all their soft stuff hidden under a shell? Edgar grimaced. It would've been nice if there were someone he could talk to about this kind of thing. It was probably for situations like this that most boys had fathers.

As he turned the dildo around, it suddenly began to vibrate. He could feel the tremors travel up his arm and hum through his entire body. It was kind of funny, actually, the way the thing was wriggling in his hand like a charmed cobra. *Waaa waaa waaa* went the little motor, and the snake rolled its head as if it were drunk. Edgar laughed and let his body go slack. For a moment all worries vanished from his mind. He even barked—a sound he'd not made since the night he'd watched his mother get ready for her date with the butcher.

But today his mother was staying at home. He'd have her to himself. He stood, shut off the penis, and stuffed it into his pocket, using his shirt to cover the several inches that remained exposed. He pushed at the taped front door and ran into the house.

"Ma?" He adjusted himself a bit. "Ma! I'm back!"

*   *   *

Lucy was kneeling in the garden, a smear of dirt across her cheek. She'd found nothing.

What did she expect? A love letter, a box of chocolates, an explanation? She was a fool to have made any effort at all. Frank had left nothing because that's all there was. She felt a wave of nausea and vomited into one of the holes.

She was empty now—a sensation that was strangely hopeful. For the first time in her life she had no fear of death. She'd already died in that other story, hadn't she—so fuck it. She stood, wiped her filthy hands across her chest, dragged her thoughts back to Earth: a beer, a shower. She'd been maudlin for too many days, and she wasn't going to let herself get sucked back into something that was finished. She kicked a clod of dirt from her shoe so hard it flew against the back wall of the house.

Maybe she and Edgar could sell the place and drive away. Really drive away this time, though. Start again.

If that was the plan, she had a lot to do. Fix the front door, call a Realtor. But first she'd give the kid his pill, change his bandage. Get him some dinner. Edgar liked Old Peking. She'd order from there.

"Hey, buddy," she said, because there he was. He had a bright red leaf in his hand and a pornographic bulge in his pants.

"Hey," the boy said happily. "I brought you a—"

He stopped, taking in the state of the yard, the shovel resting on the ground beside his mother. There was a big hole in the middle of the lawn, some smaller ones by the trees, but the most terrible thing was the tomato patch. His grandmother's plants had been completely dug out of the ground and were lying in a tangled heap, their dirt-clodded roots horribly exposed like giant chicken feet.

Edgar was speechless. He touched his stomach.

"Don't shoot me," Lucy said. "I can explain."

Tears came to Edgar's eyes.

"You could have waited." The leaf in his hand fluttered to the ground.

Lucy knelt down in front of the boy and hugged him. "I'm sorry."

At her touch, Edgar's tears came in earnest.

"It's okay. It's okay, baby." As Lucy pulled him closer, she felt the disconcerting hardness in his pants. "What is that?" she asked, moving her hand toward it.

"Nothing," said Edgar, pulling away. He wiped his nose, adjusted his shirt. "It's mine."

28

Biggleberry Island

Egg-Flower Soup. Szechwan String Beans. Triple-Delight Chicken. Edgar requested chopsticks, but then used them like tweezers, eating one grain of rice at a time.

After the meal he sat quietly, tracing with his finger the embroidered outline of a fleur-de-lis on the tablecloth. When Lucy offered him her fortune cookie, he eyed her suspiciously. "You don't want it?"

"I know you like them."

Edgar cracked both open and, as he nibbled, slowly warmed to his mother. "Fortunes?" she said. "You wanna read them to me?"

Edgar shrugged and picked up the tiny scrolls. " 'Success is made of ten thousand little pains.' "

"Ow," said Lucy. "What about the other one?"

" 'Soon new addition to your family.' "

"Ow," Lucy said again—and this time Edgar smiled.

"You can have one if you want." He held out the fortunes toward his mother, success in his left hand and the new addition in his right.

Lucy declined. She'd begun to trace a fleur-de-lis herself, as if it were the other end of a telephone by which she might better communicate with her son.

"Do you like it around here?" she asked, tossing off the question as breezily as possible.

"Around where?"

"This town. This house." Lucy gestured dismissively. "All of it."

Edgar was still chewing on a fortune cookie. "Yes," he said tentatively. "I like it."

The truth was, he wasn't really sure. So much had changed lately.

"Why?" he asked.

"I don't know. Just curious," Lucy said. "Just curious."

Edgar could tell his mother was in a mood. When she repeated herself, it meant she was having thoughts. "Do *you* like it here?" he asked her.

"Not really," she replied.

Edgar felt a flutter of panic.

"I mean, I like *you*," she said.

Edgar traced the fleur-de-lis harder. He didn't care for this conversation; it was making him sad again. "Do you want to watch TV?" he said.

"Or we can rent a movie?" suggested Lucy.

"*Predator*," Edgar said immediately. "There's a new one."

"No, that gives you nightmares."

It was true, but he still wanted to see it. "We can just fast-forward when the monster is feasting."

* * *

At the rental box there were no copies of the new *Predator,* and Lucy chose a well-reviewed romantic comedy about a group of extremely fat women who visit a magical island in hope of becoming skinny.

Lucy, drinking beer as she watched, was unimpressed. It turned out that the magic was learning to love one's self. In another move of stunning implausibility that made Lucy mutter, *Are you fucking kidding me?*—an international conference center on another part of the island was hosting a group of overworked wealthy men in candy-colored Bermuda shorts. Summer-camp hookups led to moonlit walks and poolside betrayals, and ultimately to a large group wedding. Even as Lucy rolled her eyes through most of *Biggleberry Island,* she kept reaching under her T-shirt to test her belly fat.

Despite her padding, Lucy was still a beauty. But, because no man had said so lately—at least not directly to her face—she felt distinctly in need of a few shimmering pink biggleberries. Even Ron, who seemed to like her curves, would eventually crave something more miniature. No way was she going to let the butcher seduce her, only to betray her later. She shifted position on the couch. It would have been more relaxing to have watched *Predator,* and seen skinny women being eaten alive.

Edgar enjoyed it, though. He laughed innocently at the fat jokes. The women's puffy ankles reminded him of Florence. At the end of the movie, he had another minor attack of tears—which Lucy treated by attempting to divert the boy's attention.

"Oh, your bandage!" she said. "Let's change it."

"It's already changed." He held up his hand.

"Oh," Lucy said, confused. "Who—"

"I did it myself," Edgar said quickly.

"That must have been hard."

"It was."

Lucy winced. "How'd it look? Your finger."

"I've seen worse," said Edgar.

"Okay, well, we see the doctor on Thursday."

"Wednesday," corrected Edgar. "The appointment card is on the refrigerator."

Lucy craved another beer. "Probably time for your pill, sweetie."

Edgar glanced at the clock. "Not yet. In one hour I can take it. You can only take so many a day."

Lucy tried to smile. "You know everything, huh?"

"No. Not *everything*."

"More than me, apparently."

Edgar shrugged.

"Biggleberry," Lucy said, but Edgar didn't laugh.

"It's not really funny," he said.

"What's not funny?"

"Fat people." His thoughts had returned to Florence. "They were *her* tomatoes."

"Enough on the tomatoes. I said I'm sorry."

"What were you looking for?"

"Treasure," said Lucy. "*Gold.*"

"But I gave it to you already. I gave you *all* of it. She didn't put any money in the backyard."

"You know what, Edgar? You really don't know everything."

"I know I don't. That's what I *said*."

"Okay, I think someone's tired."

"I'm not at all tired. I'm the opposite of tired."

She touched the boy's face, brushing his bangs to the side of his forehead.

Edgar bristled. "The next time you give me a haircut, Ma, you have to do a better job."

"Do I really?"

"Yes. You need to do it shorter, so I look more like me."

"What does that mean?"

"More like a boy. I don't want people to be confused."

"Who's confused?" Lucy pushed her son's hair behind his ears. "I like how you look with your hair like this."

"But you know me," he said. "What if you didn't know me?"

"Hard to imagine."

"But try. If you saw me on the street and you didn't know me. Or like if you had a store, and I came into your store."

Lucy closed her eyes and leaned back on the couch. Sometimes he exhausted her. "I don't know, Edgar. I'd just think you were Edgar."

"No, but I'm saying if you didn't *know* Edgar. I mean, if I wasn't *your* Edgar. Say I belonged to someone else. Like if I had a different name and everything."

Lucy laughed nervously. "Where's the switch?"

"To what?"

"Your *brain*."

"No, but really. Pretend you didn't know me, Ma. What would you think?"

"You know, it wouldn't kill you to take your pill a little early."

"Don't change the subject."

"I just don't want you to get wound up before bed."

"It's not even bedtime. Where are you going?"

"I'm getting your medicine."

"It's not time."

"Half a pill. You'll feel better."

"I don't feel bad—and you're not a doctor, Ma. You're not even a nurse. You're not even *married* to a nurse."

"*Stop it,*" Lucy said. "Do you hear me?"

"What am I doing?"

"You can't just let your mind go wherever it fucking wants. You have to control it, Edgar."

"I am in control. What I was saying is very *logical. If* you didn't know me. It's *hypothetical.*"

Lucy shook her head and went into the kitchen, straight to the refrigerator. She opened the freezer and stared at the bottle of vodka. Sometimes the boy's anxious intelligence reminded her of Frank.

Edgar appeared in the doorway. "Are we mad at each other?"

"You know what, Edgar—you do look like a girl. Get a towel, and get my scissors from upstairs."

"Now?"

Lucy closed the freezer door. "Or you wanna wait?"

"No," Edgar said bravely. "Now is good."

* * *

Afterwards, he stared at himself in the mirror. His mother had started with scissors, but then she'd taken up the electric clippers. He was all head now, topped with a short dense bristle.

The boy had said nothing while his mother removed a polar bear of white fluff. She'd been silent, too—serious. Though she'd caused him no physical pain, Edgar sensed that she was angry—that, under the pretext of cutting his hair, her real motive was to cut the thoughts from his head. She hadn't liked it at all when he'd suggested that there might be two Edgars—one of whom she might not know. When she was finished cutting, she'd swept up the hair— but instead of putting it in the garden, as Florence would have done, she'd opened the cabinet under the sink and thrown Edgar's thoughts into the trash.

It was odd: even with a crew cut, he still didn't look completely like a boy. Something about the cheekbones, the lips, the corn-silk eyelashes beating time over the sea-glass eyes. He looked like a girl *playing* a boy. Somehow, the haircut only increased his androgyny. Before, he would have been more quickly pegged as a girl. Now, he existed more disconcertingly between the poles.

* * *

Lucy sits on the couch to make a phone call—the bottle of vodka sweating on the table in front of her. Edgar leaves her alone. He swipes a photograph from the top of the piano and brings it up to his room.

Using the mirror, he conducts a test: his face beside the face of his father—who's seventeen and grinning under a tasseled cap. Even with long hair, his father is clearly a man. What makes it so? Edgar goes back and forth between the photo and his own face, but fails to solve the mystery—why similar elements (similar nose, similar ears, similar brow) have conspired toward masculinity in the one, and against it in the other.

Edgar wonders what his father looks like now; if he's changed a lot. He only knows him from blurry photographs and he wonders if he'd recognize him if he saw him on the street.

Maybe he's already seen him. Mr. Levinson, Edgar's science teacher, said a dead person's hair continues to grow. And so it wasn't impossible, scientifically speaking, that a dead person might have a beard—even if he'd left the world without one.

* * *

Lucy's still on hold. She's called the Friendship Hook and Ladder Company and asked for William. "I think he's playing pinball," another fireman comes on the line to tell her. "Let me dig him up."

As she waits, she can hear the sounds of the station: men laughing, forks against plates, a television, a dog. She can picture the place—brightly lit, convivial, the men slapping each other's backs or throwing mock punches; someone sliding down the fire pole in boxer shorts. She wonders if they have private rooms.

"Yup," a voice says.

"William?"

"Yeah. Who's this?"

"Lucy. We, uh . . . you came to my house the other day, for the fire. Well, there wasn't a fire but . . . anyway I just thought—"

"What was the address?"

"Cressida Drive."

"Yesterday, you said?"

"Lucy," Lucy says, somewhat irritated. "The redhead?"

"Oh, fuck, yeah . . . the one with the kid, right?"

"Yes."

"Right on. No, no, I'm glad you called."

"You said to give you a ring, so . . ."

"Right on. Absolutely."

It's awkward—he sounds sixteen. Easier if they'd just run into each other at a bar, already a little oiled.

"No, no," William says. "I definitely remember you."

Lucy hears more laughter in the background—and she suddenly imagines the other men gesturing to William, something crude, and William gesturing back in the same way.

"I'm off at midnight," he says. "Where are you?"

"I'm at—home," Lucy says, the word catching in her throat.

"Cressida near Laurel, right?"

"Yes, but . . . I have to go, I'm sorry."

"Are we on, though? You want me to pop by when I'm done?"

"You know, I just realized I have to . . . can I call you later?"

"Why don't you just text me?" the boy says, sounding annoyed. "Before eleven-thirty so I know what's up."

"It's just that I have the kid here. I can probably get a sitter tomorrow and meet you at Mickey's or . . ."

"Yeah, just text me."

Lucy hangs up the phone and reaches for the bottle of vodka. She presses it to her forehead—the iciness doing little to numb the feeling of foolishness. She senses herself growing fatter and fatter, an overweight joke with big tits. What's happening to her?

Slippage. Frank's word comes at her out of nowhere. When the doorbell rings, she doesn't hear it.

It rings again.

"Lucy!"

She starts, jumping from the couch. Someone's pounding on the door.

"Luceee!"

Shit, she thinks, hearing in the raspy shout the fury of her father. No doubt he's been brewing ever since being kicked out of Florence's wake. What does he want, though? Once, as a child, he'd broken her wrist. Sometimes she still dreams about his drunken rages.

"Edgar," she shouts from the hallway. "Stay upstairs and lock your door." She picks up a marble ashtray and moves toward the foyer.

* * *

Edgar is lying in Florence's bed when he hears the car. Out the window, he sees it parked crookedly at the curb, sees the words painted on the side. *Let us MEAT your needs!*

Edgar panics as the butcher lumbers from the van. The only lock on the front door is a strip of duct tape—and his mother is downstairs alone.

He rushes about the room, wondering what to grab. On Florence's vanity he sees the bottle of Chanel N° 5. He could throw some in the man's eyes—though it would be a shame to waste the stuff.

He picks up the headless Virgin and runs downstairs.

* * *

Lucy leans against the broken door. "I have a gun," she lies.

"I just want to talk," the man says.

"Ron?"

Lucy peels back the duct tape and opens the door—the ashtray still held above her head. "What the fuck are you doing here?"

The butcher's a mess, obviously drunk. His half-opened shirt shows a plunging triangle of dense black curls. He stumbles forward.

"Don't," Lucy says. "You can't come in."

The butcher leans against the door frame. "Why don't you ever answer your phone?"

"I'm busy, Ron."

"Busy? Too busy for *this*?"—he moves his meaty hand in the space between himself and Lucy.

"What?" Lucy snaps. "What is 'this'?"

"This," the butcher says again—the gesture of his hand more forceful now. *"Us."*

"Us?" Lucy parrots. Her only defense against sadness is cruelty. She laughs in the man's face.

"What we did and everything," the butcher says. He paws his hairy chest, as if remembering Lucy's touch. "Just how we . . ."

"We had sex, Ron. We fucked."

"I know." He looks up at her as if she's named the source of all things. His eyes are hopeful.

Lucy is frightened and makes a move to shut the door.

The butcher moans and forces it back open. Lucy's been in spots like this before. She brandishes the ashtray.

"What are you gonna do? You gonna hit me?" The man pushes his way into the house.

Edgar screams from the dark at the bottom of the stairs, and Lucy drops the ashtray.

The butcher squints his eyes, but he can't locate the child in the gloom. "I'm not gonna hurt her," he says to an invisible Edgar. He holds up his arms. "I'm not gonna hurt your mom. I love her." He snatches Lucy's hand. *"I love you."*

It's worse than she could have imagined.

"Shit," he slurs. "I don't know."

"Ron—" Lucy tries to pull her hand away.

"You're so fucking beautiful, you're fucking amazing. And I just think we can like . . . *be* together."

With a scoff, Lucy reclaims her hand. Who wrote this man's material? It reminds her of the lies she'd told herself once—romantic bullshit. She can barely stand to look at him.

Edgar, on the other hand, watches mesmerized as the butcher confesses his love to Lucy—saying the exact things that Edgar often wished to say. Except he didn't know that it was allowed to say this kind of stuff, especially to a person like his mother. She hated mushiness. How was it possible that this horrible giant could be stealing Edgar's words—and even Edgar's tears? Because the giant's crying now; his voice grows softer. "Beautiful, and *fuck*, I just wanna, I don't know, like take care of shit . . . like a promise and everything."

"Ron, *shhhh.*"

Edgar watches as his mother reaches out the hand she's just won back and uses it to lightly touch the Chia Pet of the butcher's chest.

The man closes his eyes and moans. He places his watermelon of a head on Lucy's shoulder, giving her a kiss that travels slowly toward her ear.

"Mom?"

"It's okay, Edgar. Go upstairs."

The boy steps into the light so she'll remember him. "I can stay with you," he says quietly.

But Lucy doesn't seem to hear him.

"Mom, I can stay with you."

The butcher turns his head away to give the woman and her son some privacy.

"I'm fine," says Lucy. "Mr. S and I are just gonna talk."

"*Talk,*" the butcher slurs, nodding.

"I'm gonna sleep in *her* room," Edgar says with an edge of threat.

But Lucy only tells him, that's fine, and to keep the door shut, and to take half a pill if he feels any pain at all. And then she kisses him on the top of his head.

*   *   *

He can hear them now. They sound like animals. If that's what lonely people did, he wants no part of it. From what he understands, though, he was made from something like this. But with a different man—and a long time ago.

I came out of *her* belly, Edgar thinks. Sometimes the thought makes him happy, and sometimes sad.

Tonight it makes him angry.

But maybe he deserves what his mother's done. Because, for a long time, he'd chosen someone else, too. Someone other than his mother.

"Nana," the boy whispers—using the name he called her when he was little.

He says it again—and when she doesn't answer, he tries not to cry. He picks up a rubber alien from his desk, but then puts it down and moves toward the closet. Inside, at the back, he crawls behind the trunk that holds his winter sweaters. It's a tight fit, but that's why he likes to lie there when he's upset. The pressure calms him down. He snakes his arm into his pocket and pulls out the little pink pill he's stashed there.

With these berries I conspire.
Give me the one thing I desire.

The words from the movie come back to him.

Though what *did* he desire? He didn't really need to get skinnier; he was skinny enough. If he ate a biggleberry he might disappear completely.

He swallows the pill without water. A terrible bitterness lingers on his tongue.

In the dark he moves his hand around until he finds the penlight he keeps at the back of the closet. He clicks it on and directs the yellow beam toward the rack of clothing above him. He pulls down the red quilted jacket. From the breast pocket, he removes the little piece of paper.

When he steps into the hallway, he takes the headless Virgin with him. In his grandmother's room he sits on her bed and looks at the grocery list. *Eggs, Tampons, Frosting*—followed now by ten numbers. He hesitates only briefly before picking up the telephone.

BOOK FIVE

THE PINE BARRENS

I like children. If they're properly cooked.

—W. C. FIELDS

29

The Seventh Day

Edgar had been missing for six days when Lucy discovered she was pregnant. Though she'd felt nauseous for weeks, she'd assumed it was stress. The recent jolts had been significant: Florence's death, Frank's letter, followed by the sickening vertigo of Edgar's disappearance. But when her period failed to arrive, she immediately understood that the universe's plot to destroy her was far more intricate than she could have imagined. A peed-upon test strip confirmed her condition.

How could this be happening? One baby was gone; another was on the way. It seemed a cruel trick, a sinister fold in the grid of time. Edgar wasn't here, but every morning she woke overcome by the same physical sensations she'd experienced when pregnant with him.

In the matter of the larger concern, the police had wasted no time—though their reaction was not as militant as Lucy would have liked. They'd contacted the school, the hospitals; Edgar's image had been disseminated to other law-enforcement agencies; there'd been an unsuccessful local search. During a forty-five-minute interview with a young, granny-bunned detective, Lucy had felt—largely in response to the woman's manner—like she'd been called to the principal's office. As if the situation were somehow *her* fault!

It was true, she'd been slightly lit when she'd arrived at the station (a few late-afternoon beers while waiting for Edgar to come home from school, and then a few more when he didn't show; it had been after six when she'd finally contacted the police). Every question from the female officer seemed expertly designed to poke a hole in the lifeboat of Lucy's wave-tossed existence.

The boy's relationship to his father?

Any problems or changes at home? At school?

Suspicious behavior on the child's part?

New friends or adults in his life?

Psychological issues? Peculiar mannerisms?

In responding, Lucy had felt cornered, and had softened the truth when she felt it to have no bearing on the situation or to be none of the woman's business. "I'm a good mother," she'd said defensively at one point. "I'm sure you are, Mrs. Fini," the woman said. "We're not questioning that." When she asked if Edgar had taken anything with him, like a toothbrush or clothing, Lucy said she'd have to check. "Why is that important?"

"Children run away," the woman had replied, as if she were saying *birds fly* or *dogs bark.* Ultimately, Lucy had been told it was just a matter of waiting. "They often turn up in a few days."

"And if they don't?"

"Then we'll get concerned."

"I'm concerned now," Lucy said. "I'm not gonna just sit on my ass and wait."

"Of course not. While we do our job, there's a lot you can do, too." At which point, the woman pushed forward a batch of stapled pages with a pale blue cover: *For Parents of Missing Children: An Informational Overview.* There was a teddy bear in the upper left corner and a bicycle in the upper right—childless relics floating like pieces of space junk.

Lucy's heart had caved. "Oh God."

"But think how easy he'll be to spot," the woman said, reaching across the table to pat Lucy's hand. "Not every child is so distinctive."

* * *

Tip number one: start in your own house. Look everywhere. Under all beds, tables, piles of laundry; inside storage chests, closets, car trunks. Check doghouses and large appliances; under raked leaves or shoveled snow, depending on the season. Don't consider any place unlikely. If a child might fit, even if it seems a tight squeeze: LOOK!

* * *

The first night Edgar was gone, Lucy tore apart the house. In the backyard she looked under single leaves, as if Edgar had somehow managed to reduce himself to the size of a beetle. She went into his closet and sat on the floor.

When they come, if they come to hurt you, they will look like anyone, you will think you know them. Sitting in the closet, Lucy regretted burning Frank's letter, thinking it might contain clues. She barely checked her logic when it struck her that Frank might be responsible for Edgar's disappearance.

Later, Lucy discovered that the Virgin's head was gone, as well as two tubes of sunscreen and the boy's bottle of pills. There also seemed to be a photo missing from the top of the piano.

"That's good," the woman at the police station said when Lucy mentioned the items. "That helps us rule out certain things."

"Don't rule out anything," Lucy replied. "What are you ruling out?"

The woman paused. Never use the word *abduction,* her superior had told her. "Packed items," she informed Lucy, "suggest premeditation."

"I already told you. He's not the runaway type."

"You'd be surprised what goes on in kids' minds. We'll do another search by the school tomorrow. And we'd also like to take another look at your house. Ten-thirty okay?"

"Fine," said Lucy.

"If you could have an article of Edgar's clothing handy, that would be great. Preferably something unwashed."

"Dogs?" Lucy asked, her voice rising a notch. "Are you using dogs?"

"Yes," the woman said flatly. It wasn't something she liked telling parents.

"Bloodhounds?"

"No," the woman replied. "German shepherds."

* * *

"*German shepherds?*" the butcher said. "Are you kidding me? German shepherds are crap, they need to use hounds." Ron was now the self-appointed expert; he'd done some research, made some calls. Lucy was grateful for his help. In addition to everything he was doing to assist in the search, he'd found time to take care of a few things at the house. Already he'd fixed the front door, raked the yard, scraped and repainted the burnt wall in the old woman's bedroom. Lucy had laid out drop cloths, and while Ron painted she'd put a number of Florence's possessions into a box (the blackened wedding photo, the night-light with the angel and the bridge, the blue glass votive cups, the body of the Virgin). At first, she'd planned to throw these things out, but then she'd thought of Edgar. With a black marker she wrote *Florence* on the top of the box before setting it at the back of a closet. Afterwards, the butcher helped to rehang the old woman's dresses the boy had piled on the bed.

Of course, Lucy recognized that it might be unwise to let Ron spend time at the house. Edgar wasn't a fan. *What if the butcher was the reason the boy had run away?* Even as Lucy thought this, she was conscious of the thought's attempt to shift blame off herself. Still, the idea of Ron's culpability offered some relief. There were only so many hours a day a person could condemn herself before she wanted to rip off her own head. Lucy drank a lot of beer.

* * *

Take good care of yourself. Your child needs you to be strong. As hard as it may be, force yourself to rest, eat nourishing food, and talk to someone about your tumultuous feelings. Don't be afraid to ask others to take care of your physical or emotional needs.

* * *

Ron was still babbling about the dogs. ". . . sixty times the tracking power. Plus, a bloodhound can pick up the scent in the air as well as on the ground. So, say if Edgar was, like, *carried* or—"

"Ron, *stop*—they're using German shepherds. What am I supposed to do, pull some bloodhounds out of my ass?"

"I'll call ALFJ tomorrow," he said. He'd been using a lot of acronyms lately. ACIM, NCIC, NCMEC. The police had issued a BOLO. Lucy found none of this comforting. One morning, on the pad by the phone, she'd seen the telephone number 1–800–THE–LOST.

Feeling a wave of nausea, she dashed toward the bathroom.

"Are you okay?" the butcher said.

"Nerves," said Lucy—still unaware, at this point, that she was pregnant.

For the first few nights, Lucy slept no more than an hour or two. She found herself going through the dark house with a flashlight—as if a small beam trained on the blackness might be the best way to find something that was hiding. Turning on all the lights would only frighten hope, which seemed, to Lucy, a timid thing. When she took her daily walk between the house and Edgar's school, the butcher sometimes came with her, hanging a hand-made sign on the door of his shop. FAMILY EMERGENCY.

* * *

When the Ferryfield Police conducted its first search at 21 Cressida Drive, it had been cursory, little more than a formality—since, in the opinion of Rebecca Mann, the inexperienced search coordinator who'd interviewed the mother, the situation seemed nothing more than the obvious: a careless, self-involved parent and a sensitive, confused—now runaway—child. Very likely, the boy was still mourning the loss of his paternal grandmother—with whom, from all accounts but the mother's, the child had been quite close. When Ms. Mann had visited the school, the boy's science teacher, Daniel Levinson, had showed her a morbidly obsessive paper handed in by Edgar only days before his disappearance. The boy seemed to be fixated on dead people. *Check cemetery,* Ms. Mann mental-noted to herself. *Is father buried there, too?*

The more Rebecca Mann thought about it, the more she was certain she'd find the boy in a day or two, with a tear-stained face and a melted candy bar in his pocket. A quiet child, as she herself had been, he was very likely acting out by hiding from his mother—if not at the cemetery, then perhaps in the wooded area behind the house. Nothing she'd learned at the boy's school or from neighbors had led her to believe she was dealing with anything worse. Still, an eight-year-old runaway was a legitimate concern. She wasn't taking any of this lightly. Rebecca Mann was a serious woman.

When the mother had first brought in photos of the child, as requested, Ms. Mann assumed they were overexposed. She'd sighed audibly at what she considered yet another example of the mother's inadequacy; but then she recalled the child's congenital disorder. Now, Ms. Mann had one of the photos of the angelically pale boy on her bulletin board. She felt a surprising amount of affection for him. He was her first missing child.

After several days, when Edgar still hadn't been found, Ms. Mann jumped up the search and investigation. She held to her hunch that the mother lay at the root of the problem. A second, more penetrating excavation of 21 Cressida Drive, though revealing no evidence of foul play, did bring up some oddities. An electric dildo in the boy's sock drawer; a sketch pad featuring eccentric doodles, including flying teacups and numerous studies of men with beards. Ms. Mann picked up a pig-person made of modeling clay into which the child had stuck a tiny plastic sword. A search of the boy's computer revealed only a single visit to a porn site—a surprisingly low number these days, even for an eight-year-old. *Supersluts,* Ms. Mann jotted into her notebook. Other recently visited pages included several offering recipes for meatballs; a "How to Draw Fruit" video tutorial; and the Wikipedia listing for Mount Vesuvius. An alien abduction website, GreenRabbit.com, over-flowing with first-person accounts ranging from the horrific to the sublime, had received the most hits.

"He seems like a very interesting young man," Ms. Mann said later, to Lucy. And then, not flinching from her practiced smile: "It would be great if you could come down to the station this afternoon, and we can chat more. And maybe we'll have you take a finger-flutter test."

"A what?" asked Lucy.

"It's what we use now instead of a polygraph. Just standard procedure." A dildo, a stuck pig, the broken front door, now shoddily repaired with plywood—not to mention the collection of beer bottles scattered around the house and the fact that the mother couldn't even remember what the child was wearing on the day of his disappearance. Ms. Mann had suspicions. "Why don't you come to the station at four," she said to Lucy.

Phone records had revealed one item of interest: a call made from the house's landline to a temporary, disposable cell. Untraceable. The mother didn't rec-ognize the number—and when checked against the woman's address book, as well as the grandmother's, still no match was found. The number had been called only once; the night before the child's disappearance.

The boy didn't have a cell. "How do you keep track of him?" Ms. Mann had asked, and Lucy had stammered, "Some-someone else used to do that. I'm just, uh . . . it was on my list of things to do."

The German shepherds, middle-aged sisters Nora and Dora, had found nothing. But now it seemed that Ms. Mann was going to have to initiate another sniff-search. The mother's buttinski boyfriend had contacted a na-tional organization for missing persons—and a few hours before Mrs. Fini's scheduled polygraph, representatives of the national organization arrived like prophets: stepping out of a white van, wearing white sweatshirts, flanked by two enormous bloodhounds. The depressed-looking animals seemed ridicu-lous in white collars embossed with the same gold letters that emblazoned the representatives' sweatshirts: ALFJ (A Light for Jimmy), named for the boy who'd made the organization famous, Jimmy Papadakis, a politician's four-year-old son. He'd been found after a seventeen-week search, miraculously alive at the bottom of a drainage ditch (the ditch had contained a shallow pool of potable water and a sustaining scum of blue-green algae). Jimmy was now twenty-nine, a vegetarian, and a salaried spokesperson for the organization.

Ms. Mann didn't believe in miracles; she believed in a job well done. A job she could handle on her own. She was not, by nature, collaborative. Plus, ALFJ had a history of stirring up a storm, making a national circus out of small-town tragedies to promote its own name. Still, she agreed to the blood-hounds and sincerely hoped for the best. It had been three days already, and if they didn't find Edgar soon, she knew—even if ALFJ liked to pretend otherwise—the light of hope dimmed considerably.

"It's better if you don't come with us, Mrs. Fini."

The bloodhounds were in the boy's bedroom, sniffing one of his T-shirts. They sniffed his bed, his sneakers; they sniffed the pale blue carpet across which his tiny feet had rasped, countless times, to produce small sparks of electricity. The dogs became full of Edgar. He became their sole reality—a promise, a being undoubtedly wonderful to lick. The dogs now longed for him as much as anyone.

On the lawn in front of the house they tried to pick up a scent they could follow. The creatures looked confused and kept returning to Edgar's T-shirt in the hands of the houndsman. "Give them a minute," he said. "They're two of our best."

Hopeless, Ms. Mann thought—too much time had passed. But then one of the dogs stiffened, his nostrils flaring. It was obvious he'd picked up some-thing in the air. "Oh my God," Lucy cried. "Is that him?" She moved toward the empty space where both dogs were now sniffing.

"Could be," said the houndsman. And now the dogs were moving with visible purpose around the side of the house. "Yes, yes," the man said. "We've got him."

Lucy faltered, and Ron held her.

"Keep her here," Ms. Mann said to the butcher.

"No," Lucy said, crying now, following the dogs, who were following Edgar, some part of him she couldn't see.

"*Really*," Ms. Mann said with some force. "You need to stay here."

"Lucy," Ron said, stopping her—and Ms. Mann, too, touched Lucy, add-ing with some gentleness: "You don't want to confuse the dogs. Let them do their job. Okay?"

In the yard, Ms. Mann watched the fierce determination of the animals as they circled three times a mound of dead tomato plants, then headed off into the trees at the back of the property. In the woods, the dogs barked and yanked the houndsman forward. Ms. Mann's heart raced, pumping into her body equal doses of dread and hope. She didn't want to fail—and as the animals moved across the ground, following an emptiness that had the grandeur of faith, the detective experienced a wave of gratitude toward the eerily sensitive beasts.

Through the trees, over beds of fallen leaves; past scattered acorns, chestnuts, pinecones, rooms of light and shadow, and finally emerging again onto pavement. Onward the dogs went, pausing before a candy store, racing down sidewalks, around corners, across lawns, until they arrived at a supermarket, pulling the houndsman to the side of the building, to the back: a parking lot, a dumpster, before which the barking grew frantic. Ms. Mann herself climbed up and opened the container, a recycling bin full of flattened boxes. Immediately she saw the arm. "Oh no," she said, turning on her flashlight to reveal the puffy sleeve of a red quilted jacket. "Gloves," she cried to her assistant, who handed them over. She snapped them on and touched the arm of the jacket. Empty. She pulled it from between the boxes, along with a yellow shirt so small that she understood, finally, the preciousness of the child. She dug among the boxes, but there was no body.

The dogs were crazy now. As Ms. Mann climbed down from the dumpster, the animals rushed at the clothing, breathing it in as if it were air at the surface of water. Reinvigorated by the child's essence, they immediately set off again, racing across the parking lot until they came to the street, where they slowed, and then stopped. They looked left and then right—and finally upward, toward the sky. The dogs seemed confused, as if they'd lost not only Edgar, but themselves as well. "No, no," Ms. Mann said. "Keep them going."

The houndsman shook his head. "Sorry. They've lost him."

Everyone, even the animals, breathed in silence, standing at this place where the boy ended. When the larger of the dogs walked in a circle and made a plaintive sound of distress, the smaller one turned and licked his companion's face.

*   *   *

Lucy waited alone at the police station, having encouraged Ron to take care of his own business. While looking through some mug shots, she came across the young man who'd attacked her outside Slaphappy's. She decided not to mention it, though. It would only make her look worse. Plus, it had nothing to do with what mattered—and that was her son.

When she was finally shown into the conference room and presented with photos of the red jacket, the yellow shirt, she felt wobbly. Yes, they were Edgar's. Yes, she was sure. She kept staring at the Polaroids, which made the clothes seem even more miniature than she knew they were. "Why can't I see the actual clothing?" she asked.

"We're still examining them," Ms. Mann said. "But a preliminary test has revealed no blood or semen. So that's—"

"Semen?" Lucy said, confused. "He's eight."

"Yes," Ms. Mann said, swallowing. "I meant, someone else's . . ."

"Oh God." Lucy closed her eyes. "It's too cold."

"What is?"

"For him to be naked."

"Well, someone may have provided something."

"Who?"

"That's what we need to find out."

Ms. Mann had done some research on Lucy Fini. Not pretty. Currently unemployed, husband a suicide, lived with her in-laws until they died, still lived in the same house. Numerous outstanding parking tickets, poor credit rating, possible alcoholic, arrested twice—once with her husband for public indecency (backseat coitus); once for shoplifting at fifteen, when she was still Lucy Bubko of West Mill, New Jersey. The same Lucy Bubko who'd had an abortion at seventeen and was married a year later. Not long before her husband's death, she produced a son—the albinoid, now missing, Edgar.

A hard road that, surprisingly, had not turned the woman into a hag. Certainly she was chunky, but she was also, Ms. Mann allowed, fingering the top button of her Ann Taylor oxford, what men called a *hottie*. The woman was clearly impulsive, reckless. And though there were no prior reports of Lucy Fini abusing the child, Mann did find a number of complaints filed by a teenaged Lucy Bubko against her own father, on behalf of her mother, Elena Bubko. ("He beats the fucking crap out of her," the girl stated in one report. When questioned if she was beaten, too, the girl replied, "No fucking way.") The officer that had taken the report noted that the girl was "foul-mouthed, dressed in a halter top, and possibly inebriated." A call to the Bubko residence at the time of the complaint had resulted in the mother's denial of her daughter's allegations. No recommendation had been made to investigate further.

And though it would be inaccurate to say that Ms. Mann had no sympathy for Lucy Bubko, the fact was: the boy was her priority now. What had to be faced was the sad truth: abuse breeds abuse. The detective had no evidence of this yet in the Fini case, but considering what she'd learned about such families in her training, she had a hunch about what was going on.

Lucy had abused the boy, and the boy had fled.

"Why is there a sexual novelty item in your son's sock drawer?"

"A what?" Lucy said.

"A dildo," clarified Ms. Mann. "A *vibrator*."

The detective pulled out the device, condemned to a Ziploc bag.

"Is that . . . ?" It looked familiar. "Where did you get that?"

"It was found in the boy's room. Does it belong to you, Mrs. Fini?"

"I have no idea."

"You have no idea?"

Ms. Mann pushed the bagged penis across the table.

"I mean, I do own a similar . . ."

"So, it could be yours?"

"I—I guess."

"You guess? Okay. And the reason it was in your son's room?"

"I don't know."

"You didn't put it there?"

"Of course not."

"Have you ever used it in the boy's room?"

"What are you implying?"

"I'm not implying anything. I'm just trying to—"

"Edgar picks things up."

"He picks things up?"

"He's interested in things."

"Like dildos?"

"What does this have to do with finding my son?"

"I'm just trying to gauge his state of mind."

"*Sad,*" Lucy snapped.

"Why sad?"

"His grandmother."

"But I thought you said they weren't really that close. Mrs. Fini?"

"When did I . . . ? I don't know why I said that."

"So they *were* close?"

"Yes." Lucy nodded. She felt the air rising in her chest like a bubble, and though she kept down the sound, the tears came.

Ms. Mann pushed a box of Kleenex toward Lucy and paused for the recommended five seconds before recommencing. "Okay, Mrs. Fini, just a couple more questions. If you could . . ."

Lucy no longer cared to look at the woman's face. "What?"

Ms. Mann shifted some papers, aware of the official sound she was generating. "I have a hospital report here. Apparently, Edgar suffered a serious injury about a week—"

"What happened?" Lucy interrupted, frightened. "Are you not telling me something?"

"Not at all. If you'd let me finish. He sustained an injury *before* his disappearance."

Lucy felt dizzy, confused. "He did?"

"You don't remember? It seems his finger was—"

"Oh, yes. Yes."

"Cut off," Ms. Mann said, calmly finishing her sentence.

Lucy looked down at her own fingers, whose tips were covered in tiny silver rings—the rings attached by wires to a computer capable of detecting the subtle flutters that supposedly accompanied lies.

"My hands are shaking," she said. "This is pointless."

"The machine can tell the difference. You're doing fine. Let's talk about the child's injury."

Lucy shook her head and deliberately pushed a stream of air from her nose. She could see where this idiot of a woman was heading. "He was cutting a tomato. It was an accident."

"You let him use sharp knives?"

"Yes," Lucy said, ". . . and dildos. You stupid—" Lucy pulled the flutter receptors from her fingers. "You don't know what the hell you're talking about."

"Mrs. Fini—"

"Don't 'Mrs. Fini' me. Why are you wasting time with this shit when you should be looking for Edgar?"

"I *am* looking for—"

"Actually, I don't think you know your ass from your elbow."

Ms. Mann squeezed a pen, speechless.

"You know what?" And here, Lucy snatched up the metal rings and pushed them back onto her fingers. Ms. Mann watched, mesmerized, hoping for a confession.

"Maybe I haven't been the best fucking mother," Lucy continued. "But I have never, *never,* hurt Edgar physically, or . . . not physically." Here, a small sob escaped from her. "If anyone has a sick mind, it's you."

Ms. Mann touched the neck of her oxford.

"And do yourself a favor and unbutton the top of that shirt before you choke to death." Lucy pulled off the wires and grabbed her jacket from the back of the chair. "If you'll excuse me, I have to find my son."

* * *

Stay calm. Your stress will not help you find your child. Of course, you will want to remain vigilant and participate in the search, but don't sacrifice your own health and well-being. Though you may feel that suffering is the only option, this is never true. A positive attitude, though often difficult to achieve, is always the best strategy. Are there calming rituals that please you? Baths? Massage? Music? A favorite movie or food or leisure activity?

* * *

That evening, after the finger-flutter test, Ms. Mann ate Mallomars for dinner and overfed her cat. Propped up in bed, with the animal curled at her side, she read *Missing and Abducted Children: A Law Enforcement Guide to Case Investigation and Program Management.* She hadn't been aware that such a guide existed until Mrs. Fini's boyfriend had called the station and suggested she order one from NCMEC by calling 1–800–THE–LOST.

When the cat vomited on the comforter, Ms. Mann stared at the offensive matter and once again felt chastised. Not only had Mrs. Fini passed the flutter test without any indication of wrongdoing, but also she'd vindicated herself with a passion that made Ms. Mann sense that there might be more to the woman than she'd previously imagined. Lucy possessed a kind of terrifying intensity that made Ms. Mann feel both superior and inadequate. It was the terrible passion of the working class, the violence of whose lives often made them into monsters. Though here, a rare specimen, with gorgon-like red hair and pale skin. Ms. Mann had wasted time, it was true. Perhaps, if she wanted to solve this case, it would be wise to ally herself with the fierce Mrs. Fini and her oversized, jaggedly handsome boyfriend. Though these people were like animals, they were also, Ms. Mann allowed—cleaning up the cat spew—touchingly human.

* * *

Lucy was vomiting too, sick with herself. She was not good at tests. She'd been failing them her whole life. Though that Mann woman was a bitch, Lucy knew she'd overreacted. But how did people control themselves? It was a mystery to Lucy, who had the misfortune of being born under a greedy red star that required constant payment by fire.

Of course, over the last few years, the red star seemed to have dulled to a state of mordant disinterest, requiring little from Lucy. But Mann's accusations had Lucy lit again. There was a job to be done, and she'd do it, without anyone getting in her way. She felt a stirring in the very cells of her body, a defense against chaos she'd experienced before, and one that always contained a trace of Walter Bubko. Lucy had survived a father who'd despised her; she'd survive this. Hell, she'd do more than survive; she'd win. Prove her worth to those who thought she was nothing but a piece of trash.

She cleaned up the beer bottles, picked up her clothes, changed the sheets. She called Ron and told him not to come over, claiming some girlfriends were stopping by. She made toast and tea, instead of crackers and vodka, and settled down on the couch with the photocopied pamphlet.

Children tend to gravitate toward water (rivers, lakes, ponds, drainage ditches). Wooded areas also offer a place of adventure for a wandering child.

The language was strangely comforting—as if the story could be framed as a fairy tale, one in which Edgar would reappear as easily as he'd vanished. It was mercifully impossible to imagine him harmed, or dead.

Over her thin pajamas, Lucy put on Florence's black wool coat. She'd grabbed it from where it still hung on the rack in the foyer, without thinking anything except that it seemed the warmest. As she walked into the woods behind 21 Cressida Drive, she meticulously swept the ground with the beam of a flashlight. After several hours, she'd found nothing but chestnuts—which now filled the pockets of Florence's coat.

Back at the house she got her car keys. *Rivers, lakes, ponds.* She drove to the park Edgar liked, with the ducks and the swans. The gate was locked, but Lucy climbed over it. When she shone the flashlight on the dark water, she spotted no birds. She walked past the rose garden and the merry-go-round and approached the zoo, housed behind a faux castle. The drawbridge was raised, though, and she couldn't reach it. From across the moat she could hear the low rustling of the animals—distant swishings and squawks and brays. It was then she felt afraid. On the way back to the car, she passed the placard of Hansel and Gretel with empty ovals instead of faces. She and Edgar had once stuck their heads through the holes, and someone had snapped a photo.

* * *

A few days later, after the green color bloomed on the peed-upon test strip, Lucy asked Ron as breezily as she could manage: "Listen, you always use a condom, right?"

The butcher was silent for a few seconds before he said, "Why, do we have a problem?"

"No," Lucy lied. "I just want to make sure we're being safe."

"Of course." The butcher distractedly pushed a bottle cap across the table. "We just did it once without a rubber." Without looking at Lucy, he reminded her of the night she'd come to his house with her knees cut up. "You said you'd tripped in a parking lot or something?"

Lucy's back went cold from the sudden memory of the butcher on top of her in his bathtub.

The butcher, on the other hand, recalled a sensation of warm, blissful expansion. "But, you know, if we ever did have a problem . . ." He paused and offered a small shrug. "I guess I'm just saying, it wouldn't necessarily be a problem for me."

"Well, it would be one for me," Lucy said—and the butcher, seeing her point, looked down: "Yeah, yeah, of course."

* * *

The next day marked a week since Edgar had gone missing. Lucy peed on a second test strip. Again, it showed green. When she stepped outside the house into the bright cold, the wind lifted the flaps of her short pink bathrobe. She watched the shivering trees and bushes, feeling a sudden hatred for the child inside her, a hatred for the butcher. These people were not her family.

She marched into the house and made the call. The number was still in her phone book. The woman who answered said they'd just had a cancellation; Lucy could schedule the procedure for that very afternoon. "Have you visited the clinic before?" the woman asked, and Lucy said that she had.

"We'll want you to meet with a counselor first."

"Sure," Lucy said.

Her decision was made, though.

She understood now that it was physically impossible for the two beings to exist simultaneously—a problem of physics that made her head spin, but which her gut solved immediately.

For Edgar to live, his usurper must die.

30

Extra Credit

Science, Period 3, Mr. Levinson

"Can you come up with ten questions that have not been answered by science?"

1. How long does it take a dead person to get to where they're going? Do they get there instantly or does it take a long time?
2. Do dead people keep the same age and the same face?
3. Do they even have bodies?
4. Do they know they're dead, or just think they are lost?
5. Do they remember things from when they weren't dead, like other people?
6. Can they call you on the telephone, like in movies?
7. Why do people die in the first place? Is there not enough room on Earth, like when we talked about overpopulation?
8. Is it dark where they are?
9. Is it cold?
10.

Edgar, this is very interesting. I was hoping to receive questions about a variety of subjects, but I will give you credit for the obvious effort you put into this. Perhaps we might say these questions come under the banner of physics. I am curious about the lack of a tenth question, since you seem to have no shortage of thoughts on this particular subject.

I have recommended that you meet with Mrs. LeBreck. She is very nice and just a good person to talk to if something's bothering you. Your mother has been notified.

Good job!

Mr. Levinson

31

Goodbye, Toni-Ann

A yellow fish with ruffled wings hovered above the turret of a sunken castle. Edgar stared at it while the dog sniffed his ankles. The situation seemed a little less terrible now that he'd taken his pill. Earlier, in the small bedroom the man had given him, he'd poured out the pink tablets and counted them. If he kept breaking them in half, taking only four halves a day, he'd have enough for eleven more days. His finger didn't really hurt so much anymore, but something deep inside him remained steady in its request for the Percocet.

He'd spent the first few days crying in the other boy's bed. "It's okay," the man kept saying. "It's normal to cry when you go away. Even astronauts cry." He brought Edgar juice and milk and cream cheese and jelly sandwiches, leaving them on the nightstand.

Sometimes, in the dark, Edgar woke, afraid. It wasn't clear to him exactly how he'd ended up here. A lot had happened since his grandmother had died. He tried to understand how one thing had led to the next; to understand what had been his fault, and what the fault of others. But he made no headway; all thoughts and attempts at logic seemed to tatter and tear and float away like tiny pieces of ash, as if his mind were a fire burning everything that passed through it. Several times he'd asked the man if he had a fever, and the man had touched his forehead and cheek like Florence used to. And though the man's hand made him tremble, it felt nice, too. It seemed, to Edgar, that he couldn't trust even his own body to tell him what was true, or what he wanted.

The day after he'd arrived, he'd gotten out of bed while the man was outside the house. It was early, a terrible coldness seeping up from the floor. In the living room, a neat stack of logs burned in the fireplace. Edgar found the man's cell and attempted, twice, to call his mother. Both times, though, the pig-killer had answered the phone. "Who the fuck is this?" the butcher had snarled in response to Edgar's stricken silence—and Edgar, distraught, had hung up. When, seconds later, the cell began to ring, the boy panicked and, in a fit of confusion, threw the small phone into the fireplace. When the man came back inside and sniffed, Edgar started to cry. "I burned your phone," he said, too frightened to lie. The man told him not to worry—he had lots of them. "Did you try to call someone?" he asked, and Edgar nodded, releasing a fresh burst of tears. "It's okay, *shhhh*," the man said. "Remember what I told you. If you want to go home, all you have to do is ask."

Edgar felt sick over the fact that he hadn't yet.

Staring at the fish, he wondered if the butcher was living at his house, using his grandmother's pots and pans and making his mother sound like an animal. Edgar felt a furious jealousy that was indistinguishable from hatred. His brow furrowed—but only for a moment. Confronted by the equanimity of the fish and the complete dispersion of the Percocet into his bloodstream, he leaned forward and let his nose touch the glass of the aquarium.

"Fish kiss," the man said from behind, and Edgar closed his eyes.

*   *   *

The man had never expected the boy to get in touch. He'd offered his telephone number more as a gesture of goodwill. It was also, he recognized, a gesture in the direction of his own destruction. More and more, he felt compelled to take such risks. He was as impatient to be condemned as he was to be saved. When the boy had called, the man had felt a disastrous flutter of hope.

"I don't know if you remember me," the boy had said on the phone, "but you punched the fat kid who was hurting me and then you changed my bandage and we talked about stuff and just like . . . talked about stuff." The boy had sounded drunk. When he'd finished his nervous spiel, he concluded quietly, "So I'm just calling."

The man waited a long time before he asked if the boy was still there.

"Yes."

"That's good. Is everything okay?"

"It's just noisy. Because my mother has a friend over."

"Oh, okay." The man paused, the empty space feeling like a delicate glass flower he had to be careful not to break. "Did you maybe want to take a walk?"

"Where?"

"We could meet somewhere." A tiny translucent petal began to crack. "Maybe our spot behind the supermarket?"

"It's nighttime, though."

He could hear the boy sigh, and waited for him to speak again.

"I don't know what's happening."

"At your house?" the man asked. "What's happening?"

"I don't know," Edgar repeated. "They sound like *animals*."

* * *

It was too easy. Not only had the boy called, but he'd shown up in the parking lot in his little red jacket, with a fresh crew cut and a blue backpack over his shoulders. At that point, the man doubted his own sense of reality. The boy's arrival, his disturbing willingness, so perfectly matched the man's hopes that it was as if he'd invented the child. He was like something from one of those implausible tales the man used to scribble in notebooks when he'd fancied himself a writer. The child was convenient, a character.

Still, it had taken a while to get him into the truck. They spoke for several minutes through the rolled-down window—the boy, shivering.

"I don't think your clothes are warm enough, soldier."

"It's quilted," said Edgar, touching his jacket.

"Is it?"

"Yes. It has feathers inside."

"*Squawk, squawk*," the man said, but the boy didn't laugh.

"Are you just fooling me?" he said.

"Fooling you how?"

"Are you just pretending to know me?"

The man was taken aback. "Are you just pretending to know *me*?"

"No," Edgar said innocently. "I *don't* know you."

"Guess I'll have to give you a test then."

"What kind of test?"

"What's my dog's name?"

"I know. Jack."

"Right. And was I ever married?"

"Yes."

"To whom?"

"To a nurse."

"And what's in here?" the man said, patting the glove box.

"First-aid kit."

"Correct. And let's see, final question . . . what's my nickname for you?"

Edgar paused. How was it that he knew all the answers? A faint pride pulsed inside a knot of apprehension. "Kevin."

"Bingo." The man reached beside him and pulled some clothes from a bag. "And you know what? I don't think Kevin would wear a red jacket."

"Why not?"

The man shrugged. "How do you feel about costumes?"

"Like for Halloween?"

"For Halloween, sure. Or just for fun."

"I was a vampire last year," Edgar said shyly.

The man smiled. "I bet you were perfect."

"Not perfect, but my grandmother made me a cape and I . . . I put a drip of blood here," the boy said, touching the right side of his lips.

*   *   *

After the boy had been sitting in the truck for a while, warm and sleepy from the heat, the man asked him if he'd like to go for a drive. When the boy said that maybe he should go home, the man asked if it was safe there, and then watched, inspired, as the boy's lips condensed into a marvelous pout of uncertainty. His confusion seemed all the more precious with his little head poking out of the larger boy's denim shirt and down jacket.

"Have you ever been on a camping trip?" the man asked.

Edgar shook his head.

"Did you know there's a place where the trees don't grow any bigger than you are?"

"Like in a story?" Edgar said, and the man said, "No, for real. I have a house there."

The boy's pale face absorbed this information with a series of nervous blinks. "But I have to go home."

"Of course." When the man shifted into gear, the boy flinched. The truck sounded like a helicopter. "You okay, soldier?"

Edgar didn't like loud things. He touched his pocket to make sure the diamond was still there. He'd made sure to transfer it from his jacket to Kevin's when he'd made the switch.

As the man drove, he glanced at the backpack on the boy's lap. "I see you brought a bag." He'd purposely not commented on it before, but time was running out now; they were almost at the boy's house.

Edgar looked down at his schoolbag with no recollection of what he'd put inside—let alone why he'd brought it with him in the first place. When the truck turned onto Cressida Drive, he felt afraid. The lamppost in front of his house was dark. The only light came from his mother's room, a dim red haze, which meant she'd placed her fringed Indian shawl over the lamp— something she did when she had a headache or wished to be left alone. But she wasn't alone now. The white van was still parked in front of the house. *Let us MEAT your needs!*

His grandmother had been gone less than two weeks and his mother was already letting a suitor stay over. Edgar shook his head like a clockwork miniature of the old woman.

"Last stop, soldier."

"Why do you call me that?" said Edgar.

It was something Florence sometimes called him after she'd combed his hair or cleaned a cut or wiped a smudge from his cheek. *All done, soldier.*

"I won't say it anymore," the man said.

Edgar closed his eyes, too tired to say that he liked it.

And the word made sense. A soldier was someone who fought in a war— and there had always been a war at 21 Cressida Drive. Edgar could feel the red haze from his mother's bedroom seeping into every room of the house. Slowly, he began to rock, letting the air rush from his nose with each thrust forward.

"What kind of trees are they?" he asked.

"Where?" the man said.

"The little ones. Where you live."

"Pines." The man spoke quietly. "Pygmy pines."

Tears dripped from behind Edgar's closed eyes.

As the man pulled away from the house, and Edgar realized that he was still in the truck, he understood that he must quickly get a message to the two women he was leaving behind. But it was an impossible feat. He was too angry to say goodbye to one, and too sad to say goodbye to the other.

He turned his eyes to the house next door.

Goodbye, Toni-Ann, he thought, offering his farewell to someone he didn't love at all.

But it was a trap. Because, as soon as he'd thought it, he realized that he loved her, too.

* * *

"Pit stop," the man said. "I'll be right back."

They'd been driving for barely twenty minutes when the truck pulled into a dark driveway. Edgar watched sleepily as the man approached an expensive-looking brick house with a weedy, overgrown lawn. From inside, a dog was barking.

A few minutes later, the man emerged with a duffel bag and a long silver case with a black handle—both of which he put into the bed of the truck. He whistled, and the dog bolted from the shadow of a bush.

When Edgar turned, he could see the dog looking at him through the narrow window behind the seats. The animal wagged its tail and barked.

"Don't let him scare you," the man said, back at the wheel. "He's a pussy-cat."

Edgar's eyes fluttered. He knew what was coming. Soon, the finger-pill would drag him down like water into a drain. "How far to the . . . ?"

"A ways," the man said. "But you rest, okay? Lie down if you want. There's plenty of room."

* * *

On Percocet, Edgar had troubled dreams with the forced perspective and feverish light of medieval paintings. He moved through rooms in which every fold of fabric, every floor tile, winked with rumors of some dreadful ecstasy; landscapes in which the uniform leaves on miniaturized trees seemed like insignia torn from the lapels of a thousand perished soldiers.

The man watched the boy sleep and reached out to touch his face. A car horn recalled him to the road, where he'd begun to stray into an adjacent lane. Though there was little traffic on the Parkway at this hour, each car he passed—or that passed him—seemed a kind of invasion, or accusation. He gripped the wheel to steady his shaking hands.

He knew that what he was doing was unforgivable, but this thought had little effect. He didn't wish for forgiveness; no longer believed such a thing was possible. His main desire was to be destroyed, but first—if only for a little while—to exchange something, some sweetness, with the child he'd stolen. The whole transaction, he hoped, could be finished in a few days. He didn't want the boy to suffer.

The man wasn't a sociopath; did not possess a mind unfettered by the pain of others. In fact, every step he'd taken toward the child, each bid for the child's trust, was matched by a stabbing awareness of his own selfishness.

Still, he'd done it; had not stopped himself. Perhaps he was even worse than a sociopath—with a mind that tended toward the poetic. He felt too much, swerved dangerously and often into metaphor. Such a state of mind was not unreasonable, considering the scope of his tragedy—a tragedy that he'd both suffered *and* inflicted. Plus, as a writer—albeit a failed one—he understood how one could bend the contours of reality to suit one's desires, as well as to fulfill one's pain.

If the man was ill, he had no sense of this. He only knew that he wished things to be different. He wanted dead things to live again, and living things to perish. The current state of reality was horrible.

Kevin was gone.

What choice was there now but to enact some story by which he might redeem himself. Yes, he was using the child, but it was obvious the child needed something, too. That's why they had found each other. Why it had been so effortless.

We belong here, the man thought as he drove into the Pinelands National Reserve. He felt a hot sickness in his chest—to be here again, in the place his son had died.

But the story made sense now. He saw exactly what would happen— imagining, like every poor writer, that he alone was in control; that all outcomes would be a factor of his own design.

32

The Pine Barrens

The man and the boy walked along a narrow road of sugar sand, flanked on both sides by far-reaching plains of dwarf pine. It was the first time Edgar had been more than a few yards from the cabin. The sky, massed with slender lenticular clouds frozen in place, seemed like a parking lot for spaceships. The improbable terrain, and the fact that they'd been walking for half an hour without seeing another house, caused the boy to suffer another fit of breathlessness. He considered running into the trees, but a deep tiredness made any real effort at flight impossible.

Besides, these woods were nothing like the woods behind his house. This landscape was enormous. One could feel, even without having walked very far, the oceanic distances. The shrieks of birds rang out from a silence that seemed an echo of infinity. Plus, the man had warned of feral dogs that roamed the forests of pygmy pine. Which was the reason, he said, he liked to keep Jack in the house or tied to a post in the yard. The man said the wild dogs were normal people-dogs that had run away, centuries ago, from the old bog-iron towns of the Pine Barrens. But they were no longer normal people-dogs; they'd become something else.

Edgar had been in this strange place for a week now (he kept track with his pills). It might have seemed much longer were he to judge by other means, such as the flickering inconsistency of his mother's face, or how quickly the hair she'd shorn from his head was growing back. At night, in the glass globe of the old-fashioned lamp beside his bed, he pretended he saw her—like in a magician's crystal ball—standing on the lawn of 21 Cressida Drive, calling his name. He knew, of course, that this was nothing more than an image borrowed from a movie. In reality, his mother was probably in bed with the butcher, a red shawl draped over the crystal ball of her own lamp.

"Wait." The man stopped on the sandy road and slowly pointed. In the distance, among the tiny trees, a deer lifted its head.

"But I don't want to learn yet," Edgar whispered anxiously. The man was carrying his gun. Just this morning, he'd talked again about teaching Edgar some new skills, things a person had to learn if he was going to live in the woods. In the cabin, two mounted deer heads, with blind glass eyes the color of tar, searched for each other futilely from opposite sides of the living room.

Gun control is hitting your target.

The man's bumper sticker made sense now. He was a hunter. And though that didn't seem so different from a butcher, the bearded man was somehow nicer; he didn't kill animals and put them in a glass case to sell to strangers. "Only for my family," he'd explained this morning—after which he'd abruptly stopped speaking and excused himself to his bedroom.

"Season doesn't begin for a few weeks," he said now, still pointing at the deer. "I just wanted to make sure you saw her."

"How come it doesn't run?" asked Edgar.

"She won't move until we do. If we don't make any sudden moves . . ." The man slowly lifted the gun into position. "I'm not going to do anything," he said. "I'm just showing you."

Edgar's hands began to shake. When a sound erupted from his mouth, it was less a scream than a bark. The deer bolted.

"I'm sorry," said Edgar, his cheeks flushing red.

"No worries. But it's probably better if we don't make too much noise."

The boy nodded. "I just make sounds sometimes. When I'm nervous."

The man smiled and resisted the urge to touch the boy's face. He was a peculiar child. Twice, the man had heard him talking to himself in his bedroom—little murmurs that reminded him of the sounds Kevin used to make when he struggled over his math homework: the grunted half-utterances of thought overflowing into speech. But the boy's sounds were odder—squeaks and coos, small animals escaping from the underworld of the boy's anxious dreaminess. That Edgar had arrived confused, even damaged (the finger, the death-white pallor), provided an opportunity, the man felt, to offer comfort, and clarity. The man recognized, though, that the manageable tensions of the last week might become something far worse when the boy's medication ran out. He might start barking in earnest.

"Come on," the man said, moving from the road into the dense scrub of trees. "I want to show you something."

Among the tiny pines, the man looked, to Edgar, like a giant. The boy followed at a distance, his shoulders rubbing against the shoulders of his arboreal brethren. Being his size, they seemed even more alive than normal trees, and more plaintive. They were not Christmas tree pines, but more like bonsais, twisty and tortured, with blackish branches that gestured with the panic of fleers from Vesuvius. Edgar had a feeling that Florence was nearby.

"Do you know what's underneath us?" the man said. He turned back to look at Edgar, who offered an obedient schoolboy shake of his head.

"A gigantic lake," the man said. "We're basically floating on top of a melted glacier."

Edgar stopped walking and looked at the dusty, desert-like earth.

"Purest water in the world," the man said. "Right under our feet."

Edgar knew from Mr. Levinson that what the man was saying could be true. Mr. Levinson had once spent a whole science class talking about how the world was shaped—the mountains and caverns and lakes—a great cataclysm that had made so much of what we now consider beautiful.

"From the Ice Age?" asked Edgar, and the man said, "Very good."

After another ten minutes of walking, the ground began to slope downward. The plain of pygmy pine slowly descended into a cooler, darker terrain—the trees growing progressively larger. No longer even pines now, but maples and gums and magnolia, and in the distance tall stands of oak and cedar. Edgar stopped again—a sudden gut resistance to going any farther. He longed for the confraternity of the pygmies, and the open sky, which was gradually closing now under the latticework of lengthening branches. When he looked back, he could still see the edge of the plain lit by the sun.

"Are they really that small?"

"What are you looking at?" asked the man.

"The trees up there. The ones we just walked through."

"Do you think your eyes are lying?"

"No, but I mean . . ." Edgar paused. He wasn't sure what he meant. "I mean, will they get any bigger?"

"They will not," the man said. "They're a very special case."

"But are they babies?"

"No. Most of them are fully grown."

As the boy continued to stare at the pygmies, the man felt a hot flash of impatience. He grabbed the boy's arm to wake him. *"Kevin."*

At the touch, Edgar doubled over and vomited onto the ground—and then, as he'd been doing for days, he apologized. So much of the mess he was in seemed his own fault.

"You don't need to keep saying you're sorry. You haven't done anything wrong." The man knelt down to fix things. "I didn't mean to yell. I'm the one who should apologize."

Edgar shut his eyes to the stranger's closeness. "I'm supposed to eat something when I take my pill."

"Come on, if we walk just a little more, there's a nice spot for you to rest."

With each step, the ground became softer; Edgar could feel his feet sink into the soil. The smell, he noticed, was different, too. The dried paintbrush tang of the pines was replaced by the must of a just-watered flowerpot.

As the man continued talking, the understory grew thick with shrubs and bushes. He named each variety as he passed it. It calmed him down to repeat the lessons he'd learned from his father—who'd loved this place, and whose *own* father had built the cabin. But as the names of each species of flora came out of the man's mouth, he realized how worthless it was to parse things into categories, to separate each thing by its name. A bush was a bush; a child, a child.

Edgar wasn't sure what the man was saying. Some sort of poem, an assemblage of gibberish like the one by Lewis Carroll they'd read in English class. *Staggerbush and dangleberry; swamp azalea, leatherleaf; bracken fern, fever bush.*

As the pair pushed through, branches snapped, releasing the scent of coffee and chocolate and black pepper. Edgar's uncannily sensitive nose twitched like a rabbit's. He wished the man would stop speaking, because his words were somehow making the forest darker. Now they were standing before a large pond. As Edgar stared at the reflection of a leafless tree reaching for him from the other side, the man's stream of words continued. Plants had become animals. *Pickerel, mudminnow, swamp darter, pirate perch.*

"We used to fish here," the man said.

Edgar wondered if the water before him was the melted glacier seeping through. Water was the Earth's vitality, Mr. Levinson had said. It was healing. Edgar looked at his freshly bandaged finger (the man changed it every morning with a military precision). Inside the wrapping he could almost hear his body ticking. He knew the mechanics of this had something to do with his heart.

* * *

The man stopped speaking and turned to Edgar, who was standing on a carpet of crimson leaves—which seemed not to have come from a tree but to have fallen from the boy. Why else would he be so pale? The red leaves were like blood. The color had drained from the other child's face in the same way.

This was the spot where it had happened. The man sat on the ground, unnerved by the sound of his own whistling.

Edgar nervously fingered the dried flowers of an orchid growing near the water.

"Lady slippers," the man said.

The boy considered them more closely, noticing how the dead flowers did, in fact, mimic the shape of puffy shoes. He thought of his grandmother's dried and cracked feet. When a frog jumped from a rock into the water, Edgar felt the splash inside his chest.

"I want to go home," he said quietly.

The man said nothing as Edgar knelt among the leaves.

"People are waiting for me," he cried. "And I have school and I have home-work and—*people are waiting for me.*"

The man reached for the child's hand.

Edgar pulled away and shook his head.

"You know me," the man whispered.

"I thought you were someone else," said Edgar.

The man retreated and took hold of his beard to steady himself. "Okay, listen to me, I know you're scared and you miss your family and—"

He stopped. The boy wasn't listening. He had curled up on his side and was emitting a high-pitched drone like a mosquito—a terrible, keening sound.

"Shhh, listen to me. I don't want you to be afraid. Why don't we start all over again? Okay?"

"My name is Edgar," the boy cried.

"Okay, okay. Look. Edgar, look." The man unstrapped the gun from his shoulder, double-checked the safety, and laid it beside the boy. "I'm putting this here for you."

"I don't want it."

"Well, I'm giving it to you anyway."

"Why?" The boy was shivering.

"It's a present."

Edgar stared at the gleaming wood of the rifle, a grainy red-brown as per-fectly polished as a chestnut. "I'm not allowed," he said. "It's dangerous."

"Only if you don't know how to use it. But you'll learn. How old are you?"

"Eight."

The man swallowed. So young; four years younger than his son. "Well, at eight, it's time to . . ." He felt his mind caving to clichés he'd heard as a child from his own father, things he'd repeated by rote to Kevin. He took a breath and began again. "I bet you're angry at some people, huh? And you're afraid of things—it's okay. I'm afraid of some things, too." The man grimaced and pulled at his beard. "I'm afraid of you."

Edgar didn't see how this was possible. "I'm *eight*," he said again.

"Well, that's not a baby. That's old enough to know."

"Know what?"

The man picked up one of the crimson leaves and traced the veins with his finger, as if trying to find a place on a map. "Sometimes you think people are waiting for you, but then you find out that nobody's there."

"Where?"

"At home or . . . just in your head or . . ."

The man put down the leaf, with full awareness of his own monstrosity. "I just wish you'd stay with me for a few more days, that's all."

It was only due to shame that Edgar had been holding back, but now he closed his eyes as another glacier broke free from its wall of ice.

"It's okay. Let it out." The man touched the boy's head. "Just imagine what it'll be like when you're not afraid of anything. When you can take care of yourself."

"But I should call her and tell her where I am," the boy cried.

"You said she had a friend."

"Yes, but—"

"And now you have a friend."

Even in his distraught state, Edgar knew the man was simplifying things unfairly; but he was too tired to argue.

"I'll do whatever I can to help you, Edgar." The man took a green plaid blanket from his pack and placed it over the boy. "And then maybe you'll help me, sometime."

Edgar pushed his clenched fists under the carpet of crimson leaves. "I need my sunscreen," he said sleepily.

"I have it," said the man.

Briefly, before closing his eyes, the boy looked up at the white tree that had caused the reflection on the pond. He knew it was his grandmother, and he understood now how easy it was to die. A person might do it almost by accident. Like walking too far into a forest, and then not being able to find a way out.

33

Soon New Addition to Your Family!

Lucy's feet were already in the stirrups. It was an accomplishment, she felt, to have gotten this far. Even when one's mind was made up, going through with it was something else. She closed her eyes and tried to breathe. Waiting was the worst part. The actual procedure, she recalled, took less than five minutes.

"You're all set," the nurse said, making a final adjustment to the IV. The tranquilizing drip of fentanyl was optional, and Lucy had opted for it without hesitation. She planned to put the whole thing on her credit card.

"You have someone to drive you home, right?"

"Yes," Lucy lied.

"Good. You comfortable there?"

"What do you think?"

The nurse smiled and patted Lucy's uplifted leg. "The doctor will be in in a minute, hon. Try to relax."

Alone, Lucy could still smell the faint fruity sweetness—a lingering trail from the nurse's perfume or hand cream. Fragrances shouldn't be allowed in here, Lucy thought with an uncharacteristic puritanism. The judgment propelled her backwards: a dim memory of Frank complaining about a mailman who wore too much cologne.

Though there was no pain, Lucy clutched her belly and tried to drown her awareness in the sea of beige surrounding her. Everything in this damn clinic was beige, offset by green plastic plants cowering in corners. The wicker pots in which the plants lived were filled with heaps of shredded cellophane that looked, to Lucy, exactly like the fake grass Florence had always used to decorate Edgar's Easter basket. Again, the phantom pain: a jittery silent movie flickering against the inside of her body. Images of the boy, images of Florence—spliced footage some conscientious demon had

meticulously preserved. Lucy glanced at the bag of fentanyl. Her head was
spinning.

It was Easter again. Florence in one of her ridiculous bonnets; the heavy
scent of Chanel No 5, an indulgence the old woman seemed to allow herself
only on holidays. Lucy could picture the white chocolate cross that looked
like a gravestone and that always went into Edgar's basket, along with marshmallow bunnies and dolled-up dollar bills folded into fans and flowers.
Sometimes, on the night before the holiday, Lucy would sit at the kitchen
table and watch as the old woman composed her Italianate architectures of
sugar and cash. Florence was never happier than when she was doing something for the boy. Her Easter baskets had been surprisingly artistic. Lucy had
said so once, and Florence had been so tickled that she'd accepted Lucy's
offer of a small glass of wine. "I used to fancy myself an artist," Florence had
admitted.

The pain was impossible to locate, yet all-encompassing—a ravaging, as
if memory were some kind of autoimmune disease. Lucy adjusted her right
ankle in its stirrup and took a deep breath, reminding herself that she was
doing this for her son. It was a deal she'd struck with the unfathomable.
This fractional child's life in return for Edgar's. Maybe it was a deal she
was making with the dead. Lucy was willing to enlarge the scope of what
she believed in, if it would bring Edgar home.

She tapped her fingers against the onionskin rolled down over the exami-
nation table. For Christ's sake, how long were they going to keep her waiting? She scowled at the door, which the nurse had left ajar as if for a child
prone to nightmares.

Even with the freshly painted walls and the new artwork and the addition of plastic greenery, it was hard for Lucy to forget that she'd been here
once before.

Twice, actually.

The first time, over fifteen years ago. The outside of the building still
looked the same: a pleasant little brick house in which the architect—perhaps
a blind man—had neglected to put any windows. The clinic was located on
a flowerless street named Bluebell Avenue—a designation Lucy could only
interpret as mockery; when in fact the street, during the days of Florence's
youth, had been a favorite stroll for people who wished to take in the purple
hyacinths that flourished in the spring in the tiny John Paul Preedy Public
Garden. By the time Lucy was born, the garden had become a strip mall—
now mostly inhabited by fast food chains, including the wildly popular

Wings and Things. Only an hour before, en route to the clinic, Lucy had pulled her red coupe up to the drive-through window to purchase a Diet Coke and one of the establishment's Things—which were donuts.

On her first visit to the clinic—seventeen years ago, to be precise—Lucy had arrived on a bicycle, a fake ID in her pocket, with which she'd successfully jimmied the lock of parental consent, a requirement back then for girls under the age of eighteen. An unlucky Lucy had become impregnated on her first go at intercourse—though, really, one could hardly call it a *go;* Lucy had given the boy no green light. Technically, there'd been no *intercourse;* it had been an indisputably one-sided affair—Lucy drunk, and the boy, a fuzzy blond with an alligator on his shirt, doing his business on top of her like some mechanical pony outside a supermarket. And though she'd tried to push him away, her hands had dissolved into the air like useless fins.

Afterwards, Lucy was afraid that if her father found out he'd kill both her and the baby—a fear that was not in any way an exaggeration. The least she could do was to save herself. She did the awful thing at the clinic and then, having told the same lie about having a ride home, walked the half block to where her bicycle was chained. When she'd tried to mount it, her stomach had cramped. She'd left the ten-speed leaning against a fence—and as she trudged toward her parents' house, it was in a haze of anger and shame. All of New Jersey appeared to be one giant cliché—an ugly sprawl of pizza and traffic and sleazeballs; green lawns lorded over by Marys on the half shell, and women who forced their hair into unnatural acts of aggression. Lucy, at seventeen, was no exception, with her glitter T-shirt and overblown mane. She stopped on the pavement at one point, noting her reflection in the window of a butcher shop. Within the ghostly transparence of her chest hung a huge hunk of meat—exposing her, it seemed, for what she was: an animal.

New Jersey was a terrible place, the worst place in the world—and a teenaged Lucy knew that it would only get worse. She could see every part of the Garden State growing fatter and fatter—the people, the buildings, the cars, the hair, until, finally, there was no space between any two things and a mass suffocation ensued. As Lucy stared at her seventeen-year-old self in the window of the butcher shop, it suddenly made sense where the real pain was coming from. It was coming from the future.

There on the street, she began to cry, bending over as if to trap the pain inside, prevent it from fleeing into the rest of her life.

Or maybe she could outrun it. Steal her father's car and drive to Los Angeles.

She headed in the direction of home, and then, confused, turned back toward her bicycle, uncertain if she'd put the chain back on.

Fuck it. She was too old for a bicycle, anyway. She turned again the other way.

"Are you lost?"

Lucy wiped her eyes.

"Where are you trying to get to? Miss? *Hablas inglés?*"

Lucy turned to the boy framed in the open window of a gumball-blue Camaro. "Do I look Spanish?" she said, mustering a little attitude.

"You look confused. If you need directions, I can—"

"I'm fine," Lucy said, straightening her back. "I live here."

The car purred at the side of the road. Lucy could feel the vibration in her chest.

"Were you in a fight?" asked the boy.

"No. Why, am I . . . ?" Lucy glanced down at her legs—a sudden mortifying fear that she might be bleeding.

"Just the way you were holding your stomach, I mean. Like somebody punched you."

"What, were you like staring at me?"

"Kind of, yeah. Sorry."

"Well, maybe you should mind your own business."

"I should," the boy said, still staring at her. "You're absolutely right."

"And do I look like the kind of girl who gets into fights? *Do I?*"

"Uh, *yeah.*" The boy was smiling now.

Lucy noted the nice lips, the perfect teeth. She turned away.

"Don't go. *Hey,* come on, wait up." The boy got out of the car.

"Stay away from me!" Lucy wielded a lavender fingernail with a white daisy painted on it.

"*Whoa whoa whoa,*" the boy said.

"You don't just jump out at people," scolded Lucy.

"Who's jumping? I'm not jumping. You must be thinking of the other guy."

The boy's dark, elaborately lashed eyes seemed capable of reading her mind. "What other guy?"

"I don't know. Whoever got you all like . . . defensive and shit."

Lucy caught her breath and pushed some hair behind her ear.

"I wasn't trying to freak you out," the boy said. "Honestly, I just, when I saw you, I don't know, I was just . . ." He trailed off and shrugged.

"Whatever," Lucy said, leaning awkwardly on one leg now.

"Whatever, but like . . . *something*," the boy replied.

He was older than her, maybe around twenty, with a voice like scrap metal wrapped in velvet. His skin, burnished olive.

"I have to go," mumbled Lucy.

"Don't go." The boy's come-on swagger was undercut by a strangely intense earnestness. His wavy black hair matched his eyes. An adorable pout transformed his lips into two small throw pillows.

Lucy was furious at New Jersey again, this time for its uncanny success at producing so many beautiful boys—brusque and over-blooded and slightly baffled, like shipwrecked princes suffering from concussions. They lingered everywhere, at the edges of the ugliness, like billboards making false promises.

"What if I'm here to protect you?" the boy said.

"I don't need—" She couldn't even say the word. *Protection*. It was what she needed more than anything. She began to tremble.

"Whoa," the boy said. "You don't look so hot."

Lucy raised an eyebrow—her vanity pricking up like a periscope, even as the greater part of her was sinking.

"I mean, you don't look *well*," the boy said. "You definitely look *hot*."

Lucy felt the wrong kind of heat rising through her body.

"Here, come on," the boy said, "lean on my arm."

"I'm fine."

"You're really pale."

"I'm always like that. It's genetic."

"Are you like part Chinese or something?"

"What?" Lucy peered more closely into the boy's night-gathering eyes. "Are you *stoned*?"

"No," the boy said. "A little."

Lucy sighed. "I'm Polish."

"Right on, right on," the boy said. "I'm Italian."

"No kidding," Lucy said sarcastically.

"You're not a racist, are you?" the boy asked with an artfully crooked smile.

"No," replied Lucy, "but I was raised by one."

"Me, too," said the boy enthusiastically. He extended his hand. "I'm Frank."

Lucy, intrigued by the formality, extended her own hand. "Lucy."

They shook.

The touch stopped them both. A lifetime passed, it seemed, before the boy continued.

"But if you ever want me to find this guy . . ."

"What guy?"

"The other guy, the one who—"

"Why do you keep saying that?" Lucy interrupted. "There is no other guy."

"Okay. But if he ever shows up, you just let me know, and I'll give him a nice knuckle sandwich."

"Oh my God." Lucy laughed. "Who says things like that? That expression's like a million years old."

"Sorry. My father's been giving me that line since I was like thirteen." The boy raised a fist and delivered an impressive cotton-mouthed Brando. *Shut your mouth, Frankie, before I give you a nice knuckle sandwich.*

"Sounds like a charmer," Lucy said of the old man she'd not yet met, but in whose house she would live long after the boy standing before her was dead.

"I have to get home," she said.

"Let me drive you."

"I should probably walk."

"Listen," the boy said. "I don't know why I jumped out at you but—"

"Oh, so now you're admitting you jumped?"

"Yeah. I jumped."

They both smiled.

It was disgusting that flirtation could feel this good, sallying through the air with no respect for the greater tragedies of life, or even the smaller one Lucy had suffered less than an hour ago. She tried to remind herself that he was just a boy, and she was still in New Jersey; it was the same old story. But flirtation had a way of tricking you into thinking that, this time, the ending could be different.

Plus, the sense of a beginning—even if ultimately leading nowhere—seemed the perfect antidote to the unforgivable finality she'd just inflicted on some faceless twitch of consciousness.

"Sometimes you just do shit, right?" the boy was saying. "Jump out at a hottie on the street."

Lucy looked into the boy's eyes, attempting to get a fix on his game. He seemed sincere.

"You've got glitter on your face," he said.

"Oh." She brushed her hand across her cheek. "From my T-shirt, I guess. It was a gift," she added quickly, embarrassed suddenly by the stretchy top with its twee motif of heart-shaped vines.

"Wait, you missed it." He touched her face, and then together they stared at the tiny silver square on his finger—as if into a mirror that might predict their lives.

The boy blew at the glitter, and it angled away invisibly.

"The imp of the perverse," he said.

"The what?" Though the boy was still speaking, Lucy perceived nothing but the nimbus of his moving lips.

"It's from this story I'm reading by—well, he mostly writes horror stories—you know, the 'Pit and the Pendulum' guy—but he also writes these great science fiction pieces—well, some of them, I guess, are more like essays or whatever."

"Okay," Lucy said, trying to keep up. The boy was suddenly speaking very fast.

"Anyway, in this one there's this *force* or—the *imp,* basically—that makes the guy do certain things, mostly bad shit, but I think it's probably the same thing that makes us do other stuff, too, stuff that's not necessarily *bad* but just different from what we would normally do if we were in our right minds or whatever. I mean, it's not really about right or wrong but like, you know, why did I *have* to get out of the car when I saw you, you know, these *impulses* or . . ." He paused and rubbed his face. "Am I like completely boring you here?"

"No, no," Lucy said. "Not at all."

Though she didn't understand everything the boy was saying, what she did grasp seemed to make sense. She herself sometimes did things a normal civilized person would never do.

"Like a voice in your head," she suggested.

"Or even more than a voice," the boy said. "Like another person almost."

"Totally," Lucy said. "Like a couple of weeks ago, I broke all these beer bottles for like no reason."

"Done it, too," the boy said, touching his chest. "I love breaking shit."

"Or like when I tried to stab you before with my fingernail."

"Exactly," the boy said.

They nodded self-consciously. A bird yakked boisterously above them in a tree. The boy looked up. "Right on," he said—maybe to the bird; Lucy wasn't sure. "You know, you should really let me drive you home." This part, definitely to Lucy. "What do you say?"

She looked away and then looked back at him. "Let me ask you something."

"Anything," the boy said.

She asked him if he owned any shirts with alligators on them.

He asked her, in reply, if he looked like a loser.

"Too early to tell," she said.

When, at last, she was sitting inside the gumball-blue Camaro, her stomach began to flutter. Maybe this was a bad idea. The leather-hushed interior of the car was like another weather system, with its gentle hum of cool-flowing air, the cloud cover of tinted windows, and the clean scent of pine blooming from a Christmas-tree-shaped air freshener hanging from the rearview mirror. Dangling there, as well, like a real ornament on the fake tree, was a religious medal of some kind. The inside of the car seemed more manicured than man cave.

"It's so clean," Lucy said.

A smile emerged like a ninja from the corner of the boy's lips. "My mother always says, you have to be ready for company."

"Uh-huh." Lucy rolled her eyes. "You get a lot of company in here?"

"No one of your ilk," the boy replied.

Lucy didn't know the word. Maybe it had something to do with the *imp*. She glanced at the odometer: just under fifty thousand miles. The Camaro still had a long life ahead of it. Once again, Los Angeles flickered through her mind.

"Where do you live?" the boy asked—and then, using his obnoxious telepathy again: "Unless you want to go somewhere else?"

"No," Lucy said quickly. "Just home. I live in West Mill."

"Cool. I'm in Ferryfield. We're practically neighbors."

The boy was smiling at her again.

"The key goes in there," she said, pointing. The longer they sat in a parked car, the more likely the boy was going to get the wrong idea.

"How old are you anyway?" he asked.

"Twenty-two," Lucy said, the lie delivered with confidence, fresh from its successful debut at the clinic.

"Yeah, right," Frank said.

"I can show you my ID."

"Okay, show me."

Lucy pulled it out and handed it over before realizing that the boy would now know her last name *and* her weight, both of which she hated.

"Terrible work," the boy said of the ID. "Who made this for you?"

"It's real," Lucy protested.

"I can get my cousin Vincenzo to make you a better one."

"I'm good," Lucy said, snatching it back. "I really need to get home."

"And what, may I ask, do you need a fake ID for, Lucille Bubko?"

"You know what? I think I'll walk," Lucy said, reaching for the door.

"*No no no,* come on." The boy started the car. "I'm sorry. Just tell me how to get there." Carefully he pulled out onto the road. The religious medal came to life, swaying and ticking.

"Which way?"

"Straight," Lucy said. "For now."

The boy did as he was told. "Lucy Bubko," he said quietly, nodding to himself, as if the name were a memory and he were trying to recall the story that went with it.

Lucy, without warning, began to cry.

For a while, the boy said nothing. He didn't seem troubled by the girl's tears, neither embarrassed nor angry. He didn't pretend it wasn't happening, as Lucy's mother would have done; nor did he shout, *Shut the fuck up,* in the parlance of her father. When the boy did speak, it was only to offer a simple "Yup. Yup yup yup," nodding his head at the girl's tears, as if familiar with the idiom.

"Left here," Lucy managed.

There was something oddly liberating about crying in front of a stranger. She'd never done anything like that before. Of course, she'd never killed a baby before, either. It was a day that for the rest of her life would always seem like a dream.

"I'm sorry," she said, wiping her face.

"No worries," said the boy. "You want me to put on some music?"

It seemed a kindness. "Sure."

"The Pogues," Frank said, slipping in the CD. "They're like from the eighties."

"That's okay," Lucy said.

A snarling dirge blasted through the speakers, eliciting another rush of tears.

I met my love by the gas works wall
Dreamed a dream by the old canal

"Do you want me to turn it off?" asked the boy, and Lucy shook her head.

Cats are prowling on their beat
Dirty old town, dirty old town

For a moment it seemed Lucy was singing along, muted dog-howls to round out the cats. The car was nearing her house, and it was probably a good idea to get the last of it out. By the time the song was over, she felt better—her body strangely calm, and her mind clear.

"Oh my God." She manufactured a fairly convincing laugh and covered her face. "You probably think I'm like insane."

The boy turned off the music. "The opposite."

"That's me over there." Lucy pointed to a squat two-story with dingy yellow aluminum siding. "But don't pull in the driveway," she instructed. "They'll see you."

The boy stopped by the curb, a short distance away. "I live in a house like that, too," he said. "Eyes everywhere."

Lucy reached for the door, but didn't open it. The two of them sat for a while without speaking. Late-afternoon light crashed through the windshield like a cataract.

"It was just a really weird day," the girl began. "I'm not usually so . . ." Her voice was suddenly false.

The boy waited, desolately, for the girl to reduce herself to just another boring chick feigning frilly empty-headedness.

"Why am I apologizing?" she continued. "It's your own fucking fault for picking me up."

Frank relished her attack. "It's the imp's fault."

She asked if he had any more pot—and then, in reply to his endearingly nervous face: "I really am twenty-two."

"Dream on, little sister."

"I am."

Frank sighed, to register that what he was about to do went against his better judgment. He looked both ways out of the car, and when he'd ascertained an all clear, he opened the ashtray and pulled out a half-smoked, pinky-thick doobie.

"What about the eyes?" Frank said, gesturing toward the yellow house.

Lucy shrugged. "Fuck them."

"You've got a mouth on you."

"You picked up your knuckle sandwiches, I picked up my fucks."

"I've got a foul mouth, too," Frank said.

"It's not a contest," said Lucy. "Are you going to light it or what?"

"Maybe I should kiss you first."

The boy leaned in and placed his lips on Lucy's cheek. Despite its G-rated positioning, the kiss was more familiar than any the girl had ever known. He lingered there, breathing into her ear.

"I hate my family," she whispered. "My parents."

The boy answered with more breath in her ear.

"Do you hate yours, too?" she asked.

He kissed her again before pulling away to light the joint.

"My parents, *shit,* they're from like another world," the boy said. "Literally." The rolling paper flashed red as he took a deep drag. "And they're total pains in the ass." He inhaled again. "But, yeah, I don't know, I guess I love them."

Lucy saw how it was sad either way with parents. Love or hate. When the boy held out the joint, she took it and sucked in the smoke until she began to choke. "Skunk!" she cried, slapping her chest.

"It's good shit," the boy concurred.

In five minutes, they were banging their heads to the Pogues and laughing hysterically.

"Hey," Frank said, "why don't you come over to my house for dinner?"— and Lucy, thinking the invitation the most ridiculous thing in the world, accepted. "Why the fuck not?"

"Why the fuck not indeed," Frank proclaimed, setting off more laughter. Machine-gun bursts of it they fired at everything and nothing—the hilarity carried straight into the house at 21 Cressida Drive, where the boy's stout, crucifix-wearing mother asked them what was so funny, had they swallowed a box of feathers?

Which only made them laugh more.

Until eight years later, when Lucy found herself, at twenty-five, in the same windowless clinic on Bluebell Avenue, married to Frank and carrying his child. Her plan had been to get rid of it. Now, under the drip of fentanyl, Lucy began to mumble—apologizing to Edgar for what she'd almost done to him.

Lucy had never wanted a baby. And besides, Frank was too far gone by the time she'd gotten pregnant. Sometimes he'd disappear for days, come home looking like an African Jesus fresh from the desert: sun-darkened skin, wild hair, the whites of his eyes shocked by visions. Lucy hadn't told him she was pregnant. When she'd made the appointment, she'd done so in secret, from Tricia Migliorisi's house. But then Tricia had ratted her out, and while Lucy had sat in the waiting room, flipping through the pages of a fashion magazine, in stormed Frank, wearing nothing but a pair of ripped jeans. No shoes, no shirt.

He'd knelt in front of her, pleading. The other girls had stared—the younger ones with envy, and the older ones with pity.

"*We need him, Luce.*" Begging. Putting his head on her lap.

"It's not a *him*, Frank," she'd tried to explain. "It's not anything."

But Frank had said he could feel what it was. "It's a boy," he shouted. "It's me."

When a security guard approached, Frank had grabbed Lucy, crying, "*Please don't kill me.*"

It was too much. Lucy had stood. "It's okay," she said to the guard, to Frank, to the other girls—to herself. She kept saying it, like some idiotic robot, as she held on to her husband and walked out of the clinic onto an impossibly sunny street. *It's okay it's okay it's okay,* like she'd lost everything but the ability to utter a profoundly ridiculous lie.

"Where are your shoes?" she asked Frank, but he wasn't listening. He was pushing her into the car—the gumball-blue Camaro now replaced by Pio's gold LeBaron—telling her they had to get home, she had to rest. "He'll save us," Frank said. "You'll see. This baby was sent for a reason."

Lucy's foot cramped in the stirrup. She turned to look at the tan walls and squinted, as if still on that sunny street with her husband.

But he wasn't her husband anymore, was he? Were you still married to someone after they died? Lucy felt a stab of anxiety. Dead wasn't dead. Frank was forever, and here she was, carrying the butcher's baby. She was a whore; Florence had been right.

Where was the fucking doctor?

She closed her eyes and saw Edgar barking, Edgar oinking. The thing growing inside her suddenly seemed half human, half pig.

Or was it Edgar, playing a game? Lucy touched her belly, confused.

Drip drip drip, ticked the fentanyl, as time moved back and forth like the shuttle of a loom, weaving fantastic cloth: maybe Edgar hadn't been born yet.

Maybe the reason no one could find him was because he was still inside her.

Was it possible, Lucy wondered, to have the same child twice?

She fumbled for the IV and pulled it from her arm. She couldn't do this again. This was something a woman could do only once. Plus, she didn't wish to bring further punishment on herself. It was entirely possible that Edgar had been stolen in retribution for the fact that, once, she'd tried to destroy him.

But she hadn't *known* him then. When she'd made the decision to kill him, he was nothing but a bunch of cells she'd conceived with a lunatic.

In fact, it seemed that she hadn't known him until this past week, after he was gone. A boy with the glowing eyes of a sea monster. Who ate one pea at a time. Who saved the fortunes from cookies in a demitasse cup. Lucy had pored through them just a few days ago. *You always bring others happiness. People are attracted to your delicate features. Soon new addition to your family!*

Lucy tried to stand, her hand tearing the onionskin covering the table.

"Mrs. Fini, sorry to keep you— What's wrong?" The doctor rushed over and grabbed Lucy's arm to keep her from falling. "What are you doing? I need you to sit back down."

"I have to go."

"Please, Mrs. Fini, you're in no state to—"

But Lucy ignored him. She took her clothes from the hook and began to dress. It was like putting on cobwebs.

"Change your mind, hon?" The fruity-smelling nurse was back. "I'll take care of her," she whispered to the doctor. "You can see Ms. Ramirez in room three."

"Where are my shoes?" asked Lucy. *"Where are my shoes?"*

"Right there." The nurse pointed. "But I want you to rest for ten minutes, okay? And then we'll call your ride."

"He's waiting outside."

The woman tried to lead her back to the table.

"He's waiting," shouted Lucy. "I have to go!" She picked up her shoes and arranged her face carefully for the nurse. "I'm fine."

Passing through the outer room, she saw the other girls, bored faces in beige chairs, as if waiting for pedicures. One little blonde was smiling, texting into a rhinestoned iPhone. A child—she could almost be forgiven for her stupidity. Lucy had no such luxury.

As soon as she emerged into the shock of daylight, she knew where she had to go. She had to drive to the bridge at Shepherd's Junction. In her drug-shadowed state, dressed in cobwebs, it seemed the obvious place to look for the boy. Possibly he was still there. In the berry bushes at the side of the road, where she'd left him, all those years ago.

BOOK SIX

NINE MONTHS

Times are bad. Children no longer obey their parents, and everyone is writing a book.

—ATTRIBUTED TO CICERO

October

34

Withdrawal

Thwok. Thwok. Thwok.

It was like a clock—louder, though, and with the ticking slowed down. Edgar woke to the sound. He rolled from under the comforter and peeked out the window.

Thwok!

Conrad was splitting logs. Conrad was the man's name—and though Edgar felt funny calling him that, it was better than the other suggestions the man had made as to how Edgar might address him.

Edgar mostly just said, "Excuse me." It was important to be polite when you were a guest in someone's house. Conrad had said, "It's your house, too," but, of course, it wasn't. The situation was still confusing—in some ways more so now that Edgar had finished his pills. To be without them had proved disastrous.

In addition to the unaccountable horror Edgar had felt, five days ago, when faced with the empty bottle, there had been physical repercussions, as well. A ringing in his head had left him unable to sleep for more than a few hours at a time—and when he did drift off, it was on a wave-tossed raft, from which he'd crash ashore with his limbs shaking and his skin drenched. Fever, delirium. For three days the boy's awareness skittered through a blinding lexicon of water and bones. Plus, there'd been a terrible twelve hours of constant running to the bathroom. Worse than all of it, though, had been the sadness—a walled-in, suffocating grief that left no room for tears. It was as if Florence had died all over again.

Ironically, the man—Conrad—had tended to Edgar exactly as Florence would have done—setting up a chair beside the boy's bed, always at the ready with a cool rag or a soothing pet. Whatever words he'd whispered—and there'd been lots of them—had arrived in the boy's ear as nothing more than

mush, a steady stream of background noise, void of sense. If they had a meaning, it was only in their quality, which Edgar had been able to recognize
even from the depths of his shudders. It was the quality of kindness—
something of which, one might say, Edgar was a connoisseur. For most of
his life he'd sipped from an excellent vintage.

Thwok.

Of course, kindness only made the situation *more* confusing. What was
clear was: big things, like time and place, had shifted. It was odd to be awake
again after a long dream under the powder-pink thrall of Percocet-Demi,
and to find oneself living a completely different life. The oddest thing was
how familiar it all was—as if during the powder-pink dream Edgar had been
learning things, or rehearsing them, and now, finally shoved onstage, he
found he knew how to go about his business. He knew the ins and outs of
the set, and where the props went.

He knew where to find the cereal bowls and the spoons, and he knew
what time Jack took his breakfast and how much wet food and how much
dry to give him. He knew to use extra force to turn on the hot water in the
bathroom sink—but not too much, or the fixture would come loose.

Thwok.

He knew that even though there was electric heat in the cabin, the man
liked to make a fire first thing in the morning, and then again after dinner.
The stone floor in the living room was often numbingly cold, and the fire
was the only thing that helped to warm it. As for keeping one's body warm,
Edgar recalled that the man had shown him a good trick: how to sit close to
the flames, but facing away, and then after a few minutes, when you could
barely stand the heat, to quickly lie on your back on one of the little rugs. It
was amazing how the heat from your back bloomed into your entire body—a
warm liquidy unfurling that was almost unbearably pleasurable.

Still, Edgar, being Edgar, often found himself cold. And though he'd
been given permission to turn up the thermostat ("Anytime, anytime," Conrad had said), he was timid. Whenever he did bring himself to adjust it, he
only notched it up one or two degrees—and, even then, proceeded with a
distinct feeling of stage fright.

Thwok.

Edgar watched the axe come down and the wood crack—after which he
looked at his finger. It had pretty much healed. The bandage was gone, and
Edgar studied the little Frankensteiny rimple surrounding the tip of his left
pointer.

"Battle scar," the man had called it—and the boy had silently agreed. Because that's how he remembered it, too. It *had* been a battle. Conrad may have said some things along this line, about how lucky Edgar was to have gotten away—but Edgar was pretty sure that most of the story had come from his own memory.

First and foremost: the way the butcher had cut off his finger.

Edgar dwelled on the incident. It was like some horrible bedtime story— except no one had told it to him, had they? It had actually *happened*. Edgar could follow his mind back to the brightly lit kitchen—and, if he was brave, force himself to see the exact moment when the butcher's hand had come down with a malicious, air-bending whack.

But why would a person do such a thing? And why would his mother have just stood there and let it happen? The Schlips—Henry and Netty, Florence's friends—had been there, too.

Was it a dream?

No. Edgar clearly remembered how the butcher had put the fingertip in a plastic bag and tried to steal it. But, somehow, Edgar had gotten it back. Maybe the Schlips had interceded on his grandmother's behalf. Edgar suspected that Conrad might have helped, too.

What stood out, most of all, was the image of the butcher standing beside Florence's tomato plants, laughing, shining a flashlight onto his oversized face. Edgar could remember his mother laughing, too—and then suddenly there'd been a lot of blood.

Thwok!

Edgar instinctively touched his throat where Florence had once put a crucifix on a chain. It had had to be removed because the metal caused a rash on the boy's sensitive skin. Now, at the cabin, he wished for something charmed: one of his grandmother's Saint Christopher trinkets or a little white candle in a blue glass cup; maybe even a dab of Chanel N⁰ 5—something to protect him from evil, a job that had always been Florence's. His grandmother had been an expert at discerning what was good from what was bad, whether it concerned towels or artichokes or people. Edgar would now have to figure out such distinctions for himself.

He looked away from the window, toward the bureau. The Virgin's head rested on top. Edgar had hoped her body might grow back, like a lizard's tail. But there she lolled, useless, facedown next to the empty bottle of pills.

Luckily, he still had the diamond.

In one corner of the bedroom, where the floorboards were slightly rotted, there was a small splintery hole. He knelt before it now and pulled out his treasure. He slipped Florence's ring over his Frankenstein finger and kept it there for several minutes. The idea was similar to recharging a battery from a power source—Edgar being the battery, and the diamond being the source. He did this every morning. If it weren't for the ring, he probably wouldn't have had the strength to get out of bed.

Cold air sometimes came up from the little hole. It was coming up now, making Edgar shiver. From the bureau he got one of the other boy's sweaters and pulled it over his head. The waistband fell nearly to his knees. The clothes were all too big, but at least there were lots of warm things, including bulky turtlenecks that made Edgar feel burrowy and safe. The only item he didn't care for was the reflective orange vest. It looked to Edgar like something worn by garbagemen—or by the prisoners who picked up litter on the sides of roads. But the man had explained that it was for hunting. He'd also said that when it came time to practice for real, Edgar would have to wear the orange vest.

Hunting season started in November, according to the man. Edgar wasn't sure how soon that was. He'd lost all sense of time. When he'd searched the cabin for a calendar and found nothing, he wondered if he should start making marks on the wall.

Conrad would have noticed them, though. Other than some splintery wood here and there and the faulty fixture in the bathroom, the cabin was in excellent condition. If it had once been the house of a poor person, this was no longer true. The man said the place was over a hundred years old, but that a lot had been done to fix it up. The windows were new and tight, each with two sheets of glass—the double panes keeping out not only drafts, but also sound. The trees beyond the windows tossed silently, appearing less like trees and more like current-swept vegetation at the bottom of the ocean. Edgar would not have been surprised to see one of the fish from the man's aquarium disappear into the submerged stone tunnel, only to reappear outside among the trees. The silence was so profound at times that Edgar had the uncanny sensation he'd gone deaf.

The fish had miraculously appeared a few days after his arrival. "I got them while you were sleeping," the man had said. Edgar, it seemed, slept a lot. Only recently had he started to wake up enough to see the cabin as something more than a foggy wooden box; to see it as a house.

The place was a weird mixture of old and new. There was an antique cuckoo clock with little figures that trotted out twice a day; hulking pieces of wooden furniture: towering wardrobes and rough-hewn chests, intricately carved throne-like chairs. But then, interspersed among the heavy old furniture, space-age lamps rose like silver ferns—and in one corner of the living room stood a spotlit sculpture, a delicate floating staircase that seemed to be made from translucent paper. In the kitchen there were chipped cups of blue enamelware, alongside a set of expensive-looking white china. The stove was an old gas top whose oven made a loud tinging sound whenever the man used it, as if he were cooking up a hailstorm instead of a chicken. Across from the seventy-year-old stove, though, lived a new dishwasher, as well as a robotic refrigerator that scolded you if you failed to properly close one of its doors.

The strangest thing in the cabin was a small round window of pink glass, embedded high in the living room wall, above one of the mounted deer heads. In the late afternoon, there was a brief period when a beam of colored light fell nearly to the floor. On several occasions, when the man wasn't around, Edgar stood directly under the channel of pink light. Unfortunately, it seemed not to function as a teleportation device.

Not that Edgar knew where he would go. Home was complicated. To make going home okay, he'd need more than a teleportation device; he'd need a time machine, as well.

For now, he had to stay where he was. His anxiety was lessened slightly by the fact that the cabin was clean. The man was nearly as fanatical as Florence had been when it came to housecleaning. Even when they'd first arrived, Edgar's perceptive nose had picked up a lingering scent of bleach, as if the place had been scrubbed down before it was last vacated. Conrad was always washing or polishing something. Several times a week, he scoured the kitchen faucet with an old toothbrush. He kept good care of the outside, too, and had recently started to dig a series of holes. For a fence, he'd said. The man's constant activity seemed a kind of nervousness—and this made Edgar feel a little less ashamed about his own fears. Sometimes he was even able to approach the man without shaking. He once asked him if he had a job, and Conrad said he didn't need one, he was busy enough. When the boy then asked him what he *used* to do, Conrad only smiled. "I'm retired now," he said. "I'm writing a book."

Edgar didn't think the man seemed old enough to be retired—and as for writing a book: when did he find the time to do it? When he wasn't working around the house or attending to Edgar, he mostly read. Sometimes, at night, you could hear him talking in his bedroom. Possibly, that's when he was writing. The boy knew, from his own experience of doing compositions for school, that it was sometimes necessary to say one's words out loud to see if they were good, or true.

Having a life meant having a story.

Edgar wondered if he should be writing, too. Even though he had a pretty good memory, he worried about forgetting stuff. His grandmother and his mother had forgotten tons of stuff, especially about his father. Maybe it was important to keep notes so you'd have them when you were older. Lately, Edgar had the sense that there was a hole in the middle of his brain; that important thoughts were slipping away.

Clearly, he'd let his head get lazy. It'd started with the little pink pills, but the effects seemed to linger even now, especially at night, when he had the most confusing conversations with Conrad. What did it mean when a stranger said he needed you, or wanted to know if you hated him? Edgar tried to give the right answers. Still, he often felt like he was drowning.

If the ship is sinking, better start thinking, Mr. Levinson had always said in science class. Edgar liked Mr. Levinson; he was smart—and he thought Edgar was smart, too. But recalling him now only flurried the boy's breath. Ever since he'd run out of Percocet, he'd grown more and more anxious about missing school. How would he ever catch up on his homework? One day he'd mustered the courage to ask the man for some paper—but instead of practicing fractions or trying to remember the dates of historic events, he'd only doodled. While he was jig-jagging some lines into the shape of a Christmas tree, the man had walked up behind him and said, "You're pretty good. Maybe we should collaborate."

Edgar, who knew the meaning of the word, but not the context, had looked up quizzically.

"I can do the story," Conrad said. "And you can do the pictures."

In response, Edgar had only shrugged sufficiently to imply a polite *maybe*—but, later, he tore up his drawing, promising himself that the next time he asked for paper, he'd use it to write a note to his mother.

Besides, if he ever decided to write a book, he'd do the whole thing himself. Words *and* pictures.

* * *

A sleepy Edgar ventured out into the living room. He knew he had a little more time alone. After Conrad chopped the wood, he always swept the back patio. And sometimes he cleared branches off the roof or went around collecting the tall bitter greens he used in salads. He didn't seem to worry anymore about leaving Edgar by himself. Once in a while, Conrad even drove to a store and was gone for more than an hour. Straight out, he'd tell the boy, "I trust you." And though Edgar wasn't sure exactly what might make him *un*trustworthy, he knew it was important to live up to the faith the man had put in him.

He'd already promised not to make any more phone calls or wander off alone down the sugar sand road. Even if he hadn't promised, he would have given up anyway. A second attempt to call home had led to the same problem as before: the voice of the butcher. Once again, Edgar had hung up without saying a word. He was furious with himself for not knowing his mother's cell. But the only number he'd ever needed—the one that was always put down for "call in case of emergency"—had been Florence's landline.

Every time the butcher answered in the old woman's stead, a peculiar terror seized Edgar's heart. He wasn't sure he could bear calling again—and anyway, Conrad didn't leave his phones lying around anymore.

As for running off into the woods, it was pointless. Whenever he tried it, he only got lost—somehow always ending up back near the cabin, as if the small wooden house were following him or existed in more than one place. Plus, the woods were dangerous—not only because of the feral dogs, but because of the snakes. At first Edgar had thought Conrad was exaggerating, but then he'd seen them: a timber rattler and a puff adder—the latter of which Edgar had nearly stepped on one day, causing the animal's neck to expand like a pharaoh's headdress and its mouth to gasp open to enormous size.

It seemed safer to stay inside. Besides, Conrad had assured him again that whenever he was ready to go home, all Edgar had to do was ask. It was obvious, though, that the idea of his leaving made the man sad—a baffling sentiment that Edgar didn't know how to factor in with his own desires: wild slashes of feeling that went in every direction, but cut no clear path through to his heart.

Sometimes he wondered if he wished to punish his mother. Maybe that's why he'd run away—if that was even what he'd done. Not once, at this point, did Edgar consider *abducted,* or *imprisoned.*

In regard to his mother, he realized that he didn't have it in him to punish her. Maybe all he wanted was to *test* her. In some ways of looking at things, she should be the one trying to find *him.*

If she even realized he was missing.

Possibly she'd become distracted by the black hair curling from the top of the butcher's shirt. She might even be touching it right now, slipping her fingers inside the slits between the buttons, as Edgar had seen her do. It wasn't difficult to picture the two of them sitting on the sofa, smoking cigarettes, sipping from the freezer-frosted bottle of vodka—after which the butcher might slide a cold hand between his mother's legs. Edgar had seen that, too.

A lot had changed at 21 Cressida Drive. It was no longer the kind of place that Edgar could imagine his grandmother living. Not that that really mattered, considering the fact that she was dead. Still, ghosts sometimes wished to return to the places where they'd once lived. Edgar had seen the evidence (actual video footage) on *Ghost Patrol*, as well as on *Haunted Habitat* (shows, incidentally, that he'd sometimes watched with Florence).

Clearly, though, his grandmother would be upset if she somehow managed to swoop into her old house and see what was going on. But then it dawned on Edgar that, were Florence to come back, she'd probably come to the woods, where he was. In fact, he was pretty sure he'd seen her once— but then she'd disappeared behind a tree. Sometimes, when the man was sleeping, Edgar stood outside and waited for her.

* * *

Conrad, too, believed in ghosts. Edgar had heard him mumble some things about dead people. When he'd said, one night, that nothing really died, he'd looked at Edgar so steadily that it had made the boy blush. Sometimes, though, the man's stares brought forth the sickening ooze of octopus ink inside Edgar's belly. He often felt strangely paralyzed. He rarely spoke, especially about Florence or about his mother and the butcher, but sometimes the man drew out little things. Speaking, though, often caused Edgar to become upset—and, even through his tears, he could see that he was upsetting Conrad. Lately, Edgar had been trying to do most of his crying while the man was out of the house.

Sometimes he rolled himself into a little ball and hid behind a leaning bookshelf shaped like a ladder. It wasn't as good as the spot at home, behind the trunk in his closet; it wasn't as tight. Still, it helped—the self-imposed constriction somehow allowing his breath to slow and his mind to blur into whiteness. Claustrophobic conditions had the opposite effect on Edgar from what they had on most people: rather than causing panic, they cured it. Pressure in general, whether from tight sheets or a dictionary put on his chest, felt nice. Another good technique from his old life had been to lie on his stomach, and then to ask Florence to put her foot between his shoulder blades. "Silly boy," she'd always say, but she would do it—until her foot got numb or she claimed she was getting dizzy. Sometimes Edgar thought he wouldn't mind spending the whole day like that, under the warm pressure of his grandmother's foot. It was something he wouldn't dare ask Lucy to do—and, of course, he'd never ask Conrad. For now, the narrow spot behind the bookshelf ladder was the best comfort he could manage.

Whenever Edgar hid there, it didn't seem to bother Conrad. He seemed to understand the boy's need to withdraw; to limit his tiny body even further: tucking his white head down and his legs up, expertly making an egg of himself. He could stay like that for several hours, perfectly still.

At home, Lucy had never liked it if she found Edgar in his closet, behind the trunk. Even Florence, who didn't mind lending her foot now and then to apply a little pressure, had absolutely no tolerance when it came to the closet. "Out, out," she'd say. "There's no air back there—you'll suffocate. Out!"

In his new habitat, the only one who occasionally rustled him from his hiding place was Jack. Which was interesting, Edgar thought—because in the old days it was Jack who'd first brought him *into* little hiding spots, and now it was Jack trying to get him *out* of one. Of course, they weren't the same Jack. The old one had been imaginary, and the new one was real. Also, one was human, and the other a dog.

Sometimes, when Edgar was behind the bookshelf, he could feel the animal panting above him. Occasionally the dog used its paws to gently prod the boy's side. More often than not, the egg would open—exposing its pale green eyes to the animal.

"Hello, Jack."

The boy's words, the sweet tone, were always perfectly understood by the dog: *Permission to lick, granted.*

35

Jack

The boy tasted wonderful, like fresh snow—his white face smooth as a bone. He was different, less like the man and the other slow-movers. He was more like the little ones that had been taken away—her own babies.

Jack was a girl—*Jackie*—though everyone seemed to have forgotten this. Jackie had been fond of licking the other boy, too. Even at the end she'd tasted him—one last lick, after his face had become as white as the boy in front of her now. She'd tasted the red, as well, until the man had pulled her away. When she'd howled, the man had muzzled her with his hand. If he'd not been howling, too, she would have bitten him.

* * *

"Why do you say *he?*" Edgar once asked. After consistently noticing Jack doing number one like a girl, he'd finally peeked between the animal's legs.

"Just habit," the man had replied. "Dogs always seem like boys, don't they?"

Edgar didn't agree.

"She can't make babies anymore," the man added.

"She's fixed?" Edgar remembered the terminology from something his grandmother had once said about Toni-Ann, how people like her shouldn't be allowed to have children.

"Yes," the man said.

"We should probably say *she,* though," Edgar suggested meekly.

"And what should I call you?" the man asked.

Edgar blushed, nervously touching his hair, which was getting long again.

"I'm just teasing," the man said. "You still want me to call you Edgar?"

"Yes, please," said Edgar.

* * *

Whenever the boy stepped out of his room, Jack trotted over and immediately began to lick. She preferred his face, but if the boy was standing she usually went for his left hand. Edgar noticed the way she gave particular attention to the once-damaged finger, as if she could taste something different there, or wished to soothe whatever hurt remained.

If Florence were here, she would have done something similar. Kissed the tip of his finger every morning. Kisses were another kind of medicine.

But that was more for a baby, and Conrad had said, *Eight is not a baby.*

Still, Edgar often knelt before the animal and hugged her as if she were someone he loved. Sometimes he rested his forehead against hers and let his breath condense into a small moan. When he was alone in the house and feeling brave, he'd bark, and Jack would bark back. It was a kind of screaming.

Soon Edgar learned that Jack had more than one kind of bark; he'd isolated seven varieties thus far. Plus, in addition to barks, there were whines and yelps and squeals, as well as howls and chirps and sighs. Edgar was a good listener, a good student. He came to understand that a dog's body— the way it moved—had a lot to say, as well.

This morning, as Edgar stood in the living room yawning, Jack tested him:

The licking was finished and now she was moving in a circle (*I want to play*), followed by a peculiar tilt of the head (*I have an idea*), and then the animal's circle widened and became more of a figure eight—this last movement, combined with a short repetitive squeal, could only mean one thing: *I want to show you something.*

As Edgar approached, the dog offered a small yelp of approval and skittered away. The boy followed until he was standing beside the dog in front of Conrad's bedroom door. Jack knelt, lifted a paw, and began to scratch.

"No," whispered Edgar.

The dog whined.

"No," the boy said more firmly.

But the dog contradicted him, lifting her head in a regal snap and uttering a brief, sharp demand.

"*Shhh.*" Edgar looked up. He could hear Conrad on the roof—removing branches or clearing the gutters of pine needles.

"You're messing up the door," said Edgar, noticing the white lines the dog's paws had made on the dark wood. When he knelt down to examine the marks more closely, he saw there were lots of them—more than what Jack could have made in the last minute. Some of the marks were deep grooves that preserved what seemed to be a long history of the dog scratching at Conrad's door—of wanting in, but being refused.

"Are you not allowed?" asked Edgar. The dog answered by licking his face.

The boy had always assumed that the dog slept in Conrad's room. If that wasn't the case, Edgar wondered if he might ask if Jack could sleep with him. His bed was small, but there was room enough for two, considering the size of the two in question. He and Jack were around the same length. Jack was thicker, of course, but together they would still be less than one full-sized person.

Jack was scratching at the door again. It didn't seem right to deny her. *It's your house, too,* Conrad had said.

Edgar stood and tried the handle. It turned, but the door wouldn't move—it seemed to be stuck. He would have left it at that, had Jack not offered a sustained squeal of encouragement. The boy pushed again and the door popped open with a twang. Instantly Jack flowed through the foot-wide opening.

Edgar couldn't see much of anything, but resisted the impulse to open the door wider. "Don't make a mess in there," he whispered through the crack (the dog had become suspiciously quiet). "What are you doing?" asked Edgar. "Okay, come on—come out. *Jack.*" Edgar pushed open the door a little more. The curtains in the room were drawn; there was very little light.

When his eyes adjusted, he could see the animal moving with her head down—sniffing the carpet, the man's slippers, the bottom of the heavy curtains. She lifted her snout to smell the seat of a chair, and then the edge of the quilt hanging from the large bed. The dog even put her head *under* the quilt—burrowing with a slight thrashing motion that began to mess up the neatly arranged sheets.

Suddenly the dog seemed to Edgar like no one more than his mother. Sniffing around a room that wasn't hers; trying to root out something of value. The way she'd rummaged through his grandmother's private papers, stolen her money—it still made Edgar furious.

"It's not your room," he scolded the dog. He went to smack her behind, but only lightly patted it—his anger, as always, drawing back at the brink of cruelty. The butt-pat did make the dog emerge from under the quilt, but only

in expectation of play. She looked up at the boy, barked, and then jumped
up on her hind legs as if she wished to dance.

"No," Edgar said—"*down.*"

The dog uttered a thin mewl of disappointment before leaping onto the
bed and settling there with a sigh.

"We can't stay in here," Edgar whispered. *"Jack."*

The animal rested her head on her front paws and peered upward with
the sad hope of a saint on a prayer card. The boy uttered his own sigh; took
a moment to catch his breath. The small jagged crack between the curtains
let in a frail rivulet of flickering light that traveled across the floor. When
Edgar followed it to the window, he did so with only slight trepidation: the
room didn't face the woodpile—and anyway, from the sound of it, Conrad
was still on the roof.

Larger pines pressed in close to this side of the cabin. Edgar spread the
curtains a few inches and saw the dense cluster of trunks—medium thick
and muscular. They seemed joined in a common task, collaborating to create confusing pathways of empty space. They were maze-makers, these
trees—hypnotists. Outside the window was the beginning of the mirrorland,
a place that, should you enter it, you might find yourself—as Edgar had—
right back where you'd started.

It was beautiful, though—the forest. Edgar looked up into the rustling
green. Sundrops pinballed down through the needles—though very little
light actually made it to the ground, which remained densely shadowed.

He glanced back toward the bed. Jack was staring at something, and Edgar's
heart leapt. He clenched his fists and turned, expecting to see Conrad.

Instead he saw a small table near the door, from which two tiny sets of
eyes returned his gaze. He hadn't noticed the photographs when he'd first
come in. "Are you looking at those?" he asked the dog. He moved closer,
and immediately understood who it was. It was Kevin and the nurse.

Conrad's son. Conrad's wife.

Each was consigned to a separate photograph—though both images were
obviously taken in the same place. Behind each figure, the same curved background of tall summer trees. The boy looked to be around twelve, and the
woman not much older than Lucy. Both were dressed in shorts and T-shirts.
They seemed happy—though that was probably no longer true.

"They're gone now," the man had said.

Edgar had known better than to ask the man to clarify the nature of their goneness. Whenever Conrad mentioned them, he always looked ill, and his right leg would often start to jitter as if it had a motor inside it.

Edgar put himself in front of the two smiling faces. The boy was handsome, and the woman pretty. Mother and son, standing among the trees. *Mirrorland.*

Edgar felt dizzy. In his own family, it was the father who was gone—the son and the mother still here. But in Conrad's world, it was the mother and the son who were gone, and the father who remained. It seemed to be a problem of mathematics. Edgar's solution was to divide the people into two separate families: one family of the living (Conrad, Edgar, Lucy) and one family of the dead (Frank, Kevin, the nurse).

But then he realized his error. The nurse wasn't dead. Only Kevin was dead. The nurse had simply gone away in a car. Edgar wasn't sure how he knew this, but sometimes it seemed that, while he slept, Conrad lingered by his bed, telling him stories. When Edgar had nervously asked one day if the nurse was coming back, Conrad had replied in a tone more forceful than usual: "No one's coming back."

An exchange after which the man had suddenly embraced Edgar. The boy had stood there, frozen.

Edgar peered closer, scanning Kevin's face, trying to see some sign of whatever it was that had killed him—some sickness or disease perhaps. Conrad hadn't said how he'd died.

Edgar sat on the bed, beside the dog, and closed his eyes.

Why was there so much sadness everywhere? And what could be done about it? *Frankie,* his grandmother had sometimes called him, without even noticing she'd done it. It had seemed to help her somehow—to lessen a sadness that lived inside her, but that Edgar had never managed to understand. He felt ashamed now, as if he'd failed her.

Maybe he *should* let Conrad call him Kevin—not all the time, just once in a while.

The boy laid his head on the quilt, pulled himself closer to Jack's warmth, and tumbled into sleep.

*   *   *

"Kevin."

Edgar heard the word, but only barely, a snowflake landing on his ear, dissolving instantly. He curled himself into a tighter ball. When he felt the dog beside him, he realized with a start that he was still on Conrad's bed. He continued to breathe, feigning sleep.

"At least open one eye," Conrad said, "so I know you're alive."

Edgar did.

The man stood in the doorway, pine needles clinging to his blue plaid shirt. In his hand was a plastic bag filled with something lumpy.

"I fell asleep," said Edgar. "I didn't touch anything," he added. "Jack wanted to come in."

"It's fine," said the man. He set down the plastic bag beside the small table of photographs.

When the boy attempted to speak again, no words came—only a sharp garble of sound somewhere between human and animal. Jack pricked up her ears.

The boy swallowed and tried again—pushing out the words. *"Where are we?"*

"Please don't shout," said Conrad.

Edgar breathed. "I want to go back to New Jersey."

"Where do you think you are, kiddo?"

"Pinelands," squeaked Edgar, remembering what the man had told him.

"That's right." Conrad was smiling, using his Mr. Rogers voice. "Almost a quarter of the whole state is the Pinelands."

"But *what* state?" asked Edgar.

The man's smile was stuck on his face. "New Jersey."

Edgar couldn't see how that was possible. New Jersey wasn't a *wilderness.*

Conrad shuffled over to the window and threw open the curtains. "And do you know how much of it belongs to me? Nearly nine hundred acres. Pretty amazing, huh?"

In his head Edgar rounded off the number to something just shy of infinity.

"I know it doesn't seem like paradise now, but wait until the spring. There are flowers here, Edgar—orchids—that don't grow anywhere else in the world."

The boy closed his eyes and whimpered. Spring seemed a million years away.

"You know what we need?" Conrad said brightly.

"What?" the boy said, close to tears.

"A miracle," whispered Conrad.

Edgar could feel his heart hurtling through space. Florence had often said the same thing. "What's in the bag?" he asked, gesturing toward the plastic sack by the door.

"Apples," said Conrad.

Edgar's mouth watered. He'd hardly eaten anything for several days. He asked if he could please have one.

"These aren't for eating." Conrad retrieved the bag and pulled out a deformed little bulb covered in black spots. "They're crabapples. I thought we might play a game with them. Put them on top of some posts, see how many we can knock off."

Edgar didn't think this sounded like fun. He asked if, instead, he might write a letter.

"Of course," said Conrad. "Breakfast first, and then a letter. Here, let me give you a lift."

As the man swooped in toward the bed, Jack lifted her head and barked.

Conrad immediately pulled back. "What's the matter, boy?"

"Girl," Edgar said quietly, before informing the man that the dog didn't like it when people moved too fast.

"Is that right?" said Conrad.

Edgar nodded. When he climbed down off the bed and headed into the living room, the animal followed.

If the man felt a twinge of jealousy, it passed quickly. What lingered in his mind, though, was the realization that the boy might be more willful than he'd seemed at first.

Which was a good thing, really. Two weeks had already passed—and though Conrad was happy to have this sweet interlude with the child, it was time to get down to business. Business that would not be served by trying to gain Edgar's affection. Wasn't the whole point to get the shotgun into the child's hands?

Conrad pulled a small notepad from his pocket and jotted down the words.

I am to be despised.

He wrote it repeatedly, until there was no room left on the page.

36

Signs and Symbols

Driving home one afternoon, Lucy saw a boy with an axe stuck in his head. He was walking casually on the sidewalk, swinging a large orange shopping bag.

An hour later, as Lucy was stepping out of the bathtub, the doorbell rang. She quickly wrapped a towel around herself and ran downstairs, leaving wet footprints on the carpet. The doorbell had lately become a poisoned arrow tipped with hope. "Coming," she cried.

A child stood on the stoop. He was covered in a white sheet—pink lips flashing through a crudely cut mouth hole.

"Trick or treat."

The voice was high, like her son's—and he was the right height.

Lucy could feel the water dripping down her legs. When she reached out to touch the sheet, the child retreated, and a woman in a purple tracksuit emerged from the shadows of the lawn. "What are you doing?"

"I just . . ." Lucy's hand moved again toward the sheet.

"*Miss.* Would you please not touch my kid?"

Lucy pulled back as the mother approached, her thin face sketched with whiskers and crowned with two triangles of black felt. She glared at Lucy. "How could you even answer the door like that—*half naked*—when you know there's gonna be children?"

Lucy apologized. She stood there, sweating, as the revelers scurried off.

But then the hope-like fear shot through her again, and she dashed across the lawn. At the sidewalk, by the hydrangea, she came up behind the child and pulled at the white sheet.

"What the hell are you doing?" The woman gave Lucy a shove, but Lucy somehow managed to keep hold of the sheet. She nearly had it off when it snagged at the neck, where some elastic had been sewn in.

"Ow," squealed the ghost.

"Are you crazy?" the woman hissed.

Lucy used both hands now, freeing the child's head.

A little girl in white leggings and a thermal undershirt stared up, terrified.

Not Edgar.

The words repeated themselves in Lucy's head like some cruel mantra. Everything in the world, it seemed, was *not Edgar*. The greatest cruelty being how everything in the world somehow still *referred* to Edgar.

The woman in the tracksuit continued to shout, threatening to call the police. Lucy barely heard the words—nor did she feel the towel slip from her body.

"Oh my God," the woman said with disgust—marching away with her daughter.

Lucy watched them go, as other children gathered on the sidewalk—all of them keeping a safe distance from the naked woman. Two boys—one in a black cape, one in a hockey mask—were laughing.

Lucy didn't feel the cold. She was looking at the sky now. The storm clouds had blown through, and the stars were coming out, clear and bright— close and far at the same time. She felt their light falling into her eyes. The stars were pulsing, speaking in code.

Not Edgar.

When the butcher's van pulled into the driveway, Lucy saw it only peripherally. She had a sense of standing on a bridge, waiting for an ambulance. But when she felt a coat being wrapped around her, she recognized the voice. "Come on, babe," the butcher said, leading her back toward the house.

"Get out of here," he barked to some of the lingering children. "There's nothing to see."

To which the hockey mask crudely replied: "We already saw it!"

As soon as the butcher had Lucy settled on the couch, he grabbed one of the flyers with Edgar's picture. He flipped it over to the blank side and wrote in large block letters: NO CANDY SORRY. PLEASE DON'T RING BELL. He taped the note to the front door, turned on the porch light, and told Lucy to close her eyes and rest; he was making pork chops.

November

37

The Waiter

Under the influence of fentanyl, she'd driven erratically, but with no doubt that she'd find Edgar waiting for her on the bridge or by the berry bushes. The closer she'd got, though, the more frightened she'd grown. Shepherd's Junction existed on a plane of reality that was bent—the rules of gravity, different. One could easily be torn apart, or crushed.

Still, it drew her. Every few days she found herself heading in that direction.

She never made it more than halfway, though. A force field of grief kept her from returning. Parked at the side of the road, she'd try to breathe while sucking the venom from a cigarette. Sometimes she had to pull over because she couldn't see what was in front of her; it was a disastrously rainy autumn. But even when the sky was clear, there were the blinding effects of tears.

Still, she refused to stop looking. Every morning, after the butcher had left for his shop, Lucy got in her little red coupe and made random circuits around the state, sometimes for up to four or five hours.

"Babe," Ron said. "What are you doing? You think you're going to find him standing by the side of the road?" Always in measured tones, never unkindly, he'd tell her that she was being foolish—that the kid was probably inside somebody's house. "They're not gonna let him run around in the street."

A comment that made Lucy furious. "Are you suggesting someone's got him tied up?"—the question brandished before Ron, daring him to join her in imagining the worst.

She was thankful when he refused the bait. "Of course not," he replied. "Who could hurt a kid like that? He's a friggin' angel."

Lucy relied on the butcher's steadiness, his seemingly unshakable conviction that Edgar would return. Still, she had no one else to lash out at.

"What am I supposed to do, get out of the car, knock on people's doors? Look in their fucking windows?"—to which Ron replied that she didn't need to be doing the police's job. A bogus answer, because he knew as well as she did that the police never seemed to be doing enough. *Everything possible,* they constantly said—but there was never any news.

Still, Ms. Mann, the detective, was in touch with Lucy almost every day. "Please, call me Becky," she often said—but Lucy preferred not to reduce the woman heading the search for Edgar to a name that brought to mind pigtails and braces.

Ms. Mann was less of a bitch, though, than she'd been at first. Lucy suspected the softening was due to the fact that the woman had failed to pin the boy's disappearance on maternal abuse (some sort of dildo cult hosted in Edgar's bedroom). Lucy hadn't completely forgiven the detective for her insinuations early on in the case, but what choice did she have other than to accept Mann as an ally. In regard to the investigation, she did seem to be the one police person who'd remained persistent, always following some new lead—even though each prior lead had led nowhere. The mysterious phone calls the butcher had received had come from disposable cells—but now, with the technology in place to trace future calls from such devices, there was only silence.

Some boys from Edgar's school had come forward about a man outside a convenience store. Fairly tall, light brown hair, a beard. He'd helped Edgar escape the clutches of a bully. "I think he was a cop," one boy said. "But like off-duty." "Yeah," another agreed. "He said he had buddies at the station." None of the boys could recall if he'd had a car. Ms. Mann, remembering the doodles in Edgar's sketch pads, was looking into cops with beards. As for the bully, the boys claimed not to have recognized him ("some fat kid"). The detective suspected the boys were reluctant to name the bully for fear of reprisals. She gave each of them her card and said, "If you think of anything, call me anytime, day or night." Two of the boys had tittered as if she were proposing a date. "This is very serious," she scolded them. "Your classmate could be dead."

A teacher of Edgar's had been brought in for questioning. Daniel Levinson, Math and Science. When employees of the school had first been interviewed, the man had been unabashedly verbal about his fondness for the child. "A delicate boy," he'd gushed. "Such a commodious mind." He'd used words like *beautiful, special;* had admitted that, like Edgar, he himself had grown up without a father. "I know what that's like. I tried to be a mentor to him, you know. A friend. People often misunderstand children like that." "Like what?" Ms. Mann had asked—to which Daniel Levinson had replied, "Brilliant, but—with issues." By the end of the interview, the unattractive forty-year-old man had confessed to sleepless nights of worry over poor Edgar Fini. When Ms. Mann ordered a search of Mr. Levinson's office, as well as the small house he shared with his mother, the man made no protest— only blushing slightly, saying, "I'm not like that."

Though nothing was found to warrant further investigation, Ms. Mann claimed she was keeping an eye on the man. When she talked about these things to Lucy—offered details from the search—Lucy felt the conversations went beyond an official exchange. Mann told her too much, describing the dusty interior of Mr. Levinson's house, how she'd unrolled his tube socks and poked around inside, only to find postage stamps. It seemed, to Lucy, that Mann shared such details because she wanted approval—needed someone to tell her she was doing a good job. Perhaps it wasn't easy being a female detective, but Lucy often wished Mann had more confidence.

"You're doing great," Lucy would say. "I know you'll find him."

"Thank you." Here, Mann would nod one too many times. "I will."

Luckily there were days when the detective's enthusiasm seemed genuine. One afternoon, she proudly informed Lucy that Edgar's image and profile had effectively been entered into every law-enforcement and missing-persons database in the country, and that the information was going out internationally, as well.

It seemed miraculous at first: Edgar's little white face appearing on computers and phones all around the world. But, that night, when Lucy lay in her son's twin bed and stared up at the glow-in-the-dark stars on his ceiling, she felt the extent of the search to be inadequate.

"He's everywhere," Ms. Mann liked to proclaim, in regard to the proliferation of the boy's image. "We should definitely be getting some reports soon." Lucy tried to remain hopeful, pushing down her glow-in-the-dark fears of an abduction that had little to do with the lines on a map. *Slippage*, Frank had called it. A slow falling from this world.

Lucy began to have unpleasant dreams in which her body rumbled across the sky with the deafening roar of a helicopter. Her eyes were spotlights— though they found nothing on Earth but strangers. When she woke in a sweat beside the pneumatic hiss of the mouth-breathing butcher, she would slip her toes between his hairy legs and try to remind herself of some scrap of pamphlet wisdom: *Be calm. Remember: even as you sleep, much is being done to find your child. You are not alone.*

Lucy pretended this was true.

Visualize your child sleeping in his bed. See yourself tucking him in.

When she tried, though, she could never see her own hands at the boy's chin—only Florence's.

* * *

Recently, Ms. Mann had started to collaborate with the Light for Jimmy people to help bring more attention to the case. The organization that had provided the bloodhounds employed a creative team that exploited everything from pop stars to public art. The latest news: Edgar's face would appear on a large screen in Times Square, between 5:42 and 5:43 P.M., on the first Wednesday of December. "One minute?" snapped Lucy—to which Mann replied, a minute was good, and that no missing child was getting more time than Edgar. "How many faces are they projecting?" asked Lucy, and Mann said, "About twenty thousand."

Slowly, the hunt for Edgar lost most of its real-world components (dogs, search parties, flashlights) and became more and more relegated to the virtual (e-mail, images, data). It no longer seemed a hunt at all—the whole project largely reduced to a matter of information dissemination and waiting. This was intolerable to Lucy. A working-class girl to the bone, she knew that if Edgar were to be found, it would be through effort—physical effort. She committed herself more fully to grueling drives around the state. Slowly, her circles widened to include New York and Connecticut—and soon she planned to drive farther south, as well.

One morning she took the Parkway to Seaside Heights—a route that, just past the exit for Toms River, swept through the northern edge of the Pine Barrens. She paid no mind to the scrappy trees at the side of the road; her destination was the ocean.

Walking along the cold deserted beach, she experienced a gasping relief at being able to shout the boy's name as loud as she wanted, without anyone telling her to calm down. On the way home, when she was only a few blocks from 21 Cressida Drive, she made a detour and drove to her father's house. She parked on the street and watched for signs. It wasn't inconceivable that the old man might have stolen the child. She shuddered, thinking of his sodden thrashings at Florence's wake, his crocodile tears and greasy desire for reconciliation. When she tried to step out of the car, her bad leg buckled. After all these years, she was still afraid of him. She drove home, telling herself it would be better to let Ms. Mann look into it.

But when Lucy ran into the detective the next day, she said nothing about her father. In a cavernous King's Drugs, Lucy had just grabbed a large bottle of Tylenol PM when she saw Ms. Mann shuffling down the aisle with a red nose and two boxes of NyQuil.

"I'm off duty," Mann said, as if to apologize for the bathrobe-like felt coat she was wearing. Her unbunned hair revealed crinkled filaments of gray Lucy hadn't noticed before.

"Are you sick?" Lucy's question came out unkindly, almost an accusation. Edgar's life was in this woman's hands, and here she was, looking like a wraith in need of a dye job.

"I'm fine," Ms. Mann replied. "Just a few sniffles." She sniffled lightly and shrugged—the effort causing her to collapse into an alarming fit of coughing.

"Oh my God," said Lucy.

"Let me just get these," Mann croaked, holding up the NyQuil, "and then we can sit in my car and chat."

* * *

"Is something wrong with your leg?" the detective asked, after Lucy was settled inside the blue Honda.

"What do you mean?"

"I notice you limp sometimes. I was wondering if maybe it was an injury from childhood."

"No," Lucy said coolly.

"I don't mean to pry, I'm just—"

"You just what? You read a file about me and now you think you know me? I did it to myself, okay?"

"Why are you getting testy?"

"This is not about me. This is about Edgar. Do you have any news?"

Ms. Mann seemed not to hear the question. She busied herself with ripping open one of the boxes of NyQuil.

"*Rebecca?* Is there any news?"

Mann shook her head.

In the silence that followed, Lucy closed her eyes. The detective poured herself a shot of NyQuil and quickly downed it.

"Why am I sitting here?" asked Lucy.

"It's important we talk."

"About what? My leg?"

"I was just asking out of concern. As a friend."

"We're not friends. You're looking for my son."

Mann coughed and poured herself another shot.

"You probably shouldn't drink any more of that shit until you get home," said Lucy. "It's like twenty proof." She stepped out of the car, and then leaned back in. "Listen, Ron said he had some questions for you."

"Of course. Just have him give me a call."

"Or if you want to stop by the house sometime, he's usually home by six."

"I'll look at my schedule."

Lucy nodded. "And just so you know—I'm not really a big *friend* person."

Before Mann could say anything in response, Lucy slammed the door of the Honda and dashed across the wet parking lot. It was only then that the detective realized that Lucy Fini wasn't wearing shoes.

Mann shivered, and downed the second shot.

* * *

A lot of people were trying to help—but, to Lucy, they seemed useless. They came to 21 Cressida Drive bearing casseroles and cookies, cellophane-wrapped baskets of fruit. Genuine kindness, but what did it mean in the absence of information? None of these people *knew* anything.

At least Lucy always had someone to station at the house while she was out driving and Ron was at work. Edgar might show up at any moment—and an empty house might confuse or frighten him. Mann also said it was important to keep one's eyes open for anything out of the ordinary *outside* the house—strangers on the street or an unfamiliar vehicle.

The home guard was comprised almost entirely of women. Netty Schlip was often there, waiting in Florence's chair, knitting an apple-green sweater she hoped to give Edgar for his birthday—only two weeks away. When Lucy asked her if she wouldn't mind, every now and then, sitting outside to keep an eye on the street, Netty said, "Of course not. I'll just fix myself a thermos of tea."

Netty had first learned about Edgar's disappearance from a sign outside the post office. At first glance, she'd noticed only the words SMALL and WHITE and MISSING, and had assumed the flyer was for a cat; but then she'd moved closer and seen the photo—the boy's face made paler than usual by a copy machine low on ink. For the last few weeks—despite the rainy weather—she found it impossible to wear her new rain bonnet, troubled as she was by the memory of her old one filled with ice and Edgar's fingertip.

Occasionally, when Netty was needed at the dry-goods store, another woman, who claimed to be an old friend of Florence's, filled in. Lucy vaguely remembered her from the wake: a praying mantis in vintage attire who'd obviously had her fair share of plastic surgery. When she'd first come to the house she seemed trustworthy enough—but, one day, Lucy had returned to find the woman in Florence's closet.

"Straightening up," she'd explained. "Too much clutter, darling. If you ever want to get rid of some of these old dresses, I'd be happy to take them off your hands." But Lucy had replied that she was keeping them. It had been necessary to tug twice before the woman relinquished a yellow silk evening-length. "Don't rip it, dear, it's one of a kind," the woman had scolded.

*　*　*

Honey didn't mention that she'd recently had a dream about the boy in which she'd seen him sitting on a lily pad, wearing Florence's engagement ring—though, oddly, not on his finger. He'd had the damn thing in his nose, like some Hindu princess.

Of course, her diet pills often gave her funny dreams—but this hadn't felt like a dream. It had had the shock of life. Honey had woken up sobbing, deciding on the spot that she'd visit the child's mother. Plus, she'd wanted to get inside Florence's bedroom—not only to see the dresses, but to make amends for certain cruelties.

Make amends—well, they were cheap words. Still, every little kindness helped at a time like this. She sat on the dead woman's bed and said things she hoped would clear the air. A request for forgiveness was directed earnestly toward the ceiling. When no reply came, she removed her pearl dangles and put them in the pocket of one of Florie's plainest frocks. All she took in return was a small embroidered hankie. *F.F.*

Friends forever—wasn't that what the young girls said these days? The little fools! Clearly they knew nothing about life. The pearl earrings had been a gift from Pio, a gift he certainly couldn't afford. What a hussy she'd been to accept them. Why, she'd probably taken food right off Florie's table.

* * *

A day didn't go by without someone ringing the doorbell.

Celeste, Lucy's ex-employer from the salon, showed up early one morning in a sequined baseball cap. She brought some homemade wine in a clear plastic bottle, at the bottom of which lurked twigs and leaves and what appeared to be gravel. "Not to drink," she informed Lucy. "Pour it out in the front yard, and write the boy's name with the drippins." The explanation of the custom summoned a missionary intensity in Celeste and pushed her Jamaican accent full tilt. "Now listen, girl, make sure you go slow, so you have enough for every letter. You want da *Edgar* and you want da *Fini*." She tilted the sealed bottle toward the carpet to illustrate—"drip drip drip, right on da grass."

Other girls from the salon dropped by, too, with cards and flowers and teddy bears, as if it were Valentine's Day. Even Audrey Fenning, the client whose ear Lucy had nipped, appeared at the door one afternoon. She handed Lucy an intricately folded five-dollar bill—a belated tip to make up for the one she'd withheld on what she referred to as "the day of the prick." As Lucy stared at the folded square, Fenning flushed and reached into her purse to pull out a twenty.

The most unexpected visitor, though, was Anita Lester. Lucy hadn't seen her in years. Anita had been there when Edgar was born. In fact, she'd served as midwife. Frank had been too afraid of hospitals, and despite Florence's protests, Edgar had been delivered at home. "A black woman?" Florence had whispered to Lucy. "Are you sure?" The interracial hippie-like birthing ceremony, in which Frank had worn carnelian beads and burned sage, had been a source of shame for Florence. When Edgar was older, she'd told him that he was born in a clean room at Holy Name Hospital—and Lucy, not wishing to argue with the old woman, had gone along with the story. Lucy had even embellished it with a traditional slap on the behind and a little glass box in which, she informed Edgar, he'd slept for a week. She'd added the detail about the incubator not to scare her son, but to please him; she knew how fond he was of curling up in tight spaces. Still, she wondered now if there was a single thing she'd ever told the boy that wasn't an outright lie.

Since Edgar's disappearance, Anita Lester had come to the house three or four times. When Lucy asked if she was still midwiving, she shook her head. "I got my nursing degree a few years ago. I'm at the hospital now." Lucy had always liked Anita. When she'd come to 21 Cressida Drive on the day of Edgar's birth, she'd brought her own son with her. The boy—Jarell—couldn't have been more than five at the time. Florence had given him almond cookies and a glass of milk. Pio, squeamish about childbearing, had rushed off to the racetrack to calm his nerves—and Frank, of course, was in the bedroom with Lucy. Florence had waited in the living room with the black boy until it was over. When Anita came down the stairs and announced, "You're a grandmother, Mrs. Fini," a teary Florence had leaned over and kissed Jarell on both cheeks.

"Do you think he still remembers?" asked Lucy.

"I'm sure he must," said Anita. "And I know he's heartsore about Edgar, same as everyone."

* * *

In fact, several days after Edgar's disappearance, Jarell Lester deleted Thomas Pittimore's name from his digital contact list. It was a strange thing to do, because he'd known Thomas a long time and deleting him from the phone was sort of like killing him.

It had to be done, though. Pitt had changed. He'd always been insanely funny, like a clown on crack. But recently he'd become mean. It was amusing, at first, what he'd done to Edgar in the woods—forcing him to watch porn. But then Thomas had gone sado and incised the little boy's arm with a ballpoint pen. Jarell had just stood there and watched.

He knew that his lack of valor showed him to be the exact opposite of what his mother always told him to be—which was a stand-up man. *You don't hurt things smaller than you,* she'd once said to him. It hadn't meant much to Jarell at the time, but now it seemed profound.

* * *

When Toni-Ann sat at the house (always Lucy's last resort), she drew pictures of tiny snowmen in Edgar's sketch pads. It made her feel less terrible.

On the day of Edgar's disappearance, the police had stood in Toni-Ann's living room and asked her mother if she'd seen anything suspicious. "No. Nothing," Mrs. Hefti said. "Of course, it's always been a circus next door."

Toni-Ann had wanted to tell them about the green truck, but as soon as she began to speak, her mother had shushed her. "Not now, honey— Mommy's talking." Finally, a nice policewoman turned to the girl and asked if there was something she wanted to say. Toni-Ann only had to glance at her mother's hard, impatient face to know the correct answer: "No. Nothing."

Maybe it wasn't such a terrible lie. She'd only ever seen Edgar get *out* of the truck, she'd never seen him go *away* in it. Still, it bothered her. Whenever she drew the little snowmen, she often decorated them with flowers— mostly yellow daisies. Flowers could protect a person. It was the least she could do to keep Edgar safe. Sometimes she tried to put a rose in the snowman's hat, but roses were hard to draw—they always ended up looking like snails.

When Lucy returned home from one of her drives, Toni-Ann would hug her. "I waited all day, Mrs. Feen," she'd whisper as if it were a secret. "I'm the waiter."

* * *

"I'm Janet," said the woman at the door. "From ALFJ." A Light for Jimmy regularly provided volunteers to assist families in crisis.

"I don't really need anything," Lucy informed the woman. "I've got a lot of people helping."

"Oh, that's okay. We can just talk."

This was the fourth woman the organization had assigned to Lucy. One had spent the afternoon making chocolate chip cookies and banana bread, until the whole house smelled like a bakery. Another had dusted and vacuumed and put Ron's variously scattered beer and wine bottles into the blue recycling bin. A young woman of about twenty-six, dressed in pink overalls, had spent several hours tending to the yard. She'd even cleared away Florence's dead, uprooted tomato plants, which she then stuffed into plastic bags and stowed in the trunk of her car.

In another situation, Lucy might have felt grateful for these women. Basically, they were free servants: cooks, housecleaners, gardeners. The problem was, they often wished to be therapists as well—and, even worse, "friends." The problem was that these woman had once been in Lucy's position. Each of them was the mother of a child who had disappeared. At first, when Lucy heard about the volunteers, she assumed they offered their time out of gratitude for ALFJ's help in the return of their children. Soon enough, though, Lucy learned that all of these women were still waiting; had been waiting for years—most of their cases ancient history. A Light for Jimmy somehow kept them going.

"Going into my eleventh year this December," Janet said at one point, sipping the coffee she'd made for herself in Florence's kitchen. "Yup." She nodded, staring into a chipped white mug. "And you know, honest to God, I still feel her. I feel her on her way back to me. This . . ."—she patted her chest—"this feeling of hope, you know. With every heartbeat it's like, *yes yes yes*."

Bullshit, Lucy wanted to scream.

But she held her tongue and tried to smile as Janet pulled out the photographs, like they all did eventually. "She's cute," Lucy said of the dark-haired, bespectacled child, six years old. The child would be seventeen at this point—practically an adult. She'd have a different face.

As if she'd heard Lucy's thought, Janet flipped to a second photograph. "And this is her now."

Lucy was confused. "How do you . . . ?"

"Oh, I had it made. It's an age-progression shot."

"I didn't know they could do them that far," Lucy said. "I thought they did them, you know, just a few years . . ." She rolled her hand to signify the ghostly wheel of the future.

"No no no," Janet said with determined enthusiasm. "They have really good computer programs these days. Really accurate. You know, because they test the programs on children who aren't missing, to refine the technology. I mean, this is probably *exactly* what Olivia looks like now." Janet stared at the hypothetical face of her daughter. "I kept her in the same color shirt. She's always been crazy about pink."

"Maybe she has pink hair now," Lucy said lightly, not meaning any offense—only thinking of the blue hair she'd tried on herself, as a teenager.

"No," Janet said. "I don't think so. No, she definitely wouldn't do that. She played the flute."

Lucy didn't know what else to say. She gently pressed her fist above her stomach while Janet moved her finger slowly back and forth between the two photographs. "And supposedly, you know, they can just keep going. They can progress them into their thirties and forties. At which point she'd probably start to look like me. I mean, a face can only do so many things, right?" Janet turned to Lucy with a thin, nervous smile.

Lucy nodded, thinking of the face of the child inside her—its features becoming less like Edgar's, and more like a stranger's. She still hadn't told the butcher she was pregnant.

"Are you all right?" asked Janet. "Tummy ache?"

"What? No." Lucy moved her hand away from her gut.

Janet slid the photographs back inside their protective plastic sleeves and closed the booklet. Lucy was relieved not to have to look at more. God knows what else the woman had in her little album: Olivia photoshopped into a graduation gown or a wedding dress.

Edgar in his thirties. Edgar in his forties. "Would you excuse me a minute, Janet?"

In the bathroom, Lucy experienced a wave of fury that obliterated any obligation to sympathy. It was disgusting how these women lied to themselves. Lucy suspected their husbands, the fathers of the children, weren't as stupid. The fathers were probably gone—remarried, with new families under which they could bury their sadness. These women had no one to torture but themselves—and now Lucy.

She looked at her tired face in the mirror. She'd never become one of these Light for Jimmy circus freaks who juggled machetes over their heads and called it hope. Besides, Edgar would be back soon. It wasn't necessary to think about the future. The future was dangerous. That's where doubt lived. It was only necessary to stand where she was standing, in the here and now, and make demands. There'd be no need for age-progression. Edgar would progress at home, right under her nose.

Besides, if he didn't come back soon (this sudden doubt she blamed on Janet) . . . well, then she'd just have to get on with her life. That's what people did. That's what she'd done with Frank—hadn't she? She didn't carry around pictures of her husband and show them to strangers. And she wouldn't do that with Edgar. If Edgar ever became part of the past . . .

She leaned over the bowl and vomited.

Eleven years! Oh my God! She could never wait that long. If time were to play such a cruel trick on her, she'd simply make herself forget Edgar—even if the only way to forget him was to rip out her own heart.

Again, she vomited.

"Are you okay in there, Lucy?" Janet's voice was close to the door.

"Morning sickness," Lucy croaked without thinking.

Immediately, though, she sensed her error. She could see Janet's face, as if the door had become transparent. She rinsed her mouth and emerged from the bathroom to find Janet as she knew she'd find her: with tears in her eyes.

"You're very lucky, Mrs. Fini"—a sudden formality in the woman, as if Lucy's good fortune had put some distance between them. "I had Olivia late, and so I couldn't . . ."

Lucy held the woman's gaze and took her hand—closing the gap.

"Only child?" Lucy asked, and Janet nodded.

38

The Headless Woman

When the butcher came home, Lucy told him everything. She told him about Janet and Olivia and the imaginary photograph. She told him about the curly hair and the black spectacles, the pink blouse. She told him about the eleven years. The words rushed out of her, and before she knew it she was talking about Frank—and what it was like waiting for him on the nights he would disappear from the house; how, sometimes, she'd even prayed.

She didn't look at the butcher as she spoke; she looked at her hands, or at the walls. Though she hadn't been drinking, she felt drunk. Her voice moved about the room like a frightened animal. There was no sense of time. She began to speak about her childhood, about her father—landing squarely on the facts. "He liked to hit me in the face." She was not complaining or looking for sympathy. It was simply information.

Ron, who was sitting close to her, nodded. It was clear to him that he wasn't to say anything—only listen. She was talking about her husband again. Ron knew the story, same as everyone, from the news reports and the papers. Well, he knew the *end* of the story—but only in a general way. Lucy was providing a few more gruesome details—how she'd fallen on the bridge, trying to make her way to Frank.

"That's why I walk the way I do," she said.

"I never noticed," Ron lied—and Lucy made a sound that seemed, at first, like laughter.

She grabbed a bunch of her hair and pulled it. "I can't do this again."

"Do what?"

When the butcher touched her, she pushed him away. "I'm not a good person. Is that what you think?"

Ron knew better than to answer.

"Remember that night I came to your house with my knees all bloody?

I wasn't out with my *girlfriends*. I didn't *trip*. Some kid knocked me down after he stole my wallet. I was trying to pick him up, Ron. I was hoping he'd *fuck* me." She made the strange laugh again. "I'd just cashed my paycheck. *I* was the one who was going to run away."

Lucy felt the past few weeks rise up inside her like a toxic wave. *The argument with Florence the night before she'd died, tire burns on the driveway, cutting off the boy's hair, killing the tomato plants*—black water that finally crashed against Janet and Olivia.

"Eleven years," Lucy muttered. "Oh my God."

In her confusion she let the butcher take her hand.

"Slow down, babe—breathe."

She told him that she had no right to fucking breathe. She touched her chest and closed her eyes. A thousand vipers sped downward into her body. "I'm pregnant," she said.

"Holy shit. Are you serious?"

Lucy nodded. "When we fucked in the bathtub."

Ron squeezed her hand tighter—and then even tighter when she tried to pull away. He got down on his knees and put his head on her lap.

"Please," she begged, her voice no more than a whisper. "Please don't be happy."

When the crash came from above, Lucy jumped to her feet and dashed toward the stairs.

"*Stop,*" yelled the butcher. "Somebody could be up there."

Lucy's thought exactly, as she raced toward Edgar's room.

But there was no one. In her own room, the same.

It was in Florence's bedroom that Lucy saw what had caused the sound. On the floor, nestled in the fibers of the new cream-colored carpet, lay the body of the Virgin.

Lucy approached the broken figure and then looked toward the ceiling, as if to understand where the thing had come from. She was certain she'd put it away in the closet. Perhaps Honey Fasinga had pulled it out when she'd been messing with the dresses.

But from where had it fallen? The Virgin was in the middle of the room, a good three feet from the bed, and at least the same distance from the bureau.

Lucy picked up the headless woman and traced a finger against the broken seam. A sharp edge pricked her, drawing blood.

Ron came up from behind.

"I think we should see a psychic," he said.

Lucy turned to look at Florence's bed—the bare mattress sagging in the middle, as if someone were still sleeping there.

39

Consolidated Laundry

Incoming material had to be sorted. There was a hierarchy of stains, from the simple to the profound—the superficial grimes of dirt and dust, below the deeper invasions of grease, wine, makeup; above which came blood—not to mention all the other effusions of the body, the yellows and browns and occasional greens, often drying into crusts. Sometimes the stained items seemed like paintings made by children or lunatics. On napkins, on towels, facecloths, sheets—all of them white, and so exceptionally vulnerable. Each piece a blank canvas marked by accident or passion or illness, by violence or impatience, or simply by people who, in Florence's opinion, didn't seem to know how to properly use a bar of soap.

Consolidated Laundry took care of the linens for a large number of hotels, including upscale establishments such as the Hyland, Hotel Calarco, and the Mattheson House. Upscale whites arrived in better crates, but were no less soiled. Dirt was dirt. Florence, at seventeen, started as a sorter—a disgusting job for which she doubled up on the rubber gloves. Items needed to be placed in various carts, depending on degree and type of soil.

Later, Florence was moved down the line, as a soaker—a promotion, technically, but no less disgusting than sorting. Here, items with difficult stains were placed in large vats of hot water with bleaching agents, where they were mashed for a while by a mechanical agitator before being passed along to the official washers. Sometimes, before being deposited into the chemical vats, a soaker was required to rub particularly offensive items with special powders, or spray them with steam.

The smells made Florence reel; the fumes made her dizzy. At day's end her face appeared sunburned. Even with protective gloves, the powders irritated her hands, turning them as red as her cheeks. At night her mother

rubbed the raw skin with olive oil. Plus, the heat from the vats was so intense that she sweated through her uniform daily, requiring more laundry
at home, more bleach. She wouldn't be caught dead going to work, especially
a laundry, with yellow stains under the arms of her shirt.

When she was promoted, yet again, to head washer, she was pleased, but,
in her modest way, wanted more. She hoped to move, eventually, to the other
side of the operation. Consolidated Laundry had a "soiled side" and a "clean
side," separated by a wall. Only the clothes crossed over, moving through
the tunnels of the giant cylindrical washers. Florence loaded the dirty
linens, set the dials to allow for the correct speeds and times, the appro-
priate levels of detergents and bleach and bluing agents. After which she
shut the great silver door and pushed down the latch as if sealing the
hatch of a spaceship. She wasn't permitted to open the door again until
the light above the machine turned from red to green—which meant that the
linens had been removed from the "clean side" of the tunnel, and that the
door over there had once again been sealed. There could be no communication between the two sides.

Sometimes, though, through the tunnel of the washer, Florence caught
glimpses of the other shore: blurry figures in white uniforms moving about
what seemed to be a version of heaven: a well-lit room where the clean linens were dried and pressed and folded; arranged neatly in stacks; after which
they were wrapped in stiff brown paper to keep them free of dust. The parcels (still warm, like loaves of fresh bread) would be driven in trucks, back
to the hotels.

Florence was doing her part to help return the world to whiteness.
The project, though, was not always a success. There was an inspection at the
other side. Items not sufficiently clean had to be washed again, and if the
stains still couldn't be dissolved, the damaged linens were stored in a special
closet. Mildly stained items were sold off in bulk to some of the cheaper
hotels, while the more noticeably ruined towels and sheets were put on pic-
nic tables at the back of the laundry, where working-class people could buy
them for ten cents apiece.

The days inside the plant were long and loud—too loud for conversation
with fellow employees. A person did her job quietly, focusing on the tasks at
hand, trying not to get burned or mangled. Sometimes it was even pleasurable to stare into the suds (which seemed like the sea or clouds) and think
about the future.

Florence was going to get married soon—or so she hoped—to a boy named Pio. He worked in a tunnel, too—tiling the walls of a great engineering feat that allowed cars to travel underwater. She would get married to him; they'd have children; they'd be happy. Being happy was another way of crossing over. Florence knew she'd make a good mother. Even in the reeking, sweaty laundry, she kept her heart on the future.

Every now and then, she could see a woman at the other side of washer number 3. Whenever this happened, Florence wondered if the woman was really there—or if what she was seeing was her own face reflected in the glass door at the far end of the tunnel. When Florence smiled, the woman smiled back. It made Florence happy, as if, in some way, by some miracle, she had already crossed over. Sometimes, though, the woman on the other side seemed much older, with gray hair—but maybe that was just a distortion from looking through water and suds.

It was mesmerizing to watch the whites turning in the foamy current. Occasionally, a napkin would slide across the glass window like a pale carp. Sometimes, a towel or a sheet leapt like the ghost of some elegant animal, a deer or a fox—or there'd be a face, a human face, with eyes and lips and a nose, flashing for no more than a second in the soapy tumult. Like the face of the clever little baby she knew she'd have one day. A white dress, a wedding cake. Sometimes a sheet that had become knotted opened like a huge flower inside the spinning tunnel, and Florence would feel something like she often did in church: that she'd been touched by the hand of God.

At times, late in her shift, she grows tired. Like now. The phantasms in the tunnel are no longer lovely. In the machine, she sees there are still stains, black lines like tire tracks on a white road. Smudges, imperfections—it will have to be done again. She's exhausted as she stares into the enormous snow globe of the washing machine.

It all looks so strange. Winter. Great mounds of snow and ice, shifting and falling. Trees smothered by a blizzard. The machine squeaks like a dog whining, or a child crying.

She wants to go home and climb into bed, to wrap herself in her own white sheets that smell like milk. She wants to soothe her red hands; to sleep.

But her work isn't finished. What's been entrusted to her is not yet clean. The black streak that moves across the glass window feels like danger, defilement. The black streak turns red.

Panic.

She puts her hand against the machine and closes her eyes. It makes no sense to feel this much heat in December, in the middle of a blizzard.

December

40

A Hunting Accident

The snow fell like a kind of confusion, piling up outside the cabin, obscuring logic. Conrad tried to understand what was going on. There was a child in his house, a creature so tiny and pale it was sometimes terrifying. The boy's delicacy had started to make Conrad's entire world seem like something made of glass. Nearly three months had passed—and nothing had gone as planned. Of course, the passage of time did have its advantages, one of which was the way it allowed Conrad's memory to take some license with the situation.

How had the boy gotten here, exactly? It seemed impossible to Conrad that he would have brought Edgar to the cabin—plucked him away from his home, his family; lied to him. More likely, the boy had followed him here. He *wanted* to be here. This being the case, Conrad found it confusing when the boy cried and said he wanted to leave. He did this less than he'd done at first—but, still, the situation was not as it should be. When the boy was upset, he appeared even more translucent. Even on good days, life proceeded at an odd tilt.

Someone, either he or Edgar, was thinking about things in the wrong way.

If he calmed his mind, though, he remembered that he had a plan. But the plan seemed ludicrous now. Grief had fucked up his head—its effects oddly similar to those of certain hallucinogens he'd experimented with when he was younger. Everything was fluid, provisional, chimeric. Nothing was real. This had been true ever since Kevin had died—but the feeling, which everyone said would diminish, had only grown stronger over time. Maybe it was a bad idea to prolong his involvement with this other boy. Conrad was torn.

While he still wished to be destroyed, he'd also become greedy. He'd become a father again, experiencing a disturbing facsimile of love. He knew it was a lie—but sometimes the motions of domesticity were sufficient to create a world. Feeding the dog together, the fish; watching television; drying someone's tears; sharing breakfast every day—these were the things that made up a life, that made people a family. Conrad and the boy were no longer strangers. They were blood. What ran through their veins and made them inseparable was the same hallucinogen. Grief.

For all their struggles and fraught negotiations, hadn't they also had some wonderful days? Conrad found himself caught between two impulses— the first being to antagonize the child, so that the child might rightly despise him. But, at the same time, Edgar had come to depend on him, and Conrad felt compelled to provide assistance.

The most miraculous thing, though, was that Edgar had found the strength to offer kindness, as well. At first, Conrad was suspicious, not being able to see beyond the context of his own manipulations. But then he came to understand that the boy's compassion was authentic. He seemed to be equipped with an empathy bordering on the pathological—a febrile intelligence uncannily attuned to the pain of others. Conrad felt *known,* sensed how his every thought and feeling drifted like spores of pollen onto the boy's invisible antennae. Edgar's whiteness seemed the outward sign of an unencumbered, and possibly self-damaging, receptivity.

The way, only a few weeks ago, he'd said it would be okay if Conrad wanted to call him Kevin. "Not all the time," the boy had clarified—adding, cryptically, "Just when you have to." At that point, though, it was Conrad who couldn't allow it—recognizing, with a cold shock, how effectively he'd dismantled Edgar's former existence. It had been a slow process, accomplished by a steady casting of long shadows backwards onto the boy's mother and the man who was conveniently called *the butcher.*

Conrad's best option might be to portray the better man. Taking the higher ground would not necessarily stand in the way of his own destruction. If Edgar were to erase Conrad, couldn't the boy's act be one of love, instead of hatred?

Conrad wished he could sleep, but his mind stayed lit with a kind of Christmas Eve electricity: outrageous desires rubbing up against the fear that he might get exactly what he deserved. The steady down-drifting of snow only added to this sense of laden expectation. Something was waiting outside the cabin, where visibility was compromised. It was often necessary to stay indoors. Much of the hunting season had passed. Conrad had gone out only once, alone, bagging a twelve-point buck, which he'd dressed discreetly in the woodshed while the boy was sleeping. The meat would last them a few months.

On clear days, during the brief hours of sun, Conrad would give Edgar his lessons in the yard. He was progressing nicely—though he still refused to shoot anything but crabapples or tin cans.

At night, in bed, Conrad tried to reconstruct the chain of events that had brought him here; tried to arrive at what he wanted. Sometimes it was helpful to jot things down in his notebook. Words weren't a solace, but they focused one's emotions into something more tangible; they were splinters that could actually be pulled from the heart and placed on a table, regarded.

Kevin is dead.

It was amazing that such a thing could be written down. It took Conrad's breath away.

A year ago he'd died. A year and twenty-six days. Since then, there were long stretches of time Conrad couldn't recall. Certain things, though, came back to him easily, mercilessly preserved, like clips from a film made without his consent.

The first few weeks after Kevin had died—Conrad recalled clearly. He and his wife had barely risen from their bed. They slept, or didn't sleep. There was no talking. They didn't touch. Eventually, Sara drifted to one of the guest bedrooms and stayed there. Conrad didn't blame her. If it had been possible for him to leave his own body and sleep in another room, he would have done it. At that point, his vague desire to abandon himself had not yet condensed into the more practical thought of suicide.

It was clear from the beginning (the beginning being Kevin's end) that Sara would never forgive him. From now on, it would be a new life—one in which every open door, every song, every glass of water, would be clogged with unconquerable regret.

Not being particularly brave or inherently brutal, Conrad was unable to act when the idea of taking his own life presented itself, like an envelope slipped under a door. He picked it up, turned it over—but found himself unable to open it.

It was not as if there were no encouragement.

Three weeks after Kevin's death, Conrad's shotgun was returned to him— the investigation complete; closed; the father deemed of stable mind, with no intention to inflict harm.

Innocent. An accident.

* * *

Sara had stood by Conrad's side at first—holding his hand during the questioning, kissing his cheek at night after he'd fallen asleep. She tried to be kind, understanding that his pain might be greater than hers.

Still, her son was dead—and her husband, the boy's father, was responsible. At first, the fury she felt toward Conrad was a distant planet, barely visible at the outer limits of her grief. But, by the time the gun was returned, the planet had moved closer. Her hands would shake whenever Conrad approached. She knew he hadn't shot Kevin on purpose, but reason played no part in this. In her mind, she parsed her fury into endless questions.

Why did Conrad have to *hunt*? Why did a rich man need to kill animals for food? Because his father had done it? She'd never liked Conrad's father. The idea to hate all men seemed reasonable. She didn't include Kevin here; Kevin was a boy. Why did Conrad feel compelled to turn him into a little soldier? Take him to that horrible cabin every year? Teach him things! Teach him to be a man! Why couldn't men leave children alone? Leave them to their mothers?

Even Conrad's grief began to infuriate her. It smacked of drama. She supposed it was genuine, no different from her own, but sometimes Conrad displayed it too fervently, as if he wanted her to approve of it or give him some kind of comfort she was incapable of giving. Maybe what he really wanted was for her to openly condemn him—take time away from her own grief and punish him. As if the tragedy were all about him.

Infuriating, to see him at the kitchen table, writing in his journal—his pen scratching violently, nearly ripping the pages. She used to love the fact that he was "creative"—it seemed to soften some of the shit Conrad had picked up from his father. But now he seemed a fool, a weakling. All these years trying to write a book! And what was he doing now, when he scribbled—working on his never-ending novel or writing about Kevin? Was it all one thing to him—all part of his fucking "process"? What writers did with their minds seemed offensive to her, the way they messed things up, mixed the real with the imaginary. As if one could escape from the facts, or change them. Writers were selfish. Conrad wrote at the kitchen table, in tears, and it repulsed her.

She no longer loved him. Nothing was left. Whenever she was at home with Conrad she found it difficult to breathe. Luckily she'd kept her job as a nurse after getting married. She wasn't the type to sit around all day like Conrad and do nothing. Writing was not a job. Who was he trying to kid? A man with a four-million-dollar portfolio, and he dressed like a gas station attendant. Drove that shitty green truck. What a phony.

She inwardly condemned her husband to mask a deeper sadness: that she'd never really understood him. Grief should have brought them together, exposed them to each other; instead, it turned her chest into a plate of armor, outside of which Conrad skulked nervously, unpredictably, a stranger more than ever—possibly an enemy.

He'd given her a child, though, a beautiful boy. But that was over, too. She'd loved them both so much, Conrad and Kevin, that she now felt it within her rights to hate with equal intensity.

She would leave. Stay with Anita, a friend from the hospital; eventually get her own place. Start over.

She'd already decided to let Conrad keep the dog. Kevin's dog. The poor beast was always wandering around the house, looking for the boy. She'd never be able to bear it.

* * *

For Conrad, the return of the shotgun was significant. It meant that he was to be trusted. Trusted to do the right thing. He would sit in his bedroom for hours—lifting the gun to his mouth and then lowering it. Everyone, the living and the dead, waited for the sound. He left the door cracked in case Sara cared to see what he was up to.

She never came to the bedroom, though.

If he just had a little encouragement. If someone would just say, *Do it.*

There was an edge, black and breathless. It was right there, right in front of him. Crossing it would require no more than a click—a beetle closing its wings.

But he was afraid.

How did other people do it? Conrad wondered. Those who'd managed it certainly could not have had more sadness than he did. More regret, more self-loathing. What secret power did they possess—these suicides—what charm against fear? They must be like gods, he thought. Unable to finish himself, Conrad felt the sting of his mortality as never before. Did he secretly want to live? It was disgusting.

He saw shadows. Sometimes the dog came into the bedroom and stared at him or pushed her head against his leg. He refused to touch her.

One afternoon, he took the shotgun into the living room—where Sara was sitting on the couch, picking lint off the sleeve of her sweater. He placed the gun on her lap and knelt before her—a little to her left so that the barrel of the gun was facing him.

He didn't expect her to do it, of course. He only wanted her to look at him. To *see* him.

Air streamed audibly from his wife's nostrils, a slow deflation; her body slumped. When she looked at Conrad, it was with an expression that began as sadness, but quickly bloomed into contempt.

"You think you can just . . . ?"

She looked down at the gun. The corners of her lips stretched so far into her cheeks it almost seemed she was smiling. From her mouth came a stream of garbled sound Conrad couldn't decipher.

She swallowed and tried again, setting down each word as if it were a heavy stone pulled from her chest. "How can a person look like an animal?"

Conrad closed his eyes.

"Tell me—how can a twelve-year-old boy look like a fucking deer?"

The question contained no sarcasm; it was not rhetorical. She wanted to know.

But what could he say that he hadn't already said—to her, to the police, to himself—a thousand times?

A boy can look like a deer if he has dark hair and is wearing a brown jacket.

A boy can look like a deer if he's running.

A boy can look like a deer if it's late afternoon and the light is fading.

Conrad was an excellent hunter. He always put safety first. Kevin was supposed to have been behind him. *You stay behind me*—he'd drilled that into the boy since he was eight, when he'd given him his first rimfire. What the fuck had gotten into the kid's head? Why had he wandered off and circled around to the pond? Why had he taken off his orange vest? Sometimes Conrad found himself so angry with Kevin he would punch the wall—a consuming rage that confused his grief and made him wonder if he *was* capable of murder.

But, no. It was an accident—a hunting accident. Those were the words on the report.

Conrad rehearsed the phrase. It seemed odd, code for something else, as if it should be in quotes. He scrawled the words at the top of a blank page, where they floated hopelessly, like the title of a story that would never be written.

A Hunting Accident.

Over the next several weeks, Conrad, delirious with exhaustion, would sometimes spot the entry in his notebook. Eyes fluttering, he would stare at the words—troubled by the sense that they bore some relation to something that had happened in his own life.

* * *

When Sara left, she kissed him—but when he tried to embrace her, she pulled away. She'd packed only a small bag. She was crying. She wished him good luck, as if he were a stranger. But then she said two things that made Conrad feel that she still loved him—even though she refused to look him in the eye.

"It's not your fault," she said.

And then she said, "I hope you finish your book."

A few weeks later, when the paperwork came, making their separation a legal matter, Conrad signed his name and returned the papers without delay. Soon after that, a woman named Anita, another nurse at the hospital, came by the house to pick up a few of Sara's things. She brought along her son, a tall healthy boy—thirteen, fourteen—named Jarell. Conrad could barely stand to look at the strapping kid in torn jeans.

The things Anita and Jarell collected from the house seemed strange to Conrad. Sara had made a list. *Electric toothbrush, neck pillow, passport, running shoes, inversion table.* It was the teenage boy who carried out the large contraption that allowed Sara to hang upside down to stretch or do sit-ups. It made no sense to Conrad why she would want that now. He pictured his wife hanging upside down in the black woman's living room. How was that going to help? Did she think her body was an hourglass; that she could reverse the flow of time? He was surprised that Sara wanted nothing of Kevin's.

The boy's bedroom, all its sunken treasure, was left to Conrad. Sometimes he would lay out Kevin's clothes and stand before them. It took no effort at all to play it differently—Conrad forgetting his orange vest, and Kevin blindly shooting.

*　*　*

For a while, in the quiet house he'd shared with his wife and son, he lost all
sense of his body. Minutes, hours, days—they varied little in length or quality. When he returned, several months later, to the here and now, it seemed
that he might be slightly better. He was able to eat, bathe, take Jack for a
walk instead of just letting her relieve herself in the yard. One morning, Conrad found himself tucking in his shirt and sensed that he might actually
survive; might *want* to survive.

But then he started watching the children. He would drive around until
he found an active spot near a school or a park or a convenience store. What
struck him as he watched them was the disconcerting fact that they were all
beautiful. It was like an assault—each face flying into his body like an arrow. Whereas before it had always been obvious that certain young faces
lacked charm or grace—now it was impossible to find an ugly child. The
homely, the ill-fated, the plain, joined hands with the gifted and the comely.
They all seemed to possess a secret trove of light that they carried, threaten-
ingly, just under their skin. They were beautiful, but dangerous. They brought
back Conrad's desire to be loved, destroyed.

Each child, no matter how awkward, moved as if they were supported
by invisible nets or wires; they floated rather than treaded. When an adult
walked by, you could see how out of joint he was with the natural order of
things. Conrad, sitting in the truck, felt the weight of his own spine, its an-
tagonism with the Earth, like a drill grinding against an impenetrable layer
of stone. It was as if there were two realities, side by side: children here, and
adults there. They coexisted, but only in an illusory way. The same was true
of the happy and the sad. The living and the dead.

There was one child, though, who seemed to exist somewhere in between
these contradictory realities. He was the most luminous and, at the same
time, the most deadly. And now that child sat across from Conrad every
morning, eating a bowl of cereal.

*　*　*

"Good morning, Conrad."

"Good morning, Edgar."

Sometimes the boy's politeness unnerved the man. Despite everything,
they were friends now.

"A little more milk?"

"Yes, please."

The most casual exchanges felt profound to Conrad, and would make him break out into a sweat.

"I'm just putting on a little sugar," Edgar said—sprinkling half a teaspoon onto his cornflakes.

"Go for it," said Conrad with a wink.

That's what the cabin had always been about. Boys being boys. A place to eat junk, stay up a few hours later—a place a young man could do all the things he wasn't allowed to do at home with his mother.

Conrad tried not to watch the boy too closely—the thin, white fingers clutching the spoon.

"A can of soda has like ten times more sugar," Edgar said, glancing up to find the man looking at him the same way his grandmother used to look at him. It made Edgar feel less nervous. "I know some kids who have soda for breakfast," he continued. "But I'm not allowed."

"The rules," Conrad said, and Edgar, feeling understood, nodded.

The man got up and poured himself some coffee. He noticed the sunlight on the walls: a nice day to be outside. "After you eat, we'll go out and practice."

Edgar finished chewing. Swallowed. "Okay." He lifted another spoonful—stopping it just short of his mouth. "But with the little gun, right?"

"Yup." Conrad quickly sipped the hot coffee, intentionally burning his tongue. It was unpredictable what he might say—feeling himself ambushed suddenly by an unpleasant rush of gratitude. Some mornings, the boy didn't scream or cry or hide, but actually seemed content, even happy.

"I think the little gun is better for me," said Edgar.

Conrad mumbled agreeably and poured more coffee into his already full cup. He put a dishtowel over the spill and looked out the window. At this point, the boy was only using Kevin's old Daisy air gun, shooting pellets. During an early lesson, when Conrad had used the larger Remington to shoot a crabapple off a stump, the sound had frightened Edgar.

Just take it slow, he thought. The same way he'd taught his son. Start with the pellet gun, which had no recoil or muzzle blast to upset the child. When he was comfortable with that, move him up to the Rossi, which had been given to Kevin when he was around Edgar's age. It was a good youth gun, but still did a man's job. In a few years, when Edgar was older . . .

The man stopped, reminding himself that the boy wouldn't be here much longer. This was temporary. Everything was temporary. Conrad most of all. He'd always planned to leave the guns, the cabin, to Kevin. As things stood, Sara would probably just sell it all to strangers when the time came.

"I don't think they taste terrible," said Edgar.

"What's that?" asked the man.

"The little apples. You said they tasted bad. But I tried one, and it was definitely edible."

Conrad laughed. He rubbed his eyes and asked the boy to please excuse him; he needed to write something down.

*   *   *

With very little practice, the kid had become a surprisingly good shot. Whenever he pinged a hole into a can, his mouth fell open in surprise, his natural humility preventing him from shouting *Yes!*—as Kevin would have done. After a successful shot, Edgar would sometimes turn to Conrad for approval. "Perfect, kiddo," was the man's standard reply. Only then would the boy smile shyly and say, "I guess I'm sort of getting the hang of it."

The Rossi would be more challenging. Especially with moving targets. Conrad would make sure to always follow behind with the Remington.

Follow behind. Or drift ahead.

The boy was by and large still tentative, even with the pellet gun, but there were days when he fired it with an eerie focus and precision. Often these bouts of somnambulant accuracy occurred after a night of crying, or after Edgar had emerged from his hiding spot behind the bookshelf. Sometimes, when the boy pulled the trigger, Conrad could detect a trace of fury in the pale green eyes.

At such moments, Edgar didn't turn to the man for encouragement; nor did he smile. Conrad understood; remembered. Sometimes a can was more than a can. When you hit it, it was like hitting your father.

*   *   *

After breakfast, Edgar made three good shots in a row—and Conrad felt something strange. He felt his heart go cold and leap against the boy. This boy who had his whole life ahead of him. For a moment, Conrad imagined a different outcome—one in which no child would be granted things his own son could never have.

Not that he wanted to hurt Edgar. Hurting Edgar was the worst thought in the world.

But someone was always hurt, someone was always in pain.

He watched the boy closely, waiting for clues.

Don't think you know how it will end, he wrote in his notebook.

And then he wrote: *Sometimes I feel I can't wait much longer. I feel sick, almost hopeful. But it has to stop. It has to be over by Christmas.*

41

First Wednesday of December

At 5:42 on a freezing afternoon, Honey Fasinga and Dominic Sparra were making their way across Times Square, having just seen a revival of *Annie* at the Palace. Several months before, the pair had reconnected on the steps of St. Margaret's after Florence's funeral. They looked quite the item now, dolled up despite the miserable day. With one hand, Honey clutched her hat against a strong wind; with the other, she clutched Dominic Sparra. She'd left her cane at home, knowing she'd have a man to keep her steady. The man, though, was slightly tipsy. Dominic had downed two Dewar's and water during the interval, to soften the assault of another hour of screeching orphans.

They crossed the plaza slowly—Honey, warm in her fur, and dreamy. She was lightly humming "It's the Hard-Knock Life" when the wind took its advantage and her crimson pillbox harrumphed upward like a startled pigeon. *"Crap,"* she cried.

"It was," said Dominic, recalling the play. "Too much stomping."

"No, darling—look."

Honey pointed, and Dominic followed her finger to a small blur of red spinning above them. "What is it?"

"My hat."

"How'd it get up there?"

"Magic," Honey replied crabbishly, as the hat flew higher. It was a Florence, and damned if she didn't want it back. The tottering couple craned their heads skyward. Dominic felt dizzy.

Others were watching now, too. A pack of fat Germans, led by a woman with a rainbow flag, began to snap pictures.

"It's mine," announced Honey, prophylactically. Some little fashionista in the crowd might get ideas. *Finders, keepers*—that sort of nonsense.

But the hat seemed to have disappeared—sucked higher into the air, or perhaps it had already fallen into the hands of a stranger. Dominic and Honey saw nothing now but the large glittering screens. The advertisements in Times Square were out of control, thought Dominic. Two-hundred-foot televisions jangling with images. On one loomed a pretty, young model with flawless skin.

"Ah," gasped Honey, recognizing the face.

"Oh my God," said Dominic. "That's . . . what's-his-name."

Words on the screen faded up to assist.

Edgar Allan Fini. Nine years old. Missing.

Honey reached for Dominic's hand. He squeezed her fingers—the pair of them thinking, in different ways, how they'd wronged Florence: Dominic and his failure to woo her; Honey and her disastrous affair with Pio. At their ages, it was hard not to see the knottiness of time as some horrible work of macramé, a mass of connected tangles, of which you were one—knitted into its plan like a fly entombed in silk. They were all in this together, the living with the dead—and so much had been done badly, so many mistakes had been made, maybe it was only right to be trapped in the web and let the spider eat you.

For a brief moment Florence's hat (crushed velvet and honeycomb lace) flashed before the huge white face and then vanished. Honey experienced a wave of nausea and regret. Terrible things had happened; were happening still. Edgar's face faded out and another child bloomed onto the screen. A brown girl with strawberry lips and crooked teeth.

Benita Cardenza. Six years old. Missing.

Dominic shook his head. "It's a sick world."

Honey stared at the screen. "I guess we're lucky we never had children."

"We didn't love the right people."

"No, we didn't," agreed Honey. She watched the little girl's face for a bit more and then patted Dominic's hand. "You're freezing, old man. Let's catch our bus."

"I hate going through that friggin' tunnel."

"I know, darling—but it's the only way home."

Entry #4

Seeing how they suffer, she's not without sympathy, remembering how she, too, had suffered once. How, even with faith, she had hung her stars in the sky with wires. Had she really not believed, as they do not believe? They might find the boy more easily by giving up and facing the greater void his missingness implies. But they're afraid of that.

What they desire is something like forgiveness, though that's not quite the right word. They're playing at stories they have to finish. She watches—and though she wants to swoop down and shepherd them home, the patterns of their chaos prevent it. Patterns they're forced to play out. She still remembers her own patterns, her own chaos; remembers who had betrayed her and who had loved her.

It's all the same to her now, though.

Now that she's shed the coil of her own wrongdoings.

She understands, of course, that, for them, it's not as easy. So much gravity down there, so little faith. Remembering again how, every year, she'd set up the little house with Mary and Joseph and the baby—and how, when the prong to hold up the Magi's star had broken, she'd used a bobby pin to keep it in the sky.

42

The Holiday Season

Edgar's birthday had come and gone. Thanksgiving, too. Lucy had spent the first occasion in bed. On the second, the butcher had dragged her to his sister Izzy's place: a bleak condo with a view of Route 46, furnished with faux antiques—the dining room table done up with baby pumpkins and paper maple leaves. "Do you want me to turn up the heat?" Izzy had asked when Lucy sat down to dinner wearing Florence's black wool coat. "She gets cold," the butcher had explained, and everyone had nodded and smiled. No one mentioned Edgar.

Lucy liked the old coat, realizing that, during her whole adult life, she'd never owned a proper winter jacket. She'd always been too vain—often wearing, even during the coldest months, only a short leather bolero or a shearling-lined vest. Now, she found herself putting on the bulky black shroud whenever she left the house, caring little for the fact that it added twenty pounds to her appearance.

Most days she wore no makeup, nor did she fluff her hair with spray or foam, but simply pulled it back in a ponytail. Ron thought she looked beautiful but learned to keep this opinion to himself. The last few times he'd said it during sex, she'd requested that he just fuck her quietly. If Lucy cried—which she sometimes did after she came—Ron held her, though he knew not to do it too tightly, or she'd buck.

* * *

There were no baby pumpkins or paper maple leaves at 21 Cressida Drive. The place was a mess. Neither Lucy nor Ron were good housekeepers. They threw clothes on the floor and hung plastic grocery bags on the coat rack. Lucy often ate cookies in bed, the crumbs biting her at night like insects.

And though she'd stopped smoking, the butcher's habit lingered. He indulged in the yard, throwing butts into a coffee can.

Florence's kitchen was a disaster. The butcher cooked flamboyantly, over-heating the olive oil and spattering the wall with grease. After his culinary performances, Lucy always offered to clean up—but she'd often leave the larger pots and pans in a half-submerged scrap heap in the sink. The old woman's arsenal of cookware was vast; it was possible to let the pot pile build for days. When Netty Schlip was stationed at the house, she wiped a rag here or there, but knew better than to fully attack the problem—understanding that people got attached to their messes, like pets.

The only order at 21 Cressida Drive existed on the dining room table—where Lucy kept, in neat piles, the flyers with Edgar's face. She and Ron put them up tirelessly. The ones on telephone poles and in shop windows had to be replaced often, because they faded or tore or—appallingly, to Lucy—were postered over by weight-loss ads or babysitters seeking employment. Ron attached a flyer to every package of meat sold at his shop. At St. Margaret's, the boy's face was framed in cedar, and sat near the entrance on a small table. Recently, though, Lucy had had to start again from scratch with the posters, because the facts had changed. Ron had suggested they simply cross out the eight and write in a nine for Edgar's age, but Lucy had insisted on printing a revision. Somehow that seemed less awful.

On the new flyer, Lucy had added the word *reward*—planning to use the four hundred dollars from Florence's teacup. The butcher had offered to throw in some money, as well. It wouldn't add up to much—but Ms. Mann said that even a small amount might encourage someone to come forward with helpful information.

So far, there was nothing. It was as if Edgar had ceased to exist. When Ms. Mann came to the house now, it was more of a courtesy—bringing a box of crullers instead of a handful of leads. Sometimes Lucy asked her to stay for dinner. After several refusals, the detective finally agreed. The butcher baked ziti and opened a bottle of zinfandel. At one point, Lucy watched, amazed, as Ron trotted out a few crude jokes and Mann laughed stiffly, like a mannequin come to life. *It's okay to laugh,* one of the pamphlets stated. *A good laugh can be as cleansing as a good cry.*

But Lucy couldn't do it. She pushed back her chair and stood. "This damn baby makes me have to pee every ten seconds." In the bathroom, she turned on the faucet to drown out Mann's polite chuckle. Lucy tried smiling in the mirror, but wasn't convinced by her upturned lips pinned into place. All her life, people had commented on her laugh. An explosive cackle that had always reduced Edgar to giggles, even if he didn't know what she was laughing about. Merely the sound of it would infect him—an inoculation against sadness, to which the boy was prone. Lucy hoped it was still inside him, a shard of her laugher, protecting him. If a person couldn't laugh, he was as good as dead. She tried to picture the boy giggling, his elfin ears turning pink.

In the mirror she smiled, as her eyes filled with water.

*   *   *

Around the second week of December, Lucy's mood began to drift toward mania. She marked up maps before going out to look for Edgar, but then followed none of her plans—driving instead by instinct, often exceeding the speed limit. When she came home, she chewed off the ear of whoever was stationed at the house. She even rambled on to Toni-Ann, telling the girl about the albino she'd spotted in Dover, outside a diner—not Edgar, of course, but surely it was a good sign. During another flash of hopefulness, she agreed to see a psychic (Ron had not stopped pestering her).

Lucy crumbled, though, on a frigid Wednesday (windchill 12 degrees), when she walked in the door and saw the Christmas tree. Ron had come home early to put it up. It was decorated with red bows and white twinkle lights. The effect on Lucy was stunning.

They were all there suddenly: Frank, Pio, Florence. Edgar, at two months, in a Santa hat; Pio unwrapping a plush puppy; Florence kissily jiggling the toy in Edgar's face.

"We can't stay here." Lucy shook her head and turned to the butcher. "Not for Christmas."

A few days away is all she needs, she tells him. Just until after the holiday. They can go to his place.

"We'll go tomorrow," Ron says, but Lucy insists on driving there that evening.

Before they leave, she asks him to take down the Christmas tree and makes him promise not to put up any decorations in his shop, or in the apartment above, where they'll be staying. Lucy throws a few things in a shopping bag—clothes, toiletries, a hairbrush. She wants some of Edgar's things, too. From the top of his bureau, she grabs a handful of tiny farm animals, the rubber alien. She takes the demitasse cup of Chinese fortunes, along with the plush puppy his grandparents had given him. After carrying the stuff downstairs, though, Lucy has second thoughts about leaving. She calls Ms. Mann to ask if it's okay to spend the holiday at Ron's.

"You don't need my permission," says the detective.

"But I mean, what if . . . ?"

Mann is silent. Three months have passed, and she feels it's best not to offer too much encouragement.

"Should I have someone stay at the house?" asks Lucy.

"During the holidays that'll be tough," says Mann. "Just leave a note on your door with all your information—and I'll have an officer keep an eye on things."

"We'll be gone only a day or two. Christmas is just hard."

"Get away," Mann says. "It'll do you good."

Edgar, Lucy writes, *I'm at Ron Salvatore's house. Call me at the number below. I love—*

Ron hands her a tissue. He takes the note and pens in the final *you,* along with his telephone number.

Lucy tapes the message to the front door.

"Should I lock it?" she asks—and the butcher says, "Yes, you probably should."

43

Everyone's Guilty

Thomas Pittimore, of course. In the shower, unable to masturbate, thinking, *I did it, I made him run away*—the thought progressing: *I hope he doesn't come back. I hope he dies.* Shame becoming anger becoming fury. Why should Edgar be getting all the attention? It's like he's famous now—his face everywhere.

I'm a genius compared to him, Thomas thinks, punching, in the shower, his own fat belly. *I should be famous.*

Instead he's mocked now. At school, everyone knows about the man outside the Mark-O-Market—how he'd called Thomas a pervert, slapped him down to the pavement, made him run away in tears. "Move your fat ass," boys say, imitating the man.

The world is upside down. Thomas feels like he's falling.

He stands behind some trees at the edge of the football field where no one can see him. It's nighttime. Practically the whole school is gathered on the dead lawn for a candlelight vigil. Pretty girls crying, holding pictures of Edgar. There's even singing. Jarell is there. He's been ignoring Thomas lately, which makes Tommy's anger sometimes feel like sadness. Jarell is with Bethany Harvow; they're holding hands. They probably think they're in love—it's disgusting.

What makes Tommy madder than anything is not the boys mocking him—it's not even Jarell's treason. The greatest outrage is that faggy little Edgar Fini could have a father who loved him *that* much—enough to go apeshit on Thomas, just to protect his stupid disease of a son.

Not knowing Edgar's family history, Thomas has never assumed that the man outside the Mark-O could be anyone other than Edgar's father. Who else would care enough about the kid? Edgar's parents were probably the type to be like, *Oh my goodness, we just feel so blessed to have a little diseased baby like you. We're just so lucky!*

"What's the matter?" Thomas's mother asks him. "Why are you eating like that?"

"*Lah wah?*" he says, his mouth full of food. Some of it falls back onto the plate.

His father slaps him. More food goes flying.

When Thomas's brother laughs, he gets it, too—though not as hard as Thomas.

Someone once said, *Love makes the world go round.* Thomas isn't sure where he's heard it—it might be a song. The singer keeps saying the words over and over like he's insane. It's like circus music. The only way to stop it would be with a gunshot. For Halloween this year, Thomas's costume was a white hockey mask—which means mass murderer.

He knows the truth, though. That he's a coward. He'd like to go to the police and tell them how Edgar Fini's father beat him up on the street.

But what if the police laugh, too?

He wishes he had some great plan to get back at the world. He puts on his hockey mask.

When other people were mean to you, you had to be meaner. If that wasn't your philosophy, then you should get out of New Jersey and move somewhere like California. New Jersey wasn't for wimps. It wasn't for *lovers.* Look at a map, for Christ's sake. The state was shaped like Frankenstein's head. New Jersey was a *monster.*

Sometimes Thomas googles the boy.

Edgar Fini Ferryfield New Jersey

Immediately a line of photos pops up—plus links to articles that go on for pages and pages. Local girls sob about Edgar on their blogs; he's a hot topic in at least a dozen e-prayer circles. One site (A Light for Jimmy) offers a ready-made poster with a high-res pic they ask you to "kindly print and put up in your local coffee shop, place of worship, or community center."

Every week there are more pages, more links. Once you get to around page twenty of the listings, it's necessary to use the translate function. Edgar in France, Spain, China—even *Turkey*! When Thomas turns a Bangladeshi site into English, the translating wizard seems more like an idiot.

> *The white child is missing.*
> *Have you seen the white child?*
> *If you see him, he is lucky.*
> *See him!*

Around Edgar's picture there's a frame of red roses and glittery golden stars, like he's the frickin' Dalai Lama. When he googles his own name, *Thomas Pittimore*—the search engine rudely asks him: *Do you mean Thomas Mattimore?* It's like he doesn't even exist.

At least he still has *Supersluts.com*. He can always go there when he needs to relax. Of course, when he's finished, he often feels strangely weak—as if all his power has been drained from him.

He cries sometimes—it's stupid. The world is so stupid. He doesn't *really* want Edgar to die.

44

Liars

Ping!

"Beautiful."

Ping!

"He's on a roll."

Ping!

"Holy baloney." Conrad used his funny voice here, but Edgar didn't laugh.

"I'm trying to concentrate," he said, taking aim.

"Sorry, maestro."

The next shot whistled past the cans, making a muffled *thuff* in the carpet of pine needles. Edgar unstrapped the BB gun and sat on the ground. He grabbed a handful of dry weeds and slowly crushed them. "I'm just going to be quiet now, okay?"

"Okay," said Conrad, who by this point was familiar with the boy's moods, which fluctuated wildly. At any moment, he might stop what he was doing and—there was no other way to put it—*play dead*. When he exhibited such behavior (lying on the ground for long periods without moving) Conrad often felt that the boy was taunting him. He was curled up now on the damp moss—his right hand clutching some bog asphodel, while his left rested delicately across the barrel of the air rifle. The gun was properly turned away from him, the safety latched, as Conrad had shown him.

"Take your time, kiddo. I'll go and fix us some lunch."

Edgar sprinkled the leaf dust over his corduroys, watching the tiny flakes fall between the wales. "I didn't feed the fish this morning," he called out.

Conrad shouted back that he'd take care of it.

The ground was cold; Edgar could feel it sneaking into his bones—a slow paralysis that made him want to sleep. It was a coldness that almost felt warm. It wasn't so different from the feeling he had when Florence would visit him;

which she did occasionally—always in the same spot: a small clearing among the pines, less than thirty yards from the cabin.

The boy stood, slapping the dried leaves from his legs. Hearing Conrad in the kitchen made him angry. Something wasn't right about the way the man had been talking to him the past few days. Even when he was being friendly, he often sounded impatient—and sometimes it seemed to Edgar that Conrad was making fun of him. It was hard to know for sure.

The boy looked at the shot-up cans, the rotting crabapples, the two guns: his own pellet gun and Conrad's larger one. The light in the sky was indecisive. Edgar wandered toward the clearing, though he knew his grandmother wasn't coming. She never came when he was angry, but seemed to pop up only when he was staring into space and not thinking so much about his problems. Whenever she appeared, neither of them cried or made a fuss. They only stood there quietly, sending bits of themselves back and forth. Edgar could stare at her face for hours. She didn't look dead at all. She looked the same as she had in life—her hands still red, her feet still cracked. You could even smell the perfume.

Unfortunately, she could never be tempted inside the cabin—preferring the violet shadows among the trees. Often, when she came, the pines trembled and whispered. Today, though, the trees were silent, which made Edgar wonder if more snow was on its way.

If that were true, then he'd better do something now. Once the snow started, it might be a while before the roads were clear again. With the tip of his boot, he dug up a half-buried stone and then kicked it.

He was mad at his mother, too.

She hadn't answered any of his letters. Just a few days ago he'd sent another one, bringing the total to ten. It was a depressing number—almost irrefutable.

Edgar picked up the gun.

Ping!

Right through the window of 21 Cressida Drive. How could she just ignore him? He'd said a lot of nice things. He'd even apologized.

Edgar closed his eyes against the light. The short days, the angle of the sun—for a while, he'd known something awful: his birthday had passed. He didn't say anything to Con, who would have made a big deal out of it, maybe even given him a party.

Edgar didn't want a party, though. He wanted a letter from his mother.

But his mother was an alcoholic. Conrad had explained this after Edgar had told him about the daily six-packs and the vodka in the freezer. A lot of her behavior made sense now. Conrad was smart about other people—though sometimes Edgar wished he hadn't told the man so much about 21 Cressida Drive. Maybe he'd given Conrad the wrong impression about his mother.

What did it matter, though? Why should he care about protecting a person who hated him? Conrad hadn't used the word *hate;* he'd only said, "It sounds like she doesn't like you very much."

Edgar shot again and missed.

How could he be *nine* years old? It was unbelievable. Nine wasn't a man, but it wasn't a child, either. Conrad was always telling him it was time to *act.*

Letters were not acting. Writing one was fine, but waiting for one back required a kind of patience that was beyond Edgar. E-mail would have been better, but there was no computer. And the cell phones were long gone; Conrad said the waves were dangerous, they could give a person cancer. He had a tendency to exaggerate—though, lately, Edgar had the impression that Conrad was doing more than exaggerating. He might actually be lying.

When Edgar first suggested writing to his mother, Conrad agreed it was an excellent idea. "Just to let her know where you are."

"Of course," he added, "there's always a chance her boyfriend will read it first."

"He's not her boyfriend," Edgar protested, blushing.

"Oh, I thought you said he was?"

"I don't know *who* he is. Anyway, I'm not going to address it to *him,* I'm going to address it to *her.*"

"Some people don't respect that, though," Conrad said.

Edgar knew it was true. He'd seen his mother go through Florence's private papers, some of which had been letters.

Another problem was that he didn't have a very good return address.

Edgar Fini
c/o Conrad Billings
Pinelands National Forest
New Jersey

Not even a zip code. And the Pinelands was over a million acres. But Conrad said it was fine; it would work. If she wrote a letter back, he assured Edgar it would get here.

Still, the boy was worried. Christmas was coming (the telltale light hid nothing), and everyone knew what mail was like during the holidays. *Slow as molasses,* his grandmother had always said.

Christmas had meant a lot to Florence. She loved decorating the house. Mistletoe and twinkle lights. She took great care in arranging the Nativity set under the tree. Delicate hand-painted figures with rosebud lips; they even had eyelashes and pale pink flecks for fingernails. Florence would sometimes let Edgar put the little glass star on the barn's roof—and then it was all done except for the manger, which was always left empty until Christmas morning.

"Where do you keep the baby before then?" Edgar often asked—and Florence's answer was always the same: "I'm not keeping him anywhere. He hasn't been born yet."

People who loved you often lied. If Conrad lied, maybe it was the same sort of thing. A way of protecting you from the truth, or trying to help you believe in something better. For the most part, though, it seemed that Conrad was honest. Many of his comments were properly directed against the butcher. "After what he did to your finger, there's no way of knowing what he's capable of. You're safer here." Of course, it was always implied that Lucy was in cahoots with the butcher.

Conrad had even suggested that Edgar might get in trouble if he tried to go home. Running away was a punishable offense. There was no guarantee he'd even be allowed to stay at 21 Cressida Drive. He might be sent away to live in a foster house, or in some shelter with dozens of other runaways.

But what if Conrad was wrong? What if the butcher was holding his mother prisoner—even hurting her? Such thoughts had only recently occurred to Edgar.

A prisoner. It made a lot of sense.

The boy sighed and set up some fresh cans on the stump. While he was making sure they were evenly spaced, a deer emerged from the trees. It was rust-colored, with white spots—which meant it was still a baby. It stared at Edgar, but said nothing.

Gleaming fur, twitching ears. It was beautiful.

After a moment, it disappeared.

But that didn't mean it wasn't still there. From church, Edgar knew that invisibility was not equal to absence. "Ask," the old woman had often said, holding the boy's hand in the pew at St. Margaret's. "Ask Him to help us." And she wasn't just referring to the half-naked man hanging on the wall;

she was referring, as well, to something you couldn't see, which was the Holy Ghost. She said it could change a person's life. When the Holy Ghost went inside you, it opened your eyes. Like swallowing the red pill in *The Matrix*, supposed Edgar. You saw everything. And you knew exactly what to do.

*   *   *

"But you never get *any* mail." The screen door slammed behind Edgar. "Do they even deliver mail here?"

Conrad was pressing a spatula onto a grilled cheese, making it sizzle in the frying pan. "It's our constitutional right to receive mail, Edgar."

"But what if it got lost?"

"It's possible. I'll check if there's anything at the ranger station the next time I go out for supplies."

Edgar looked down at his muddy boots. "Maybe I could drive with you."

"That's an idea," Conrad said, flipping the sandwich in the frying pan.

"We could even go today," suggested Edgar—his eyes still focused on his boots.

"Well, it's already two o'clock—and you haven't watched your video yet."

Edgar made a small sound—half resignation, half annoyance.

Conrad had purchased dozens of DVDs—*National Geographic* specials, science programs, documentaries about animals and artists and music. Edgar was supposed to watch at least one DVD every day. It was Conrad's idea of "school." In some ways it was preferable to real school. Edgar got to sit alone; there was no risk of someone spitting on your shoe or slashing your arm.

"I could watch it when we get back," offered Edgar.

"Today's not a good day. Can you wait until I go out for supplies next week?"

"On Monday?"

"Monday or Tuesday. Let's just see how the weekend goes."

Edgar pulled out his chair with a scrape and sat down heavily.

"What?" asked Conrad. "Are you mad at me?"

"No. But I think you're burning that."

"It's perfect." Conrad slid the sandwich onto a plate and brought it to the table. "Is that perfect or what?"

When Edgar didn't respond, Conrad asked him if he wanted a hug.

"No, thank you." He felt like screaming.

"Come on. Come here." Conrad knelt beside the boy's chair.

"I'm not really in the mood to be touched." Edgar kept his eyes on the plate.

"Okay. That's okay. Eat your sandwich while it's hot." Conrad stood and walked around the table.

Edgar dutifully picked up his knife and sliced the grilled cheese in half. "I should probably *see* her," he said. "Talk to her."

"Who? Your grandmother?"

Edgar looked up. That's not who he'd meant. Why was Conrad trying to confuse him? He'd come in the door with a plan, but suddenly he was feeling funny, almost feverish.

"Let's just get through the weekend," the man said again. "Plus, tomorrow, I was going to let you use the Rossi. Be great going home with a new skill, right?"

"I don't like the sound." Edgar pressed on the warm sandwich, making orange goo seep from the sides. "And I doubt I'll even be able to do it."

"Do what?"

Edgar stared at the bread.

"Do what?" the man repeated, banging his fist against the table.

It took a few seconds for Edgar to catch his breath.

"Kill the devil," he said quietly.

45

The Devil

Not only were there snakes and lizards and eagles, feral dogs and swamp frogs with orange stripes—but there was a devil, too, in the Pine Barrens. It had two legs, with hooves, and it could fly. Its wings were similar to a bat's. Conrad had shown Edgar pictures from a book—drawings based on descriptions from people who'd actually seen it. To Edgar, the creature looked like something from outer space—but Conrad explained that it had been born right here in the Pinelands. The devil's mother was a bad woman from one of the old bog-iron towns. Conrad had used the word *whore*—looking at Edgar sympathetically, as if it were a word the boy would understand and that might cause him some distress. The whore made booze from crab-apples; was a drunk—and because she'd had so many babies with so many different men, God had punished her. Her thirteenth child was cursed. As soon as it was born it killed her—clawing her neck, before escaping up the chimney and flying off into the pines.

Edgar had no trouble believing that such a creature could be real. First of all: if aliens were real (and they were), there had to be secret creatures on Earth, as well. In fact, one of Conrad's DVDs was all about the bizarre animals that lived in the deepest part of the sea. Some of them were even stranger than the Jersey Devil; one looked like a transparent brain with Christmas tree lights inside.

Besides, how could Edgar *not* believe in impossible creatures? He was one himself—his unnatural color often inspiring fear and derision. *Casper* and *Snow White* were only the tip of the iceberg; there were colder words, as well—*freak, creepy, midget of the living dead*—some scrawled on his locker, some said straight to his face. Being different from other people was exhausting. Other people's dread became your own; you ended up haunting yourself. Mirrors were awful.

Only once had Edgar seen another person as pale as he was—a girl. But she was blind, so she hadn't seen him back. It had made Edgar sad. "You're very lucky to have such good vision," a doctor once told him. "People born like you often have terrible eyes."

The Jersey Devil, for all its grotesquery, had beautiful eyes. In one of the drawings, the artist had given the creature an exotic feline squint, with dotted lines emanating from the pupils like mystical rays. "What are those?" Edgar had asked, and Conrad had said, "Bad intentions"—explaining how, over the last three hundred years, the Devil had killed not only animals, but humans as well. His last victim had been a child—just a little over a year ago.

Edgar now had a jacket and a baseball hat. On each, stitched in red thread, was the official insignia of two horns—and, between the horns, stitched in black: *Devil Hunters Club.* Both the jacket and the hat were too big, but Edgar liked them; he'd never been in a club before. This one had been founded in 1735. The members, mostly men, largely hunted deer— but they were always on the lookout for the Devil. In fact, members had to take an oath. Traditionally, it was signed in blood, but Conrad had let Edgar use a pen.

I have not entered into any secret pacts with the Devil. I swear him to be my enemy and to oppose him in both thought and action.

As he wrote down the words and then signed his name, Edgar had the feeling he'd taken a similar oath before. Living with Florence, there'd been an unspoken accord Edgar had agreed to; it was almost as if there'd been a sign hung on the door of 21 Cressida Drive—*"Keep Out!"*—directed against all things evil. And though the old woman's devil was vaguer than the creature of the pines, it was no less real. At times Edgar sensed that his grandmother had actually seen the beast, had possibly done battle with it. Apparently, though, she'd never been able to kill it. The threat remained.

Florence's weapons had been candles, crucifixes, holy water—padlocks and rosary beads. She hadn't had a gun. But Edgar had no trouble imagin- ing her using one. Often, when his grandmother came to him in the pines, she made a gesture like the one Jesus made when he pointed to his bleeding heart—forefinger and thumb in the shape of a pistol.

In the kitchen, Edgar kept his head down. Conrad had just slammed his fist against the table. Eventually the boy picked up the grilled cheese sand- wich and took a bite. The man was saying something about going outside to practice some more after lunch. "Time to prove yourself, little man." His voice was unpleasant, almost mean. Edgar could hardly swallow. The cheese tasted sour in his mouth.

He wished his grandmother were here to tell him what to do. When he took another bite of the sandwich, his stomach lurched. He stood, ran into the yard, and vomited.

Jack was outside now, too—barking into the trees.

"She's not there," said Edgar.

The dog licked his hand. When Conrad stepped outside, Edgar immediately picked up the gun.

A few seconds passed before the man said anything. "You think you're ready for that?"

Edgar was holding the larger shotgun. It suddenly felt heavier, as if Conrad's question had put a hex on it.

"I thought you wanted me to," the boy said in a barely audible whisper.

"I do," said Conrad, just as quietly.

After this, everything moved in slow motion, but there were gaps in time, which gave the impression of quickness. Edgar was shaking. He looked into the trees to see if his grandmother had returned. Jack stood by him.

"Do you want to try it?" Conrad had moved toward the stump and had picked up one of the rotting crabapples.

"Try what?"

"The apple game."

"No," replied Edgar—confusing himself by raising the gun into position.

"Listen," said Conrad. "There's nothing to be afraid of, if you do it properly."

Edgar had stopped listening, though—distracted momentarily by the sense of something moving above his head.

"Do you want the ear plugs?" said Conrad. "Put the gun down for a second and—"

"You gave it to me," protested Edgar. He had a funny feeling that if he put down the Rossi, the man would rush at him.

"I did give it to you," said Conrad. "I just want you to wear the plugs— or you'll be crying about your ears again." Conrad imitated the sound of a whining baby.

The boy could feel the color flood into his face. He stared at the apple in the man's hand—like Jesus' heart, only rotten.

Something was definitely flying overhead, passing back and forth. The breathless sound of flapping wings.

"You know what I think, Edgar?"

The boy's nose twitched from the smell—a sharp tang of black bananas and gasoline. Hoppe's No. 9. The oil used to clean the gun.

"I've been thinking about this a lot, little man."

It was an awful smell. The boy's nostrils were burning. The more he tried to understand what was happening, the more his vision closed to a single point of reference: the red crabapple shining against Conrad's yellow shirt.

"I think you're a coward, Edgar."

"I'm just cold," the boy said, trying to explain why he was shaking. He looked directly into the man's eyes—so blue they seemed inhuman. Edgar could see the dotted lines coming toward him. His arms trembled violently now, and with each breath he drew in more of the rancid smell.

None of it made sense. Conrad had been so kind, taking such good care of him when he was sick and frightened. Giving him a place to stay when no one else had wanted him.

But maybe everyone lied to you, betrayed you. His mother had done it, too.

"Shoot, for Christ's sake," said Conrad. "What are you waiting for?"

"Do you *know* me?" shouted Edgar.

The man said nothing. His burning eyes didn't seem to understand the question. Edgar shouted it again. "Do you *know* me?"

Conrad's lips parted. "No," he said, strangely smiling. "I don't."

The sound that came from Edgar's mouth was terrible. The world seemed to be turning. The sun slid from a cloud like a concealed blade.

Everything happened at the same time now. The boy's scream indistinguishable from the dog's barking; the blade of the sun shattering into blinding pins; the gun suddenly light as a feather.

No one's going to die, his grandmother had once told him.

But it wasn't true.

Everyone died.

When Conrad yelled the other boy's name, the wings descended, blocking out the sun—the talons, even in mid-air, reaching for the apple.

Edgar closed his eyes and pulled the trigger.

46

Alpha Orionis

A ringing in his ears. A silver thread of sound, almost a keening. It seems to be coming from inside his head—but Frank knows better. He knows that the sound is coming from far above him, from the stars. A time-traveling sound. High-pitched, painful.

eeeeeeeeeeeeeee

Like an alarm. Meaning *death;* meaning *danger.*

He's outside, in the dark. Outside is safer than houses. The sound falls from the sky, but is less terrible tonight because of the baby in his arms. His *son*—though Frank doesn't like to use this word. It's dangerous—like *wife* or *love,* like *mother, father, family.* Too general, too absorbent—and, at the same time, too reflective.

Better not to think; just hold the baby. He's so white—more so under the stars. "Edgar," Frank says. "Look." Pointing toward the sky.

He feels almost calm tonight. No one's yet discovered his nighttime thefts—snatching Edgar from his crib. Frank likes the yard at this hour; it's even better than the closet. As dark—but with all these pricks of light. So many tonight. Even the red one is there, screaming the loudest.

The baby smiles. *So brave.*

Frank looks from the white face to the red star. Alpha Orionis. He tells Edgar its proper name, as well as its common one: Betelgeuse. Some nights, he uses other names (this isn't the first time he's taken the baby outside for lessons). *Lucy,* he sometimes calls the red star, so that the baby will always be able to find her.

Frank has loved these stars a long time. He's studied them, observed them—recently more than ever. Lately he can't seem to sleep. His mother's dreams, his father's—even Lucy's—keep him awake. He can see the pictures falling through their minds, filling the house with quicksand. Even when they're sleeping, they're scheming. They're keeping secrets.

Well, he has secrets, too.

He tells Edgar not only the names of each star, but also the constellations—though Frank's arrangements defy tradition. He doesn't see bears and bulls and Egyptian queens. He sees a motorcycle and a man with horns. In the western sky: a raven, a pistol (he's bought one recently from his cousin Vincenzo). To the south: a neat parallelogram of stars he calls the Machine. Even Alpha Orionis—a.k.a. Betelgeuse, a.k.a. Lucy—is unstitched from its Greek tapestry. It no longer signifies the shoulder of Orion, the hunter, but is part of a more self-evident constellation known as the Bridge.

Everything is personal when it comes to the stars. That's what the astronomers don't understand. There's no single story, no universal law. How one connects the dots—whether in the heavens or on Earth—is a choice. *You write your own story.* This is what he wants to tell the child. Whatever you think, whatever you *choose* to think—that's what's real.

Frank's getting excited. The stars move, illustrating his enthusiasms.

"Even the gun," he says—"I might not use it, I might go *there* instead"—pointing to the constellation that involves him and his wife.

I'll leave it for you, he thinks; *I'll bury it in the yard*—conversing with the baby telepathically now so that no one can overhear them.

Maybe you'll never find it. Maybe you'll want to live.

"What are you doing out here?"

The voice comes from behind him. He tries to hide the baby in the folds of his coat.

"What's that? What do you have there?"

"Nothing,"

"Francesco."

He turns. His mother—ridiculous, almost beautiful tonight, in her purple flannel.

"Oh!" she cries, seeing the baby. "Give him to me." She rushes across the lawn.

Frank gently steps away. "Ma—*please.* I've got him."

Florence relents. She doesn't want to make a scene in the backyard; give the neighbors more to yap about. She adjusts the baby's coverlet. "Just don't drop him."

It's comments like this that kill Frank.

"Let's go inside." She pats his arm. "I'll make you something to eat."

He shakes his head.

"At least let me fix you a cup of tea."

Frank can feel her anxiety—wriggling into his gut like worms.

"*Il mio amore*—please. Come inside."

You're sick, you're dangerous, is what she's really saying.

Frank checks the sky to ensure that everything's still in order.

Florence follows his gaze. "What are you looking at?"

Frank whispers into Edgar's ear.

"What are you telling him? I don't want you telling him stories."

Frank grimaces.

Florence knows that face—and she's afraid of it. "Come on," she says. "It's warmer in the kitchen."

"We're going to stay out here a little longer," he says.

"I'll stay with you," his mother chirps.

Frank can see the effort she's making. And though it's not an easy thing for him, he leans down and kisses her.

It stuns Florence. She starts to cry.

"You know I love you, Frankie? And your father loves you—and your wife."

"Yes," Frank says dutifully. He touches his ear and looks up at the Machine. "Ma."

"Yes, *caro—dimmi*."

But how can he tell her?

He begins by pointing at the stars. "A lot of them," he says, "are dead."

"Nothing's dead," she assures him.

"The stars," he mumbles.

"Don't be silly," she says. "I can see them."

Frank grunts. "Just because you can *see* them doesn't mean they're up there." He jabs again at the sky. "Some of them died like a thousand years ago."

"Quiet," Florence says. "You're upsetting the baby."

Frank hands over Edgar, knowing that's all his mother cares about.

But then, once she has the child firmly against her chest, she reaches out to caress Frank's cheek. It confuses him. Usually it hurts when she touches him like this, but tonight there's no pain whatsoever. It's a good sign, he thinks. It means he's already gone.

Stella stellina, la notte si avvicina

It's his mother—singing.

"You understand?" Frank says—and Florence, understanding nothing, says, "Yes, Francesco, of course."

La fiamma traballa, la mucca é nella stalla

Frank knows this song.

Edgar does, too. He raises his white fist and shakes it at the stars.

47

Tomb

Edgar was thrown backwards—a hot pain in the crook of his shoulder. The explosion, a horrific bang, lingered in his ear like an enraged mosquito.

eeeeeeeeeeeeeeee

He staggered sideways and was about to put down the gun when he saw Conrad kneeling beside the stump. The crabapple in his hand was gone, but a second one had appeared: a distinct bloom of red on Conrad's yellow shirt.

Breathing. I'm.

Even as this thought passed through the man's mind, he was afraid to open his eyes. A moment ago he'd felt the ferocious spray of buckshot whiz past him. Though the boy had missed, a stray pellet had pierced Conrad's flesh; the pain was stunning.

"Don't pretend you're dead! I can see you breathing!"

Conrad's eyes were still shut.

"Get up," the boy was shouting.

When the second shot came, Conrad hoped that it had entered his heart. He sank closer to the ground.

"Stop joking," screamed Edgar. "I'm not even shooting you."

When Conrad looked, he saw the boy holding the gun, the barrel raised to the sky.

It was not anger alone that caused Edgar to shout; he was compensating, as well, for the fact that he couldn't hear his own voice. The ringing in his ears

was so profound that even the barking dog mimicked the drone of the enraged mosquito.

Conrad, too, was speaking in the same way—*eeeeeeeeee*—gesturing now,
as if he wanted something.

The boy thought quickly, with a clarity that shocked him. "Get in the
truck!" he shouted—managing, even as he trembled, to hold the gun in a
convincingly aggressive position.

Conrad stood and touched his chest, begging Edgar to shoot again.
Please.

It terrified the boy to see Conrad's lips form the word.

"No—*go over there.*" Edgar pointed the shotgun toward the green pickup
parked inside its lair of latticed branches. The more he shouted, the dizzier
he felt. "Stop crying," he ordered Conrad.

How many times had people said that to him? All his life, it had been
the same: *Don't be a baby. Stop bawling. Take a pill.* These had been his
mother's words. Conrad preferred, *No whimpering. Be strong. Be a man.*
Moments ago, he'd called Edgar a coward.

Now the boy moved behind Conrad with the gun. It felt to Edgar like
something he'd seen on television. His trembling increased, but he steeled
admirably when the man made a sudden move.

"No—don't turn around!" Edgar pushed forward the tip of the shotgun.
He was careful to keep his finger off the trigger, knowing there was only
one shell left. He'd seen Conrad load the gun—filling it with the legal number of shells permitted in the state of New Jersey. Edgar was always watching, always listening. Nothing slipped past him.

"I don't have the keys," Conrad said, standing before the truck.

"Yes you do," said Edgar. "They're in your left pocket."

When Conrad was behind the wheel, the boy climbed into the bed of
the pickup.

"It's too cold back there," said Conrad. "You'll freeze."

Edgar wondered if he'd been shivering like this all along. Why wasn't he
wearing a coat? His mind felt blank. He looked around at the jigsaw puzzle
of snow—scattered patches under the trees.

"Sit up front with me," the man was saying. "You'll be warmer."

"Don't try to confuse me," cried Edgar, his voice hoarse from shouting.
"Just take me home."

"Okay, but listen to me for two seconds." The man reached for the sliding window that separated the cab from the bed.

"No," said Edgar, banging the gun against the glass so hard that a crack appeared.

Conrad flinched, and pulled the keys from his pocket.

Edgar was sick of other people—sick of their lies, their tricks. If you weren't careful you could spend your whole life tossed from person to person, like a toy—barely human. Only human because you reminded them of someone else. Someone from before.

"Quiet!" yelled Edgar. Someone was making a racket. When the boy turned and saw the dog, his heart lurched. He strapped the gun to his shoulder and climbed down. When Jack licked him, he pressed his face into hers.

I'll come back, he wanted to say—but that would have been a lie.

"I have to go." When he moved away, the dog followed.

"No—*stay.*"

Jack did as she was told, but her legs twitched from the effort. She barked.

Edgar didn't look back. A tunneling sadness roared through his chest. White flakes began to fall from the sky. Conrad was right: it was too cold to ride in the bed. Edgar took a deep breath and opened the passenger door.

"I don't want to talk," he warned, unstrapping the gun and sitting as far from the man as possible. With his back pressed to the door, he positioned the Rossi so the barrel was just a few inches from Conrad's thigh.

It was painful, being unkind. How other people did it so easily, Edgar couldn't fathom. He glanced at the blood on the man's shirt. The spot was getting bigger.

When Conrad put the key in the ignition, Edgar told him to wait. He opened the glove box and removed the first-aid kit. Pushed it across the seat.

"You don't want me to die?" asked Conrad.

Edgar, bravely, said nothing.

The truck rocked as it moved down the rutted road. Conrad felt dizzy, watching the snow fall onto the sugar sand. It had never been more beautiful. Fresh snow on old snow, like polished marble. Sheer white veils over the pygmy pines. Almost a tomb.

After the boy had handed him the first-aid kit, Conrad had opened his shirt to inspect the wound. He'd seen the silver pellet lodged in his flesh, just below the clavicle—and though it would have been easy to remove, he'd neglected to do so. He'd cleaned away the blood, sterilized the wound, and covered it with two gauze patches. Edgar had handed him the white surgical tape—the same tape Conrad had used to change Edgar's bandage when they'd first met. What a history he and the boy had. Conrad could feel the pulse of blood around the silver pellet, like a second heart. With each rut in the road he winced.

Edgar asked why they were driving so slowly.

"The bumps," said Conrad. "We'll be on the main road soon."

Of course, the man's preference would have been to stay in the Barrens, to keep driving through the pines for the rest of his life—the snow endlessly accumulating on the white road. He wouldn't change a thing: the weather, the pain in his chest, the boy with the shotgun. The story could end like this, as an image: the child holding him eternally at gunpoint. Conrad grimaced.

"Why are you smiling?" asked Edgar.

"Why are you crying?" the man asked in turn. "Isn't this what you wanted?"

Edgar held his lips firmly shut to keep his emotions from escaping.

Anyway, why should he feel any confusion about leaving? He almost felt sad.

The man was quiet now, slumped at the wheel as he drove, breathing audibly.

Heat raged from the vents. Edgar was flushed. He needed fresh air but was afraid to roll down the window. Conrad had said they'd be on the highway soon, though it seemed they were driving in circles. The road was still sandy, still bumpy. Nervously Edgar touched the smooth flank of the Rossi. How enamored he'd once been of its elegance—the chestnut sheen of the wood; the polished metal appearing almost blue.

He hated it now. Hated holding it against Conrad.

He looked out the window, at the little trees, and felt, with a tilting anxiety, that he was leaving something important—that he was leaving not only the land of the pygmies, not only the man and the dog, but also Florence.

Because she'd followed him here—and maybe now she'd want to stay in the woods. Maybe she wouldn't want to go back to her other life at 21 Cressida Drive.

Edgar's life in Ferryfield would now be a life without Florence. A life without Conrad. And though these two people were in no sense equal, they were in some ways similar. Both had wanted Edgar to the exclusion of everything else.

It wasn't easy being loved like that. Sometimes it was like being in prison.

Was he really going home? He couldn't understand why it had taken so long. Someone or something must have been holding him back.

But when he looked in the side-view mirror, no one was there. Neither Florence nor Jack was chasing the truck. There was only the snow falling, the same as everywhere. The only difference was that the snow behind the truck changed color every time Conrad applied the brakes: when each falling star turned from white to red.

48

In Flanders Fields

Conrad could hear the boy talking to himself. An unnerving habit of his—though merely one among a stunning panoply of quirks. Gestures and twitches that suggested some serious dysfunction—but seemed also to imply a shadowy devotion to a world Conrad couldn't see.

Several times, he'd spotted Edgar in the yard, talking to the little doll's head he'd brought with him. Conrad often had the feeling that the boy was plotting his escape. Talking to his mother or to the police—or even to Kevin.

It made Conrad furious. He'd never had any success communicating with the dead.

Possibly because he didn't believe in such things.

He drove slowly—the buckshot in his chest sending out rhythmic flares of electric current, almost like music. There was no reason to rush. Edgar didn't seem to have noticed that they'd driven past Thompson's Grove twice and were now approaching it a third time. The snow-topped pygmies stretched splendidly toward the horizon, reminding Conrad of a poem he'd learned in school.

Short days ago, we lived, felt dawn, saw sunset glow.

The lead pellet tapped along brightly like a metronome.

Loved and were loved, and now we lie in Flanders Fields.

Conrad held tight to the steering wheel. If he turned left, just ahead, he could take the road to the Blue Hole. It was a place children loved. You could swim there. You just had to be careful not to drift too close to the places that might suck you down—a warning that had come from Conrad's grandfather, who'd explained that the Blue Hole was where the Devil lived. It had made swimming there a profound experience, a test of one's bravery. A young Conrad had been frightened of the place before he'd learned to love it. It had been the same with Kevin.

The water was a stunning cerulean—so different from the ubiquitous brown lakes of the Barrens, sullied by bog iron and tannic acid. The Blue Hole was pure—a clear pool surrounded by dense forest. Bottomless, according to legend.

Of course, it would be too cold to swim there this time of year. But that also meant they'd have the place to themselves. "Are you feeling warmer?" he asked Edgar.

The boy pointed his chin toward the dashboard. "You'll need gas soon."

Conrad looked. "First thing when we get to the highway."

He turned left onto another dirt road. He could show Edgar the other holes, too. The seeping marshes and the slurpy patches of quicksand. And the holes his grandfather had called *swallets*. Subterranean caves whose roofs had collapsed. Open doors into the Earth, exposing hidden waterways. It was to one of these limestone pits that Conrad had been coming, for months now, to deposit Edgar's letters.

Sometimes, with a broken branch, he mashed the envelope into the murky sludge. Occasionally he let the paper float on the surface until the weight of the silt pulled it under. Just at the edge of the waterline, you could see the very top of the cave's mouth, into which all surface matter eventually flowed.

There were times he'd actually considered posting one of the boy's letters. In November, around the holiday, he'd actually stuck his hand into the maw of a blue mailbox not far from the ranger station. And then it would have been over. They would have come—the guns, the flashing lights. Part of Conrad longed for that.

But he was a coward. He knew this. Despicable, to put one's destruction in other people's hands. The truck jolted over some stones and he winced. His yellow shirt was soaked with sweat. He could hear each snowflake detonate as it touched the ground.

He was ready now.

In his mind he saw it. Saw the Blue Hole—saw himself taking off his shoes, wading out to the icy center. His body was on fire. The cold water would be a relief.

Conrad's reveries were so consuming that he was shocked when another car zoomed past. Shocked, as well, to hear the zing of the truck's tires on the paved road. Just ahead was the sign: YOU ARE LEAVING PINELANDS NATIONAL FOREST. THANKS FOR VISITING!

"Why are we stopping?" asked Edgar.

Conrad looked at him, but said nothing.

"Is that the highway?"

A blur of mechanical life in the distance. Conrad felt an old sadness. He'd always hated leaving this place when he was little. In the car with his father, after the weekend—or at the end of summer vacation.

"You don't like it here?" asked Conrad. Kevin had never liked it much, either.

Edgar was crying now. "I just . . . I can hear the highway."

To Conrad, the sound of cars on a wet road—that endless *shoosh*—was the sound of a Sunday night. Why was it always raining or snowing when one was leaving? Tires on wet blacktop—was there ever a more depressing sound?

He shifted gears and began to accelerate. Just beyond the trees: the world. Infuriating, that it could be there again, after this.

The pellet in his chest was burning.

Everything would fall apart now. Everything would be lost. Though in what direction it was hard to say. Nothing was set in stone. Ferryfield was over an hour away—practically a lifetime.

Another hour with the boy: that was something. Some children lived for no more than a minute after being born. Some children were never born at all. Life was precious, no matter how short.

"You have to go right," said Edgar, gently nudging the Rossi against Conrad's leg. "We have to get on the part that goes north."

"Yes," Conrad said quietly, checking his rearview mirror before crossing into the correct lane.

49

Maria di Mariangela

"Are you kidding me?"

"What?" asked Ron.

"That's her name?" Lucy sneered. "It sounds made up."

"It's not."

"I mean, why doesn't she just call herself *Shazam?*"

"Why are you being mean? She's very respected."

"I'm not being mean. I'm just saying, what kind of name is that?"

"It's Italian."

Lucy rolled her eyes. "So—what?—does she, like, 'talk to the angels'? And what the hell am I supposed to wear?"

"She's a friggin' psychic, Lucy, not the fashion police. Just throw on some jeans."

"Nothing fits, if you haven't noticed."

"Wear one of those maternity things Izzy sent over."

"I'm not *that* big yet."

"Well, put on something or we're gonna be late. I'll wait for you downstairs."

"Ron."

"What?"

"Nothing."

"*What*—are you worried? I'll be sitting right next to you." He tried to take her in his arms.

"Stop. I said, I'll go—so I'll go. I'm just not getting my hopes up."

"Why the hell not?"

* * *

The butcher's question made her want to cry.

A lot of people thought Edgar was dead. Even Ms. Mann, Lucy sensed. Whenever the detective discussed the case now, she could barely make eye contact.

Often, in regard to Edgar, Lucy wasn't sure of her own feelings. She was living in a world unlike anything she'd ever experienced. It was no longer a world one could call *home*; it was more like a tree house, something made from sticks and mud and leaves—wind-rocked, provisional. Whenever hope bubbled up, Lucy watched it with fascinated horror, unsure whether to squash it like a bug or to shelter it in cupped hands to protect the frail creature from her own fury.

It was a funny thing, hope. Those who had it baffled her. Take the Schlips, for instance—Henry and Netty—who called Lucy once a week and who regularly sent over baskets of fruit, always with a note attached. *Any day now. Always in our prayers.* "What am I supposed to do with all this fruit?" Lucy complained one day to the butcher. "Make a pie," he'd replied. When she said she didn't know how to make a goddamned pie, Ron kept his cool and calmly said, "I do."

And he did. With all his work at the shop, he found the time to cook. Lucy was eating a lot of pie. Red meat, too. The butcher said she needed the blood. She had to think of the baby.

Eating was a kind of hope, wasn't it? Ron was an excellent cook. He was kind, too, like the Schlips. She had no right to be mean to him. He was letting her stay at his house, for God's sake. She planned to go back to 21 Cressida Drive in a few days, right after Christmas. By then, she hoped, the ghosts would be gone.

"Stay as long as you need," he'd said. "I like having you here."

It was incomprehensible to Lucy that such a thing had happened to her not once, but twice. Hadn't Pio and Florence been this kind? When she was seventeen and had nowhere to go?

Still, there was a problem with kindness. Sweet things, sweet thoughts, mostly led to sadness, which implied death—while rage seemed to imply life. Lucy felt she needed to keep a balanced perspective. For example: the woman who'd taken her in at seventeen was the same woman who, years later, had called her a whore—the same woman who, the day before her death, had actually slapped Lucy in the face.

It was important to keep one's rage alive. She'd been lazy, lately—mostly sleeping for long hours in the butcher's bed. She no longer took her car on long hauls across the state. Of course, at least once a day she did drive to 21 Cressida to inspect the house and to ensure that her note to Edgar was still attached to the front door. Even when the mailbox was empty, she banged her hand around inside, just to be sure.

Ron called from downstairs and asked if she was ready.

Lucy quickly slipped on one of Izzy's gifts: a yellow-flowered maternity smock and a pair of powder-blue drawstring pants. When she saw herself in the mirror, she winced. She looked like a clown. Her cheeks were flushed, glowing—though, due to her agitated state of mind, she didn't attribute the ruddy color to the healthy heat of her pregnant body. The red seemed, instead, the residue of Florence's slap.

"Lucy!"

"One second!" She went to the closet and pulled out the sack of Edgar's possessions she'd brought from the house. She wanted to take something with her, maybe that little rubber alien. Not that psychics were like bloodhounds; they probably didn't need something to sniff. What the hell, though—it couldn't hurt. She put the toy in her pocket.

"You look nice," Ron said when she came down. "Put on a hat, though. It's snowing."

*   *   *

The psychic's house was a dump—the outside overgrown with large clackety weeds, and the inside an obstacle course of high-piled newspapers and magazines. Lucy pictured the woman poring over the various papers, hunting for tidbits about people's lives—stockpiling her intuitions. Surely, she'd read some things about Edgar. Maybe even seen that YouTube video the kids from his school had made, with the boy's photo spinning over mountains and rivers and then landing in a pair of outstretched hands. "I see mountains and rivers and hands," the psychic would probably tell them.

When they'd first arrived, Lucy was confused by the sound of the doorbell—multiple chimes that rang out what seemed to be a sluggish version of "Hava Nagila." A tall, thin, middle-aged man wearing denim shorts had answered the door. "Pete," he'd informed them. "I'm the son." His impeccably parted beetle-black hair was clearly a toupee.

Four matching lamps with fabric rosettes on their shades imbued the living room with a pleasant pinkish light. The temperature, though, was stifling. Ron instantly began to sweat. "I'm baking cookies," Pete said festively. "For my friends. Let me show you in to Mom."

Lucy, who'd decided in the car that she wouldn't remove her coat, had no choice but to do so when they reached what Pete referred to as "the reading room"—a chamber no bigger than a walk-in closet, and where the heat was even more oppressive.

"You're late!"

It seemed to be the armchair speaking. The room was underlit (apparently all the lamps had been exiled to the living room). What illumination there was came from a cluster of electric candles, whose wicks flickered with migraine-inducing persistence. Perhaps that was why Maria di Mariangela was wearing large black sunglasses. Ron and Lucy could see her now as they moved closer—a small woman practically absorbed by the lemon velvet armchair in which she was sitting. Her doll-like feet, which did not reach the floor, were bundled in fluffy green socks with a pattern of tiny candy canes.

Ron apologized for their tardiness. "The weather is terrible out there."

"Be that as it may," Maria di Mariangela shouted with the rude pomp of the hearing-impaired, "I cannot give you extra time. Please sit."

Lucy hesitated before what appeared to be lawn furniture.

Edgar wouldn't like it here, thought Lucy. Shouting made him nervous, and he was sensitive to smells. Now that she was seated before the little woman, Lucy could detect a distinct odor—not offensive exactly, but not pleasant, either. A mixture of licorice and Ben-Gay.

"I'm so glad to have this opportunity to visit," shouted Maria di Mariangela, fussing with the tie of her terry-cloth robe.

"Yes, we are, too," Ron shouted back.

Lucy closed her eyes.

"Are you tired?" asked the psychic.

"She's just—" began Ron.

"*Not you.* I'm talking to the young lady."

"I'm fine," said Lucy.

"You are hiding something?" suggested Maria di Mariangela.

Lucy opened her eyes. "I might ask the same of you."

"You might, yes." The old woman adjusted her sunglasses. "Now, as Peter may have explained, I can record this session and you pay only ten dollars more. Okay? Then you can listen again later, at home."

Ron nodded. "That's a good—"

"No, thank you," said Lucy. "I have a good memory."

Maria di Mariangela frowned, skeptical of this good memory of Lucy's. "I do not do this for profit, young lady."

"Of course not." Lucy offered a curt smile. Her heart was racing.

"You are afraid?"

The wicks of the electric candles were now flickering in synch, their seemingly random patterns exposed as programmatic. "Not at all," said Lucy.

"Even in death," said Maria di Mariangela, "there is nothing to fear. Let me tell you something you may not understand. Most people are idiots when it comes to death. When I look at you, you know what I see right away?"

Lucy reached into her pocket and retrieved the alien.

"I do not permit food in this room!" shrieked the psychic.

"It's not—" Ron attempted to explain.

"Please, young man." Maria di Mariangela held up her hand. "You are not the husband—is that correct? You are not the father! You must please be quiet."

Lucy extended the toy. Immediately, the psychic snatched it up—bringing the rubber humanoid to her nose and lips. She grumbled contentedly and then kissed the figure. "Edgar, yes?"

A small sob, like the coo of a pigeon, broke from Lucy's mouth.

Ron handed her his handkerchief. "It's okay, babe."

"Shhh," Maria di Mariangela reprimanded, before turning sharply toward the wall.

Lucy and Ron turned, too—squinting at the ill-lit wood paneling.

"You are welcome here," Maria di Mariangela said to the paneling. She leaned closer to the wall and seemed about to fall from her chair when she pulled back with a gasp.

"What is it?" demanded Lucy, sickened by her own curiosity.

"So many." Maria di Mariangela touched her head as if she, too, felt sick. The little alien was locked in the woman's fist. "All are welcome," she proclaimed—her head turning in slow circles as she moaned in discomfort.

Lucy hoped it was arthritis and not some kind of funny business. She glared at Ron, while offering a gesture toward the head-roller *(What the fuck?).*

"Trance," whispered Ron.

"I can hear you," scolded M di M. She rolled her neck three more times and then stopped, mid-roll, leaving her head hanging oddly to the left. "One at a time, please," she beseeched the wall.

Lucy looked again at the paneling—knotty pine planks that did seem to suggest a multitude of eyes.

An unwholesome sound was coming from the psychic's mouth. She was grinding her teeth. After a few seconds she turned to Lucy with a dolorous smile. "They want me to touch you. May I touch you?"

Lucy shook her head. "No. Who wants you to—"

"Give me your hand."

"Can't you just tell me about Edgar? If he's—"

"Edgar is not here." Maria di Mariangela waggled her fingers in Lucy's direction. "Please, my dear."

"What do you mean, he's not here?"

The woman huffed and grabbed Lucy's hand. Her grip was formidable.

The room was unfathomably hot. Lucy could feel a line of ants trailing down from each armpit.

"Stop resisting," ordered Maria di Mariangela. "They don't always come this easily. Tell me—who is this woman I see? The fat woman."

"That would be me," snapped Lucy.

"Not you," snapped back Maria. "The woman with the red hands."

"I don't—"

"The woman with the burned hands."

"*Ow,*" cried Lucy. Maria di Mariangela's hands were on fire.

"The old woman. Only recently passed."

"Florence," whispered the butcher.

"Shut up, Ron. Don't help her."

Once again, Maria di Mariangela kissed the alien. "She says she's the boy's mother."

"I'm his mother," declared Lucy.

"No, another boy." The psychic spoke as if her mouth were filled with gravel. "This other boy is with us, too."

"I'm only interested in Edgar!"

"*Shhhh*—what is this word she's saying? She's saying this to you. *Lucille,* she calls you."

"What did I just say? I don't want to talk to her." Lucy tried to free her hand. Maria tugged back. "If you want Edgar, you must speak with her."

Lucy felt certain she was going to pass out.

"This word she's saying is inside you. Even from your father, you know this word."

Lucy pulled away. All she could hear now was her last argument with Florence. Condemnations from both sides—though Florence's had been the harshest. *Unfaithful. No respect for the dead. A drunk, a—*

"Whore," hissed Maria di Mariangela.

When Lucy's hand moved quickly in the dim light, it seemed to Ron a pale bird. He gasped when the bird crashed into Maria di Mariangela's cheek.

Oddly, the slap brought a smile to the psychic's face, even as tears rolled down from under her black sunglasses. "Yes yes yes," she cried.

"Oh my God," said Lucy. "I'm sorry, I—"

"No." The old woman silenced her. "You must forgive *me,* Lucille."

The voice was familiar. Lucy felt something break inside her chest.

"The door is open!" proclaimed the psychic.

As Lucy leaned forward, Maria did, too, until the two women were touching, forehead to forehead. Lucy was reeling. The flickering candles, the scent of Ben-Gay replaced by the scent of Florence's perfume. If Lucy was crying, it was nothing compared to the sound coming from Maria di Mariangela's mouth—a keening whine that condensed into a wolf-like howl. "There is a dog," she shouted.

"No," said Lucy. "We don't—"

"His father," spat Maria. "With his father."

Lucy swallowed, unable to speak.

"And who is this Rosie?" demanded Maria, squeezing Lucy's hand. "Tell me."

"I don't—"

"Rosie," repeated Maria, dragging the word through the gravel inside her mouth. "Rosie—Rossie—*Rossi. Ahhhh!"* She detached her hands from Lucy's. The alien fell onto the table.

"You must leave!" shrieked the psychic.

Ron glanced at his watch. "I'm sorry, didn't we—I think we booked a thirty-minute—"

"The boy is in danger. Go!"

"Where?" cried Lucy.

"Twenty-one," croaked the psychic, before expiring in a crumpled heap on the yellow armchair.

"Oh my God," said Lucy.

"Pete?" called the butcher. "Peter!"

When Maria di Mariangela's son appeared, he brought the scent of chocolate and butter—his hands and T-shirt dusted with flour.

"She just—" Ron gestured toward the slumped psychic.

"Oh, don't worry," replied Pete, "that happens. She'll be fine."

"Should I pay you?" Ron fumbled for his wallet.

"*Go!*" shrieked Maria in a stunning, though brief, reanimation.

Lucy grabbed the rubber alien and ran from the room.

A moment later she was standing, confused, outside the house. It seemed as if Pete had been baking out here, too. The trees, the parked cars, the pavement—everything was covered in flour.

"It's really coming down," the butcher said, leading Lucy carefully across the white ground.

As they drove away, neither thought to call the police. Their only wish was to get to 21 Cressida Drive as quickly as possible. At the first turn in the road, the van slid, and Lucy's heart lurched. "Be careful, Ron."

"I think Tulaney Avenue will be quickest," he said. "I can probably get to the house in ten minutes."

The words seemed familiar to Lucy—some lie she'd told Florence once. The day she'd driven away with Frank and the baby. *We'll be back in ten minutes.*

"Hurry," she said, feeling frightened now as she looked at the snow. It was falling too slowly, as if it had all the time in the world.

50

Homecoming

Edgar was shivering so violently he could barely keep the blanket over his shoulders. The snow had stopped, but there were deep drifts on the ground. He proceeded slowly, every footfall a collapse, after which he could retrieve his leg only by force. Snow was getting into his shoes. Everything felt slippery. He hoped there were no animals around that might smell the blood on his shirt.

In the distance, through the bare branches, he could see houses. On some of them were Christmas lights—the glow of the tiny bulbs magnified in the misty air. Edgar felt sick with excitement—so much so that he had to stop to vomit.

He picked himself up and trudged on. Soon he'd be able to see the Heftis' house and then, just past the knife-carved oak *(Frank loves Lucy 4-ever),* he'd be in his own backyard. Every few steps he looked behind him, but no one was there—his relief marred by fury.

Conrad had not even said a proper goodbye.

For most of the drive to Ferryfield they'd barely spoken. At one point, Conrad had suggested Edgar take a nap, and Edgar had told Conrad to please not speak to him like he was a baby. Also, how was he supposed to take a nap with the Rossi in his hands? Once you picked up a gun, you couldn't just put it down like you'd made a mistake.

He and Conrad were enemies now. It was awful.

When they'd finally pulled off the Parkway and the truck was moving through neighborhoods familiar to Edgar, the boy had felt an abrupt confusion. In the end, the man had parked in their old spot behind the supermarket, telling Edgar he'd have to get out and walk the rest of the way.

Then, he'd said, "Wait," just as Edgar was reaching for the door. "Take this."

He'd unbuttoned his flannel shirt and strained himself out of it. Edgar was horrified to see that the bandage on Conrad's chest had soaked through and was beginning to leak. "There's a blanket in the back of the truck," Conrad mumbled. "Take that, too."

When Edgar put down the gun, he placed the barrel on the floor, next to his feet.

"No—that's yours now," insisted Conrad.

"I don't want it," said Edgar. The gun had belonged to Kevin. "You can't just give it to *everyone*."

Conrad grimaced. When he asked what he should do with it, Edgar said he didn't care. "Why don't you just—"

The boy stopped. He could hear something funny in his voice—something he didn't like. Something mean.

In the dark, with the snow rushing silently under the beams of the streetlights, Edgar was too tired to pretend to be someone else. Someone brave. A man. What did it matter if he made a fool of himself now? He leaned across the seat and kissed Conrad on the cheek.

Conrad stiffened, and said nothing.

When Edgar slammed the door, a black bewilderment kept his tears at bay.

Now he stood behind 21 Cressida Drive. It seemed to be moving—swaying on a sea of blue snow. Florence's garden was covered—her metal bench upholstered with delicate pillows of ice. Above the backyard, huge swaths of the sky were clear, exposing huddles of stars. The red one was there. Someone—Edgar couldn't remember who, maybe Mr. Levinson—had taught him about that star, which had a funny name, like a monster. Supposedly it was going to die one day, and people on Earth would be able to see the explosion for weeks, like a second sun.

Supernova was the word.

Edgar thought about the stars because it was better than thinking about the house, which was very dark and very quiet. It was too early for his mother to be sleeping. Unless she'd been drinking. On the ground, by the back door, was a coffee can filled with cigarette butts—not his mother's, though; there was no lipstick on them. Still, he reached for the doorknob.

It was locked—and since Edgar couldn't bring himself to knock, he turned and headed toward the garden bench. He knelt before it and stuck a bare hand into the snow; mushed around until he felt the stone under which his grandmother kept the spare key.

The panic he'd felt outside only increased when he was standing in the kitchen, beside the yellow Formica table. There were crumbs on the surface, crumbs on the floor. In the sink was a small tower of food-crusted pans. Tiny insects like particles of dust floated over a cluster of overripe bananas.

Edgar's anxiety accompanied him into the living room, where at the end of December there was no Christmas tree, no lights. On the coffee table, beer cans and road maps. A dirty hairbrush. He called out to her and ran up the stairs. On the floor of his mother's room, and all over the bed, were clothes—including a pair of black boxer shorts the size of a television.

"Ma," he called out again.

In Florence's room he clicked on the light. Not only was no one there, but the room itself seemed to have gone away. The eggshell walls and pale blue carpet had switched places. The walls were now blue, and the carpet cream. The night-light of the angel on the bridge was gone. The body of the Virgin, the Chanel N° 5, the wedding portrait—gone, too. Not a candle was lit.

He ran to his own room, but there was no safety there. As in Florence's bedroom, important things were missing. The little cup filled with fortunes; his figurines; the stuffed puppy from when he was a baby. How could she have thrown these things out? He'd been gone only a few months.

Sometimes you think people are waiting for you, but then you find out that nobody's there.

That's what Conrad had said. Maybe he hadn't been lying about the letters.

Edgar felt sick. He put his hand in his pocket to touch Florence's ring. When he stuck his other hand in his other pocket, he began to utter a peculiar panting sound. He dug his fingers deeper, even as he knew. He'd left the diamond at the cabin—in the little hole where the floorboards were rotted. Suddenly it was hard to breathe.

In the hallway, he stood at the top of the stairs, paralyzed by the sight of the piano below—the framed photographs drifting like sailboats across the black lacquer. As Edgar descended, he heard a noise—and then he saw her, standing by the back door, letting in the cold air. She was shivering in purple pajama bottoms and a white cardigan adorned with holly leaves.

"Ed-guh?"

"Toni-Ann?"

To each, the sight of the other was incomprehensible.

Toni-Ann, though, took action. She rushed forward.

Edgar stepped back and leaned dizzily against the table.

"*Oh my gah*—what they do to you?" She touched the dried blood on Conrad's shirt.

Edgar immediately started to cry. "Where's my mother?"

"*Oh,*" Toni-Ann exclaimed. "Oh my gah!"

"What?"

"She's going to have a baby!"

Edgar felt a sickening heat as Toni-Ann breathed into his face: "And they have to get married now, my mom say, or the baby have problems."

Edgar's legs turned to jelly. "Why are you *lying*, Toni-Ann?"

"I'm not."

"Does he live here?" asked Edgar. "Mr. Salvatore?"

"Sometimes. They on vacation now."

Edgar was trembling as he picked up the army blanket that had slipped to the floor.

"I go call them," said Toni-Ann.

As she moved toward the phone, Edgar grabbed a dirty glass from the counter and threw it down.

Toni-Ann turned.

"Kiss me," she said implausibly.

Edgar looked up from the glittering shards.

"Like we're married." Toni-Ann's eyes glowed like a panther's.

Edgar was speechless as the girl tiptoed toward him around the shards.

"It's just our lips," she said.

When Edgar asked again about his mother, Toni-Ann said the same awful things, even when he asked her to swear to God.

"Kiss me," she persisted.

"No."

"Please, Ed-guh."

Since she had tears in her eyes now, Edgar said: "Only if you promise."

"What I promise?"

"That you won't call them."

"Okay," she said, leaning in with her purple lips.

When it was over, both were blushing. Both were crying.

"We're just dreaming," said Toni-Ann, looking down, chastened.

Edgar, too, stared at the broken glass.

"I call them now, okay?"

"No."

"It's my job, Ed-guh."

"*No.* If you tell them, Toni-Ann, I won't love you anymore."

The girl scrunched up her face, confused.

Edgar's face changed, too. He turned away and began to move like he was dancing.

But Toni-Ann knew he wasn't dancing. He was doing that thing he did when he was upset. She'd seen him do it before. He was making funny sounds, too, like a bird.

"Don't cry. I promise, Ed-guh. Look." She made an *X* over her heart. "You my husband now. I promise, okay?" Gently she petted the boy's arm. "Okay?"

Edgar nodded as Toni-Ann wiped his cheek.

It was too terrible to stay here.

When the boy slipped out the door, Toni-Ann wondered if somehow she'd been tricked.

"You coming back?" she called, pulling anxiously at her lips. It was so dark she couldn't see him. "Ed-guh?"

The cold air smelled like smoke.

"Mess," said Toni-Ann.

She knelt down to gather the broken glass—but when a car squealed into the driveway, she panicked and ran into the yard.

51

The Shell

He'd walk to the clearing, he decided, and then turn around. He wasn't as cold now. Over Conrad's yellow shirt was a jacket he'd found hanging by the back door—an enormous fleece-lined windbreaker, no doubt belonging to the butcher.

Edgar wondered if they already had a name for the baby.

And were they planning to put it in *his* room? Use the same cradle *he'd* slept in—the wicker one covered with lace from Florence's wedding dress?

He was tired and wanted to lie down. But falling asleep in the snow wasn't a good idea. In the spring, Conrad had said, there'd be lots of flowers. He'd said the Pinelands would be like a fairyland.

Spring was far away, though. Winter lasted a long time. Especially in the woods.

Of course, Edgar knew things now. How to build fires, how to forage. A lot of plants people called weeds were actually food.

Still, how long could a person survive without other people? Probably not forever.

Edgar's thoughts unraveled, taking him past the clearing. He didn't realize that he'd been following his own footprints until he saw the torn-up fence at the edge of the woods. He saw the dark lot and the green truck still parked there. He kept walking in the only direction he could understand.

Something was wrong, though. Conrad wasn't in the truck. Instead there was an animal with a long snout—or a beak. It was trembling. It made no sense, even when Edgar was just a few feet away. Only when he leaned his face against the passenger window, and the animal's eyes met his own, did he understand.

Conrad was leaning back, holding the gun toward himself—the tip of the barrel inside his mouth.

"No," said Edgar—though the word was barely audible. He was inside the truck now, kneeling on the seat. Conrad's thumb was on the trigger, and Edgar traced his hand delicately along the flank of the shotgun until he found the safety. He clicked it—and then slowly, slowly, lifted the gun up and away.

Conrad's teeth chattered against the metal.

When Edgar had the gun at a safe angle, he opened it, removed the last shell and tossed it out the window, onto the pavement.

The man, who was shaking like a puppet now, began to cry. A horrible sound.

Edgar was uncertain what to do.

After a moment, he touched the man's arm and said what his grandmother always said after a bad dream.

"I'm here."

But Conrad only wept all the more.

January

52

Pilgrims

The persimmons were lovely, with smooth orange skins bright as Chinese lanterns—each one wrapped in pale blue tissue. Netty had found just the right basket for them: a crafty little thing in which the weaver had incorporated random plaits of silver ribbon.

She suggested to Henry that they walk to Lucille's house. The trip, she estimated, would take no more than twenty minutes. And though the day was cold, the sun had come out—and besides, the exercise would do them good. The two of them had been cooped up in the house for days. That miserable storm, and then a frozen pipe had burst at their shop. A new shipment of area rugs, as well as some luxury sheet sets, now had noticeable water damage and would have to be put on discount.

"I should like to tell Edgar," said Henry, as they set out on their walk.

"What's that, dear?"

He reminded his wife how the little boy had once asked if *everything* at the dry-goods store was, in fact, dry. "Not anymore," boomed Henry.

"Yes," agreed Netty. "He'd like that."

Then they were quiet for a while. The streets were empty, bordered by huge piles of snow. There were sizeable drifts, as well, on people's lawns. They walked as if in a kind of maze. It was lovely, but disorienting.

After five minutes, Netty handed the basket of persimmons to Henry. "Your turn."

The drifts of snow were growing larger, as if the worst of the storm had fallen on the west side of Ferryfield, where the Finis lived. When they were just a few blocks away, the sun slunk into gray clouds. Immediately it turned colder. Netty looked at the persimmons for comfort. Fruit was the least she and Henry could do.

When Edgar had first disappeared, all those months ago, there had seemed more they could offer Lucille. During the first terrible days, Henry had suggested he call his buddies at the VFW. "What can they do?" Netty had scoffed, and Henry had said, "*Puuh,* they can do a lot."

And they had. They'd gone though the woods with sticks and flashlights, like something out of a Sherlock Holmes story. They'd knocked on doors with Edgar's photo hanging from their necks (Netty had printed the photos with card stock and attached them to loops of string so the old codgers wouldn't lose them). They'd worn suits on their rounds, like missionaries. They'd stapled posters to telephone poles with their shaking arthritic hands.

Nothing, of course, had come of it.

Netty had played her part, as well—sitting in Florence's chair, waiting for Edgar while Lucille was out. But she hadn't done that in a while. Truth be told, no one seemed that frantic anymore. It didn't seem absolutely necessary that someone stay at the house twenty-four hours a day. Not that anyone believed the child was dead—of course not!—but people were simply being practical. Also, Lucille didn't go out much anymore. She did most of the waiting herself. And of course she now had that Italian man to help her. He had better stick around, that's all Netty had to say.

At first, she'd assumed the pregnancy was just a rumor, but then she'd run into Lucille after not seeing her for a while, and, lo and behold, there it was—the pudding-proof of the girl's belly.

The persimmons in the silver-threaded basket would be, without having to say it, for both Edgar *and* for the baby. Fruit suited any occasion.

"Do you want me to carry that?" she asked Henry.

"I won't say no," he replied, handing her the basket. "Like bowling balls, these things."

Within two minutes, they reached Lucille's street.

They walked on—the snowdrifts like white hedges along the side of the road. They couldn't see the Finis' house in its entirety until they were directly across the street from it, standing in a driveway that had been cleared. When they stepped into the road, Netty began to slip. Henry grabbed her arm.

"Watch the fruit," she cried.

"The fruit?" scolded Henry, once he'd stabilized his wife. "The fruit is not my number one concern."

"I'm fine."

They stood at the edge of the street and caught their breath. Henry grasped

Netty's hand to lead the way. Not two steps later he began to slip, and it was now Netty's grip that kept him, just barely, on his feet.

"It's that damn basket," said Henry. "It's throwing us off balance."

But Netty's eyes were sharper than his. She saw the dull glint on the road, which was covered in a thin layer of nearly invisible ice. "Don't move," she said.

"What? We're going to stand in the street?"

As soon as he moved, though, he understood the merit of Netty's warning. The ice was so slick that he slipped away from her and began to sail forward. He progressed steadily, like a mannequin on a conveyer belt, until he stopped in the dead center of the road. Miraculously he didn't fall.

"Oh my God," said Netty.

"If we take baby steps," began Henry—but Netty said, "*No*. Don't move a muscle." At her and Henry's age, a fall was no laughing matter.

At the sound of an approaching car, Netty gasped—but when she looked there was nothing, only the wind.

Henry gazed at the white house they were planning to visit. The porch light was on, though it was only mid-afternoon. The air around the property seemed suffused with smoke—a miasma of winter and palpable defeat. What was the point of going there? Henry closed his eyes against the futility. Florence had been right, getting out of the game. She was lucky not to have to live through another winter, another tragedy. Already she was in the land of forgetting. *Sheol*. The dwelling place of the dead.

As soon as he thought this, though, he saw her, sitting on the porch, eating one of the persimmons. As he leaned forward to get a better look, he realized that his eyes were closed. When he opened them, Florence was gone.

He sighed. All those sheets, ruined. Even the ones with the nice satin trim. He thought of his own daughter, Helen—the lesbian.

End of the line.

The words echoed in his head. Helen was their only child and would no doubt sell the store when he and Annette were gone.

He could hear his wife moving behind him. "What are you doing?" he asked.

"Give me one minute." Netty had crouched down on the frozen street. "I'm coming for you."

As she began to crawl forward, pushing the persimmons before her, she could feel the cold boring into her kneecaps. Her arms wobbled. When she'd reached Henry, she grasped his ankle and told him to slowly—*slowly*—get down.

When Henry was beside her, on all fours, the Schlips proceeded, crawling like toddlers, until they and the persimmons had reached the edge of the Finis' driveway.

Henry was breathing heavily. Netty only a little less so. They rested for a moment, and then proceeded in the same way, on their hands and knees, all the way to the steps of the porch. From the bottom, they could see the sign on the door. It was more of a plaque, offering, in very neat block print, instructions for Edgar, along with some telephone numbers.

Henry sighed. "I guess she still . . ."

"Of course," Netty said sharply.

They pulled themselves up onto the steps and rested again.

"We'll knock in a minute," said Netty.

"Pull ourselves together," agreed Henry.

Netty was glad to have her back to that awful plaque.

What terrible luck the Finis had. It was like a curse from a fairy tale; it never ended. Suicides and bridges and a child with marble skin. And though Netty never liked to think that anyone had worse luck than she and Henry, the truth was, the Finis did. They had very peculiar stars.

Even just recently, less than a month ago, someone had broken into Lucille's house. Luckily the girl and her boyfriend had arrived home before the burglars had stolen anything. Crazy kids, no doubt, hopped up on drugs. One of them had smashed a glass in the kitchen.

Apparently the incident had stirred up Lucille, who was convinced that the break-in had something to do with Edgar. Unlikely, thought Netty. Still, the police were taking it seriously. A shotgun shell had been found not far from the house—in the same parking lot where Edgar's clothing had been discovered that first week he'd gone missing.

Netty didn't know where to put her heart.

When she took Henry's hand, he said, "What?"

"Nothing," she said. "What?"

After a moment, he said, "We should call Helen. Have her to dinner."

When Netty reminded him that their daughter lived in California, Henry reminded Netty that there was such a thing as airplanes.

53

The Goofers

When Toni-Ann saw the old people crawling across the road, she was afraid they were coming for her. She closed the curtains and, after several moments of turmoil, put on one of her Goofers sing-along CDs. The Goofers wore their hair as if it were cotton candy—in towering pastel puffs. They had jumpsuits to match. Their music always made Toni-Ann happy.

> *Give me that G, G, G, that O, O, O.*
> *When the light turns green, you GO GO GO.*

As she sang along, her voice was shaky. It was confusing when the things that always made you feel better somehow made you feel worse.

The trouble was, the old people in the road were friends of Florence's— and Toni-Ann had been worried lately that Florence might be angry with her. The police had been at the Finis' several times during the past few weeks; they'd come to Toni-Ann's house as well, asking more questions about Edgar. The girl, keeping her promise, had said nothing.

> *Give me a YELL, not loud, make it LOW LOW LOW.*
> *When the sign turns yellow, it's SLOW SLOW SLOW.*

Toni-Ann locked her bedroom door. From the top shelf of the closet she took down her Magic 8 Ball. It was the size of a Florida grapefruit and made of black plastic. A little window exposed the inky fluid inside. Answers lived in that ink until you needed them.

"Magic 8 Ball," she asked, "should I tell them about Ed-guh?"

She shook the ball and then turned it over. It took a moment—always heart-stopping—for the response to rise to the surface of the dark liquid.

Reply hazy, try again.
"Magic 8 Ball, should I tell them about Ed-guh?"
Shake, shake, shake.
Concentrate and ask again.
Toni-Ann groaned.
"Magic 8 Ball"—and this time she asked *very* slowly, so that whatever it was that was inside the ball would not misunderstand her. "Should I. Tell them. About Ed-guh?"
Shake, shake, shake.
Better not tell you now.
"Oh, don't be stupid!" cried Toni-Ann.
By now the Goofers had circled back to the main verse of the "Rules of the Road" song.

Now Ss and Ts and Os and Ps.
When it turns to red, the Goofers say FREEZE!

It suddenly occurred to Toni-Ann that she'd like to drive a car one day. Maybe a cherry-red zoomer like the one Mrs. Feen had. And since Ed-guh was now married to her, Toni-Ann pictured him in the car, too. The two of them driving home to wherever they lived. Maybe a farm with chickens.
She held the 8 Ball close to her chest.
"Should I tell them about Ed-guh?"
She shook the oracle vigorously, in time to the Goofers' music, and then peered down at her fate, which was also the fate of others.
My sources say no.
Toni-Ann scrunched up her face. What did the ball mean? And who were these sources, exactly?
Toni-Ann suspected it had something to do with Florence. Though how the fat old woman could have gotten inside the 8 Ball was beyond the girl's reckoning. Maybe dead people shrunk.
"Are you mad at me?" she asked it.
You may rely on it.
"But will Ed-guh come back?"
Cannot predict now.
The ball was obviously tired. Toni-Ann shoved it under the pink sham of her canopy bed.

The Goofers were singing about manners now, about *thank you* and *please* and *excuse me*. Toni-Ann grimaced and clicked off the music.

Anyway, she had to do a report for school.

It was supposed to be a story about herself, but Miss Hussein said it could be made up. "Nothing shorter than five sentences," Miss Hussein had said— "but try for ten."

My name is Toni-Ann. I have a purple coat.

But wait—that was true. Maybe it would be better to make something up.

She crossed out the words and started again.

54

The Farm

My name is Toni-Ann. I live in the farm with chickens. The chickens lay the eggs, it's a lot. You can't put chocolate chips in a omelet but on the farm it's allowed. I make it for Edgar. One chicken is black but he's not the bad chicken. The bad chicken is green. That's the shut-up chicken.

Edgar and I live here a long time.

This is the tenth sentence.

We have tomatoes and corn on the cob in the garden. If someone planted a gun we don't find it. It never snows. This is in the future. Edgar stays small but he's a man now. Everyone is happy for me when he comes back.

February

55

The Golden Rectangle

Edgar sat at the table, drinking chocolate. He'd used two packets of mix, so the liquid was thick as mud and blindingly sweet. With each sip he closed his eyes.

More trees. Inside, outside—it didn't matter; even his mind was overgrown with pines. He walked through them as best he could. The path was dark. The sugar helped.

Today, something moved among his thoughts like a snake. A flash of greenish gold weaving in and out of the boy's larger concerns. This snake-thought—always the same color—had plagued him all his life, surfacing at intervals, but moving too quickly for Edgar to catch or understand. Sometimes he saw a golden rectangle floating on water. Saw it clearly, the gold against the blue—but then the rectangle would always vanish, swallowed by the blue water. Certain thoughts, it seemed, had minds of their own; they wandered away from their thinkers and lived wild unchained lives.

Edgar tilted back his head to drain the last of the sweet mud. He knew it was wrong to have used two packets of mix. He promised himself that, tomorrow—and from then on—he'd only ever use half a packet.

He set the cup on the table and looked at the clock. It was nearly two, time for Conrad's pill. He'd also bring some crackers and jam, which always looked nice on a plate—and besides, it was the sort of thing that went down easy when you were sick.

Of course, lately, no matter what Edgar fixed, Conrad refused it. Nearly eight days had gone by, during which Conrad had taken no food. Edgar decided to put some peanut butter on the crackers. There were only so many days a person could live without eating. Water was even more important. Edgar ran the tap and filled a tall glass. He put everything on a tray—the crackers, the water, a paper napkin, and a pinecone. The pinecone only because it was winter, and there weren't any flowers.

*   *   *

Conrad had been very sick after they first got back. The hole in his chest had become infected, yet he'd done nothing to take care of himself, even after the wound began to resemble a swollen eye with a slimy yellow pupil. It had been left to Edgar to clean it. Of course, every time he'd done this, Conrad had said to leave it alone. He'd consistently pushed Edgar away. But Edgar had pushed back. The idea of Conrad being sick terrified him. Edgar couldn't afford to be squeamish.

Besides, much of this was his fault. Though it hadn't been his intention to hurt Conrad, he had—and perhaps seriously. The first time he'd wiped some cotton across the wound, he'd discovered a sizable shard of buckshot still lodged there. He'd immediately gotten the tweezers, and—as Florence had once done when Edgar had stepped on some broken glass—he'd pecked gingerly into the man's flesh. It wasn't easy to get the shard out—Conrad's skin seemed to have grown around the metal; it was like pulling a tooth. It came out bloody—strangely shaped, and sharp—less a tooth than a fang.

Edgar had already taken the guns and buried them in the backyard, behind the woodpile. He'd dug nearly two feet down—and once the hole had been filled back in, he'd used his boot to cover the grave with pine needles. As for the fang he'd removed from Conrad's flesh, he'd stuck it into the bark of a pygmy, a warning against whatever it was that was trying to hurt everyone.

But none of it had worked. Because afterward came the fever—Conrad sweating and shivering and babbling, crying sometimes, even shouting. And though Edgar had been frightened, he'd proceeded without hesitation. He knew exactly what to do. All his years of exquisite care at Florence's hands had made of him a mirror, in which the old woman still lived, and through which he reflected her spirit back into the world.

Lukewarm washrags on Conrad's arms and chest and legs. A cooler one on his forehead if he was sweating. An extra blanket if he was shivering— but only a light one. You didn't want to kill the fever, Florence had always said. The fever was your friend.

Probably the most important thing was sitting next to the person so they didn't have to be alone. It didn't matter if they were delirious and didn't know you were there, or thought you were someone else. Sometimes just putting your hand over theirs made the sick person feel calmer. It was calming for Edgar, as well. He was afraid to be alone. Now more than ever.

When they'd first returned to the cabin after the horrible night in Ferryfield, Edgar had cried for two whole days. He'd run into the woods—not to escape, but to scream without disturbing Conrad. Jack sometimes followed the boy, and they howled together.

But then Conrad had gotten sick. After that, there'd been no time for tears.

The boy had gone through the medicine cabinets. There were some old prescriptions, but none of them seemed right. There was a bottle of Elavil with Conrad's name on it, but Edgar knew from television commercials that such pills weren't for infections or fever. Another bottle contained something called Ritalin—but that had Kevin's name on it. Aspirin had been Edgar's only option.

In the first-aid kit from the truck, he'd found half a tube of antibacterial cream and a pack of sterile bandages. Supplies had dwindled quickly, though—and when the bandages and surgical tape were gone, Edgar had had to use paper towels held down with Scotch tape. The flimsy tape had barely stuck to Conrad's skin. Edgar ended up cutting an old sheet into strips, and then tying the strips around Conrad's chest to keep the paper towels in place. It had been a complicated setup, reminding Edgar of a picture book from his old bedroom. Gulliver tied down by the Lilliputians.

One morning, toward the end of January, Edgar noticed a red line emanating from the wound. Each day the line grew a little longer, closer to Conrad's heart. When it was nearly four inches long, and Conrad's fever at its worst, Edgar had insisted that the man get up and go to a doctor. When he refused, the boy took action. He'd had no choice but to make the man suffer through something he himself had suffered through more than once during his own bouts of illness.

From the bottom of the kitchen pantry, he'd taken the little wire basket of garlic—and every day, for nearly two weeks, he'd chopped up a large clove and boiled it in a little water, which he then made Conrad drink. When the antibacterial cream had run out, Edgar mashed up more garlic and put the paste directly onto the wound. Florence had always mixed it with honey, but there was only sugar at the cabin. Edgar even wrapped two cloves of garlic in a bit of tissue, and then put them in the man's ears while he was sleeping. Florence had done that, too.

Sometimes it seemed that Conrad wanted to be sick—or even worse. But why would a person want that, especially if it meant having to leave behind people you loved? It was a stupid idea—and Edgar wasn't going to let Conrad be stupid. With lukewarm rags and aspirin, hot tea and garlic, he'd managed to save Conrad; the wound had closed, the fever had vanished.

It was intolerable to Edgar that Conrad was making himself sick a second time, by not eating. Sometimes Edgar wanted to slap him, to wake him up. A few months before, in a grove of yellow aspens, Conrad had told Edgar that he loved him, and Edgar had told Conrad that he wasn't allowed to say that. Now, in winter, with snow padding the roof of the cabin, Edgar hoped Conrad would say it again.

But he barely spoke.

"I'm not angry anymore," Edgar would tell him.

He had no time to be angry. It was a lot of work taking care of someone who was ill.

The hours passed quickly, though. And the work took your mind off other things—such as your own life. Edgar was pretty sure he never again wanted to think about the baby inside his mother, the one she'd made with the butcher. The baby that would grow up in Edgar's old room and look at its face in Edgar's mirror. The baby that, one day, would pull *Gulliver's Travels* from Edgar's bookshelf and think it was just some made-up story.

It was better to think about Conrad.

Plus, there was a lot to do at the cabin—and only one person strong enough to do it. Cleaning and cooking and laundry, and of course he was responsible for Jack. The fish, too. Twice a day he made a fire. The snow had not let up—six storms since the blizzard in December—and Edgar often needed to clear a path to the woodpile. By evening he was exhausted and would fall into a sleep so deep that his unhappy dreams stayed in the underworld, and had little effect on his waking life.

*　*　*

When he carried the tray into the bedroom, Conrad turned away. His eyes were red.

"I'll drive you back soon," he mumbled—and then he said something that sounded like *mistake*.

Edgar set the tray on the bedside table. "I have crackers."

"No, thank you, Edgar." Conrad was very polite lately, as if he and Edgar had just met. It made the boy sad.

He held out the glass of water.

But the man shook his head and pointed weakly to the left. "In the desk. I want you to get something."

"Just have a little," persisted Edgar.

Conrad pulled the boy's hand to his mouth.

Edgar shifted nervously. "A cracker would be better."

He didn't mean it to be funny, but Conrad smiled. The light from the parted curtains fell like a plank across the bed. Conrad was so skinny he looked unreal, like a cartoon.

Edgar could smell the peanut butter, the strawberry jam. He felt hungry.

It wasn't right, though, to take Conrad's food—and besides, Edgar was trying not to eat too much. Not that he ever did—but lately he'd been trying to eat even less, since there wasn't a great deal left. For several weeks now, there'd been no fresh fruit or vegetables. In the pantry was still some canned stuff; cookies and crackers; two boxes of cereal—cornflakes that, without milk, tasted like sawdust. There was peanut butter and sugar cubes, a half jar of fish flakes, a week's worth of kibble for Jack.

Edgar reached for the bottle of aspirin and shook one out.

Conrad waved it away. "I want to give you something," he said, pointing toward the desk. "Top drawer."

Edgar got up and opened it. The first thing he saw was the cell phone.

"I don't need it," he said quickly, his voice rising in anger.

Conrad gestured impatiently. "Under the notebook."

Edgar looked, and saw the key.

"Everything you need," Conrad mumbled, closing his eyes. "Won't be long."

* * *

It was the key to the shed.

Edgar had never been inside. The only thing he knew about the little building beside the woodpile was that it was where Conrad had taken the deer after he'd killed it.

Edgar looked out his bedroom window. Maybe he should have taken the phone, too.

But all that was over, wasn't it? He lived in the Pinelands now; it was no longer Mars. He knelt on the floor, and from the rot-hole in the corner he retrieved the diamond. He laid it on his bed, beside the key. He added the Virgin's head—and then the photo of his father, the one he'd brought with him when he'd first come away with Conrad.

The key was worn in spots, and shiny—not so different from the color of the floating rectangle he sometimes dreamed about. Maybe the rectangle had something to do with his father. Edgar placed Frank's photo on the nightstand as he slipped under the covers. It seemed that one's own life could be a secret. There was a plan beyond what you could understand.

Maybe that's why the future was important. To figure things out.

Edgar was sad beyond measure, and frightened—but, unlike Conrad, he would not let go. He was bound to this world by a chain of wonder, each link an unanswered question that surely only a long life would be able to undo. Always one had to ask: *What happens next?*

Maybe the answer would come in a dream. Mr. Levinson had once said something about Einstein figuring out relativity after dreaming about cows.

Was it cows?

Or was it a snake?

Edgar drifted off, feeling very confused.

March

56

Expecting

The Gospel Shoppe looked from the outside as if it sold fudge. A canvas aw‑
ning of blue and white stripes fluttered over a large window on which the
store's name was painted in golden curlicues. Hanging from the door, below
a lace valence, was a heart that chimed as Lucy entered.

The proprietress, dressed like an usher, looked shocked to have a customer.
When Lucy asked for a Saint Christopher medal, the woman presented six
options, including one rimmed with tiny misshapen diamonds, like a mar‑
garita glass dipped in salt. Lucy made a show of examining it before choos‑
ing one costing $6.99, made of nickel. Then, feeling guilty, she grabbed a
small bag of Communion wafers from a rack beside the register. "I'll take
these, too."

"They're not consecrated," the woman said.

"Good to know," said Lucy.

She hung the tiny medal from her rearview mirror, to replace the one
she'd lost outside Slaphappy's, the night she'd been attacked in the parking
lot. The same night she'd ended up in the butcher's bathtub and had let his
sperm enter her body.

As she drove, she was annoyed by the preponderance of green lights—
the signals utterly indifferent to the trepidation she felt about her destina‑
tion. She looked at Saint Christopher, an old man bent over a walking stick
who somehow managed to carry that child on his back. She touched the
medal, set it swinging. Ever since she'd slapped the psychic's face, Lucy had
felt a little less frightened; often had the odd sense that she was working in
collaboration with Florence.

On the earthly plain, she still had the support of the butcher. He was
doing a lot—though sometimes he had funny ideas about what Lucy might
need. Now and then he'd bring home some ridiculous book or DVD. The

latest offering was a three-part series entitled *Fireheart: Overcoming Emotional Trauma*. It came with a workbook in which Lucy was supposed to write down her thoughts and feelings. *Do you remember the first time you experienced fury as a child? What caused you to feel that way?* After these questions, the workbook offered a single blank page. As if that would be enough room! Lucy could write a fucking novel.

She left the page blank. Rather than write about things, she preferred to deal with her problems head-on.

That's what she felt she was doing now, as she parked the car outside her father's house. Somehow, this place where she'd been hurt as a child seemed inseparable from what was happening with Edgar.

Ms. Mann and the police had come up with nothing, after nearly six months. Just a few weeks ago, three missing boys had been found in Mississippi, all in the same house—all alive. Lucy asked Mann if the police might be encouraged to search the house again, reminding the detective that Edgar was tiny and had a habit of jamming himself into tight spaces. Ms. Mann didn't rise to the occasion, though—claiming blandly that the authorities in Mississippi had surely done a thorough job.

A boy who'd been bullying Edgar had finally been identified. He'd cried through most of his interview, claiming that he, in turn, had been roughed up by a man he assumed was Edgar's father. When Ms. Mann asked Lucy if she was sure Frank was dead, Lucy said she was no longer sure of anything. Ultimately, it was the detective's opinion that the man who'd assisted Edgar was just an overzealous Good Samaritan. Neither he nor the bully was deemed worthy of further investigation.

Back in December, the break-in at 21 Cressida Drive and the discovery of the shotgun shell had seemed promising. Especially in light of the fact that the shell was found in the same parking lot where Edgar's clothes had been discovered right after he'd disappeared. Plus, there were two sets of partial fingerprints on the cartridge—one of them small enough to be a child's. Unfortunately the prints, compromised by weather, were deemed illegible. The shell itself was of a generic type that could be used in any number of 20-gauge shotguns—and since the shell was unfired, there were no markings capable of connecting it to any specific gun.

Still, Lucy couldn't understand why every person in New Jersey with a 20-gauge shotgun wasn't being investigated. Mann replied, again blandly, as if she were losing interest, that it was a pretty standard hunting firearm—the list would be a mile long.

But a mile didn't seem very long to Lucy. "Where do people hunt?" she'd asked the butcher. He'd told her that, as a kid, his father had taken him up to the Kittatinnies or the Catskills. But he had cousins who hunted up at Ramapo, and an uncle who liked to go south to the Pine Barrens or around Fort Dix. When Lucy started to write down the locations in her notebook, the butcher gently stopped her pen, explaining that those were only a few of the hundreds of places folks hunted in New Jersey—and there were hundreds more where people hunted illegally.

Her father had been a hunter. Though it wasn't animals he'd been after. He'd preferred his wife or daughter. As Lucy sat in the car, munching nervously on Communion wafers, she wondered if he'd already be drunk. It was nearly lunchtime. They tasted like shit, the wafers, like glue. She opened the door and spit a mouthful beside the curb.

As she walked down the flagstone path, she buttoned up Florence's coat—a gnarly bear of a thing with tremendous faux-fur lapels. It had become a sort of armor, useful as much for protecting herself as for intimidating others.

Lucy paused before ringing the bell, thinking, *He'll have time to prepare, time to hide things*—though as to what these things might be she had only a vague sense. All she knew was that she needed to think strategically.

She moved her ungloved hand from the bell to the doorknob. It was cold as she turned it. The door opened easily, as if in a dream.

Everything as she remembered it—but so exactly the same that the preservation seemed malicious. There was the little egg-shaped lamp on the foyer table. There was the green plank studded with yellow plastic coat hooks. The water stain on the ceiling like the outline of a cloud. And here—she was standing on it now—the pale blue entrance rug with its border of smashed daisies.

She passed through the hallway into the main part of the house. Again, its spiteful accordance with her memory made her freeze—each piece of furniture like a dog commanded to sic her.

When she took a deep breath to dispel her fear, she began to hear the clocks. There had always been too many of them in this house—the brief silence of one always filled by the tick of another nearby. A constant, overlapping argument about time—pointless because, sooner or later, all the clocks would arrive at the same conclusion. For those under their spell, as Lucy had been for the first seventeen years of her life, it was only a matter of waiting as, second by second, the little machines brought you closer to the things you dreaded most.

Finally, as if each sense wanted its own moment of tyranny, the experience of the house was suddenly its smell. Her mother in the kitchen, frying potatoes, boiling cabbage. A kind of nauseating hope filled Lucy.

Voices. A television from upstairs.

He was sitting in a chair in his bedroom, his back to the door. She could see the pill bottles and the framed photographs on the bureau. There was one of Edgar—but something wasn't right about it.

"What is that?" she said to announce herself.

Walter Bubko, who could not see behind him, gasped and reached for his cane. He fell back into his chair as he tried to stand. It took him nearly thirty seconds to get up and turn sufficiently to see who was there.

He said his daughter's name quietly.

He looked awful. When Lucy had seen him at Florence's wake, it was after not seeing him for nearly fifteen years—and, though older, shakier, he'd looked essentially the same that day, with his greased-back black hair and his powerful little body stuffed into a brown suit. Now, several months later, half the stuffing it seemed had been knocked out of him; his skin looked singed. There were distressing black patches on his cheeks and on his forearms. His hair, without pomade, was thin and weeded with gray. Even his smell was different. Lucy could detect no alcohol, but rather a deeper, more pungent scent, swampy and rotten. He was clearly ill.

"Is everything okay?" he asked.

She responded to his absurd question by walking over to the bureau and picking up the strange photo of Edgar. She could see now that it wasn't a real photograph—only the boy's face cut from one of the flyers she'd put up around town. The black ink that described Edgar's features had faded a bit.

"I meant to get in touch," said her father.

She put down the framed photocopy. "These are meant to be outside—for people to *see*."

The old man coughed for a bit—and then grunted, as if to silence the animals in his lungs. "You did a good job with the posters," he said. "I saw them everywhere."

He attempted to smile. Lucy watched his lips carefully. He'd always been a man of easy smiles, ferociously mean. He could have killed her as a child if she'd been weaker. She should have taught Edgar how to fight. Why hadn't she?

For the boy's whole life, she'd kept him away from this man. She'd told Edgar that her parents were dead, had made up stories about them. Just as she'd made up stories about Frank. A shell game, but it had worked. Her lies had protected the boy. She'd managed to keep the men out of his life.

Lucy glanced at the pill bottles. It made her sick that she wanted to ask her father if he was ill. She turned, looked around the room to see if she could spot the real bottle, the proof that nothing had changed.

"What are you looking for?"

She went to the closet where he used to keep them.

"What are you doing in there? Lucille—whatta you need? Come downstairs, I'll make us some coffee."

With her foot, she pushed aside some boxes at the back of the closet. She finally found it in the bottom drawer of the nightstand. Bourbon. Half a fifth. She poured the stuff into an empty glass and brought it to him.

He waved it away. "I don't—"

"Drink it."

"I can't with my—"

"Drink it."

He shook his head and suggested she have it.

Lucy stared at him without blinking, and downed the shot.

Immediately she felt sick. Other than the handful of Communion wafers, she'd eaten nothing this morning; nor had she taken any alcohol since October. An overwhelming heat gripped her inside Florence's coat.

"Where are you going?" her father asked her. "Stay."

He followed her into the hallway. She could hear the clicking pursuit of his cane—*tick tick tick*—as if the terrible thing that lived inside the clocks had broken free and was coming to get her.

The brown threadbare carpet in the hallway, the gauntlet of photographs. Lucy couldn't help herself from looking—her mother in a Mets cap, obscenely young. Pale skin, red hair—a real beauty. After Lucy had left this house at seventeen, she'd sometimes see her mother on Saturdays. They'd sit in one or the other's car, eating hamburgers. They'd talked about nothing— never about the bruises on her mother's arms, or Lucy's happiness with the young man she'd met. Since they both had jobs, cutting hair in different salons, there were always other women to talk about. Elena Bubko's beauty was long gone by the time of the hamburgers. Lucy always picked the two bread-and-butter pickles from her sandwich and gave them to her mother.

Now, as she ran from her father, habit propelled her into her old room at the end of the hall. It was the same as the rest of the house, perfectly preserved. Lucy had forgotten how much she'd left behind, and it was confusing to see her things still here, to see the bed made and the stuffed animals peaceably arranged on top.

"Who did this?" she asked.

She slid her hand across her old desk, across her music collection, a long shelf of jewel cases. There was no dust.

"Who cleans this?" It was disgusting to her, such order. It was deceit.

"I do," her father said from the doorway.

Lucy knelt and looked under the bed, and then went to the closet and threw open the doors. Her clothing still there. She pushed apart the hangers. "Where is he?" She bit her lip to keep back the tears.

Her father said nothing as he watched her.

Lucy was sweating. Without thinking, she unbuttoned the black coat—revealing the red spandex top, tight against her body.

Her father made a small sound of shock.

"Are you expecting?"

Lucy looked down at her belly.

Expecting. It was a word Florence had used when Edgar was inside her. It was then she began to cry.

Her father grimaced and came close enough to strike her.

She almost wished he would. Because maybe she'd been punished as a child not for who she was, but for what she'd become. A terrible mother.

"Lucille, Lucille"—his hand was clutching her arm. "What can I do?"

She shook her head and moaned, waiting until her father's hand fell away of its own will.

April

57

The White Child

Jimmy Papadakis often signed the checks personally. He never rushed—preferring to use a slow, schoolboy penmanship that made his signature perfectly readable. He understood that when families saw his name it gave them a lift; he was still a celebrity of sorts—at least in the missing-persons game. He'd been kidnapped at four—missing for seventeen weeks before being found nearly dead in a drainage ditch, less than twenty miles from his home. His parents' efforts to locate him had been well funded and well publicized (his father was a politician). A Light for Jimmy was now a multimillion-dollar organization. Still, it was important to offer a personal touch.

The amount of the current payment, to Lucille Fini, was for just over twelve thousand dollars—sixteen percent of what had been collected on behalf of the woman's son. The remaining eighty-four percent had gone toward the search efforts, as well as toward preexisting programs such as prevention education. And of course there were salaries, fund-raising costs, publicity. Bloodhounds were expensive, too, and ALFJ had the finest—descendants, supposedly, of the famous Saint Hubert hounds of Europe.

The winter event in Times Square, in which the children's faces were transformed into goliaths on huge screens, had run more than two hundred thousand in production costs alone. Luckily one child—that little Spanish girl, Benita something—had been found as a result of the project. The Board, though, had hoped for more. Jimmy's father, Dimitri Papadakis, had said that in a perfect world, the organization would be able to claim one recovered child for every fifty thousand spent. But everyone agreed that cost-effectiveness was a tricky issue when it came to missing children.

Usually the public sent donations to ALFJ in a general fashion, but over the past few months quite a lot of funds had come in with notes requesting that the money be used specifically in efforts to find the Fini boy. For some reason, he'd become one of the most popular missing children in years. Possibly since Jimmy himself. The boy was cute as a button, heartbreakingly pale; he captured the attention of even the most jaded types.

Twelve thousand bucks. Jimmy hoped it would be useful to Mrs. Fini. There were never any restrictions placed on the money sent to the families—many of whom had to take time away from their jobs, because of stress or to stay on top of the search efforts. Though, at seven months, which is how long it had been with the Fini boy, there was little one could do. Jimmy understood that the money he was sending to Lucille Fini was more of a consolation prize.

He'd never seen a case with a more stunning lack of leads, nor with a more inept chief detective—a novice female, neurotically prideful, who seemed to resent ALFJ's assistance. Of course, had there been any real hope, such personality clashes wouldn't have mattered. ALFJ would have persisted. As it stood, though, the Board had decided that it was best if the organization eased out of the case.

In addition to the bad business of pouring resources into what was essentially a black hole, there were other reasons a withdrawal seemed prudent. ALFJ's reputation might be sullied by remaining involved in a case that had been co-opted by a distinct fringe element. Certain segments of the public were reacting to the boy's plight in bizarre ways—taking it out of context, turning the story of a missing child into something fantastic, often blatantly spiritual.

Jimmy, who had no religion per se, could understand, though, how this Edgar kid had been turned into a saint. The photo the family had provided was amazing: the pale boy captured against a dark wall, so that his face popped like a full moon before a black mountain. On his forehead and then extending onto the wall behind him was an odd striated reflection, perhaps from an unseen chandelier—rays of colored light whose point of origin seemed to be the boy's eyes, which were beguilingly upraised and shyly turned to the side. Even in black and white the photo was noteworthy—but when reproduced in its original color, it had the quality of a painting. The boy's skin the white-pink of a magnolia petal, and his eyes a watery peridot.

As was standard with all abducted children, Edgar's image had been disseminated widely—moving swiftly through official channels to the agencies that dealt with the issue. But at some point Edgar's likeness had been hijacked by Internet sites not strictly geared toward the recovery of missing children—though one could argue that the electronic prayer circles that

Edgar had grown popular in were, in their own quaint way, attempting to do so. These online prayer circles were a global phenomenon, primarily Christian. But as Edgar's image traveled around the world, he soon began to slip beyond the bounds of Christendom. Every persuasion of god-botherer seemed interested in the albino boy's plight.

Of course, on the slop heap of the Internet, information quickly became misinformation. There were willful distortions, bad translations. Soon it seemed that people were not only praying *for* Edgar, but *to* him. Just recently, three boys in Cesky Krumlov, in the Czech Republic, claimed they'd seen Edgar Fini outside the Church of the Three Snails, eating dandelion greens. When the boys had approached, Edgar reportedly disappeared into the clouds. "Edko up, Edko up" was their tearful refrain, repeated numerous times on the video that Jimmy and the ALFJ Board of Directors had watched online.

Edgar's story was out of control—wrested away from the pragmatists who wished to find the child and tossed to the birds, into the hands of people who seemed to want to use the child for their own agendas, or to support their own fantasies. Edgar was a prophet, he was an angel, he was—as one New Age blogger from New Hampshire put it—"the child of our inner light." It made Jimmy want to spit. Having been a missing child himself, having lived through such horror, he felt personally violated that Edgar should be reduced to metaphor.

There were poems and stories about "the white child" all over the Internet, in at least sixteen languages. There was no doubt which child they meant, since the text was nearly always accompanied by the haunting photograph of Edgar.

No longer a real child, but a viral image, something to be "trended," Edgar effortlessly leaped between the sacred and the secular. Someone in L.A. was already writing a screenplay. Edgar, sadly, had entered the marketplace. His ceaseless repetition had all but obliterated the original. Did these people even remember, Jimmy sometimes wondered, that there was an endangered child behind all this nonsense?

As he put the check to Lucille Fini in the envelope, he considered adding a personal note to go along with the official letter. Perhaps he should even drive down from Greenwich to hand-deliver it. But the truth was, he always felt sick when he met the families. It brought too much back.

Not that he remembered very much about his own abduction—though perhaps a bit more than he'd ever admitted to the press, or even his parents.

He rarely spoke of those seventeen weeks he'd been gone, so who could know that he thought about it all the time. Even now, almost twenty-five years later. Those terrible days existed for Jimmy as a highly specific blur, like a cloud—a shape that could be drawn sharply only as an outline, empty within.

He'd been four years old. Outside a department store with his mother. She'd been packing bags into the trunk. When something had knocked into Jimmy, he didn't immediately understand that it was another human. He was lifted off the ground and then put in a car. It seemed a long time before he started screaming.

The man—again an outline—was tall and thin, though his hands always appeared, in Jimmy's memory, absurdly large, like Popeye's fists. He'd been strong—but what grown man wouldn't be to a four-year-old? Jimmy had been hurt, but the pain was part of the cloud. It had grown larger over the years, but less distinct, less part of his body. It had turned into something like shame. "No one touched me," he'd always told his parents—because that's what people like them needed to hear. He'd had to protect them. Over the years, Jimmy had seen other children come back with that happy-to-be-home grimace he understood to be a mask over terror.

Children who'd been to the underworld.

When, after several months, the man was finished with Jimmy, he'd left him, nearly starved, in that slimy ditch. Apparently he'd not expected Jimmy to live.

Luck was a funny thing. Jimmy's abductor had had his share, as well. He'd never been found. It seemed odd to Jimmy that the man who'd taken him was still missing. It seemed dangerous. Jimmy's nightmares persisted to this day. At twenty-nine, he remained with his parents, in the house he'd grown up in. He was not married, and had no children.

"You're back now, you can do anything," his father used to tell him. But Jimmy hadn't ever felt like he'd come back. Part of him would always be missing. When he thought of a sweet kid like Edgar Allan Fini, gone now for nearly thirty weeks, trapped with who knows what kind of man—because it was *always* men—Jimmy hoped for only one thing. He hoped that Edgar was dead.

58

The Shed

In the last week of February, as Conrad was approaching his death, he'd found barely a moment of peace. Things had leapt toward him constantly out of the shadows. Some of these things had the feeling, if not the form, of people. There were often doublings. Sometimes both boys were in the room simultaneously—each holding a glass of water to Conrad's lips. Every sip had made him feel like he was drowning.

His wife had come, too, asking questions—but not like her former interrogations, or those of the police. She didn't ask about the shotgun or the woods or how the fuck could a deer look like a twelve-year-old kid. Sara's questions had little to do with the past; they seemed to be more about Conrad's plans for the future. *Did he have any? Was he taking traveler's checks or cash?* But when Conrad had attempted to think about money, of which he had a great deal, the thoughts dissolved like candy floss—a momentary sweetness followed by a distinct bitterness that burned his tongue. You shouldn't eat that shit, his father scolded, rots the teeth.

Conrad had not wanted to talk about candy with the dead man; didn't he and his father have more important things to discuss? He'd needed guidance from his father just then; a road map. How about a swim in the Blue Hole, the old man had suggested. But Conrad declined, claiming it would be too cold. After that, his father had stood quietly in the corner of the room, whittling a small piece of wood—each flick of the blade signaling his disappointment. As the pine chips had flown toward the bed, Conrad had closed his eyes against the assault. Still, he couldn't help but to wonder what kind of animal his father was carving, and, more importantly: *will he give it to me when he's finished?* Never in his life had Conrad coveted something more. He'd wanted his father's carving even more than he wanted the child—wishing somehow he could give back everything he'd stolen, asking in return only the small wooden toy.

A wolf had come into the room at one point, looking for food. It had been difficult to keep it off the bed. The man's slow starvation attracted only more of what was ravenous. One night, the thing with hooves and wings had appeared in the window. *Liar,* Conrad had shouted, furious that the tall tale he'd told the boy had had the audacity to come to life.

The most forceful presence had been an olfactory invasion. And though the scent was sweet—like jasmine and baby powder—it had made Conrad anxious. At first he'd thought it was his mother, because the smell was exactly like the French perfume she used to wear. But when this presence had stood beside the bed, he knew it wasn't her. It was too kind—a kindness so extreme that it seemed almost diabolic. Sometimes the scented presence had put things inside him—a warm liquid, like blood, straight into his veins. Someone else's blood, though. Someone else's memories. Conrad could not understand the nature of the woman's mercy. "I want to die," he'd told her one morning—and with a shocking jab she'd put more of the liquid into his veins. A warning, it had seemed, against such language. Conrad had felt ashamed.

It had gone on like this for weeks. Dying, it seemed, was work. Litanies of recapitulation, committees of approval, the final tortures of persistent affections.

But, in the end, it had come. The gates had opened for Conrad—and, as he'd hoped, there were flames.

* * *

When Edgar first used the key, he'd hesitated before entering—opening the heavy plank door only an inch, and sniffing. At that point, all he'd known of the shed was that it was the place where Conrad had taken the dressed and disassembled buck he'd shot during season.

Inside, it was dark (there were no windows) and Edgar had had to jump three times to snag the chain that clicked on the light. The first thing he noticed was the food.

Against the back wall, floor-to-ceiling shelves were lined with cans and jars—each shelf long enough to hold (Edgar counted; counting was calming) twenty-seven cans across, and wide enough to stock them around three deep. Rather than thinking about the meaning of the food, Edgar did the math. Twenty-seven times three equaled eighty-one; times twelve shelves equaled—(Edgar blinked)—nine hundred and seventy-two cans of food!

The boy's first impulse had been to run and tell Conrad, tell him that there was nothing to worry about, they could both eat as much as they wanted; Conrad didn't need to deny himself, which he'd been doing for weeks, and which was making him sick. But as Edgar turned to leave the shed, he'd realized that Conrad would already know about the food. It was Conrad who'd given him the key. In light of this new thought, the boy felt afraid.

Even Florence, who'd always liked to have a good store of canned goods, had never thought *this* far into the future. The shelves of food suddenly seemed to have everything to do with time. These cans might last Conrad and Edgar for years. More winters, more birthdays—Edgar's passing in the Barrens, while the baby inside his mother grew up at 21 Cressida Drive. When Edgar heard a low humming, he thought, at first, it was coming from himself—it was not unlike the sound he made right before he started to cry. But then he turned and saw the freezer—an enormous white casket, its moan distinctly human.

Edgar knew what was inside. More time. That's what an animal was, after you broke it down. It gave you what you'd stolen from it; let you live that much longer. Edgar could hardly believe he'd ever eaten a dead animal. Pieces of meat wrapped in plastic. He looked down at his finger and remembered how the butcher had once tossed it into an ice-filled rain cap. Conrad had done something similar to a deer.

Edgar curled up on the floor. Jets of warm air streamed audibly from the bottom of the freezer. Edgar moved closer and hummed along, telling himself that it was wrong to abandon someone who needed you. He told this to himself over and over, until the world fell away.

*   *   *

When he opened his eyes, some time later, he sensed, even in the windowless shed, that it was night. He didn't remember having closed the door and worried for a moment that someone had locked him inside. He got up and pushed at the heavy plank, which swung outward to reveal the dark yard. The lamp was burning in Conrad's bedroom—but Edgar knew he'd be sleeping. In the morning, when Conrad woke up, Edgar would *force* him to eat. It didn't matter that he no longer had a gun. A man could act without one.

As Edgar stood outside in Kevin's jacket, Kevin's hat, and Kevin's gloves, he looked up at the stars and hardly felt the cold. When he turned and walked back into the shed, he examined things more carefully. He noticed the small folding table and the splintery schoolhouse chair. The table was bare except for a coffee mug filled with pens, but just above it was a tiny shelf crammed with notebooks. Most of them (twenty-two, to be exact) were blue; three were red. All were labeled. The red ones said *Golden City,* and were numbered; the blue notebooks had only dates.

Edgar pulled down a red one. He didn't worry that he was betraying Conrad's trust. When Conrad had given him the shed key, he'd said, *everything you need.* No doubt he'd meant the food—but Edgar felt it was within his rights to look further.

He peeled back the cover of *Golden City #1* and read the first few sentences. A man in a jungle was running toward some ruins. He seemed to be in some kind of danger—maybe someone was chasing him; it wasn't exactly clear. There were so many words it was hard to find the story. Also, there were a lot of cross-outs. Edgar skipped ahead, only to find more long sentences, by the end of which he could barely remember where he'd started.

If this was the book Conrad was writing, it didn't seem to be very good. By the time Edgar returned *Golden City #1* to the shelf, he had no interest in volume #2. He reached, instead, for one of the blue notebooks. He half expected to find the man in the jungle again, and was startled to find someone else.

Kevin, the notebook said, *was born today. 8 lbs, 6 oz. I'm so happy I can't sleep. Black hair, brown eyes. Perfect. When I called Dad he said, welcome to the club.*

Edgar stopped, walked in a circle. He took off Kevin's hat and threw it on the ground. When he pulled another blue notebook off the shelf, it was with genuine hope that he chose the one labeled with the year of his own birth.

But, again, it was Kevin. He was five years old.

Kev and I went to Hammonton and picked blueberries. He fed half of them to Jack.

From across the yard came the faint cry of the cuckoo clock inside the cabin.

Sara didn't think there was enough for a pie, so she fixed a cobbler. Afterwards Kevin refused to wash his face. It was still blue when we put him to bed.

Edgar grimaced. Maybe he'd seen enough. His hands were shaking. And the cuckoo clock had said it was ten—well past his bedtime.

Still, he longed to see his own name—even just once. He pulled down six more notebooks and sat at the table. The light was terrible. It had been easier to read standing in the center of the room, under the hanging bulb. Edgar thought to bring the notebooks into the cabin—but then he saw the lantern and the box of matches.

When the room was glowing, he opened a blue notebook dated just a few months prior—but most of it was hard to understand. Some of the words seemed like gibberish. *Mullica. Shamong.*

On the last page, though, was a numbered list—and though it was hard to make out what the items were (the entries were often illegible), beside each item was a clearly printed name in parentheses. Sometimes the name was *Sara;* sometimes it was *Edgar.* As for the things to which each person was attached—even when the boy could decipher them, they made no sense.

Chase (Edgar)
Fidelity (Sara)
Wells (Edgar)

The boy had hoped for more. Somewhere, surely, Conrad must have explained what the two of them were doing in the woods, and why it was necessary they stay.

A blue notebook from two years prior offered somewhat better penmanship—though here Edgar would have wished it otherwise.

<u>*A hunting accident*</u>

The three words underlined at the top of the page, like the title of a story.

A hunting accident. Is that correct? I suspect you're watching me as I write this, so I won't lie.

Here, the words began to slant, crossing the blue line as if dipping under water. Edgar felt the octopus ink seep into his belly.

When you asked to go out, I told you to leave me alone, let me work for an hour.
   When you asked again ten minutes later, I said we'd go the next day and you said there is no next day, Dad, it's the last day of season.
   I said, stop whining, and you made a face just like your mother.
   I remember thinking, why did I have a child?
   And then I said, fine, get your coat.

It was the end of the page.
Edgar hesitated—and then turned it.

59

Confession

Edgar followed Conrad and Kevin into the forest. It was late afternoon and the light wasn't good—but Edgar saw everything. Conrad leading the way, and Kevin, in his brown coat, a few steps behind.

Or so Conrad thought.

When the gunshot came, Edgar immediately closed the notebook. He began to rock his body back and forth. Inside the blue notebook, Kevin was lying on the ground, bleeding.

It was terrible. Still, Edgar wanted to look again.

I brushed my teeth!
   You were already gone, wrapped in a blanket. I brushed them three times before I carried you into the truck.
   I'd had two drinks.

Edgar found it hard to breathe. Kevin was wrapped in a blanket while Conrad cleaned his teeth.

As if it were part of the same story, Edgar saw the bottle of vodka his mother kept in the freezer. When she drank it she became someone else—her limp more pronounced and her voice deeper, her aim unsteady. She could barely get a key into a door, or a cigarette into her mouth.

I said I was sober. I was sober by the time they questioned me.
   I still want to blame you for wandering away, for sneaking ahead. You said you'd seen a large buck by the pond, you were anxious to get there. I wasn't thinking about the buck or the pond. Do you know what I was thinking about? I was thinking about my book. It wasn't two scotches that killed you. It was a fucking book. A piece of shit not worth a single

strand of your hair. Why didn't I keep a lock of it? One day they'll be able to remake people and I won't have any of your body.

I go back with you every day, to the pond. I live there now. That moment you died.

The moment I killed you.

Edgar closed the notebook, and his mouth opened as wide as a puff adder's. The sound, too, was not unlike the muted hiss of a snake. It came from deep inside the boy's throat—as violent as anger or terror, though it was neither of these things.

It was grief.

Edgar looked toward the food and tugged at his hair. Surely Conrad wouldn't hurt someone again. He only wanted to hurt *himself.*

Edgar's body trembled as his hand lurched out to push away the notebooks. When he realized that he'd pushed the lantern, too, he watched, paralyzed, as it crashed to the table—the clear liquid pooling across the surface, and the modest lick of flame summoning a blinding flash. Edgar stood, knocking over the chair. He backed away until his body was pressed against the twelve shelves of food.

The lantern, as if moved by an unseen hand, continued to roll across the table. When it fell and shattered, the lamp oil that had dripped to the ground ignited, and a line of fire was written across the room, blocking the door.

Edgar leapt forward to grab the notebooks, but the heat stopped him. He slid to the floor, the foul-smelling smoke above him like storm clouds. He held his breath, which made his next intake of air more desperate. Smoke entered his mouth. The door and the wall around it trembled in monstrously gleaming fur.

When the wooden shelf above the table gave out, the remaining notebooks fell with a whomping crash into the flames. Black moths of ash flew into Edgar's eyes.

When he called for help, it wasn't to Conrad. There were faces in the smoke. He searched for her among them. He knew she was close because of the scent. When he took a deep breath, it filled him with a mind-altering heat.

Then, through the flaming doorway, he saw her crossing the yard.

His grandmother was so skinny she looked like a skeleton. When she stepped into the shed, the boy reached out his arms. And when she lifted him, she was not herself. She was half naked, with a hairy chest and a beard.

Edgar closed his eyes—and as he and the man passed through fire, his skin felt stung as if by hornets. Inside his head, darkness flashed white. Then they were outside in the wet air. They were on the ground.

The man was breathing heavily, moving his hands over the boy's clothing, patting it down as if looking for something. Jack had run out of the cabin and was barking at the flames. The man was already moving back toward the fire. Edgar tried to speak, but only coughed.

The shed was wavering; it appeared more liquid than solid, almost transparent. Conrad's form was visible inside the flames. Edgar's eyes were blighted by light and smoke. Someone was screaming.

Yet, despite the chaos and the vile odor of burnt hair, there remained a subtle undercurrent of the beloved—powder and flowers and sweat.

Edgar took a deep breath, and ran back into the shed.

60

Spring

Bearberry, leatherleaf, staggerbush; the blueberries and the huckleberries, the sparkleberries and the top-hat dwarfs; golden heather, bird's-foot—they were all in bloom. All white, as are the first flowers of spring. Delicate flags of surrender, brave poppers risking a late frost. The blossoms seemed whitest at dusk. The early crocuses of course were pink, but you couldn't see them unless you were clever and thought to look under the fallen leaves of scrub oak.

The butterflies, too, were beginning. Pine Elfin, Mourning Cloak, Hessel's Hairstreak in the white cedar swamps. The birds were not yet here in mass, though the pine warblers and some gray catbirds rustled about, making their nests. Chuck-Will's-Widow had been crying for weeks. It was April. The wood frog and the peepers had renewed their chant at the end of March. Fowler's toads were just coming to life out of the mud. Spring was here, though sometimes only in spirit. Winter lingered, especially in the mornings, leaving a thin footprint of ice or breathing out its death in chilly vampire-castle fog. The bog asphodel had come up but was too sluggish to bloom. The public lakes were restocked with trout—brook, brown, and rainbow. They darted, dazed, in the frigid depths.

It would be weeks yet—months—before life was free of all danger. Still, even on the coldest mornings, people went out without sufficient clothing. It was a cold that humans could survive. It excited them. They knew it was not the kind of cold that killed. Enthusiasts prowled the Barrens, hoping to spot an early colony of white-fringed orchids. Under the pine needles, the lady slippers were stirring, and in the ashy ground where the shed had been, dandelions thrived, bringing the snails.

May

61

Carnation

On a Tuesday afternoon, at the Ferryfield Municipal Court, Lucille Wilhemina Fini (née Bubko) married Ronald David Salvatore. She did not take his name. She'd told him, weeks before, that she couldn't afford the extra syllables—and the butcher, though disappointed, did not insist. He understood that, even though he loved this woman and she, it seemed, loved him, there were certain things she'd never give him. At 4:15 the couple entered the courthouse holding hands and went straight to the second floor, room 17. The civil ceremony was brief, performed without fuss by County Clerk Lanny Ho, a diminutive man with a large birthmark on his left cheek that everyone later agreed looked exactly like an Oscar statuette. Lucy wore a pale green shift dress she'd found in Florence's closet. Though simple in design, it was pretty, with a band of darker green at the hem, and on the sleeves a delicate iridescent embroidery suggesting fairy wings. The choice, Lucy convinced herself, was not sentimental, merely practical; the shift dress was roomy and did a fair job of covering her mounded belly.

Of course, the baby was no secret to anyone that mattered. And they did matter, even Lucy had to admit. All these months, everyone had been so kind. Still, Lucy would have preferred not to have seen them at the courthouse. She'd wanted it to be just the two of them—and by necessity Ron's sister Izzy, who was the witness. But the butcher had called a few people, and then word got around. On Tuesday afternoon Mr. Ho's smallish office bustled with the breath of twenty-six people, many of them aged.

The Schlips, of course, were there, wearing nearly identical brown suits of spring wool (Netty's was a bit more scalloped at the collar). The moth damage was minor, but duly noted by Honey Fasinga, who'd come to the courthouse sporting the same dress she'd worn to Florence's wake—black crepe silk, with a pink butterfly bow at the waist, and on the shoulders the designer's signature embroidery. Honey immediately noticed that the bride was wearing a sister creation—though it was clearly a lesser beast from a later period, something Florence must have made for herself after she'd run to fat. Honey was accompanied by Dominic Sparra, a man she would not categorically refuse should he ask one day for her own hand in marriage. She had no idea what Dominic was waiting for; he was a good ten years older, could croak at any moment. She was extremely fond of him. Though somewhat arthritic, he'd proved to be a flexible man, bending to Honey's tastes sexually and sartorially. Today, she'd put him in blue seersucker and tawny calfskin loafers.

A few of Ron's cousins were present; two aunts, one uncle—all quite beefy. Lucy's former employer, Celeste, stole attention in her island bangles and op-art headscarf (Honey approved). Mary Hefti would not have stood sweating in a polyester pants suit had it not been for Toni-Ann's fit of begging the day before. The girl was sullen, though, during the ceremony, often thinking about Edgar, her own husband, with whom she shared so many secrets. It was Mr. Ho's voice, rather high-pitched, with gently popping consonants like bursting bubbles, that eventually brought a smile to Toni-Ann's face. "And the 'Cademy 'Ward goes to . . . Mr. Lanny Ho!" she kept saying on the ride home, using the registration card from the glove compartment as the secret envelope.

Some of the folks in room 17 were people Lucy had first encountered only after Florence's death. They weren't exactly friends now, but they certainly couldn't be called strangers. Mr. Wong from the fish store, Mrs. Collucci from the bakery. The peddler, the cobbler, the Fortunato brothers who sharpened knives. And though there was no poetry to the ceremony, no music, no banks of flowers or references to God and eternity, everyone, at some point or another, cried—even if sometimes these tears fell only inward, a private weather like post-nasal drip.

Lucy could hear them sniffling behind her, but refused to follow them there. She gripped Ron's hand and held her mouth in a pose of rigid determination, wishing to appear intrepid. She carried no bouquet. The only flower present was a white carnation pinned to her pale green dress. The modest corsage had been a gift from the butcher. He would have preferred to have given his bride a flaming orchid or a red velvet rose but, knowing how adamant she was about keeping things simple, he settled on the small white flower. It was a nothing flower, but honest—its aroma not so much sweet as clean. When Lucy had first leaned down to sniff it, all she could smell was the Chanel N° 5 she'd patted between her breasts. An indulgence, stolen like the dress, shaken from a bottle blackened by fire.

Honey was disappointed that no rings were exchanged. She'd rather hoped for an appearance by Florence's diamond—the one she'd helped Edgar filch from the coffin. The theft was not, Honey would be the first to admit, her most shining moment. She would have liked to have seen some good come of the crime.

Lucy, though, had specifically requested that there be no rings. ("We'll do it later," she'd demurred to Ron—meaning, essentially, never.) On the subject of everlasting promises she wished to be conservative, recalling that the wedding bands from her first marriage lay underwater—Frank's at Shepherd's Junction, and her own at the bottom of the Hudson River, where she'd chucked it two months later.

It was a history so savagely carved on Lucy's existence that it reduced room 17 to a mere suggestion of reality. She floated through the afternoon on the edge of hallucination. The ceremony (certificate number SB–32287) was done by 4:30, and ended, like all good beginnings, with a kiss. Afterwards, Mr. Ho clapped his tiny hands and smiled prodigiously, as if he'd just watched two tigers leap through a flaming hoop. Toni-Ann, taking her cue, clapped along. Mary Hefti whacked the girl's back, but by then it was too late. The whole room had burst into applause—humble in its restraint, respectful, the sound as mournful as unexpected rain. At least to Lucy's ears. She turned and smiled at all of them.

The first person she approached was Anita Lester, dressed in nurse scrubs. "I just came on break," the woman said, and Lucy said, "How nice"—and then she found herself touching her belly, asking Anita if she'd consider coming to the house when it was time. "Looks soon," said Anita, swallowing, and Lucy said, "About a month." She knew Ron would want her in a hospital, but she'd work on him. "What do you say?" asked Lucy, and Anita (who'd delivered Edgar at home, and who could not imagine delivering this new baby in the same house), scratched her arm and said, "Of course. I'd be happy to."

Lucy kissed Anita's hand and then quickly excused herself. There were others with whom she needed to speak. Unbelievably people were thrusting envelopes at her. Ron intercepted them, stuffing his pockets. The bride briefly closed her eyes: how had this turned into an Italian wedding? Of course it wasn't just the Italians throwing money around. Henry and Netty gave an envelope, Mr. Wong, Celeste. The woman in the ball gown was coming close, and Lucy asked Ron to please deal with her. "I'll take care of the two by the door," Lucy offered in return. Ron looked up and saw to whom she was referring. He wished her luck.

A man and a woman lingered just outside room 17 like timid party crashers, though both had been invited—or at least not barred from coming. The two people were separate issues, but fate had stood them side by side. Lucy's father rubbing shoulders with Detective Mann.

Mr. Bubko's diminishment was profound. Every time Lucy saw him (not much; only twice since she'd first gone to his house in March), he looked more and more like someone had taken an eraser to his body, scratched away swaths of his flank and his face. Soon he'd be gone. Why didn't this make Lucy happy? She held up a one-minute finger to Ms. Mann and approached her father.

"Thanks for the chops," he said.

A few weeks before, Lucy had asked Ron to send over a care package from the shop. "You ate them?" she asked. "You're eating?"

"You look nice," he replied—glancing in the direction of the butcher, hoping he wouldn't join them. Ever since the giant wop had evicted him from Florence Fini's memorial, Walter Bubko had remained on alert. For months, he'd wondered how close this guy was to his daughter, how much he might know about her past. Now they were husband and wife, signed and stamped, a nipper on the way. She'd probably told him everything.

Lucy thanked him for the compliment, and Mr. Bubko nodded, said he was a little tired; he was looking forward to sitting down.

"We're not having a party," Lucy quickly informed him. She offered to call a cab, but he said he had his car.

"Really, no shindig?" he chirped, an attempted playfulness that did not play well with rotten teeth.

"Really," answered Lucy.

He felt sure the girl was lying.

"I'll send more meat," she said. "If you want."

He couldn't digest it anymore. Still, he hungered for whatever scrap of kindness she might offer. "Sure," he said. "Thank you."

For Walter Bubko, the hope remained—that, although he'd seen his grandson only once (a flash of white by the old woman's casket), he might get to know this new kid better.

"All right then," he said, reaching forward. "I'll just . . ."

Lucy accepted her father's hand, though steered clear of his kiss.

She told him to take care of himself, before turning away toward the detective. "Rebecca. Why don't we . . . ?" She took Ms. Mann's arm and led her into the hall, halfway down the corridor. She could see her father at the far end, descending the stairs. Part of her wanted to call out to him, but what could she say?

She waited until he was gone before meeting Ms. Mann's anxious gaze. Lucy knew then not to ask the question, the only question that existed. In lieu of that, there was nothing to talk about. They smiled at each other like old lovers.

That's really what it was like, sad and strained. They'd been so close once, or so it had seemed. These days, Lucy knew, Mann was giving most of her attention to other cases. Lucy couldn't help but feel resentful, even jealous. Mann, it was clear, felt guilty. Now they were standing together in an over-lit hallway. Why had Lucy dragged the detective out here as if there were important business to discuss?

"I just came to . . ." Mann began.

"I'm glad you did."

When an official type walked by with a sheaf of papers, Lucy looked down, waited. "I always feel like I'm in trouble in places like this."

Mann knew the history. "Well, not today," she said.

It was awkward. Ultimately, Lucy couldn't help herself. "So? Is there any . . . ?"

The detective shook her head. "No. Nothing." Adding, a moment later: "I shouldn't have come."

"It's fine," said Lucy. "I wasn't expecting news."

Ms. Mann fidgeted, brushed the back of her head. She'd dyed her hair, all the gray was gone. Brown locks, unbunned, fell to her shoulders. She looked smart and trim in beige slacks and a tight black sweater. "New look going," Lucy observed.

"What? No. Just spring, I guess." Mann blushed. Everything out of her mouth was wrong. She looked at her watch.

"Don't look at your fucking watch," snapped Lucy.

Ms. Mann swallowed, said nothing. When she began again, it was quietly, her eyes no longer on her wrist but on the floor. "I did everything I could. I'm still doing what I can. I haven't—"

Lucy stopped her. "No. It's my fault. I say shit, you should know that by now."

The imp, Frankie had called it. That wild thing inside her.

"What's that?" asked Mann.

"Nothing." Lucy shook her head and laughed, placing her hand on her belly.

The detective noted the gesture, felt a sudden rush of heat—or was it anger? She adjusted her sleeve. "I don't know if I ever mentioned it . . ."

Lucy looked up. "Mentioned what?"

Ms. Mann took a deep breath and met the woman's eyes. "I can't have children."

Lucy Fini didn't seem to understand. The detective elaborated. "Physically, I mean. I'm not able to—"

"Wait wait wait," stammered Lucy. "Why are you telling me this?"

Mann said she wasn't sure. "Edgar was important to me."

Lucy clenched her fists, furious at Mann's choice of tense. But she let it go, and when she embraced the detective it was quick. As they said their goodbyes, both women smiled and waved, pretending that this was not the end.

*   *   *

Outside the courthouse she avoided looking at the sky, which was very blue. A ragged cloud like the pelvic bone of a large animal drifted south. The newlyweds headed in the same direction, straight home. There was no rented hall to go to, no party; Lucy hadn't lied to her father.

Ron, of course, had wanted one. He'd wanted a church, a priest, the banks of flowers. He'd wanted the rings, the mentions of God and eternity, the whole shebang. Give him a glass of champagne, a smear of wedding cake, he knew he could bang the future into shape. For the first time in his life he understood what it must feel like to be an artist. The desire to make something beautiful, lasting. He was poised, ready.

Yet he didn't push his luck. He'd agreed to everything Lucy had wanted (which was nothing). He'd even said, "Fine, babe," when she'd told him, the day after accepting his proposal, that there could be no honeymoon.

Still, it was their wedding night. He wanted to give her something extra. Something more than just a good pounding. He wanted to show her what was in him, what was possible. This wasn't just another Tuesday night, this was—(he looked up; it was the sort of thought you could only share with your dead mother)—this was fate. This was *Fortuna*. In time his wife's other story would fade. Especially after he took her away from this house where the ghosts still had a hold on her. In fact, he didn't want to spend their first night in any bed upstairs. He had a plan.

"Why don't you take a bath?" he suggested. "Relax for half an hour."

They were standing in the kitchen. Lucy noted something funny in his voice.

"What are you up to?" For the past few days she'd observed the growing collection of twist-tied plastic sacks by the back door, a duffel bag, a small pile of boxes—and now there was a large nylon case long enough to hold fishing poles. Ron had said they were supplies for the shop, and Lucy, believing him, hadn't bothered to snoop. Now she was suspicious. "Those better not be presents."

"Take your bath."

"Or suitcases."

He gave her a little push. "Bath. Bubbles. *Go.*"

She headed toward the stairs, reminding him of their no-honeymoon agreement. "Least of all, a fishing trip."

"I don't know what you're talking about. I'm a butcher," said the butcher. "I hate fish."

* * *

The hot water was a relief, slowing Lucy's mind and expectations. She stayed in the tub until she was puckered. Before a fogged mirror, she dusted herself with powder, and then put on a new maternity nightgown—a short black number, with a slight ruffle. It was supposed to be sexy, but made her look like a chambermaid stealing a watermelon. She pinned the carnation to one of the shoulder straps, knowing it would make Ron happy.

But when she went downstairs he wasn't there. The bags in the kitchen were gone, as well. The watermelon shifted position, and Lucy was afraid that the butcher had had second thoughts. She ran to see if he might be in one of the other bedrooms. All she encountered, though, were the footprints of a ghost, the faint trail of her own powdered feet. Back in the kitchen she leaned nauseously against the counter. It was then she saw something moving outside the window.

There he was, in the yard.

She was so relieved she laughed—even after she realized that he'd put up a tent. It was huge, with a peaked roof like a log cabin.

A long time ago, Frank had stolen a tent from a garage sale—but of course they'd never used it. Never made it to any of the places they'd dreamed of going. Venice Beach, Machu Picchu. A backpack full of almonds and dried apricots.

Lucy stepped outside and watched Ronald David Salvatore, not with anger, but with a soft confusion that allowed for tenderness. He was fussing inside the tent, his butt sticking out, and when he emerged it was with an extension cord that he dragged toward the house.

"So this is it?" asked Lucy, and Ron said, "Hold your horses." He moved toward the outlet by the back door.

"Wala!" he crooned in Pepé Le Pew French.

The tent, lit from within, glowed like a paper lantern. The sun was setting; the air was already getting cool. Ron took Lucy's hand, telling her she looked gorgeous. The tent flapped in a steady breeze; it seemed impatient, unnaturally luminous. If Lucy was remembering correctly, Ron had set the thing directly over one of Frank's holes. Filled in now, of course—but memory was a tireless excavator. Lucy could picture her lunatic husband holding Edgar over the freshly dug earth. She'd found him there, eyes blazing, at five in the morning. He'd been reluctant to hand over the child, claiming he needed to show Edgar where the river was. Later that day, Frank had been taken back to the hospital.

"Would you like to go on a little trip?"

It was only Ron, though, whispering in her ear.

"Sure," she said, serving up a smile, and together they walked over the weedy, dandelion-dotted lawn and entered the tent.

"Christ Almighty," sighed Lucy.

An air mattress draped with purple satin sheets took up nearly half the space. The remainder of the floor was covered by a faux-fur rug the color of squirrel.

"Are we filming a porno in here?"

"You want to?" The butcher flashed his very white teeth. "We can do it on my phone." He kissed her neck and then poured her a glass of non-alcoholic champagne.

The walls undulated, the belly of a whale. Lucy extended her foot and toed the watery edge of the satin sheets.

Superslut.

The word arrived in her head not as sound but as picture—faint blue lines scrawled across Edgar's forearm.

But that couldn't be right.

Lucy suspected she wasn't thinking straight; felt dizzy. "Are you sure this stuff's non-alcoholic?"

"Positive," said the butcher.

When she went to put down the drink, she noticed the glasses—matching flutes etched with slender flowering branches. Florence's wedding set.

"Where'd you get these?"

"From the china cabinet. In the dining room."

"Those aren't yours, Ron."

"Don't pull away." He was trying to rub her shoulders.

"I just don't want you rifling through the house."

The butcher said he was sorry, meant it, continued his kneading.

Lucy huffed impatiently. His touch felt good, but she couldn't let him in—couldn't accept the advice that constantly came her way.

As heartless as it may seem, your life must go on.

Isn't that what one of the pamphlets had said? Or maybe the phrase was something she'd heard at that ghastly meeting she'd attended back in February. Parents of Missing and Murdered Children. POMMC. "Welcome to Pom-C!" everyone had shouted in greeting, pronouncing the acronym as if it were some friggin' sports drink.

The butcher's breath traveled down Lucy's neck—slow wet kisses.

She forced herself to keep still. She'd made this marriage, this bed—and, despite the tacky purple sheets, she now had to lie in it. The butcher helped her down, arranging her like an invalid against a small mountain of pillows. He'd thought of everything. Beside the mattress, on a linen-covered box, white bowls and silver spoons shone in the poisonous yellow light of an electric lantern. On a hotplate a pan of beef stew was just coming to a simmer. Lucy reached over and turned it to low, saying that it smelled good, but she wasn't hungry.

"That's okay." The butcher kneeled, put his lips between her breasts. She leaned back onto the pillows as he drifted south—his big hands pushing up the black nightie, tugging down the low-rise maternity panties.

"Don't rip them," she said. They hadn't been cheap. Maternity gear was highway robbery. With Ron at her thighs, she let her thoughts drift to the envelopes of cash thrust at her at the courthouse. There was no greed in these thoughts. The truth was, she wanted nothing to do with the money. Why did people think that they could buy her sadness from her? Like the check she'd received from that Jimmy Papadakis. Twelve thousand, one hundred and six dollars, and forty-seven cents. A Light for Jimmy hadn't even had the decency to round it the fuck off. As if Edgar's value could be calculated down to the penny.

Lucy moaned. She was furious. The butcher's tongue entered her. She spread her legs to give him better access.

Maybe she'd tear up the checks. Maybe she'd burn them.

"Oh my God." Her muscles were already beginning to shake. It took so little these days to get her going—her body pitifully sensitive, always ready for dissolution, oblivion. She looked down from her stack of pillows. The butcher's head was hidden below her swollen belly, but she could hear him licking. She imagined the sound coming from her womb, from the child who was clearly going to be a giant, like its father. Her stomach was enormous— so different from the modest bump that had been Edgar. The memory made her want to pull away.

But oh he was good! He was a genius with his tongue, goddamn him. Lucy was in the hole now, in the dirt, moving through the soft pliant earth. *A hole that keeps going is a tunnel,* Frank had said. But where would it take her? Frank's father had worked underground, too, building a tunnel, a passageway connecting two cities separated by water.

"Ahhh," she cried, wishing to forget, knowing very well that forgetting was a kind of remembering—it only made room for something else.

"Deeper," she instructed the butcher, reaching down around her belly to find the thick swag of his black hair. She pushed, forcing his head into a more animated conversation with her vagina. She wanted him to scream, wanted his voice to carry all the way through to where the light was.

"Yes." The word hammered out as she thrust her pelvis upward. The butcher slid his hands under her buttocks to assist. When her neck tilted back, she saw the tiny pins of light and could not understand how the sky had gotten inside the tent.

A clear plastic rectangle was sewn into the ceiling. Through it the stars were visible, though blurred. It reminded her of the last glimmer she'd had of Pio's car—the roof of the LeBaron, a golden rectangle vanishing into the water with Frank. "Shut the lamp," she instructed the butcher—who, without stopping his fervent flicking, reached out his arm to click off the lantern.

So many stars—a swarm, flying into the tent, into her eyes, between her legs. Long needles piercing her body. She squinted them into finer points. *The Machine, the Bridge, the Slip.* Frank had had such peculiar names for the constellations, but Lucy had barely listened—refusing to understand her husband's calculations until it was too late.

Where was the red one, though? Frank had said the red star was important. Would die one day, he'd said, but its death would be beautiful. As Lucy's head rocked from side to side, she knew that her son was gone. She tried to stop herself from coming, but it was impossible. *Let it happen,* she thought, *let it go*—and as the hot liquid rushed into the butcher's mouth, Lucy knew, in her bliss, that she could never be forgiven.

62

The Bridge

The Earth turned. Above the tent the stars shifted position. The red star, Betelgeuse, had already slipped below the horizon. Later, during the day, it would drift invisibly overhead, camouflaged by sunlight. Lucy wouldn't see it again until October, when it reappeared in the night sky over New Jersey.

Betelgeuse was dead, though no one on Earth knew this yet, as its light still traveled here. The star had died over five hundred years ago—and its death had been spectacular.

One day, humans will witness how it had ended—the supernova burning for weeks, visible even at noon. Of course, the star's earthly death will be merely a delayed broadcast—ghost fire. Still, it will enter human history as a day of great importance, this old death happening as if it were new. The celestial catastrophe with its expanding halo of light will seem profound to those who witness it, an echo of their own story. Death remembered as life.

Lucy Fini will not survive to see the show.

Long life is wished to those that come from Lucy Fini's womb.

* * *

She woke, shivering. The butcher had stolen the covers—the satin, greased by moonlight, pulled up to his neck. Lucy tugged down her nightie, could feel the pin of the carnation scratching her flesh. She tried to reclaim some of the sheets, but Ron had rolled in them, was firmly wrapped—his head sticking out of what seemed a huge purple cocoon. The beef stew was congealed and the bottle of sham champagne had toppled, wetting the faux-fur rug. The tent smelled meaty, sweet. Florence's wedding flutes were empty.

Carved with a diamond, the old woman used to brag whenever she showed anyone the garishly etched glasses.

When Lucy sat up, her head swam. The light inside the tent was grainy, like an old photo—the air filled with infinitesimal dots. Lucy swatted them away, only causing more to appear. It was funny: in all her years of drinking she'd never really felt drunk. But now that she was sober, she felt sloshed half the time—the world at an odd tilt. Her bad leg ached as she crawled toward the zippered door—the black line in the fleshy nylon like a scar, like stitches. She saw the blood again on the kitchen floor; Edgar's finger.

"Where you going, babe?"

"Nowhere, I just . . ." She didn't turn. "I have to pee. I'll be back."

The butcher, slit-eyed, dream-tapped, admired her wide ass wriggling out the door. "Bring back a blanket," he called after her. "I took the day off, we can lounge all morning." He lifted his head. "Luce, you hear me?"

She had, but was unable to reply. The silence in the yard was too heavy, a plank over her chest. Her bare feet took small shocked steps in the wet grass. The house was dark, the hour indeterminate. The back door seemed a hurtful distance away. Something was wrong with the light. It was barely there—the not-quite mind of it watching her. Halfway to the house she stopped, snagged by a crooked bone of déjà vu.

The light wasn't wrong at all, but exactly right. The same predawn crepusculence, the trees dusted with dregs of moonmuck, ravenous shadows taking their last licks. It was the same darklight in which she'd found Frank at his holes. The same season—the angle of the unhatched sun a perfect match. The light was like a map, and Lucy realized that when she'd come out here in October, after finding Frank's note in Florence's room, she hadn't dug in the right spots. Her excavations had been wildly off target.

This knowledge didn't inspire her, though. She no longer wished to get on her knees and claw at the ground. She passed over the filled-in holes, over the gun she didn't know was buried there, and entered the house, unarmed—her mind pulsing with the words from Frank's note.

Your mother and I are gone now.

She passed through the kitchen, headed upstairs.

We were your parents, Frank and Lucy Fini.

Why had she refused to go with him? Her error lay here. Even with Edgar: why had she hidden him in the berry bushes? It would have been better had they all stayed in the gold LeBaron. There'd be only silence now, only blackness.

She went straight to Florence's room and pulled the box from the back of the closet. The Virgin's headless body, the silk-lined case with its braid of hair, the burnt wedding portrait. Wrapped in newspaper, she found the night-light with its frosted panel of molded glass. She ran her fingers over the angel, the bridge. She even dared to plug it in. As she stared at it, whatever pain there was was tempered by the weightless sensation that none of this was real. How could it be? Someone must have made it up; a story. She had every right to leave it behind, go back to the tent, back to the drowning lips of the butcher.

She stood, drifted into the hallway, found herself downstairs, but moving in the wrong direction. She opened the front door.

There was no sun yet, though the darkness thrummed nervously, the last stars biting through the gloaming. Lucy stepped onto the porch. Some idiot had parked in front of the house. In the beginning there was always a policeman stationed there—and then, later, reporters, do-gooders, tragedy hounds. Now it was just disinterested strangers taking the free space.

As Lucy turned away, the car's lights flashed—a brief disturbance she sensed only from the corner of her eye. She spun around, looked in error toward the sky. When the vehicle's lights flashed again, Lucy's heart jumped. She took a step back, squinted.

A truck, an old pickup.

"What do you want?" What she'd meant to shout came out as whisper.

The truck shuddered to life, its motor turning like a sluggish helicopter. Lucy could just make out the figure behind the wheel. Tall, skinny, an oddly shaped chin—maybe a beard.

It couldn't be. She said his name quietly, and then listened for a long time to the ratchet of her own breath. When she moved forward, the truck pulled away—but only slightly, into the middle of the road.

Lucy was in no mood for games. Particularly at five in the morning, or whatever hellish time it was. This is why she liked to sleep in. Early mornings were minefields, mindfucks. Still, she steeled herself and made a dash forward.

Instantly the truck rumbled away.

"Stop, asshole!" yelled Lucy, with no desire whatsoever that the man respect her wishes. She watched the truck tear down Cressida Drive—and then halt, halfway to the corner. It stood, without apology now, under a streetlight. Pale green, freckled with rust, the license plate covered with black paper. Lucy felt an incomprehensible stab of hope.

For several seconds neither she nor the truck moved. And then, without turning away, she stepped slowly backwards toward the house, thinking she had better wake the butcher.

As if the truck had a better idea, it flashed its lights again and rolled forward a few inches.

Lucy felt her face burning in the chilly air as she continued to backtrack toward the house, saying, *Ron, Ron, Ron,* in a pathetically quiet voice. Without taking her eyes from the truck, she blindly stepped up onto the porch and then dashed inside—but only far enough to grab her car keys, along with Florence's coat hanging by the door.

"Ron!"—and though she shouted now at the top of her lungs, there was no time to wait.

Outside, a strange relief that the truck was still there. Lucy got into her little red coupe. As soon as she'd pulled out of the driveway, the pickup began to move. Lucy followed, glancing only quickly toward the house, where the butcher was standing on the porch, waving his arms. A moment later she turned from Cressida onto Laurel, free to give her full attention to the tar-papered license plate.

She kept her eyes solely on that. It gave her a point of focus, and it made her decision to follow the truck seem somehow more logical. She wasn't following a bearded man at five in the morning, she was simply following a small black rectangle, the signifier of all she didn't know.

* * *

Without looking at the buildings or the signs, she could tell that she was no longer in Ferryfield. Peripherally glimpsed shadows informed her that she was passing through West Mill, where she'd grown up. She now noticed the scribbled-over bumper sticker on the rear fender of the truck. She squinted, could almost make out a word. *Control.*

The truck sped up.

Now they were inside other towns, where the light was better or the hour later—Lucy couldn't tell which. Time was locked down, held in stasis by the glitch of Lucy's heartbeat. When she saw the sign for Bluebell Avenue, she was confused, thinking that the man in the truck might be leading her back to the abortion clinic. But he didn't turn there; he drove onto some wider roads where there were more cars. Lucy cut ahead of a few sluggish drivers to stay with the truck. Her rising nausea was tinged with giddiness, that peculiar sloshed sobriety. She found it difficult to swallow. Near the entrance to the Parkway, in a pocket of congestion, she lost sight of the pickup.

North or south? She pressed on the horn to clear her thoughts, startling a raven from a maple. The bird flew to the left, and Lucy followed it. *North.*

On the highway, though, she couldn't find the man—or couldn't be sure which vehicle up ahead was his. The sun, just risen, was hampered by clouds. She stepped on the gas, and after a while she saw the truck flash its lights in her rearview mirror. Strangely, the man was behind her now, a distressing distance away. Lucy was unable to slow down, locked in a freight train of aggressive commuters.

She flashed her own lights to let him know that she'd seen him. In the semi-darkness, communication seemed enhanced—and as she moved swiftly in the flow of traffic, it produced an exotic effect. The Parkway itself seemed conscious—each driver a part of its brain. So what if the man was behind her? She'd beat him there.

A funny thought, since she had no idea where she was going.

Still, she kept driving. Humming a song she didn't know. She covered a great distance with a startling absence of thought—startling because she sensed her blank mind was only a curtain, behind which everything was set: elaborate scenery, all the props in place.

She's felt like this before, a frightened spider, architect of her own web.

She drives, humming; she drives in silence. Ten minutes, an hour. She checks the mirror regularly; the truck is still a ways behind her—though now she isn't sure if it's the same one. When its lights flash again and an arm emerges from the window, pointing, Lucy tries to understand the gesture. She sees an exit ramp just to her right and takes it—a last-second turn that sends Saint Christopher swinging.

She's so sure she's correctly interpreted the man's directive that she fails to look behind her, to see if he's taken the exit, as well. The angle of the emerging sun is distracting. Breaking clouds, a twisting narrow road, a sudden increase in the number of trees. It's a lot to take in, but when she rolls down the window, she can smell Edgar.

Never stop looking.

You will want to dedicate part of each day to your missing child. And though your grief is likely to come unannounced, don't dwell on it. Remember: You have work to do!

When Lucy finally looks for the man in the mirror, she doesn't see him. All she can see are trees. She adjusts the rearview. An approaching car blares its horn. Lucy moves quickly back to her lane, and when she speeds around a rib-contorting curve, she sees the two bridges.

She doesn't make a sound. Her shock is not the choired shock of revelation, but the silent shock of terrors recalled.

She's been tricked. The man or the raven. She should have driven south. The truth is, she hasn't been sure of the green truck since right before the Parkway. She races ahead anyway. The *thump thump thump* of the first bridge rocks her body like gunfire. On the other side, she slows, looking for the berry bushes, the spot where she'd laid Edgar on the ground.

The wild field's been paved, though—the bushes ripped out. Some kind of warehouse or storage facility has been put up. A series of padlocked doors Lucy can't stand to look at.

Not everything has changed, of course. There's the second bridge, the slatted guardrail grinning. She drives as close as she can, stops the car. She gets out, walks to the rail—though walking is the wrong word. She feels *carried*. There's no pain in her leg, as if the injury hasn't happened yet.

She climbs over, works her way down to the small rock ledge high above the water—knowing now that she's been tricked by no man, no raven. She's done this to herself. The river moves swiftly. The baby kicks. She raises her arms to something she doesn't understand, wanting to scream but able to eke out only dry pebbles of sound.

Had Frank's pain been this great? Had Florence's? To have lost her only son. Why had Lucy never realized how terrible it must have been for the old woman?

She leans forward into the void. The sound of the canyon like a huge seashell pressed to her ear; the river a cold blue flecked with white. She only wishes she could detach her belly, leave it safely on the ledge. All she wants to do is to swim in the river, to understand it. Frank said it might be possible to find each other again under the water, even in the darkness. Edgar's face, he said, was the light. *Swim toward that.*

It's only a matter of how to get down there. She takes a step forward, uses her toe to envoy a stone. It falls silently—the reverie interrupted by the sound of wheels on gravel. Lucy turns and sees the truck.

Except it's white now, like before. An ambulance.

Like the one that took her away with a bleeding broken leg, a sunburned Edgar in her arms. *No,* she'd pleaded with the men that day—telling them she needed to go back for her husband. But somehow they'd managed to silence her. By the time she'd regained consciousness, they'd set her leg, encased it in plaster, the police outside the room asking if there was anyone she needed to call.

Just—just take me back, she'd stammered, throwing things until they'd relented. They'd put her in another ambulance after that.

They didn't drive her back to the bridge, though, but to 21 Cressida Drive—the old woman rushing outside at the sight of the white truck. When Lucy was wheeled from the back, the baby in her arms, it was someone else's turn to scream.

"Where's Frankie? Where's Frankie?"

Lucy shakes her head, covers her face. Florence goes white, runs down the street.

Runs until she falls, sobbing. Pio goes to her, pulls her up, drags her back.

When the old woman approaches the wheelchair and takes the baby, Lucy doesn't resist. She knows she can't be trusted. It begins here—the boy no longer hers, but belonging to his grandmother.

Even now, Lucy senses, she would be made to keep her promise. Edgar would be Florence's even unto death.

"Lucy!"

She opens her eyes to the truck.

Not an ambulance, though. A white van painted with red letters.

Let us MEAT your needs!

"Don't move," he says.

She takes a step back—though that's the wrong direction. She doesn't care, though.

The butcher climbs over the rail.

"Don't!" commands Lucy. "I don't want you—"

"Goddamn you." His massive body engulfs her. "Goddamn you," he cries, clutching her.

When she tries to pull away, the water breaks from between her legs and slaps against the rocks.

63

Laughter

The man placed his hand on the boy's head, shaved clean after the fire. The dog was sleeping on the bed, which made it seem safe to close one's eyes; the boy did so, and barely sighed when he felt the man's thumb caress the singed eyebrow. There was no pain. All things, lately, had escaped the grip of what should have destroyed them.

Even the pygmies.

The little pines behind the shed had been horribly charred—black daggers, dead to the core. A few weeks later, though, seedlings appeared in the ash. It seemed a miracle, but it was merely science. Fires, the man had explained, were common in the Barrens—and the pygmies had learned how to survive them. In fact, it was the heat of the flames that caused the pinecones to open and the seeds to fall. While it often killed the tree, fire was good for the tree's children. Evolution required sacrifice.

The boy thought a lot about the pygmies while lying in bed. He only wished he could tell Mr. Levinson—though Mr. Levinson, being a science teacher, probably knew all about the fire-foxing trees. Besides, it was unlikely, the boy realized, that he'd see Mr. Levinson again. Mr. Levinson was part of the dream of before.

If this was sad, it was folded up, put away in a drawer. The boy's spring-roaring blood turned him manic; roiled the darker concerns of his plight into the general mud of his native melancholy. Anyway, things weren't so terrible now at the cabin. Life seemed almost normal.

Which is not to say the boy was happy—though he knew he should be. He was lucky to be alive. There was even plenty of food. The stocks from the kitchen were long gone, but some cans from the shed had been salvaged.

Everything else had burned—the shed itself a pile of black bones. The boy was glad the notebooks were gone, though he hated himself for feeling this way, knowing the man must have spent a lot of time working on his stories—most of which were more than stories. It was terrible what people said when they thought no one was listening.

When the boy remembered what he'd read, it seemed like something from another planet.

Private stuff about people named Sara and Kevin and Edgar.

Names were a funny thing. They, too, could be burned away. For several days after the fire, the man and the boy had slept in the same bed—not as Edgar and Conrad, but as something else. The fire had changed them, cooked them, making them less who they were, and more who they might be.

Shock. That was the word Conrad had used. This shock had somehow corrected them.

They'd slept, it seemed, for a long time—every now and then one or the other stumbling into the kitchen for a glass of water or something to eat. Kibble for Jack, flakes for the fish. Brief excursions, after which they returned to the dark cave of Conrad's bedroom. For days they'd smelled like smoke, and their hair had been horrible. Later, when they were awake for real, the man had used his beard trimmer to shave their heads. It was almost funny, then, the way they'd resembled each other.

"The baldies," Conrad had said, and Edgar had found himself smiling.

Every now and then, it happened again—Edgar's lips going up instead of down. It didn't happen often, but when it did, it was disturbing.

Sometimes Edgar wasn't sure who he was. Even his face had changed. At first it was a bright red—a raw color that reminded him of his grand-mother's hands. "Superficial burn," Conrad had said, whose own skin had been the same.

But as Conrad's burn had faded and healed, Edgar's had turned flaky. Pieces fell off, translucent curls like the molt of a snake. What was under-neath made no sense. The boy's skin was noticeably darker.

"Do you think something's wrong?" he often asked.

"You're fine," Conrad assured him.

"But why is it like that?"

"Like what? It looks normal."

Edgar shook his head. "Don't you remember what I looked like before? When you first met me?"

Conrad said that he did.

"Well, that's how I look," persisted Edgar. "I was born like that. It doesn't go away. It's a *condition.*"

Not that he'd ever liked his shock-white skin, but he'd gotten used to it; it was one of the things that made him who he was. Now, he looked different somehow—and not just his face. His chest, too, his legs, the whole run of him like someone in makeup.

"Come away from the mirror, Edgar."

"I'm getting darker." He rubbed his cheek as if it were smudged, as if the real boy might be underneath. There was too much blood in his face, too much color. He looked down at his painted hands.

Conrad took the boy by the shoulders and turned him around. "Stop. There's nothing you can do."

"But why would it happen?"

The man said he didn't know. "People change, Edgar."

* * *

Sometimes the man watched the boy as he slept. The color disturbed him more than he let on. Plus, the boy seemed taller, stronger. Surely the color was a sign of health—a disturbing thought in its own right. Edgar looked more real than ever before. Conrad's fear took a new turn. The boy had been at the cabin long enough for Conrad to witness, once again, the miraculous horror of a child growing up.

Edgar's face, emboldened, seemed that much more corruptible. There was more responsibility, more danger. It had almost been better when the boy had looked dead.

When spring came, Conrad felt as if he were coming out of a long dream. So much had changed. The most frightening thing was that he, too, was alive—and he was actually happy.

It was a happiness, of course, like glass. Sometimes he wondered if he should break it, be done with it. It would break eventually, anyway.

Time flashed, shimmered. It was almost summer. Conrad didn't want to squander the days. There'd been enough of that. The gun, the refusal to eat—ridiculous, juvenile. Wasted opportunities. A wasted life.

"What are you doing out there?" he called to Edgar, who was in the yard, chasing Jack—the two of them more than ever like siblings. The boy spoke the animal's language and even had the audacity to answer the man's question with a bark.

"Is that so?" said Conrad.

Edgar turned away and ran in a circle.

Sometimes the boy ignored him, which was only natural. A child that age, they started to go away. Still, the boy's odd habit of barking, the frantic hoopla, his whisperings to empty air—all of it seemed to have increased recently, and Conrad was unsure what was play, and what was acting out.

"Are you okay? You mad at me?"

Edgar shook his head and barked again.

"I thought we could go to a café," said Conrad. "Get some pie."

The man had made no plans for such a thing and surprised himself by suggesting it.

The boy stopped and turned. The dog was quiet, too.

"What do you mean?" asked Edgar.

"Pie. It's when they take fruit and put it inside a—"

The boy tilted his head adorably. "I know what pie is."

"Well, do you want some?"

The boy's face went blank, then seemed perturbed. His eyes grew glassy.

"I thought you'd want to."

Edgar sat on the ground.

"What?" said Conrad.

Edgar grabbed up some pine needles and spread them across his thigh. "But where are we really going?"

"I told you, a café. We'll drive to Shamong."

"Is that a place?"

"Yes, it's a town."

"But you never took me there."

"That's true," said Conrad, not really understanding what the boy meant.

In the silence that followed, the man further considered his plan. Shamong, not Hammonton, is where they'd go. Hammonton was closer, but people knew Conrad there. It's where he went for supplies, made calls, put gas in the truck. He'd picked blueberries there with Sara and Kevin. He'd eaten at Daisy's with them. He'd eaten there with his father. There was too much history in Hammonton.

Shamong seemed the right place to take the boy. There was a decent restaurant—nothing like Daisy's, but Edgar would enjoy the statue.

"There's a sculpture there I think you'll like."

"What is it?"

"You'll have to see."

Conrad stepped into the yard and held out his hand.

Edgar hesitated. Which made Conrad wonder if he were lying to the boy.

Shamong. A café. Was that really where he planned to take the kid? He checked the corners of his mind to see if anything might be hiding there.

"A couple of hours, and then straight back."

"I should do my homework," said Edgar.

Conrad smiled. The boy was slowly making his way through every book in the cabin. "It's practically summer, kiddo, if you didn't notice."

"I noticed," Edgar said sharply.

Conrad waited. He understood. With love came anger.

The boy looked at the dog. "Why don't we go next week?"

"I thought you'd be excited. We can hop in the truck right now."

Edgar said it wasn't a good idea; it would be dark soon.

Conrad took in the yard, the blossoms of swamp azalea phosphorescent in the late light—tiny bells hot and silent.

"They look like whipped cream," said Edgar.

"What's that?"

"The flowers."

Conrad nodded, squinted—the clustered blossoms like soft round dollops. "I'm thinking you're hungry."

"A little," said Edgar.

"Come on." Conrad offered his hand again.

But the boy stood on his own, made a shrill whooping and ran toward the trees. He pulled a handful of flowers from the azalea and stuffed them toward his mouth—after which he thrashed viciously at the bush, knocking more blossoms to the ground.

"Edgar. *Edgar, stop*. What are you doing?"

Jack was beside him now, sniffing the fallen flowers.

The boy calmed. Conrad watched, saying nothing.

Watched the child who'd spent hours curled up behind the ladder bookshelf, withdrawn, silent—but who, lately, was more likely to be found roughhousing with the dog, throwing things, digging holes as if he owned the place.

"You're right," Conrad said. "It's too late. We'll go tomorrow. Or next week. Whenever you want." He was suddenly grateful for the boy's resistance. It would be better, anyway, to drive there in daylight, innocently. "We'll go for breakfast one day."

"But I'll still have pie," Edgar said solemnly.

"Me, too," said Conrad.

*   *   *

After the boy had fallen asleep—in his own bed now—Conrad sat in a corner of the living room and looked through Edgar's books and DVDs: a makeshift schoolroom the boy kept obsessively neat. Conrad had originally assembled the materials to distract the child, but was surprised by how studious he'd turned out to be. Edgar read voraciously, and was religious about watching at least one DVD every day—educational programs that seemed to pacify the boy's anxiety about missing school. Just a week ago, though, he'd suggested that, come September, it might be a good idea for him to go back to a real school. Conrad had smiled without a twitch and said, "Absolutely."

Quite a collection of books the boy had. Conrad surveyed them. Kevin's old school texts and science fiction, mixed with things Sara had left at the cabin—Jane Austen, Margaret Atwood. There was a small black Bible, probably Conrad's father's, which Edgar must have found somewhere in the cabin. The cover was filthy. *Read me,* a small finger had written in the dust.

Conrad flattened his hand and wiped the slate clean.

*   *   *

The damage was done, though. Irreversible.

When Conrad had driven to Ferryfield, it hadn't been planned. Unable to sleep one night, he'd got in the truck, ended up on the Parkway. It had seemed important to see her. To know that she existed.

He'd parked in front of the house. When she'd come outside wearing a tight black negligee, ridiculously short, Conrad had felt contempt. The woman looked exhausted, blowsy—and though he'd been surprised by her beauty, she looked in every other way as he'd imagined. Like a slut. The most shocking thing was that she was pregnant.

It seemed unforgivable—and obscene—the huge bulge in the black nightie.

Of course, the woman did look genuinely sad. He'd flashed his lights. It was then that she'd started to shout. Conrad had wondered if she might be drunk. Screaming, *fuck, asshole,* waving her arms like a madwoman. The whole encounter illogical, like a dream.

But by the time she was following him on the road it seemed natural that it had come to this—though of course he had no idea what he'd do when she arrived at the cabin. At one point, overcome by nausea, he'd vomited in the truck. He'd felt like he'd been on this road before with this woman. Maybe because he'd imagined it for so long. Imagined giving everything up. Crashing, burning. End of story.

And then, suddenly, his mind had flipped. Because there she was, drunk and pregnant, following him in that trashy little car. Conrad had felt a distinct sense of superiority. How could he give the boy back to someone like that? She was driving recklessly, an unfit parent. The red hair, a sign of her cruelty. She'd not answered a single of the boy's letters. She was a stranger to him now.

He'd sped up, and at some point it seemed he'd lost her—though it was hard to tell for sure in the glare of dawn. It wasn't until he'd entered the Pinelands again and saw no one behind him that he'd managed to take a deep breath—the air rushing in like poison, burning his lungs.

A green truck: they'd know that now.

But only that. He'd been smart enough to cover the license plates with tar paper. Still, he'd given these people so many chances. Why hadn't they come for the boy already? *Idiots.* He'd pulled to the side of the sugar sand road to compose himself. It was only then that he'd remembered. He'd never sent the boy's letters; he'd thrown them into a swallet. Sunk them in mud.

So what? Was he any worse than the woman in black spandex? He didn't know her, yet he judged her. Half naked, screaming obscenities.

It was all so confusing. Conrad felt like a child, trapped by the unknowable hearts of everyone around him. The boy, especially. By the time Conrad had returned from Ferryfield, it was light, full morning. Edgar had come outside to greet him—sleepy-eyed, shielding his face from the sun.

"Where were you?"

"I wanted to get some bread," replied an empty-handed Conrad.

Inside, in the bathroom, he'd vomited again—the little voice outside the door. "Are you okay?" The boy's kindness seemed a curse now.

After the woman's face.

"All better," Conrad had said, coming out of the bathroom.

"I was worried," said Edgar.

* * *

Weeks had passed, with no sudden knocks on the cabin door. No red-haired madwoman had shown up. No police. Conrad's agitation, though, remained constant. His impatience was overwhelming, but, being connected to no clear desire, was a kind of torture.

Don't just sit there, do something, his father had always insisted.

Conrad had given the same advice to the boy—and he'd taken it to heart, made Conrad proud. Now it was Conrad's turn to do something brave. Not to frighten the child, but to earn his respect. Show him that freedom was still possible—the two of them driving in the truck, buddies, as before.

Just like how it had been with his own father. The windows open, sizzling static of the AM radio, the old man yodeling along with Hank Williams. A warm pizza box on Conrad's lap.

The memory fell clear as rain, as the man stepped into the yard. A promising light-spattered morning. Edgar was playing again—this time carving something on a tree, using the pocketknife Conrad had given him. It was a gorgeous little knife with a wood veneer that when opened halfway looked like a sailboat. It had belonged to Kevin.

Edgar was past the cleared edge of the yard, about twenty feet into the larger pines. Between the trees, strands of spider silk flickered like glitches in reality. The dog was there, too, watching the boy as he picked at the bark.

Conrad didn't approach them.

Edgar worked for a while on whatever he was carving, and then stopped. He stared at the tree, almost seemed to be speaking to it. Conrad's heart lurched; he touched his face where the skin was still tender. After the fire, when he'd told Edgar, "You saved my life," the boy had only replied, "We were very stupid"—and Conrad, chastened, had nodded.

He watched now as the boy and the dog ran back toward the yard. When Edgar was past the woodpile, he threw himself onto the ground and rolled. Jack pounced, licking the boy's face, making him laugh—a high-pitched giggle, triumphant, like an eagle. The dog seemed to be laughing, too.

Abruptly, though, the laughing stopped—and the boy turned toward the trees as if he'd heard something. Conrad looked, but saw nothing.

What Edgar heard was his mother. It was the thing about her he loved best, the way she laughed. After a moment, he jumped to his feet and dashed toward the cabin, where the man was standing.

Jack barked, and when Edgar crashed into Conrad it was with a punching embrace that knocked a little air from both of them. Another savage burst of laughter erupted from the boy's throat. He gripped Conrad so tightly that the man had no choice but to return the hug.

When Edgar looked up and saw Conrad's frightened face, he immediately pulled away.

"Why don't you laugh?"

Conrad tried to smile, but failed. And when Edgar asked again, the question shot out like an accusation.

"Why don't you laugh?"

Conrad opened his mouth, but said nothing. And then: "I'm just feeling a little . . . Maybe I'm coming down with something."

"Don't lie," said Edgar. He wasn't going to let Conrad worm his way out of this one. "You can't laugh, can you?"

For several seconds Conrad's face twitched—and when finally he apologized to the boy, he didn't recognize his own voice. He sounded like a robot; even his movements were mechanical as he turned away and walked into the house. He felt heavy and light at the same time, a metal shell with lots of hollow space. Where there'd once been blood, there was only air.

"Conrad!" shouted Edgar—but the name fell on nothing.

Entry #5

She was glad for the sound. Even if mined from chaos, the child's laugh was a step forward. It was conceivable that she might be finished soon. Not only with this story, but with all stories.

For now, though, she's still caught in the in-between, snagged like a leaf in an eddy, doing the same work she'd done all her life. Trying to straighten things, make them clean. How long had she spent, some mornings, positioning the photographs, just so, on top of the piano? They'd never seemed quite right—the angles of the faces or the space between the frames.

Perfection; how she'd wanted that. *Ha.*

Yes, the laugh was progress. The wheel was turning. When the boy laughed, he thought of his mother. He was thinking less and less about the old woman—who, in the boy's mind, had blended into other things: into the trees and the deer, the stream and the fox, the yellow birds and the hairy orchids. She was part of everything now, and he tended to forget her. She no longer had to appear to him in her old form, in a purple paisley robe, with her cracked feet and her red hands; no longer needed to prove herself, as she'd done before, in a clearing among the pines. The boy had turned the wheel of grief and was headed in the right direction, toward the living.

Which is not to say he was out of danger. Only to say: he no longer called out to her or asked her to intervene. As he'd done from the shed. A prayer she'd answered using the man's body. Since the fire, though, she's been of less use to him.

In some ways, it was a relief to be forgotten. In fact, when she'd watched the boy carve *Edgar* on the tree, followed by the word *loves*, she had no desire that her own name be the summation of that equation.

* * *

Still, she watches him. He's in the house now, reading a book.

If I loved you less, I might be able to talk about it more.

And, of course, he thinks of many people when he reads this. More people than before. It's good.

A good book, too. *Emma.* Jane Austen. Florence (funny to say the old name now) didn't read much when she was alive; could hardly read at all. But dying is an education. She's read them all now.

The boy, though, moves slowly through the words, hoping for wisdom or guidance.

He looks up from the page and sees the man who can't laugh. The boy goes to him and takes his hand. Seeing that, she almost wishes she could be human again.

They don't speak, the two beings in the cabin, but they're afraid, knowing everything must change. The child, in particular, senses, as never before, the sadness of the two deer heads mounted in the living room. His thoughts and feelings are huge shifting patterns of light and shadow, for the most part wordless—but she wants you to understand them, and so, as she's been doing all along, she translates. The child's feelings into words.

To some extent, she's been translating for all of them. Even the man, who's thinking about a boat on the Mullica, about taking the boy there.

It's unlikely either will survive.

Of course, the dead don't know everything. The living, too, invent the future.

She alights at the edge of the couch, where she catches drifts of the old scents: milk, dirt, dust.

Live, she says to them. *Live!*

(If it's even her voice.)

June

64

Madwoman

Though they didn't tie her to the bed, they rarely left her alone. Someone was always in the house, exuding good cheer, pretending not to be concerned.

How little they understood.

She was done. She was gone. Which meant, she was *here*. She was staying put. Giving up. I mean, what did they think: that she'd meant to jump off the bridge?

To be honest (and why not be, when you were talking to your own lying heart?), she had, for a moment, considered jumping. For more than a moment, maybe.

What a joke it would have been, too. Following Frank, eight years later, hauling ass toward oblivion in a slutty black maternity getup. How pathetic.

Surviving, though, was pathetic, too. It seemed that if you lived long enough your reward was humiliation. Survival was embarrassing—though probably a riot for the folks in the good seats, watching from above.

The dead, it turned out, were useless.

Still, she prayed to them.

At this point, it was simple: let the kid survive. The one inside her—a fat little kicker who'd recently become unnervingly still. Plus, it was pulling a Howard Hughes, refusing to come out. Even after Lucy's water had broken at Shepherd's Junction, labor hadn't started.

Premature rupture of membranes, the doctor said. Stress, physical strain, the likely cause. The baby wasn't quite ready, he said—though he could induce labor, if she wished. But she told him, No, she'd wait.

Bed rest was advised. It would happen soon, everyone said. Or hoped. There was so much talk of delivering this baby safely, perfectly, that Lucy felt a stultifying pressure. It was clear that everyone considered this kid the solution, the cure. Sometimes Lucy felt like the frickin' Virgin Mary, being asked to pop out salvation.

How unreal, to lie on your back all day while people stared down into the Cyclops of your belly. Confined, waiting on a star—or whatever cosmic force it would take to draw out the child. Maybe it was Lucy's fear, the sense that she'd mess things up, get it wrong, that kept the baby from coming.

Plus, she wasn't sure she was ready to see its face. Ron was hoping for a boy, but Lucy refused any offers of disclosure in regard to the baby's sex.

Premature rupture of membranes. The phrase stayed with her; seemed like something Frank would have said, some condition to be feared. Lucy often felt confused, woozy, her mind spiraling for hours as she lay in bed beside the manger. She wondered if they were putting something in her food. Something to keep her calm.

But she *was* calm, she told them; she was fine.

She got up sometimes, while no one was looking, and closed the curtains. Morning always came too quickly, the rah-rah of the sun like some demonic cheerleader. But even with the curtains drawn, it was still too bright. She half considered going into the closet.

*   *   *

It wasn't for a baby—the manger. It was for Ron. He'd set up a cot beside the bed, claiming he didn't want to injure Lucy. "How are you gonna injure me?" she'd asked.

"I toss," he'd replied.

When he kissed her goodnight, he did so from the side, pecking her cheek, steering clear of her belly. Ashamed for having grabbed her with such force on the bridge, he wished to cause no further harm to the endangered Cyclops. He was careful, timid, treating Lucy as if she were some other kind of woman, patting her shoulder, avoiding obscenities, speaking softly—another man entirely. It made Lucy want to scream.

And it was too ridiculous: the butcher's hairy bulk lying across the flimsy fold-up mattress, while she floundered in the queen.

"This is silly," Lucy often said. "Come here." When she said that she missed him, he smiled, but stayed in the cot. Sex, for the butcher, was out of the question—and Lucy, for the first time in her life, was ashamed to ask.

All she wanted was that he lie beside her, kiss her mouth, her breasts, put his hands on her thighs.

Soon, he said, he'd be back in the bed. Back on top of her. Soon, it would be like new. A new house, too. He was already looking, he told her.

How could she tell him she could never leave?

Sometimes he kissed the eye of the monster, Lucy's bellybutton, and whispered things that Lucy made an effort not to hear.

* * *

"Summer's just around the corner," Netty said, opening the curtains, the window. "Enjoy the nice air while we have it, dear. We'll be melting in a few weeks."

"The sun hurts my eyes," said Lucy.

"I'll make some tea." It was Netty's solution for everything, including Lucy's complexion, which the old woman deemed peaked.

Lucy's face was as pale as Edgar's now. Paler, in fact, if one were to judge by the posters around town, which had yellowed, giving the boy's death a semblance of life.

While Netty made tea, Lucy put on her sunglasses and tiptoed downstairs, out the front door. She only wanted to sit on the porch—to watch the grass bend and the shadow of the dogwood inch its way toward the street. She'd become a great starer, observant in a way she'd never been. The shadow of the dogwood wasn't black, but dark dark purple.

She looked up every now and then when a car passed. But there were no green trucks.

Not that she expected one. Ron had practically convinced her that there'd been no pickup; that she'd been following air. "You had a little flip-out," he said. "Let's forget about it, okay?"

When she'd telephoned Mann to discuss the five A.M. visitor with the blacked-out license plate, Mann had said she'd look into it—asking Lucy why she thought this was related to Edgar.

"You said anything out of the ordinary."

"Yes," conceded Mann. "So, what kind of truck was it?"

"Green," said Lucy.

"And the make? The model?"

Lucy, deeming the question a scold, had wanted to hang up the phone—angry with herself as much as with Mann. She couldn't remember the make or the model.

When the detective confessed it wasn't much to go on, Lucy added, in her new faraway voice, that it was a pale green, sort of minty.

* * *

In a chipped pot on the porch, yellow freesia was in bloom. Florence, no doubt, had put down the bulbs in the fall—possibly one of the last things she'd done. Bumblebees bobbed in the blossoms. Sometimes Lucy thought about bringing flowers to Florence's grave. But she was afraid she might see other names carved on the stone. Her own. Or Edgar's. Who could tell what was real anymore, or what time was up to? Sometimes she stared into her phone for hours, swiping through photos—and occasionally she even dared to watch one of the white-child videos on the Internet. It was like sneaking a cigarette, flashes of sweet bright poison.

When a drunken bee knocked Lucy's face, she scooted away from the freesia. She checked the shadow of the dogwood, which had moved nearly an inch.

It wasn't the only thing creeping, though.

"I can see you," said Lucy.

The girl was hiding behind the large hydrangea, the pink blossoms like candied brains.

"What you doing, Mrs. Feen? You just sitting?"

"You can sit with me if you want."

Toni-Ann immediately marched over, doing a terrible job of hiding her glee. She plopped herself down, her bare and sweaty arm rubbing against Lucy's. She smelled like warm milk, nearly sour. When she put her sticky hands under Lucy's blouse, to touch the sleeping Cyclops, Lucy allowed it. She liked the girl's boldness; so unlike the others.

"I'm petting it."

Lucy could feel the catlike purr of the girl's body. She tried to imagine that the vibration was coming from inside her frozen belly. Toni-Ann's sticky fingers now played a light bongo against the taut skin. It felt nice.

Toni-Ann, too, liked being next to Lucy; it helped. After a while, she took back her hand and put it in her mouth. She looked at the street, where she'd once seen Edgar get out of a green truck.

"We're still waiting," she said—and Lucy nodded, not wishing to discourage the girl.

* * *

Not long after they'd been called inside (Lucy, by Netty, to take her tea; and Toni-Ann, by her mother, who didn't like the girl hanging around the funny farm next door), the purple shadow of the dogwood reached the street, and in a cocoa-colored room in Villa Maria Hospice, Walter Bubko turned his head toward the bright chaos of a television and died.

At the nurse's station, a light blinked; a buzzer buzzed. One of two women playing rummy put down her cards and sighed. "Number thirty-four."

"Out the door," her companion rhymed—intentionally, but without malice.

* * *

When a nurse arrived at 21 Cressida Drive, it was only Anita Lester, there to examine the mother. She put a Pinard horn against Lucy's belly and listened for the heartbeat.

"Okay?" asked Lucy.

Anita nodded abstractly. She removed the horn and put her hand and cheek against the mound. She'd need to stay there for nearly half an hour, counting the movements. Since Lucy refused to go to the clinic or the hospital, older techniques were required. Anita didn't mind. She got to practice skills she'd learned but rarely used.

Plus, there was time to chat—though Lucy and Anita said little. Small talk. Still, it was nice. Lucy was not a woman Anita would have ever considered a friend. But here they were. And the truth was, people changed.

"Kick," said Anita.

"How come I don't feel it?" asked Lucy.

"He must have his slippers on."

Anita timed the intervals between tremors. It seemed slightly long.

"I'd like you to come in tomorrow for a Doppler."

"Is everything okay?"

"Yes. I just want to double-check with the machines. Can you come tomorrow at eight?"

Lucy said she didn't like the machines, they were too loud.

"It'll be quick," Anita said brightly. "You'll be home by nine."

Lucy watched her belly rise and fall with each breath. Anita was still listening—her head floating like a buoy.

"How's Jarell?" Lucy asked after a while.

"He's good," said Anita. "In fact he's waiting downstairs. We're going to a movie afterwards."

"What are you gonna see?"

"Zombies, I think. On a spaceship. He loves that stuff."

"Boys do," said Lucy. "Does he like *Predator*?"

"Oh my God," said Anita. "He even has the dolls. Of course he doesn't play with them anymore. He has a *girlfriend* now. You know Bethany Harvow?"

"I've seen her. She's pretty."

"Yes, well, I don't think her father's happy about it."

"Fuck him," said Lucy—and though Anita didn't like such language, she felt the truth of it here and laughed.

"It's nice that Jarell still makes time for you," remarked Lucy. "That's impressive."

"The girl's at French camp. He's pining."

"He's such a handsome kid."

Anita grunted. "Don't I know it." She moved her hand a bit higher.

"I really appreciate what you're doing," said Lucy. She could hear the kindness in her voice, and it embarrassed her.

At least she was still a bitch when she talked to herself.

"Kick," said Anita.

"Damn right," said Lucy.

*   *   *

"Would you like some tea?" Netty asked Jarell.

"No, thank you, ma'am."

"A cookie?"

Jarell declined. "Thank you, though."

Such a polite boy, thought Netty; she hardly minded that he was black.

"You can put on the television if you want, dear."

"Okay," said Jarell—and did.

He felt weird being in Edgar Fini's house. You couldn't help but think of it as haunted. He was glad his mother was helping, though. His mother was a really good person.

Maybe he should surprise her, tell her they could skip the zombies, go to that romantic thing she wanted to see. The one with what's-her-face, about the couple who keeps falling in love—but as different people, and over, like, a thousand years. It was the kind of crap she liked.

When the Finis' phone rang, Jarell was startled.

So was Netty, who had the sense that a large bird had just flown into the house.

"Hello?" she said brightly, certain it was bad news.

65

Star of Bethlehem

Outside the café, pixie moss was in bloom, along with some other star-shaped flowers Edgar knew to be sandwort. He'd become a near expert on Pine Barrens flora—having spent a lot of time looking through *Great God! Flowers of Field and Swamp,* an enormous watery-smelling book with lurid photographs and the occasional pressed blossom. In another life, it had belonged to Conrad's grandmother. Her name (Frances Billings) was written (curly script, purple pen) at the top of the first page. Most of the saved blossoms were little more than crumbs. Which is what happened to flowers—people, too—over time. Conrad's family had been coming to the cabin for more than a hundred years. "The castle," he sometimes called it jokingly—though Edgar could tell it was more than a joke. It was easy to see how much Conrad loved the place.

When they'd left, that morning, Edgar was astonished once again how long it took to get to the main road. Jack had barked at the truck, but couldn't follow because she'd been tied to her post. The first vehicle they'd passed had been another truck, brand-new, with gigantic wheels. The driver, an old man with a white ponytail, had waved, and Conrad had waved back. "Do you know him?" Edgar had asked, and Conrad had shook his head. "Just being friendly." The odd squeak in the man's voice, plus the rat-tat-tat routine against the steering wheel, had made Edgar feel queasy. For a long time they'd said nothing, as if they were driving to a funeral. Edgar had tried counting a flock of chimney swifts, but they'd disappeared before he could finish. He was glad when Conrad turned on the radio, even if it was mostly just static, like a broadcast from Mars.

* * *

Being in public again, among strangers, frightened Edgar, and he focused on the flowers. The hostess taking names at the door had said it might be a while before she could seat them. The normally quiet spot was hopping; a tour bus was parked at the side of the road.

"Star of Bethlehem!"

The voice was loud, and Edgar, startled, turned. A huge woman in stretchy shorts and yellow plastic sunglasses was so close he could smell her lunch-meat breath.

"I try to grow them at home," she said, "but they never take. They come up a little bit and then they"—she made a fart sound, by which Edgar assumed she meant *die*.

Luckily she wasn't talking to him, but to another woman, also in stretchy shorts. Edgar looked again at the flowers. They were definitely not Star of Bethlehem. He moved away, closer to Conrad, who was sweating under a tree, pretending he wasn't scared. But Edgar could tell that he was. "Walk around," he'd encouraged the boy after they'd got out of the truck. Edgar wondered if it was some kind of test.

To the side of the café, behind a white metal fence, was a huge statue of a gorilla. There was a sign on the gorilla's chest, but the text was too small to read from the distance—and since a crowd was gathered there now, taking photographs, Edgar and Conrad stayed away. The gorilla was over twenty feet tall, his face frozen in an unconvincing scowl. Tall pines, twice his size, loomed at his back. He looked trapped, confused, behind the white fence. "We'll check it out after we eat," said Conrad, pushing down Edgar's baseball cap.

"They can still see me," said Edgar.

But Conrad said he was only adjusting the hat because of the sun—and besides, he told the boy, they weren't doing anything wrong.

Edgar nodded and, as he'd been doing a lot lately, grabbed Conrad's hand. Each could feel the other's heartbeat. After a moment, Edgar, pretending to have an itch, took his hand away. Conrad whistled blithely, tapped his fingers against the tree. "Did you put your sunscreen on?"

"Yes," said Edgar—though he'd put on only a little, considering the fact that his skin hadn't returned to its former paleness and therefore seemed less vulnerable. Possibly the darker pigment was a reaction to the fire, or to spending so much time in the sun, but Edgar wondered if it might have something to do with God. He'd recently seen a documentary about churchgoing people who fell on the ground in fits of shaking until they were no longer themselves. Being *born again*, they called it. Supposedly, in a single life you could be more than one person.

Edgar needed this to be true. Why else would he be standing among all these strangers and not screaming for help? Why, when the fat woman had pushed past him, saying, "Excuse me, hon," had Edgar let her pass without grabbing her arm and whispering his secret into her ear?

His silence troubled him. He knelt down to pick up some pebbles to distract himself.

And, anyway, what *was* his secret? He hardly remembered.

Of course he remembered! But it was too painful to think about. Edgar threw the pebbles, surprised by how hard they struck a tree not far from Conrad.

Why had they come to this horrible place? All the people outside the café seemed phony, like actors. They were dangerous, too. Not dangerous as if they might hurt him, but dangerous as if they might break the world into a million pieces. Only recently had it come together again.

Edgar wanted to go home, wanted just the three of them. He and Conrad and Jack.

Still, he found his attention drawn to the phone—an old-fashioned one with a slot for money and a big black handle. It reminded him of the one in his grandmother's bedroom, from which he'd first called Conrad. His mother and the butcher had been making terrible animal sounds that night. It was distressing to think about it even now. Edgar hummed to drown out the memory—though the sound that came from his mouth was more of a grunting.

"Is that the ape?" said Conrad.

Edgar shook his head and walked distractedly toward the phone. CALL ANYWHERE IN THE U.S.A. FOR $1.00! He lingered there, stuck his fingers into the coin return.

Conrad drifted over. "What? Do you want some change, buddy?"

Was he joking? Edgar wasn't sure. "No," he said. He didn't want to hurt Conrad's feelings. Conrad had not been well lately. A person who didn't know him might think he was fine, the way he cooked and cleaned and worked in the yard just like before; the way he played checkers and told funny stories. But Edgar knew him and could tell that he was going away again. His voice had changed. His hands, too—which, when they weren't tapping, were quivery, like guinea pigs.

Edgar moved into a shady spot free of strangers. On a low bush there were huge blossoms, like hairy cupcakes the color of a sunset. He leaned in toward one. It smelled amazing. He motioned for Conrad to come over.

"Wow, pretty cool."

"Smell it," said Edgar.

Conrad did. He put his nose deep into a blossom and closed his eyes.

Edgar was glad the man was taking the flowers seriously. "What do they smell like to you?" he asked.

Conrad took a moment to consider it—and then said, "Butterscotch."

Which was exactly right. When Edgar turned his back to Conrad, it was to hide his tears.

Once, at VanDervoort Park, he'd asked his mother if they could go into the rose garden. They were all in bloom, and Edgar had said how nice it would be to smell them. But his mother had said no—and when Edgar had asked why not, she'd replied, "Because I already know what they smell like."

Which Edgar had thought a funny thing to say. Of course a person knew what roses smelled like. *Knowing* was the exact reason a person would want to do it again. But, instead, his mother had pulled him over to a bench and told him to sit still while she made some phone calls. This was long before Mr. S, the butcher, but Edgar knew she was talking to one of her initials, the way she whispered and giggled while sipping the beer she'd smuggled into the park in a paper bag.

Edgar wiped his eyes and turned back to the hairy cupcakes. People were coming close again—including the fat woman in stretchy shorts. With her thick North Jersey accent and her whipped hair and yellow-daisy decals on pink fingernails, she was particularly bothersome, reminding Edgar of another life. Plus, it was hard to ignore Conrad's hands—going a mile a minute as if a bomb were about to explode.

"Billings! Party of two!" someone shouted.

Edgar felt dizzy.

* * *

The day before, the boy had been sitting cross-legged on the floor of the living room, bathed in pink light. He often sat there in the afternoon when the sun came through the little rose-glass window.

The boy's eyes had been closed, and Conrad had watched him—the shaft of sunlight illuminating countless mites of dust, brilliant sparkles that might have been stars, the little boy a giant among them. To Conrad the boy had seemed like the Creator Himself—imagining the pink light, imagining Conrad, who was feeling thin, not quite real. He was at wit's end, without strategy. He wanted to end things; start again. He wanted Edgar to open his eyes and stop dreaming.

Suddenly he'd laughed, feeling drunk.

Maybe he was drunk. On the last shopping trip, he'd bought a couple of liters. It had been nearly two years since he'd taken a sip. He'd gone cold turkey right after Kevin.

When he joined Edgar in the pink light, the boy made no comment about Conrad's laughter—saying only, "I can smell you." After Conrad curled up on the floor, Edgar stood and walked away. A moment later, he was back with a blanket.

Conrad said he wasn't cold, but Edgar covered him anyway, suggested a nap.

"Do I need one?"

"Yes," said Edgar.

Like a distractible child, Conrad sat up. "Do you still want to go to Shamong?"

The boy didn't answer. He stood there like a statue, inscrutable—and when Conrad said, "Would you rather I tie you up?" Edgar's lips began to quiver.

"Why are you acting like this?"

"Like what?" asked Conrad.

Edgar shook his head; said he was going outside with Jack.

"Just sit with me a minute," said Conrad.

The boy hesitated. He had a pine needle in the cuff of his jeans, and Conrad reached out to remove it.

"They always get in there," said Edgar, moving away, promising he wouldn't be long.

"We'll go tomorrow," Conrad called out. "For real. Okay?"

"I didn't ask to go," Edgar shouted back, as the screen door slammed.

The next morning, though, when Edgar came into the living room dressed like a Mormon (white shirt, blue pants, a backpack slung over his shoulders), Conrad's heart had lurched.

"You're wearing your new outfit?" He'd bought it for the boy a few weeks before in Hammonton.

Edgar asked if the shirt was too big, and Conrad said it looked pretty good.

"What's the backpack for?" It was the same one the boy had arrived with.

"I always take it when I go out."

When Conrad asked what was inside, the boy said there was a book and a sketch pad, some pencils. "So I can keep myself busy if you need to do things."

Conrad felt confused as to what the boy meant. An unpleasant thought came to mind, but was interrupted by the cuckoo clock. Both he and the boy turned to it, watched the bird squeal and the woodchopper chop—the little figures putting on the same show they'd been doing since Conrad was a child, assuring him that certain things were eternal. "Let me get my coat," he said.

"You won't need a coat," the boy replied. "It's only cold in here. It's warm outside."

"Right. Plus, we're not going far." Conrad clenched his fists. Why did he keep saying this?—that the café wasn't far, that they'd be back in a few hours. It was true, of course, but the boy was smart and might think it wasn't.

Outside, Jack was whining at her post. The boy petted her and told her not to bark.

She did, of course—and as they drove away they could hear her, it seemed, for miles.

* * *

"Welcome to Mighty Joe's," the waitress said, handing them the menus.

They were in a corner booth by a window, from which Edgar could see a chicken coop, as well as a bit of the gorilla's left arm.

"Coffee?" asked the waitress.

Conrad nodded.

"And for you, young man?"

Edgar swallowed, tried to say *milk.*

"What's that?"

"He'll have some milk," said Conrad.

"You want chocolate milk, babe?" For the first time, Edgar looked up at her. She had bushy black hair with white stripes running through it. She looked like a zebra. Around her eyes were starbursts of wrinkles. She smelled soapy, but also like she had a body. She was smiling.

"Yes, please," said Edgar.

When she walked away he stared after her until he realized Conrad was saying something.

"I just need to use the restroom." Conrad looked pale. He scooted out of the booth.

Edgar stood. "I'll—"

"No, you wait here. I'll be right back."

Edgar watched the man enter the bathroom, and felt a twinge when he heard the bolt turn. Sitting down, he pushed his backpack closer to the wall, patted his pockets: in one was his fold-up knife; in the other the diamond ring. He'd wanted to take the Virgin's head as well, but it would have been noticeable in his pocket. Also, if he'd brought three things for luck, it would have made him worry even more that something bad was going to happen. Taking two things seemed almost normal.

"What'll you have, babe?" The waitress was back, setting down the drinks.

"He—he's in the bathroom," sputtered Edgar. "But . . ."

The Zebra smiled, patient.

"I—I think I know what we'll have." He'd known for weeks. "Blueberry pie, please."

"Oh, sorry, not yet," said the Zebra. "It's a little early. We've got a nice cherry, though—or I can do you a piece of strawberry-rhubarb."

Edgar wasn't ready for the change of plans. He looked up toward the overhead lamp—the light reflecting beautifully on his face. It was then that the waitress noticed something familiar about him.

"I wanted blueberry," he said quietly—seemed to be saying it to the light above him.

"I tell you what," the waitress said. "Come back in two weeks and I'll cut you an extra-big slice."

Edgar pressed down on the diamond in his pocket to keep himself from crying.

"I'll have cherry," he said.

"Good choice. And for the old man?"

"The same," said Edgar. He looked again toward the ceiling.

"Been in here before, babe?"

When Edgar said, "No," she wondered if maybe she'd seen him on television.

"You're not an actor, are you?"

Edgar turned to her, confused. "I'm not lying."

"No no no," she said. "I'm only saying you've got a nice face."

Edgar blushed, and the Zebra winked, wrinkling her eyes even more.

Star of Bethlehem, he thought. All he said, though—and very quietly—was "Thank you."

*   *   *

When Conrad came out of the bathroom, he noticed the waitress chatting with a man behind a counter, both of them looking over at Edgar.

Conrad intruded with a tight smile. "Is there a problem?"

"No," said the waitress. "Just getting your pie."

"We didn't order yet."

"Your boy did. Cherry okay?"

"His name is Edgar," Conrad said boldly.

The waitress nodded, unsure why the man was telling her this. "Can I get you something else? Oh, there he goes."

Conrad turned just as Edgar slipped out the door.

The waitress laughed at the man's startled face. "It's okay. He's probably just going out to see Mighty Joe."

"Fuck," hissed Conrad—apologizing immediately. "I just—I should check on him." He tried to walk slowly as he crossed the room, uncertain now why he'd brought the boy here. Was it this—what was happening now? Exposure. Loss. To let the world steal back what he'd refused to relinquish.

Or was this supposed to be the beginning? Day One. Father and son at a café, eating pie, immune to doubt. *Your boy,* the waitress had said.

Conrad proceeded cautiously, but as he neared the door he began to run, shoving aside an old man.

"Watch out," someone scolded.

Outside there was a crowd. Conrad tried not to push, but he did. "Have you seen a little boy?" he asked. His tone was sharp, though, so no one answered. When he was in the clear, he stopped.

There was Edgar. Not gone, not running. He was standing by the white fence, looking up at the gorilla. Conrad laughed, turned to the crowd and offered a belated "Excuse me." They stared at him. The waitress he'd been chatting with had stepped outside, too. "Everything okay?"

Conrad nodded. As he moved toward the boy, he noticed the fresh paint on the statue. Someone had touched it up since the last time he'd been here. The lips too red; the teeth too bright. Edgar was perfectly still, looking up at the sculpture. Conrad didn't wish to disturb him yet. He was no doubt reading the sign on the gorilla's chest.

Hello, my name is Mighty Joe.

The simian had once stood on the boardwalk at Wildwood. The family who owned the café had bought the monster at auction, put it up as a memorial to their son. Conrad was pleased by Edgar's interest.

Joe was the boy's name. A boxer. *Who now lives in the kingdom of heaven,* the sign read. Or something to that effect. Conrad moved closer.

Joe was not only mighty in his appearance, but also in his courage. He is truly missed by his family and friends. He is always in our thoughts and prayers. My job is to look up to heaven from time to time and say, "Hey, Joe, we will always love you!"

Vulgar, Conrad had always thought—death by Walt Disney, working-class horseshit—and yet, walking toward the ape grave, he felt deeply moved. He knew that Edgar would feel the same. Together they would stand in silence, seal their vows. Conrad stepped into the shadow of the ape and put his hand on the boy's shoulder.

Edgar spun around—his eyes aflame.

"Terrible," Conrad tried to say, but before the word was halfway out, Edgar was upon him, knocking his tiny fists against Conrad's stomach and ribs. Screaming, too—a horrendous bird screech, not unlike the sound he'd made the first few weeks when he'd been locked inside Kevin's bedroom. The memory paralyzed Conrad. For several seconds he let the boy strike, even though the blows were painful.

Conrad sensed the crowd watching. He grabbed Edgar's arms. "Enough!"

The boy swung his legs, kicking. Whatever words were coming from Edgar's mouth Conrad chose not to understand. After such generosity on both their parts, it was impossible that the boy could be saying, *I hate you. I hate you!*

"Are you all right, son?" someone said, coming close.

"I'm not your son!" Edgar shouted viciously.

"Apologize to the man," ordered Conrad—and when Edgar's only response was a prolonged howl, Conrad slapped him. The boy stumbled and fell.

Then there was silence everywhere—in the crowd, but most profoundly from Edgar. Conrad turned to the onlookers, assured them that everything was okay.

He turned back to the boy—who wasn't moving. "Edgar? Stop playing." He touched the boy with his foot, and only then saw the stone near the child's head.

"It's fine," Conrad said to no one. "It's fine." This was nothing like what had happened before, he told himself. There was no blood. *"Edgar?"* He knelt down and picked up the boy, whose face had drained of color.

Muttering intruders gathered round. "He's fine," said Conrad, moving toward the truck—and though the ground was level, he had a sense of falling. A falling that, if he were lucky, might go on forever—no bottom, no crash. The body still warm in his arms.

"Stop pretending," he said to a limp Edgar. And then to the crowd: "He's just kidding. He does that. *Edgar!*"

The waitress with the black-and-white hair was there—her hands glued to her face.

"His stuff!" she said, dashing back into the café. But, by the time she'd made it outside again, it was too late. The truck was pulling away, trailed by a ghost of exhaust.

She unzipped the backpack, pulled out the sunscreen, the Jane Austen, the sketch pad. Her hands shook as she rustled through the pages.

Sara Billings was written on the inside of the paperback—and, in the sketch pad, below a drawing of an orange moon and a scattering of red stars: *This book is the property of Edgar Allan Fini.*

"Holy shit," said the Zebra, fumbling for her phone.

66

Keep It Clean

The room was too bright, the dim Victorian lamps pointless below ceiling panels of lightning-strike fluorescence.

Lucy tried the lid, but it was locked. Not that she wanted to see his face; she just wanted to be sure he was in there.

"Of course he's in there," said Ron. "Sit down."

He'd made her come to the wake in a wheelchair.

"I have an appointment with Anita," she said, confused.

"That was yesterday," said Ron.

Lucy tried the lid again. It was absurdly large. Why did he need such an enormous casket? The last time she'd seen him he'd been so small. It seemed a waste to put him inside a giant refrigerator. She wondered if someone had at least combed his hair. Slicked it back with grease. Her father had always used a goop that smelled like cinnamon and motor oil. Sometimes, when he'd come too close, the grease had smeared against her cheek.

Her father, she had to keep reminding herself. It was her father inside the box.

She sat in the chair and glanced behind her, scratching a weary eye across the room. Hardly anyone had shown up to bid the old man goodbye. A few withered truckers from the union; none of their wives. Some neighbors from West Mill—a handful of which Lucy remembered from her childhood. She nodded, kept her distance.

"What do you have there?" asked Ron.

"Nothing," said Lucy, not recalling why she'd brought the little rubber alien. "I just need a few minutes alone—okay?"

Ron let go of the chair, and Lucy wheeled herself closer to the casket. Some other Lucy might have spit on it. Even the lilies were screaming, sticking out their tongues. Lucy's fire was gone, though. She was a dead star, a giant piece of lint.

In some ways it was a relief. It had been a long fight, a long fucking fight. The great resistance. Everything, always, a battle, her whole life. It had started here, with him. He'd given her her rage. Rage that had somehow found its way to forgiveness—but too late.

You're a good girl, her mother used to say afterwards. *It's not your fault.*

Lucy reached out a hand to wipe a smudge off the silver casket, but only made it worse—leaving a smear of sweaty fingerprints.

Why did the same things keep happening? You loved people and they went away. She wasn't thinking of her father—whom she couldn't claim to love, even now. Neither was she thinking of Edgar. She was thinking of her mother, Elena, who'd made, on her deathbed, a single request: that Lucy visit her grave and keep it clean.

"Yes," Lucy had said. "I promise."

Not once, though, since her mother's burial, had she gone to the cemetery. She'd been a child when she'd made that promise. What had she known then about loyalty or time?

The butcher stepped forward, held her arm while she wept.

Her parents were gone. It hurt more than she would have expected—and then it *really* hurt. A painful contraction that made her jackknife forward. *"Ahhh."*

"Is it? Are you?" babbled Ron. "Is it the baby?"

"Motherfucker!" cried Lucy, holding her belly.

Some old neighbors from West Mill shook their heads, remembering the foul-mouthed girl running from Walter and Elena's house. It seemed, to them, that nothing had changed. This girl, that girl: one and the same.

"Motherfucker!" she cries again, as Ron wheels her out the door.

67

Seven Bridges

Conrad drove north, toward Tabernacle. He knew of a small shop there called the Black Bear, run by a slack-jawed geezer who never got up from his chair, pointed at things, only accepted cash. The road was clear of traffic, and Conrad took his liberty, hard-pedaling the gas until the old engine sounded like a helicopter. A rising wind tattered the clouds. Shadows jumped, and little gray birds burst in and out of the light like buckshot.

"Shhh," Conrad said to the boy, though the boy had said nothing. He was lying peacefully across the seat, jostled now and then by ruts in the road. Conrad turned left at the old wooden sign nailed to a creosote-drenched telephone pole: SODA AND SUNDRIES. He'd buy a blanket, some snacks, a few bottles of water. Sunscreen, maybe a tarp. He had plenty of gas.

"Fuck," he said as he came to a stop—the panic flashing hot and white like a migraine. He bit the insides of his cheeks and stepped out of the truck. "Right back," he said, gently closing the door.

* * *

After Tabernacle, he drove east, and then dipped into the Wharton Forest— but not toward the cabin. The boy was covered with one of the blankets. Conrad had always wanted to show him the Mullica, that great snake of a river. Had imagined a day trip on a canoe, all the way down to where the Ice Age waters emptied into the Great Bay.

There was no time now, though, for such meandering. Conrad swung back up to Old Barnegat Road and headed toward Chatsworth. He should take the boy to a hospital. But perhaps they'd already blocked the major exits—Route 9, Route 72, certainly the on-ramps to the Parkway. Of course, within the Barrens there were a million little roads, and no one knew them better than Conrad.

This was *his* place, *his* land. He'd been brought up to consider himself a kind of lord here. His family had once owned much more than nine hundred acres. They'd had thousands. They'd owned mines, too—bog iron, and later titanium and rare earth minerals. They'd owned sand pits. So much of the concrete in New Jersey and New York had started with gravel owned by a Billings. Hadn't some of it been used to build the Lincoln Tunnel?

"Did I tell you that?" He touched Edgar's leg.

The Billings family were part of this land's history. They were Pineys through and through. His great-grandfather had been at Lakehurst when the *Hindenburg* had crashed. In fact, he'd been holding one of the tethers when the dirigible had burst into flames. As a child Conrad had seen a piece of the charred rope, which his great-grandfather kept in a cloisonné box. When he'd first shown the relic to Conrad—asking him, "Do you know what this is, little man?"—Conrad had started to cry, thinking it was his mother's hair, which she sometimes wore in braids.

* * *

Past Chatsworth, there were more cars—most of them coming from the opposite direction. Tourists, no doubt, going home. Conrad found himself annoyed by the traffic. So many of the people who came here for the day did nothing but sully the place. They left behind trash, stole orchids, poisoned the birds with potato chips.

As Conrad drove through sparkling pines, he was unsure where he should go. The Blue Hole wasn't far—the place his grandfather had forced him to swim, testing his bravery. For all its beauty, the Barrens was an underworld, a desert over demon-infested waters.

Maybe he should drive to one of the great pygmy plains, with its stunted trees and blue sugar sand. The plains tended to spook people and were nearly always deserted. There were also the tunnels under the old brick factory near Batsto. Conrad unfolded the map in his head. All he wanted was to find a sweet spot where he could be alone with the boy for a little while longer—maybe just for the night.

Whatever time remained was grace.

It was not divine grace, though; it was cold and bureaucratic. Like the grace his family might give to debtors who couldn't pay their bills. *Thirty days.*

For Conrad it was much less. He could hear his luck running out. Something stuck to one of the tires was clicking like a roulette wheel.

Near Tuckerton, Conrad winced at the huge boxy houses, with their fountains and lawns and mechanized wrought-iron gates. Sickened by the blight of humans, he drove south, toward the bay. The bay was pure, protected. As he pulled onto Seven Bridges Road, the sun did a sly trick—oozing from a cloud like honey from a broken jar.

* * *

He'd done so much wrong. Impossible to undo—or simply too late.

After he'd driven over the first three bridges and was heading into the marshlands, where terns were diving for silversides, he began to cry. At one point, he had to stop the truck for a diamondback terrapin crossing the road. Upland were cherry trees, their wilting white blossoms dripping with caterpillars.

When he pulled into Tammy's Pedals and Paddles, it seemed effortless. It was late in the afternoon; there were no other customers. He rented a simple aluminum jon boat—an eight-footer with oars.

"Life preservers?" asked the teenaged girl running the store.

"Sure," said Conrad.

"How many?"

"One."

"It's extra," the girl said. "And you have to leave a deposit."

Conrad handed her his credit card.

* * *

The fifth bridge was a narrow wooden one, single lane—and so was the sixth. The truck thudded over the planks, and at each crossing Conrad put his hand on the boy to keep him steady. Out on Crab Island, you could see the ruins of the Stinkhouse.

There was no seventh bridge. Conrad remembered this now as he came to the end of the road. The seventh bridge was an imaginary one—never built. The idea had been to let drivers cross over to Dog Island, giving them access to the beaches north of Absecon. But the engineers could never get it right. When Conrad was a child, there'd been half a bridge here, ending in the middle of the bay. Now there was nothing.

Conrad dragged the boat to the water, and then went back for Edgar. After setting him in the space between the two seats, he gave the boat a good push to get it through a snag of eelgrass. He watched it rock on the waters of the inlet, which separated the bay from the ocean.

Across the water, past Brigantine, Atlantic City rose in the hazy late-afternoon light like a fairy town. Edgar would like that. The boat, pulled by a current, was already ten feet out. Conrad let it go a little farther, before wading through the shallows to join the boy. The tide was slack, and Conrad had no trouble rowing from the inlet into the bay.

A few fishing boats were heading back to Mystic. When Conrad reached the center of the bay, he pulled in the oars and steeled himself with a slug of bourbon he'd purchased at the Black Bear. He took off his shoes, and as he swung his legs over the side of the boat, Edgar opened his eyes and said, "What are you doing?"

68

Rest

At first, he thought the tattered clouds were part of the dream he was having about rags in the window of a washing machine. Then, he turned and saw Conrad, who was climbing down a ladder—maybe after picking crabapples.

But it wasn't any of these things. Edgar lifted himself on his elbows, even though Conrad said, "Careful," and tried to stop him. They were on a boat in the middle of a huge circle of greenish water. You could see weeds at the bottom, as if through a magnifying glass. You could even see some fish. In the distance, a fin broke through the surface. Edgar touched the side of his head where there was a fierce throbbing, and discovered a bump. "Oh," he said, confused.

He recalled the zebra and the ape, though not much else. When he tried to ask Conrad where they were—and why—the question came out wrong.

"Did we have our pie?" he said. And then: "Why are you crying?"

Conrad shook his head, pretended he wasn't. He hid a glass bottle in a bag, and then pulled out some water.

"I can do it," said Edgar, when Conrad tried to hold his head and put the bottle to his mouth like a baby.

The water was warm but tasted good, and Edgar drained half the bottle in a single slug. He wiped his mouth and looked around again. When he breathed he could hear himself doing it. It was like they were in some kind of auditorium where sounds were amplified—and there was something about the rasp of his breath and the slap of tiny waves against the metal boat that seemed to be coming from far away and close at the same time. It felt like church, or Percocet. Plus, the light was huge, doubled by the water—and somehow this made it hard to speak.

"I'm glad you're okay," said Conrad—a comment that only added to Edgar's confusion.

"Why are we . . . ?" The question was absorbed by the glare. Edgar squinted, tried to see the shore. "Where's the truck?"

Conrad was quiet for a long time, and then said, "Edgar."

Edgar, being right there, didn't feel the need to answer.

"I thought . . ." said Conrad.

After another spell of silence, the man seemed to wake up. He started digging again in the paper sack, as if whatever he wanted to say had fallen in there. "We didn't—we didn't eat." His hands were awful, rattling some wax paper as he unwrapped two slices of pie. "Blueberry."

Edgar recalled the lady at the café telling him there wasn't any blueberry, and when he mentioned this to Conrad, Conrad said he'd bought it somewhere else. "You were sleeping."

It was only then that Edgar noticed the blanket over him. He pulled it off because he was hot. But then immediately he felt cold.

Conrad pushed the pie toward him.

Edgar desperately wanted to be back in his room, or rolled up in a ball behind the tilted bookshelf—a thing he'd stopped doing, but which his body hungered for now.

They both took little bird bites of the pie, which wasn't very good. Edgar pushed his away. "I don't want to be here." The sun was slipping down, dragging color from the clouds: pink streamers and orange patches of gleaming fish scale. Edgar was still trying to understand the water. Toward the horizon the circular bay narrowed, and then there was a ruffly white line, after which the water opened again into an immense field of blue.

"What is that?" asked Edgar.

"What are you pointing at?"

"That white line." Even from a distance, you could hear it hissing.

"Breakers," said Conrad. "It's the ocean."

Edgar didn't understand. "What do you mean, the ocean?" He touched his head where the bump was. "I want to go home. Can we go home? Conrad? We should go home."

Edgar, realizing that he'd said this three times, fell silent. He waited, and then waited some more, but Conrad didn't pick up the oars, which seemed to be how the boat worked. "Where's my hat?" He suddenly realized it wasn't on his head. It was his Devil Hunters cap, and he didn't want to lose it. "Is it in the truck?"

"I'm sure it is," said Conrad, as if he weren't sure at all—or didn't care.

Edgar squinted against the light, feeling dizzy. He asked Conrad to check his forehead. "I think I have a fever."

"Me, too," said Conrad. He dipped his hand into the water. "Maybe we should take a swim."

Edgar ignored this comment, even as Conrad began to unbutton his shirt.

*   *   *

In the sky the colored streamers had multiplied—all of them pointing toward a single spot on the horizon. "Sit down," said Edgar, because Conrad was standing now, taking off his pants. The sharp light cut his face into angles—long shadowed creases. He looked like a piece of origami.

He held out his hand. "Come in with me."

Edgar shook his head.

Conrad stared at the shore and then turned away and dove, rocking the boat. Edgar could see his wobbly form moving through the weeds. When he came up, he was farther out, closer to the inlet. Edgar shouted, but Conrad went under again—and when his head popped up a second time, it seemed no bigger than an orange. He was swimming toward the breakers.

Edgar kept shouting, even though it made the bump on his head more painful. When he took up the oars and tried to row, he went in a circle before he managed to get his arms in synch and navigate in the right direction. Conrad had turned and was waving—either saying hello or goodbye or gesturing for Edgar to stop. And then he was gone.

Edgar rowed as best he could, but a willful current kept turning him. When Conrad suddenly appeared beside the boat, Edgar's breathlessness succumbed to tears.

The man's breath was jagged, too. "I was just swimming, kiddo."

Edgar shook his head furiously. "I saw a shark."

"No," said Conrad.

"Yes. *I saw it.*"

"Probably a ray."

"What's a ray?"

"Manta ray." Conrad spread his arms. "They have wings. Pointy. Sometimes they break the surface."

"Fish don't have wings."

A few lights had come on at the shore, which made Edgar realize how low the sun was, and how much of the world was already in shadow. He told Conrad to get in the boat. He held out his hand.

When Conrad didn't take it, Edgar said, "Please."

"I'm fine here."

"Conrad—*please.* I want to give you something."

"I can't come with you," Conrad said.

"Where am I going?" asked Edgar—and when he got no answer, he asked if they were in trouble.

"No."

"Yes we are."

"Yes," said Conrad.

"I don't care," said Edgar—and this time when he extended his hand, Conrad took it and climbed aboard.

"We can row in now," said Edgar.

"What is it you wanted to give me?" asked Conrad.

Edgar blushed. He didn't have anything. It had been a trick to get Conrad back in the boat. "I don't . . ."

"It's okay."

"I left my backpack at the restaurant."

Conrad nodded.

"With my book. With my name in it."

Edgar was crying again.

"It's okay. Look at me. It's okay."

The surface of the bay was now painted with splashes of color—confusing and unreal. Conrad's eyes seemed very blue—and he had that face of his, almost too sad to look at. Edgar wished he had something to offer. He touched his pocket where he had the little knife.

But since the knife had come from Conrad, it wouldn't be a real gift.

He reached into his other pocket and pulled out the diamond—which he clutched in his fist for several seconds before holding it out toward Conrad.

"No, that's yours."

"Really. I want you to have it."

"*Shhh,*" said Conrad.

"I'm not crying because I don't want to," said Edgar. "Take it." He shook his hand, not caring if his generosity looked like anger. "*Take it.*"

* * *

The water was dark now, and Edgar understood that they wouldn't be row-ing to shore. The lights around the bay were sparse and seemed to have no effect on the blackness of the water. Buoys with reflectors bobbed in Little Egg Inlet, catching the stray beam of a faraway lighthouse.

Edgar's head was throbbing, and he was still worried about the breakers. In the darkness they seemed much whiter. Louder, too. They were definitely closer than before.

"I think we're drifting."

"Tide maybe," said Conrad. He was lying down and didn't sound con-cerned. He told Edgar to lie down, too.

But the toy world back on land was impossible to turn away from: tooth-pick trees; traffic lights small as earrings; tiny cars moving across a faraway bridge. Closer, there were flashing red lights, like something bad had hap-pened. Every once in a while you could hear a voice or a dog—but the sound was echoey and insubstantial.

"What about Jack?"

"He'll be okay."

"Because we'll go back soon." Edgar made this a statement, to limit Con-rad's authority.

Little waves rocked the boat—but it wasn't calming like the rocking Edgar sometimes did with his own body; it was more like someone pushing you, or slapping you in the face. Edgar felt his mouth filling with saliva. He leaned over the side of the boat.

"Are you okay?"

"I don't know."

"Lie down."

"Maybe I'm sick from the waves."

"Come here."

Edgar didn't resist as Conrad pulled him down to the floor.

* * *

Edgar clenched and unclenched his fists, silently counting each squeeze. He was small enough to fit comfortably between the two raised planks that served as seats—but Conrad had to pass his feet under the lower planks like shackles. They both lay on their backs, looking up at the sky. Sleep came and went in starts—sudden fallings and sharp awakenings that seemed to follow a set pattern, but was as indecipherable as some foreign language. The stars were jumpy, shifting position, and Edgar couldn't tell if the buzzing he heard came from them or from inside his head. It was very confusing—and at the same time familiar, as if he'd been here before.

Now and then Conrad spoke, talking about serious things (his grandfather, his father, Kevin), or just little things, like the fish in the bay (gobies and wrasses and bluefish). Sometimes he hummed a song that he'd sung to Edgar when Edgar had been sick from the little pink pills.

If it weren't for the leaping confusion inside the boy's heart, being here with Conrad might have seemed almost normal, like a scene from some movie about fathers and sons. Maybe even the leaping confusion was normal. How would Edgar know, who'd only ever had a ghost for a father?

"I'm sorry," he said.

"What for?"

Edgar wasn't sure. Instead of answering, he reached out his hand.

He should just have left it at that—gone to sleep holding Conrad's fingers. But he couldn't stop thinking about the breakers. When he lifted his head to look, he was sure they were closer—and he said so.

"Really, Edgar. We're fine."

"We're not fine."

Conrad grunted and crawled to the stern of the jon boat. He opened a little box and pulled out a piece of metal shaped like a mushroom—which he dropped into the water.

"Is that an anchor?"

"Yes. Happy now?"

Edgar was not—but at least they would stay in one spot. "I can say things," he said defensively. "If I'm scared." Conrad's hands were dripping with dark water—that in some other story might have been blood.

"Yes. Of course." The man's fingers touched the back of the boy's neck. "You can say anything, kiddo."

"I'm not a coward."

"No," said Conrad. "You're not."

Edgar tried to breathe, gauging the truth or untruth of this. He closed his eyes, and when he was settled again on the floor Conrad clutched him. Edgar didn't pull away. He could hear Conrad crying, so he clutched him back.

Maybe it was right and maybe it was wrong—Edgar wasn't sure.

Either way, it was all pretty terrible.

* * *

The clouds had blown offstage, and the stars were brighter. Edgar held his hands above his face. They were white again, like before.

He wasn't another boy. He was only Edgar.

And he was selfish, the way he wanted people to love him. He blushed now with a ferocity like fever—his whole body burning with shame. Was it possible a person could have too much love in his life? Could you get sick from it, like from eating too much sugar? As the boat lifted on a swell, Edgar could hear the metal mushroom scraping the bottom of the bay. They were still drifting.

Edgar wondered how far out they were, but he didn't get up to look. Not because he wasn't allowed, but because an invisible weight held him down. Maybe it had something to do with his head, which seemed to be getting heavier and heavier the more he thought about things.

"Are you asleep?"

Conrad said he wasn't.

"Do you know what that one's called?" Edgar pointed toward a pulsing star in the center of the sky.

Conrad aligned his eyes with the boy's finger. "No—what is it?"

"I don't know," said Edgar. "I thought you knew."

"No—sorry. Rest," said Conrad. He pulled the boy closer.

And though the man's body was a mystery, Edgar folded himself into it, as he'd folded himself into those other bodies—which had been mysteries, too.

When he told Conrad that his head hurt, the man caressed his hair. "Go to sleep."

But Edgar's heart was racing. "What happened?" he said.

"When?"

"At the restaurant."

"You hit me," said Conrad, turning his face toward Edgar.

"No I didn't."

"Yes. You said you hated me."

Edgar had once said the same thing to his mother. The memory made him sick. The tears fell, as before.

"I won't tell them, Conrad."

"Okay, *shhh*."

"If they come, I mean. We don't have to say goodbye."

"Who said anything about goodbye?" whispered Conrad. "You rest."

* * *

The boat moved steadily on the waves, like the burrowing snout of an animal. Everything was quiet now. Even the sound of the anchor scraping the sand had stopped—which must have meant that the water was deeper. Conrad had pulled the blanket up too high; it was over their heads.

Edgar shut his eyes. He was supposed to rest.

To rest, his grandmother had said, was to go home.

Everything was fading. If there were sirens, the bay blew them back toward shore. When Conrad made a small sound like a baby, Edgar sleepily patted him—meaning, *I won't let them hurt you.*

69

Beauty

Lucy sat by the window, with the curtains open. Her pink robe glowed—and in her arms the little body wriggled. It was hungry again, its dumpling fist knocking against Lucy's ribs.

She looked away.

In the mirror, she saw a painting—a stony-faced woman with one breast exposed. She'd seen something like it before, in a museum with Frank; had shrugged it off as Old World porn. But Frank had disagreed, saying, "No, babe, it's not just a tit. She's potent and she's not afraid to show it."

Lucy, though, felt frightened, sitting in the plush nursing chair by the window. What frightened her wasn't the child's coloring (Mediterranean skin, black honey hair) or its willful shrieks; what frightened Lucy was how much she had to offer it, how her milk flowed freely, like wealth.

Words slipped from her mouth, too, before she could stop them. "You hungry, beauty?" Though part of her wanted to ignore the child, she found it impossible to be unkind.

The suckling felt good, and she caressed the baby's head.

Learning kindness late in life was a kind of torture. The pain often came from the past, from kindnesses withheld. The knife was particularly sharp when those who most deserved your kindness were long gone. And unless you wanted to die of sorrow, you had to give this unspent kindness to those you loved less.

Lucy tried to keep the people from her life in separate camps, keep *now* from *before,* the living from the dead. It wasn't easy, though—nearly impossible, really, when your body was mostly fluid, and the sun touched the skin of something impossibly lovely.

This impossible loveliness didn't have a name yet. Lucy had agreed to a christening, though, and needed to come up with something soon.

The butcher would have liked *Angela*, his mother's name, but didn't suggest this to Lucy. "Whatever you want is fine," he'd told her. "But hurry, or the boys won't know what to tattoo on their arms"—nuzzling his face against the baby's as he'd said this. "Isn't that right, gorgeous? *Yes, you are. Yes, you are.*"

The child had Lucy's pale green eyes set in the butcher's proud swarthiness.

Now he appeared in the doorway of the bedroom. "I'm off to the shop," he said, catching Lucy's eye in the mirror—and then her breast. "That looks nice."

"Pervert," she said.

Ron smiled and told her to watch her language, or his daughter might end up with a mouth like her mother's—a mouth he stepped into the room to kiss.

"Look at that hair," he said, touching the baby's black curls. "Look at those fingers." When the little hand grabbed his meaty thumb, he sighed, and his eyelids dipped as if he'd just been shot with heroin.

The drug, though, was blood—something Lucy, growing up as she had, had never really understood. But Ron was another Italian; his métier was family. Sometimes Lucy was so grateful to him that she could hardly bear it, and was glad for the hours he spent at the shop.

"See you tonight, babes"—after which he left them with a chaste kiss to Lucy's breast.

* * *

Thank God it was a girl.

A boy would have been harder. A boy would have made the central fact more glaring—the central fact being that the child was not Edgar.

Not Edgar. Those words, with Lucy for so long now, in response to every kid on the street, every star, every crumb on the table, had now found their final resting place. Had they come to rest in a boy, how would she have been able to love it? The green eyes were bad enough. In addition to being Lucy's, they were also Edgar's.

A girl seemed less of a thief.

Lucy had planned to parse out her love, deliver it in increments—but it had happened all at once. As soon as you fed one of these things, you felt the clever red thread that bound you to it eternally.

As Lucy nursed the girl, she noted that it looked a bit like Frank, even like Florence—something about the brow—and it was a shock when she realized her error. The child shared no blood with either of them.

Still, she'd decided to make the nursery in Florence's old room. Not that they were staying here much longer. Ron wanted them in a new house by Christmas.

Maybe they should reconsider, though. There was something here—in the walls, in the floors, in the white tiles stolen from the Lincoln Tunnel. *History* was a terrible word, but it had to be faced. Lucy recalled how, after Frank's death, the old woman had performed a kind of miracle. Their world had been destroyed—and while Lucy and Pio would have been content to burn down what little remained, the old woman had somehow rebuilt the house. The foundation had been Edgar. Maybe it could be done again, with this child.

Not *start over*—but *continue*.

*　*　*

The early white blossoms had withered, and Ferryfield was purple with lilac and azalea. As summer staged its miracles, the dramatis personae arrived, one by one, to visit the baby.

Anita Lester came. She'd of course been there for the delivery. It had been a difficult labor, with a fair amount of blood. The butcher had fainted. Hard to believe that it had only been a week ago. But Lucy and the baby were healthy now—and when Anita came by it was mainly to bring crumb cake or gossip.

Henry and Netty, hearing of the messy delivery, had brought a new set of sheets to replace the birth-stained ones—and then they'd stayed for tea. "Good she doesn't have red hair," Henry had remarked of the baby.

Lucy had lifted an eyebrow. "Why is that?"

Henry simply said, "Unlucky."

"Your luck begins now," chirped Netty, in an attempt to deflect Henry's faux pas. She reached for a shopping bag. "Look! We brought you towels, too."

There were other gifts, as well—some of them surprisingly intimate—from women with whom Lucy was not particularly close. Celeste from the salon arrived with a homemade salve for sore nipples, and Florence's old friend Honey Fasinga brought an expensive cream for stretch marks. "I thought you never had children," Lucy said—and Honey said, "That's right," explaining that she used the cream on her face.

People were clueless and—it couldn't be avoided—kind. In addition to the cream, Honey bestowed a velvet bed jacket with a faux-fur collar—something, Lucy imagined, Joan Crawford would have worn. Either that or a pole dancer. Honey assured Lucy that such jackets were *in again*.

"Plus," said Honey, "it's so much better to receive visitors in something like this than in *that*. What do you call that?" She stuck a bony finger into one of the holes in Lucy's moth-bitten Pogues T-shirt. When Lucy explained that the T-shirt had sentimental value, Honey said, "Be that as it may, fashion imprinting begins at birth."

* * *

"You could have died," Anita had told her. "It was a very dumb thing not to go to the hospital."

"I know," said Lucy.

"Now you have to think about . . ."

"I know," said Lucy.

The *future* was a difficult word, too. There was no need to rub it in.

Anita pushed back the baby's curls. "She's a looker."

"Yes," agreed Lucy. "God help her."

* * *

The girl had sucked like a pro and was sleeping now. Lucy put her in the crib.

The house was so quiet. Lucy wandered in pretense of aimlessness, though she knew where she was headed.

In Florence's room, she stared at the old black telephone. She picked it up and listened to the dial tone—the sound like a tunnel. Sometimes she could hear indistinct voices, faraway conversations, laughter. She sat on the old woman's bed where she'd delivered the baby. It had been an exhausting six-hour labor; Lucy had been delirious—glimpsing Edgar in the doorway. She'd seen other children, too—kids from the billboard in Times Square. She'd seen Olivia—the dark-haired, bespectacled girl, whose mother had shown Lucy not only a picture of the child at six, but also an age-progressed one at sixteen.

Of course, Olivia in the doorway had still been six—Edgar still eight. Every child had been white—and they'd just stood there, silently, as Lucy had screamed and pushed. By the time it was over, though, the ghosts had cleared out, leaving behind only flesh and blood.

Lucy hung up the black telephone and went to the closet—pulling out the cardboard box marked *Florence*. From it she took the blue glass cup, along with a new candle.

The old woman and her flickering votives, her saints, her girlhood hair in a black silk box—she suddenly seemed, to Lucy, more than what she'd been in life. Not just a balding, semi-illiterate biddy in a faded housedress. She seemed wise—some kind of sad genius whose art had had something to do with those tiny fires.

Of course, the dead tricked you. They came back, telling you they were someone other than who they'd been; tried to improve themselves in your eyes.

Still, why not wish them well, even if you had no hope of seeing them again?

Lucy's affection for the dead, though, was not distributed equally. When she told Ron that she loved him, she said it loudly, so that Frank would hear it—and when she said the same words to the baby, it was quietly, so that Edgar would not.

The bureau was dusty, and Lucy wiped the surface with her T-shirt, before setting down the candle and lighting it with one of the chopstick-length matches Edgar had liked to play with. She held her palm over the flame, and had no idea what her life was, or meant.

Not two seconds later, she heard a strange sound—*Chuk! Chuk! Chuk!* It sounded like a chicken or a held-in sneeze. When she went to the window, she saw the squirrel in the tree. *Chuk! Chuk!*

Then, she looked down and noticed the police car in front of the house. "No."

She didn't want to know. She returned to her bedroom and grabbed Beauty—after which she ran downstairs, and out the back door.

70

The Fish

Edgar woke to a bang, but could see nothing. He shielded his eyes against a chaos of light. Against the bottom of the boat, Conrad's foot was flailing desperately. Edgar reached out to help and immediately pulled back.

It wasn't Conrad, but a silver oblong the size of a flattened football. Slits by its head opened and closed, and it was flopping with such force that it flew into the air. There was blood by its mouth.

For a moment the creature was still, and Edgar noted the terrible glass eye staring at him. Then it flipped again, as if trying to cook itself against the warm metal. When Edgar grabbed it, it slipped away and slammed into the side of the boat.

"Stop," shouted Edgar. He couldn't help the thing unless it calmed down.

The fish seemed to understand. Only the mouth moved now, releasing a thin stream of red. Edgar spotted the hook—which he deftly removed by holding the fish down.

When it thrashed again, Edgar scooped it up and tossed it over the side. It darted under and away with a graceful flick, as if it had become another creature entirely. A red thread trailed behind it, dissolving instantly.

It was only then that Edgar realized he was alone in the boat.

He looked into the water where he'd thrown the fish. A panic seized his throat.

"Conrad?"

Everywhere was boiling light. As Edgar wiped the blood from his hands, he noticed the rope at the front of the boat. It was cut, and the anchor was missing. Edgar touched his pocket. The knife was gone, too. The diamond, though, sat on the plank, beside Conrad's shoes.

When Edgar looked out at the water, it took him a moment to understand that the glittering oval in the distance was the bay, and that he was on the other side of the breakers.

"Conrad!"

Edgar grabbed the oars. And though he rowed furiously, some invisible conveyer belt dragged him backward, farther into the ocean. He screamed, squinting into the glare.

He howled and barked and worked his arms, until a huge black shape materialized on the water. It cut across the glittering surface, blocking the sun. Edgar's tiny jon boat fell into shadow. The black thing roared and came closer. It was as big as a house. Someone waved from the porch.

Edgar let go of the oars, sobbing.

The house hovered above him now—and a voice said, "Come."

He felt like a baby again at the bottom of the world. He stood and reached out his arms, just as the person on the porch of the floating house leaned down to raise him up.

71

The Clearing

Far above her, black birds glided through a white haze. At her feet, a cluster of yellow mushrooms. Ron was shouting from the house.

Lucy didn't answer, though. She wanted to stay here with the baby a little longer.

"What you doing, Mrs. Feen?"

Toni-Ann stepped into the clearing, breathing heavily. Like Lucy, she'd run into the woods when she'd seen the police car.

"Why are you following me, Toni-Ann?"

"Not following you. I didn't know you were here." Toni-Ann looked down. She looked at the leaf dust and the yellow mushrooms—but she refused to look at the baby.

"Lucy!" Ron's voice was louder.

Toni-Ann banged her fists together anxiously. "They arrest me?"

"No, sweetie." Lucy tried to smile, but already she could hear the footsteps.

Toni-Ann made a sound like an owl. Possibly she was crying.

Lucy only shook her head.

72

Chicks

Edgar said nothing to the fisherman. He was unable to speak.

The floating house had turned out to be a boat, and the person on the porch an old man who smelled of sardines. The man had sandpaper hands and a calico beard like the pelt of a guinea pig. When he'd first lifted Edgar aboard, Edgar had hugged the man, thinking it was Conrad.

The next thing he remembered was something awful under his nose, like ammonia. Edgar had pulled away, but the man had persisted, saying it was only spirits of hartshorn. "From deer bones," he explained, making things worse.

The boy was grateful, though, for the blanket and the tea, and for the fact that the man had turned the boat around and was headed toward shore. When he asked if Edgar was alone out here, Edgar looked back at where he'd been. The abandoned jon boat was barely visible—a flash of silver lost in the sword-fight light on the surface of the water.

"What's your name, young fellow?"

"You live around here?"

"Where are your folks?"

"Are you deaf? *Boy.* Can you hear me?"

Edgar was mortified that he couldn't answer.

"It's okay, just breathe," the man said, because someone—Edgar slowly realized it was himself—was gasping.

The man poured out more tea. It tasted like smoke and moved inside the tin cup like it was part of the ocean.

Edgar watched the old man steer. His fingers were unwashed parsnips, and now and then he used one to scratch inside a tufty ear. Florence had said that Jesus was a fisherman.

At the thought, Edgar checked his pocket. The ring was still there. He gripped it as a tangle of birds circled overhead. Nothing seemed real. The first words he spoke cracked in his throat.

"Twenty-one."

"Twenty-one what?"

The man patted the boy's face. "Tell me."

But Edgar could manage no more.

* * *

There were police and lights and plain-clothed men with guns; people talking on phones and into radios; static and briefcases and rustling paper. A woman with a thermos and a clipboard sat with Edgar inside what seemed to be a makeshift trailer. The woman's hair was wet and smelled of shampoo. She tried to calm the boy, to stop him from rocking. What she said was friendly, but seemed recorded. The main questions, repeated again and again: "Have you been hurt?" "Who were you with?" "Can you describe him?"

A man in a yellow T-shirt examined Edgar's clothing, and then his hair and hands and fingernails—even inside his mouth. There were tweezers and scrapers and popsicle sticks. Invisible things were placed inside baggies. Edgar understood that they were looking for Conrad—as if Conrad's body were somehow still here.

"He's not . . ." Edgar tried to explain.

"Who? You can tell us."

"Tell us," repeated the woman with wet hair.

But, again, Edgar fell into rocking silence.

The man in the yellow T-shirt stood. "We need to do a full exam."

"No, we're transporting him. They'll do it there."

Another friendly-sounding person—this time a black woman—escorted Edgar to a car. Within, a metal grate separated the front from the back. "For your protection," she said when the boy hesitated. "Don't worry, someone will sit with you."

Edgar rubbed his nose. He could still smell the deer bones.

Other people approached; often they spoke in numbers. "We have to do a fifty-seven." "Call in a four-nineteen." Someone was talking into a radio, saying, "Echo, Delta, Golf."

Edgar was in the cage now, sitting beside a bald man in glasses.

"My name is Mike. I'm going to stay with you the whole time."

His voice was fragrant and wet. Edgar could see a white button on the tip of his tongue.

"Would you like a peppermint, buddy?"

Edgar shook his head and curled up against the door.

"Let me lock that," said Mike, reaching over Edgar's body.

"Don't touch me."

"I'm not touching you. I'm not touching you." Mike held up his hands as if Edgar had pointed a gun.

The two people up front, who'd been chatting, fell silent.

Edgar pressed his face against the tinted window. Outside, a man in blue shorts leaned against a tree. A German shepherd, also dressed in blue (a padded vest with buckles) waited patiently at the man's feet. When the car began to move, Edgar tensed.

"What's wrong?"

"I have to—we have to get the dog."

"Don't worry, hon," a woman murmured through the grate. "Everything's going to be fine."

Edgar shook his head. "He's in the water."

"The dog?"

"No." Why didn't these people understand? "I—I'm—"

"It's okay," Mike said. "*Shhh.* We know who you are."

* * *

Edgar had been given an aspirin—but maybe it wasn't an aspirin, because he fell asleep and when he woke up he had a tummy ache and someone in rubber gloves was carrying him down a hallway.

When he woke up a second time he was on a narrow cot. His clothes were gone and he was wearing a flimsy blue gown. The room was small, with walls of gray cement. There was a window, but the glass was dark, almost a mirror, and gave the impression of being in a house at night. In one corner, on the linoleum floor, was a pile of old toys—mangy stuffed animals and scattered pieces of a plastic castle. On the wall: a framed poster of baby chicks.

A man with a nametag was sitting near the toys in a too-small chair. He lifted his hand in greeting and was about to speak when a woman entered the room. She wore a blue suit and clicky heels. Her hair was neatly pulled up and sat on her head like a biscuit. Edgar couldn't understand why she was smiling.

He didn't smile back. When she said, "Hello," he asked where his ring was.

"Your what?"

"It was in my pocket."

"We've got everything," the woman said. "We just have to look at it." She sat in a chair beside the cot. "I'm very glad to see you, Edgar. I'm Rebecca."

"And I'm Evan," said the man in the corner. "I'm here for your safety. If you feel uncomfortable about anything, you just let me know."

Edgar closed his eyes. The lights were too bright. Plus, he didn't like the way the woman was staring at him.

"We've called your mother, but we just need to—"

"Where are my clothes?"

"Are you cold?" asked Evan. "Maybe he's cold."

"Are you cold?" said Rebecca.

"Where am I?"

"You're home." When she reached for Edgar's hand, he pulled away.

"How do you know my name?"

"It's all right, Edgar—I'm a friend. I just need to ask you a few questions, and then you can see your mother."

At the second mention of this word, Edgar felt dizzy—and then frightened. He turned toward the wall and began to rock.

"You're upsetting him," said Evan.

"I'm not upsetting him. *Edgar*," the woman crooned. "Edgar—come on, look at me."

When Edgar didn't, she told him again that she was his friend. "I've been looking for you for a long time. This is a great day." She told him that he should be happy. "Don't you want to see your mom?"

Edgar looked at the poster of baby chicks and noticed the cracked eggshells in the background. The jagged edges were all the same, and Edgar wondered if the eggs were fake.

"You don't have to be afraid." The woman spoke slowly, almost in a kind of rapture. "I know it must have been terrible, Edgar, but we found him. Do you understand? We found him."

The boy was crying now. Evan stood and walked over. "I think we need to wait until the family is here."

"The family's here," Rebecca whispered. "I just have to ascertain his safety."

"Well, do it quickly," said Evan.

The woman pushed a sprig of hair off her forehead and leaned toward the cot. "I'm not going to ask you about what happened out there, Edgar—okay? We can talk about that later. I just need you to tell me a couple of things before I can bring your family in here—all right?"

"I want . . ." Edgar couldn't get the words out.

"Rebecca—he's not up to this. You need to stop."

"I have to ascertain what's going on. He's clearly unhappy about something."

"Of course he's—"

"Please, Evan—just let me do my job."

The man backed away, and the woman opened a folder. She placed a photograph on the cot.

Edgar felt something awful come over him—a sickening wave of shame.

"Do you know this person, Edgar?"

It was a blown-up photo from a driver's license.

"You know this person—yes?"

Edgar nodded.

"Who is it?"

A bark-like sob erupted from the boy's mouth.

"This is your mother, yes?"

The boy's voice—"yes"—was as small as a grain of salt.

"And has she ever hurt you? Or—"

"Hasn't this already been settled?" interrupted Evan.

"It's just procedure. I have to ask." The detective turned back to the boy and smiled, as if his tears were invisible. "You can tell me, sweetheart."

Edgar shook his head. He wasn't going to let this woman trick him. When she started to speak again, he screamed.

The woman flinched and dropped her folder.

Evan stood. "Just—just calm down, Edgar. We're going to bring her in." He moved hastily toward the door.

"Stop," ordered the detective. "I will get her." Her hands were shaking as she adjusted her collar. When she looked at the boy again, it was to apologize. "I know your mother's a good . . ." The woman's voice caught in her throat. "Please forgive me, Edgar."

* * *

In another room, down the hall, Lucy waited with Ron. The baby was at home with Netty. Lucy paced beside a small table. "I don't understand—is he here? Why can't we . . . ?" She was only half certain she wasn't dreaming.

Ron was confused, as well. The police had called him at work, claiming that they were at the Fini residence, but that no one was there. When Ron had shown up, an officer explained that the boy had been found and that he'd escort them to the station. They would've arrived there sooner, but it had taken a while to find Lucy, who'd been traipsing through the woods.

Neither understood why Edgar hadn't been brought straight home. The policeman had said something about procedure. Also something about having to *identify* the boy. It was a disturbing word—but since the man hadn't offered any condolences, then surely the boy was alive. It was not a question, though, that Lucy could bring herself to ask.

When she'd asked if Edgar was hurt, the officer had said, "Someone will talk to you at the station." The man was a mumbler and not particularly friendly. Ron was offended by his manner, but took Lucy's lead and remained silent. He didn't wish to upset her further by making a scene, or by demanding information that might prove deadly.

In the back of the police car, Lucy had clutched the butcher's arm. As they'd proceeded, unreally, at five miles under the speed limit, she'd silently counted the lampposts on summer lawns. Edgar had always liked to count things; now she understood why. The abstraction of numbers was helpful, reductive, a pretense of order. *Twenty-six. Twenty-seven. Twenty-eight.*

In the waiting room, though, there was nothing to count. A little pressboard table, some folding chairs. The door had a small window with a cross-hatching of embedded wire. The fluorescent light seemed to suggest insects.

"What did they say again?" asked Lucy—but Ron couldn't remember now. He was so furious at the Ferryfield police that he wanted to bust a wall. Seeing the same anxious rage growing in Lucy, he made an effort to stay calm. He tried to take her hand, but she was moving too fast.

"They can't just ignore us."

"Why don't you sit down, babe?"

"This is—this is—I'm not waiting. Fuck this." When Lucy marched toward the door, Ron made no attempt to stop her.

As soon as she stepped into the hall, she heard the commotion—someone screaming.

She moved slowly, as if through tar—down the cement hallway, past identical metal doors, and then there was Ms. Mann—face drawn, dressed for a funeral.

"Oh my God—tell me."

The detective touched Lucy's arm. "He's okay. He's okay. We just—"

Lucy made a garbled sound and fell to her knees. When she looked up, she saw the man standing by an open door, gesturing toward her with an odd formality, saying, "Please," like a maître d'.

Why couldn't she stand? She felt something like terror. How would she be able to look at the boy without dissolving? Ms. Mann tried to help her up, but Lucy refused. Ron was there now, lifting her. Ceiling vents shuddered with air-conditioning, and as Lucy moved toward the little room at the end of the hall, her vision blurred.

Cold walls and stinging lights. The smell of burnt coffee and too much human breath.

My mother was so close I could hear her footsteps. I could hear her breathing. I could hear the slow pity of a large black clock and the man from Child Protection and Permanency saying, "Come in, Mrs. Fini."

I remember it as if it were yesterday.

She was crying when she came into the room, and I was crying. Other children's toys on the floor, strangers watching us, Ron in the corner like a timid bull. My mother's mouth a shape I'd never seen before. We kept our distance for what seemed a long time, as if a river raged between us.

"Your feet," she finally said—I suppose because they were bare. She was trembling and her voice came out in bits. I looked away, at the floor. Covered my face.

"I'm sorry," she said, taking my words. Our sobs like the cries of dogs.

Still, we didn't go to each other. We waited, shivering—both of us understanding that the river was real, and that, like before, it had the power to carry us away. We were frightened, and ashamed.

But my mother was brave. She stepped into the water—and I stood to receive her.

BOOK SEVEN

HOME

If I loved you less, I might be able to talk about it more.

—JANE AUSTEN, *EMMA*

73

Time

For a long time I didn't talk about him—not in any detail. Not to the police or to my mother. Back then I could only say meaningless things. "I got lost." "I'm sorry." "No, he didn't touch me"—when of course he had, though not in the way everyone feared.

My first days at home were a slow-moving dream filled with too much light. It was summer still, and I didn't have school. I spent a lot of time in my room, where I tried to reacquaint myself with my figurines, many of which didn't seem to recognize me.

My mother and I kept a polite distance, though we were always in danger of crying when we looked at each other. At night, I often had terrible dreams and finally was brave enough to go to her room. "You okay, pal?" the butcher asked, and I could only say, "Yes"—even as I moped closer to their bed. When my mother opened her side of the sheets, I crawled in.

After that night, our bodies began to remember, and then it seemed that every time we saw each other—even if we'd only been apart for five minutes—we embraced. Soon it became almost a joke, and if the butcher caught us failing to perform, he'd say, "What, no hug?" My mother and I would then go through the motions—sometimes hammily—and Ron would always applaud.

The lies I'd accumulated about the butcher fell away with alarming haste. And though these lies had been expanded upon by Conrad, they'd originated in me, out of fear and jealousy—things that were by no means gone in regard to my mother's husband, but were greatly lessened by the fact that I better understood now how to be with men. My heart didn't stop when Ron boomed, "Eddie, my man!" or when he banged around my grandmother's pots and pans, or when, one night after dinner, he picked up my hand to look at the tip of my finger and said, "You wouldn't even know it was ever missing."

"Poor Netty," my mother said, recalling how Mrs. Schlip had had to wrap a piece of me in her rain cap. Ron nodded at the memory, and a lightness fell over us—I suppose because it's a comfort to pretend that the heaviest burdens are never your own.

When I first saw Henry and Netty, it was at their shop. Netty cried so hard that somehow she knocked over a box of jelly jars, which made everyone laugh, even Henry, who declared the broken glass "very good luck." Whether this was guile or superstition on his part, I don't know—but we all accepted it.

Luck. The word was mentioned often. My mother and I were on television. We watched ourselves, eating popcorn. *Fini boy found. Missing albino safely at home.*

It wasn't over, though—my life in the Barrens.

A few weeks after I was back, my mother received a call from an animal shelter in Hammonton. The police had brought Jack there, and since she was quite old—something I hadn't realized at the time—it was implied that she'd soon be destroyed.

My mother was upset, but not about the dog. She couldn't understand why these people were calling us. She'd hung up on them. When I asked her to call back, she refused.

I'd barely spoken a dozen words in those first few weeks—I mostly slept or stared at the baby—but now I argued with my mother and I wasn't satisfied until she and Ron drove me to Hammonton, where, it was agreed, I was only to say goodbye to the dog, but where, once we were reunited, there was no parting us.

When I asked where the fish were, the woman at the shelter said she only had cats and dogs. "But there was an aquarium," I explained. "There were eleven fish." I looked at my mother and the butcher, hoping they would join my cause, but they only smiled stiffly as if I were Dorothy back in black-and-white, mixing things up.

"You had a pretty bad bump on your head," my mother said. When it came to the Barrens, she seemed to prefer that the greater part of it be assigned to silence. And since this was my proclivity, as well, I was easily lulled back into secrecy.

It was strange, at first, having Jack in the house, drinking water from one of Florence's old mixing bowls, or curled up under the piano gnawing bones from the butcher shop.

I couldn't quite figure out what it all meant. It seemed both wonderful and terrible—and often, just past the edge of my happiness, I would glimpse the tattered orange clouds and the jon boat. Seven bridges and not a single angel.

* * *

That anyone dies in water is terrible. You can't see it. It happens behind a curtain, in darkness. It has to be imagined.

Drowning. For a long time I couldn't even say the word—let alone write it. I couldn't imagine it. But then it became the one necessity, to go back to the bodies and make a bed for them, a story. What they must have felt—what you imagine they must have felt.

I think my father, at the end, believed in eternity. Conrad, only in oblivion.

Sometimes I wonder if he watched the boat for a while before he went down with the anchor; if he watched me sleep. Was it night still, or morning already? If it was night: was the water cold? If it was morning: I wonder if he could see the edge of the Barrens in the first light, the mouth of the Mullica, the faraway plains of pygmy pine. His papers were in order—I know that. He was, according to himself—and like my father—thinking clearly when he went down.

And I want him to go down, I want him to die—and at the same time I know this isn't quite the truth.

When I remember him, sometimes it's with terror, sometimes with grief. Certain days, there's a wishful melancholy, like when you look through a discarded photo album in a thrift shop and think, *I know these people.* That compulsion—almost a sense of duty—to carry these strangers home.

* * *

About a month after my return, I discovered a little card in the pocket of the suit I'd worn to my grandmother's wake. *Honey Fasinga, Bon Vivant.*

It took me another two weeks to get up the guts to call. "I've been meaning to visit," she said when I finally did. "Why don't I stop by on Friday?" She asked if she could bring her boyfriend.

I told her my mother and the baby had a doctor's appointment on Friday, and she said, "Good. Babies are boring. And you're the one I want to see."

When she came to the house, she was wearing a frilly white top and a silver skirt that looked like it was made of metal. Her boyfriend was the man I'd seen kiss my grandmother in her coffin. "Dominic Sparra," he said, shaking my hand. He poked his head into the downstairs bathroom and cried, "Ha!"—after which he told me, "You know, we stole those tiles, your grandfather and me."

"They were bad boys," said Honey, and Dominic said, "We were young." He nosed around some more. "I spent a lot of time in this house."

"He wanted to marry your grandmother."

"Honey!"

"Well, it's true. You always had the hots for her."

"We were just good friends," he said, resting his hand on the piano. "She played like an angel."

When Dominic went into the kitchen to toss back some beers with the butcher, Honey and I sat in the dining room. She'd brought a tin of fancy tea with flower petals in it, which we drank using my grandmother's good china cups.

"I still have it," I whispered.

"The diamond?" Honey whispered back.

When I nodded, she winked at me. "It was your lucky charm."

Later, in Florence's room, I said she could pick out a dress, if she still wanted one. I hadn't meant to make her cry. She chose a lavender sheath with orange rosettes and the signature butterfly-wing stitching.

We sat on the bed and she told me stories—things I'd never known about my grandmother. That she'd played "Clair de lune" at her mother's funeral, and that, one Fourth of July at VanDervoort Park, she'd sung the national anthem in a yellow turban.

When I showed Honey the silk box with the braid of black hair, she smiled. "Oh, Flo." She stared at it for nearly a minute with her strangely catlike eyes.

"And *you*"—she finally said, turning back to me. "You're quite the little man now, aren't you?"

I told her that I'd turned nine while I was gone, and she said, "Yes. It happens."

"What happens?" I asked.

"Don't you know?" She raised her chin slightly, as if posing for a photograph. "Time, my dear. Time."

74

Tree of the Year

In September, when the letter arrived from Robert Penny, Esq., my mother hid it and didn't mention anything for nearly a week. Though it was addressed to me *(Master Edgar Allan Fini),* my mother had kept it away, she said later, only to protect me.

When she finally threw the cream-colored envelope on the table, it was open. Ron pulled out the letter and read it. "We're supposed to see him tomorrow."

"You don't have to go," my mother said, turning to me. "They can't make you go."

Then, after a pause, Ron explained quietly: "It's about that Billings guy."

I was eating a cookie. A crumb fell to the floor. I had the urge to run and hide.

All I could manage, though, was to bend down and pick up the cookie crumb. Over the last several months, my mother and I had made an unspoken pact: we'd make my disappearance disappear. Suddenly it was in the kitchen.

Jack, sensing danger, lifted her head from the doggy bed by the back door.

My mother was standing behind Ron now, looking at the letter. I walked over and took it from them.

"Don't read it," my mother said, as if doing so might contaminate me.

The paper was cream-colored like the envelope, and felt rough, almost hairy.

"Why do they call me *Master?*"

"Because you're a kid," said Ron.

This made no sense to me.

Then I remembered how Conrad had sometimes called me *Maestro,* and I felt queasy—as if the letter had somehow come from him.

"I'll go talk to this Penny myself," the butcher said.

"No," I surprised myself by saying.

"He's right," my mother said. "Let's just ignore it."

But she'd misunderstood me. I hesitated before quietly correcting her. "I want to go."

My mother snatched the letter from my hand. "Why? What could you possibly want from him?"

Upstairs, the baby began to scream. We all looked at the ceiling as if at our own thoughts. Then my mother tossed the letter in the sink and ran some water over it, as if the thing were on fire.

* * *

In the van the next day, the butcher said, "You have to at least be curious."

My mother said the obvious—that it killed the cat.

"Well, I don't know about you," the butcher replied, "but Eddie and I are dogs." He winked at me in the backseat.

I was wearing new clothes—a stiff pink oxford and hard-creased khakis. I'd grown nearly an inch while I was away, and my arms were slightly longer.

My mother looked different, too—and I knew that I'd done this to her. There was something in her gaze now that reminded me of Florence. It wasn't sadness, exactly. But there could be no lies now, no pretense that we were the same people as before.

"You have reached your destination," the GPS said.

The butcher pulled over and parked under the shade of an elm, which according to a plaque near its base was *Tree of the Year, 2001*. I knew that something had happened then, something terrible I'd learned about in school—though I couldn't recall what.

* * *

Someone was talking, but it seemed to be another language. I traced circles on my palm and stared at the wall.

The office was dark brown, with wainscot paneling that looked like segments of a chocolate bar. Behind a desk made from the same recipe sat Mr. Penny. His enormous ears and gleaming bald head somehow seemed obscene—and though there were no wrinkles on his face, I could tell he was very old.

"I don't understand," my mother said—the baby asleep in her arms.

Mr. Penny smiled patiently. He read the sentence again.

"The eight hundred and seventy-six acres in the Pinelands National Reserve, including the cabin and all its contents, are left to Edgar Allan Fini."

"How does he . . . ?" My mother hesitated. She turned from Mr. Penny to me. "How does he know your middle name?"

My face was burning and I was too ashamed to speak.

Silence, and then a business-like cough, after which Mr. Penny continued.

"Yes, well, this is simply disclosure. The next step, of course, is probate, which can take some time. At this point, no one is questioning the authenticity, and I'd be more than happy to—"

"We're not hiring you," said my mother. "We're not interested."

"Lucy." Ron put his hand on my mother's arm, before turning back to the lawyer. "We really can't afford legal counsel."

"Yes, I gather that. But if I might just finish." Mr. Penny tapped the pages on his desk. "The boy—"

When the old man met my gaze, I looked away.

"The boy has also been left a sizable sum of money."

In the absence of any response, Mr. Penny spoke agreeably to himself. "Yes, indeed."

And then: "The investments represent . . . well, as far as we can determine . . ."

He stopped, understanding perhaps that his words were going to waste. He turned around a sheet of paper and slid it forward, so that Ron and my mother might look. "Right there." Mr. Penny's finger quavered like a compass needle. "Quite a substantial sum, as you can see."

My mother pushed the paper away.

Mr. Penny grimaced. "Given the circumstances—"

"Do you know the circumstances?" my mother interrupted.

"I do," said Mr. Penny. "I'm very aware of the complications here." He touched the knot of his tie. "Still, it's an incredibly generous gift. The property and the investments come to well over three—"

"The property? You mean where my son was tortured?"

"I can't—I can't speak on that, Mrs. Fini."

"Tell him, Edgar."

I was overcome with panic. Had I been tortured? All I knew was that my nightmares hadn't let up—dreams of guns, of fire and water and blood-soaked bandages. Still, I was in no position to say what it all meant.

Ron put his hand on my shoulder because I was crying now. I wondered how much Mr. Penny knew. He must have known that another boy should have been sitting here. I made an effort not to look at any of the papers—afraid I might see Kevin's name crossed out and mine inserted.

"I have no tissues, I'm sorry." Mr. Penny spoke exclusively to the butcher now. "Let's try to put this into less emotional . . ." He sighed, looked helplessly at the walls. "Of course, I don't mean . . . I'm sure it's all very difficult for you. I only want to suggest that this would be helpful for the boy's future. And for your other child, as well."

"I guess we're just confused," said Ron. "We don't know this man."

"Yes," said Mr. Penny. "I understand. But you must try to think of it as . . ."

He seemed not to know how to think of it, though. He tilted his head and sighed again.

The light coming in the window fell equally on all of us. I could see through my hands. I could see the blood. My mother was strangely quiet. Bubbles formed at the baby's mouth, and she wiped them away.

Mr. Penny closed the leather-bound folder on his desk. "What has happened is beyond terrible—Mr. Salvatore, Mrs. Fini—and I'm not here to defend anyone." He paused, shook his head. "I knew Mr. Billings's father. I've worked for the family for many, many years. Mr. Billings—the younger—was always quite impulsive and—"

"Is this a eulogy?" asked my mother.

"No," said Mr. Penny. "Not at all. This is strange for me, too. It's just . . . it would be silly to refuse this. For Edgar's sake."

I made a sound—but no one seemed to understand it.

"What's that, young man?"

Though I was looking at my hands, I could feel everyone's eyes on me.

"You have something to say? Edgar?"

I wanted to crawl into the earth, where no one would ever ask me to tell the truth—where I might live among stones and be silent.

"He has a wife," I said.

"Yes," said Mr. Penny. "Ex-wife." He seemed to know what I was driving at. "She's been very well taken care of. You're a good boy, to ask. But she's not contesting this."

"What about other family?" asked Ron.

"No," said Mr. Penny. "No other family."

"I saw her picture," I said—my voice barely there.

"Listen to me, Edgar," Mr. Penny said. "I've spoken with her at length. She wants you to have this."

No one said anything for a while—or if they did, I didn't hear them. Finally I heard Mr. Penny say, "She's lovely. What's her name?"

He was talking about the baby.

"I don't mean to pry," he said, because no one had answered him.

"Emma," I said.

I was proud of the name. My mother had let me choose it. But now she looked at me as if she'd just heard it for the first time.

"That's what you used to call your grandmother."

"I never called her that."

"Yes." She smiled to stop her tears. "When you were little. You couldn't pronounce *gramma*. It always sounded like *emma*."

"It's a good name," said Mr. Penny—and my mother agreed, kissing the baby's head.

75

Blue Music

She lived longer than anyone had expected, and when she died it was in her bed by the back door. Emma, who was five, said we should bury her in the yard, but Ron said no—it was illegal.

Emma, being Emma, persisted. "Jackie's *my* dog. So it's kind of up to me, Dad."

"We're having her cremated, honey."

"What's cremated?"

Ron explained, and when he was finished, Emma said, "I know exactly where we can put her—next to the fish pond."

"I just told you, honey, we can't put her back there," and Emma said, "Not *in* the fish pond, but *next* to it."

And so it was decided.

My sister, who always called Jack by her proper name—Jackie—presided over the interment. The plastic Ziploc of ashes was put inside a pink Giga-byte Girl lunchbox—which Emma wanted to upgrade anyway, she admitted to me, to a Terabyte Teen ("I'm older now").

When my mother suggested wrapping the lunchbox in a garbage bag, Emma said that it would ruin the whole thing, to cover up the pink, and my mother said, "No one's going to see it once it's down there," and Emma said, "*I'll* see it because I'll *think* about it. Plus, God will see it."

"Deeper," she instructed the butcher as he dug. "Wait, Daddy." There was a worm. "Eddie, get it out and move it over there." She pointed toward Ron's vegetable garden.

The spot Emma had chosen for Jack's grave was a sober corner of the yard with a patch of snarled yellow weeds. "Devil's grass," Florence had called it. I'd often seen my grandmother on her knees, tearing it out. I think Emma chose the spot because Jack liked to pee there.

The shovel made a sharp sound on what we all thought was a stone, but which I quickly recognized, even half obscured by dirt—the sculptured snout, the crescent moon of the trigger. Smaller than Conrad's, but the same animal.

"Oh my God," said my mother.

"Oh my God," repeated Emma.

"Don't touch it," said Ron.

"I'm not," said Emma.

Despite the octopus ink filling my belly, I knelt before the hole.

"*No,*" my mother and the butcher cried in unison.

"It's okay," I told them. "I know how." I picked it up from the grip, turned the muzzle away from us, clicked the safety, and opened the chamber. There were six bullets. I shook them out into my hand, and then placed them in my pocket.

"How do you know about guns?" my mother asked me.

"I'm fourteen," I said—which was easier than explaining that I'd learned at nine.

"Okay," said Emma. "I don't like this. Can we finish with Jackie, please? Put the gun down, Eddie."

I was more than happy to oblige.

Emma turned toward her father with an authoritative nod.

The butcher placed a bone in the hole, after which Emma added a dirty tug rope Jack was fond of. She arranged it, just so, around the lunchbox. Then she stood, took a deep breath, and began.

"She was a very good dog. There really wasn't another dog like her. She was very funny, and also she was very . . ."

She struggled for the word.

"Loyal," I suggested.

"Yes. She was pretty great." Emma took another breath and was quiet for a bit, contemplating the lunchbox. "I guess we have to cover her now. But do it slowly, Daddy."

The butcher picked up the shovel.

"Don't cry, Mommy."

"I'm fine, baby."

I could see, though, that she wasn't. Her eyes kept drifting away toward the trees at the edge of the yard.

Frank loves Lucy 4-ever. I wonder if she was looking at that.

* * *

"Who put that gun in there?" Emma asked later, at dinner, and my mother said, "Probably whoever lived here before us."

"And who was that?" asked Emma.

My mother said that she didn't know their names, and to stop talking and keep eating.

"They were probably criminals," said Emma.

"I'll bring it to the police station," said Ron.

"No," said my mother. "We don't want them asking questions."

"What questions?" said Emma.

"I'll take care of it," my mother said.

"Mommy doesn't like the police," Emma explained to me. "If they drive behind the car, she gets nervous."

"Here," said the butcher, giving Emma more cavatelli and broccoli.

"This always made Jackie throw up. It's not really meant for dogs."

"Yeah, and I wonder who gave it to her?" said the butcher.

"Well, she liked it. It's not our fault you're a good cooker."

*   *   *

It was still dark when my mother woke me and asked if I wanted to go for a drive.

"Sure," I said. In those days, I refused her nothing.

It was too early for conversation, so we drove in silence. I saw the paper bag on the backseat and didn't question it. On the highway we listened to the radio—my mother's station of whining electric guitars and frantic drums. Occasionally she sang a refrain in her awful singing voice that was like someone talking in their sleep.

We drove for a long time, maybe two hours. At one point, moving through a stretch of woods, I felt what I hadn't in years—a vision-doubling panic. My mother seemed to sense this and patted my knee. We drove across a small bridge and then pulled over just before a second, larger one.

We sat in the car for a while more, the radio still on. "You don't smoke, do you?" she asked.

I told her no. "Why—do you want a cigarette?"

"I stopped when you disappeared," she said. "But if you had one, I'd take it."

Parked at the side of a road, in some kind of canyon, with a river below us, I felt myself grow calmer. I've always loved sitting in a car with my mother—the hushed interiority, the twinship of it. We talked a bit about school, and then about Emma and Jack. I could tell that there were other things she wanted to discuss, but I was patient. Now and then she repeated herself, and I realized she was nervous. She pointed out the sign: SHEPHERD'S JUNCTION. "Funny name, huh? I mean where're the sheep?"

"Maybe they're hiding," I said.

She smiled. "Maybe." Her hand found my knee again.

This wasn't the day, though, when she told me the story of what had happened here. It wasn't until years later, when I was in my twenties, that she began to speak of it.

That day, when I was fourteen, we just walked on the side of the road, stood at the railing of the bridge and looked at the water.

"It's pretty," I said.

"Yes," my mother said. "I thought so, too."

She fished the six bullets from the paper bag and gave them to me. She gestured with her head. Again, I didn't question her. I threw the bullets, one by one, into the water.

"Wait," she said.

There was one left. She took it from me, and then removed the gun from the bag.

"What are you doing?" I said.

"Trust me," she said.

Her hands were shaking and she couldn't get the chamber open.

"Stop." I took it from her, loaded the bullet, and then raised my arm to throw the gun.

"Let me do it," she said.

"Ma."

"Trust me," she said again.

When I gave her the gun, she told me to stand back.

"Ma, be careful."

She pointed the muzzle toward the water and pulled the trigger. The chamber was empty.

My heart was racing, but I had no compulsion to stop her. She pulled the trigger again—two more dry shots until on the fourth the horrendous sound startled us both. The ring echoed like the cry of a dying animal. It entered our bones and lingered there.

"We're done, baby."

She held out the gun, as if to see it against the sky. Then she dropped it into the water.

* * *

Over the next few years, there were parties at the house—as there must have been when Pio and Florence were young and had just bought the place. A few friends, some neighbors. There was always too much food, always wine. Sometimes the furniture was pushed aside and there'd be dancing.

The parties were never large, but I was still shy and often hid in the kitchen or at the foot of the steps, from where I had a good view of the living room. Emma, up past her bedtime, was easy to spot—walking around proudly in pajamas, controlling the music with her wrist-rover, which was the latest rage—and with which she seemed to rule the very spirit of the house. "Blue music," she'd command. "Now, red. Now, pink!" No one understood her categorizations, but she kept the room hopping—often dancing herself in a way that never failed to make me laugh, like she was being shocked silly by electricity. On the dance floor she often gravitated toward Toni-Ann Hefti, who shared an equally expressive style. Toni-Ann must have been around nineteen or twenty then. She worked part-time at the Container Store and often gave Emma tiny colored boxes that Emma adored but in which my sister would never put anything. "The *box* is what matters," she explained to me.

When Emma got tired, her dance became a slow rocking of her hips that seemed only to make her sleepier. She would dance until her eyes began to close and it was often me who put her to bed—in Florence's room, which was now my sister's.

She always said her prayers out loud, without shame. In fact, it seemed she recited them with a savvy awareness of her audience. The night-light of the angel on the bridge was back in action. It still baffled me sometimes that Emma and Florence shared no blood. This truth never seemed quite right.

"The old lady in the pictures?" she'd say, if ever I brought up Florence.

"Yes," I would say. "My grandmother."

"I don't have any grandmothers," she'd tell me. "But I have you, and I have parents. There's a girl in my class named Fung who doesn't have any parents—only guards."

"Guardians," I told her.

"Yes, but not like angels—just like normal people."

* * *

Eventually, I went away to school. Money wasn't an issue.

My mother, of course, never asked for a penny. Still, I convinced her to fix up the house—repair the roof and the faulty plumbing. Over time we added all the new technologies, according to Emma's specifications. Florence's house became wired for transcendence. A skylight illuminated the historically dark staircase.

For a while, there'd been talk about moving—but something in the house wouldn't let us go, and we didn't fight it.

When my mother turned fifty, I took her and the butcher on a trip to Italy—mostly to look at the paintings. At one point, in the Uffizi, the butcher took my hand. We were standing before a depiction of the abduction of Ganymede—the boy in the wings of a large black eagle.

The butcher turned to me, and I blushed.

"I'm okay," I said. "I'm better."

Of course, the sadness still came and went—and the panic.

It was the same for my mother, who suffered a migraine every time I had to go away again. Often I'd delay my departure a day or two, sit with her in a dark room, stroke her head.

I never stayed away for long—never for more than a few months. Summers we were always together. It became our season. We traveled everywhere, slept in good hotels—from which my mother regularly stole the soap. She said, "I dreamed of doing this with your father."

My mother died when she was eighty-six—just two years after the butcher passed, at eighty-nine.

I never married. Neither did Emma. There are no children.

Forgive me for rushing, but I want you to feel it as I did—the way the years flew, masquerading as minutes.

21 Cressida Drive is gone now. There's some kind of warehouse there that I don't understand, don't have any desire to understand.

Things dissolve, they disappear, and if you want to keep them, it takes some practice. These days, I mostly stay in my room, trying to remember. I always have a notebook close at hand. My greatest pleasure has been writing the ghosts.

* * *

You're that boy who was missing.

More than once, when I was young, people would come up to me and say something to this effect. It wasn't uncommon to learn that these strangers had prayed for me. Such interactions were always brief. People seemed compelled to approach, but soon realized that there wasn't much to say. And of course my one-word answers or silent nods did little to put them at ease.

Everyone's lost something—some people quite a lot, some people everything—and I suppose these strangers saw me as a bit of luck. A happy ending.

"Well, I won't keep you," they'd often say. "I'm sure your mother is waiting for you."

"Yes," I would inform them, trying not to gloat. "She is."

MIRRORLAND

After Emma died, Edgar returned to the cabin.

It was the same as before: the tricky floorboards, the pink glass window churched by sun, the old clanging stove. The Barrens were the same, too: the towering pines and the pygmies, the milk snakes streaming through fallen needles.

Winters were colder now, of course, and Edgar always had a fire—though gathering wood at his age proved to be a heart-thundering chore. Often he stood baffled before mirrors. How could he be an old man when for most of his life he'd been a child? It seemed a riddle.

Now and then he found himself staring at words carved on a tree. *Edgar loves . . .*

Still unfinished. Sometimes he took a knife with him, intending to complete the sentence.

But what had he meant to write, all those years ago? Who was the object? An old woman in a paisley robe, with workhorse hands and feet like the skin of an orange? Or maybe it was the redhead with the house-burning laugh. There had been others, as well—but they'd come later.

Edgar decided to leave the carving as it was. All he did, with a slow turning of the point of his knife, was to add a period.

Edgar loves.

He'd consider it an honor should he be deemed worthy of such a tombstone.

But not yet. He'd like to sleep and wake for a few more months. He'd like to see spring again—hear Fowler's toads in the mud and Chuck-Will's-Widow in the trees, glimpse Hessel's Hairstreak in the cedar swamps. He'd like to eat one last sparkleberry.

Soon, these nine hundred acres will be part of the National Reserve—Conrad's private estate given back to nature. Edgar has it all on paper.

Sometimes he's too excited to sleep and he sits in the yard, listening to the night birds doing their invisible work. He makes tea and folds himself over the kitchen table, takes a few more notes. He still rocks his body, but only when he's writing and trying to find his rhythm—the old habit cleansed of anxiety; it's a kind of freedom now, a breaking through. He works every day. The book is nearly finished.

Mid-afternoon. He's kneeling by the woodpile, gathering greens. Above him, a light unlike anything he's ever seen.

The light explodes, expands. Edgar wonders if a war has begun—and when he tries to stand, he falters. The light in the sky grows larger—an orb half the size of the sun. From its burning surface emerge brilliant bluish tendrils—a living, jellyfish luminescence. Edgar recalls the ships he dreamed about in his childhood, vessels powered by diamonds.

All day he lies on his side by the woodpile, watching the light—and when night comes, it's still there, brighter than the moon. With the stars out, the sky is a map Edgar can read. The pulsing jellyfish has replaced the shoulder of Orion, the Hunter.

Someone had told him that this would happen. Someone had held him up to the sky, some long-ago night school. He can smell the greeny green scent of tomato vines.

Edgar nibbles a dandelion leaf and rolls onto his back. He once knew all about red giants and white dwarfs and dark matter. He's forgotten most of it. Something with a *B*—that was the name of the star. A name that had always made him think of a monster.

He's no longer afraid, though.

This thing he's watching—this death—happened a long time ago. There's no pain. It's ghost light. Still, it's hard not to imagine it as something just being born. Lying on the ground, in the wet weeds, it's as if the dog were licking his face.

The supernova will burn for weeks yet before collapsing into darkness. It's almost bright enough to write by. If only he could crawl to the house and get his notebook.

He's too weak, though.

And what would he tell you, anyway?

This is how it ends.

When, really, there's no art to it. It just happens.

Like the deer, who's appeared in the pines.

Is it a deer? Maybe it's a fox. It almost looks human.

Edgar lifts his hand and waves, as the ship throws off its streamers.

ACKNOWLEDGMENTS

I wish to thank the following people for their invaluable assistance—and for their kindness and generosity.

The living: Bill Clegg, Elizabeth Beier, Nicole Williams, Dori Weintraub, Olga Grlic, Austin Brayfield, Richard Lodato, Daniel Mahar, Janet Neipris, Steve Johnstone, Adam Geary, Marilyn Edwards, Michele Conway, Karson Liegh, and Chris Rush.

The dead: Josephine Lodato, Sophie Lodato, Teresa D'Auria, Jetti and Louis Ames.

For the gift of time and a beautiful place in which to write, I am grateful to Pietro Torrigiani and Maddalena Fossombroni at *Castello in Movimento,* Italy.

—V.L.